Praise for L. E. Modesi̇ P9-AGM-557

Of Tangible Ghosts

"Possibly Modesitt's best book, it's certainly highly recommended."

—*Booklist*

"A mystery with an other-worldly difference. Modesitt deftly works out what the political and social consequences might have been had ghosts actually existed. Recommended."

—Jack McDevitt

"There is excitement and tantalizing near-familiarity on every page. *Of Tangible Ghosts* is a delightful read."

—Alfred Coppel

The Ghost of the Revelator

"I found it easier to suspend disbelief in this tale, to concentrate on spies, politics, and the intricacies of Modesitt's alternate history, even to enjoy it more in important ways. May you also."

—*Analog*

"Modesitt's intriguing, flavorsome alternate-world yarn where ghosts are real and America doesn't exist . . . Appealing characters, agreeably labyrinthine plotting, a fascinatingly detailed backdrop."

—*Kirkus Reviews*

Tor Books by L. E. Modesitt, Jr.

*Forthcoming

Ghosts
of
Columbia

L. E. Modesitt, Jr.

A TOM DOHERTY ASSOCIATES BOOK

New York

TOR®

GHOSTS OF COLUMBIA

Afterword, copyright © 2005 by L. E. Modesitt, Jr.

This is an omnibus edition comprising:
Of Tangible Ghosts, copyright © 1994 by L. E. Modesitt, Jr.
The Ghost of the Revelator, copyright © 1998 by L. E. Modesitt, Jr.

Omnibus edited by David G. Hartwell

Map by Mark Stein Studios

A Tor Book
Published by Tom Doherty Associates, LLC
175 Fifth Avenue
New York, NY 10010

www.tor.com

Tor® is a registered trademark of Tom Doherty Associates, LLC.

ISBN 0-765-31314-6

EAN 978-0765-31314-0

First Edition: June 2005

Printed in the United States of America

0 9 8 7 6 5 4 3 2 1

CONTENTS

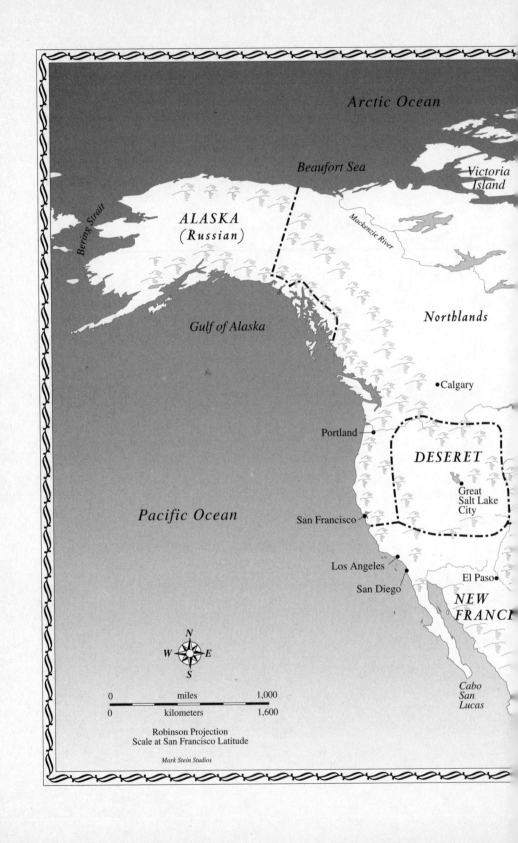

Arctic Ocean

Beaufort Sea

Victoria
Island

Bering Strait

ALASKA
(Russian)

Mackenzie River

Northlands

Gulf of Alaska

•Calgary

Portland

DESERET

Pacific Ocean

Great
Salt Lake
City

San Francisco

Los Angeles

El Paso•

San Diego

NEW
FRANCI

N
W ✦ E
S

Cabo
San
Lucas

| 0 | miles | 1,000 |
| 0 | kilometers | 1,600 |

Robinson Projection
Scale at San Francisco Latitude

Mark Stein Studios

Of
Tangible
Ghosts

For Kevin,

his mother,

and Toffee and Triscuit

CHAPTER ONE

• • •

One ghost in my life was bad enough, but when you have two, an inconvenience can become a disaster. That Saturday night in October, I wasn't really thinking about Carolynne—the family ghost—disasters, or any other ghost. All I wanted to do was lock the office door and get back to the recital hall for Llysette's concert because I'd lost track of time.

My mind was on Llysette when I left my office and walked down the stairs and through the Natural Resources Department offices. I stepped out onto the covered porch and the almost subsonic shivering that tells you there's a ghost around hit me. I thrust the key in the lock, feeling uncomfortable and hurried, without knowing why at first.

Then I pulled out my key, and the shivering went up two notches before the sobbing began.

"No . . . no . . . I wouldn't tell . . . wouldn't listen . . . no . . . no . . ."

The light on the porch of the old Dutch Republican that had been converted to the offices of the Natural Resources Department came from a low-powered permanent glow square. The glow square made seeing the ghost a lot easier because she didn't wash out under the light. Ghosts, even fresh ones, aren't that substantial, and this one was a mess, with white streaks and gashes and droplets of white ectoplasm dripping away from her figure.

I swallowed, hard, because the ghost was Miranda—Miranda Miller, the piano professor—and you don't usually see ghosts like that unless someone's been murdered. Murders aren't that common in the Republic, especially at universities located out in the hinterlands. Miranda was an easy grader, so it couldn't have been a disgruntled student, although that has happened, I understand, but not at Vanderbraak State University. Llysette was more likely to be a target of some burgher's pampered daughter than Miranda.

"No . . . no . . ." The ghost's hands were up, as if trying to push someone away.

"Miranda . . ." I tried to keep my voice soft. The books all say that you have to be gentle with ghosts, but since I come from a pretty normal family, I'd never seen a ghost right after it had been created by violent death. Grandpa's ghost had been pretty ornery, but he'd been ornery enough in life, and he'd faded before long. Most ghosts did, sooner or later.

"Miranda, what happened?"

"No . . . no . . . no . . ." She didn't seem to recognize me. She just projected that aura of terror that felt like subsonics. Then she was gone, drifting across the faculty green toward the administration building—a stone and mortar horror, what the first Dutch settlers had called native-stone colonial. Campus Security had offices there, but I doubted that they were really set for ghost handling, nor were the county watch, even though Vanderbraak Centre was the county seat.

Almost as an afterthought, I closed the door and pulled the key out. I started walking, then running downhill toward the watch building—not even taking those long wide stone steps that led past the car park and down to the lower part of the campus. Halfway down the hill, I skidded to a stop on the browning leaves that the university zombies hadn't been able to sweep up as fast as they fell and looked down at the town square. I was across from the new post centre. The old one had burned down forty years ago, but in Vanderbraak Centre, a forty-year-old building is practically new.

But that wasn't why I stopped. I was going to claim that someone had stabbed Miranda because her ghost had drifted by me, sobbing and incoherent? That might have gone over all right in New Amsterdam, or some other big city like Columbia City, where the feds understood ghost theory, but not in Vanderbraak Centre. The watch were mostly old Dutch stock, stolid, and you seldom saw Dutch ghosts. Don't ask me why, but that was the way it was. The odds were I'd end up in one of those cold iron-barred cells, not because I'd seen a ghost, but because they'd more likely believe I'd committed the murder and claimed I'd seen a ghost.

So I gritted my teeth and turned around to walk back up the hill to the old Physical Training Center that had become the Music and Theatre Department when old Marinus Voorster donated a million guilders to build the new field house—all out of spite with Katrinka Er Recchus, now the acting dean. Then she'd been running the strings program, even before she became department chair. Rumor had it that she'd been more than friendly with old Marinus, hoping for a new performing arts center she could run.

I glanced farther uphill at the Physical Sciences building that held the Babbage centre, but only the outside lights were on. My eyes flicked back to the Music and Theatre building. All the old gym doors were open, since it was a warm night for mid-October. I stopped, straightened my damp collar and my cravat, took some deep breaths, and wiped my forehead on my sleeve before I walked up the stone steps into the building.

As usual, even though it was less than ten minutes before the recital started, only a handful of people walked across the foyer and down the side corridor in front of me.

"Good evening, Doktor Eschbach."

"Good evening." I took the one-sheet program and nodded at the usher, a student whose name momentarily escaped me.

The recital hall had actually been a lecture hall, the only one in the old PT building, so that the "renovation" that had turned it into a recital hall had consisted of adding a full stage, taking out several rows of seats, and removing the lift-tilt desktops attached to the sides of the seats. The seats were still the traditional Dutch colonial hardwood that made long recitals—even Llysette's—tests of endurance.

Miranda Miller—dead? Why Miranda? Certainly, according to Llysette, she whined a lot in her mid-south English dialect. I could have seen it had it been Dean Er Recchus or Gregor, the theatre head who bellowed at everyone, or even Llysette and her perfectionist ways.

The program looked all right:

Llysette duBoise

Soprano

In Recital

Featuring the Mozart *Anti-Mass*

She was doing mostly standard stuff, for her, except for the Britten and Exten. She'd protested doing the Mozart Anti-Mass, but the dean had pointed out that the stipend from the Austro-Hungarian Cultural Foundation had come because they were pushing their traditional musicians, even Mozart, even the later ultraromantic stuff composed after his bout with renal failure, even the weird pieces no one sings much anymore, if they ever did. She'd wanted to do Lady Macbeth's aria from Beethoven's *Macbeth* or Anne's aria from his *Heinrich Verrückt,* but the Austro-Hungarians were pushing Mozart's less popular pieces, and the Foundation had suggested either the Anti-Mass or the love song from *Elisabet*.

You don't turn down a two-hundred-dollar stipend, nor the dean's suggestion, not if you're an academic in up-county New Bruges. Not if you're a refugee from the fall of France trying to get tenure. And not, I supposed, if you were linked to the suspicious Herr Doktor Eschbach, that notorious subversive who'd been forced out of the government when Speaker Hartpence's Reformed Tories had won the elections on a call for a clean sweep of the ministries. So Llysette had opted for the Anti-Mass as the least of the evils.

I settled into a seat halfway back on the left side, right off the aisle, and wiped my forehead again. I was definitely not in the shape I had once been. Yet it hadn't seemed that long since I'd been a flying officer in Republic Air Corps, and my assignments in the Sedition Prevention and Security Service had certainly required conditioning. So what had happened? I shook my head and resolved to step up my running and exercises, and I wiped my forehead once again.

By the time the lights went down, Llysette had a decent crowd, maybe a hundred fifty, certainly not bad for a vocal performance. The Dutch have never been that supportive of vocalists. Strings, strings, and more strings, with a touch of brass— that's how you reach their hearts, but, as Katrinka Er Recchus found out, not their pocketbooks.

Llysette swept onto the stage, all luminous and beautiful, dark hair upswept and braided back, bowed, and nodded at Johanna Vonderhaus, her accompanist, seated at the big Steinbach.

Llysette was in good voice, and everyone thought she was wonderful, so wonderful that they gave her a brief second ovation. I hadn't heard that in New Bruges in the three years I'd been there, except for her concert the previous spring when she had proved that a singer could actually master oratorio and survive.

I should have brought her chocolates, but I only brought myself backstage, and came to a sudden stop as I reached the open wing—the dressing rooms were down a side hall toward the practice rooms and studios—where she stood, pale and composed.

Two watch officers were there in their black and silver, and one was talking to her, one to Johanna. I listened.

"When did you see Doktor Miller last?"

Llysette shrugged in her Gallic way. "Perhaps it was mid-afternoon yesterday. I went home early to prepare for the recital. Preparing for a recital, that is always hard."

"You went home alone?"

"Ah, *non*, monsieur. Doktor Eschbach there drove me in his steamer. Then we ate, and he drove home. This afternoon he drove to my home, and brought me to his house for an early dinner. Then we came to the hall together, and I prepared for the recital."

"Did you see Doktor Miller tonight?"

"*Mais non*. I even sent Johan away while I was dressing and warming up."

"Was anyone else here?"

"Johanna." Llysette inclined her head toward the slender accompanist. "Before the hall was opened, we practiced the Exten."

"Did you see anyone go down the halls toward the studios?"

"*Non*. You must concentrate very hard before the recital."

"Were you alone here at any time after Doktor Eschbach left?"

"I could not say." Llysette shrugged wearily. "Worried I was about the Exten and the Mozart, and people, they could have come and gone. That is what happens before a recital."

There were more questions, but what else could she add? We'd left early on Friday, and on Saturday afternoon we had been together until she started to warm up and dress. That was when I went up to my office.

The tall and chunky watch officer, of course, had to question me then.

"Doktor Eschbach, what did you do when you came back to the university tonight?"

"When we came back, I dropped Doktor duBoise off in front of the theatre building. I parked the steamer in the car park between the theatre building and the library. I walked into the building to make sure Doktor duBoise had everything she needed. When she said she needed to warm up, I went to my office to check my box for any messages, and then I did some paperwork for a new course for next semester. After that I came back and listened to the recital."

"Did you see or hear anything unusual?"

I frowned, on purpose, not wanting to lie exactly, but not wanting to tell the whole truth. "I *felt* a low sound, almost a sobbing, when I left the department office. I looked around, but it faded away."

"Ghost formation," said the other watch officer, the young and fresh-faced officer I hadn't seen around Vanderbraak Centre before. He reminded me of someone, but I knew I hadn't met him before.

"Ghost formation?" I said almost involuntarily, surprised that the locals were that up-to-date on the mechanics of ghosting and equally surprised that the younger officer would upstage the older.

"There was an article in the latest *Watch Quarterly*. Subsonics apparently often occur during and immediately after ghosting occurs." The younger officer blushed as the tall chunky man who had questioned me turned toward him.

"What time did you feel these vibrations?" asked the older watch officer.

"Mmmm . . . it was about fifteen minutes before the concert. Quarter before eight, I would say."

"How well did you know Doktor Miller?"

"Scarcely at all. I knew who she was. Perhaps I'd spoken to her a dozen times, briefly." I wouldn't have known her at all if I hadn't been seeing Llysette.

The questions they posed to me went on even longer than those they had posed to Llysette, but they were all routine, trying to establish who was doing what and where and if I had noticed anything unusual. Finally both officers exchanged glances and nodded.

"We may need to talk to you both later, Doktors," added the taller officer— Herlingen was his name. When I'd first come back to Vanderbraak Centre the year before, he had suggested that I replace my Columbian national plates on the steamer with New Bruges plates as soon as practical.

They bowed and departed, leaving the three of us—me, Llysette, and Johanna— standing in the wing off the recital hall stage. I wiped my forehead.

"Are you up to walking up to the steamer?" I asked Llysette, then looked at Johanna. "Do you need a lift?"

"No, thank you, Johan. Pietr is waiting outside." The tall accompanist smiled briefly, then shook her head. "Poor Miranda."

"*Moi,* I am more than happy to depart." Llysette lifted her bag with her makeup and other necessities, and I took it from her.

Outside, a half moon shone across the campus, and between the moon and the soft illumination of the glow lamps, there was more than enough light to make our way along the brick wall to the car park and the glimmering sleek lines of the Stanley, a far cry from the early steam-carts or even the open-topped racing steamers of early in the century.

Llysette fidgeted for the minute or so that it took for the steam pressure to build. "Why you Columbians love your steamers—that I do not understand. The petrol engines are so much more convenient."

"Columbia is a bigger country than France." I climbed into the driver's seat and eased the throttle open. Only two other steamers were left in the car park, and one belonged to the watch. "Internal petrol engines burn four times as much fuel for the mileage. We can't afford to waste oil, not when Ferdinand controls most of the world's supply, and Maximilian the rest."

"I have heard this lecture before, Johan," Llysette reminded me. At least she smiled.

"That's what you get from a former subminister of Natural Resources." I turned left at the bottom of the hill and steered around the square and toward the bridge that would take us to my house. The breeze through the steamer windows was welcome after the heat of the concert hall.

"More than merely a former subminister. Other worthwhile attributes you have, as well." She paused. "With this event, tonight, is it wise that I should stay with you?"

"Wise? A woman has been murdered, and you want to stay alone?"

"Ah, yes, there is that. Truthfully, I had not thought of that."

I shook my head. Sometimes Llysette never considered the obvious, but I supposed that was because, no matter what they say, sometimes singers are just unrealistic. "Why would anyone want to kill Miranda? She whined too much, but . . . murder?"

"Miranda, she seemed so, so helpless." Llysette cleared her throat, and her voice firmed. "Still, there are always reasons, Johan."

"I suppose so. I wonder if we'll ever know."

"That I could certainly not say."

The breeze held that autumn evening smell of fall in New Bruges, the scent I had missed so much during my years in Columbia City, the smell that reminded me of Elspeth still. I swallowed, and for a moment my eyes burned. I kept my eyes on the narrow line of pavement for a time. Sometimes, at odd times, the old agonies reemerged.

Once across the river and up the hill, I turned the Stanley left onto the narrow lane—everyone called it Deacon's Lane, but that name had never appeared on any sign or map that I knew of—that wound up the hill through the mortared stone walls dating back to the first Dutch settlers. The driveway was dark under the maples that still held most of their leaves, but I had left a light on between the car barn and the house.

I let Llysette out under the light, opened the barn, and parked the steamer. It was warm enough that I didn't worry about plugging in the water tank heater.

She was waiting under the light as I walked up with her bag. I kissed her cheek and took her chin in my hand, gently, but she turned away. "You are most insistent tonight, Johan."

"Only because you are a beautiful lady."

A flicker of white appeared in the darkness behind her, and I tried not to stiffen as I unlocked the side door and opened it for Llysette. She touched the plate inside the side foyer, what some called the mud entrance, and the soft overhead glows went on.

"Do you want a bite to eat? There's some steak pie in the cooler, and I think there's still some Bajan red down in the cellar."

"The wine, I would like that."

I closed the side door and made my way down into the stone-walled cellar and to the racks my grandfather had built. There was still almost half a case of the red. I picked out a 1980 Sebastopol. It's not really Bajan, but Californian, and a lot better than the New French stuff from northern Baja, but I wasn't about to get into that argument with Llysette, and certainly not after her recital.

"No Bajan, but a Sebastopol."

"If one must."

"It's not bad, especially now that Ferdinand has cut off real French wines."

"The Austro-Hungarians, they have already ruined the vineyards. Steel vats and scientists in white coats . . . bah!"

I shrugged, then peeled back the foil and twisted the corkscrew. The first glass went to her and the second to me. I lifted the crystal. "To a superb performance, Doktor duBoise."

Our glasses touched, and she drank.

"The wine is not bad."

That was as much of a concession to a Columbian wine as I'd get from my Francophilic soprano, and I nodded and took another sip. The Sebastopol was far better than "not bad"; it was damned good.

We made our way to the sitting room off the terrace. Llysette took the padded armchair—Louis XX style, and the only mismatched piece in the room, but my mother had liked it, and my father had thrown up his hands and shrugged his wide Dutch shoulders. The rest of the room was far more practical. I sat in the burgundy leather captain's chair, the only piece in the room that I'd brought back from Columbia City.

"Still I do not like the later Mozart."

"You did it well, very well."

"That is true, but . . ." Llysette took another long sip from her wine glass. "The later Mozart is too, too ornate, too romantic. Even Beethoven is more restrained."

"Money has always had a voice in music."

"Alas, yes." She lifted her left eyebrow. "It still talks most persuasively. Two hundred dollars—a hundred crowns—for a single song and a line on the program. I, even I, listen to such talk. It is almost what little I now make for half a month of hard work."

"Don't we all listen to that kind of money talk?" I laughed and got up to refill her glass. I leaned down and kissed her neck on the way back to my chair.

"It is sad, though. Gold, gold and patience, that is how the Hapsburgs have conquered Europe. My people, the good ones, left for New France, and the others . . ." She shrugged. "I suppose they are happy. There are no wars in Europe now."

"Of course, a third of France is ghost-ridden and uninhabitable."

"That will pass." She laughed harshly. "Ferdinand always creates the ghosts to remind his enemies of his power." Abruptly she tilted her head back and swallowed nearly all the red in one gulp. Then she looked at me. "If you please . . ."

I stood and refilled her glass. "Are you sure?"

"To relax after a performance, some time it takes. The wine helps. Even if it is not true French."

Not knowing what else to say, I answered, "You sang well."

"I did sing well. And where am I? I am singing in a cold small Dutch town in Columbia, where no one even understands what I offer, where no one can appreciate the restraint of a Fauré or the words of a Villon—"

"I do."

"You, my dear Doktor Eschbach, are as much of a refugee as I am."

She was right about that, but my refuge was at least the summer home of my youth.

I had one complete glass of the Sebastopol, and she drank the rest of the bottle. It was close to midnight before she could relax and eat some of the sweet rolls I had warmed up. I left the dishes in the sink. Most days, Marie would get them when she came, but she didn't come on weekends. I decided I would worry about dirty dishes later.

At the foot of the stairs, I kissed Llysette, and her lips were warm under mine, then suddenly cold. She stepped back. I turned around in time to see another flicker of white slip toward the terrace and then vanish.

"Someone was watching. Your ghost. That . . . I cannot take." Llysette straightened the low shawl collar of her recital dress. I tried not to leer, at least not too much. "Perhaps I will go home."

"No. Not until we know more about what happened to Miranda. We've been over that already."

"Then, tonight, I will sleep in the . . ."

"Just sleep with me. I'd feel you were safer." I glanced toward the staircase up to my bedroom.

"Just sleep?" She arched her eyebrows, as if to imply I couldn't just sleep with her.

"Just sleep," I reaffirmed with a sigh. At least, I wouldn't have to fire the steamer up and drive across to the other side of the river with the local watch running all over the township.

At the same time, I was scarcely enthused about Carolynne's appearance, but what could I say? Carolynne never spoke to me, hadn't since I was a boy, not since that mysterious conversation she had had with my mother . . . and neither would talk about it. Since I couldn't force answers from either a ghost or my mother, I still didn't know why.

CHAPTER TWO

• • •

S ince, for a nonbeliever in a believing society, the worth of any church depends on the minister, I attended the Vanderbraak Dutch Reformed Church. Father Esterhoos at least understood the need to make theology both practical and entertaining. Besides, I'd gone there when the house had been my parents' summer retreat from the heat of New Amsterdam. Now my mother lived with her younger sister Anna in Schenectady, when they weren't visiting some relative or another.

When we'd spent the night together, Llysette and I usually went to church together, perhaps because Klaus Esterhoos, unlike Philippe Hague, the college chaplain, treated us more as old members or potential converts than scarlet sinners. Who knows? He could have told the deacons that saving us was worthwhile, not that I really believed that either of us could be saved.

On Sundays, we took my steamer. Although I still kept the Stanley's thermal-electric paint polished, after more than a year the flaxen-haired children walking up the mum-lined gray stone steps to the church no longer pointed at the car as my normally bright red Stanley glided around the square toward the church. It didn't have to be red, but that was the color when I left the thermal switch off. Without the red paint, the steamer would have appeared almost boring, a staid dowager of vehicles. That didn't include the actual engine or the suspension or the extras, of course, just the smooth-lined and sedanlike appearance. Columbia City had taught me the value of misdirection, although what I'd learned had barely been enough to engineer my escape from my past and the intrigues of the Federal District with a whole skin.

That Sunday was different. I guided the Stanley across the one-lane stone bridge over the River Wijk and around the square toward the church. On the west side of the square, adjacent to the campus, was parked a single dull-gray, six-wheeled steamer, all too familiar—the kind you normally saw in Columbia or the big cities like Asten or New Amsterdam, the kind the Spazis used.

"Mother of God!"

"God had no mother, not for you, Johan, you virtuous unbeliever." Llysette's voice was dry as she straightened the dark blue cloak around her shoulders and against the chill breeze that crossed the sunlit square, ruffling leaves on the grass by the bandstand.

"That is a Spazi steamer."

"Spazis?" She shivered. "Are they—do you think they are at the church?"

"With the Spazis, who knows?" My own thoughts were scattered. The steamer had to have come from Schenectady or Asten. The Spazis had a regional headquarters on the naval base outside of Asten. The last time I'd been there was when I'd been the Subminister for Environment, to see if the ruins of a house from the failed English colony at Plymouth should have been saved under the new Historic Preservation Act. That poor colony had been doomed from the start, with the Dutch bribing the *Mayflower*'s captain to land in New Bruges, rather than Virginia, and with the plague among the Indians that had left the shore scattered with bones and the forests littered with ghosts. One of the women had jumped into the ocean and drowned, and her ghost supposedly still haunted the ruins.

I'd never understood why the Congress gave Natural Resources the historic preservation program or why the minister had decided it came under environmental protection, but you don't argue with either Congress or your minister if you want to hold your position in Columbia. I hadn't argued, not that it had helped me keep my job once newly elected Speaker Hartpence set the Congress after Minister Wattson. My background certainly hadn't helped, not with the Speaker's distrust of the intelligence community and not my not-hidden-enough background in it.

"You must know, Johan. You were in government. Aren't the Spazi government?"

"Former subministers are the last to know the plans of the Sedition Prevention and Security Service."

"Government ministers, they do not know what their own security service plans?"

"Good government ministers have to use all their contacts to discover that when they're in office. You may recall that I haven't exactly been in office anytime recently, and the Spazi aren't about to go out of their way to tell an ex-minister." And they hadn't. Since they hadn't, and since the only strange thing that had happened was Miranda's death, more than a little was rotten in the Dutch woodpile, so to speak. Simple homicides didn't trigger Spazi investigations, and that meant Miranda's death wasn't simple.

The bells ringing from the church tower forced my thoughts back to the mundane business of parking the Stanley.

Even before we reached the steps to the side entrance of the gray stone church, another couple joined us. Alois Er Recchus was more than rotund; he wore a long gray topcoat, a cravat of darker gray, and a square goatee, nearly pure white, and dwarfed the still ample figure of his wife. His suit was a rich dark brown, typically somber Dutch.

"Ah, Llysette. I heard that you sang so beautifully last night." The dean of the university, Katrinka Er Recchus, smiled broadly at us above an ornate lace collar. "I did so wish to be there, but . . . you understand. One can only be in so many places."

"The demands of higher office," I murmured politely, tipping my hat to her. Out of deference to tradition I did wear a hat to church, weddings, ceremonial occasions, and when my head was cold.

"But you would so understand, Doktor Eschbach, from your past experiences in government."

I almost missed the slight stress on the word "past." Almost, but not quite. "I find those in Vanderbraak Centre are generally far less caught up in artificiality than people in Columbia City." I accented the word "generally," and received a polite smile as she turned back to Llysette.

"I do so hope you will be able to favor us with another recital before long."

"I also, honored dean, although one must take care in ensuring the composition of a vocal program, that it is, how would you say, appropriate to the audience. I would be most pleased to know if you will be attending such a recital."

"One would hope so, with such a distinguished visiting performer." Dean Er Recchus glanced toward the growing clouds overhead. "I do hope the rain will hold off until this afternoon."

The slight emphasis on "visiting" was almost lost—almost.

We nodded and continued our progress into the church. The pews were filled with the local burghers and their spouses, all in rich browns, blacks, or an occasional deep gold that verged on brown. There were more than a few wide white collars among the women.

"That woman," murmured Llysette. "She believes herself so clever."

"All politicians do, until we learn better."

"A politician I am not."

Except she was better at it than I was. While I could recognize the interplay between the two women, one quick comment was all I had managed. Sometimes I couldn't manage that much. Perhaps that was why I had not been totally averse to the forced early retirement from the government. Still, the pension was welcome, and with the investment income from the family holdings, the scattered consulting, and the income from teaching, I was comfortable financially.

We sat down near the rear, the third pew from the back, waiting for the old organ to begin the prelude, still the recipients of covert glances from a few of the older Dutch families near the middle of the church.

I grinned at a little blonde girl who grinned back above a white-collared dress. She waved, and I returned the gesture.

"You are corrupting the young, Johan," whispered Llysette as the organ prelude began.

"I certainly hope so. You can't corrupt the old, not in New Bruges."

The prelude was a variation on Beethoven's *Ode to Joy;* at least that was what it sounded like.

I waved back to the little girl. She reminded me of Walter, although they didn't look the slightest bit alike, except for the mischief in their eyes.

"Johan." Llysette whispered again. "Are you enjoying yourself?"

"Immensely."

All good things must come to an end, unfortunately. The young matron smiled pleasantly at us and turned her daughter in the pew.

"Beloved of God, we are gathered together . . ."

I straightened and prepared to listen to Father Esterhoos.

CHAPTER THREE

• • •

After my eleven o'clock class on Monday, Environmental Economics 2A, I crossed the upper green from Smythe Hall to stop by my office before lunch.

Gertrude, a blonde zombie who worked for the university's grounds staff, was carefully clipping the dried marigolds at ground level and putting them in her basket. Snip and place, snip and place, snip and place—I stopped and watched, almost mesmerized by the dreadful and precise rhythm.

"Do you enjoy your work, Gertrude?"

"I like to work, sir." As she spoke, the continual smile remained on her clean and clear face, young looking, for all that she was probably well over thirty. Snip and place, snip and place . . .

I repressed a shiver, offered her a smile in return. "Have a good day, Gertrude."

"Every day is a good day, sir," she answered unfailingly.

Another zombie—a gray-haired man with the same cheerful smile as Gertrude's—was digging small weeds from the cracks between the walkway bricks. I smiled, but did not address him, since he was new and I did not know his name.

I stopped by my office, ignored the university mail—all circulars and announcements—dropped my leather case on my desk, and walked out into the coolness and down to Delft's, the café a half block below the eastern end of the university. The café smells like a cross between a *pâtisserie* and a coffeehouse, more French than Dutch, despite the name, and that might have been why I liked it. Dutch food is like everything else Dutch, heavy as lead bricks, if tastier.

As always, I got there before Llysette and found a table on the covered porch that overlooked the square. I was seated not all that long after the clock in the post centre rang out the noon hour. The single Spazi steamer remained in the lower car park, looming over the smaller steamers used by the locals and the few students well-off enough to afford private transportation.

The breeze swirled more leaves from the trees in the square. Several women leaving McArdles' Produce fastened their broad-brimmed hats with scarves, and Constable Gerhardt retrieved one young woman's hat with a flourish and a broad smile under his sweeping mustaches. I'd never be a good burgher. I like my hair short and my face clean, and that will always mark me as an outsider in Vanderbraak Centre, even if the house has been in the family almost a century.

While I waited for Llysette, I sipped my iced tea, something I enjoy all year round. After a year back in Vanderbraak Centre, Victor, the owner of Delft's, had condescended to make it for me, even in October. We'd see about December.

As usual, Llysette was late, and her wine waited as I started on a second iced tea. Delivering lectures is a thirsty business. I rose to seat her just as the post centre clock struck half past twelve. Monday was the only day we both had free for luncheon.

"So nice to see you this afternoon, Doktor duBoise."

"You are kind, Johan." She settled herself in the oak chair, its light finish glistening. "That Jaccardy girl stopped me. Complaining she was about her recital preview. Why do they not understand that singing is true labor? To sing, it does not just happen." Llysette carefully pushed back a strand of hair that had escaped from the tight bun she wore when she taught, piled up on top of her head to make her that much taller. She paused, took a sip of the red wine, and made a slight face.

"It's just a New Ostend wine," I reassured her. In Vanderbraak Centre, you did not have to worry—I hoped—about knowing the exact bouquet of whatever you drank. East Coast wines, even I have to admit, aren't that wonderful. But I applaud their spirit, especially given the cost of Californian or smuggled French vintages.

"That I can discern." She set the glass down for a moment, and I half wondered whether she had a lithograph strip to test for poison, but it wasn't twenty years earlier when I had had to worry about such matters.

"What have they found out about Miranda?" I asked.

"They have found little. The piano studio is closed off, and the technicians come and the technicians go." She shrugged. "The ghost, it is sometimes there, and sometimes not, but it says little. At times, when it is quiet, and when I leave the studio and it is in the hall, I can hear the screams. So I must stay in my studio or depart. It is most disturbing. Some of my students will not come." She took a sip of the wine. "Doktor Geoffries, he says that the studio may not be used for some time. It is a pity."

"How did she die?"

"She was stabbed, many times. The person who murdered her wore a large overcoat from the prop department. They found it with blood on it."

"Did they find a knife?"

"I do not know. Doktor Geoffries thinks it was a prop knife, but no one has said."

"That makes it sound like someone familiar with the building."

"One would think so."

"Still . . . there must have been two hundred people in the building. Why didn't anyone hear anything?"

"In the studio, Johan?"

"Oh." I understood. The reason they insulate all the studios is so that no one can hear students and performers practicing. So poor Miranda could have been screaming her lungs out, and no one would have heard. "It had to be someone who knew that."

"Most certainly." Her lips quirked after she sipped her wine.

I understood her expression. Although the music faculty was not large, there were still a good dozen full- and part-time professors and lecturers, and that didn't include nearly a hundred music and theatre students. It also didn't include another few hundred people around the university and Vanderbraak Centre who also knew the Music and Theatre building. Besides, anyone with a motive could have scouted the building during the week when classes were ongoing. Just wear a dark coat and cravat and walk around looking preoccupied.

"You would like?" asked Victor, appearing at Llysette's elbow and winking.

"La même, comme ça," she answered, offering him a smile but not a wink in return.

"Oui, mademoiselle," he answered, except he pronounced it "mam'selle." He turned to me. "And you, Doktor Eschbach?"

"The soup and cheese, with the shepherd's bread."

Victor bowed.

"You like Victor?" I asked after the owner had departed.

"His French is not that good, but it is a help, Johan. The others, except you, for them France is an embarrassment."

"People don't like to admit their weaknesses."

"Not for us poor French. Your government did not wish to lose a single ship to Ferdinand's submersibles. Nor one of your few precious aircraft carriers. Not in 1921. Not in 1985."

"That was after my time in service."

"You do not talk much of it." Llysette downed the rest of her glass, and Victor appeared to refill it. He also set a small salad in front of Llysette and a side plate with the shepherd's bread in front of me. Behind her back, he shook his head sadly at me, as if to say that it was a pity she did not savor the wine.

"What is there to talk about? I flew reconnaissance for several years during the time Ferdinand did nothing." My throat was dry, somehow, and I swallowed the rest of the iced tea and signaled for a third, hoping Llysette would drop the subject, but she continued as if I had never spoken.

"And the English and the Irish? What could they do? Now they must wait for the inevitable. You Columbians will wring your hands. You will talk in the League of Nations. You will not act." She took a forkful of greens and glanced toward the square, where Constable Gerhardt was admonishing a hauler for bringing his twelve-wheeler into the square, either that or for the plume of unhealthy black smoke from the steamer's burners. "His panzerwagens, they rolled down the Marne road and through Troyes, and you did nothing. Even at the gates to Versailles, nothing." Llysette sniffed.

"Speaker Colmer was not known for his love of overseas adventure, and Europe is still far away, even with the new turbojets. As for Speaker Michel . . ." I had to shrug.

"Did not the pictures—" Llysette broke off. We'd had the discussion before, and nothing we said would change the past. Finally she said, "I prefer the comfort of the dirigibles. They are less stressful on the voice."

"And far less crowded, but expensive."

"Once I would not have had to worry," she pointed out.

Victor's son set my soup in front of me and a cup of chilled consommé before Llysette. I nodded, and he departed.

"Still . . . Johan, when will you Columbians act?"

"When it is too late." I laughed, not without a bitter undertone. "We believe in letting each man go to the devil in a coffin of his own making. Or each nation."

"And women also?"

"That is becoming more popular, although some still suggest that women's coffins be made by their fathers and husbands."

"My own coffin I must make. For alas, I have no husband, and Ferdinand's regiments killed my father, old and ancient as he was."

There was little I could say to that, not at the moment. So I took a small spoonful of the soup, a properly flavorful Dutch broth. The cheese was a white New Ostend cheddar, extraordinarily sharp, the way Victor knew I liked it. I nodded at the tang, then broke off a piece of the crusty bread. Llysette took the consommé in precise spoonfuls, interspersed with the red wine.

"Johan, why is it that you showed no interest in Professor Miller? She always wished to talk with you."

I finished chewing the bread before answering. "I could not say, not exactly. But she seemed to show a certain lack of discipline. In any case, she appeared far more interested in Gerald Branston-Hay." The first part was certainly true—I couldn't say exactly why I hadn't been attracted. The second part was a polite way of saying that she was a lazy and round-bottomed widow who was required to support herself in any way she could, but who was really looking for a husband. My background and hers certainly would not have fit.

"Considering that the good Doktor Branston-Hay is thoroughly married," Llysette laughed, "you retain the manners of a public servant."

"At your service, my lady." I gave her a head bow. Like Llysette, I had wondered about Miranda's more than passing interest in Gerald Branston-Hay, as conveyed by Llysette. The man must have had some charm, although I had seen more manners than charm in my assorted conversations with him. I refrained from mentioning that I knew Llysette had spent more than a luncheon or two with him. "Professor Branston-Hay is indeed a gentleman of the old English stock." I finished my soup.

"Ah, yes. He is very polite." Llysette's voice was measurably cooler.

"And far more reserved than Professor Miller, I presume."

"She is, she was, not reserved, I think."

I glanced at my watch, my father's old Ansonia that still kept perfect time, and rose.

Llysette glanced at the clock on the post centre. "Do you not have a half hour before your two o'clock?"

"Ah, yes, dear lady, but duty calls. I must stop by the post centre before class because I must attend a meeting of the curriculum review committee after class."

"This is the committee which nothing does?"

"The very same."

"Yet you attend when nothing will be done; is this not so?"

"Absolutely. Then we can claim that we have met, and that the best course of action was to do nothing."

"Like your government."

"Exactly. Except it appears that people get killed at universities, while I cannot recall the last time a public servant was murdered, not when it was apparent. Will I see you for dinner?"

"Not this evening, Johan. I must complete previews for student juries."

"I had hoped . . ."

"You always hope, Johan. One of your best traits." She smiled.

"Thank you." I bowed and turned.

Although I had hoped that the monthly pension cheque had arrived, the only item in my postbox was a long, narrow brown envelope, the type I had seen too many of in Columbia. Of course, it had no return address. I took a deep breath and locked the box.

"Ye find anything interesting?" asked Maurice from behind the counter.

"You know better than I would. You saw it first." I grinned at the post handler. He grinned back.

I hurried back to my office, grateful for the cool breeze.

I smiled toward Gilda as I passed the front office, but she was engaged in a conversation about nouveau-Dutch painting with Andrei Salakin, and with his accent, listening alone was a full-time occupation. Once back in my office, I closed the door firmly.

Except for the clipping from the *Columbia Post-Dispatch,* the brown envelope was empty. I laid the short clipping on the desk.

Columbia (RPI)—Representative Patrice Alexander (L–MI) announced a shadow investigation into charges that the Austro-Hungarian Empire has infiltrated Columbian universities. "Through such blatantly transparent ruses as the Austro-Hungarian Cultural Foundation and the Global Research Fund, Ferdinand VI is encouraging the dissemination of pro-Hapsburg values." Congresslady Alexander also disparaged "so-called scientific research aimed at undermining traditional Columbian values." She claimed the investigation will bring to light a de facto collusion between Speaker Hartpence's "trained liberals" and Ferdinand's "pandered plunderers." Neither the Speaker nor President Armstrong was available for comment, although the president is known to have received a visit from Ambassador Schikelgruber shortly after Congresslady Alexander's announcement.

Schikelgruber, one of the few political ambassadors from the empire, was always sent to smooth things over. He was supposedly captivating and charming, and cultured. His mother had been a fair actress and his father a landscape painter.

I didn't need a detailed explanation. Schikelgruber was there to put pressure on the president to put pressure on the Congresslady, since they were of the same party, and Ralston had sent me the clipping to highlight his concerns about such "infiltration."

Ralston McGuiness was the president's special assistant for budgeting—no one special to anyone outside the Presidential Palace, just the one man who not only recognized the growing, almost tyrannical, power of the Speaker but also knew how to use the few powers of the presidency to check that power. Now he finally had a president willing to try and good old idealistic Johan, willing to offer a little observation, a little assistance.

I was beginning to wonder if my idealism were going to be my undoing. Ralston's clippings were showing an increasingly effective campaign against the Speaker, a power struggle that had so far gone unnoticed in the press but, clearly, not by the Speaker nor by the Spazi who worked for the Speaker. I folded the clipping back into the envelope and placed it in the left breast pocket of my coat, then picked up the leather folder which held the notes for my two o'clock class. Gilda was still listening patiently to Andrei when I left, but I made a point to wave and flash her a smile. She probably deserved it.

My two o'clock class, Environmental Politics 2A, was in Smythe 204, a hot room on the southwest corner of the second floor. I always had to open the windows. Peyton Farquharson taught Ecology 1-B immediately before me, and his Louisiana heritage was always clear enough by the temperature of the room. He was leaving as I entered.

"Good afternoon, Johan. Terrible business about Miranda Miller."

"Absolutely awful."

"Did you know her? Was she close to your 'friend'?"

I smiled politely, ignoring the reproof implied by his choice of words, knowing that, with his Anglican-Baptist background, he really was being as tolerant as he was able. "Llysette and Miranda were colleagues, but not what one would call close."

"And at her recital, too, I understand."

"It was upsetting. At least Llysette didn't find out until after she finished singing."

"Yes, it would be difficult to sing right after a murder. Do you have any idea how it happened?"

One of my students, Peter Paulus, nodded to me, and stepped back. I was sure he wanted to ask the reason for the low grade on his first paper. None of them were used to my requirement for short papers throughout the term. Most academics simply lectured all term, then required a single massive research project or logical proof and a final exam that was more regurgitation than thought.

"The rumor is that she was stabbed, but the watch officers did not tell me." I inclined my head. "I have a student with a problem, I can see."

"Good luck with young Paulus," concluded Farquharson. "He is inclined to inflate the magnitude of his difficulties."

"I have noticed."

I waited for Paulus, but he was scarcely bashful.

"Professor Eschbach, could I trouble you to explain this comment?" He pointed to the brief phrase I had written in the margin of his greenbook—*"Mere assertion."*

I held a sigh. "Mister Paulus." They hated my use of English formality, but it worked, at least for me. "As I have explained a number of times in the course of the past few weeks, when you make a broad assertion, you must prove it with either example, fact, or logic. You have left this statement dangling in the breeze, so to speak."

"But, Professor, it is true that Speaker Taft's failure to adequately capitalize the Environmental Subministry—"

"I know, Mister Paulus. I spent considerable time in Columbia City, and a fair amount of it supervising the Environmental Subministry. You never explain how much funding would have been adequate and why, or the actual results of such underfunding. Did you mention any programs that were reduced? Or initiatives that were canceled? You just wrote that it contributed to the rise of Speaker Hartpence's Reformed Tories. How? What demographic trends did the new Speaker tap? Did the president play a role as titular head of state? Was the environmental funding issue merely a political ploy between the two? What changes in funding have happened under the new government?"

"I see, Doktor Eschbach. Thank you." He nodded and walked to his desk in the rear of the classroom. His tone indicated that he hadn't really the faintest idea of what I meant. Someone had told him, or he had read, that the environmental funding issue had led to the fall of the Taft government, and that was that. Black or white. It was in the book, so it must be true. Never mind about why it happened, or even, heaven forbid, if it might not be true. Thank God I only had him for Environmental Politics.

But I supposed people in every country are like that. So long as the trains run on time and the lights go on when they press the switch plates, how many really understand the power base of their system? After all, who really cared that the presidency was the only remaining check on the power of the Speaker? Or that the only real tool the president had was his budget examiners and their ability to uncover blatant favoritism? Who cared that the Spazi obtained more and more real power every decade? After all, they didn't really bother most people, just those involved in treasonous acts. But when the Speaker controlled both the Congress and the Spazi, and one defined treasonous acts and the other had the right to detain and punish such acts, that power could become very disturbing, as Elspeth and I had found out when I had applied for permission for her treatment in Vienna.

By the time I had opened the windows, I was perspiring. I wiped my forehead on the soft linen handkerchief I carried mainly for that purpose and surveyed the room. About a dozen of my twenty-three students had arrived. All the men, except mister Jones, wore cravats, but not all wore jackets, and the women wore knee-length skirts or trousers. Most wore scarves.

I opened the case and took out my notes, waiting for the rest of the class or the chimes of the post centre clock. I tried not to think of the president's special assistant or the Spazi steamers, but I couldn't escape the conviction that they were both waiting for me to make some sort of mistake.

CHAPTER FOUR

• • •

Lysette had indicated rather clearly that she was tied up for the evening, although student previews would not last *that* late, but I certainly had no claim on her, not unless I wanted to formalize our relationship, and I did not feel all that comfortable about that at present. So I reclaimed the Stanley from the faculty car park as the post centre clock struck five and headed down Highland toward the square and home.

After deciding against stopping for a case of ale from McArdles', I turned past

Samaha's and pulled up at the west side of the bridge to wait for another steamer, a bulky Reo, to finish crossing. For some reason I recalled the time in London when I'd driven a steam lorry. I suppose it was the waiting. You always wait in those assignments. People think intelligence and undercover work is glamorous, but it takes a lot of patience.

Marie had left before I arrived home, as usual, but the table was set, and there was a veal pie in the oven, with a small loaf of bread and some sliced cheese. I fumbled together some lettuce, peppers, and carrots with some oil and vinegar for a salad. The table gleamed, as did the white-enameled windowsills.

I forced myself to eat slowly and not to wolf down my food. After I washed the dishes and set them in the rack, I walked into the main parlor and glanced at the videolink, then shook my head. None of the three channels available in Vander-braak Centre offered much. In fact, none of the eight in the capital offered much. I walked on into the study, wondering if I should get to work on the article I had promised the *Journal of Columbian Politics* on the reality of implementing environmental politics. After the editorial controversies over my recycling article, I was faintly surprised that they wanted another one.

In the dim light I glanced toward the difference engine. Mine was one of the newest electric-fluidic types, not the mechanical monsters that hadn't changed that much after Babbage invented them, but one of those based on Bajan designs. I never have had much of a problem with using a New French concept, not so long as the manufacturer was a solid Columbian firm, and Spykstra Information Industries, SII, is about as old-line Columbian as you can get. Of course, Bruce had added more than a few frills, both for the extra fees he got and because we went back to the old days, when he was a techie and I a mere expendable. He was smart and got out early, but for some reason he has a warm spot in his Jewish heart for me.

SII makes its machines about twice as heavy and twice as tough as they probably need to be, and that means twice as much power, and an equivalent monthly bill from NBEI, not to mention the cost of having the house rewired and breakers installed in place of the old Flemish fuses. I even had a no-flicker screen and a non-impact printer, again on recommendation from Bruce.

Under the desk, tucked right into a bracket behind the front leg, was a standard watch truncheon, a lot more effective against intruders, most of the time, than firearms. Also, you don't have to go through the license business. I still retain some occupational paranoia.

The whole system sat on a low table beside the antique Kunigser desk my father had obtained from somewhere, but from either the desk or the Babbage engine table I could see out the double eight-pane doors across the veranda and down the lawn to the sculpted hedge maze.

I still hadn't quite restored the maze, but another year might see it back close to its original condition. Gardening does help heal the past, I had found, at least sometimes.

Because I was restless and did not feel like writing, I finally opened one of the double doors and slipped out onto the veranda, so welcomingly cool in the autumn. When I had been with the government, when I had been free from assignment for several weeks, my family had enjoyed taking holidays, infrequent as such occasions had been, not only in the summer, but even in the fall. I had liked winter, but Elspeth had been a southern girl and spent her days before the fire or the big woodstove, while Waltar and I skied on the long grassy slope down toward the river. Hiking back up, to me, had even been pleasurable. Waltar would have been ready to enter college by now.

For a time I stood and watched the purple twilight drop toward black velvet above the hills across the river, watched the lights of Vanderbraak Centre blink on, some reflecting in a patch of the River Wijk. As the chill built, I realized that I did not stand on the veranda alone, that a white figure stood in the shadows closer to the house.

Slowly I sat down on the white-painted wrought-iron chair, but the floral patterns felt like they were cutting right through my trousers. So I sat on the stone wall, but Carolynne had not moved.

"Carolynne . . ."

She drifted across the stones until she stood almost by my shoulders. Her hair was in a bun, as always, and she wore what Llysette would have called a recital gown, an old-fashioned one that covered her shoulders and upper arms, the kind they still wear out in Deseret.

"You used to talk to me."

An indistinct nod was her sole response.

"I am an adult. Elspeth is dead, and so is Waltar. Whatever—however—my mother bound you, that should not hold you now."

Only the whisper of the breeze through the ancient oaks and the pines planted by the builder of the house, the English deacon, greeted my request. My father had said there was more to the story than her murder by the deacon's wife, and more to Carolynne, and that someday he would tell me. But he died in a steamer accident while I was in Columbia, at my time of troubles, and he never did. He never left a note, not that I found, but Mother had sorted through his papers.

"Please, gentle singer, why are you here? Why do you linger? Why do I dream of you?"

Just a sense of tears, perhaps three notes sung so softly that even the breeze was louder, and she vanished, leaving me alone in the twilight on the old stones of the porch. For a time longer I watched the lights of the town, and some winked out, and some winked on, just like life.

Finally, when the breeze turned even colder, I walked inside, closed the door, and went upstairs to go to bed alone.

CHAPTER FIVE

* * *

Good morning, Doktor Eschbach." Marie Rijn swept into the house with her usual smile and bustle of gray working skirts.

"Good morning, Marie. This time I do believe most of the dishes are clean, and—"

"You leave me little enough to do, Doktor Eschbach. Be on your way, and leave my work to me."

"Things are fairly clean."

"Fairly clean is not clean, Doktor." Marie insisted on re-cleaning everything until the house shone, and then, I think, she went home and did the same there. Good, clean Dutch stock.

I shrugged. Being alone for the past three years, I'd had enough time to clean up and do laundry—especially at first, in the Federal District. Even if my efforts weren't quite to Marie's standards, my houses had been clean, probably because without sisters I had learned enough growing up. Besides, after the accident and Elspeth's death, it had helped to keep busy. Yes, anything to keep busy.

"As you wish, Marie."

"And for dinner, Doktor?"

"Tonight for one. Perhaps two tomorrow night."

"Someday, will you marry the French woman?"

"I have not thought that far ahead."

"But perhaps she has." Marie gave me a sidelong look, one that warned me about scheming women preying on lonely men, as if I needed more warning. Still, Llysette had not pressed me, and she had shared my bed, offering warmth in a chill world.

Although my breath steamed in the morning air as I opened the car barn, it was measurably warmer than when I had awakened and run to the top of Deacon's Lane and along the ridge and back. The chill had been especially welcome after the run, when I had stepped up my exercises.

I tossed my leather case into the Stanley and clicked the lighter plug, then sat and waited until the warning light flicked off before backing out of the car barn onto the hard bluestone of the drive. I put on the brake, closed the car barn door, climbed back into the steamer, and turned it around before heading down the long driveway to Deacon's Lane.

In the field across the lane from the house, Benjamin's sons were harvesting the pumpkins that had grown between the last rows of corn. The squash had already come in. I waved, and Saul waved back, but Abraham didn't see me.

Most of the thin layer of frost had melted in the morning light by the time I drove across the River Wijk and stopped outside Samaha's to pick up my copy of the *Asten Post-Courier*. The sign outside the cluttered display window says that the store has been there for over a century. So had some of the inventory, but Louie— he refused to be called Louis—was the only shopkeeper left in town who had special narrow paper boxes for his customers. I do have a fondness for some traditions.

Samaha's Factorium and Emporium is dark, with wooden counters and rough-paneled walls that contain fine cracks older than any current living souls in Vanderbraak Centre. Even the modern glow panels in the ceiling do not seem to penetrate the store's history.

I walked past the bakery counter that always featured breads and rolls heavy enough to sink a dreadnought or serve as ballast for a dirigible and pulled my paper from its slot, fifth down in the first row, right below the empty slot labeled "Derkin." In the year and a half since I returned to Vanderbraak Centre, I'd never seen mister Derkin.

"Here you go, Louie." I left my dime on the counter. The *Post-Courier* was only seven cents, but the other three I had pressed on Louie on principle as a fee for saving back issues for me when I was away.

"Thanks be ye, Doktor. Have a pleasant day."

"The same to you."

The front-page story below the fold caught my eye, and I read it even before I left the store.

SAN FRANCISCO (RPI)—A fire of undetermined origin destroyed the entire Babbage center of the California Polytechnic Institution late last night, killing one professor and a night watchman. Arson is suspected, but the destruction was so thorough that it may be weeks before federal investigators can determine even where in the massive complex the fire began. The dead professor is believed to be the Babbage research coordinator, Elston Janes.

CPI has been the site of recent protests against psychic phenomena duplication studies. Webster VanBujirk, speaking for the Roman Catholic Diocese of the Pacific, denied any church involvement. "Although we have expressed grave concerns about the direction of Babbage research [at CPI], such widespread destruction is reprehensible."

Selkirk Means, Anglican-Baptist bishop of California, released a statement which claimed in part that "all devout Anglican-Baptists deplore such wanton destruction." Even so, Bishop Means added that he hoped that after rebuilding the facility the Institution would reconsider its policy of accepting federal research contracts on psychic phenomena.

The Alliance for World Peace asked Speaker Hartpence to begin an investigation into charges that the CPI research was in fact disguised Defense Ministry research. This allegation was denied immediately by the Defense Subminister for Procurement and Research.

Speaking on behalf of Minister Gore, Subminister Allard Reynard stated, "The federal research conducted at CPI was exactly as contracted. It was research of purely psychic phenomena. . . ."

I folded the paper into my case and climbed back into the Stanley for the short drive to the faculty car park. As I turned up Highland Street, the clock on the post centre struck half past eight.

Only a handful of spaces remained, but then, the car park only contained four dozen places, and twice that number of faculty lived outside of easy walking distance. The rest parked where they could, but not, of course, around the square. The parking issue almost had had Dean Er Recchus and the town elders before the magistrates, and might yet again.

I vented the Stanley before locking the doors and walked to the Natural Resources Department's offices. Gilda had not arrived, and there were only two messages in my box. One was from my esteemed chairman, the most honorable Doktor David Doniger—a reminder of the faculty meeting, on the special memo paper he used as chairman. The other was a note from the Student Affairs office that Corinne Blasefeldt would be absent because of her father's funeral. I wanted to send a note back that I would have been surprised if she had been in class, but the dean's office would not have appreciated the humor.

Once in my office, I read the *Post-Courier* from front to back, but there were no other stories related to the California Babbage center fire. The Asten Braves had finally decided to move to Atlanta as a result of falling attendance and the failure of the city fathers to allow hard liquor in the old stadium. Then again, soccer has always been a participatory sport for the Dutch, unlike the English, and Atlanta was far more English.

I read the CPI story again. Finally I dug out the student file I needed and looked up Gerald Branston-Hay's wire number in the faculty directory. I should have remembered it, but I never did. Then I picked up the handset and dialed the numbers.

"To whom do you wish to speak?"

"Gerald, this is Johan Eschbach—"

"Ah, Johan. How might I help you? Or should I ask, what might be the problem this time?"

"You know, you Babbage types always create problems." I laughed.

"So you insist." His voice was dry.

"I have a rather delicate problem with one of my advisees, a Peter Paulus. I'd rather not discuss it on the wire. Is there some time you might be free for a few moments?"

I waited.

"Ah . . . I was checking my schedule. How about eleven o'clock?"

"I am sorry, but I have a class then."

"Well . . . it's a bit short, but I could do it now. I have an appointment at ten."

"It shouldn't take that long. In ten minutes, then?"

"That would be fine."

While I did have a problem with Peter Paulus, I really wanted to talk to the good Doktor Branston-Hay again before there were any more fires of suspicious origin, particularly in the vicinity of Vanderbraak State University.

Gilda had claimed her desk by the time I headed out. Bulking over the corner of the desk in his black suit and maroon cravat was the junior member of the department, Wilhelm Mondriaan, some shirttail relative of the painter. The young Doktor Mondriaan had received his doctorate from The University—Virginia— and had yet to realize that most of us had ceased to worship unquestioningly at that altar of higher education, Thomas Jefferson notwithstanding.

"Please do not let any of the students see the exam when you duplicate them." Mondriaan attempted to cultivate a rumbling bass, but a mild baritone was all he could manage. He turned to me. "Good day, Johan. What is the festive occasion?"

I looked down. My jacket was light gray, but the cravat was a maroon brighter than normal by Dutch standards. "No special reason. I suppose I felt cheerful." I looked at Gilda. "I am headed over to the Babbage offices to see Professor Branston-Hay about a student whose problems we share. I won't likely be too long."

"Dare I guess?" she asked.

"I'd rather you did not. You might be correct."

Mondriaan frowned at my levity. He'd learn, unfortunately, that levity was often the only escape from academic insanity.

The brick-paved walkway to the additional steps up to the hillside building containing the lords of the difference engine was nearly untraveled, since it was between classes. I passed only Gregor Martin, and he scowled indifferently.

Gerald Branston-Hay was not even the department chairman, but his office was twice the size of Doktor Geoffries's—Llysette's chairman, who had a Steinbach upright in his spaces—and easily three times the size of Doktor Doniger's, although David had neither difference engines nor pianos to worry about.

More interestingly, every Babbage man or woman I knew was surrounded by stacks of paper, piles of disk cases, or pieces of hardware, or, more usually, some combination of all three. Every surface in Branston-Hay's office was always clean and had been every time I had come to see Gerald. Even my office isn't that empty, and with my government experience, I knew the danger of loose information.

He did have a modern electro-fluidic difference engine—although mine was probably close to his in capability. Both our machines probably made most recent machines look as obsolete as Babbage's original mechanical model, the one that sat unrecognized for its capabilities for nearly fifteen years after his death, until it fell into the hands of John Ericson.

"Please have a seat."

I took the chair across the desk from him and opened the file I had brought. Best to begin with the ostensible reason for my visit. It might even offer an opening. "I noticed that young Paulus received a warning in your introductory class. From what I recall, this is not a difficult course, assuming one does the work."

Gerald offered a quick smile. "While I would not characterize the course as particularly easy, virtually any student who matriculates here should be able to master enough of the material to turn in acceptable work. The reason Mister Paulus received a warning is relatively simple. He seems to be one of those few students with an inability to understand a series of logical commands. To use a difference engine requires using Babbage language or one of the newer programming systems. All are based on logic. While Mister Paulus has demonstrated the ability to memorize the structure and commands, he seems unable to fathom anything which requires either logical analysis or construction." He shrugged. "There it is, I'm afraid."

"Hmmmm," I temporized. "That would seem a serious flaw. I am surprised that it's not more widespread, in some ways."

"There are always a few students like that, but most seem able to grasp the use of logic."

"Do you suppose that . . . doctrinal background has anything to do with it?"

"Doctrinal? Oh, I suppose you're referring to the religious fundamentalists."

"They do seem to oppose logic. Did you see the *Post-Courier* this morning?"

"I haven't read it."

"Apparently some fundamentalist group burned the entire Babbage center at the California Polytechnic Institution. Didn't you do some graduate work there?"

"No. I did work with Immanuel Jobs, who now runs their program. Burned the entire Babbage center, you say? So," he mused, "I thought I heard something about that on the videolink this morning, but I really didn't pay much attention."

"One group claimed that CPI was actually doing Defense Ministry work on psychic phenomena." I shrugged. "Why is it that people want to link Babbage research with ghosting?"

"They have since before I got my doctorate." Gerald shifted his weight in his chair and looked toward the door.

I ignored his hint and went on. "We've talked about this before, but aren't most university Babbage people doing some work on the psychic side?" I waved off his objection. "I know you can't tell me exactly what you're doing because of the government contracting rules and all that. That's not what I'm talking about. But you Babbage people have both the expertise in correlating data and the most expertise in electrical fields, particularly those of a transitory or almost nontangible nature. That makes it pretty hard to avoid this sort of speculation, doesn't it?" I smiled broadly and, I hoped, in my friendliest manner.

"Johan, as you well know from your own past experience in government, people will always speculate."

"It looks like those speculations are growing, not to mention some strong objections, particularly from the Anglican-Baptists or from Deseret, to researching ghosts as transitory electrical phenomena."

"They're certainly transitory, although there seems to be some evidence that magnetic fields enhance their duration. Sellig-Ailes actually plotted ghost duration phenomena along the strongest lines of the earth's magnetic fields. The data were rather convincing." Branston-Hay shifted his weight in the chair again.

I continued to appear oblivious. "It would take a large difference engine to do that, I can see. Has anyone tried to replicate the effect with a magnetic field in a laboratory?" I watched the tightening of his face before I added, "Do you suppose they were doing something like that in California? That would certainly have upset a great number of souls." The pun was intentional, although I suspected it would be lost on Gerald.

"Unless we attempted murder in the laboratory, which no one in his right mind would do, Johan, it would be rather difficult to study a ghost here or in any Babbage center. Ghosts don't just appear at will in our laboratories. That's one of the reasons studying them is so difficult and why so many projects work on simulations—I mean simulations of ghost behavior, not simulations of ghosts," he added hastily.

"Of course." I laughed. "I didn't mean that." I stood. "I really didn't mean to go off like that, but when you mentioned logic I thought of the religious types and the mess in California." I shrugged, then bowed. "I appreciate your clarifying Mister Paulus's problem. I must confess that I had a similar experience with the young man, but I had thought it was more related to stubbornness than to logic."

"I have also found Mister Paulus stubborn." Branston-Hay stood up. "Lack of logic and stubbornness often go together, often, as we have discussed, even within the government of the Republic."

"So right. So right." I nodded. "Perhaps at some point we should have lunch."

"I would like that."

"So would I. Thank you again for the explanation about Mister Paulus." I nodded again and left, offering yet another nod to the clerk in the outer office, a square-faced older woman in the somber hues of brown that declared her Dutch origins more surely than a sign painted on her forehead could have. She reminded me of the government clerks in Columbia City. Her nod was barely more than perfunctory, but I bestowed a broad smile on her before I headed back toward my office.

The smile I bestowed on Gertrude, cheerfully sweeping the steps down to the middle of the campus, was more genuine. I even smiled at Hector, who is one of the few somber zombies I've seen. Surprisingly, he smiled back.

I was still wondering about the smile when I entered the department offices and Gilda gestured at me. "Doktor Eschbach?"

"Yes?"

"Someone called from a Deputy Minister vanBecton's office." After a glance at David's closed door, Gilda grinned at me from her desk. "They asked for Subminister Eschbach. I told them that we had a very distinguished Herr Doktor Professor Eschbach."

"You can't really add all those honorifics together."

"I know, but I hate government, and the clerk who placed the call was snooty." Gilda extended a piece of paper.

"Most federals are, even down to the clerks." The name on the paper was Gillaume vanBecton, and the number on the paper was a federal exchange. I didn't recognize the name, not that I would. When Speaker Hartpence had been elected, he'd removed all the old ministerial appointees, and I had recognized very few of the new names then. Two years later, especially after Waltar's and Elspeth's deaths, I recognized even fewer. Unfortunately, I did recognize the number, and I tried not to sigh. "I'll return the call."

"I'll place it for you." Gilda grinned again, and I returned the grin, since we both knew it was returning snobbery with snobbery. Still, I'm petty enough to be able to enjoy that and was grateful to Gilda for offering, since I never would have asked. And it was better that she place the call, rather than have me retreat to my office, if the message were what I thought it might be.

She picked up the headset and dialed. I waited.

"This is Doktor Eschbach's office, returning a call from a Herr vanBecton." Gilda raised both eyebrows. "Just a moment." She looked at me. "They're connecting him."

"I'll get it in my office. That way I won't tie up your wire."

By the time I lifted my handset, Gilda was saying, "Just a moment, Minister vanBecton."

"I have it, Gilda. Johan Eschbach here. I understand you had called."

"Bill vanBecton here. I do appreciate your prompt return of my call, Doktor Eschbach." At that point, there was a click as Gilda left the wire. "I regret the necessity of the call, but I was hoping you could pay me a visit here within the next few days. The return of the prodigal son is a mixed blessing."

I stiffened at the deadly words recalling me to service, but only said, "Mixed indeed. I could be there on Friday afternoon."

"That would be more than adequate. Call it a consulting assignment based on past services. Of course, as in the past, we will pay your daily fee and expenses, and a bonus upon completion of your work."

"I thought I recognized the number."

"If so, you'll know my office. I look forward to seeing you on Friday."

"And I you. Good day, Minister vanBecton."

"To you also, Doktor Eschbach."

I set down the handset slowly and looked out into the graying skies and swirling leaves. Being recalled to service in the Spazi was scarcely what I had expected. While it was technically possible, I'd never heard of it happening before. And why now? Were Congresslady Alexander's charges of Austro-Hungarian infiltration correct? Or did vanBecton know of my work for Ralston?

I took a deep breath as the leaves swirled beneath me on the green. Nothing was ever simple, and nothing ever ended. I took another deep breath.

CHAPTER SIX

● ● ●

Wednesday started like Tuesday, with a smiling Marie Rijn.

"Today I intend to wash and press the curtains, Doktor. They're dusty, and the windowsills are a disgrace. You may be neat, but . . ."

The implication was that I wasn't clean enough, and that the white lace curtains—did any truly Dutch residence have anything besides shimmering white lace curtains?—weren't either.

"I do appreciate it, Marie."

"I know, Doktor. Long hours you work and there being no family to be as clean as it should be . . ."

I nodded and searched out my overcoat, leaving the house to her.

The day was gray and windy. I didn't see mister Derkin at Samaha's, not that I probably ever would, and I did get to my office early.

After reading and discarding David's rewriting of the minutes of the last faculty meeting, I picked up the wireset and tried to reach Llysette. She answered neither her home number nor her office extension. Perhaps she was in class, although she usually managed to avoid teaching before nine-thirty.

I rummaged through my case and laid out a draft of the test for Environmental Economics. Was the question on infrastructures too broad? Would they really understand—There was a rap on the door.

"Johan?" Young Grimaldi stood in the door of my office. In his European-cut suits he was always chipper, and I suppose I would be too with that much money, even if his family had been forced to flee from Ferdinand. "Do you have a moment?"

"Almost an hour, if you need it." I grinned. "What's on your mind?"

He slipped into the hard chair across the desk from me with that aristocratic elegance. "They reopened Monte Carlo—the casino."

"Ferdinand did? When?"

"Sometime last week. There's always some delay in the news coming out of the Empire."

"At times I have thought it would be nice if our reporters had some delays imposed. Then a lot of trash wouldn't make it to print."

He looked appalled. So I added, "I don't mean Ferdinand's kind of censorship—just delays. Does it really matter whether an aging movie star like Ann Frances Davis could never forget her one great love, an obscure football announcer named Dutch? Or whether Emelia vanDusen is going to wed Hans van Rijssen Broekhuysen and unite the two largest fortunes in New Amsterdam?" I took a deep breath. "The reopening bothers you?"

"It shouldn't. I've lived almost half my life in Columbia." He glanced toward the window and the gray clouds before continuing. "Sometimes, Johan . . ." He offered a self-deprecating grin. "It would be easier to forget the past."

I understood, although I didn't know that he knew that. "Sometimes . . . but without the past we wouldn't be who we are."

"I suppose. And I suppose that things could be worse."

"There is always the issue of progress," I offered.

He frowned. "Do you really think the world is a better place now? That progress in technology has meant anything more than better ways to kill?"

"Medicine is better. Women don't die in childbirth, and that makes for happier homes with fewer tormented ghosts."

"It also makes for bigger battles with fewer ghosts to remind us of the horrors of war."

"That's true enough. On the other hand, we don't see civil wars in the Balkans. There aren't any pogroms in the Polish and German parts of the Empire. The Greeks stopped killing the Turks generations ago—"

"That's probably because Ferdinand's father killed most of the Greeks, like his grandfather killed off most of the Serbs." Grimaldi snorted. "And that left the Croats with all the land."

I shrugged. "Some rivalries only end when one group is exterminated."

"You approve of genocide?"

"I didn't say that." I forced a laugh. "I have noticed, however, that peace among human beings tends to exist only as a condition of some sort of force, and some groups seem destined to fight forever—like the Irish and the Brits, or the Copts and the Muslims."

"Or Japan and Chung Kuo? That could get nasty—maybe nastier than Ferdinand's March to the Sea—although I don't see how."

"Don't say that. From what Llysette has told me, it was pretty horrible." I paused. "Still, things can be horrible anywhere. DeGaulle's efforts to push New France's boundaries right up to the Panama Canal haven't been exactly bloodless, and the Panamanian Protectorate is effectively a Spazi police state."

At the mention of the Spazi, Grimaldi glanced toward the open door.

"I've said far worse." Still, I changed the subject. "You said that the story about the casino upset you."

"I don't know," Grimaldi mused. "The story about the casino—I can recall running for the dirigible, and hearing the roar of the panzerwagens. My father never opposed Ferdinand. He even offered to accept an Austro-Hungarian protectorate. Ferdinand didn't even bother to respond. The armored divisions just poured out of San Remo. What could President Bourbon-Philippe do? The Spanish had already caved in, and Columbia . . ." Grimaldi shook his head.

"I'm sorry."

He laughed harshly. "There's not much you can do, Johan. Not more than fifteen years later. At least they had to wait almost twenty years for my father's ghost to fade."

There wasn't too much I could say about that. So I nodded.

"Everything's so quiet—here or in what remains of France. So clean, so efficient. Even Ferdinand's gas ovens are environmentally safe—except to the Gypsies and the outspoken Jews. Everyone just goes to sleep and doesn't wake up. It's a hell of a quietly efficient and environmentally sound world, Johan." He looked at me. "Why did you leave the government?"

"It got harder and harder to do my job. Let's leave it at that."

"I think I understand." He shook his head and stood up. "Time to face the well-groomed and empty-minded masses."

"All young in any culture tend to be empty-minded," I pointed out. "I suspect we were."

"We were probably happier then." He gestured from the door and was gone.

I looked at the test for a while, made some corrections, and packed up my leather folder for my first class.

As I walked across the green, absently waving to Hector, bagging leaves in a dun-gray canvas bag, I wondered how many people like Grimaldi and Llysette were tucked away in the back corners of Columbia, unable to protest for fear of losing their last sanctuary. Even I had looked to the door at the mention of the Spazi.

The wind, almost warm, blew through my hair, but I shivered anyway.

CHAPTER SEVEN

• • •

Miranda's memorial service was on Thursday afternoon at four o'clock. When I had talked to Llysette on the wire in the morning, after trying to reach her for nearly two days, she had indicated she would not be free until close to dinnertime. She had been almost curt, with a student waiting. So I had called Marie on the wire and told her not to prepare anything for dinner.

I had also refrained from telling Llysette about the trip to Columbia and decided to go to Miranda's service alone. The watch had released no information on Miranda's murder besides a perfunctory statement on continuing the investigation, but after vanBecton's call, it was clear I was going to be involved through more than mere curiosity.

Following my two o'clock class, I put on a black armband I had dug out of my armoire that morning. From the office I headed to the Bank of New Bruges to deposit the errant pension cheque that had arrived on Wednesday, and then I walked down to the small Anglican-Baptist chapel two blocks off the main square. No one saw the mourning band because it continued to drizzle and I wore my camel waterproof. I've never liked umbrellas, perhaps because they tied up one hand, and in the past that could have been a real problem.

After slipping in the side door at a quarter before the hour, I sat near the rear of the church on the right-hand side. I eased out of the waterproof as soon as I sat down because, despite the drizzle, the day was warm for mid-October. Watching as people drifted slowly into the small church, I was not entirely surprised to see Llysette. She wore dark blue flared silk trousers and a white blouse with a loose blue vest that matched her trousers. She carried an umbrella, but had not worn a coat. She entered through the main door, carefully closed the umbrella, and sat halfway back. I bent down to check my boots before she looked in my direction.

The pipe organ began with something suitably somber, and a young and clean-shaven man and a woman walked down the aisle and sat in the front pew on the right. Presumably he was one of Miranda's sons, and she was his wife. They both wore black, and she had a heavy veil.

Behind them, on both sides of the aisle, were a number of people from the university, including Doktor Dierk Geoffries and his wife Annette; Samuel Dortmund, the brass instructor; Wilhelm Mondriaan; and Johanna Vonderhaus. I didn't quite understand why Mondriaan was there, except as a matter of courtesy, and he did have the Dutch penchant for courtesy—not to mention the somber clothes that fit in so well in mourning situations.

The crowd was small, less than a hundred souls, not even half filling the small chapel, and the faint scent of perfume was overwhelmed by the pervading odor of damp stone.

Philippe Hague, the college chaplain, stood up to conduct the service, although he was of the Dutch Reformed persuasion.

"In God is our salvation and our glory; the rock of our strength, and our refuge, is in God. Praise be to the Lord, for our world, our souls, and our salvation. Let us pray. . . ."

Although the liturgy was not exactly familiar, I opened the book, found the words, and bowed my head with the rest.

The service was standard, commending the soul of the dear departed to the care of a merciful God, praying that God would cause her murderer to repent of his sins, and saying what a wonderful person Miranda Miller had been. No one mentioned that she had been somewhat tight, even by old Dutch standards, but I did find out that she had been widowed young. Her husband had died in the confusing mess that had marked the abortive Columbian intervention in the rape of Singapore by the Chinese.

Good Chaplain Hague did not call the incident by any of the commonly accepted terms, instead characterizing it as "that sadly unfortunate involvement" in Asian affairs. Maybe that was symptomatic of the reasons I casually detested him. We might be too weak to get involved on the far side of the Pacific, especially with the limited range of our electric submersibles and the lack of fuel depots for our handful of aircraft carriers, but the only thing unfortunate about our attempt to forestall Chung Kuo's annexation of Malaysia was our inability to stop the Chinese. Of course, we hadn't been able to stop the Japanese from taking over half the islands in Southeast Asia, either, and the Philippines seemed likely to fall any day. Since we'd left them to the Aussies as a protectorate after taking over Cuba in the Spanish-American War—no one had wanted American ghosts in faraway Asia back then—it wasn't a Columbian problem.

Philippe seemed to think that pacifism was a workable philosophy. Ghosting may have reduced conquest, but it has never stopped it. In fact, I suspect ghosts gave a slight but significant advantage to nations with policies of accretion, or small conquests.

The eulogy was all too long. When the time came I hoped mine would be shorter, or nonexistent. That Miranda deserved better than being murdered didn't excuse gross beatification of what had seemed to me a small personality.

I slipped from the pew just before the final blessing and out into the heavier rain. I got wet, of course, because I didn't try to put on my waterproof before I went outside.

After waving to the fresh-faced watch officer who had known all about ghosting and shouldn't have, I sloshed back up to the department offices to check my box for messages. Even the main door was locked, and everyone had left. So I used my key. There weren't any messages, except for a note from David Doniger, as chairman, requesting that we keep photoduplication to an absolute minimum in view of the energy costs to the department and to ensure the department set a good example. Why hadn't he just brought it up in the departmental meeting?

I left David's pedantic sermon in my box and locked the main door behind me. Then I trudged back across the south green to the steps to the Music and Theatre Department and along the corridor. Unlike the Department of Natural Resources, the building was filled with people. Sometimes I wondered how the music professors ever got the reputation of laziness. They worked longer than almost anyone else, except maybe the poor library staff, and they got paid less.

Martha Philips was still at her desk in the main departmental office. I stepped inside.

"Martha."

"Doktor Eschbach, Llysette is in her studio." Martha was stolid, square, open, and seemed honest.

"I think I'm early." I glanced at the wall clock. "I saw Doktor Geoffries at the memorial service. How is he taking this?"

"We are all in shock, I think. You read about murders in Asten or New Amsterdam, but they are cities. You don't think it could happen here."

"I know. It must make things hard for Dierk."

"You don't know how hard. Between Doktor Branston-Hay and the watch, and Miranda's ghost—sometimes it—she—drifts by here, but she never stays, and all she says is something about not listening and screaming no. It must be hard on Llysette, because her office is one of the closer ones, but at least it never enters her studio. One of her students ran off screaming yesterday."

"That must have upset Dierk."

"It upset everyone."

"I can see. Has the watch said anything about coming close to a suspect?"

"Not to any of us. The way they keep asking questions, I don't think they know."

I shrugged and glanced at the clock. Martha smiled, and I headed out of the main office and down the hall. Before I went to Llysette's office, I turned toward the piano studio. The glow strips outside the studio were off, and the hall was dim there, almost gloomy. I stopped when I saw the video camera mounted and trained on the padlocked door.

I retraced my steps and took the outside doorway, then walked along the wall of the building until I could look in the studio window. Despite the dimness, I could see the covering on the piano—and what looked to be a Babbage console, a small video camera, and a cable running between them. I wasn't sure, but I thought I saw a flicker of white, but I kept walking. A ghost and now Babbage engines connected with the ghost? Just what else was Gerald hiding?

When I reentered the building, I made my way back to Llysette's studio, where, by placing my ear against the door, I could barely hear the piano and her voice. After she came to a break, I opened the door.

Llysette lifted her hands from her studio piano when she saw me inside the door. "Johan . . . I did not expect you here . . . so soon."

"I went to Miranda's memorial service," I said.

"I also. She had few true friends, I think." Llysette frowned. "I did not see you there."

"I was in the back. Philippe was not all that eloquent."

"He did not seem so." She cleared her throat before asking, "And why are you here?"

"Because time is short." I smiled. "An old client called me up and offered me a consulting job. I must go to Columbia tomorrow morning."

"You did not tell me this morning. I had thought . . ."

I tried to smile apologetically. "You sounded so rushed, as if you wanted me off the wire, and you said you would not be free until now. If I had known, we could have gone to the service together."

"Ah, yes. That I would have liked. I knew so few there."

"I thought we might at least have dinner."

"But then, then you must drive back . . ."

"You at least deserve a dinner at Cipoletto's."

"Johan, the food, it is good, but it is not . . ."

"I understand. But I am tired, and so are you, and we do require some form of bodily sustenance, even a little luxury. I could follow you home. That way you could leave your steamer, and we would only take one."

For a moment her green eyes were hard, as if she were looking straight through me. I smiled apologetically once more and waited.

"Ah, well, it is not as though we were children. I will be but a moment."

She began to pick up music and stack it on the old wooden desk in the corner. Her office was really a studio, with the old Steinbach in one corner and bookcases on the inside wall. The glass in the three windows was all graying, except for the two panes that had clearly been replaced recently. The hardwood floors sagged slightly, even after last year's refinishing. A rag rug beside the piano added a touch of warmth, but it should have, since I'd offered it to her when I'd turned the old parlor into my study.

"I am ready." Llysette carried her coat over her arm.

"No music? No umbrella?"

"The umbrella, if I do not keep it here," she lifted her shoulders and dropped them, "then I do not have it when most I need it."

The rain had diminished to a scattering of droplets by the time we emerged through the side door and walked up to the car park. She climbed into the tiny Reo runabout. As usual, she didn't wait long enough for the steam pressure to build fully, and the Reo lurched out onto Highland Street.

I followed Llysette up Highland and out old Hebron Road until we reached the stone-walled and white-windowed cottage she rented. As in almost every other Dutch-owned house, the front windows showed lace curtains. She put the Reo almost right in front of the porch.

I set the brake and stepped out onto the damp packed clay. "Do you need anything?"

"A moment I will just be." She was already unlocking the door.

"I'll just wait here." Somehow Llysette's cottage depressed me. It was neat, although she had a tendency to stack her music in piles. Perhaps it was just that it was so modest, so little, really, for a woman who could have been a great diva in old France, had Ferdinand not annexed it.

The top branches of great oaks behind the cottage waved gently in the wind, barely visible in the growing darkness, and a few more droplets caressed my face as I waited and watched. Llysette left on the porch glows.

"Voilà—I am not long."

"Not long at all."

I held the Stanley's door open for Llysette, then closed it and walked around and climbed in myself. As I turned back onto the old Hebron Road toward Vanderbraak Centre, I asked, "Have any of the watch been back to talk to you?"

"Yesterday, the young one, he stopped by to ask a few questions."

"About you, or about Miranda?"

"First, about where she lived he must know. Then about her working hours he wanted to know. Then he asked why Professor Miller was working late on a Saturday."

"Did you know why she was there? That does seem strange." I edged the steamer to the right edge of the road to avoid a fast-moving Williams that was taking the big turn too fast.

"They should not travel so quickly."

"Not on wet roads. Did you know where she lived?" I prompted after I turned back onto Highland.

"I did not know where she lived. And as I have told most, the hours she worked were . . ." Llysette shrugged. "They were not terribly long. I told the watch officer I did not know why Professor Miller was there that night."

After another silence, I turned right at the edge of the square and continued past the Anglican-Baptist chapel toward the south end of town.

"Perhaps she was waiting for someone?" I eased the throttle down as we neared the edge of Vanderbraak Centre and the bend in the river where Cipoletto's overlooked the weirs. Only a handful of steamers were parked outside the restaurant, but it was early for the college types and late for the burghers.

"How would one know?" Llysette pointed out reasonably. "If one had meant to meet Professor Miller . . ." She shrugged again.

"Then that person either killed Miranda or would be afraid to admit the meeting because of being accused of the murder." I pulled up beside another Williams, this one a racing model that few in New Bruges could afford and fewer still would want.

"This is most kind of you, Johan," she said as I helped her out of the Stanley. "You do not need to pack?"

"It's a one-day trip, perhaps an overnight. Clients never like to pay extra, and I'm certainly not in the mood to pay federal city prices." I offered my arm, which she took, and we crossed the brick-paved courtyard with the light wind flicking the faint odor of woodsmoke around us. I held the door for her.

"You have not a good opinion of your capital city?"

We stopped by the raised table where Angelo waited with his book and list of reservations.

"Not of its prices." I nodded to Angelo. "Two, in the red room." The red room was for nonsmokers.

"Doktor Eschbach, of course. I even have the table where you can see the river." He bowed, and I nodded back.

"You would like some wine? Red or white?" I asked as we walked through the main room toward the small corner red room.

"White, I think."

Angelo gestured to the table set in the bay window. A brass lamp cast a flickering light over the red tablecloth. He pulled out Llysette's chair.

"A bottle of your house white, Angelo, if you would."

"Of course, Doktor Eschbach." He smiled, and gestured to the slate propped on the stand against the wall. "Tonight's fare."

In the flickering lamplight, we studied the slate.

"Fettucini alfredo again?"

Llysette pursed her lips. "I think the pasta primavera."

"Then I will have the fettucini."

Angelo returned with a green-tinted bottle. I did not recognize the label, but it was from California, and most of his wines were good. So I nodded, and waited for him to pour some into the glass. I sniffed, and then tasted. "Good."

He filled both our glasses and set the bottle in the holder by my elbow.

I raised my glass, and Llysette followed. The rims of our glasses touched, and we drank from our glasses without speaking.

A waiter I did not know appeared. "Have you decided, sir and lady?"

"The pasta primavera, with the tomato rice soup," said Llysette.

"I'll have the fettucini alfredo with the barley soup. Two of the small salads with the house dressing."

Llysette nodded in confirmation.

After the waiter left, I took another sip of the white. I liked it. So I looked at the label—San Merino. While I was looking, Llysette finished her glass, and I refilled it.

"I saw Miranda's ghost," I volunteered.

"This ghost you saw recently?"

"No. I meant the night she was killed."

The waiter placed warm cranberry rolls on the butter plates and set our soups before us.

Llysette took another solid sip of the San Merino. "You did not tell the watch." She lifted her soup spoon.

"I walked out of my office, and there she was. She mumbled some meaningless phrases, and then she was gone." I tried the barley soup—hot and tangy with a hint of pepper and basil, an oddly pleasing combination.

"That woman, always was she talking meaningless phrases."

"How is your soup?"

"*Comme ci, comme ça.* Less of the tomato, I think, would be better. How do you find yours?"

"Quite good. Would you like a taste?"

She inclined her head, and I held the bowl so she could try the barley soup.

"Better than the tomato," she confirmed. "You should see."

I tried hers, and she was right. The barley soup was better, fuller. I broke off a corner of the cranberry roll, still almost steaming, then finished my soup.

"I really never knew Miranda," I said, after the waiter removed the soup bowls. "Was she always talking nonsense?"

"Nonsense, I would not say. She always repeated the small . . . the trivial. One time, she spoke at a meeting four times about the need to revoice the concert Steinbach. And Doktor Geoffries, he had agreed to approach the dean for the necessary funds after she spoke the first time." Llysette finished her second glass of the white. My glass remained about half full, but I refilled hers.

I frowned. "Did she keep confidences?"

"Confidences?"

"Secrets. If you asked her not to repeat something . . ."

"*Mais non.* A tale she knew, everyone knew."

"Still, it is very sad."

"Very sad," Llysette agreed.

The waiter arrived with our pasta, and another cranberry roll for me. Llysette had scarcely touched her roll.

The fettucini alfredo, especially with the fresh-ground Parmesan, had that slight tang that subtly lifted it above the mere combination of cheese, cream, garlic, and pasta.

"How is the primavera?"

"It is good. You would like a little?"

"If you could spare it."

"I eat all of this, and into no recital gown will I fit."

I didn't have a witty response. Instead I leaned over and tasted some of her dinner. The primavera was as good as the fettucini, but you expected that when you paid Angelo's prices.

"It is good," I said. "Would you like some of the alfredo?"

"*Non.* I will not finish what I have."

Several minutes passed before Llysette wiped her mouth on the red linen napkin and took a swallow of her wine. Then, glass still in her hand, she asked, "Johan, what was it—did you miss something the most when you left the capital?" Her eyes were thoughtful.

I finished a small sip of my own wine before answering. "Most times, when you leave a place, you do miss things, especially at first. I thought I might miss things like the museums, or that something was always happening. At first, I missed the newspapers. I missed the up-to-date radio and even the stuffy television news. But I noticed something after a while. I started missing items in the news, and nothing changed. I mean, the names change, but the problems continue, and they go on and on." I shrugged. "What do you miss about France?" I grinned. "The food?"

"Ah, yes, the food I miss." Her eyes clouded for a moment, and she swallowed more wine.

"Or the singing, the culture?" I prodded gently.

"Johan, you understand . . . and still . . . you are here. She shook her head. "That I do not understand."

"There is little more culture in the Federal District of Columbia than here in Vanderbraak Centre. The most popular play at Ford's Theatre is the updated revival of *The Importance of Being Earnest*. The most popular classical music is either Beethoven's Ninth or the *1812 Overture*. Yes, there is more to choose from, but given the choice . . ." I let the words drop off.

She finished her wine, and I poured the last of the San Merino into her glass.

"You sing better work than often appears in Columbia."

"And yet, I am here, forced to teach spoiled Dutch burghers who believe one note is much the same as another."

After looking at the remainder of the fettucini, I nodded to the waiter, who removed both plates.

"Some coffee?"

Llysette shook her head.

"Perhaps a brandy?" I asked.

"Not this evening, Johan. Perhaps we should go. You must rise early."

"The check, please?" I beckoned, and the waiter nodded. He returned as Llysette drained the last of the wine.

I left a twenty and a five, and we walked to the front, past a scattering of couples in the main room.

"How was the dinner?" Angelo stood by the door as we left.

"Very good, as usual. The barley soup—I'd like to see that more often. And," I winked at Llysette, "perhaps a shade less tomato in the tomato rice potage."

"What can I say, Doktor? Your taste in wine, women, and food is impeccable."

"The lady is even more discriminating in wine and food, but more tolerant in men, thankfully." I nodded.

Angelo bowed to Llysette.

Once we were in the courtyard, Llysette glanced back toward the restaurant, and then toward me. "Here, no one believes a woman has taste—except you."

"That's because few men or women have taste."

"Johan, sometimes you are more jaded than I."

"Only sometimes?" I helped her into the steamer.

A light rain began to patter on the roof of the Stanley as I drove back out the old Hebron Road to Llysette's cottage. Her tiny Reo runabout was still parked in front of the porch, and her trousers got damp when we scurried up to the front door, despite my trying to keep the umbrella over her.

"Thank you for the evening, Johan."

"Thank you."

I bent down and kissed her. Her lips were warm, welcoming, but not quite yielding. I did not even suggest I should come in. The next morning, I knew, would come all too early, and I had an hour-and-a-half drive westward to the Blauwasser River to catch the train in Lebanon.

"Good night, dear lady."

"Good night, Johan."

I stepped back into the rain, and to the Stanley, but I waited until she was inside before I pulled out of the graveled drive and onto the road back to Vanderbraak Centre.

CHAPTER EIGHT

• • •

I caught the early-morning Quebec Express in Lebanon and took it into New Amsterdam, and then the Columbia Special from there to the capital—the Baltimore and Potomac station just off the new Mall. Even with stops, it took only a bit over six hours, and the sun was still high in the autumn sky when I stepped into the heat and looked toward the marble obelisk on the edge of the Potomac.

I still couldn't believe that they'd finally finished the Washington Monument after more than a century of dithering. Now they were talking about a memorial to Jefferson, but the Negroes were protesting, especially Senator Beltonson, because they said Jefferson had been a slave owner, not that there had really been that many slaves after the horrors of the *Sally Wright* incident. Speaker Calhoun's compromise had effectively led the way to civil rights for the Negroes, and Senator Lincoln's Codification of the Rights of Man had set an amended compromise in solid law. Personally, I still thought Jefferson had been a great man. You have to judge people by the times they lived in, not the times you live in.

The same drizzle that had enveloped New Bruges the day before had reached the Federal District of Columbia, except it was warmer, steamier, unseasonably hot, even in the former swamp that was the Republic's capital.

I wiped my forehead on the cotton handkerchief, sweating more than I would have liked. At least I didn't have to go to the congressional offices. Electric fans were their sole official source of cooling; only the White House was fully air-conditioned. That had been one of Speaker Roosevelt's decisions—that air conditioning would only make the Congress want to spend more time than was wise in Columbia.

As ceremonial head of state, of course, the president was obliged to stay whether he liked it or not. So he got the air conditioning, and so did the rococo monstrosity that housed his budget examiners. His budget reviews and public criticisms were about the only real substantive powers the president had. I had seen a lot done with budget reviews, and members of Congress didn't like to seem ridiculous.

As for the heat, the Congress made do with fans or left Washington, and the civil servants sweated. Of course, ministers did find ways to cool their individual offices, but no one talked much about it, so long as they spent their own money. In the 1930s, Speaker Roosevelt had also insisted that the growth of the various ministries would be restricted by the heat. I hadn't seen that—only a lot of sweating civil servants. Anyway, how could one imagine a government much larger than the half million or so on the federals' dole?

I hailed an electrocab outside the station. "A dollar extra for a single ride."

"The single is yours, sir." The driver opened the door. "Where to?"

"The Ministry of Natural Resources, Sixteenth Street door, north end."

We passed the new Smithsonian Gallery—Dutch Masters—built to contain the collection of Hendrik, the Grand Duke of Holland. At least he had been Grand Duke until Ferdinand VI's armies had swept across the Low Countries.

Columbian Dutch, the oil people, had paid for the building. The Congress had approved it over my objections to the design—heavy-walled marble, stolid and apparently strong enough to withstand the newest Krupp tanks, even the kinds the Congress had shipped to the Brits and the Irish to discourage Ferdinand from attempting some sort of cross-channel adventure. Not that a gross of metal monsters had ever stopped any would-be conqueror.

Besides, Ferdinand was through with conquests. The Austro-Hungarian empire was nothing if not patient. England would not fall until Ferdinand VII took the throne. By then, most of the ghosts in France would have departed, and the remaining French would be dutiful citizens of the Empire, happy with their taxes and the longest period of peace and prosperity in their history—bought only at the cost of thirty percent of their former population.

Ghosting worked both ways—but basically too many ghosts hurt the locale where they were created. That was why ghosts almost stopped William the Unfortunate's conquest of England, but not the Vikings or the early Mongols. They also stopped a lot of murders and slowed early population growth—second wives didn't take too well to a weeping female ghost who had died in childbirth.

I was probably being too cautious, but strange wire messages recalling former agents to duty and promising stranger assignments have a tendency to reintroduce occupational paranoia all too quickly. I could feel my chest tighten even as I thought about it.

"Here you be, sir."

I nodded and handed him two dollars and a silver half-dollar.

"Thank *you,* sir."

After offering my identification card to the guard—I'd never surrendered it—I walked to the corner of the building and took the steps to the basement, and then those to the subbasement. A guard sat at the usual desk around the bend in the tunnel.

"Your business, sir?"

He wasn't a problem, but the armed sentry in the box behind him was.

"Doktor Eschbach. I'm here to see Subminister vanBecton."

He picked up the handset, and I waited.

"You are expected, Doktor."

I nodded again and walked down the tunnel under Sixteenth Street until I came out in the subbasement of the Spazi building. Another set of guards studied me flatly, but I just nodded. They were there to keep people from leaving, not entering. Officially, it was called the Security Service building, but it was still the Spazi building, with the flat gray ceramic tiles and light-blond wood paneling designed to hide the darkness behind each door. The smell of disinfectant was particularly strong in the subbasement.

VanBecton's office was on the fourth floor. I walked up, in keeping with my recent resolve to improve my conditioning, but I was still panting, and stopped a moment on the landing to catch my breath. Even on the fourth floor I could smell disinfectant, common to jails and security services the world over.

The disinfectant odor vanished when I opened the landing door and stepped onto the dark rust carpet on the corridor leading to his office in the middle of the floor. Corner offices, for all their vaunted views, are too exposed.

His clerk, though young, had a narrow pinched face under wire-rimmed glasses, and presided over a large wireline console. "Might I help you?" Her eyes flickered to the bearded man in the loud brown tweeds perched on one end of the leather settee. The bearded man glanced at me impassively.

I extended a card to the clerk. There was no sense in announcing my name unnecessarily. "Minister vanBecton invited me for a meeting."

"Yes, Doktor." She picked up one of the handsets and dialed. "The doktor has arrived." She listened for a moment, then added, "Yes, sir."

I smiled pleasantly as she turned toward the bearded man. "Your meeting may be delayed slightly, sir."

The other's eyes narrowed slightly, but he nodded. I returned the nod.

"Doktor, it may be a moment. If you would be so kind . . ."

"Thank you." I took the straight-backed chair in front of the dark mahogany bookcases. I picked up the Friday *Columbia Post-Dispatch,* since the fellow in brown

English tweeds clearly had either read it or had no interest in doing so. There was another story on religious protests against psychic research, and more speculation about the full extent of Defense Ministry funding of such projects. I also enjoyed the story which speculated that Senator Hartpence's private office in the Capitol had seen some very private uses, and which suggested that, improper as such uses might have been, a politician's private life remained his own. How could it not be? Then again, perhaps even the mention of the incident might be a disturbing trend. Would the masses decide that they would buy more newspapers if such tidbits were more frequent?

"Doktor? Minister vanBecton will see you."

She opened the door in the blond-paneled wall to her left, but did not enter, and closed it behind me.

The office was almost the same, except that vanBecton had added an Escher oil in place of the copy of the *Night Watch*. It looked like an original, not that it surprised me much.

"Good afternoon, Doktor Eschbach." The man standing behind the wide, dark English oak desk gave me a half-bow.

"Good afternoon, Minister vanBecton." I returned the bow, and he gestured to the straight-backed leather chair facing the desk. I slipped into it, and he sat back down in the slightly overpadded burgundy leather swivel chair. The office was still that combination of Dutch and English—dark Dutch furnishings and English lack of spark—that created an impression of bureaucratic inertia. The windowsills were dark wood, not dusted frequently enough, reflecting the less astringent standards of the English-settled south.

Gillaume vanBecton was a particular type of man raised from money and boarding schools. They are the ones who wear tailored gray pinstripes, their cravats accented in red, their graying hair trimmed weekly, their gray goatees shaped with that squarish Dutch cut to imply total integrity, and their guts almost as trim as when they once jumped over those lawn tennis nets they now only reach across in congratulating their always vanquished opponents. As they get older, they take up lawn bowling with the same grace as tennis, and the same results.

I've always distrusted the vanBectons of the world. I hadn't liked Hornsby Rogers, either, when he'd been seated behind vanBecton's desk.

If he had actually done a tenth of what he'd probably ordered, Gillaume vanBecton would have been a bright-eyed, ex-ghosted shadow—a zombie cheerfully pushing a broom for the city or hand-sorting glass for the recycling bins. Instead, he was the honorable Gillaume vanBecton, Deputy Minister for Internal Security of the Sedition Prevention and Security Service, in short, the number-two Spazi, the one responsible for all the dirty work.

"I am at your disposal."

"I am pleased that you recognize that." VanBecton smiled briefly.

"I try to be a realist."

"Good."

"What is this 'consulting' assignment, if I might ask?"

"It has to do with your Fräulein duBoise—"

"Doktor duBoise?"

"We have some concerns about who she really is."

"You don't know? Perhaps I can help you. Her name is Llysette Marie duBoise. After obtaining her degrees, she apprenticed at the Académie Royale, then premiered in Marseilles, where she eventually sang and bedded her way into the roles she deserved and needed to support her family. Her mother died, and later her father was killed by Ferdinand's troops. Because she had some stature, and because of some intervention by the Japanese ambassador, who had heard her sing, she was allowed to leave France—although not without, shall we say, some detailed interrogation." I inclined my head politely.

"How detailed, Doktor Eschbach?" VanBecton's voice remained smooth, and he leaned back in the heavy swivel chair.

"Enough to leave scars where they are not normally visible."

The subminister leaned forward again, but his eyes did not hold the smile of his mouth. "That would certainly seem to provide some indication that she has no love of Ferdinand. But . . . how do you know she isn't an agent of New France? Maximilian VI—"

"He's a fifteen-year-old boy. We both know Marshal de-Gaulle runs New France." I shrugged. "These days anyone can be working for anyone else. But, even assuming Doktor duBoise were an agent of New France, why on earth would she be in New Bruges?"

"At first glance, that would seem odd." VanBecton continued to smile. "Although Maurice-Huizenga has been known to recruit other . . . refugees." He covered his mouth and coughed, and his hand brushed the top drawer. That was where Rogers had kept his gun, and probably where vanBecton kept his. Stupid of him, since, if murder had been anyone's objective, including mine, vanBecton would have been dead before he could reach the weapon.

"At first glance?" I decided to oblige him.

"Don't you think this whole business is rather odd, at least from the federals' position? A former New Tory subminister returns to teach at a mere state university in a small town in New Bruges where he once spent summers. All very innocent until we consider that his position as a subminister was essentially to fatten his pension for his previous services to his country and to provide some consolation for the personal trials occasioned by his service. Then a refugee from the fall of France appears, a lovely and highly talented . . . lady, and she immediately becomes close to this widower, a man possibly—shall we say—vulnerable . . . Then another academic with a past better left not too closely inspected is murdered for no apparent reason."

"And might you tell me why Professor Miller's past is better left not too closely inspected? Was she an agent of Ferdinand? Or perhaps of Takaynishu?"

VanBecton smiled politely. "We actually are not sure, only that she was receiving laundered funds and instructions."

"What instructions? I'd rather not get in the way of a murderer trying to find out what you already know."

"She was instructed to find out what you were doing and to try to compromise you in a way to cast discredit upon the government."

"Someone seems to have looked out for me."

"No one that we know of," vanBecton said blandly.

"Perhaps it was fortuitous." I offered another shrug. "Murders occur, but rarely are they openly investigated by the Spazi. That was just obvious enough to show your interest."

VanBecton steepled his fingers together. "A nice touch, I do believe. I trust that it will make Doktor duBoise more reliant upon your protection."

I didn't have to force a frown. "I doubt that you are paying expenses merely to encourage Doktor duBoise to rely upon me. If anything, my traveling here right after the murder would make her somewhat suspicious."

"You will have to work to allay her fears, Doktor." He smiled broadly, fingering the standard-issue pen.

"But of course." I returned his smile with one equally as false.

"You can be quite convincing." VanBecton cleared his throat before continuing. "According to Colonel Nord."

I held my temper. "Considering my patriotism cost me my son and later my wife . . ."

"I am certain that Minister Reilly handled it as well as he could."

". . . and that the Spazi blocked further treatment in Vienna, treatment she wouldn't have even needed . . ."

"You knew the risks. As we know, Doktor Eschbach, the Austro-Hungarians only *claim* to have an effective treatment for degenerative lung fibrosis."

"The Health Office of the League of Nations has verified it."

"The League of Nations also verified that General Buonoparte used no poison gas on the French strikers in Marseilles."

I forced a shrug of reluctant agreement. Nothing I offered would convince van-Becton. He was one of the true believers, and nothing existed beyond his narrow vision of the world. In a way, his attitude reinforced my reluctant support of Ralston, though I suspected Ralston, in his indirect way, was the more deadly of the two.

"Does it really matter, Doktor Eschbach? We're men of the world. Only perceptions count, not reality." He smiled again.

"And what else do you want?"

"If you could trouble yourself to find out why Professor Miller was murdered, and why she wanted to discredit you—certainly in your interest—it would be helpful."

"It's also clearly in your interest not to have me discredited."

"Not so much as you think, Doktor Eschbach. It could be merely embarrassing for us."

"I so appreciate your concern. I presume I will be hearing from you again."

"As necessary." He stood.

I followed his example.

"I assume you know the way out." He gestured to the rear door.

"I have been here once or twice."

"I look forward to seeing you again."

"And I, you."

The narrow corridor had two one-way doors, both steelcored in steel frames, before it opened onto the main hall. The second door looked more like a closet door than one to an office. Overkill, in a way, given the guards in and around the building.

Just to make matters a shade more difficult for whoever might be following me, I retraced my path back to the Natural Resources building, except I had to show my identification to the guard on the Spazi side of the tunnel. Then I went up to my old offices on the fifth floor.

Estelle was there. She smiled as I walked in. "Minister Eschbach! It is so good to see you." Turning to the black-bearded young man beside her, she added, "Doktor Eschbach was the subminister before Minister Kramer."

"Pleased to meet you, sir." He edged back ever so slightly. Clearly, he had heard of me.

"I should only be a bit, Stephan," Estelle said brightly. "We don't get to see Doktor Eschbach much anymore."

"I'll check back in a few moments." Stephan looked at me once more before he stepped past us and out into the main hallway.

"How do you like being back in New Bruges?"

"It's definitely a change." I laughed. "But not so much as I'd thought. The teaching is interesting. Other things aren't that different. What about here?"

Estelle glanced around, then lowered her voice. "It hasn't been the same since you left. Everyone worries about whether the Hartpencers will go after them."

"Hartpencers?"

"The Speaker put his own people everywhere—" She broke off and forced a smile as the door to the right opened. "Minister Kramer—do you remember Minister Eschbach?"

"It's good to see you, Kenneth. I hope the job is treating you well." I gave a half-bow.

"It has been an education," my successor offered. "And Estelle has been most helpful." He glanced toward her.

"I understand. Perhaps the next time I'm in the Federal District . . ."

They both nodded. I stepped into the corridor, then made my way to the Seventeenth Street exit. From there I took a cab up to the Ghirardelli Chocolatiers right off Dupont Circle. Llysette would enjoy some chocolates, even as a peace offering. The cab waited, for an extra dollar, then eased through the heavy afternoon traffic in a stop-and-go fashion.

Up New Bruges Avenue, I could see the rising-sun flags where the massive Japanese embassy stood on one side of the avenue, less than two blocks above DuPont Circle. While I could not see it from the cab window, the embassy of Chung Kuo stood across from it, just as the two Far Eastern empires squared off across the Sea of Japan. I also could not see the cordoned-off section of the sidewalk where the ghosts of ten Vietnamese monks still wailed fifteen years after they immolated themselves there in protest. Still, I knew they were there, and so did the Chinese—not that it seemed to stop them. They seemed to like the reminder of the futility of protest to their endless expansion.

Although the Chinese Empire was far larger than the Japanese, even the Chinese understood that Japan was unconquerable, especially because the Japanese were fortifying every island and creeping ever closer to isolated Australia. Once the Low Countries had fallen to Ferdinand, the Chinese and the Japanese had intensified their efforts to annex the former Dutch possessions in Southeast Asia. Again, I wondered how long the Philippines would last.

It wouldn't be in our lifetime, but what would happen when the Chinese, the Japanese, and the Austro-Hungarians finally assimilated Asia and what was left of Russia?

The cab jerked forward and around the circle, turning back onto New Bruges and thence back to the Mall and directly to the B&P station. Although I would have liked to have made some other stops, the stops would not have been fair to those people. So I caught the five o'clock to New Amsterdam.

CHAPTER NINE

• • •

A fter my breakfast, exercise, and shower, I dressed and took the Stanley down to the post centre to see what had arrived in my absence.

As always on Saturday, the square was crowded with steamers, the flagstone sidewalks filled with dark-clad shoppers. I had to park over by the church and walk across the square.

"Greetings to you, Doktor Eschbach," offered the young watch officer who had known about ghosts.

"And to you, Officer Warbeck," I said politely enough, finally close enough to read his name plate.

He smiled politely and walked past, up toward the college, while I continued north to the post centre.

"Good day, Professor Eschbach," offered Alois Er Recchus with a broad smile as I went up the steps to the post centre. His dull-gray work jacket was thrown open by the expanse of his abdomen, and he wore bright red braces over his gray work shirt and trousers. I hadn't thought him the type for red, even in braces.

"Good day. I don't see the dean."

"She's off to some conference in Orono. Something about the need for inter-linking among women in academia."

"Interlinking—that must be the latest term."

Alois shrugged, smiled, and waddled down toward the hardware store. I went inside and opened my box. Besides three bills and an announcement from the New Bruges Arts Foundation, there was an invitation. The return address was clear enough: the Presidential Palace.

I closed the box, preferring to wait until I got home before opening anything. After another handful of casual greetings, I retreated to the Stanley and headed back across the river, waiting for several minutes at the bridge for a log steamer to cross.

Of course, once at home and in my study, I dropped the post offerings on the desk and opened the invitation first. It was standard enough—the envelope within the envelope, the inner envelope addressed to the honorable Johan Anders Eschbach, Ph.D. The wording was also standard:

> *President and Mrs. Armstrong*
> *request the honor of your presence*
> *at a state dinner*
> *honoring his excellency, Yasuo Takayama,*
> *ambassador of*
> *the Imperial Republic of Japan,*
> *Thursday, October 28, 1993,*
> *at seven o'clock.*
> *Répondez s'il vous plaît.*

A nice gesture, certainly, and my presence might be listed as one of many in the *Columbia Post-Dispatch,* if that. The timing of the invitation indicated I was a late addition to the guest list, since it was for the coming Thursday. I didn't have much choice about going, since Ralston had clearly had the invitation sent to get me to the Presidential Palace for further instructions. Things were moving. David would not be averse to my going, even if I had to cancel classes on Thursday and Friday. My students would certainly like the break.

I set aside the card announcing the New Bruges String Quartet's performance at the university for Llysette to see; their presence resulted from the dean's infatuation with strings of any sort. After leafing through the bills, I stuffed them into the top drawer to do all at once later.

For a time, I sat behind the Kunigser desk and just looked out over the veranda into the patchy clouds in the deep blue of the fall sky. Finally I picked up the handset and dialed in Llysette's wire number.

"Hello." Her voice was definitely cool.

"Hello. Is this the talented and lovely Professor Doktor Llysette duBoise of the enchanting voice and the charming manner?"

"Johan. Where are you?"

"At home. Where else would I be? I took a late train and got home rather late last night—or, more accurately, early this morning. I slept as long as I could, then got up and did chores. I do have a few, you know. Then I called you."

"Your trip to the capital? How did it go?"

"I got paid, or I will. But I'm afraid it may be a dead end. This client wants a great deal, but he isn't really very specific." I laughed. "I've told you about the type. You know, the ones who want the world, but they only say something like 'find out what you can.' Whatever you find is never enough. In any case, if you want to know the details, I can tell you later . . . assuming that you would be interested in company later."

"Johan, I am not feeling terribly well, but it will pass—as these feminine matters do. I would be more appreciating of your company perhaps tomorrow."

"How early tomorrow? Perhaps right after midnight?"

She did chuckle for a moment, I thought, before she answered. "Dear man . . . you are impossible." She pronounced "impossible" in the French manner.

"That's my specialty—impossibility."

"At three, would that be agreeable?"

"Of course. Have I taken you to the Devil's Cauldron?"

"*Mais non.* The Devil's Cauldron—what is that?"

"That is a place up the river valley where the river has hollowed out a cauldron. They say—but I will tell you that tomorrow."

"As you wish . . ." Her voice trailed off.

"Then I will see you at three o'clock tomorrow, for a drive to the Devil's Cauldron." I paused. "I have one other problem. Perhaps you could help."

"And so?" The suspicion resurfaced in her voice.

"Miranda. I remember that she loaned me a book, something she thought I should read. I never did, and now I can't remember what it was. I think Marie must have reshelved it."

"Ah, Johan, and never in all those shelves could you find it. So polite you are . . . but no one would know if you kept it."

"Alas, I would—even if I don't remember what it was." I laughed. "I feel rather . . . rather stupid. Did I ever mention it to you? I hoped I might have."

"*Non.* But outside of the music, I think—I do not know, you understand—but once she asked me to read something by a Doktor Casey, excepting he was not a real doctor."

"An Edgar Cayce? Perhaps that was it."

"That may have been. I do not know."

"I thank you, and I trust you will be much improved by tomorrow afternoon."

"I also. But also see to your own sleep, dear man."

"That I will, even if I must sleep alone in a cold bed."

"You will survive."

"Cruel lady."

"You think the truth is cruel?"

"Sometimes, and sometimes you are a truthful lady."

"*Point toujours,* I hope. Some secrets I must keep."

"Well, keep them until tomorrow, and take care."

"You also."

I set down the handset and leaned back in the chair for a moment, my eyes flicking across the massive Dutch Victorian mirror set between the windows overlooking the veranda. With its overelaborate gilt floral designs and bosses, it was one of the older items in the house. I kept thinking about replacing it, but since it was literally built into the wall, I had put off undertaking such a chore, and had instead replaced the lace curtains and about half the paintings. I didn't have to have lace in my study, and even Marie hadn't said anything about that—but she had washed and pressed the box-pleated blue curtains.

With a head shake at what I had yet to do, I slowly got up and walked over to the bookcases, starting at the far right. I always go through things backwards. It's faster for me that way. I tried to find a book that would suit my purpose, one that would fit the psychic mold, one that Miranda was unlikely to have had.

When I saw the title after having scanned nearly two hundred books, it didn't exactly leap out at me: *The Other World—Seeing Beyond the Veil.* But I pulled it out and studied it. It was a sturdily bound book, published by Deseret Press, but not an original, written by Joseph Brigham Young, a former elder in the Church of the Latter Day Saints and later the Prophet, Seer, and Revelator of the Church.

After leafing through *The Other World,* I decided it would do. An entire section dealt with the spirituality of music and the role of music in "piercing the veil." While it was a gamble, the only one who was likely to call me on it was dead.

I found some brown paper in the kitchen and wrapped the book in several layers of paper, tying it carefully with twine I had to fetch from the car barn. I debated writing something on the paper, but then demurred. The whole point was not to leave the book, but to talk to young Miller and his wife.

The day was sunny, and I decided to sit on the veranda and catch up on reading. I had several potential texts to review, although I was dubious about the authors, since they had spent little time in the federal city and not that much time dealing with the environment. I didn't want to write a text, and the Carson text I was using was badly outdated.

Comfortably ensconced in the canvas sling chair, I struggled through thirty pages of the Edelson text, but it was too journalistic, sacrificing accuracy to a golly-whiz crusading spirit. After discarding Edelson, I wandered back to the kitchen, made iced tea, and finally walked back out to the veranda, moving my chair into the shade by the dining room windows.

The Davies text wasn't much better. While the environmental science was good, he didn't understand even basic Columbian politics. After forty pages, I set it aside and got more tea. Then I just sat and enjoyed the view and the scent of the fallen leaves, listening to their rustling as the light wind occasionally picked them up and restacked them.

The more I learned about Miranda's murder, the stranger it seemed. Why would anyone murder Miranda? There could be reasons to murder Llysette, me, probably Gregor Martin, certainly Gerald Branston-Hay, and those reasons didn't count normal jealousy, either personal or professional. It was also clear that van-Becton intended to set me up to discredit the president in the undeclared struggle between the Speaker and the president. That meant trouble and more trouble, unless I could come up with a solution fairly soon.

Could vanBecton have had Miranda murdered, just to set me up? It was possible, but who did the actual deed? I shivered. Who was on whose payroll, and why? I knew the dangers of being on Ralston's "payroll," although I'd never received a cent directly, just an early retirement indirectly arranged. I doubted vanBecton had known all the details—until now, when his agents certainly could have found enough to point indirectly at my involvement with the Presidential Palace. There was nothing on paper, but both vanBecton and Ralston were old enough hands to know that by the time you had real evidence, it was too late. That was my problem— if Ralston or vanBecton wanted me framed for something or out of the way, by the time I could prove it, someone would be digging my grave and Father Esterhoos would be saying the eulogy.

After a deep breath, I drank the last of the iced tea as the sun dropped into the branches of the apple tree halfway down the lawn.

After a light supper in the kitchen—cold leftover veal pie—I drove the steamer down Emmen Lane, out to the bungalow owned by Miranda Miller, noting the lights in the window. The curtains were white sheers, not the white lace of New Bruges. I pulled into the paved area beside the house next to the steamer that had been Miranda's. Knocking on the door, the wrapped book in hand, I waited until the young, clean-shaven man I had seen at the memorial service opened the door.

"Doktor Miller? I'm Johan Eschbach. I teach in the Natural Resources Department. I saw you at the service, and I wanted to return this." I held up the package. "I would have just left it, but since you were here, I didn't want to slink away and leave you with something else to worry about."

"Please come in, is it . . . Professor?" He stepped back.

"Technically, Doktor or Professor, but . . ." I slipped into the small foyer, but waited for an invitation to go farther.

"I'm Alfred." He turned to a young woman in slacks and a cardigan sweater over a synthetic silk blouse. "This is my wife, Kristen."

"Pleased to meet you." I bowed. "I wish it were under other circumstances."

"So do we," she answered in a calm but strong voice.

"You are Miranda's younger son?" I asked, again lifting my package as if unclear what to do with it.

"The medical doctor," he acknowledged with a brief grin that faded almost immediately.

"She was proud of you," I said. After a brief pause, I added, "But I am wasting your time, and I had just meant to drop this off."

"What is it?" asked Kristen Miller.

"It is a book she had suggested I read, that I might find interesting. Something called *Seeing Beyond the Veil.*"

"Mother—she was always looking for something beyond." Young Alfred shook his head as he took the wrapped book. "I appreciate your kindness in returning the book." He gestured toward the sofa and chairs. "At least sit down for a bit. You don't have to run off immediately, do you?"

"No. I would have returned the book sooner, but I had to take a short trip yesterday—I do some consulting in addition to teaching. I did not think it would have been appropriate to descend on you Thursday night." I took the couch, since it was lower and left them in the more comfortable superior position.

The couple sat across on a set of wooden Dutch colonial chairs on each side of the copper-bound table.

"Could you tell us anything else about . . . about . . ."

"Perhaps a little," I offered over his hesitation. "I was leaving my office that night when I felt something strange, and I thought I saw a ghost. I heard, I think, the word 'no' whispered, and then her ghost was gone." I shrugged. "I do not know if that is much help. I cannot say I knew your mother well, except that once or twice she and I and others shared a luncheon." I frowned. "Do you not have a brother? Is he not well, or his business . . . ?"

"Frederick." Alfred glanced at Kristen. "I suppose it's no great secret. He is—was—in the electronics import business in San Francisco. He liked to import the latest Bajan designs. The last time he went to Los Angeles . . . he did not come back. He was imprisoned for some form of export violation."

"When did this occur?" Despite my best resolve to appear disinterested, my eyes scanned the room, and I noted absently that the white enamel of the windowsills had begun to chip and appeared soiled. No, Miranda had not been Dutch.

"Almost a year ago. It was September 17. I remember because it was the day after Mother's anniversary."

"That must have been doubly painful for her."

"It was," said Kristen.

"The entire episode does not sound . . ." I shrugged. "Your mother struck me as a careful person. Was not your brother much like her?"

"Rick? Of course. I mean, he did have some wild ideas about electronics, but he knew what sold, and Rick was very careful. It's some sort of excuse, something."

"It doesn't make sense," added Kristen. "Rick reported *everything*."

"He was almost paranoid about being careful," confirmed Alfred.

"These are strange times. I would never have thought of a murder here." I shook my head. "That makes no sense, either."

"A jealous lover—or would-be lover, do you think?" asked Kristen, looking intently at me.

"Kristen . . ." muttered Alfred.

"One never knows, lady. But in response to the question you never asked, I was widowed several years ago. Currently I am attached to Doktor duBoise, and she is the only one with whom I have been, shall we say, intimate."

Alfred blushed, and Kristen nodded.

"How did Doktor duBoise and Mother Miller get along?"

"They were professional colleagues, but not friends. They seemed friendly."

"Were there . . . other men?" asked Kristen.

I liked the young lady's directness, and I answered directly. "I know Professor Miller had luncheon occasionally with Professor Branston-Hay, but I was led to understand that such was merely friendship. He is a Babbage type and, I think, thoroughly devoted to his wife, or as devoted as any Babbage type might be to mere flesh and blood. There are few unattached men here in Vanderbraak Centre," I added.

"So Mother wrote," commented Alfred.

"But it makes no sense," protested Kristen. "No one had any reason to kill her, not that the watch or anyone we've talked to can discover. She was lonely, but not totally alone. She could be a shade self-pitying—"

"Kristen . . ." murmured Alfred.

She glanced at him. "Mother Miller is dead, and I loved her, but there's not much point in sugarcoating her character. She was raised to be wealthy, and that all came apart when your father died. She worked hard, and she got you and Rick through your educations, and if she had a trace of self-pity, well, I think maybe she deserved it." She took out a plain white handkerchief and blew her nose, then continued as if she had never stopped. "Besides, no one ever murdered someone for feeling sorry for themselves. There has to be a reason. She had friends and men friends, but no lovers that anyone could even hint at. She was not robbed, or attacked in . . . untoward ways."

"Murder is untoward enough, I fear," I said, and added, "but what you say makes sense. Did she have enemies from where she came from?"

"How?" asked Alfred. "She's been here for almost fifteen years. The teaching was her life after I went to Louisiana and Rick to California."

"It does not make sense," I agreed. "I assume the watch has questioned every member of the music faculty."

"They still are." Alfred sighed. "But everyone was miles away or with someone else—usually two others."

"I am afraid I have taxed your hospitality at a trying time." I rose. "I did not mean to intrude so long, only to return what should be returned."

"And perhaps," added Kristen with a faint smile, "to try to make some sense out of something you also find senseless?"

"You are perceptive, young lady. Yes," I admitted, "that also. But there is no point in overstaying my welcome when you are as baffled as I." I extended a card. "If there is anything with which I could help, please do not hesitate to ask."

"Thank you." Alfred belatedly rose and took the card. "We appreciate your concern." He grinned briefly. "And your forthrightness." He looked at the card, and frowned. "You aren't *the* Johan Eschbach?" He handed the card to his wife.

"I'm afraid you have the better of me."

"The former Subminister of Environment that the Hartpencers went after, I mean. Why are you here?"

"In Vanderbraak Centre?" I smiled—wryly, I hoped. "My family had a home here, and there really was nowhere else to go. I had the doctorate, and I still needed to make a living."

"Even stranger," he murmured.

"How so, Alfred?" asked Kristen, except her words were too matter-of-fact.

He shook his head. "Mother once wrote about you. She said you were the only honest man in a den of thieves, carrying about a lantern looking for another honest man. I'm sorry. I just didn't connect. I guess I am not thinking very well."

"Your mother must have been mistaken." I wouldn't have characterized myself as a Diogenes.

"No." He looked at me. "She also said that you were looking for a ghost in Doktor duBoise, and she—Doktor duBoise—was all too willing to oblige you, as desperate women often are."

I must have staggered, or reacted, for Kristen stood at that point. "Forthright-ness is all very well, Alfred."

"No," I demurred. "I would hear more, if there is more."

"There's not much. She just wrote that she felt that all the recent arrivals at the university carried secrets too terrible to reveal and too heavy to bear. She meant the newer faculty, I think."

"Was your mother psychic?"

"Sometimes we thought so. But most of the time she kept her secrets—that's what she called them, her little secrets—to herself."

"It's amazing what you never know about people."

"I can see that." Alfred's tone was friendlier, for some reason. "How many people at the university really know your past?"

"You probably know more than most. I have said little, and most of the older Dutch do not ask. I would not, certainly."

"You would characterize yourself as older Dutch?" asked Kristen.

"By birth, but not by inclination." I frowned. "But how did your mother know? I cannot recall providing so much detail."

"I fear I'm the guilty one." Kristen grinned. "When Mother Miller wrote about you, I was skeptical, afraid that you might not be quite so honest. So I had a Babbage search done on you."

"She's a librarian," Alfred explained.

"The articles on you were interesting," Kristen added.

"You are too kind."

"Not much seems to have happened in your life," she continued inexorably, "after you got your doctorate from the University of Virginia, not until you were appointed deputy subminister of natural resources."

"I was a midrange government employee who did his job, got married, had a child, lost a child, and lost my wife."

"Murder is rare in Columbia," she said. "Yet a number have occurred around you. Why do you attract them?"

I shrugged. Anything I said would only make things worse in dealing with a very bright young woman who was clearly sharper than her husband.

"Do you know what I think, Alfred?" She turned to Alfred. "I think Mother Miller was right. Doktor Eschbach is an honest man, but, since there are so few left in our world, many people are afraid of his honesty. Yet killing him would create an uproar, perhaps bring to light the very things people want to hide. So whenever someone learns too much from the doktor's honesty . . . they die."

I shuddered. Could what she said be partly true? If so, it was even more horrible than the truth I knew.

"You've upset the doktor, I believe," Alfred remarked.

"It shows his honesty." Kristen inclined her head. "I apologize for my directness." She extended a card to me. "If you find out more that you can share with us, please let us know. We have to return to Lake Charles on Wednesday."

"That I will," I promised, taking her card. "I was sorry and have been deeply troubled by your mother's death."

"That is obvious."

"We appreciate your kindness and honesty," added Alfred as he held the door for me.

"And I yours."

By the time I fired up the Stanley and drove back in to town on Emmen Lane, I was almost happy to have escaped Miranda's children without revealing more than I had. Young Kristen Miller would have tied both Gillaume vanBecton and

Hornsby Rogers in knots, I suspected, except that she was too direct to have survived in the Spazi organization. I almost hadn't, the Lord knew, especially once I'd left field work.

When I got back to the unlit house, looming like a monument on the hillside, I pulled off my coat and hung it on the knob of the stair railing, intending to take it upstairs when I got ready for bed. Then I went to the study, turned on a single light, and sat down at the old desk, looking into the dark. The more I knew, the worse it got.

How long I sat there before Carolynne appeared beside the desk, I didn't know, and really didn't care. In the dimness relieved only by the single lamp behind the stove, she appeared almost solid, in the recital gown that she always wore. It must be hell for a female ghost to always appear in the same clothes, I mused.

"Is it, Carolynne? Is it difficult to always wear the same gown?" I didn't expect an answer, but I got one. As I watched, she flickered, and appeared in another dress, high-necked and lacy.

"I didn't know ghosts could do that." Then again, there was probably a lot I didn't know about ghosts. "Can a ghost really say who murdered her?" I was thinking about Miranda, not Carolynne.

"Murder most foul . . ."

Her voice sent shivers down my back, but was that because of the fact that I heard her voice in my thoughts as much as in my ears? Or because I had not heard her speak in more than thirty years?

She drifted next to the window, seemingly more solid there. "A little water clears her of this deed . . . what need we fear who knows it . . . Macduff, Macbeth . . . damned be he who first cries . . ."

I considered her words. Who was the woman to whom Carolynne referred? What did the murder have to do with Macbeth? Was murder the deed or the cause of the deed? How did that apply to Miranda Miller?

". . . that death's unnatural that kills for loving."

Death's unnatural that kills for loving? Like Wilde's words about men killing the one they love? Or was it a question of not being strong enough to love? Was that why Llysette and I never got too close? But who wasn't strong enough to love? That brought up another thought.

"Do we always kill the ones we love? I didn't fire the shots that killed Waltar and ruined Elspeth's good lung. I might as well have. Spazi field men shouldn't have hostages to fortune." My eyes flicked to my sleeve, as if I could see through the pale cotton to the white scars beneath that ran from arm to shoulder.

Carolynne said nothing. Neither did she flicker or depart. So we remained for a time, ghost and the ghost of a man.

CHAPTER TEN

• • •

Before I left the house to get Llysette, I walked down the lawn to the remnants of the orchard and picked half a basket of apples and the few pears that actually looked decent. I carted them down to the root cellar, except for a handful of each which I put in the fruit bowl in the kitchen.

With the box of chocolates on the seat, I waited for the steamer to warm up, then headed down Deacon's Lane toward town. Vanderbraak Centre was its usual sleepy Sunday afternoon self, with only students passing through the square.

After passing but a single steamer on the old Hebron Road, I brought the Stanley to a halt beside Llysette's Reo at almost precisely three o'clock, according to the pocket Ansonia that was nearly a century old. Llysette was not waiting breathlessly on the porch for me, but that was always to be expected. I shut down the steamer and stepped up to the door, holding the chocolates behind my back.

After lifting the heavy brass knocker and letting it fall, I waited, and waited. Finally the sound of footsteps neared the door, and the lock clicked.

"Come inside, Johan. Only a moment will I be."

As I watched her figure, shapely even through the robe she had thrown on, retreat to the hallway leading to her bedroom, I doubted her estimate of the time.

Rather than sit, with a drive up the valley ahead, I wandered to the table that served for both filing and food. I put the Ghirardelli chocolates on the corner. On the other corner, the one closest the small kitchen, was the same stack of old-fashioned vinyl discs I had seen the last time. Beside them were piled various music publications— *Musical Heritage, Opera News, Main Line Musical.* A higher stack of letters, notices, circulars, and the like spilled around the dried floral centerpiece and came to rest against the dog-eared news magazines—*Look, Life, Newsweek,* and *Columbian World Report.*

I picked up the latest issue of *World Report,* which I had not seen, since subscribing to two news magazines and a daily still seemed extravagant. In some matters, my Dutch heritage did linger.

Newsweek arrived in my postbox, perhaps because *World Report* had always seemed somewhat more liberal in its speculations on the meaning of the news. Flicking through the pages of *World Report,* I caught a glimpse of red and stopped to read the article.

The ghost of Pope Julius Paul II appeared before the College of Cardinals last week, prompting speculation that his death earlier this month had not been from the natural causes announced by the Vatican. "The Pope clearly wished to convey his blessing upon the college and offered the traditional benediction before his shade vanished," stated Cardinal Guilermo Moro, spokesman for the Vatican.

Julius Paul had been thought to favor easing the absolute Roman Catholic ban on psychic research. Earlier this year, he had remarked in a small audience that the "true mysteries of God are not so easily solved by mere mortals."

After that audience, Pope Julius Paul had been visited by the ambassadors from both Columbia and Austro-Hungary, and later by Archbishop Konstantin from the Apostolic Eastern Catholic Church . . .

Psychic research seemed to be an increasingly touchy subject. Why now? Ghosts had been around forever.

"Johan?"

Llysette stood there, in stylishly quilted blue trousers and a matching jacket, carrying a heavy quilted down coat and an overnight case.

"You are ready in a moment, indeed. Are we headed for the Arctic?"

"You a polar bear are. I am not. The wind is blowing from the north, is it not?" She arched both eyebrows.

I grinned in submission and set down *World Report*. "You know best for you." Then I glanced toward the table, and her eyes followed mine.

"Oh . . ." She moved to the table and looked at the box. "You are very sweet."

"Those are because I care, and because I never did bring you something at your recital."

"Would you mind if I had one now?"

"Of course not. Instead of lunch?"

She smiled and opened the box, but she offered it to me. I guessed, looking for a caramel, and was lucky. Llysette actually had three before we walked to the door. I waited on the porch while she locked up.

After seating her in the Stanley and setting her case in the back seat, by the time I was behind the wheel and had lit off the steamer, the wind made me glad that I had worn a sweater and the heavy Harris Tweed jacket. I wondered if young Ferdinand would let the Scots continue with Harris Tweeds when he overran the isles in the next century.

The center of town was nearly deserted, even by the students, except for a few steamers gathered around the Reformed Church, when we circled the square and headed north on Route Five.

The winds had ripped away the last of the leaves, and the birches, oaks, and maples were bare, stark, letting the evergreens stand out against the brown and gray of the harvested fields and leaf-stripped woodlots. The white enameled windowsills of the colonial stone houses stood out more, too.

"It is quiet," noted Llysette as we passed the empty car park at Vanderwerk Textiles, the sole remaining mill north of Zuider. The sign read VANDERWERK TEXTILES, A DIVISION OF AZKO FIBERS. The plant had been expanded a decade earlier when Azko bought it and a number of other facilities. That had been when Azko had moved the last of its operations out of the Low Countries before Ferdinand's final push to the English Channel.

Sometimes I bought sweaters and heavy work shirts at the factory store, but not often, since their woolens generally lasted forever.

"It's Sunday, and even the industrious Dutch like time off."

We passed the road that led to the Wiler River covered bridge and beyond to Grolle Mountain and one or two other smaller skiing slopes. The Covered Bridge Restaurant was out that road, as well. Llysette smiled.

"Stop smiling," I commanded sternly.

She smiled more broadly, and I smiled back. What else could I do? Our second dinner, I had actually run out of fuel coming back from the restaurant—and who could I tell that I hadn't even planned it?

North of Vanderbraak Centre, Route Five generally follows the River Wijk, at least until you get near the top of the notch. The wind rose as we climbed northward, and heavy gusts rocked the Stanley when I pulled off the main road.

The parking lot for the state park that holds the Devil's Cauldron was nearly empty, and the wind blew down from the notch, past the craggy Old Dutchman jutting from the mountain, picking up force as it swept southward. Had I worn a hat, it would have blown halfway to Asten or Haartsford.

Llysette tightened her scarf after she stepped out of the Stanley and onto the blacktop.

"The wind, it is energetic today."

That was one way of putting it.

We walked past a battered Ford petrol car—there weren't many around—and then past a Reo and a Williams and a long six-wheeled Packard limousine with registration plates from New Ostend. It even had the dark-tinted windows that made me think of the high-tech trupps of Asten.

The damp clay path, lined with matched and stripped logs, wound through the nearly bare birches and maples and the pines along the high side of the stream. A jay became a flash of blue, and even the stiff and cold breeze couldn't quite dispel the odor of damp leaves.

The river twisted over a flat bed of rock before it turned and shot at an angle into the Devil's Cauldron itself, a circular hollow in the rock that extended nearly twenty feet beneath the surface of the swirling and foaming water. In spring, the Cauldron literally spewed water in all directions.

We stopped at the vacant overlook.

"They say that the Pemigewasset Indians called this the cauldron of the seasons, where the spring waters washed away the ice and dank water of the old season, mixing the old and the new."

"That story, Johan, it sounds as though you just made it up."

"Perhaps I did. Don't we all make up history to suit the present?"

"You are cynical this afternoon." Another gust of cold air blew past us, and she shivered, even in the heavy quilted coat.

"Just this afternoon?" I tried not to shiver. I should have brought the heavy tweed overcoat that would have stopped a midwinter blitzwehr.

"Johan, cynical you are not. That is why the government, it was hard on you."

"You are kinder than you know."

"*Mais non, je crois.*" She smiled crookedly, and added, "This, it is fascinating, but it is *seulement* a river, and I am cold."

"It is cold," I admitted, taking her arm.

Even just getting out of the wind and into the Stanley warmed me enough, but Llysette kept shivering until the heater really got going and I was sweating. By then we were passing the turnoff for Grolle Mountain.

"Do you want to stop for some fresh cider?"

"If you wish."

I decided against stopping.

Whitecaps actually dotted the surface of the River Wijk when we crossed the bridge and headed up the bluff road toward Deacon's Lane. The trees were bending in the wind when the Stanley rolled to a stop outside the house.

I brought in her case and took it upstairs. The house was cold, despite the closed and double-glazed windows, and a trace damp. Llysette stepped inside, but did not take off her heavy coat.

Since I had laid the fire, with shavings and paper, in the solid Ostwerk Castings stove that dominated one wall of the main parlor, it took only a moment and a single match to start it up.

I offered Llysette the tartan blanket in place of her coat, which she surrendered reluctantly. She immediately huddled under the blanket.

"In a bit, the chill will begin to lift."

"I'm sorry, Johan." Her teeth chattered.

"Don't be sorry. It's damp out there. It's a bit damp in here. Coffee or chocolate?"

"Chocolate, I think." She continued to shiver under the wool blanket when I went into the kitchen and lit off the stove, bottled gas, which is good in the winter, since the new oil furnace doesn't work without electric power.

While the milk and chocolate were heating, I turned on the oven and took the pork loin from the refrigerator. I managed to get it sliced, stuffed, rolled, and in the oven by the time the chocolate was ready.

Llysette took the chocolate, and I set a tray with biscuits on the hearth by her feet.

"Biscuit?"

"Yes, thank you."

I ate two biscuits to her every one and was back in the kitchen for refills before I finished half my chocolate. That might have been because I hadn't bothered to eat since breakfast.

"Another biscuit?"

Llysette took two.

"No lunch, either?"

"No. I was sleeping."

I let that lie, and had another biscuit and took another sip from my mug, finally feeling warm from the chocolate and the growing heat from the woodstove.

"What about tomorrow?"

"A working lunch with Doktor Geoffries I must have, and the afternoon session with the choir, and we begin the opera rehearsals in the evening, until ten. And I must complete the schedules for Herr Wustman. Arranging the students and their accompanists, it is difficult. Most nights this week, except Thursday, I am busy. And you?"

"Thursday, I am going to Columbia once more. I was asked to a presidential dinner." I laughed. "A gesture for old times' sake, I guess."

She lowered the mug from her lips. "Do you want to attend this dinner?"

"I have very mixed feelings, but I think I should."

"Pourquoi?"

"For the consulting—it helps to maintain a profile in high circles within government. And this sort of thing allows me to do it without living anywhere near the Federal District. Besides, I imagine that it will give Dean Er Recchus something else to boast about."

"That woman . . ." Llysette snorted, then bit into a biscuit.

"I take it that you are not enamored of our dean."

"Would I consider developing a new course? A course in singing for instrumentalists and actors," she asked.

"Instrumentalists and actors?"

"Gregor, he wanted a course in singing for actors. That I understand. But she, she felt that the instrumentalists, especially those of the strings, should also be included."

I shook my head.

"That also, I understand. But now, she wants to share my next recital. She had Dr. Geoffries suggest that I ask the dean to play for me. She sounds like . . . like a dance fiddler."

Clank. Her cup almost bounced off the stone hearth, so hard had she set it down. "She does scheme a lot."

Llysette glared at me. "Like saying the hog is sometimes not so neat, that is."

While I wasn't sure of the comparison—or the metaphor—I got the idea.

"What does Doktor Geoffries think?"

Llysette squared her shoulders, letting the blanket slip away. "He says that if there is any way to make the dean happy, it would be better. Better for him, I think."

I nodded. "I wonder why they all bow and scrape."

"Because they are men."

"You're saying I'm not?" I raised an eyebrow.

"Different you are."

I decided not to pursue that line of inquiry further. "Excuse me. I need to finish working on dinner."

"With you I will come." So she dragged the blanket into the kitchen and sat at the table while I worked.

I sliced some of the fresh apples and set them aside in a pan to make fried apples—better than applesauce any day, and chunky, not pureed baby food. Then I dragged out the butter, some cinnamon and nutmeg, and the raw sugar.

"You cook well."

"Experience helps." So did growing up in a household without sisters and a mother who insisted that no man should be slave to helplessness and his stomach. That had worked fine for food, but not so well in other areas.

Beans from the lower garden, via the root cellar, with almonds from McArdles', were the vegetable, and I'd mixed batter for some drop biscuits.

"Cooking I did little of," she admitted.

"I know."

"Johan!"

I grinned. "I'm not primarily interested in your cooking."

"Men! No better are you than . . . than all the others."

"In some things, I'm better." I tried a leer, but she wasn't looking. So I dug a pale cream linen cloth from the butler's pantry, not that we'd ever had butlers, and spread it on the dining room table. I even used the bayberry candles and silver instead of stainless.

Then I dropped the biscuits into the oven, and fried up the apples. After the biscuits came out, and the apples went into the covered bone china dish, I dashed back down to the cellar for a bottle of Sebastopol. Somehow I got all the food on the table warm, and both wine glasses filled.

"In France, you would have been a chef, a great chef," Llysette said after several bites and half of her wine.

"Mais non, point moi," I protested in bad French.

"If you did not speak, that is."

"We all might be in less trouble if we did not speak, I sometimes think."

"But life, it would be dull."

"Dullness can be a virtue," I reflected. Especially compared to the alternatives.

"At times." She lifted her glass and drained the rest of the Sebastopol. "We have seen such times."

I refilled her glass, and tried the apples, just crunchy enough to give my teeth some resistance, soft enough to eat easily, and cinnamon-tart-tangy enough to off-set the richness of the stuffed pork. "Some biscuits? The honey is in the small pitcher there."

"Thank you, Johan. Perhaps it is as well we do not eat together all the time. I could get fat."

"I am."

"*Non.* Solid you are, with all that running and exercise." She took another healthy swallow.

"I need to get more exercise."

"Of what kind?" She winked slowly at me.

"You are terrible."

"*Non*—it is the wine. With the wine, I can say what I feel. Without, it is hard. The feelings, they hide."

I decided against another slice of the pork, but did take some of the apples. "Some more apples?"

"Just a few."

There wasn't any dessert, not with the fried apples and the need for both of us to watch waistlines, but we had tea, taken in front of the restoked woodstove, af-ter I had washed and Llysette had dried the dishes.

Outside, the wind continued to whistle.

"Here, one can almost forget the world."

I glanced toward the blank videolink screen. "So long as one ignores the news."

"Cynical you still pretend to be."

"Cynical I will always be, I fear." I sipped from the mug, letting the steam and scent circle my face, breathing the steam.

"*Non.* You are not cynical. You see the world as it is."

"Perhaps. I try, but what we are colors what we see. Truth is in the eye of the beholder." I laughed, more harshly than I meant. "That's why I'm skeptical of those who say they have found the truth."

Llysette nodded. "They are terrible." She meant the word in its original mean-ing.

"I think I'd rather not dwell on truth tonight. How about beauty?"

Llysette yawned, but spoiled it with a grin.

I grinned back. "You're ready for some sleep?"

"I did not mention sleep . . ."

"Fine. You head upstairs, and I'll dump these in the kitchen." I picked up the mugs.

She winked again.

By the time I took care of the dishes, damped the woodstove, turned off the lights, and got to my bedroom, her clothes were laid on the settee, and she was under the sheet and quilt.

"The sheets, they are cold."

"I'll see what I can do about that."

She was right. The sheets were cold, even for me, but the contrast between their coolness and the silk of her skin made me want to wrap myself around her. I didn't, instead just held her and enjoyed the moment. There were too many moments in the past I hadn't enjoyed, and there might not be that many in the future. Involuntarily, I shivered.

"What do you think? Are you angry with me?"

"Heavens, no. I was just thinking."

A gust of wind, moaning past the eaves, punctuated my words.

"Sometimes, too much we think."

"It's the kind of world we live in. How can you not think when there are murders, and you have to wonder why the Spazi show up in a university town?"

"You worry about the Spazi?"

"Yes," I admitted.

"Are the Spazi like Ferdinand's NeoCorps, Johan, dragging innocents from their beds?"

"All security police have their problems," I reflected. "Even those with the best intentions."

"Do you think the Spazi have good intentions?" She curled upside my arms and shivered, warm as her bare skin felt against me.

"They did once. Now, I am not so certain."

"All of them are beasts."

"At times," I agreed. "It is a hard job, and it makes hard people."

"Why do you say that?" Her lips turned toward mine, and I kissed them, gently, and for a long time. "Tell me," she prompted.

I shifted my weight so that her body did not cut off all the circulation in my arm, and held her tightly, letting that satin skin warm me, taking in the fragrant scent of Llysette and perfume. Finally I rolled back, letting my head rest on the pillow, my eyes on the white plaster of the ceiling, not wanting to look into her eyes, not then. "The world gets harder every year, and people lie more. Ferdinand claimed he would not invade France, and he did. Now he says he will not turn the Spanish protectorate into part of the Empire, but how good is that promise? Marshall deGaulle claimed that New France would not annex Belize, or Honduras, but they did. Here in our country, take Miranda. All the people who were around claim they were innocent and saw nothing. But she is dead. To find the answer, the watch or the Spazi must distrust everyone. I find that cold and hard . . . and perhaps necessary."

Llysette shivered in my arms, and I pulled the quilt over her bare shoulders. In time, she turned to me.

Later, even after she slept in my arms, I held her tightly, wondering how I could protect her when I doubted I could protect myself.

CHAPTER ELEVEN

• • •

On Monday morning, I made it through my run and exercises, and fixed both of us breakfast by seven—not bad considering that we hadn't gone to sleep all that early. While I ran, Llysette slept, or tried to. She still had the quilt pulled around her ears even after I had breakfast on the small table and the aroma of coffee filling the kitchen.

"Young woman," I called up the stairs. "Your coffee is ready. So are your fruit, toast, and poached eggs."

I thought I heard a muffled groan, and I called again. "Time to rise and shine, young lady."

"Young I am not, not this morning, but coffee will I have."

She clumped down the stairs, in slippers, and slouched into the chair on the other side of the small breakfast table, sipping the coffee and ignoring the food. I had hot chocolate, bad for my waistline, but I felt virtuous after my heavy exercise.

"What are you thinking?"

"Many things. The students, now they are getting sick, and they cough in my face. I tell them to get well and not bring their illnesses to me, but still they do. John Wustman, the pianist-coach, he will be here next week for master classes." She shrugged tiredly. "Many students do not know their music, and now come the midterms, and after that, the opera. Then I must start the rehearsals for the Christmas gala, and that music they have never opened." After sipping more coffee, she speared an orange slice, from probably one of the last oranges we would see for a while.

"They never think ahead."

"Think . . . what is that?" She dipped her toast into the half-runny eggs.

I poured more coffee into her mug, and she smiled. "Thank you, Johan. It is nice not to fix the breakfast."

I didn't comment on the fact that I doubted she had breakfast if I didn't fix it.

After we finished, Llysette took a shower while I scraped and washed the dishes. Then I raced upstairs and hopped into the shower while she struggled with her makeup.

I dropped Llysette by her house just before eight and headed back to town and Samaha's for my paper. There was a space right outside Louie's emporium, and I dashed in.

After nodding to Louie, I pulled out my *Asten Post-Courier* and left a dime, taking a quick glance at the headlines before even leaving Samaha's. The Derkin box was empty; another day had passed without my learning who Mr. Derkin was.

The newspaper headline was bland enough: "NO COMPROMISE BE-TWEEN DIRIGIBLES AND JETS." Since I could guess the content of the story, I folded the paper under my arm and walked through the blustery wind back to the Stanley.

Llysette's steamer was not yet in the faculty car park, I noted as I parked the Stanley in a vacant space closest to the Music and Theatre building. With my folder in hand, I trudged to my office. Although the main office was open and Gilda's coat was on the rack, I did not see her. There was a message from David, indicating that Tuesday's departmental meeting would start at a quarter to four instead of four o'clock sharp.

I took it and made my way upstairs to my office. There I briefly checked the paper.

There was almost nothing new in the *Asten Post-Courier,* not about Babbage fires or political gambits, except for an editorial warning Speaker Hartpence to beware of sacrificing the long-held Columbian ideal of free trade to short-term political goals. With the usual Dutch diplomacy, it did not actually accuse the Speaker of political idiocy.

Then I looked over the master class schedule. Gregor Martin appeared to be free until ten. I picked up my leather folder and headed back out. Gilda waved, and I waved back.

Gertrude and Hector were mulching the flower beds beside the brick walk. As usual, Gertrude wore the unfailing smile and Hector the somber mien, but their hands were quick, and they worked unhesitatingly, taking care to ensure that the wind did not scatter the bark chips onto the bricks of the walk.

"Good day," I said as I passed.

"Good day, sir," chirped Gertrude, and I wondered what personality disorder had rendered her a de-ghosted zombie.

Gregor Martin's office was in the side of the building away from the music wing, and probably only the same size as my office, for all that he was head of an entire area and I was only a subprofessor. His door was open, and he was pacing beside his desk as I rapped on the door frame.

"Yes."

"Johan Eschbach, Natural Resources. We met after several productions last year. I'm also a friend of Llysette's." I extended my hand.

He ignored it. "What do you need, Johan?"

"Well, Gregor, I need to know whether a student absolutely has to take Introduction to Theatre before taking the Two-B course."

"It's a prerequisite."

"Even for an arts school graduate?"

Surprisingly, Martin shrugged. "You know, I really don't care. Most of them know nothing about theatre, not in the performing sense. You have a student who wants to try, I don't care. I'm tired of protecting them from themselves."

"Is this a bad time?" I took the chair by the desk, and he actually sat down. If Miranda Miller had been right, and all the new faculty had secrets too heavy to bear, what secret weighed down Gregor Martin?

"No worse than any other." He picked up a black pencil and twisted it in his fingers.

"You came here from the Auraria Performing Arts School. I imagine it was a shock."

"You imagine?"

"I came from the capital, good old Columbia itself, and found that most of the students knew very little about politics, and cared less. Why would it be any different in the theatre? Vanderbraak Centre isn't exactly the great white way of New Amsterdam or the musical Valhalla of Philadelphia."

"You're right. But it's worse in theatre. They all have this . . . this Dutch stolidity." He set down the pencil and waved his hands, almost disconnectedly. "They can't even imagine being something other than what they are. Theatre is the art of creating a different reality. How can you create a different reality when you can't even imagine its possibility?"

"What is, is. Is that it?"

"More like what isn't, isn't—but it has to be for good theatre."

"What about a sense of wonder? Take ghosts," I offered. "We see a ghost, and whether we like it or not, it exists. You can't touch it, exactly, and you can't tell exactly when it will appear. Doesn't it make you wonder?" I shrugged. "But you talk about . . . what if there were a world where there were no ghosts? How would that change things? I asked that in a class. No one knew. They hadn't even thought about it."

"That's it. They don't even think about it. How could you envision a *Hamlet* without the impetus of his father's ghost?"

"That could be rather discouraging. What do they do when they see Professor Miller's ghost? Just look and plod on?"

He nodded. "I asked one of them to really look at her ghost before it disappeared. He's cast in *Hamlet* next term. You know what he said?"

"I'm afraid to guess."

" 'It's just a ghost.' " Martin slammed his hand on the desk. "It's just a ghost!"

"Sad about Miranda," I mused. "Now she's just another ghost."

"I don't know that the woman was ever alive—always walking around with that self-pitying air, as though the world were about to crush her."

"Perhaps it was," I said. "She was born to money, widowed young, and forced to raise and educate two children."

"Lots of people do that, and they don't carry the weight of the world around so that everyone can see."

"But was that enough to make someone want to kill her?"

"No. I doubt that." Martin leaned forward across the desk. "What did you do in government, Johan?"

"Before they ran me out, I was in charge of environmental matters. Why?"

"Because you've scarcely said 'good day' to me before now."

"I didn't have a student who had questions, and your reputation is not exactly as the most approachable—"

"Ha! Well, that's true. So why are you worried about who killed Miranda?"

"I'm attached to Llysette, and she's single and attractive, and no one knows who killed Miranda or why. Do you blame me?"

"Do you suspect me?"

"No," I answered truthfully. "But you're probably pretty observant, and you might have seen something."

"You don't trust the watch?"

"It's not a question of trust. They may even have a suspect, but they won't arrest whoever it might be unless there's evidence. The good Dutch character, you know. Without evidence, no arrest." I laughed. "Of course, once there's any evidence at all, it's rather hard to change their minds. For now, though, legalities don't protect Llysette."

"You have a point there. Not a very good one, but a point." He frowned. "You can believe me or not. I was in the lighting booth, and I didn't see anyone, except for the students. Martin Winston was one, and the other was Gisela Bars. They were with me the whole time. And I don't know why anyone would even bother with Miranda. I really don't. She tried to flirt with you, and with Branston-Hay, and with Henry Hite, but you never had eyes for anyone except Llysette, and they love and honor their wives, at least so far as I know. Me? She never looked in my direction, thank heavens. With Amy, that was probably a good thing."

"Amy is your wife?"

He nodded. "She got a job as an electronics technician with the state watch in Borkum."

"Yes." I waited.

"That's it. You know what I know. That's also what I told the watch." He stretched and stood. "Have any ideas about getting acting students to think about creating reality?"

I stood, following his lead. "Could you play-act? Make one of them a ghost, and insist that the others treat him or her like a real ghost? And start knocking points off their grades for every unrealistic action they take?"

"You believe that would work?"

"I don't know, but a lot of them live only for grades. Make it real through the use of grades—sometimes that works."

"Obviously a graduate of the school of practical politics."

"Theory often doesn't work, I've found. And Dutch students do respond to practical numbers."

He actually grinned, if only for a moment, then bowed.

I found my way back to my office, noting that the two zombies had finished mulching the flower beds along the one walkway and were working on those flanking the stairs up to the Physical Sciences building. Gilda waved as I passed her office and climbed the stairs.

When I got back to the Natural Resources building, David was nowhere around, as was so often the case, and Gilda was juggling calls on the wireset console.

"Greetings, Johan. Why so glum?" asked young Grimaldi from the door of his office. His gray chalk-stripe suit and gray and yellow cravat marked either his European heritage or natural flamboyance. I wasn't sure which.

"I just had a meeting with Gregor Martin. He actually smiled once."

"He does sometimes. He's actually a pretty good director, but I'd be grim if I had to work with our students in theatre, too. It's bad enough in geography and natural resources. One of them wrote that a monsoon was a class of turbojet bomber in the Austro-Hungarian Luftwehr."

"He's probably right."

"But in geography class?" Grimaldi laughed. "See you later. Did you get David's note?"

"Which one?"

He laughed again, and went back into his office, while I unlocked my door and stepped inside, stepping on a paper that had been slipped under the door. I picked it up—Clarice Reynolds was the named typed on the cover sheet—and shook my head. Despite written instructions on the syllabus directing students to leave papers in my box in the department office, some never got the word.

I set the folder on the corner of the small desk and sat down. After looking blankly out the window for a long time, I finally picked up the handset and dialed, listening to the whirs and clicks until a hard feminine voice answered, "Minister vanBecton's office."

"Yes. This is Doktor Johan Eschbach. I have discovered that I will be in Columbia City on Thursday, and I thought I might get together with Minister vanBecton sometime in the late afternoon."

"Just a moment, please, Doktor."

I found the tip of my fountain pen straying toward my mouth, but I managed to stop before I put more tooth marks on the case. Outside, the clouds were thickening, but it was still probably too warm for snow.

"Johan, what took you so long? You got your invitation on Friday." Again, van-Becton's voice was almost boomingly cheerful.

"On Friday, you may recall, I was in Columbia. I did not actually receive the invitation until Saturday, and I didn't think you wanted to be bothered over the weekend."

"I'm in a bit of a rush here, but what do you say to stopping in around four o'clock? That will give you plenty of time to get dressed for the reception. Where are you staying?"

"Probably with friends, but that remains to be seen."

"Many things do, but I look forward to seeing you on Thursday." A click, and he was gone.

I looked up another number in my address book and dialed.

"Elsneher and Fribourg."

"Johan Eschbach for Eric, please."

"Just a moment."

The clouds outside were definitely getting blacker.

"Johan—is it really you?"

"Who else? I called because I'll be in town on Thursday. They invited the old hack to a presidential dinner."

"You're more than welcome to stay with us. Judith would like that. So would I. Even if you have to attend the dinner, at least we can have breakfast together on Friday. Can't we?"

"I'd like that. How is Judith?"

"She's fine." He coughed. "I've got a client on the wire . . ."

"I understand. Can I stop by the house about five, before the dinner?"

"Sure. I'll tell Judith. See you then." And he clicked off.

I watched the clouds for a moment, then, before my eleven o'clock, collected the copies of the short test I planned to spring on my students, leafed through my notes, and skimmed the latest copy of the *Journal of Columbian Politics*. I tried not to hold my nose at the article entitled "Rethinking the Role of the Politician's Personal Life."

At ten before eleven, squaring my shoulders, I collected the greenbooks and the thirty copies of the test and marched over to Smythe Hall to do battle over environmental economics.

Once the class had filed in, I pulled the greenbooks from under the desk.

"Unnnnghhh . . ." That was a collective sigh.

I smiled brightly and handed out the greenbooks first, followed by the single sheet of the test. "You can answer one question or the other with a short essay. You have twenty minutes. Just answer one question," I repeated with a caution created by past experience.

"But, Doktor, this test was not announced."

"If you check the syllabus, you will note that it states that tests may be given in any class."

"Unnnghhhh . . ."

I had the feeling, from the groans, from the distracted looks on students' faces during the lecture following the test, and from leafing through a few of the green-books when I returned to my office, that not a few had neither read nor considered the assignment.

My two o'clock wasn't much better, not when half the class failed to understand the distinction between pathways of contamination and environmental media.

After my two o'clock, rather than immediately deal with either exams or the papers I had collected in my last class, I walked down to the post centre. I could have gone at lunchtime, since Llysette had been invited to a working lunch by Doktor Geoffries to discuss the student production schedule for the spring, but instead I'd spent the time trying to scan through some of the journal articles—not that I would ever catch up. Not if I wanted to remain sane.

Constable Gerhardt was by the empty bandbox in the square, chatting with the same young watch officer who seemed to turn up regularly when I was around, thanks, I suspected, to Minister vanBecton. I nodded to them both, rather than tipping the hat I wasn't wearing, since it still wasn't cold enough to wear one.

The chill wind had been promising snow for more than a week, but we had gotten neither cold rain, sleet, nor snow—just continuing cold wind—although the thick clouds to the northwest looked more than usually threatening. Despite the blustery weather and the few leaves hanging on the trees, the grass in the square was raked nearly spotlessly clean; even the hedges had been picked clean, as usual.

The lobby of the post centre was almost deserted, with only a gray-haired, stocky woman standing at the window. I unlocked and opened the postbox. Besides the monthly electric bill from NBEI and the wireline bill from New Bruges Telewire, there were two legal-size envelopes. The brown one had no return address. The other had the letterhead of International Import Services, PLC. Both were postmarked "Federal District."

I tucked all four into my black leather case, which contained, generally, my lectures and materials for the day.

"Ye find anything interesting?" asked Maurice.

"You always ask, and you always see it first." I grinned at the post handler. He grinned back, as always.

I walked quickly back to my office, my breath steaming in the afternoon air. I waved to Gilda as I passed the front office.

"Doktor Eschbach, Doktor Doniger was looking for you."

"Is he in his office?"

"For a little while, I think." She looked over her shoulder quickly, as if to confirm her statement. Her shoulders were stiff.

I knocked on the frame of the half-open door. "You were looking for me?"

"Yes, Johan. Please come in."

I shut the door behind me and looked around the paper-piled office. David believed in horizontal filing. Although he didn't invite me, I sat down in the single chair anyway.

Before he could get started, I said, "I've been invited to a Presidential Palace dinner on Thursday. So I'll have to make up Thursday's and Friday's classes one way or another."

"You always do, Johan, and I will tell the dean. She will be pleased that our faculty continues to travel in such exalted circles." He smiled.

I smiled and waited. Then I added, "Gilda said you were looking for me."

"Johan, I read your commentary in the last *Journal of Columbian Politics.* Don't you think it was a trifle . . . unfounded?" He leaned back in his creaky swivel and puffed on the long meerschaum, filling the office with intermittent blasts of air pollution, the kind I'd once been charged with reducing when it occurred at industrial sites.

"Commentaries are by nature unfounded. Of course, I could have made it three times as long and proved it with examples."

"Do you honestly believe that disposable glass is better than recycling metals? You even cited a recycling rate of almost eighty percent in major Columbian cities."

"Obviously what I wrote was not so clear as I thought." I coughed before I continued, glad that I had not followed my father's pipe-smoking habits. "My point was not that either was environmentally better. You can make a case for either. I was pointing out that the Reformed Tories used the press and half-facts to build a case against the Liberals that had no factual support. In short, that despite all the environmental rhetoric it was politics as usual. Just like the ghost business is more politics than science."

"The ghost business? That sad affair with Miranda Miller? Surely you weren't mixed up with that, were you?"

"Only to the degree that one gets mixed up when a murder occurs before a friend's recital. That wasn't what I was referring to, however. I meant all these bombings and fires in schools across the country, all in the Babbage centers, and all protesting supposed ghosting research."

David looked totally blank. "What does this have to do with the journal article?"

"They're both political. You can make a case for or against disposable glass; you can make a case for or against ghosting research. Does the voting public really pay any attention to the facts? It's a question of which side most successfully appeals to existing prejudices."

"Johan, I'm still troubled about the glass business."

"Most people don't realize it, David, but glass is structurally a liquid. A very stiff liquid, to be sure, but a liquid. It is also virtually inert, and comprised mainly of silicon and various oxides. Provided lead isn't used, as in crystal, you can bury it or dump it and the only harm it can do you is cut you. Metals aren't nearly as beneficial to the environment, and even with recycling, some are lost to the environment. So, claiming that recycled metals are more beneficial than discarded glass is misleading. Glass could certainly be recycled, and if it weren't so cheap, that could have happened long ago. It may still happen."

"Dean Er Recchus asked me if I thought that the commentary would hurt the fund-raising effort."

"Not if it's handled right. Just pretend you never saw it. Pretend that you have so many people writing in so many publications that you can't keep track, and no one will think a thing. Make an issue of it, and I'm sure you both can find a way to hurt fund-raising."

"Johan, I really wish you were not so . . . cynical."

"Realistic, David. Realistic. Besides, if the dean gives you too much trouble, point out that no one made an issue of her rather close friendship with Marinus Voorster."

"I couldn't do that."

I stood up. "Then why are you bothering me about an obscure commentary in a journal no one outside academia even reads?"

"Johan, I never meant to——"

"Good. I need to get ready for my two o'clock." I left, nodding at Gilda with a polite smile that was probably transparent. While I had some indication of David's lack of involvement with the whole ghost business, his toadying to Dean Er Recchus was inexcusable. He had tenure. Meddling much with his budget would have upset the university system budget committee. Just because he was worried that anything might upset the dean, as if he even understood what real pressures were—I shook my head at the thought as I opened my office door. And neither had even noticed the commentary until more than a month after it had been published. David was looking for an excuse, more than likely, but why? Because I didn't put up with his academic small-mindedness?

Back in my office, after I put down my folder, I opened the International Import Services envelope first. It contained an invoice and a cheque. The cheque was for five hundred dollars; the invoice merely stated, "Consulting Services." I didn't recognize the name on the signature line—Susan something or other—but it was undoubtedly genuine. International Imports was a real firm, trading mainly in woolens, electronics, and information. It had a retinue of consultants worldwide, and probably half of them were actually export consultants. I'd always fallen in the other category. Still, five hundred dollars was equivalent to nearly a month's pay as a professor, and I took a deep breath.

I studied the second envelope before opening it. Although I couldn't be absolutely sure, the slightly more flexible feel of the paper around the flap indicated a high probability that it had been steamed open. If I had looked, I suspected that I would have found that most of the envelopes with clippings had been similarly treated, at least recently. VanBecton's people had been tracking me and knew my comings and goings. Presumably they had read my post, including the clippings, untraceably posted in the Federal District, probably at the main post center. The clipping itself was short.

Sr. Louis (RPI)—A series of explosions ripped through the Aster Memorial Electronic Sciences Center at the University of Missouri at St. Louis shortly after midnight this morning. The ensuing fire gutted the building. Although no fatalities were reported, more than a dozen firemen were injured in the blaze that turned the skyline of St. Louis into a second dawn.

According to early reports, the explosions began in the Babbage wing of the center. Only last week, the chancellor of the University of Missouri system had defended UMSL's policy of accepting Defense Ministry grants for psychic research.

Governor Danforth denounced the action as that of "ill-informed zealots." Speaking for the Alliance for World Peace, Northrop Winsted added the Alliance's condemnation of violence. Similar statements were also issued by the Midwest Diocese of the Roman Catholic Church and the Missouri Synod of the Anglican-Baptists.

At the slapping of rain droplets on my second-floor windows, I glanced out to the north, but the rain was falling so heavily I could barely see Smythe Hall across the green.

I slipped the clipping and the cheque into my folder, and, with a sigh, pulled out the stack of short papers I had collected from Environmental Economics 2B. Most of the students thought they understood economics and the environment. I did, too, until I'd actually had to deal with both.

I'd graded perhaps ten of the twenty-six papers by quarter to five, and was still chuckling over one line: "Money should be no object nor price no impediment to the continuation of our priceless environment . . ." While I understood the underlying sentiment, the writer—one Melissa Abottson—had inadvertently illustrated the fuzzy thinking of her generation. What she meant was that a pristine environment was worth a great deal, but that wasn't what she had written. Priceless meant without a price, and if the environment were priceless then money was irrelevant—which certainly wasn't what she meant. Likewise, the environment means the external conditions and objects surrounding us, or the world, and in the broadest sense, the environment, in some form or another, will continue, whether we do or not.

The problem with environmental economics is not one of willingness, but one of capability. No society has infinite resources, and certainly not a Columbia faced with an aggressive New France to the south, a blackmailing Quebec to the north, Ferdinand in Europe, and the twin terrors in Asia.

With a last head shake at the naiveté of the young, and at the recollection that I, too, had been equally naive, I left the stack on my desk, pulled on my waterproof, and took the umbrella from the corner. The main office was empty, and all the other doors were closed when I stepped out into the continuing light rain. My breath puffed white, and the cold felt welcome after the stuffiness of the building.

Umbrella in hand, I walked past the brick-stepped top landing of the long stairs down to the lower campus and then around the Music and Theatre building, stepping carefully to avoid the puddles and taking my time as I passed the closed piano studio. Even through the rain I could see that the Babbage console that had been in Miranda's studio was gone.

I stepped into the main office of the Music and Theatre Department. "Martha, have you seen Llysette?"

"No. Oh, wasn't she taking some students to the state auditions in Orono?"

I put a hand to my forehead. "I forgot." I offered a sheepish grin. "She told me, and I forgot."

Martha grinned back at me. "It can happen to anyone."

"How's Dierk taking the ghosting business?"

"It's better now." Martha frowned. "As a matter of fact, no one's seen Miranda's ghost for several days now."

"I saw Dr. Branston-Hay removing his equipment. Was he studying the ghost?"

Martha looked around, then lowered her voice. "He asked us not to mention it. People get very sensitive about those sorts of things, even here."

"I understand." I nodded. "Some of the papers had stories about bombings at other universities' Babbage centers."

"Really?"

"Yes. There was one the other day in St. Louis."

"How terrible."

"You can see why Dr. Branston-Hay wants to be very careful. He probably only wanted a few people to know."

"Just Dierk and me, and the watch, of course. Their video camera is still there."

"I won't say a word—not even to Llysette."

"Thank you, Dr. Eschbach."

Instead of heading home, I went back to my office and locked the door. I pulled down the blinds and took out the thick old hard-sided briefcase, filled with a melange of older publications. The small package of tools and the special wedge came out of the false bottom easily, and I slid the flap shut and pocketed the small, soft-leather case. After replacing the publications, I set the open briefcase on the corner of the desk. I took a Babbage disk in its case from the shelf and slipped it into my pocket. It barely fit. After that I sat down and graded another dozen papers in the time until it began to get dark.

Contrary to popular opinion, nighttime is not the best time for marginally savory work. Early dinnertime is, especially on a university campus where most students are of thrifty Dutch stock and actually eat in the cafeteria.

I dialed Branston-Hay's office number, but there was no response. So I picked up the special wedge and put it in my right pants pocket. Then I picked up my black leather case, half-filled with the day's class notes, and stepped out into the hall. Once outside, I locked the door to the department, the former residence of some obscure poet—Frost, I think, was the name—and headed across the green to the west.

The main door to the Physical Sciences building was unlocked, as a number of laboratory courses ran late. There were always several early evening classes, but none, according to the schedule, involving Branston-Hay or the Babbage laboratories.

I walked to the main Babbage room and glanced inside. Perhaps half the consoles were occupied, mainly for word processing by students worried about various midterm projects, I guessed, although I did see one student struggling with some sort of flow chart.

The smaller laboratory, the one Branston-Hay used for research, was at the end of the corridor. I knocked, for the sake of appearances, and was surprised when a round-faced man with cold blue eyes opened the door.

"Yes?"

"I was looking for Gerald."

"He's not here at the moment. Could you check back later, or better yet, in the morning?"

"I'll catch him in the morning. Thank you," I said as I turned without even hesitating, knowing that I dared not.

Although the man I had never seen before had kept his considerable bulk between me and the laboratory, I caught a glimpse of it, enough to realize that I'd definitely missed more than a bet. The windows were painted black, and at least a dozen technicians were still working. There was some sort of strange apparatus that looked like a silver helmet, the kind they use to dry women's hair. Everyone, even the man at the door, wore what looked like a metal hair net.

The doorkeeper wasn't a Babbage type. The slightly thicker cut of his coat, and what it concealed, the fact that the other technicians wore no coats, and the guard's flat blue eyes told me he was more at home in vanBecton's office than in Gerald's laboratory.

After I bowed and left, I made my way back toward the office section, around two corners. When I arrived at Branston-Hay's office, I knocked sharply on the door, but there was no answer, and the thin line between the tiled floor and the heavy door was dark.

After glancing puzzledly around, as if mystified that my appointment had not been kept, and seeing no one, I slipped the lock picks out of my jacket pocket.

As soon as I had the door open, I stepped inside and locked it. Then I tapped the wedge loosely between the bottom of the door frame and the floor. The adhesive rubber would jam if anyone tried to open the door. Simple, and effective. I also unlocked the window, but did not open it. I did lift it slightly to make sure that I could. I have gone out windows before, although I would rather not.

I tried to remind myself of the old adage that you should never try to find it all out at once. Removals you do once or not at all, but information gathering requires far more patience and repetition. That's one reason good espionage is far more difficult than murder.

The first step was activating the difference engine, not that dissimilar to my own recent model. After I turned on the machine and all the lights came on, and the pointer flipped into place on the screen, I typed in the initializing command, and smiled as the substructure menu appeared. Trying not to hurry, I scanned the directories until I found what I wanted, or, I should say, the absence of what I wanted.

If you attempt to hide something, you have to leave a keyhole, and that was what I needed. Branston-Hay hadn't been that subtle. He'd assumed that any datapick would need to unscramble the keys. I could have cared less. I just wanted to copy them.

Still, it took almost half an hour before the machine began to copy what I needed onto the data disk I had brought.

While it copied, I helped myself to his desk. As I had suspected, everything— or almost everything—was strictly related to his teaching, and the office was as clean as when I had visited earlier.

I did find a folder of clippings, which I began to read.

COLUMBIA (FNS)—After meeting with departing Ambassador Fujihara of Japan, President Armstrong today suggested that the Reformed Tories would find that their yet-to-be announced initiative on reducing the VAT on tobacco exports, while desirable from the perspective of Far Eastern relations, was more of a public relations effort than a real step toward solving the growing Asian trade imbalance. Speaker Hartpence had no comment . . .

CHICAGO (RPI)—In his speech opening the National Machine Tool Exposition in Chicago, President Armstrong gently chided the Reformed Tories for even considering expanding product liability tort claim protection. According to the president, "Speaker Hartpence would strangle Columbian business to remedy a nonexistent problem." Neither the Speaker nor his press aide were available for comment . . .

COLUMBIA (RPI)—Even while the general perception of President Armstrong has been that of a vigorous opponent of the Reformed Tories, slashing publicly at their every weakness, his private meetings with members of the House have been exceedingly different.

"It's almost as though the president were running for election to the House, and attempting to line up votes for Speaker," said former Commerce Minister Hiler.

Since President Armstrong's election last year, virtually every influential member of the House has been invited to an intimate and off-the-record dinner or luncheon at the Presidential Palace. While not all members have been willing to divulge the exact nature of the conversations, all indicate that the president was unusually attentive and nonpartisan, unlike in his public appearances, generally asking questions and listening . . .

MEMPHIS (SNS)—Today, in dedicating the Memphis Barge-Railway Terminus, President Armstrong denounced Speaker Hartpence's policies as shortsighted and bankrupt. The president claimed that the Speaker is secretly considering accepting Asian revisions to the Law of the Oceans Treaty which would effectively close both the Sea of Japan and the South China Sea to Columbian traders and provide Chung Kuo and Japan with effective trade advantages in Asia in return for similar concessions to England and Columbia in the Caribbean and the Mediterranean.

"Such concessions, if true, would be ruinous," declared Cecil Rhodes, IV, chairman of the Columbian Maritime Association . . .

Speaker Hartpence angrily denied the president's charge, stating that he "has nothing to hide."

SEATTLE (NWNS)—In accepting the frigate *C.S. Ericson* for the Columbian Navy, President Armstrong proclaimed "the continuing need for a strong Columbian presence across the waters of the globe."

In a scarcely veiled criticism of Speaker Hartpence and Foreign Minister Gore, the president added, "Reducing the federal budget for ships such as this, or for the long-range electric submersibles such as the *Fulton,* is truly penny wise and pound foolish." He went on to suggest . . .

"Both Minister Gore and Defense Minister Holmbek later denied that the submersible procurement budget was to be reduced . . ."

I flipped through the rest of the clips, jotting down dates, pages, and newspapers for all twenty-odd stories. By the time I had copied the dates of the stories, the machine, faster than the human hand, had copied a far vaster volume of material. I folded my notes, slipped them into my folder, replaced the disk in its case and the case in my pocket, returned the difference engine to its previous inert state, then removed the wedge and stepped confidently into the empty hall. The only student I saw in the science building did not even bother to look up as he trudged toward the gentlemen's facilities at the corner of the first floor.

I nodded to two students I did not know on my way across the green and back to my office, where I replaced the wedge on the shelf, closed and replaced the old case in the closet, and turned off the lights. I kept the lock picks, uneasy as they made me, in my pocket. They almost looked like a set of hex wrenches or screwdrivers, but any watch officer would know instantly what they were.

Then again, if they stopped me, it would either be a formality or lock picks would be the least of my problems. I picked up my folder and locked the office, leaving the uncorrected papers on my desk. For once, the students probably wouldn't get them back at the next class.

The wind blew, and more drizzle sleeted around me, almost like ice, as I walked to the steamer. By the time I was inside the Stanley, I wished I had worn a heavier coat.

The roads were beginning to ice up, and visibility was poor at best. I was glad for the four-wheel option when I reached the hill below the house. No matter what they say about four-wheel drive not helping on ice, it does.

After I garaged the Stanley and went into the house, I lit off a fire in the woodstove in the main parlor, even before I checked to see what Marie had fixed. After unloading my pockets onto the antique desk and setting the disk case by the difference engine, I climbed upstairs, where I hung up my jacket and pulled on a heavy Irish fisherman's sweater before descending to the kitchen.

The smell of steak pie told me before I even opened the warming oven, although it was probably drier than she had intended, but it still tasted wonderful. I ate it right from the casserole dish, washing it down with a cold Grolsch, both of which actions would have horrified my mother.

I did wash the dishes, though, before I headed into the study. Some Dutch habits die hard.

After I turned on the difference engine, and as it completed its powering up and systems checks, I pulled out the Babbage disk, wondering exactly what I had.

As I expected, the files were encrypted, but, if you know what you're doing, that's not a problem. Time-consuming, but not an insoluble problem. Why not? Because most nonalgorithmic systems used on a single machine have to have a finite and relatively easy key, and because, in most systems, you can go under the architecture and twiddle it. Of course, I made copies first.

The first interesting section shouldn't have been on Gerald's machine at all—his notes and speculations. Most Babbage types fall into two categories. There are those who know the machine so well that everything is custom Babbage language shorthand. I hate those, because it's all unique. Branston-Hay was the other kind, the kind who play with difference engines, who document everything and link it all together. It's as though they have to tell the Babbage engine how important they are—almost as bad as a politician's diaries.

You can figure out either kind, because the way it's structured gives it away in the first case, and the documentation in the second is certainly elaborate.

Still, it was well past midnight before I could break through, and that was as much luck as anything.

Some of the notes were especially chilling.

> . . . headset design . . . multipoint electrode sensors to enhance the ambient magnetic field . . . A-H design overstresses basal personality . . .
> . . . Heisler ignored possibility of disassociated field duplication . . . phased array of field sensors . . . duplication of field perturbations would emulate basal personality . . .
> . . . personality implantation . . . greater density perfusion at high field strength and minimal transfer rate . . .
> . . . Babbage electro-fluidics emulate field capture parameters . . .

That one made sense, given what I knew about ghosting. Instant death doesn't create ghosts. It's a stress-related, magnetic-field-enhanced personality transfer phenomenon, and Gerald had merely quantified the electronic and magnetic conditions.

The last entry in the notes was worse.

> Empirical proof of capture—MM case. Theoretically, the psychic magneto-net should work in most conditions, since a new ghost is clearly the strongest . . . Practically the disassociator should also work . . . but the ethical problems preclude construction . . . Suspect it might not work unless the subject is in an agitated condition . . . No way to test at this point.

The rest of the files dealt with specifications. Two were actually schematics, and after reading the descriptions of the "basal field disassociator" and the "perturbation replicator" I realized I might need the lock picks again—if I weren't already too late—or a good Babbage assembly shop. The third file that looked interesting was called a personality storage file, and required what looked like a modified scanner, although it didn't look like any scanner I had ever seen.

There was also what looked to be an elaborate protocol of some sort attached to the personality storage file—again with explanations under such headings as "visual delineation file," "image structure," and "requirements for compression/decompression."

I thanked Minister vanBredakoff for the two years undercover as a Babbage programmer in the Brit's mercantile Babbage net. That and a skeptical nature helped.

Theoretically, neither the disassociator nor the replicator looked that hard to build. I began to sketch what I needed . . . and got colder and colder. Most of the components were almost off the shelf, although I'd have to check the specifications with Bruce as soon as I could. Then, almost as an afterthought, I sketched out the scanner I needed before I stumbled upstairs and into bed, leaving my clothes strewn across the settee under the window.

If Branston-Hay were doing what I thought, Miranda's murder was almost inconsequential—unless she had known.

I lay in the darkness, in my cold bed under crisp cold sheets, listening to the cold sleet. Even the faint remnant of Llysette's perfume somehow smelled cold.

CHAPTER TWELVE

• • •

Because I scarcely slept well, even as late as I had collapsed on Monday night, getting up early Tuesday was almost welcome. Or it would have been if not for the headache that had come with the morning. I treated that by skipping my exercise routine and having a cup of hot chocolate and a bigger breakfast than normal—toast with raspberry preserves, one of the last fresh pears from the tree, picked on Sunday before the ice storm, and two poached eggs. I knew I'd pay later with tighter trousers or more exercise.

A long hot shower helped, and I felt less like a ghost myself when I headed out to the car barn, carrying the empty box that had contained my difference engine. After gingerly stepping down the stone walk to avoid the icy spots, I crossed the bluestone to the barn, where, after opening the door, I put the box in the Stanley's front trunk and closed it.

I hadn't used firearms in years, and although I had a license, the last thing I wanted to do at the moment was to appear in the watch office to register to purchase one. If I used the ones I wasn't supposed to have, that could raise some rather confining issues. The government looks unkindly upon unregistered guns, especially those originating in government service—directly or indirectly.

Since any weapon would be better than none, particularly if I were considered unarmed, I thought about the professional slingshot I had used to keep the crows from my garden. I almost took it from the bracket in the barn and tucked it under the front seat of the Stanley. Then I had to laugh. A slingshot? If things got as bad as I thought they might, digging out what I wasn't supposed to have would be the least of my problems.

That thought bothered me, because I kept thinking that this minor problem or that illegality would be the least of my problems. That meant I had problems bigger than I really wanted to consider.

With all that, leather folder on the seat beside me, I was on the road south to Zuider before eight. I held my breath going down the hill on Deacon's Lane, but after that the roads were clear of the scattered ice.

Zuider sat on the southwest end of Lochmeer, the biggest lake in New Bruges, at least the biggest one totally inside the state. The Indians had called it Winnie-something-or-other, but the Dutch settlers opted for a variation on the familiar, and Lochmeer the lake became, and remained.

I turned south on Route Five, which followed the Wijk south for almost fifteen miles. Fifteen miles of stone-fenced walls, some enclosing winter-turned fields, some enclosing stands of sugar maples, others enclosing meadows for scattered sheep.

The stone walls reflected their heritage, each stone precisely placed, and replaced almost as soon as the frost heaved it out of position. Some were more than chest high, probably for the dairy herds that fed the New Bruges cheese industry.

It took me about twenty-five minutes to reach the spot where the Wijk winds west and Route Five swings east toward Lochmeer and Zuider. The well-trimmed apple orchards before I reached the three Loon Lakes reproached me. The trees made my hasty trimming look haphazard by comparison, and I felt there was yet another task awaiting me—sometime.

Most of Route Five had been redone, with passing lanes every five miles, but I always seemed to run up behind a hauler just at the end of the passing lanes, and that morning was certainly no exception.

Past the last Loon Lake, where I actually saw a pair of loons beyond the marshes, I slowed behind a spotless white tank-hauler—vanEmsden's Dairy, of course. From there I crawled past the fish hatchery and back southeast on Route Five until the hauler turned off for Gessen just outside of Zuider.

Even on the new road with its passing lanes, it took almost an hour from Vanderbraak Centre. I got the Stanley up to eighty once, about half its red line. I actually had it up close to the red line when I first got it. It was after Elspeth's death, and I took it out on the closed runway at Pautuxent. I had turned the thermals on and the Stanley had almost blended into the runway cement. They never did find out who I was, but I wouldn't recommend doing something that stupid.

Closer to Zuider, going that fast wasn't advisable anyway, but I've always had a tendency to push the red line.

Unlike some places, LBI opened at nine, and what I wanted was definitely special. Bruce had helped me with the specifications of the SII fluidic difference engine and the additional modules. Besides, we went back a long way, not in a fashion that was readily available to Billy vanBecton.

Bruce's place is about two blocks behind Union Street, where all the banks are, and there was plenty of parking in his small lot. The sign above the door was simple enough—LBI DIFFERENCE DESIGNERS. The initials stood for Leveraal Brothers, International. I'd never met his older brother, but Bruce had certainly been helpful.

A slight bleep sounded when I opened the door and carried the box into the store. Unlike most difference engine places, nothing was on display. If you go to LBI, it's either custom-made or custom-ordered. The SII logo was displayed, but not overpoweringly.

"Herr Doktor," offered Bruce, emerging from the back room, looking very bearded and academic under the silver-rimmed glasses, and very unlike a Babbage technician in his cravat and vest. "Troubles already? SII won't be happy."

"No expletives, please. I know how you feel about excessive and overpriced degrees. And there's no problem. The box is empty. I'll pick it up with my next commission for you."

"Do I really want to know what can I do for you?"

"Probably not, but I have a problem."

"We specialize in problems. Don't guarantee solutions, but problems we can certainly create."

I nodded toward the paper-stacked cubicle he called an office.

"Fine. You're paying."

He sat down, and I opened my folder, laying out the first rough schematic I'd drawn the night before. "Can you build this?"

He studied the drawing for a while. "I may have to improvise in places, but I can get the same effect. This looks like some professor's theory." He pointed. "You use that much amperage there and you'll have fused circuits here. A few other little problems like that. Nothing insurmountable." He cleared his throat. "What in hell is it?"

"It should generate and maybe project a magnetic field. Don't point it at anyone you like. As for what it really is—I don't know exactly. And you don't want to."

"Why do I want to build it, then?"

"Three reasons. First, I'll pay you. Second, I'm a good guy. Third, you want to be able to claim you have built the largest number of strange Babbage-related devices in the world."

"I may pass on the third. How soon do you need this?" Bruce took off the glasses and set them beside the blank screen of his own difference engine.

"Tomorrow."

"I can't. I just can't. Hoosler wants a system complete. It's a hard contract." He picked up the glasses and polished them with a spotless handkerchief pulled from his vest.

I sighed and laid two hundred dollars in bills on the shortest stack of papers. "That's half the bonus."

"Reason number one looks even better. Who's chasing you?"

"No one—yet."

"You think so, but you're not sure, or you wouldn't be carrying empty boxes around as if they were heavy."

I pulled out the second schematic and the sketch of the file storage hardware.

"I can't do two more—even with all the money in the world. I have to be in business next year."

"I won't need the second and third until Saturday."

"That I can do. What's this one? Or can you tell me?"

"This one I know. It's called something like a perturbation replicator."

"It replicates trouble? Why would you want something like that?"

"Not trouble. It's supposed to duplicate ghosts and suck the duplicate into Babbage disks."

"That's trouble." Bruce shook his head. "This is weird. No one would believe me if I told them." He looked at me and added, "But I won't."

"The other is some sort of electronic file conversion system." I pointed to my crude drawing. "I think it converts fields into a storage protocol."

"That looks more standard—as if anything you have is really standard."

"I like you, too." I nodded. "I'll be back tomorrow."

"Mornings like this, it feels just like ten years ago, and you know how I feel about that." Bruce's comments reflected the fact that he had never been that thrilled about being a technician for the Spazi.

"I know. Let's hope it's not."

"It really is that bad, isn't it?"

"If you don't hear anything, don't ask."

"It's that bad. You need some firepower?"

I considered. "No."

"You can ask tomorrow."

"I'll think about it."

"I take it you want this first thing portable? How much power? How long do you want it to operate?"

"A spring trigger switch, I think, and as much power as will fit."

"It's not going to fit under your coat. I can tell you that."

"I suspected." I rose. "Just like old times?"

"God, I hope not. Good luck, Johan."

"I don't know as I can rely on luck now."

"You never had the best."

I straightened up and left the drawings on his piled papers. "Tell me about it, Bruce."

"I'm sorry. That's not what I meant."

"I know. But it still hurts." I forced a smile. "I'll be back in the morning. Eight o'clock all right? I know it's before you open, but . . ."

"It'll be done then or not at all."

"Let me buy some spare disks."

"The highest-density ones, I assume."

"Of course."

He bowed, and I paid and carried the case of disks back to the steamer, not noting anyone strange. That didn't mean much, although Bruce had been a techie, and no one paid attention to the techies in government, and they generally paid less attention to them out of government. After all, what harm could a technician do? Didn't they just do what they were told?

The pair of loons had taken flight—or something—by the time I passed the Loon Lakes, and I got stuck behind another vanEmsden tanker, also spotless but puffing gray smoke, a sign that the boiler burners were out of trim.

I got back to the university by quarter to ten, later than I had hoped because I stopped by the New Bruges Bank to deposit the International Import cheque, which wouldn't compensate for what I was spending on hardware but might help. Then I rushed to the office, picking up my messages in a quick sweep.

"My, you'd think something important was about to happen," Gilda observed acerbically.

"I'm sorry. Good morning, Gilda."

"Good morning, Herr Doktor Eschbach."

"I did say I was sorry."

"Just like all men. You think a few sweet words make up for everything."

I caught the grin, and answered. "Of course. That's what women want, isn't it? Sweet words of deception?"

"You are impossible." She arched an eyebrow.

"No. Merely difficult."

"Better Doktor duBoise than me."

I smiled.

"You may go now, Herr Doktor."

"I can see that I stand dismissed." With a nod, I made my way upstairs and unlocked my office.

"At last, he's actually late," said Grimaldi as he hurried past me for his ten o'clock. "Will wonders never cease?"

"Not these days."

After I unloaded my folder, I picked up the papers I had left and finished grading the last handful, then recorded the generally abysmal marks. I swallowed hard and looked at the tests that needed to be graded.

After a moment, I picked up the handset and dialed Llysette's office/studio.

"Hello. A student I have . . ."

"This is Johan. I had to go to Zuider this morning to get some work done on my difference engine. I just got back."

"I will call you in a few minutes."

"Fine."

Click.

Preoccupied or angry? She had been the one who had been busy the night before.

I started in on the tests, which were, unfortunately, worse than the papers, and I had read perhaps a dozen when the wireset rang.

"Johan Eschbach."

"Johan. I am sorry, but the student . . . oh, I was so angry! My fault, she said it was. My fault that the music she had not learned. My fault that she had not listened."

"I'm sorry."

"Oh, I cannot stand it! It is my fault? They have no . . . no responsibility to learn? I should beat notes into their thick little Dutch heads."

"You do sound angry."

"Johan! I am not a child."

"What can I say? They're lazy. I'm grading a test, and half of them didn't read the assignment."

"Lazy! They should have been in Europe while Ferdinand's armies marched. So lucky they are and do not know it."

"I did call to see about dinner."

"I cannot, not all this week. I must beat notes and more notes. Oh, I cannot stand it!"

"Chocolate at Delft's at half past three?"

"That . . . I do not know. There is so much . . ."

"The university can spare you for a half hour."

"They are fortunate to have me."

"They are. Half past three?"

"That would be good. I must go. Another student, and I must beat notes."

I went back to the tests. More than half the class clearly hadn't read the assignment. In one way, it made things very easy. It doesn't take that long to flunk students who have no idea of the question. What takes time is determining the degree of knowledge exhibited. When there isn't any, it's quick. Half the class flunked, and only one student received an A. There were two B's, and the rest of those who passed got C's.

I gathered up both papers and exams and stuffed them into my folder, then headed back over to Smythe for my eleven o'clock.

I offered a smile to Gertrude, who was raking leaves across the green under a gray sky. She smiled vacantly back and continued raking, happy with the routine work. Hector did not even look up from his perfectly placed piles of soggy leaves.

Natural Resources 1A was the intro course, and most of us in the department had to teach it some of the time. Although it was basic, very basic, you would have thought none of the students had ever even considered the environment and natural resources.

We were working on the water cycle. Now, the whole basis of the water cycle is pretty simple. There's so much water in the world. The amount doesn't change much, and the question really is how much is usable for plant and animal life, particularly human beings, and how changes in the cycle affect that.

"There's enough water in the world that if the earth's surface were flat, which obviously it's not, we'd all be a mile under water. So why, Miss Haasfeldt, do we have drought conditions in the Saheel?"

"There's not enough water there."

I smiled. It was hard, but I smiled. "A little more detail, please. A drought means that there isn't enough water. With all that water in the oceans, *why* do we have a drought in mid-north Africa?"

"Well, it's the wind patterns . . ."

"What about the wind patterns?"

I tried not to shake my head too much. After all, they would be the ones running society before too long.

After the intro course, I ducked by the snack line in the student activities building and picked up a sandwich and tea. I ate alone, quickly, before I headed down to the post centre.

Besides two advertising circulars and the weekly edition of *Newsweek,* there was a letter from my mother.

"See!" exclaimed Maurice. "We do deliver the good material."

"Sometimes."

"Bother on ye, Doktor."

I grinned and opened the letter.

Dearest Johan,

I appreciated your letter of last week, and was delighted that you had managed to bring back the apple trees and even the old pear. While I do miss the old place, my visits to you in the warmer months are more than enough, and I certainly do not miss the winters!

Anna and I went to New Amsterdam yesterday to see *Miss Singapore.* It was good, but terribly depressing. I am glad you did not enter the Air Corps until after that sad situation was over. Your father always felt that we should have annexed the Sandwich Islands much earlier, and that having a big naval base at Pearl Harbor would have prevented much of the disaster in the Pacific. I don't know, only that the play was most moving.

I know that Llysette makes you happy—she seems very warm—but you come from very different backgrounds, and I hope you will be gentle with her. She needs much kindness, I think. I also wonder if the war in Europe took a little something out of her. I cannot say what it might be, and you can discount this as an old woman's fancy.

Here a few leaves still hang on the trees, but they will be gone before long. You were kind to invite me up again, but that week we are going to visit Aunt Elisabet in Baltimore. She is ninety-three, and I do not know how much longer she will be around. She still does beautiful needlework, though.

I enjoyed your article. The finer points were beyond me, but I did get the message. Anna liked it, too, and she made a copy for Douglas. He posted it in his office.

I hope you can see your way clear to stop by when you get a chance in that busy schedule of yours. . . .

I folded the letter back into the envelope as I finished climbing the stairs up to the lower campus.

My two o'clock was Environmental Politics 2B. Since most of them had taken the previous course from me, they knew what to expect. Most of them actually had read at least some of the assignment.

By the follow-on 2B class, we worked more on a discussion basis.

"Mr. Quellan, what are the basic trade-offs between incentive-based and command-and-control environmental laws?"

"Well, uhhh . . . When you give businesses incentives, it's in their interest to follow the laws."

"Please be more specific. Do you mean it's not in their interest to follow a command-and-control law that will fine them or put them in prison?"

"No, sir. I mean, I meant that with incentives they make money or lose less money by following the law. They will obey a command law, but they don't want to."

"Why not?"

Sometimes it was like pulling teeth. We hashed through that section, finishing up just before half-past three. I rushed down to Delft's and still got there before Llysette, but not by much.

Victor had just set the chocolate and biscuits on the table when she stepped into the greenhouse section of the cafe.

"*Bienvenue,* Doktor duBoise." Victor offered her a sweeping bow.

I did him one better and kissed her hand. "*Enchanté, mademoiselle.*"

"Johan, Victor, I have need of the chocolate."

Victor bowed and scraped away, and Llysette slumped into the chair. She sipped the chocolate, then bit into a biscuit.

"They are impossible . . . I stood on the stage of the Académie Royale, and to beat notes I must?"

"I ran a government ministry, and I have to give tests every class to get them to read their assignments?" I bit through a biscuit and sprayed crumbs across the wooden surface of the table.

"Johan . . . I did not come to discuss the students. To avoid them I came."

"Do you think that our hoopsters will win their korfball game tonight?"

"Korfball? Why do you ask such a thing?"

"Why not? Or would you rather I discussed the relative merits of postclassic Mozart as compared to Beethoven?"

"No music, please."

I sipped the hot chocolate before saying more. "David—the doktor Doniger— was worried about an article I wrote, because the dean was concerned it would hurt fund-raising. I made a politically inappropriate statement."

Tears welled in the corner of her eyes. "I hate this."

I squeezed her hand, and she squeezed back.

"Did you know that Michener's new book deals with the Sandwich Islands?"

We discussed literature until the clock struck four, and Llysette looked up. "My time . . . it is gone." She took a last bite of her biscuit and drained the chocolate, then rose and pulled her cape around her.

As I stood and left three dollars on the table for Victor, I suddenly realized that I had missed at least fifteen minutes of the departmental meeting.

"You look disturbed."

"It has been one of those days. I forgot that David moved the departmental meeting up to a quarter to four."

"It is important?"

"David thinks it is."

"Ah, the chairs. They think . . . what is the use?" She bent toward me and pecked my cheek. "Later this week, I will see you?"

"I don't know. When you are free, I'm not, and I'm tied to the dinner in Columbia. How about Saturday?"

"Mais oui." She looked at her watch. "I must go."

She scurried away and up the hill. I followed more sedately. If I were going to be late, late I would be.

David looked up as I slipped into the corner of the seminar room.

"I thought I had made the time change clear to everyone." His voice was mild.

"You did." I smiled. "I couldn't change a previous engagement."

"As we were discussing, we are being required to cut one course from our elective load next term. Since Doktor Dokus will be on sabbatical, we will put a zero cap on registrations on Natural Resources Three-B. That's the Ecology of Wetlands course. There are no seniors who need it to graduate."

"Is that wise?" asked Grimaldi. "Why don't we cap one of the baby eco courses?"

"That's where we get almost fifteen percent of our majors," countered Wilhelm Mondriaan.

"If we cancel the wetlands course—"

"Zero-capping is not a cancellation. That keeps the course options open."

"It's the same thing," snorted Grimaldi.

I sat back and listened.

After the meeting, which dragged on until past four-thirty, I reclaimed my folder from my office, locked up, and headed to the faculty car park.

I stopped by the Stanley, unloaded my folder. Then, with an exasperated shrug, I relocked the Stanley and marched up toward the Physical Sciences building, but instead of going through the front entrance, I took the narrow walkway around the downhill side as if I were headed to the Student Center.

Since I knew what I was looking for as I walked unconcernedly toward the center, I found them—inconspicuous little brown boxlike squares, heat sensors, probably with directional scanners behind the thin cloth shields. They only covered the right rear corner of the building. The other thing I noticed was that the laboratory windows did not look like they had been painted black from the outside. They looked like the silvery gray of heat-reflective glass. Someone had gone to a lot of trouble to keep Branston-Hay's research very low-profile, so much trouble that I felt stupid. I should have seen it, and yet I had been bumbling around, transparently pumping the good doktor. I shook my head and kept walking. Where had my brains been? I circled back to the Stanley the long way, feeling more and more foolish by the moment—and more scared.

Tired as I was, I hoped I could sleep—without nightmares—but at least Marie would have left me the main course of a dinner. It was definitely a luxury having her come every day, but I felt better when the house was spotless, and she liked the fact that I didn't hold her to fixed hours so long as she got the job done.

As I drove out of the car park, I did note that Llysette's Reo was still there.

CHAPTER THIRTEEN

• • •

Wednesday morning came too soon, even for me, and I usually like mornings. But I was dutiful and forced myself through the running and the exercises. My legs still ached, and the leaves by the stone walls smelled half of fall and half of mold.

With a look at my waistline, and a groan as I recalled Tuesday's breakfast, I held myself to plain toast, fruit, and unsweetened tea. Then I took a shower and dressed. My stomach growled, and I said, "Down, boy." It didn't help.

The trip south to Zuider seemed longer than usual, perhaps because I got stuck behind a hay truck until I reached the passing zone near the turnoff for Gairloch. I ended up sneezing for another five miles, and my nose itched until I got to the outskirts of Zuider. Across the town beach I could see whitecaps out on the big lake, but at least the morning was clear and sunny. I even whistled a bit as I parked the Stanley in the lot outside LBI.

Bruce had two long boxes and a small one on the counter. One of the long ones lay open, and the gadget within looked something like a ray gun from the paperbacks, not at all like a rifle, except in general shape.

"Two?" I raised my eyebrows. "Do they both work?"

"I thought about it. You'll need two. One for show, whatever that is, and one for you." Bruce smiled. "They generate a damned funny magnetic field, enough to blow my breakers. The batteries are standard rechargeables."

I had another thought. "No fingerprints?"

"No. All the components are standard, too. This isn't signed artwork."

"And the little one?"

"That's your file gadget. Just hook it into the external port. I assume you have the programware."

"Sort of."

"One of those deals? I don't envy you."

My stomach answered with another growl. Bruce laughed. I shook my head and handed him the rest of the fee in bills.

"You sure this won't break you?"

"Money isn't the issue." The worst of it was that I meant that, and, while I may not be a totally typical Dutchman, I'm certainly not a free spender. It wasn't that I liked spending money; it was the feeling that if I didn't get ahead of the game I wasn't going to be around to do much saving or amassing of capital—the modern variety of "your money or your life."

I loaded all three boxes in the front trunk of the Stanley, and sped back to Vanderbraak Centre, hitting eighty only once. I stopped by Samaha's for my paper and the post centre for whatever awaited me there.

Only two bills—from Wijk River Oil and Sammis Pump Repair—graced my postbox. I peered around the empty post window at Maurice. "It's all junk post."

"Doktor, we just deliver. We can't improve the quality of your enemies."

"Thanks!"

"We do our best."

I got to the office not that long after Gilda, and I even managed to say, "Good day."

"Good day to you, Johan." She shook her head and grinned. "I heard that you suggested to Doktor Doniger that faculty meetings were not sacrosanct."

"I believe I was ill."

"Good. I wish more people were."

"Gilda?" David marched through the door. "Here are my corrections to the minutes of yesterday's meeting."

"Yes, Doktor Doniger." Her voice was cool and formal.

He turned to me. "Good morning, Johan."

"Good morning, David."

"We need to talk, Johan, but I'm off to a meeting with the dean. Will you be around later?"

"I'll be in my office from about noon until just before my two o'clock."

"I don't know. Well, we'll play it by ear." He turned back to Gilda. "If you could have those ready to go by the time I get back?"

"Yes, Doktor Doniger."

David swung his battered brown case off Gilda's desk and marched out the door and off to the administration building. Gilda and I looked at each other, and I shrugged. She took a deep breath and picked up the papers David had left.

Once I got to my office and set down my folder, I opened the *Asten Post-Courier*. When I saw the story below the fold, my stomach churned.

KYOTO (INS)—The Japanese Minister of the Imperial Navy announced on Monday night that Japan had successfully built and tested a new class of submersible. The *Dragon of the Sea* is an electric submersible powered by a self-contained nuclear power plant. The ship has a theoretically unlimited range without surfacing.

The Japanese ship was denounced by a spokesman for Ferdinand VI as a violation of the Treaty of Columbia . . .

Gao TseKung, Warlord for Defense of Chung Kuo, declared that deployment of the *Dragon of the Sea* in the Sea of Japan would be a blatant violation of the Nuclear Limitation Agreement . . .

Speaker Hartpence warned against the development of "naval adventurism" that could restrict international trade to the detriment of all . . .

The story on page two didn't help my growling stomach either.

MUNICH (INS)—A raging fire blazed through the difference engine center of the Imperial Research Service laboratories here last night. "Fortunately, the fire did not destroy any vital research," stated Frideric VonBulow, deputy marshal for imperial research.

Outside observers covertly doubted the deputy marshal's claim. "If that were so, why do they have hundreds of technicians sifting through the ruins?" asked one bystander.

Well-placed sources indicate that the Munich laboratories were the center of highly secret research on psychic phenomena, a claim disputed immediately by deputy marshal VonBulow. "While all research has import for the Empire and the people of Austro-Hungary, certainly the research at Munich was of no greater or lesser import than in other research centers."

The wireline bell rang. "Johan Eschbach."

"Doktor Eschbach, this is Chief Waetjen down at the watch center. I wonder if you would have a moment to come down and chat with me this afternoon."

"I could do it from one to two. Might I ask what you had in mind?"

"Just follow-up inquiries on the Miller murder. It won't take long. Quarter past one?"

"That would be fine."

I set down the handset and then leaned back in the too-stiff wooden chair. The chief had been too friendly. Why was he contacting me?

There wasn't much I could do about that. So I worked on the next set of unannounced tests for my section of the intro course, Natural Resources 1A. That was on Tuesdays and Thursdays. Then came the time to do battle over environmental economics.

The green was jammed with scurrying students, and one or two actually waved or said hello as I plowed toward Smythe.

Once my own students were seated and relative calm prevailed within the confines of Smythe Hall, I handed out the Environmental Economics papers without a word, then watched their faces. At least half of them failed to understand. That was clear from the mutterings and murmurings.

"But . . ."

"I don't understand . . ."

"Supposed to have all term for the reading . . ."

"Ladies and gentlemen. I cannot call you scholars. Not yet. Perhaps not ever. You cannot learn if you refuse to read. You cannot learn if you will not think. You cannot sing if someone else has to drum the notes into you. You cannot succeed in anything by merely going through the motions. These papers show more interest in form than substance. Almost every one is just over the minimum length." I gave a sardonic bow.

"Mister Gersten, how would you characterize the impact of unrealized external diseconomies upon the environment of New Bruges in the 1920s?"

Gersten turned white. I waited. It was going to be a long class and a longer term.

After terrorizing the students in my eleven o'clock, I announced that they would have no class until the following Monday, but that they had better have caught up on the reading by the time I saw them again.

I skipped lunch and made up another short test for the eleven o'clock—a nice present for them for the next Monday, since most of them still wouldn't believe me. After that, I went over my notes for Environmental Politics 2B, the follow-on course to my two o'clock that ran at two on Tuesdays and Thursdays.

David, of course, never did bother to stop in. Before I knew it, it was time to head down to the watch station, that gray stone building next to the post centre.

The chief was waiting in the lobby, or whatever they call the open space with a duty officer.

"Doktor Eschbach?"

"The same."

I had never met Hans Waetjen, but he looked like his name. Solid and stocky, with graying hair, gray eyes, and a ruddy skin. He was clean-shaven, unlike most older Dutch-surnamed men.

"Pleased to meet you, Doktor Eschbach. Wish it was under other conditions."

"I would guess these things do happen, not that I've seen one in Vanderbraak Centre." I tried not to wrinkle my nose. The watch station smelled like disinfectant.

"I'd guess you probably saw lots of strange things in government, but you're right. We sure don't see this sort of thing here. Must have been a good three, four years since the Adams case. Happened before you came back. Boy took an axe to his old man. Old man probably deserved it—he'd been beating both children. Still, a terrible thing it was." Waetjen shook his head and gestured toward the small office in the corner. "Coffee? Chocolate?"

"Chocolate would be fine."

A young watch officer carried two cups toward the urns on the table in the main corridor. Waetjen walked through the open door to his office and sank into the scarred gray leather chair behind the desk, not waiting for me to sit, but I did without invitation.

The younger watch officer delivered the cups, setting them both on the desk. He closed the office door on his way out, and it clunked shut with the finality of a cell door.

The chocolate was hot, and sweeter than even I liked it. Waetjen had coffee, so bitter I could smell it across the desk, mingling with the sweet-acrid odor of disinfectant.

"Just had a few questions I wanted to ask you, Doktor." Waetjen's eyes ran over me. "Fine suit you got there."

I smiled. "Just a leftover from my days in the big city."

"Don't see those that much here. You must have been an important man in government, Doktor."

I shook my head. "I was so important that I doubt anyone at the university even knows what I did."

"With all your traveling, I was wondering if you had ever met Professor Miller before you came here."

"I've met a lot of people, Chief, and I could have seen her at a reception or something, but I know I never talked to her before I joined the faculty here."

"I thought so, but I had to ask. What about any of the others that were at the concert? Do you know if any of them knew Professor Miller before they came to the university?"

"Not that I know of. She was here for a long time, according to some of the old-timers."

"What about Doktor duBoise? When did you first meet her?"

"I'd say it was six months after I started teaching."

"You didn't know her before that?"

"No. It was even an accident when I met her. She's in Music and Theatre, and I'm in Natural Resources."

"What do you know about Professor Martin?"

"Not much. I have talked to him once or twice. He seems very straightforward."

"Do you think any student could have been involved?"

"That's always a possibility, but it would probably have to be one of Professor Miller's students, and I wouldn't know one of them if they bumped right into me."

"How did the administrators regard Professor Miller?"

"I don't know. I was led to understand that she and Dean Er Recchus got along fairly well, and they certainly were friendly at the new faculty gatherings where I saw them."

Because he was stalling to keep me around, I finally looked directly at Chief Waetjen and kept staring at him. "I've answered your questions. What can you tell me about what you've found out?"

"I can't really say much."

"I know that. Let's try off the record, Chief."

He took a deep breath. I waited.

"The time of death was right around quarter to eight. We know that because of the subsonics you heard, and because Doktor Geoffries found the body just before eight. Both Frau Vonderhaus and Fräulein Matthews saw Doktor Miller at seven before Frau Vonderhaus went to check the tuning on the Steinbach." Hans Waetjen spread his hands before continuing.

"So where was everyone? You were in your office, and three people saw you on the way to and from there. Doktor duBoise and Frau Vonderhaus were on stage practicing. Doktor Geoffries and the box-office manager were together. Gregor Martin was in the lighting booth replacing the gel in one spotlight, and the backstage crew has insisted that no one went down the corridor to Doktor Miller's studio."

"That almost sounds like someone was hiding there or waiting there," I ventured.

"A prop knife was apparently used, and the knife was wiped clean on the coat. The only blood was Doktor Miller's."

I nodded. Not exactly a locked-room mystery, but close. No obvious reason for Miranda's murder and no obvious suspects. No job problems. No romantic ties. No hard evidence. Strange—you pass pleasantries with someone, and suddenly she is dead, and you realize how much you didn't know.

"So who do you suspect, Doktor Eschbach?"

I had to shrug. "Something isn't quite right, but right now I couldn't tell you what it is." Everything I said was perfectly true, unfortunately, since I don't like to lie. I have been known to resort to untruths, generally in desperation, which is where it gets you in the most trouble.

"And you suspect?" he pressed.

"Right now, I suspect everyone, probably, except for Professor Martin, but even that, I couldn't tell you why. And I could be wrong."

Chief Waetjen nodded again.

"If you haven't any more questions, I do have a two o'clock, and not much time to get there."

"Of course." He stood. "I do appreciate your coming in."

"Any time." I bowed and left.

Why had the chief asked me down? It wasn't to tell me what the watch had discovered. So I watched as I left, and, sure enough, there was a young fellow with a portable videolink waiting outside. His presence confirmed that vanBecton was telling the chief what to do—and that I was bait to bring down Ralston and the president, one way or another. How many other lines had he set? Did it matter?

"Doktor Eschbach, do you have any comment?"

"On what?" I asked, letting a puzzled expression, I hoped, cross my face.

"On the murder."

"I hope the watch is successful in apprehending the guilty party."

"Why were you here?"

"While I would suggest you talk to Chief Waetjen, my understanding was that the chief hoped I could provide some additional information."

"Did you?"

I smiled politely. "That's something for the watch to release. As I said, I am confident that they will find the guilty party."

The journalist backed away, looking puzzled. I tried not to smile more than politely as I walked back up to my office. Score one for Johan in the positioning war. Of course, vanBecton had scored a lot more. I felt like I was stuck trying to mark a seven-foot giant in korfball, and vanBecton was that giant and almost scoring at will.

The two o'clock class on Environmental Politics was almost worse than the meeting with the watch chief, and not because of the short rainstorm I encountered on the way across the green. Even more of my students had failed than in my eleven o'clock, and none of them seemed to understand. I repeated my sermon, and they still looked blank.

"Miss Deventer, what was the political basis behind the first Speaker Roosevelt's efforts at reforestation?"

Miss Deventer paled. Students looked from one to the other.

"Come now. It was in the assigned reading. Surely you have not forgotten so quickly. Mister Vanderwaal?"

"Uhhh, Doktor Eschbach, I didn't get that far."

"It was on the second page. Mister Henstaal?"

I finally dismissed them, early, went back to my office, and drafted another short test for the next Monday.

Because I had yet to pack or handle any of the details for leaving, I closed up the office and stuffed the draft of the test in my folder, along with the post and my mother's letter, and made my way to the car park.

Again, Llysette's Reo was left forlornly by itself, and I shook my head at the hours she and the other music people put in.

Marie must have figured that I was working late, because she had left on the side porch light and one light in the kitchen. The lights made driving up to the house more welcoming, and so did the odor of the stew and the crusty fresh bread she had left. I just hoped her husband got the same sort of food. If he did, he was a lucky man.

After I ate, I reclaimed Bruce's work from the steamer and carted all three boxes into the study. I set the two disassociators aside for the time being. Then I turned on the difference engine and called up the specifications for the filing gadget. Although I didn't yet have the perturbation replicator, I might as well figure out how the storage system worked. If I understood the system right, what the perturbation replicator did was capture a pattern that the field storage system converted into an electronic file. If . . .

If that were the case, Branston-Hay's notes and the president's dinners with individual members of Congress made way too much sense.

I connected Bruce's gadget, the external field/formatting device, to one of the external ports of my difference engine. Then I began to see what I could do to devise the program to make it work. My machine language commands probably weren't suited exactly to use the full capability of the device, even given Branston-Hay's notes and specs as a starting point, but it was worth a try.

A try it might have been worth, but when I stopped and brewed a cup of chocolate at half past ten I was still twiddling with the program and restudying Branston-Hay's cryptic notes, as well as the structure of his own files, looking for some more insights. One file appeared to contain the entire structure, almost a template, but there were enough parameters that trying even to plug in values was extraordinarily time-consuming.

While the chocolate brewed, I went upstairs and packed a hanging bag, basically with evening clothes for the dinner and another suit to wear back, but also some extra shirts, socks, and underwear, since I was thinking of coming back the long way, via Schenectady.

After packing I went down and sipped the chocolate at the kitchen table, munching a biscuit or two, still thinking about the proto-program. The file format I didn't have to worry about. Branston-Hay actually had those specs in his files; and so were the field capture parameters, though I didn't yet have that hardware. All I was working on was the transfer section, almost a translation section.

Finally I went back to the difference engine, and back to the files I had stolen and duplicated. I decided to look at the encryption protocol—after all, it was a translation system of sorts. One thing led to another, and it was past midnight when I installed the completed program.

A flicker of white caught the corner of my eye. Carolynne hovered in the darkest corner of the study, where the full-length bookshelves met. I pursed my lips. Why had she appeared now? Was it just because it was around midnight? Supposedly midnight had no special significance for ghosts.

Shrugging, I turned to the difference engine again, then looked up as Carolynne seemed to drift from the shelves toward me. She seemed to be resisting a current, almost swimming against an invisible river.

"No more of that, my lord . . . no more!" she protested.

I looked around the study. "No more of what?"

"The Thane of Fife . . ." She tried to pull away from me, but it wasn't me, exactly.

I snapped the switch on the difference engine. Something else might have worked as well, but usually the off switch is safest.

Carolynne curtsied and vanished.

I frowned and sat at the blank screen for a time. True, Carolynne never seemed to be around when I worked on the machine. What was it about the machine? Or had it been the new device? What was it about the device?

Not knowing why, exactly, just following a hunch, I went to the breaker closet off the kitchen and threw the master switch. Then I trundled outside, flash in hand, to the NBEI electric meter.

I had turned off everything, but the current meter wheel still turned. Even after I switched off the breakers, the meter turned—slowly but perceptibly.

Why?

I walked back to the veranda. Carolynne stood there, insofar as any ghost could be determined to stand.

"Will you tell me? Why are you still here? All ghosts fade—except those on magnetic fields. There must be a field here—somehow. I will tear up the house if I have to, but you could help."

Carolynne drifted into the main parlor. She just went through the wall, or maybe she vanished outside and reappeared inside, but I had to go around to the side door into the kitchen, since I'd never unlocked the veranda door when I came home. Then I had to go back when I remembered I had left the flash in the study. Carolynne waited in the main parlor, but she still had not spoken, as if speech were unnecessary.

I watched as she floated behind the heavy love seat and a slender ectoplasmic hand pointed to a circular floral boss on one side of the mirror and then the one above it.

I touched the boss to which Carolynne had pointed, and the mirror—that mirror I had believed mounted in the wall itself, with its back to the veranda—that mirror swung out on heavy hinges. I shone the flash into the darkness. Concealed behind the mirror was an enormous artificial lodestone, with old-fashioned copper wires wound around it in coil after coil.

"Who?" I asked, reclosing the mirror cover on the lodestone.

She seemed to shiver, as if crying, but I hadn't thought about it. Why wouldn't a fully sentient ghost cry?

"Was it the deacon?"

She seemed to pause, then shook her head. Even as I frowned, the story came back to me. After the deacon's wife had stabbed Carolynne, he had taken the knife and killed his wife. The next morning he had walked the entire way to Vanderbraak Centre and confessed. He had never returned to the house.

"But he couldn't have built this."

"Boldness comes . . ." Her voice was faint. "Like Troilus, he gathered what he did. Your father, great king Priam, the lodestone was his and hid."

"My father built this?"

". . . conclude that minds swayed by eyes are full of turpitude . . ."

I sat down on the sofa in the darkness. My father—he had built the artificial lodestone. "You were fading, and he built this?"

I got the impression of a head shake, but she said nothing.

"But why?"

"But with my heart the other eye doth see . . ."

"In a way, he was in love with you?" I asked.

"One cannot speak a word."

I sat in the sofa, looking at Carolynne, shaking my head. "Why?"

"Ah, poor our sex!"

"Did you give him a reason?"

"The error of our eye directs our mind."

"But why?"

"It is no matter . . . but now, you have it, you have me in your sight . . ."

"But," I began again, "how does that have anything to do with the lodestone?"

I only got a shrug, but a number of things began to make a crazy kind of sense. Mother had never been happy about Carolynne, but she had tried to keep her away from me, not from my father.

"Did my mother know about this?"

I got the sense of a head shake in the dark, but Mother had known.

I sat there in the darkness for a long time, accompanied by an equally silent ghost, until I finally got up and switched on the breakers and reset the electric clocks.

Again, I had trouble getting to sleep.

CHAPTER FOURTEEN

• • •

When I carted my traveling bag off the Columbia Special and out of the old Baltimore and Potomac Station—far classier than the shabbier, if newer, Union Station—I had to wait for a cab. That figured. Congress was in session, working on the trade and finance bills, and all the Dutch bankers from New Amsterdam had descended on Columbia City. Portly as most were, each required an individual cab. So I walked out to Constitution Avenue and down toward the galleries, hailing a beat-up blue steamer bearing the legend "Francois's Cabs—French spoken."

"*Ministère des Resources Naturels, rue Sixième.*" I wondered if the driver actually spoke French.

"*Oui, monsieur. Voulez-vous la porte este?*"

"*Non. Dehors la porte norde.*"

"Ah . . ."

I also wondered about the knowing "ah," but, French or not, the driver took me the back way, passing the B&P station again before turning north and back west. She muttered under her breath in French. As we waited at Eighth and D, I found myself looking at a small sign.

VLADIMIR NOBOKOV-JONES
SPECIALIST IN PERSONALITY UNIFICATION

What a scam. Only a small number of people ever suffered a personality fracture without physical trauma—and that was usually from extraordinary stress and guilt. They'd said I'd come close after Elspeth's death, but not many people go through years like that. So any quack could hang up a shingle and declare himself a specialist in personality unity, since so few ever suffered the problem—and if they did, how could they complain?

The next block held the big Woodward and Vandervaal, the downtown flagship store. The windows were filled with braided corn shucks and other harvest items, such as a scarecrow decked out in a brand-new New Ostend plaid shirt and leather knickers. I was grinning at the incongruity when a white figure darted in front of the cab.

Screee . . . The cab skidded for a moment. The driver released the brakes as the figure vanished the moment the steel of the bumper touched her white coat.

"Revenante! J'oublie . . ."

The driver went on in French, as well as I could follow, about how the ghost, a woman originally from Spain, had run in front of a full steam-bus the week before.

". . . elle croit qu'elle n'etait point la personne seule qui perdait tous!"

Did each person believe that he was the only one who suffered? Or was that a French ailment? I had seen that in Llysette, but wouldn't I have felt the same way? Didn't Carolynne, disembodied and sometimes disconnected ghost that she was, show that as well? I was still reflecting when the cab stopped at the Sixteenth Street entrance to the Natural Resources Ministry.

"Voilà!" The cab driver's words were flat, despite the French.

I handed her two dollars and a silver half dollar.

"Merci." The "thank you" was equally flat, as if she deserved a greater tip for speaking French, and she pulled away as quickly as any steamer could, but without the screeching tires possible with an internal combustion engine. Were the screeching tires why so many young Columbians sought out the older petrol-fired cars and restored them?

After proffering the identification card to the guard at the Natural Resources building, I left my bag in the locker behind his desk. Of course, I'd had to show him it contained only clothes, but all guards are much happier when strangers don't carry large objects into federal buildings. Then I headed down through the building to the basement, and then to the subbasement and the tunnel guard.

"This tunnel is not open for normal travel."

"Doktor Eschbach for Subminister vanBecton."

I waited for him to pick up the headset. He just looked at me.

I smiled, and the young face looked blank. I could tell it was going to be a long day. "I really do suggest that you pick up that handset and get me cleared into Billy vanBecton's office."

"Billy? I don't know who you are, but you don't belong here."

"I believe I do." I nodded politely. "I'm here to see Minister vanBecton."

"No, you aren't. I know his people."

Because I hate wise-asses, I reached down and picked up the handset, hoping that the sentry wouldn't get too upset. I dialed in the numbers.

"Minister vanBecton's office."

"This is Doktor Eschbach. I'm in the tunnel, and the guard seems to want to keep me from my four o'clock appointment with the minister."

"That's station six, is it not? The one from Natural Resources?"

"Yes."

"Put the handset down. We'll call back."

"Thank you."

I put the handset down and looked into the muzzle of the guard's handgun.

"I could blast you for that," he said.

"Not if you want to keep your job."

The wireset bleeped.

"Station six."

I watched as the sentry turned pale. "But . . . he didn't . . . but . . . yes, sir. Yes, sir. At five, sir. Yes, sir."

He looked at me, and if his eyes had been knives, I would have been hamburger. "You're cleared, sir."

I opened the leather folder for him to see and caught his eyes. "It's a cheap lesson, son. Don't ever make threats. And don't ever stand in front of someone older and wiser unless you intend to kill them and pay for it yourself." Facing him down was a risk I shouldn't have taken, but I was getting tired of the games.

"How many . . ."

"More than you want to know, son. We old goats are more dangerous than we look." I sighed and walked past him into the tunnel that led into the subbasement of the Spazi building. The guard there waved me on into the growing smell of disinfectant.

VanBecton's office was on the fourth floor. I walked up, still holding to my resolve to improve my conditioning. I don't think I panted as much as the time a week earlier, but I still stopped a moment on the last landing to catch my breath. The landings were empty, as always. It's against the English ethic to appear to work, and against the Dutch to engage in unnecessary work when there is so much that is necessary.

The pinch-faced clerk gave me a grin, an actual grin, as I walked into vanBecton's outer office. "Thank you, Doktor."

"Glad to be of service."

"The minister has not been happy with some of the guards, but most reports have been too late for him to act."

In short, Gillaume vanBecton had been taking it out on his staff, and the clerk was more than pleased that someone else was on the firing line.

"You can go right in."

I smiled at the clerk, then opened the steel-lined wooden door, closing it behind me as I stepped toward the desk and vanBecton.

"Johan. Already you're making your presence felt, just like in the old days, I understand." VanBecton offered his broad and phony smile, stepping around the wide desk.

"I doubt that. Your guard wants to kill me, and that's not exactly the impression I'd rather leave. I am afraid my patience has been eroded by age."

"Do have a seat." He sat in one of the chairs in front of the desk, a gesture clearly designed to imply we were dealing as equals.

"Thank you." I sat. "I thought I should stop by, since I was invited to swell the President's guest list at the last moment. I take it that a number of the regulars decided to decline the invitation after the Japanese announcement?"

"There were a few." VanBecton covered his mouth with a carefully manicured hand and coughed. "Have you had any interesting developments in your area?"

"Not really interesting. You have discovered, I presume, that Professor Miller's older son was arrested on trumped-up charges by the New French."

"We knew of the charges."

"His personality makes it highly unlikely that he would ever even skirt the law. That's what the family feels."

"How would that fit with Professor Miller's death?"

"The only thing I can think of is that someone else knew she was working for Maurice-Huizenga. Perhaps she knew too much."

"Oh?"

I shrugged. "Knowing who I was wouldn't be enough. A retired Spazi employee? Come now."

"That puts a different light on Doktor duBoise."

"Why?" I asked, trying to look puzzled.

"Now, Johan. She must be working for Takaynishu. Who else could it be? You have pointed out how unlikely it is that she would be in the pay of the Austro-Hungarians, and with Professor Miller reporting to Maurice-Huizenga . . . who else could it be?"

"You assume that she works for someone. What about some proof?"

"We have some transcripts of wireline conversations."

"Whose?"

"You are good, aren't you?"

"No. But I've played the game for a long time. Whose conversations?"

"The Miller operation was quite professional. She always received calls. She never made them."

"Sitting duck, and that sounds like the New French."

"The transmissions were always illegal—that is, someone tapped a line not far from the New French border—and the caller always said, 'Rick is all right.' "

"And what did the good professor say?"

"Many things, not all relevant to the point I raised. You understand, I know. She did say that—" he looked back toward his desk "—'Doktor duBoise pursues them all, but spends by far the bulk of her energy and charm on Doktor Eschbach. If he but knew what held her soul, he would be far less interested. Ferdinand is not even that evil.' " VanBecton smiled. "Unfortunately, Professor Miller was rather poetic; so it is hard to prove some things literally. I imagine that it must have given Maurice-Huizenga fits, but he was playing out of his depth."

"Yes, he was." I frowned. "You believe that such vague words mean that Doktor duBoise had to be working for the Japanese?"

"Was it not strange that she was released through the intervention of the Japanese ambassador?"

"Why? They do have a reputation for liking occidental music."

"And occidental singers."

"Bill," I said flatly, "you don't seem to know much more than I do. It's all spec-ulation. You have transcripts of conversations by Professor Miller. You have her son held by the New French, but you haven't got a thing on anyone else—except me."

"I didn't quite say that."

I smiled easily, hard as it was, before I lobbed the next one into his lap. "The only other thing I can add is that Miranda Miller also spent a great deal of time, a very great deal, discussing things with Doktor Branston-Hay, the Babbage man."

His eyes flickered, but so minutely that I wouldn't have seen it if I hadn't been waiting. "That is rather odd."

"Not at all. You certainly have read the papers. Something strange is going on in a lot of university Babbage centers. The New French could well be behind it, couldn't they?"

"It's more likely the religious fundamentalists, Johan. You've been in the busi-ness too long. Despite our concerns, we know there's not a conspiracy behind every tree." He laughed. "Every other one, perhaps."

"You know best." I stood. "That's all I know right now." All that I was telling, in any case.

"You mean that's all you're telling," corrected vanBecton.

I grinned. "Unlike some, I can't afford to deal in pure speculation, but I will keep working on it." I backed up, stumbled, caught the back of my knees on the edge of the chair, and knocked it against the low table, while almost sprawling across the desk before hitting the carpet. I lay there for a moment before taking a deep breath. As I pulled myself erect, I looked at a red splotch on my palm, then restacked the papers I had disarranged. "I'm getting too old for this."

"Just leave the papers, Johan. They're all administrative trivia."

"I'm certain they are, Minister vanBecton. Little of import is reduced to ink. That's one reason I avoid speculation."

"Good. Perhaps we'll see you again before too long."

"That's definitely a possibility."

VanBecton nodded and watched as I took the back exit.

After reclaiming my hanging bag from the guard in the Natural Resources building—the tunnel guard had looked the other way as I passed, although I felt his eyes on my back—I went out into the sunlight and looked for a cab. That took a while, but finally a patched Stanley with mottled gray and blue paint stopped.

"Spring Valley, Forty-seventh and New Bruges."

"That's a minimum of four."

"Don't worry about it."

"Don't worry about it? I got to worry about it. It's my living."

I set a five on the dashboard. "All right?"

"You got the money, I drive."

He didn't talk, and I didn't, either, not with what I had to think about. While he drove, I slipped vanBecton's memos—the ones I had swept onto the floor and into my coat—into my folder. They were definitely administrative drivel, but that wasn't why I wanted them. What I needed them for would come later.

I looked out as the cab passed Ward Circle and into Ward Park beyond the seminary. Within a few blocks we turned off New Bruges and onto Sedgwick, where the houses show why the upper northwest in the Federal District reeks of money, with their trimmed hedges, sculptured gardens, and shadowed stone walks.

Supposedly, in the early days, upper northwest was far enough from the capital itself that it served as an interim retreat for Speaker Calhoun, but now such retreats were much farther from the Capitol building.

Eric and Judith's home was a Tudor set on a large corner plot with walls around the entire back of the property and two Douglas firs rising over the walls and the three-story dwelling. Their car barn had space for three steamers.

I tipped the driver two dollars. "It's a long ride back."

"Thank you, sir."

"Johan!" Judith met me at the Tiffany-paneled front doors wearing a bright blue suit, with her sparkling silver hair swept into a French braid, and only the hint of wrinkles around her gray eyes.

"I did not expect you to be here."

She stepped back and held the door as I carried in the garment bag and my folder. "I left early this afternoon. The gallery and the Dutch masters can do without me. How long has it been?"

"Only a little over a year."

"It seems longer. Eric said you were here for a presidential function."

"A welcoming dinner for the new Japanese ambassador. Sometimes they remember the old warhorses, especially when the occasion is less than popular."

"Johan—I doubt that you've reached your midforties."

"Actually, I'm past that."

"You don't look even forty." She led the way up the carpeted circular staircase, past the large crystal chandelier, to the second floor. "You have the rooms on the end. We redid things a bit last year when Suzanne got married. It's now a guest suite. You're actually the first guest."

"I feel honored."

"We don't see as much of you."

"I know."

Her hand brushed my shoulder, and the scars there twinged—all psychological.

"It wasn't your fault, Johan. You did what you could. Elspeth told me that so many times, and you can't blame yourself for what you had to do. Without the government medical program . . ."

"Thank you, Judith. It's still hard." I hung the bag in the open closet and began to take out the evening wear. "It's really kind of you to be here."

"You could have called me."

"It was hard to call Eric."

"You and Eric are so alike." She shook her head. "I suppose it follows. Elspeth and I are . . . were alike, people said."

And they were, so much that it still ached when she talked, but the ache had almost faded—almost, but not quite.

"Sisters are often alike." I forced a grin. "I think they're supposed to be."

"In some ways, Eric could have been your brother."

"He's far more sensible."

"Do you have time for chocolate? I know how seldom you drink."

I pulled out the old Ansonia—five-fifteen. "Certainly. I shouldn't have to leave here until around quarter to seven. You can wire a cab, can't you?"

"One way or another, we'll get you to the president's. It wouldn't do to have you late."

I followed her downstairs again and out into the sun room off the parlor. "I should have guessed. You had the chocolate and biscuits already waiting."

"I hoped." She eased into the captain's chair on one side of the glass-topped, cherry-framed table and poured two cups. I took the other captain's chair.

"What do you think of the Japanese submersibles?" she asked as she handed me a cup with the gracefulness that recalled another woman.

"About the way you do about modern art, I suspect. Necessary, but hardly something you really want to support in public." I sipped the chocolate, steaming and with just the right hint of a bite. "Good chocolate."

"Thank you." She nodded. "You think the submersibles are necessary?"

"For the Japanese, they're more than that. The home islands either import almost all their raw materials or get them from their possessions. They have to expand through the islands. And now that Chung Kuo is building a navy to rival ours . . . ?" I shrugged.

"Everyone seems to be building more and more weapons. Where will it end?"

"Where it always has. In war." I tried a butter biscuit, probably too fattening but definitely delicious.

"I think you are even more cynical. Haven't you found someone? Elspeth would have liked that, you know. She wasn't possessive in that way."

I sighed. "I know. I've been seeing a singer."

"Another artistic type?" Judith laughed freely, and I smiled back. "Somehow, that doesn't surprise me. What's her name?"

"Llysette. Llysette duBoise."

"Not the Llysette duBoise? I thought she had died in Ferdinand's prisons."

"You know of her?"

"She was starting at the Académie Royale back when I did my fellowship there—one of the last ones before Ferdinand. Dark-haired, often piles her hair on top of her head? She was single then, and I think supporting her father."

"The same one. She had a difficult time, but they did release her. It took some diplomatic work, and she had intimated, although I didn't press, some pressure by the Japanese ambassador. He'd heard her sing."

"She was magnificent then, even that young. Why is she stuck up in the wilds? You're charming, Johan, but she would not have known you were there."

"It's a matter of economics and politics."

"Let me guess." Judith's voice turned hard. "She's a foreigner, and she probably had to have strings pulled to enter the country. No one cares if she sings in out-of-the-way places, but the dear Spazi has put out the word to the larger symphonies that they really don't want to be investigated. Something like that?"

I nodded.

"Can you do anything?"

"I haven't had much luck. Neither has she."

Judith studied me for a time. "Things are not looking good for you, are they?"

"No. That's one reason I came. Whatever happens, stay out of it. I should have spent more time with you earlier, but I didn't realize what would happen. I thought they'd leave me alone."

"They never did. Why would they now?"

I sipped my chocolate. "One hopes. Foolishly. But one hopes."

"Don't we all? Elspeth felt so badly for you, Johan, you know? If you can find happiness again, we would be happy for you."

"Thank you, Judith."

I heard steps come through the kitchen.

"Well, if it isn't the long-lost brother." Eric never called me his brother-in-law. "I hoped I'd get home a little before you left."

"You're in luck."

"Some chocolate?" asked Judith.

"Please." He sat in the middle of the love seat and looked at me. "When you're in town, there's usually trouble."

"Am I so predictable?"

He laughed. "The Japanese announced their atomic submersible. The Congress passed a tax increase, and Chung Kuo decided that Kilchu belongs to their great Manchurian heritage. In the meantime, Maximilian has decided that the export tax on Mexican crude will be upped another two dollars a barrel, and, in order not to upset the New French, the Venezuelans will follow his lead. The President is stepping up detailed budget reviews, and threatening to expose a good dozen congressmen for fraud and lying or both."

"And you're blaming it all on me?" I reached for another butter biscuit.

"Who was talking blame?" Eric took the chocolate cup from his wife with a fond smile. "Things just happen when you're around. That's probably why the Speaker was perfectly happy to let you get pensioned off into the wilds of New Bruges, up there with the bears and the cold winters."

"That's what I thought." I drained the cup.

"A little more?" asked Judith.

"Half a cup. In a while, I need to start getting dressed."

"How's the teaching?" Eric shifted his weight on the love seat.

"The teaching is interesting. Most of the students aren't. They're still in the mold of coasting through the term and then trying to cram a half year's work into three weeks."

"I can recall doing that." Eric chuckled.

"You had the brains to get away with it."

"Not the brains, just laziness."

"Hardly. Do your clients really believe that you're just a former korfball player who somehow bumbles through? Are you still cultivating that image despite the years in the Foreign Ministry?"

"Of course," laughed Judith.

"It's what makes people comfortable," admitted Eric.

"Tell me about the children," I suggested.

They did, and I listened while I finished the half cup of chocolate.

In time, I looked at my watch. "I think I had better get ready. If I could trouble you to call a cab for quarter to seven, I would appreciate it."

"Just get yourself together. We'll take care of it," promised Eric.

I took a quick shower, shaved again, and pulled on the formal wear. It was actually looser than when I'd worn it last. Was the additional exercise helping?

I didn't quite dash downstairs, where Judith met me, wrap in hand.

"You look almost good enough for me to throw over Eric." She winked, and I bowed solemnly.

"Almost, but not quite, thank heavens." He stood in the doorway. "Shall we go?"

"Is the cab here?"

"Cab? Nonsense. The least we could do is give you a lift. Besides, we'd already planned to go out."

"I do appreciate this," I offered again, as I seated Judith next to Eric in the front before climbing into the spacious rear seat.

"We were going out anyway. It's only a few blocks out of the way."

Eric wheeled the big Stanley down New Bruges Avenue, past the embassies and under Dupont Circle to where it became Seventeenth Street. Before I knew it, he pulled up in front of the Presidential Palace, right on Pennsylvania.

"Here you are."

"Thank you. I doubt I'll even be close to being late." I waved as the Stanley pulled away almost silently, then straightened and marched toward the gate. It always surprised me how quiet the federal city was, but that was because of the prohibition on internal combustion engines. Steamers only whisper along, and electrics are even quieter.

At the gate, I handed over my invitation and identification card. The guard checked both, and then put a tick mark by my name on the long list. A couple waited behind me.

"Honestly . . . don't know why we have to attend these. . . . So boring, and they even had to pad the guest list, Marcia said."

"We attend because it goes with the job, dear."

"I know . . . what one suffers in public life . . ."

She didn't know the half of it, fortunately for her.

I smiled politely at them as I walked through the gate and up the drive to the porticoed doorway.

"The honorable Johan Eschbach." The announcement carried through the foyer, but no one looked up as I stepped toward the East Room.

"The honorable David Dominick and Madame Dominick."

I smiled at the faces I did not know and made my way toward one of the bars, the one in the far corner. People always congregate around the first place to serve.

"Red wine, Sebastopol, if you have it."

"Will a Merino do, sir?"

"Fine." I took the wine and glanced around, finally spotting a halfway familiar face. "Martin?"

"Johan." Martin Sunquist extended his hand. "I thought you had retired to the wilds of New Bruges."

"I did. The president was so desperate that they dragged me all the way down here."

His eyebrows rose. "I did hear something along those lines. Still . . ." He lifted his glass. "Whatever the reason, it's good to see you."

"Are you still over with the Budget Examiners?"

"Same building, but a new job." He lowered his voice. "Now, I examine the geographic distribution of federal programs."

"I suppose that knowledge can be used by the president . . . and Ralston."

"This president, at least." Martin took a small sip of wine and glanced toward the corner of the room. "Ralston's done a lot with the budget shop. It's a lot more confrontational than in the old days . . . even your old days."

"Even from up in the wilds I've gotten that impression."

President Armstrong entered the East Room to the sounds of the *Presidential March,* the Sousa piece commissioned to complement *Hail to the Speaker.* He stepped up before the microphones on the low platform with a Japanese in a well-cut Western suit.

"Enough of that. Welcome, Ambassador Takayama." He bowed, and Takayama bowed. "I don't have a full speech, for which I know you are all grateful. I just have a few remarks."

Sighs greeted his comments, since his remarks were known to be often less than brief.

"Truly, you understand me. But I only have a few remarks this evening . . ."

That did get a gentle laugh.

"Thirty-three years ago almost exactly, in 1960, a great and terrible event occurred with the detonation of the first nuclear device at Birel Aswad by the Austro-Hungarian scientific team following the equations developed by their mentor, Albert Einstein. We, of course, followed in 1965 at White Sands, and Chung Kuo in 1970. To date, no one has used the nuclear bomb, even in 1985. With the theoretically great power of the atom to create mass death and possibly millions of terrorized ghosts, the spectre of nuclear weapons has made them too terrible to use.

"The Imperial Republic of Japan has continued to eschew the development of the atom for weapons, a courageous prohibition. Japan has pioneered the development of atomic power plants for the peaceful use of the nuclear genie.

"We share, of course, with the Japanese, a concern that the oceans of the world remain open and free to trade. Therefore, I am pleased to announce that Emperor Akihito and I have reached a general agreement in principle that Japan and Columbia will pool their expertise in peaceful uses of the atom, including the development of oceangoing power plants . . ."

The president smiled broadly into the silence.

". . . a development which I truly hope Speaker Hartpence and the Congress will follow with the necessary implementing treaty. Now . . . enjoy the evening."

As the humming rose to a near-babble, nearly half a dozen figures scurried from the room. I was surprised there weren't more. The president had clearly outmaneuvered the Speaker again, and the Hartpencers would be looking for blood.

Martin raised his glass to me, nodded, and slipped away toward the corner. His warning bothered me—was Ralston getting as bad as the Spazi?

"What do you suppose he meant by that?" asked a graying man, older and considerably heavier than I, accompanied by a slender and well-endowed younger blond woman who smiled at me as her escort asked the question.

"I believe he has obtained the agreement of the Japanese to provide us with plans and specifications to build a nuclear-powered submersible, in return for our expertise in other areas." I bowed. "That, at least, is what I heard. One must be careful in reading too much into political statements."

"I agree," said the older man.

"Why would the Japanese do that?" asked the young woman.

"Because," I answered, "we need that technology more than either Chung Kuo or Austro-Hungary, and because we can outbid Maximilian."

"You make it sound so . . . sordid."

"It is." I laughed softly. "All politics is sordid."

She made a face, and her escort tugged her in another direction.

The reception part of the dinner concluded with "Columbia," sung by a mezzo-soprano—almost good enough to be in Llysette's class—accompanied by the Marine Corps band.

> *"Our God, we place our trust in thee*
> *For Columbia, gem of freedom's sea.*
> *As humbled souls we pray to be*
> *Upholding those who make us free . . ."*

I still wasn't sure about the humbled souls part. After milling around with the others, I let myself follow the flow into the state dining room, as we were discreetly escorted by a number of dark-clad aides to seats bearing engraved place cards.

I was seated near the end of one of the side tables, about as close to the side door as possible, next to a couple slightly younger than me. Their place cards read Doktor and Madame Velski, but we exchanged pleasantries in perfect Columbian English until the main course was being cleared.

"Excuse me, if you would." I inclined my head to Madame Velski, and eased from the chair and through the doorway, heading toward the gentlemen's facilities.

I paused by the wireset, then picked up the receiver and dialed three digits.

"The Special Assistant's office. May I help you?"

"This is Johan Eschbach."

"Thank you, Doktor."

I nodded to the marine guard by the doorway to the staircase downstairs and proceeded to the men's room. When I came out, a nervous-looking young fellow raised his hand.

"Doktor . . ."

"Yes, I'm Doktor Eschbach."

He led me past the sentry and downstairs. Ralston McGuiness was waiting for me in the anteroom, the one off the oval office used for the president's ceremonial meetings, not the office where he did actual work.

"Greetings, Ralston."

"Read this, Johan. Then we'll talk." He handed me a thin sheaf of papers and walked out, closing the door behind him.

Since I've never believed in futile protests, I began to read. After a while I could skim through it, because the minutiae of the technical details were not all that relevant, and because much of the material was recently familiar to me.

> Dr. Joachim Heisler, head of psychic research at the University of
> Vienna . . . arrived in Paris to review . . . experiments in targeted psy-
> chological stress.

. . . theorized that psychic disassociation is not necessarily unitary, based on investigations of battlefield ghosting and investigations of European homicides . . .

. . . marked attempts to conceal Heisler's research and movements . . . significantly increased workloads occurring at GRI military difference engine centers . . . special helmets assembled in Bavaria . . . increased numbers of zombies processed at Imperial reeducation centers . . .

What was happening in Europe seemed almost as bad as what was happening in Columbia. I shook my head as I completed skimming through the material.

"Finished?" asked Ralston from the door to the Oval Office. He closed it behind him.

"Enough to get the gist of it all."

"What do you think?" He pulled out the chair on the far side of the small, circular conference table.

"We've got trouble."

"Tell me why?"

"You know perfectly well why, Ralston. That's not why you summoned me."

"Johan, it's been a long week. Humor me. The president lost four men getting that information. Canfield went part ghost, and he's babbling about disasters and catastrophe."

"Why not run it by Spazi research? That's more their line than mine."

"Very humorous, Johan. Perhaps we will, if we can't figure it out, and we'll attribute it to you. Or to Doktor duBoise." He smiled a smile I didn't like at all.

I cleared my throat. Just what did he want? A reason to put me in one of the dark cells in the subsubcellar of the budget building? Or was it an intelligence test of some sort, to see how obvious the not-so-obvious was? "It seems as though Ferdinand's tame psychic wizards have figured out how to create exactly the kind of ghosts they want. That part doesn't bother me nearly so much as it would bother the Anglican-Baptists or Speaker Hartpence. The other part does."

"The other part?" prompted Ralston, with only a slight delay to my cue.

"What do they have left when they've created a ghost?"

"A happy zombie, usually."

"Humor me this time. What if you could stick someone under one of Doktor Heisler's helmets and just target a few aspects of their brain? You know, facets dealing with integrity, or fear, or conscience?"

"You pass," answered Ralston.

I kept my mouth shut. Ralston hadn't blinked an eye, had been almost matter-of-fact. Despite the dates on the papers, he had already known. I asked, "Is Ferdinand creating ghost-immune troops?"

"There's at least one battalion, but the process isn't foolproof. It only works about fifty percent of the time."

"So we have the ghost-research war?"

"What do you mean, Johan?"

Did I play dumb, still treading between two payrolls? Did I have any choice? If Ralston knew what I actually knew, I'd likely have a heart attack on the spot, a fatal one. VanBecton was playing to set me up, and so was Ralston. I knew why vanBecton was, but not Ralston, unless he had exactly the same idea as vanBecton, which was certainly possible. And I hadn't liked the reference to turning Llysette over to the Spazi.

"You send me clippings that show destruction of psychic research facilities, but earlier this week I read a few clippings of my own, about the fires and explosions in the Munich Babbage center. I'm supposed to believe that's accidental, especially after what you've just shown me?"

"There is that. What if I said we didn't have anything to do with Munich?"

"We meaning the president, or we meaning Columbia?"

"Either."

"Then it looks like someone else is playing. The Turks can't afford to, and that leaves the Far East or deGaulle."

"We think deGaulle. What did vanBecton tell you?"

"Not much. He says that Llysette duBoise is an agent of Takaynishu, and he wants me to look into Miranda Miller's murder."

"I assume you have. What have you reported?"

"It appears as though Professor Miller was co-opted by New France. Her son was arrested on a trumped-up importing charge last year." I shrugged.

"Then who owns Doktor duBoise?"

"Does anyone?" I asked.

"You do, apparently, or she owns you, but I'm interested in the unsubordinated share."

"I don't know. The Japanese ambassador intervened to have her released from prison, and she was tortured by Ferdinand, but . . . I don't see any signs there, and that bothers me."

"It bothers me, too, Johan, and it bothers the president a lot. Right now, we have the Speaker on the run, but one false step and it could all unravel. VanBecton wants you to take that false step."

"But," I smiled, "if I disappeared at a Presidential Palace function, that would also unravel things."

"Yes, it would." Ralston McGuiness did not smile.

"So what do you need?"

"We need to know who Doktor duBoise works for, and we need to have a scandal involving vanBecton, one without your fingerprints on it. So please just keep to your assignment with Doktor duBoise, and report to vanBecton. If you solve the Miller murder, so much the better. Just keep things quiet, the way we like them."

"And if vanBecton falls flat on his face that would be fine—provided no one is within a hundred miles of him."

"That's too close. So don't do it." Ralston glanced toward the door. "You need to get back upstairs. One last thing. Was there any link between Miller and the Babbage center?"

"She had a lot of conversations with Branston-Hay."

"Does vanBecton know this?"

"Yes."

"I wish he didn't." Ralston stood. "Just keep things quiet."

"I'll do what I can, but it isn't going to be easy. VanBecton wants a mess, preferably with me in it."

"We know. We think you can handle it."

"What's vanBecton's clout?"

"You didn't know?" Ralston grinned. "Besides being the number two in the Spazi, vanBecton is Defense Minister Holmbek's son-in-law."

I wiped my forehead on the cotton handkerchief, wishing I weren't sweating, but your body can betray you more quickly than your mind. "Holmbek's not the Speaker, and he gave up his seniority to take Defense," I pointed out.

"He and Speaker Hartpence both belong to Smoke Hill and bowl together twice a week." Ralston nodded sagely, as if that explained everything. Lawn bowling certainly gave time for exchanging confidences, but that didn't mean that the Speaker would automatically do what Holmbek or vanBecton wanted. It did mean that what they did was probably what the Speaker wanted. At that I did shiver.

"You see?" asked Ralston.

"Thanks." I left and went back upstairs, just in time to finish a sloppy peach melba and to listen to a whole round of toasts that said even less than normal, as if the toasters had been carefully instructed by the president—or his budget examiners. Even for the ceremonial head of state, money talks, just less directly.

After the evening ended I walked up Sixteenth a bit and hailed a cab.

It was past eleven when Eric opened the door for me.

"Judith's gone to bed. Do you want to talk?"

"Just for a bit."

We walked into his study.

"How bad is it?" He eased into his chair in the graceful way that only a large athletic man can.

"About as bad as it can get before it really gets bad."

"No bodies yet?"

"One. A professor at the university was killed for no apparent reason. The Spazi moved in, with just enough presence to advertise to those who might be looking.

There seem to be disproportionate numbers of people whose backgrounds are thin, mine included."

"What's the game?"

"Everyone is out to play Pin the Tail on Johan, but I can't figure out why, at least not for everyone."

"Deep game?"

I nodded. "It might have been a setup from before I left here."

"Oh, shit, Johan. Can't they just leave you alone?"

"It doesn't look that way."

"Is there anything I can do?"

"As I told Judith, after tomorrow morning just stay out of the way. I don't think there's anything you can do, and . . . I just can't have anyone . . . anyone else . . ." I swallowed and sat there.

He actually got up and patted my shoulder, and we looked into the darkness for a time before we went to bed. At least he had Judith. Llysette was six hundred fifty miles away physically, and who knew how much further in her mind?

CHAPTER FIFTEEN

• • •

Judith, dressed in a maroon suit, and Eric, dressed in dark gray pinstripes, were at the kitchen table by the time I managed to stagger through the shower and dressing.

The broad bay window in which the solid-oak kitchen table sat revealed the kind of gray autumn day that had been all too common when I had lived in the Federal District. In a perverse way, it was gratifying to know that some aspects of life didn't change.

"Good morning, Johan. How was your presidential dinner?" asked Judith, rising gracefully. "Tea?"

"Please." I bumbled into the empty chair, dodging the knife-edged perfection of the table edge and old memories raised by a sister-in-law in a maroon suit.

After Judith poured the tea, I loaded it with raw sugar, then began to open the banana laid beside the heavy, honeyed, nut-covered sweet roll on my plate. The sweet roll would have to wait.

"The dinner?" prompted Eric.

"You saw the paper? The business about the Japanese sharing their nuclear submersible technology? I presume it was in the paper?"

"Oh, that?" Eric nodded. "It was in the paper. I'd seen some speculations about that earlier, though."

"Why would the Japanese give us that technology?" asked Judith.

"I doubt that they exactly gave it to us, dear. The question is how President Armstrong thinks he can persuade the Speaker."

I had to snort at that. "What choice does the Speaker have? With the free-traders after his head, he's going to turn down a technology that will give us the upper hand over Ferdinand's navy? At least for a little while." The tea tasted good, and the sugar definitely helped. I took a small bite of the sweet roll.

"Right," affirmed Eric. "I'm sure the Austro-Hungarians are working on their own nuclear submersibles."

"It's all so pointless." Sitting across from me, Judith nibbled on her roll, then sipped her tea. "I mean, what's the purpose in taxing people to raise more money to build better ways to destroy more people? In the end, we're all either poorer or dead."

"God, you're depressing." Eric finished off the last half of the enormous sweet roll in a single bite.

"The truth sometimes is." Another small bite of the banana was all I could manage, followed by more tea. "Maybe that's why it's hard to live here. You either face the truths and get depressed, or don't face them and let yourself be deluded."

"What does where you live have to do with that?" asked Eric as he poured a second cup of tea. "Everyone in the whole country has the same choice."

"I don't know that it's so obvious elsewhere." I finished the first cup of tea and reached for the pot.

"Then if you're looking for honesty, isn't this a better place to live?" asked Judith, her question followed by a bright smile.

I had to nod. "But are most people really looking for honesty?"

Eric snorted again.

"What are you going to do?" Judith asked quietly.

"Try to survive." I forced a grin. "Anything on a higher ethical plane is beyond me right now."

"You aren't *that* cynical, Johan."

"I wish I weren't, sometimes." I swallowed another half-cup of tea in a single gulp, almost welcoming the burning sensation. "I need to get moving if I want to catch one of the midday trains." I looked toward the wireset.

"I'll drop you off," said Eric.

"A cab might be better."

"Better for what? We're family," Eric insisted. "Anyone who's after you knows you stayed here. I'll run you down when you're ready, and that's that."

"Absolutely," Judith affirmed.

After draining the last of the tea, I went upstairs and grabbed the garment bag and my travel case. Both Eric and Judith were standing in the main foyer when I came down the stairs.

"Ready?" asked Eric.

I nodded.

Judith put her arms around me. "Take care, Johan." Her eyes were wet as she stepped back.

"I'll try, but you know how much good that's done before."

She gave me a last hug and turned away quickly.

Eric and I left and got into the big steamer silently. We were headed down New Bruges Avenue and almost to the Japanese Embassy before he spoke. "This whole business has Judith upset, you know."

"I know."

"Is there any way you can get out of whatever this mess is? I don't want a brother who's a zombie. You were pretty close last time."

"I'm trying." I didn't want to think about that. Was I already sliding off into ghost land? "A big part of the problem is that I don't know the whole picture. It's tied up with psychic research, and you know how touchy that's gotten to be."

Eric whistled softly. "I didn't know, but there have been a number of hints in the press lately, haven't there?"

"Where there's smoke . . ."

"Don't get burned, Johan."

"I'll try not to."

He let me out right in front of the B&P Station, which wasn't too hard, since the morning rush had long since subsided. As soon as I got inside the station, I stopped by the first public wireset and used my account number to call Anna's.

"This is the Durrelts'. To whom do you wish to speak?"

"Anna, this is Johan."

"Johan?"

"Your nephew? The crazy one? The professor?"

"Oh, Johan. I thought you were trying to be Johan de Waart, and you don't sound anything like him. Do you want to speak to your mother?"

"First, will you both be there if I come by this afternoon?"

"That's a long drive. Yes, we can be here."

"I'll be there around three, I think."

"Don't you . . ."

"I have to run, Aunt Anna. I'll see you this afternoon."

The next stop was the ticket window. Instead of the Quebec Special, I had to take the ten o'clock Montreal Express to get to Schenectady, and, after my visit with Mother and Anna, I would have to take a local from Schenectady northeast across New Ostend and into New Bruges and a good eighty miles into the state to Lebanon. That probably meant arriving home late on Friday night or in the very early hours of Saturday morning. I hoped I'd be able to doze on the trains.

After I made sure that I had some time before the Montreal Express left, I used a public wireset in the B&P station to call Bruce.

"LBI."

"Bruce, this is Johan. I need a gadget that does the exact opposite of the last two you did. One that can take a program file and project it into one of those fields and into the atmosphere, so to speak. Can you do it?"

"Johan . . ." There was a long pause. "I suppose so. Is it . . . wise?" He laughed. "No, of course not. Not if it's you. Yes, I'll do it. Monday?"

"You're a saint."

"Probably not. It's against my religion."

"All right, a prophet."

"You can be both, and have the grief."

"Fine. Monday. I'll still pick up the other gear as we scheduled earlier."

"It will be waiting."

"Thanks."

After replacing the handset, I walked across the green marble floor of the main hall toward the gate for platform six and then down the steps to the platform itself. The cars of the Montreal Express were gleaming silver, freshly washed.

The conductor studied me, his eyes going from the pinstriped suit to the garment bag and leather case. "Your ticket, sir?"

I offered it, breathing in the slight odor of oil and hot metal that persists even with the modern expresses.

"Club car, seats three and four."

I nodded and climbed up the steps. The seats were the reclining type, and because the train was a midday, the almost-new club car was but half filled. The odor of new upholstery and the even fainter hint of the almost-new lacquer on the wood panels bolstered my impressions of newness, despite the traditional darkness of the wood and the green hangings.

I sat on the train for nearly half an hour before it smoothly dropped into the north tunnel. We emerged from the darkness in a cut between long rows of brown stone houses, looking almost gray in the late October rain, and glided northward at an increasing pace. I was still holding the unopened case when the express paused in Baltimore, slowing so gently that the conductor's call came as a surprise.

"Baltimore. All off for Baltimore."

The doors opened, and eventually they closed, and no one sat near me.

Finally, somewhere north of Baltimore, about the time we crossed the Susquehanna on the new high-speed bridge west of Havre de Grace, I opened my travel case. As I took out the memos I had pilfered from vanBecton, rain began to pelt the car windows, hard and cold as liquid hail.

Certainly vanBecton knew I had pocketed something with the pratfall, and he had let me get away with it, thinking I would get nothing. What I hoped he didn't realize was that I wasn't after anything that concrete.

He was setting me up for removal, and he was saying, in effect, that I could do nothing about it. My own experiences had taught me one thing he hadn't learned yet, and I could only hope it would be enough.

I took out the pilfered memos and began to read. As vanBecton had indicated, they were pretty much all administrative trivia. One dealt with the allocation of administrative support funds. The second, signed by vanBecton, was a clarification of Spazi regional office boundaries. Another was on the subject of the United Charities Fund and the need for supervisors to encourage giving. There was a three-page, detailed exposition on the required procedures for claiming reimbursement for travel and lodging expenses.

The formats were virtually identical, but what I had wanted was the one with vanBecton's signature. I read it again and replaced all of them in the case. Then I leaned back and took a nap, trying to ignore the uneven rhythm of the rain.

Three stops and four hours later, I stepped out into the rain in Schenectady station, a cold rain that slashed across my face and left dark splotches on my coat.

I found a cab, a New Ostend special that gleamed through the mist and rain. The water beaded up on every painted surface, and the round-faced and white-haired driver smiled.

"Where to, sir?"

"Kampen Hills, number forty-three on Hendrik Lane."

"Good enough, sir."

Even the inside of the cab was spotless, and I leaned back into the seat as the driver wound his way away from the Rotterdam side, along the river road, and into the hills dotted with houses centered on gardens, now mulched for winter and surrounded with snow stands to protect the bushes.

In the summer, each gray house and its stonework and white-enameled windowsills would be diminished by the trees and the well-tended gardens, the arbors and the trellises. Now, the houses were stolid gray presences looming through the rain and mist.

There is always a price for everything, and that New Ostend special from the Schenectady station out to Anna's cost more than all the cabs I had taken the day before in the Federal District.

"Ten, that'll be, sir."

I paid him, with a dollar tip, and then I stood in the rain for far too long before my aunt finally came to the door.

"Johan, what are you doing out there in the rain? Don't you know that you come in out of such a downpour before you become a real ghost?"

I refrained from pointing out that entering unannounced was poor manners, and also impossible when the door was locked.

"Can you join us for chocolate?"

"I had hoped to," I answered honestly. "The local for Lebanon leaves at seven."

"Good! That's settled. Now off to the rear parlor with your mother while I get the chocolate and biscuits." Anna, more and more like a white-haired gnome with every passing year, shooed me down the hall and past the warmth welling from the kitchen.

"Your ne'er-do-well son is here, Ria," my aunt announced. "I'll be bringing the chocolate in a bit. Let him sit by the fire. He stood in the rain for far too long, silly man."

Mother stood up from her rocking chair, and I hugged her, not too long, since I was rather damp.

"I didn't expect you."

"I wired Anna when I left Columbia."

"She gets rather forgetful these days."

I took the straight-backed chair and pulled it closer to the woodstove. "Don't we all?"

"What were you doing in Columbia, Johan?"

"I was invited to a presidential dinner. I stayed last night with Eric and Judith."

"They're nice people, unlike so many in the capital. How was your dinner?" She picked up her knitting—red and gold yarn in what seemed to be an afghan. "As I recall, you never enjoyed those functions much. Why did you go?"

"It seemed like a good idea." I shrugged.

"Was it?"

"I suppose so. It appears I did not have much choice, as things turned out."

The heat from the stove was drying my suit—thoughtless of me not to have brought a waterproof, or an umbrella, English as that might have been.

"We always have choices, even if none of them are pleasant." Mother smiled.

"You are so cheerful about it."

"Johan, you survived the Spazi. I'm certain you could survive a presidential dinner. How is your lady friend, the singer?"

"Llysette? She's fine. She gave a concert two weeks ago. Unfortunately, the piano professor was murdered—"

"You wrote me about that. Dreadful thing to happen, especially right before she was going to perform."

"She didn't find out until after the recital."

"You see . . . even terrible occurrences have bright sides."

I shook my head. "The professor's ghost did hang around for a while."

"That happens. Poor soul."

"I suppose so. Aren't all ghosts?" I paused. "Speaking of ghosts, who was Carolynne? Really, I mean. Besides a singer who got murdered?"

Mother sat in the heavy rocker, the wide needles in her time-gnarled hands, the yarn still in response to my question. Finally she lifted the needles again. "You needn't bother with her. She must be gone by now. It was a long time ago."

"She's still there. I can see her on the veranda some nights. She quotes obscure sections of Shakespeare and some of the Shakespearean operas."

Mother kept looking at the red glow behind the mica glass of the stove. I waited, seemingly forever. "I told your father that reading Shakespeare, especially the plays she had performed, was only going to make her linger."

"I thought she was a singer."

"In those days, college teachers had to do more. She was a singer—the first real one at the college, according to your father. Sometimes she talked to him. He said she was stabbed to death, but she never talked about it to me. I don't know as she really said much except those same quotes from Shakespeare, but your father said the quotes made a sort of sense. That's why he read Shakespeare back."

"That means she was stabbed at the house."

"She was supposed to have been the lover of the deacon who built the house. His wife had stayed in Virginia, but she—the wife—finally decided to come to New Bruges. She didn't bother to tell her husband. I think she suspected, but she stabbed Carolynne when she found her asleep beside her husband late one afternoon."

I waited for a time, and the needles clicked faintly against each other and the yarn in the ball dwindled slowly as the afghan grew. Finally I ventured a statement. "That had to have been more than a century ago."

"I thought she would fade."

"I think she's as strong as ever."

"Your father's meddling, I dare say. Told him no good would come of that."

"She seems so sad."

"Most ghosts who linger do, son." Her tone turned wry, and the needles continued to click. "So do most people who linger."

"I suppose so."

"Here's the chocolate!" announced Anna, bustling in with a huge tray heaped with cakes, cookies, biscuits, and an imposing pot of chocolate.

I slipped up one side of the drop-leaf table for her, then poured out the three cups and served them. Anna took the other straight-backed armchair.

"Cake?" I asked Mother.

"Just a plain one."

I turned to Anna.

"I'll have a pair of the oatmeal cookies."

After serving them, I heaped a sampling of all the baked goods on my plate— about the only lunch and supper I was probably going to get, and far better than the lukewarm fare on the trains.

"We don't see you enough," offered Anna after a silence during which we had all eaten and sipped.

"I try, but about half the time when I'm free, you two are off to visit someone else."

"That's better than sitting around and watching each other grow old."

"This is the first time I've seen both of you sitting in months."

"We're resting up. Tonight we're going to the Playhouse performance of *Your Town*."

I frowned, not having ever cared for the Pound satire on *Our Town*. Then again, Pound was just another of the thirties crazies who'd never discovered what they had rebelled against. *Your Town* was the only play he wrote, if I recalled it right, and it flopped in Philadelphia just before Pound moved to Vienna. He'd finally ended up writing propaganda scripts for Ferdinand—all justifying the unification of Europe under the Hapsburgs.

"I need to arrange for a cab," I finally said.

"So soon?" asked Anna.

"I have to meet with an electronics supplier in the morning."

"What does electronics have to do with your teaching?" asked Mother.

"It's equipment for my difference engine."

"Better spend more time with your singer than the machine. Machines don't exactly love you back," said Anna.

"No. But they make writing articles and books much easier."

Mother shook her head. "Just be careful, Johan. These are dangerous times."

Anna gave her sister a puzzled look, and then glanced at me. "Sometimes you two leave everyone else out of the conversation."

"I have to wire a cab." I made my way back to the front parlor and used the wireset to arrange for Schenectady Electrocab to pick me up at six.

"Is it set?" asked Mother when I returned. She had set aside the piece of knitting she had apparently completed and was beginning another section with the same colors.

"Six o'clock." I poured another cup of chocolate and helped myself to two more oatmeal cookies, promising myself that I'd step up my exercise the next day.

"You never did say much about your singer," suggested Anna. "That murder business must have upset her."

My mother grinned and kept knitting.

"We were all somewhat upset—especially the music department. It's not pleasant to have the ghost of a murdered woman drifting through the halls. Luckily, she didn't linger too long."

"Did the watch ever find the murderer?"

"Not so far. I think they suspect about half the university." I was beginning to feel sleepy, with the fullness in my stomach and the warmth of the second cup of chocolate, and I yawned.

"You're not getting enough sleep."

"Too much traveling."

"Well, I say it's a shame," offered Anna. "Might I have some more chocolate?"

I refilled her cup. "It certainly is."

"Universities are almost as bad as government."

"It's hard to tell the difference." I stifled a yawn, and munched another oatmeal cookie. "Except universities don't have to be petty and are, while almost no one in government means to be petty, but the results almost always are."

"He's still cynical," Anna said after lifting her cup for a refill.

I understood why her chocolate pot was so large.

"He's still alive," added Mother.

What could I add to that? Mother had been the practical one, my father the dreamer, and I probably had gotten the worst of each trait.

After arriving right at six, the cab made it through the rain and back to the station by six-thirty. There I joined a small queue of dampened souls at the ticket window and purchased my twenty-one-dollar fare to Lebanon.

The seven-fifteen local back to Lebanon whined its way out of New Ostend into western New Bruges and into the hills that comprised the southern Grunbergs. As the slow train wound north and east through the continuing rain, I sat on a hard coach bench and tried to think it all through.

I'm not exactly a political genius when it comes to unraveling the intrigues of the Federal District, but one thing seemed clear enough. A lot of defense projects in Babbage centers were ostensibly out to destroy the ghosts and the basis of ghosts in our world. On the surface, it seemed plausible. Why not destroy ghosts? You know, put them out of their misery. Save them from lingering eternally and poisoning the present with their haunting gloom.

Was that bad? I thought so.

Wasn't it just possible that the slow progress of conquest was due in part to the inability of soldiers to accept ghosts on a massive basis? Supposedly the horrors of Hastings almost undid the armies of William the Unfortunate, so much so that it was three generations before his heir fully grasped even England.

Firearms had helped dispel that ghostly influence, especially for those armies with sharpshooters, like the assassin regiments of Ferdinand VI. But sometimes a good general can use horrors, as the New French general Santa Anna did at the Alamo. He was really a Mexican then, but that's not what the New French histories state. On balance, it seemed as though modern technology and medicine were slowly destroying ghosts, except in warfare, which is barbarous by nature.

But all the ghost-related projects were being fired and/or having difficulty— and that went for projects in Europe as well as in Columbia. Except there was something wrong with my logic, and I couldn't put my finger on it.

I leaned back in the hard seat of the local and tried to fall asleep in the dim light, with the *click, clickedy, click* of the rails in one ear and the snoring of the heavyset woman two seats back in the other.

In the end, I neither slept nor thought, but sat there in a semidaze until I reached Lebanon.

In the station parking lot, the dowager-sleek lines of the Stanley waited for me, half concealed in the mist created by the cold rain that had fallen on warmer pavement.

Even after two days the Stanley lit off easily, and I drove eastward through the darkness, alert for moose. The big animals had been making a comeback, and any collision between one and a steamer would favor the moose.

The rain had been warm enough that it had not formed ice on the roads, and steady enough that few were out, even on a late Friday evening.

The only real signs of life were at the Dutch Reformed Church in Alexandria, where a handful of hardy souls were leaving a lecture on "The Growth and Heritage of the Leisure Class" by some doktor. At least, that's what I thought the rain-damped poster stated. A leisure class of Dutch heritage? I almost laughed.

Marie, bless her Dutch soul, had not only left on the light, but had left a small beef pie in the refrigerator. I wolfed down all of it cold, even before I carried my garment bag up to the bedroom.

I knew I couldn't sleep until I rechecked Branston-Hay's files, the ones I had pirated, but I did change into dry exercise sweats before I returned to the study to fire up the difference engine.

Carolynne hovered by the desk.

I bowed to her. "Good evening, Carolynne."

"Good evening, sweet prince."

"My mother was surprised that you were still around."

"No more but so?"

"Were you in love with my father?" I asked, hoping her words, twisted as they might be, would prove illuminating.

"Rich gifts wax poor when givers prove unkind."

"My father, unkind?"

"O, help him, sweet heavens!"

I tried not to shake my head. "Why do you disappear so much?"

"To have seen what I have seen, to see what I see. Thy madness be paid by weight 'til our scale turn the beam and 'til our brief candle weighs out."

I pursed my lips. What did she mean, if anything? "Brief candle weighs out?"

"The more seen I, the less to see."

Was that it? The more visible a ghost, the shorter its lingering. "But where do you go?"

"Nature is fine in love, and where 'tis fine it sends some precious instance of itself."

I shook my head. "What do you do? Being a ghost has to be boring."

"There's rue for you, and here's some for me. Fennel and kennel and the old bitch went mad." She gave me a smile, not exactly one of innocence. "Impatience does become a dog that's mad. Yet your father left me some rare and precious effects, such as reading . . ."

Ghosts committing suicide? That was what Ophelia's lines were about, but where had the other lines come from and what did they mean? Reading? Did she read when she was invisible?

"You like company?"

"Wishers were ever fools. All's but naught."

Since she was talking, more than we had since I was a small boy, I asked another question. "Some people talk about ghosts taking over people's bodies. Could that happen?"

"The grave's a fine and crowded place, and none but do there embrace." Carolynne laughed. "Mad thou art to say it, but not without ambition."

I tried not to wince at the mixed language. Was everything she spoke the result of her singing and theatre training, drilled into her being so that her ghost reacted semirationally? Or were the words random?

The translation, if I understood, if the words were more than ghostly random ramblings, was that it was dangerous, but possible. "What if . . ." I paused before continuing. "What if someone were dying, and the ghost left the body, and modern medicine saved the person?"

"First it bended, and then it broke, and pansies are for thought . . ."

She drifted away, like Ophelia on a psychic river, and I watched the faint whiteness shift through the mirror, presumably to the artificial lodestone to rebuild her strength.

Shaking my head, I reached for the switch to turn the difference engine back on. Then I rubbed my forehead. I still wondered if the files I had pilfered from Branston-Hay contained any hints of what was going on, and why vanBecton thought I was so trapped.

A good hour of scanning files in my most skeptical manner passed before I found the first hint. The key lay in one almost innocent-sounding sentence.

". . . principal interest was in the economic section of the draft report . . . concerns over the elimination cost per ghost . . . laughable, given the costs of any war . . ."

I kept reading.

". . . without further progress in reducing per-ghost costs . . . termination of third extension set for January 1, 1994 . . ."

At the end of another file, I found the letter steamer, so to speak.

"RM pleased with improved replicator . . . budget review to be dropped . . ."

I leaned back in the chair. Branston-Hay had been padding his budget, and the president's budget examiners had caught him—but they hadn't turned him in. They'd asked for some applied research. It all made sense—except Miranda's murder. Branston-Hay had no reason to murder Miranda. First, he wouldn't have really understood the political ramifications, and I had to question if Miranda would have. Except her daughter-in-law had pointed out Miranda's intuitive or spiritual understandings. So what had Miranda known that was so dangerous that someone had wanted to kill her?

She probably knew that Branston-Hay had been doing secret psychic research, but vanBecton knew that, and so had everyone else—although almost no one knew the extent of that research. Branston-Hay wasn't the type for murder; at least I didn't think so. Could vanBecton's tame Spazi have murdered her to put the finger on me? Or did vanBecton already know that I had chosen to work for the president?

What about Llysette? Where did she fit in? I had a feeling, but I couldn't really prove it.

With more questions than answers, I drifted into a doze in the chair, to be awakened by the clock's chimes. It was two o'clock, so I hadn't slept that long. I turned off the difference engine, pulled myself out of the chair, and headed up to bed.

Carolynne was nowhere to be seen, but that no longer meant much, I realized.

CHAPTER SIXTEEN

• • •

Since the house was spotless—Marie did more than she should have when I was gone and less than she felt necessary, I was sure—all the housekeeping I had to do on Saturday was wash the dishes I had used for breakfast.

After I ate and did the dishes, I did get back to running and exercising. I even went over the top of the hill and along the ridge. Then I raked a huge pile of leaves into the compost pile below the garden and sprinkled lime over them.

A hundred years of work on the thin soil had resulted in soil that wasn't that thin any longer, and the grass was more like a carpet. The garden tomatoes were as good as any, and the time-domesticated raspberries and black raspberries—well, I had frozen pies, freezer jam, and whole frozen berries, more than enough to last until the next summer.

After my groundskeeping, with sweat and leaf fragments sticking together and plastered even under my clothes, I stripped, took a shower, and dressed.

Had I seen a flash of white in the study? I looked around, but didn't see Carolynne. With a sigh, I extricated the strongbox from the wall safe and pulled out another sheaf of bills for Bruce. There were still enough left, but how long they would last if I kept funding unique hardware was another question.

Outside it was sunny, but the wind was even more bitter than it had been earlier in the morning and ripped at the last of the leaves clinging stubbornly to their trees. I passed but a handful of vehicles, mostly haulers, as I drove the steamer back south to Zuider and LBI to pick up the perturbation replicator. With just scattered brown leaves on the oaks and maples, the dark winter green of the pines stood out on the woodlots higher on the low hills.

The narrow streets of Zuider were half filled, mainly with families in well-polished steamers, probably taking children to soccer practice or music lessons or the like, or headed out to shop for bargains in the new mall, the latest facet of Columbian Dutch culture.

There was another steamer in the LBI lot besides Bruce's battered Olds ragtop. He'd gotten it when the Pontiac people folded and he couldn't get decent service on his '52 ragtop.

A long-haired man was discussing musical programware. "I need more instant memory and a direct audio line . . ."

I had heard about the so-called synthesizer revolution and the predictions of Babbage-generated music or the reproduction of master concerts on magnetic disks or thin tapes. I shuddered at the thought of music being reduced to plastic. Somehow, at least a vinyl disc had the feel of semipermanence. Music on plastic tapes—that would be ghost music.

While Bruce talked with the would-be Babbage composer, I wandered around, mostly thinking. Bruce seemed able to create all this hardware from rough specifications; if it worked, why hadn't a lot of other techies done the same? Most weren't as creative as Bruce, and most had no need.

There also was another reason. Gerald's comment dropped into my mind— the point that you really couldn't murder someone in a laboratory to study the ghost. Of course, Ferdinand could—and I suspected our own dear Spazi could.

I shook my head. Then again, with all the fires in Babbage centers, I wondered if, in Branston-Hay's position, I'd even want to try freelancing. Bruce had understood it all too well—he'd stayed a techie. Nobody paid any attention to mere technicians.

Eventually the musical type left, and I wandered up to the counter. "Any specials on unique hardware?"

"No. Only on unique headaches." Bruce hauled out my difference engine box and opened the top. "Figured I might as well use your packaging for the improbable perturbation replicator."

Inside were two black metal boxes linked with cables. The bottom box had two switches on the front and Babbage cables. The top box was smaller and sprouted what appeared to be four trapezoids linked together in the shape of a crude megaphone. The top box also had two matching cable ports.

"What are these for?"

"I added those last night. I thought I could link the other gadget—I beg your pardon, the perturbation projector—to this and save some hardware. Whether it will work, I don't know yet, since I haven't built it, but it ought to. Any problem with that?"

"No."

"If you need to have the scanning antenna farther from the conversion box, you can just add more cable."

"Conversion box? I thought that's what the file protocol did."

"They're almost the same, except this is more complex. It converts an image of the field, while the other one actually removes the field and converts it."

"Oh." More pieces fell into place.

"Now . . . the other one's going to be a bear."

"I didn't think it would be easy," I admitted. "Do you need more time?"

"Do you have it?"

"I don't know." I shrugged. "Maybe."

Bruce gave me a nasty grin. "That means you don't."

"Thanks."

"I always try to be truthful. It upsets people more than lying."

"You are always so cheerful." I peeled off the bills and laid them on the counter.

"I try."

"You're very trying." I hefted the box, and Bruce held the door for me.

"The other will be ready on Monday—first thing."

"I don't know if I will be, but I'll be here."

"That's what I liked about you from the first, Johan. You're always ready—even if you haven't got the faintest idea what to do."

Since that was a pretty accurate description, I really couldn't say too much except, "Thanks."

He stood and watched while I backed out and headed back north to Vanderbraak Centre, and to the watch, and all my problems, including a ghost who had started to talk but spouted dialogue and song lyrics or librettos. Was it bad that she was spouting, or worse that I thought it made sense?

The clouds were beginning to build to the north, but they didn't seem to be moving that quickly. Neither was the traffic, once I got behind a logging steamer on the way to the biomass plant outside Alexandria. I speeded up when he took the turnoff for the Ragged Mountain Highway and Lastfound Lake.

Once I got to the house and got the box and its equipment inside, I just tucked it in a corner in the study. With the sun and the breeze I didn't feel like playing with electronics inside, especially since the approaching clouds meant snow or freezing rain later.

First I tried Llysette's wire, but she either wasn't home or didn't choose to answer. So I changed and went back outside and raked up a huge pile of leaves and began to drag and rake them down to the compost pile. The lawn was still partly green, and under the sun I sweated a lot, even with the cold wind.

Three horn toots sounded up the drive, followed by a small green Reo. Llysette parked outside the car barn and waved.

I carried the rake back up the hill and tucked it inside the car barn.

Llysette wore denim trousers and a black Irish cable-knit pullover loose enough for comfort, but with just enough hint of the curves that lay beneath. I saw her overnight case in the front seat, and a gown hung in the back.

"I wired you, but you weren't home. So I went back to working up a sweat."

"Something you must always be doing, n'est-ce pas?"

"Pretty much." Sweaty or not, I gave her an enthusiastic hug and a kiss, and got a reasonable facsimile in response.

"Would you like to stay for dinner?"

"Only for dinner?" She leered, which I enjoyed.

"If you insist, dear lady."

We laughed. Then a blast of much cooler air swept across the hillside, swirling some of my hard-raked leaves. Llysette shivered, and we turned to the dark clouds over the hills to the northwest.

"It looks like it might snow."

"I should hope not."

"Perhaps you'll be stuck here."

"I have to sing for the Anglican-Baptist chapel tomorrow."

"Why?"

"Because they will pay me."

"That's as good a reason as any." I laughed and pulled her case from the Reo and headed inside. She carried the gown and hung it in the closet in the master bedroom.

I hugged her again, but reluctantly released her when I heard her stomach growl. "No breakfast or lunch?"

She shrugged.

"I did have some breakfast, but no lunch. Let's see what there is."

I found a block of extra-sharp cheddar, a loaf of almost fresh bread, and mined some good apples and a bottle of Sebastopol from the cellar.

"Good . . ." the lady murmured after three slices of cheese and a thick slab of lightly toasted oatmeal bread.

"Of course it's good. I prepared it."

"You should have been a chef, Johan."

"I'm not nearly that good. You just need a man who can cook or who can afford a chef."

"I cannot cook, not well; that is true. But choosing a man by whether he can cook . . . that I do not know."

"You already have."

At least she smiled at that.

"Your dinner at the Presidential Palace, how was it?"

I had to shrug. "I guess it was history-making. I heard the president announce the agreement with Japan for us to get their nuclear submersible technology."

"Of this you do not sound too positive."

"It may be necessary, but I'm not terribly fond of ways to improve military technology. You might have noticed that not very many generals or emperors die in wars."

"So? They are the leaders." Her tone was matter-of-fact, as if we were discussing the weather.

"So? I have this mental problem with people who are so willing to send others off to do the killing, but who take none of the risks themselves."

Llysette gave me a sad smile. "In some things you are predictably Columbian. Always there have been rulers, and always there are soldiers. The soldiers die, and the rulers rule. Yet you think it should be otherwise. Would the soldier make a good ruler?"

"Not necessarily. That wasn't my point. I do think many rulers would not be so eager to start wars if they stood to die with their soldiers."

"You are right, but who could make a ruler face such risks? The world, it does not work that way."

"No, it doesn't." I sliced some more cheese and offered it to Llysette. "Here."

"Thank you." She pursed her lips. "You are angry with me."

"No . . . not exactly angry. But sometimes I don't understand. You've suffered a lot, and it's almost like you're defending the system that tortured you."

Llysette took a long sip of the Sebastopol before answering. "I see things as they are, Johan. Not one thing that Ferdinand or your Speaker does, not one thing I can change. You, you still dream that you can make the world better. I lost that dream." She took a deep breath. "That, it makes a big difference between us. You have lost much. I know. But you will die thinking you can change the world. Perhaps you will." She shivered.

It was my turn to sip wine and think. Much of what Llysette said made sense. Even after Minister Dolan denied Elspeth's and my request for her treatment in Vienna, even after Elspeth's death, I kept believing one person could make a difference. I guess I still did. "I suppose I will."

"I know. That is why I care for you. Yet that is also what separates us."

I shrugged. *"Vive la différence."*

"Vive la différence." Her shrug was sadder, almost resigned.

"Do you want any more cheese?"

"Non."

I packed up the bread and cheese, but did refill her wine glass before I recorked it, and we repaired to the main parlor, adjoining the study, where I opened the shades fully. The sun had begun to fade with the approaching clouds, but the day was still bright.

Llysette sat on the couch with her wine glass in her right hand. I sat on her left and nibbled her ear. She didn't protest. So I kissed her cheek, and stroked her neck.

"Feels good . . ." she murmured.

"I certainly hope so." I kissed her again, and let my fingers caress her neck, then knead out the stiffness in both her neck and shoulders.

"So easy to feel good . . . with you . . ."

I kissed her on the lips, very gently, very slowly, and returned to loosening the muscles in her neck and back. Under the sweater and blouse, her skin was like velvet.

After a while she put down the wine glass, and a while after that she didn't need the sweater—or much of anything else—to keep warm.

Later, much later, as I held Llysette, the quilt wrapped around us, and we watched the flicker of the flames in the mica glass of the woodstove, I wondered if Carolynne watched, unseen, and what she thought. Did she see us and wish to be flesh and blood again?

How could she not? I knew I would, were I locked into some place where I was bodiless and could only talk to a handful of souls across a century. But could she talk, or was I imagining it?

I shivered.

"You are cold, Johan?"

"A little chill."

"You who are always so hot?"

"It happens." My eyes flicked to the window. "It's beginning to snow."

"That is what the videolink forecast."

"You actually watch the video?"

"Sometimes. It is . . . amusing."

"Terrifying is more like it."

"Johan, sometimes . . . there is very little difference between terror and amusement." Her lips reached mine again, and they were warm, which was good because I was chilled all the way through to my soul.

CHAPTER SEVENTEEN

• • •

I cannot believe you are going to sing for the Anglican-Baptists. Especially for just ten dollars." I swallowed the last of my chocolate. Since she was not singing at the Dutch Reformed Church, I wasn't going to be particularly godly. In fact, I was going to work on the definitely ungodly business of psychic phenomena, and trust that Klaus Esterhoos didn't find out. But then I doubted that he would have cared that much.

"It is a comedown, no? But what am I supposed to do? Starve?" Llysette shrugged before picking up her coffee cup.

I tried not to shudder. Either chocolate or tea—those I could take for breakfast. But coffee? I ground it fresh for Llysette, and fresh-ground coffee smells wonderful. I love the smell; it's the taste I abhor.

"You're not exactly about to starve, even on your salary."

"Johan, my recital gowns, once they cost more than I make in a month here."

I nodded, because Llysette does have exquisite taste, and fulfilling good taste never comes cheaply. I'd also priced recital gowns, and while university administrations expect performers to make a good impression, their pay scale always falls short of their expectations of performing artists.

Cost accounting, again—a business professor can teach eighty students in a class and ten in an intensive seminar. A singer or instrumentalist can teach only one pupil at a time effectively. So a three-credit business lecture course generates over ten thousand dollars and takes less than three hours of lecture time for the professor. He generates three thousand dollars per credit. Poor Llysette or poor dead Miranda spent three hours a week with a student, got two teaching credits, and generated only a hundred dollars.

It's no wonder the performing arts have little administration or state funding support. Yet how can you develop the arts without education? I shook my head, but Llysette didn't notice my distraction.

"New recital gowns I cannot buy, and I will not count every penny which crosses my palm."

"How about silvers?"

"One does not have to count silvers."

I refilled her empty coffee cup, and then poured the last from the chocolate pot into my cup.

Outside, the wind whispered past the kitchen window, blowing a few flakes of the light snow off the Reo.

"It's still cold, but I suppose winter had to come sometime."

"Winter? It is October until tomorrow, Johan. Christmas—it is two months away. Winter I am not prepared for. Your winters are too long, far too long."

"Will you come back after you sing this morning?"

"*Non.* I cannot. Yesterday was ours. This afternoon and tonight I must prepare for the advanced diction class—my notes. It is another new class. And when I try to prepare here"—she smiled at me—"I do not prepare."

"You know the material."

"Knowing the material, that is one thing. Teaching it to these dunderheads is something else."

I sighed. "I understand, but I don't exactly like it, and I'm not rich enough to rescue you from such drudgery."

"I did not ask you to rescue me, Johan." Llysette stood. "I must get ready to perform my single solo for the Anglican-Baptists. And all for ten dollars." She sniffed.

After I washed the dishes, I followed her upstairs.

By then she was applying makeup, not that I thought she really needed very much.

"Lunch tomorrow?"

"But of course. That is one of my joys."

"What? Escaping the students?"

She raised her eyebrows. "How do you know I wish to escape all the students?"

"I forgot. You have some special baritones. Be careful, though. I'm a dangerous man . . . and a possessive one."

"I know, and that is amusing." She slipped out of the robe she left at the house and into the dark green dress, studying her reflection in the full-length mirror. "I look old."

"No, you don't."

"If I know old I look, then old I look." She straightened and lifted her cloak from where she had flung it on the bed. I'd have to make the bed after she left, but she got upset if I continually tidied up the place.

"But these . . . Anglican-Baptists, they will not see, and the money I need."

"You look good enough to . . ." I kissed her cheek.

"That you have already." She smiled, and we walked downstairs.

I took the broom and swept a path to the Reo and brushed the snow off. Then, after I watched her turn onto Deacon Lane, I wandered back into the kitchen and made another pot of chocolate. It was going to be a long day. Llysette had said it was amusing that I was possessive. Why? I shook my head, took a last look at the dark dual tracks in the snow on the drive, and closed the door. If I had thought the snow would stay, I would have gotten out the tractor and plowed the drive, but the six inches were already melting into slush.

When I went back into the study, I set my mug on the coaster on the corner of the Kunigser desk. Then I dragged out the two boxes with the LBI logo. I shook my head. Why I kept the toolbox in the car barn I still didn't know, but that meant another trip through the whitecapped slush that wasn't really snow.

Because Bruce built things that actually made sense, it almost took more time to get and return the toolbox than to physically install the perturbation replicator. Once again, the hardware was the easy part.

Trying to figure out the necessary programware was a mess, even cribbing liberally from Branston-Hay's files and notes. All I really wanted was what I thought would be about a twenty-line program. It took me almost a hundred and fifty, and it looked more like one of the Brit programs I'd developed years ago.

The sun was setting behind Vanderbraak Centre before I finished the program. Whether it would work or not was another question, but I was very glad of the Brit assignment. I'd grumbled about learning Babbage code—Elspeth teased me about that to the end—but after investing the time, I'd kept up as well as I could with the latest developments. Not only had it kept me busy through some dark times, but it had proved useful—especially now.

After installing the program, I took a break and wandered into the kitchen, where I put on the kettle for tea. I needed some very strong tea. The odds were that I'd fouled up somewhere, and I wasn't up to facing the repair job until I was refreshed.

While the kettle heated, I rummaged through the refrigerator and dug out some white cheddar. Then I cut two large slabs of oatmeal bread, just about finishing the loaf, and toasted them. Just to experiment, I used the Imperial Russian tea that Llysette had given me for my birthday, but didn't let it steep too long as I saw how quickly the boiling water darkened around the tea caddy.

One sip of the tea told me why it was an imperial blend—it was strong enough even to knock over a czar, not that the fading remnants of the Romanovs would be that hard to unseat. I dosed my mug with raw sugar, lots of it, but even before I got through half a cup at the kitchen table my heart was racing. I slapped blackberry preserves on the bread, and both slabs helped calm me down. I was jittery still by the time I walked back into the study, lit only by the glow from the difference engine screen. I turned on the lamp on the desk.

I was right. The first time I tried to execute the program, the engine locked. It took an hour to track down that glitch, one symbol on line twelve. All in all, it was nearly ten o'clock before the system *seemed* to work.

I turned off the difference engine and went back into the kitchen to fix a late supper, not that there was that much left in the refrigerator. Outside, the wind was howling, and it seemed like it was cold enough to freeze the remaining slush and water on the drive. I turned on the light and peered out, nodding at the reflections on the patches of black ice.

Finally I made an omelet with cheese and some mushrooms and apple slices, and slathered it with sour cream mixed with curry powder. Sounds barbaric, like a relic from the days before the British got pounded out of India by the Muslim resurgence, but it was tasty.

Once refreshed, I returned to the fray, except I couldn't do much without a ghost. So I turned down the lights and left the difference engine off.

"Carolynne? Carolynne?"

There wasn't any answer, or response, and not much that I could do. So I looked through the shelves for something halfway interesting to read and pulled out something I hadn't seen before—*The Green Secession,* one of those alternate-worlds fantasies. In this one there weren't any ghosts, apparently, and Columbia was called something like the United States of America.

I turned on the reading light by the leather chair in front of the shelves. From what I could tell after the first twenty pages, the United States had a president, but he had almost as much power as the Speaker. They had a two-house Congress, with lords, except they were called senators, and a lot of representatives who didn't seem much concerned with anything but reelection. Still . . . it was fascinating.

After perhaps forty pages I called, "Carolynne." But she was nowhere to be seen.

I called her name at irregular intervals several more times. By half-past midnight, I had almost finished my improbable novel about a Columbia, or United States, I guess, where status and power almost seemed to be separate.

At almost one o'clock, on the last page of the book, Carolynne appeared at my shoulder, still in her antique recital gown.

"More to know did never meddle with my thoughts."

"Didn't you hear me calling?" I turned off the reading light to see her more clearly.

She smiled coyly. "Your tale, sir, would cure deafness."

I sighed.

"Nor can imagination form a shape, yet once was I a shape."

I thought about that. For all her scrambled quotes, Carolynne was definitely a person, but had Miranda's ghost been one? What had Branston-Hay's trapping done to her? I shivered.

"Dead, what is there I shall die to want, nor desire to give?" She stopped speaking abruptly and drifted a few feet back from my shoulder and into the center of the study. "It would become me as well as it does you."

"I wanted to know if you would help me."

"I am a fool to weep at what I am glad of." She eased toward me.

Although I could sense something like fear as she neared the silent difference engine, I added, "You wouldn't have to get close. If you stay by the doorway, can you avoid being drawn to the difference engine here?"

"But this is trifling." She paused. "And all the more it seeks to hide itself."

"No, I'm not trying to hide anything," I answered truthfully. "I want to test something. It is supposed to make a difference engine . . . picture, I guess would be the closest term. If you feel yourself being trapped or pulled, let me know, and I'll turn it off like I did before."

"You may deny me, but I'll be your servant."

"I'll be more quick." I set up the device so that it was focused on her, then turned on the difference engine. As it came up to speed, Carolynne seemed to flutter, but she hovered by the doorway.

As quickly as I could, I trained the replicator on her, and entered the command lines, one after the other. "Define" was the first, and the machine typed back, "Definition commencing," then "Definition complete." "Replicate" was followed by the response "replication commencing" and then by "replicated file complete." "Structure file" came next, followed by the condensation and storage commands. When the screen indicated that the replicated file was stored, I exited the program and flipped the switch to turn off the difference engine.

Carolynne drifted closer. "Another, yet I do not know one of my sex, save from my glass."

"The other one of you, Carolynne, is more like a painting, or a picture. It is a copy of how you are now, but you will change, and it won't."

"Rather like a dream than an assurance that my remembrance warrants."

"Is all life a dream?" And I had to wonder. Were the words Carolynne spoke meaningful, or phrases for which I was inventing meanings? Was my mind threatened as well as my life?

"It is a hint that wrings mine eyes to it."

"Do you ever rest?" Why was I asking questions to an incoherent ghost?

The ghost seemed to frown. "What should I do, I do not. Rest do I not tossed upon stones."

Stones? Lodestones? Was modern technology actually perpetuating ghosts because of the electrical and magnetic fields it generated? In a strange way, it made sense. Modern technology allowed more people to live in better condition. Why not ghosts? Of course, the religious nuts would have hung me out to dry on that one, since they all believed that ghosts were some sort of divine creation and not natural phenomena.

"My other self, death's second self?" asked Carolynne.

That was a good question, and one I couldn't answer. "I don't know. Somehow, it would be wrong to destroy the file, but it would also be wrong to release her here with you."

"O, 'tis treason!"

Maybe I shouldn't have, but, like a lot of things, what was done was done. Did Ralston and the president feel any guilt? Somehow, I doubted it, although the comparison certainly didn't make things right.

"Hast thou affections?" asked Carolynne.

"You asked a good question. It's just that I don't have a good answer."

"I wouldst thou didst."

So did I.

"And with my heart in it; and now farewell." She was gone. At least, she disappeared from view.

I shook my head. I was troubled, and I was tired. Mornings were coming too quickly, and while I couldn't do much about the troubled feelings, I could get some sleep. So I turned out the lights and headed up to bed.

CHAPTER EIGHTEEN

• • •

Once again, on Monday morning, I was off and running—not literally, since I skipped my dash to the hilltop—but I did force myself through a half hour of exercise before eating, cleaning up, and driving back down south to LBI through an intermittent sleet that turned into cold rain as I neared

Zuider. Early in the winter, Lochmeer did moderate the weather, until the vast expanse froze over.

The Stanley was actually good on slick roads, despite its relatively light weight, because of the four-wheel-traction option.

I flicked the radio to KCNB, the classical station out of Zuider, and a program of postmodern music. Some of the younger composers, such as Exten and Perkins, actually developed harmonies that consisted of more than four-note tone rows. The only bad part was an Exten aria from *Nothing Ventured* sung by a tenor named Austin Hill. He just didn't have it, strained the whole way through. Maybe he should have been a conductor—or a critic.

When the "Oratorio Hour" began, I flicked the radio to KPOP, just before I entered Zuider. Outside of the *Messiah* and a few other demonstrably endurable works, my tastes for oratorio, Llysette's efforts notwithstanding, are clearly limited. Instead, I enjoyed Dennis Jackson's version of *Louisiana,* even if he weren't an operatic baritone.

After wading through the water and slush in the LBI parking lot, I pushed through the door, with its faint bleep, and up to the counter.

Without a word, Bruce emerged from the workroom and set the equipment boxes on the counter. Also without a word, I peeled off more bills.

Then I looked into the two boxes. The third gadget was simpler than the second, and looked somehow incomplete. Then I realized why. "These attach into the other gadget?"

"I believe you were the one who called it a perturbation replicator. This is the perturbation projector which attaches to the replicator. Now, if you want, we can just call them gadgets, but I defer to your nomenclature."

"You really are ornery."

"I do perfectly well on no sleep, impossible specifications for improbable hardware, and the concern that all sorts of people I haven't seen in years and never wish to see again will suddenly appear."

"But I like seeing you."

"That's true. I haven't seen this much of you in years."

"What was it that guy said in that cult second-rate movie—the beginning of a beautiful friendship?"

"Friendship is based on deception, and you destroyed any illusion of that long ago, Johan."

"So . . . I am impossibly direct?"

"No. Merely improbably less indirect than the average Columbian. You'll be all right so long as no one really figures out that you're about as direct as a sharp knife."

"Some already have. I'm supposed to stab the other guy, though, or take the fall for a stabbing that's already taken place."

"For a nice boy born of cultured parents, you've always played in rough company."

"Tell me." I closed the boxes.

"I have." Bruce picked up the second and followed me out to the Stanley, where we placed them both in the front trunk. "I was more than gratified to be a mere technician."

"Now you're a distinguished man of commerce."

"Times like this, I wish I were still an anonymous technician."

"You're better paid, and people like me don't show up as often." I shut the trunk.

"That's also true, and your presence is always welcome. It's the baggage with the clocklike sounds that bothers me."

"I'll try to leave it behind."

Bruce just shook his head as I climbed into the steamer.

The roads were merely damp on the way back to the university. I stopped by Samaha's and picked up my newspapers, which I didn't bother to read before heading up to my office. As usual, I was one of the first into the department offices, except, of course, for Gilda.

"Good morning, Gilda."

"You're polite this morning."

"Am I not always?"

"Not always, but on average. Doktor Doniger will not be in until late. He wired in that the ice on the lane was too dangerous."

I snorted. "I live on Deacon's Lane, and I got here."

"Doktor Doniger is somewhat more cautious."

I nodded, picked up a stack of administrative paperwork and circulars attempting to entice me into prescribing new texts for all my classes, and tromped upstairs.

"Good morning, Johan," called Grimaldi from his desk. "I see you were one of the hardy few."

"There was only a trace of slush on the roads." I paused by his door.

"Any excuse in a storm, I suppose. What do you think—you were in government—about this Japanese nuclear submersible business?"

"Politicians who don't have to face the weaponry they have built have always worried me."

"Politicians don't have to worry about facing weaponry of any sort. That's the definition of a politician—someone who gets someone else to pay the bill and take the bullets."

"You're even more cynical than I am." I forced a laugh.

"Amen." He stood. "I suppose I will see you later. Or at tomorrow's departmental meeting. I'm off to the library."

"Cheers."

He waved, and I opened my office. Then I sorted through the memos, ignoring David's agenda for the departmental meeting, seeing as the top item was still the business of deciding which electives to cut. Most of the papers I tossed, including the questionnaire asking for an item-by-item evaluation on the cross-cultural applicability of my courses.

All four days of the *Asten Post-Courier* were full of stories about the Japanese development, but there was little I hadn't seen already in the *Columbia Post-Dispatch*—except for one paragraph in Saturday's paper.

Among the attendees at the presidential dinner announcing the Japanese initiative was Johan A. Eschbach, a former Minister of Environment. Eschbach is currently a professor at Vanderbraak State University, recently rocked by a murder scandal and allegations involving clandestine psychic research funded by the Ministry of Defense.

I swallowed. Who had said anything about psychic research? VanBecton? His tame pseudo-watch officer? And tying the murder and the research to me was definitely unkind. After rummaging through the papers and my paperwork, I picked up the handset and dialed.

"Hello."

"Gerald, I need a few minutes with you. How about three-thirty?" I was glad to hear his voice.

"I'm really rather tied up . . ."

"This isn't about philosophy. I think you'll be interested. I'll see you at three-thirty." I owed him something, even if he didn't know he needed it. VanBecton wasn't going to let him know, and Ralston certainly wasn't. I took his "ulp" as concurrence and concluded with, "Have a good day, Gerald."

As eleven o'clock approached, I gathered my folder, my notes, and the next quiz for Environmental Economics, half dreading the still-blank faces that I would see.

Gertrude and Hector were sweeping the remnants of water and frozen slush off the bricked walk leading to Smythe as I passed. Their breathing, and mine, left a white fog in the air.

"Good day, Gertrude. You too, Hector."

"Every day's a good day, sir," she answered.

"Take care, sir," added Hector.

I almost stopped. Hector had never said a word to me before. Instead, I just answered, "Thank you, Hector."

Who was more real—the zombie or the ghost? Or did it depend on the situation? Or were they both real? Certainly, the government recognized zombies as pretty much full citizens, except for voting, but a zombie could even petition for that right, not that many had the initiative. But Carolynne seemed about as real as the zombies I knew, if eccentric; Miranda's ghost, or my grandfather's, hadn't. I pushed away the speculations as I climbed the stairs to the second floor.

Nearly a dozen students were still missing by the time the clock chimed. The missing were the ones who hadn't done the reading. So I smiled my pleasantly nasty smile and cleared my throat.

"As some of you have surmised, I have an unannounced quiz here. For those of you present, the lowest grade possible will be a D. Anyone who is not here who is not in the hospital or the infirmary will fail."

Three or four of the students exchanged glances, at least one with an "I told you so" look. While I wasn't exactly thrilled, what Machiavelli said about the ruler applies also to teachers. It is best to be loved and feared, but far better to be feared and not loved than to be loved and not feared.

I handed out the greenbooks first, then the test. "Write a short essay in response to *one* of the questions." That was also what the test said, but multimedia repetition is often useful for the selectively illiterate or deaf.

After I collected the tests, we spent the remainder of the period discussing the readings. Most of those in class actually had read the material on the economics of environmental infrastructures. Some even understood it, and I didn't feel as though I were pulling teeth. It continued to bother me that so many of them would only respond to force, even when learning was in their own self-interest.

Because I carried the tests with me, rather than stopping by the office, I made it to Delft's, predictably, a good quarter hour before Llysette, and this time got a table close to the woodstove. With the chill outside, I knew she would choose warmth over a view of bare limbs and gray and brown stone walls.

Victor had just offered the wine when the lady arrived. I nodded to him to pour two glasses and stood to seat her.

"Good afternoon, Doktor duBoise."

"Afternoon it is, Herr Doktor Eschbach. Good, that is another question."

"Perchance some wine? This time it is at least Californian."

Victor faded away.

"This is better." She took a long swallow of the Sonoma burgundy. "Not so good as—"

"Good French wine, I know." I grinned, and got a halfsmile, anyway. "What happened?"

"Forms! The Citizenship Bureau—they cannot find my residence report, and so I must complete another. They know I sent one, but . . ." She shrugged. "Perhaps someday they will let me become a citizen—when I am old and gray." Llysette swallowed the last of her wine in a second gulp.

"What would you like to eat?" I refilled her glass.

"You would like?" asked Victor, appearing at Llysette's elbow and winking, as he always did.

"*La même, comme ça,*" she answered, her voice almost flat.

"*Oui, mademoiselle,*" he answered. "And you, Doktor Eschbach?"

"I'll try the tomato brandy mushroom soup with shepherd's bread and cheese."

He nodded and slipped back toward the kitchen.

Llysette sipped her second glass of wine, looking emptily at the table.

"Bad morning?"

"Two of them—two lessons—they did not show up. No courtesy they had, and they did not even leave a message. Doktor Geoffries, he says he wants to observe my advanced diction class—and I have not taught this part before." She glared at me.

I held up a hand. "I'm not your department chair."

"I am sorry. All of this, it is so . . . so . . ."

"Frustrating?"

"Maddening it is." She took another healthy swallow of wine.

Victor brought Llysette consommé, except it was warm, and my soup and bread. "Would you like your salad now, mam'selle?"

"If you please."

Victor nodded.

"Have you seen Miranda's ghost lately?" I asked Llysette.

She gave me a half-frown, half-pout, charming nonetheless, before answering. "*Mais non.* But never did the ghost enter my office, only the hallway." She shrugged. "The ghosts, they avoid me, I think."

Victor eased her salad onto the table and deftly slipped out of sight.

The tomato brandy soup had big succulent mushrooms and was richer than a chocolate dessert. I spooned in every last morsel, interspersed with the cheese and bread.

"A good Frenchman you would have made, Johan. For the way you enjoy good food. The wine, you even appreciate."

"I trust that is a compliment, dear lady."

"One of the highest."

"Then I thank you." I lifted my wine glass. "Would you like dinner tonight?"

"Dinner, I would like that, but for the next two weeks I am doing rehearsals—except for the weekends."

"Then we must make do with the weekends." I sipped the last of my wine. "Some more?"

"Alas, I must go." She stood. "With Doctor Geoffries watching my class . . ."

I stood, nodding sympathetically. Evaluations were never fun to prepare for. "Good luck."

"The luck I do not need. I need more time." She flashed a quick smile, and left me, as usual, to pay the check, which Victor presented quickly.

Then, wondering if I would find any surprises, I walked down to the post centre, my overcoat half open because it was too cold not to wear a coat and too warm to bundle up. I was resisting wearing a hat, except to church—when I went, which hadn't been that often lately.

"No bills for ye, Doktor," called Maurice from behind the window.

"And you'll take all the credit?"

"You give me all the blame."

Two advertising circulars, a reminder card from the dentist, and a single brown envelope posted in the Federal District which I did not open but thrust into my folder—those were the contents of my box.

When I got back to my office, I did open the envelope, which contained one clipping. It was the same story I had already seen in the *Asten Post-Courier* that morning, except that it had come from the *New Amsterdam Post,* and that almost certainly meant that vanBecton had planted the first story.

After gathering up yet another short test and the greenbooks for my two o'clock, I trudged through the cold wind to Smythe Hall. I had to grin as I stepped into the room just a minute before the clock chimed the hour. Every seat was filled. Clearly, the word had gotten out about my policy on missing tests, unannounced or otherwise.

"Miss Deventer, are you ready today to discuss the political basis behind the first Speaker Roosevelt's efforts at reforestation?"

Miss Deventer swallowed. So did several others.

"I meant it, you know." I grinned. That was one of the questions on the test, not that she had to choose that one, but the others were equally specific.

Once again I handed out greenbooks and tests, and repeated the litany about only responding to *one* of the essay questions. After collecting the tests fifteen minutes later, we launched into a discussion—except it was more of a lurch.

"Why did it take the federal government nearly two decades to begin enforcement of the Rivers and Harbors Act?" I pointed to Mister Reshauer.

"Uhhh . . ."

That brilliant answer was equaled only by Miss Desileta's "I don't know."

Eventually we did have a discussion on the relationship of external diseconomies and regional political alliances to the delay in the development of the Columbian environmental ethic.

Still, by the time class was over, I had the definite feeling that an even higher percentage of the environmental politics class than the economics class was going to receive D's.

After gathering my notes, the tests, and the greenbooks into my folder, I pulled on my overcoat and trudged back through the freezing mist to my office, nodding at Gilda while I pulled another of David's memos from my box. This one dealt with something called graduate-level in-loading, and seemed to be an excuse for paying some faculty more for doing less. I carried everything upstairs and set out the two stacks of tests, starting to grade the morning's environmental economics quizzes. The first five were D's; then I finally got an honest C.

At three-twenty, I left the tests on my desk and took myself and my folder back outside and up the hill to the Physical Sciences building and Gerald's office.

He opened the door within instants of my rapping. "I don't like this, Johan."

"Neither do I, but I felt you deserved to know the size of the sharks you're fishing for." After setting my unzipped leather folder on the corner of his desk, I leaned forward, scanning the few memos on it before pointing to a picture. "That your daughter? She's an attractive young lady."

As his eyes moved to the picture, I slipped a memo with Branston-Hay's signature on it under my folder—it was only something about allocation of time on the super-speed difference engine, but the signature would do. Then I settled into the chair closest to his difference engine.

"Exactly what do you mean by all these veiled threats, Johan?" He sat in the big swivel, but only on the front edge, as if I were some form of dangerous animal. His hand brushed over his long, thin, blond and white hair, as if he were trying to recover his bald patch.

"I don't make threats, Gerald. I'm just offering some observations."

"Your 'observations' sound like threats to me."

I leaned forward in the chair. "You know, Gerald, I wonder what your next project will be. This one is going to end rather shortly, you know?"

Branston-Hay frowned at me, as I knew he would. The one thing that defense contractors—even covert ones—never understand is that all projects end.

I stood and ambled over to his difference engine. "You keep your notes on this, don't you, the ones no one else is supposed to read or know you keep?"

Even as he watched, his mouth dropping open, I sat down at the console and flipped the switches, watching as it powered up.

"Johan . . ." His voice was low and meant to be threatening. "No one would ever see you again if I said so."

"Permit me a word, Gerald. First, I would assume that this office is thoroughly desnooped, and that you ensured that?"

"Of course. That technology I do know."

"Good. Now what makes you think I would say what I just said without a reason?" I entered the sequence I needed, and tried not to grin. It just possibly might work.

"Reformulation beginning" scripted after the pointer.

I stood and walked from the console toward his desk, keeping my body between him and the screen. "I hope your desnooping was thorough. You know, your research is already being implemented."

"They said—"

"Bother what they said. Have you noticed all the Babbage centers going up in flames? I wonder how many professors just had heart attacks, or highway accidents, or drowned in swimming or boating accidents? I'll bet there are more than a few. And with all the religious fervor over psychic research, it's going to be a dead end all of a sudden."

"But Ferdinand would like to see it a dead end. He already has what he needs. So does Speaker Hartpence, and now it will be convenient for that research to stop." Branston-Hay looked smugly at me. "And then we'll get a new contract."

"That brings up something else. You never told the president's people about the disassociator, did you? You were even too timid to build it, weren't you?"

At that point the gun came out, a very small-bore Colt, wobbling enough that I knew he'd never even practiced with it.

I stepped aside so he could see the console screen. The gun wavered, and I moved and slashed it out of his hand, but he let it fall and lunged past me. "You . . . you bastard! But you don't know . . ."

I had the gun, and it didn't waver in my hand. "Sit down, Gerald. We're going to talk."

He looked at the gun, then at the dead screen of the difference engine, and wilted.

"Don't look so depressed. You have backup disks somewhere, I'm sure, and most of what was on there you could probably replicate anyway. I'm just keeping you out of bigger trouble."

"You're getting in well over both our heads, Johan." His voice was dull.

"We already are." I cleared my throat, even though I wanted to be out of his office. "Now, let's get the players straight. You had a research contract with the Defense Ministry, a fairly straight job to investigate some aspect of deghosting, probably using the magnetic basis of the electro-fluidic difference engine. That was the origin of your so-called filing protocol."

His mouth opened, and he gulped like a carp.

"That contract is really over, but you didn't want to close it out, because who else would pay you that much? Then the president's crew came in with a special request, right?"

"You seem to have it figured, Johan. Why ask me?"

"I don't have it all figured. What I can't figure is why you killed Miranda Miller."

"I didn't! I had nothing to do with it."

"Right." I made my voice as sardonic as I could. "She's an agent of New France pumping you for all you've got, and she finds out that you double-dealt the Defense Ministry—that the contract's really done. You know, sooner or later, because she's not very good, that the Spazi will find out. So you put her away."

"With a knife? I could have—"

"Built your disassociator and turned her into a zombie? Or just put her under one of those helmets in the lab late some night and then carted her back to her cottage and left her?"

"Yes. So why are you baiting me? You know the answers."

"You couldn't leave Pandora's box closed, could you, Gerald?"

"What do you mean?"

"You know what I mean. All the military types wanted was a way to suck ghosts out of an area. You did it, all right, and you're brilliant, Gerald. You saw what else was possible. So did the president's people. Now, I don't know how they got your reports, but I'll bet a check would show you knew someone in the budget review shop——and Armstrong's boys were on you in a flash. They threatened to show that you padded the contract, right?"

Branston-Hay looked blank

"You padded it, didn't you? I can get the answer from the examiners, you know?"

He finally nodded.

"And then they asked what else you could do. You didn't want to let the disassociator out. Even you could see the problems there. So you came up with the replicator and rejiggered your psychic scoop into a filing mechanism. And that's how the president keeps outguessing the Speaker. He has a data bank of tame ghosts."

"Who are you working for, Johan? Ralston will kill you if he finds out what you're doing."

I ignored the question and the threat. Any answer would be wrong. "If I were you, Gerald, I'd stick very close to your family and take a vacation, a sabbatical, anything."

Walking over to his desk, even as he stood there, I opened the top left drawer and pulled out sheets of Babbage Center, Vanderbraak State University letterhead. "You won't need these, and I do."

"But . . . why . . . what are you doing?"

"Trying to keep us both from getting killed." I put the sheets of letterhead and the memo I had slipped under my folder into the folder. Then I took out my handkerchief and wiped off the Colt, setting it on the chair farthest from where he paced behind his desk. I dampened the handkerchief in his water glass, then wiped off the Babbage console keys and the arm of the chair, fairly certain I hadn't touched anything else.

After picking up my folder and walking to the door, I used the handkerchief to turn the knob. He didn't stop me, just looked, almost dazed.

I forced myself to walk slowly out of the building and straight down the steps to the green, and then to my office. The wind had picked up so much that it blew the white steam of my breath away.

I skidded slightly on the bottom steps leading into the Natural Resources building, where a patch of ice remained, looking like someone had spilled something. Certainly the methodical Gertrude and Hector wouldn't have left anything on the bricks. Overhead, the glow strips were glowing as the day faded.

I unlocked the door and stopped by the main office to check my box, but nothing had been added. I looked out the window uphill and watched as Gerald hurried down to his old black Ford steamer, carting two data cases.

Poor bastard. Then I straightened. If I didn't keep moving, I knew who would be the next poor bastard. So I went upstairs to my office and looked at my desk and the mostly ungraded tests lying there.

I left them on the desk. Maybe I'd get back to them, and maybe I wouldn't, but I had more than a few things to do first. I slipped some blank second pages of university letterhead into my folder and headed back out to the Stanley, relieved in a way that Llysette was tied up with rehearsals for most of the week.

When I got home, I unloaded Bruce's latest creations from the Stanley before driving it into the car barn.

Marie—I blessed her industrious Dutch heart once more and added ten dollars to the check I set out for her—had left a chicken pot pie in the oven, and it was still warm. That and the crusty bread were almost enough to make me forget what I was going to attempt that night.

I also tried to forget the tests I hadn't graded. But a little part of me nagged about them. I usually didn't put off grading and returning things. After all, I was the one who believed in the efficacy of immediate feedback.

It seemed like I hadn't eaten in days, although that was probably the result of nerves. Still, I ate almost all of the chicken pot pie and a good third of the loaf of bread. I had a bottle of Grolsch instead of wine, and I promised that I'd run harder and longer in the morning.

Then I went into the study and took Bruce's latest gadgets from their boxes and assembled them. After that, I started in on the programming.

Some of it was relatively easy because I could use the first program I had already developed for ghost replications as a basis. I'd already decided to split the application into a basic system and a separate "personality creation" configuration.

The basic system didn't take that long, a mere five hours. Testing it took longer, and I hoped Carolynne wasn't watching, because I duplicated the replicate of her structure, then recoded it back to simple lines, and tried to project it.

Of course, it didn't work. Nothing I ever try to program works the first time. Or the second. Or the third. On the fourth try, well after one in the morning, the system worked. That is, the antennas indeed projected an image, and it promptly collapsed.

So did I. The system part seemed to work, and I'd have to develop a better file/support structure if I really wanted to create the equivalent of ghosts. Why I'd want to do that was a question I didn't have an answer for, except that my guts said it was going to be necessary, and I hadn't made it as far as I had by ignoring gut feelings. Most people in dangerous occupations don't. You figure out the reasons later, if you have the time.

Since I didn't think very well with headaches and bright rainbows surrounding every light I looked at, I turned them all off and lifted one foot after the other until I reached my bed.

I looked up. A white figure hovered by the end of the bed.

"What are you doing here?"

"Was that a face to be opposed against the warring winds?"

"The ghost I created? I was just trying to see if the system worked."

"Be governed by your knowledge . . . repair those violent harms . . . be aidant and remediate . . ."

"How?" I shook my head. "For most people, remediation in politics is revenge. The best seek justice, even when most, me included, would prefer mercy to such justice."

"Then dissolve the life that wants the means to lead it." With that she vanished.

Carolynne was definitely getting too familiar. It was a good thing Llysette wasn't around. But then Carolynne probably wouldn't have appeared with Llysette around. I wasn't sure they would like each other. Respect each other, probably, but "like" was definitely another question. Forget about communicating. Was I communicating, or were Carolynne's words only in my own mind? Was it her wish for me to create a ghost of remediation—or mine?

My head ached so much that I got back up and took three bayers. Carolynne did not say good night again.

CHAPTER NINETEEN

• • •

Difficult" wasn't the word for the trouble I had struggling out of bed on Tuesday. I pried my eyes open and climbed into my exercise clothes—uphill all the way.

Who would have thought that creating a ghost image for projection was so difficult? Everyone. I was just the one who thought it was possible. As for Carolynne's idea of a ghost of remediation, that was clearly impossible. Even a ghost of justice and mercy—how would I ever do that? Yes, I understood that establishing and maintaining any image was difficult, if not impossible. But the image of justice and mercy, or even of integrity? Politicians did it all the time, but they didn't have to have a logical structure to support it. And I certainly wasn't about to touch remediation, except . . . didn't I have to try?

Llysette had said I was always trying to change the world. Was that it, or was I merely trying to do the impossible until it killed me?

I sighed as I laced up the leather running boots. Some people run in lightweight, rubber-soled shoes, but that's stupid. At least in my profession it is. You don't run that much, but when you do it's under lousy conditions with the world after you, and your feet need protection and support.

Obviously, I'd have to go back to the basics—just create a totally ethical personality. Probably it would have to be a takeoff on some combination of mine and Carolynne's, because I had something to start with her image and at least I could fix in the program what went wrong with me. My mother and father didn't get that choice, and at times I suspect they would have liked the option.

I still didn't understand why my father had built the artificial lodestone. Had he been the one who read all the Shakespeare to Carolynne? Or were the lines from her theatrical background? Sometimes they made sense, and sometimes . . . I took another deep breath and stepped out into the cold.

All the way through my run and exercise, through breakfast, and through my shower, I kept thinking about how to layer the codes for a ghost personality.

Finally I shook my head. I needed to take a break, and besides, the disembodied spectre of all those ungraded tests on my desk was also beginning to haunt me. Should I have even worried about the tests? Probably not, but about some things we're not exactly rational.

So, after dressing, I hurried into the study, flipped on the difference engine and roughed out the code lines I thought might work, and then printed them out and stuffed them into my folder.

Then I pulled on my coat and went out under the cold gray sky to get the steamer started. The air smelled like frozen leaves, and there was almost no breeze, a leaden sort of cold calm.

The Stanley started smoothly, as always, and I passed Marie in her old Ford on my way down Deacon's Lane. We exchanged waves, and her smile cheered me momentarily.

After a quick stop at Samaha's for the *Post-Courier,* I parked the Stanley in the faculty car park. Llysette's Reo wasn't there, but, thankfully, Gerald Branston-Hay's black Ford was.

On my way to my office, I nodded at Gregor Martin, but he only growled something about winter starting too soon and lasting too long.

Even Gilda looked dour.

"Why so cheerless?" I asked her.

"It's like winter out, and it's too early for winter."

"That's what Gregor Martin said."

"For once I agree with him. For once." Gilda picked up the wireset. "Natural Resources Department . . . No, Doktor Doniger is not available at the moment."

Rik Paterken, one of the adjuncts, motioned as I pulled two memos and a letter from my box in the department office.

"Yes, Rik?"

"You have Peter Paulus in one of your classes, don't you?"

"Yes."

"What sort of student is he?"

I frowned, not wanting to answer as truthfully as I should have. Instead, I temporized. "Mister Paulus is able to retain virtually everything he reads. He does have a tendency to apply that knowledge blindly even when it may not be applicable to the situation at hand."

"In short, he can regurgitate anything, and he avoids thinking." Paterken pulled at his chin. "He seems like a nice young man."

"I am sure he is, Rik." I smiled politely.

"He was asking permission to take the Central American Ecology course. He never took basic ecology."

I shrugged. "He's probably bright enough to pick that up, but I'd guess he wouldn't get the kind of grade he wants."

"That was my impression."

"Then tell him that," I suggested.

"You're the one with the reputation for bluntness, Johan, not us poor adjuncts."

I shook my head and went upstairs, wanting to see what, if anything, was in the newspaper. I knew the memos couldn't contain much of value, and they didn't. The letter was a more sophisticated pitch for a new ecology text. I tossed it along with the memos.

The *Post-Courier* headlines were a rehash of the airspace battle between the dirigibles and the turbojets, and the spacing requirements at the main Asten airport. Governor van-Hasten wanted to build a jetport and leave Haguen for dirigibles, but the legislature was balking at the funds, and the federal Ministry of Transportation had indicated no federal funds were likely.

I leafed through the paper, still standing next to my desk, when my eyes glanced over the political gossip column. I froze.

> . . . One of the more interesting developments, almost unnoticed in the commotion of the ceremonial dinner where President Armstrong announced his Japanese initiative, which, incidentally, the Speaker will probably have to swallow, involved a little-known former politico—one Johan A. Eschbach. Ostensibly, Eschbach is a professor at Vanderbraak State University, but who was at the big dinner, and who disappeared somewhere in the Presidential Palace between dinner and dessert? Watch this space . . .

That was another one of those surprises you really don't like to find. Was it Ralston's doing? Why? To offer me up to vanBecton? I put the paper down and looked at my desk. I had less than two hours to grade the quizzes, and I wasn't giving any more this term. Period. As if I would be around to give any, at the rate I was going.

I plowed through both sets. Eighty percent of the grades were D's. Too bad, but I really didn't feel charitable. No one was providing *me* much charity these days.

At ten to eleven, I finished entering the marks in my grade book and set the greenbooks in separate piles to return the next day. Then I locked my door and went downstairs. Gilda was off somewhere, and I went back out into the leaden gray day. The day seemed even colder than it had at dawn. But then everything was seeming colder.

Despite the cold and the ice, Gertrude and Hector were out on the green, carefully laying a sand and fertilizer mix on the icy bricks of the walk to Smythe. While it was more expensive than salt, the mix resulted in a lush lawn the rest of the year.

I just waved, not really wanting to hear Gertrude's predictable statement about every day being a good day. They both waved back.

I smiled brightly as I walked into Natural Resources 1A. At least we'd finished the water cycle and were working on air, with an emphasis on deposition mechanisms and transport characteristics. I started right in.

"Miss Francisco, could you tell me what air deposition had to do with the Austro-Hungarian decision to require converters on internal combustion engines?"

Miss Francisco looked suitably blank.

"How about you, mister Vraalander? Any ideas?"

"Well, uh, sir . . . didn't it have to do with the Ruhr Valley and the Black Forest?"

"That's a start. Can you take it further, Miss Zenobia?"

"Doesn't acid deposition combine with ozone from internal combustion engines?"

"It does. What does it do?"

"Oh . . . tree damage," blurted out mister Vraalander. "Now I remember."

I tried not to sigh. The rest of the class period was marginally better, just marginally, but perhaps that was because my mind was half on the column in the *Post-Courier*.

Lunch was a quick bowl of soup at Jared's Kitchen, followed by another quick look at the tests I'd already graded to make sure I hadn't been too hurried. I hated the damned tests, and even more the fact that I had to give them to get the students to read the material. After that I scrawled out more Babbage code lines, amending my hastily printed beginning of the morning.

Then there was my two o'clock, Environmental Politics 2B. I had to collect papers—unfortunately, because it probably meant that very few of those stalwart souls had bothered to do the reading assignment. In turn, that meant I either had to talk a lot or badger them or surrender and let them out too early, which I generally refused to do because it might give them even more inflated ideas about the value of ignorance.

So I talked a bit about relative political values and their links to economic bases, and led them into speculation about why the Brits politically felt they couldn't afford too much environmental protection while the Irish were busy reforesting—yet both faced virtually the same threat from Ferdinand. What made the difference? Was it another hundred miles of ocean?

I was still tired and hoarse when I walked back to my office. I grabbed a double-loaded cola from the machine and went back to work on codes until it was time for David's weekly finest hour—the departmental meeting.

The less said about the departmental meeting, the better. I did not lose my temper. I only said one or two sentences, and I didn't leave. Instead, I sat in the corner and jotted Babbage codes on my notepad, trying to work out the parameters of an ethical ghost while ignoring David's long and roundabout evasions of the basic problem. I sat back and listened, half aware that the arguments hadn't changed in a week. Finally David did what he should have done two weeks earlier.

"I've heard everyone's comments and objections, but no one has a better idea. I will inform the dean that Natural Resources Three-B will be capped at zero next semester and that we will rotate between courses to be capped, but none will be struck."

Unfortunately he didn't quit while he was merely behind. "The next item on the agenda is EWE."

Mondriaan groaned. He hated the Educational Writing for Excellence program. I just thought it was useless. Most university graduates can't really write, and most never have been able to. It's a delusion to think the skill can actually be taught at the collegiate level. Polished, perhaps, but not taught. Of course, I didn't say that. Why make any more enemies? I had enough already.

After EWE, David proceeded to the department's recommendations for library acquisitions because—what else was new—our recommendations exceeded our share of the acquisitions budget.

I continued to work on Babbage codes until the end of the meeting. No one seemed to notice.

After the meeting, I packed up my folders, decided to leave the Environmental Politics 2B papers behind on my desk, and walked to the car park. My resolve about tests hadn't considered the papers I'd already assigned.

A watch steamer, sirens blaring, wailed out Emmen Lane toward Lastfound Lake. I wondered if someone had had an accident or if the locals were just testing their sirens.

At the bridge I had to wait as two heavy Reo steamers, gunmetal-gray paint and chrome trim shimmering, rolled westward across the Wijk and past me into the square. While they were from Azko, they somehow reminded me of Spazi steamers.

Marie hadn't left me dinner, just a note explaining that she hadn't been able to fix anything because I had no meat, no flour, no butter, and precious little of anything else.

I had apples and cheese, and opened a sealed box of biscuits from the basement. It filled my stomach, and my head stopped swimming, but I definitely missed that hot meal, especially after no real lunch and the way the day had gone.

Then I washed the dishes and began trying to assemble all the code fragments I had developed for a justice/mercy/integrity ghost. When I put them all together and completed the file profile, nothing happened. Nothing at all.

Then I discovered that I didn't have the handshake between the profile and the system set up right, and that meant a minor rewrite of the system program I'd only finished the night before. Why had it worked the night before and not with the new ghost profile? Because I had created a more complex profile—that was what I figured.

I tried again. The system worked, but all I got was a spiral that collapsed in on itself.

Probably I needed some sort of image. Carolynne's profile had the image tied up with the rest, but I didn't know how to do that. But . . . adding an image on top of everything else?

I turned off the difference engine and went to the kitchen for a bottle of Grolsch, probably bad for me, but things weren't going right.

Halfway through the Grolsch, I tried again. Around eleven o'clock I got an image that looked like a one-eyed demon of some sort, even though I'd inputted, I thought, the graphic image of a man with a set of scales in his hand.

So I took a break and decided to finish something I'd started over a week earlier—a transitional identity.

It's amazing what you can do with the right Babbage programs and a decent printer. A laminator helps, too, but you can get the same effect with an iron and certain plastics.

I created Vic Nuustrom—lift operator at the mills down in Waarstrom, in season. The real Nuustrom, of course, had moved out to Deseret, but he looked roughly like me, except he had been heavier. When you've been in the business, you always keep a bolthole open. I already had a complete alternate identity as one Peter Hloddn, a ledgerman who was only marginally successful at the wholesale purveying of office supplies. He had a bank account and a few bills, a credit history, and a driver's permit issued in New Ostend—all real. The depth wasn't that great, but since it predated vanBecton, and I'd never let Minister Wattson know about it either, it was relatively safe, as such things went.

Nuustrom was a transitional identity—you never go straight from one to another. There's a way to phase into a new identity.

After trimming the heavy stock, the seal printed on a transparent overlay, and setting the picture in place, I studied it, then used the tweezers for fine adjustments before setting the plastic down and lifting the iron.

I held my breath, but the lamination worked, as did the pictures taken more than a year earlier in a red plaid lumberjack shirt. They were just overexposed enough to be convincing as a vehicle operator's license. Nuustrom, of course, had a hauler's endorsement, which was no problem since I'd done that for a year in London. You drive a lorry on those roads, and you can drive anywhere.

I reburied the files in the difference engine and totally erased the actual identity section. They'd expect me to have some way of creating an alternate identity. I just didn't want them to know what it was. I also didn't know when I'd need the card, but it looked like it was going to be soon, and when I did, I probably wouldn't have time to create it.

The whole process took less than an hour, and I had something besides lines of code that didn't work. That's a trick I learned a long time ago. When you get stuck on a big project, do something smaller and concrete. It helps your sense of accomplishment and a lot more.

Then I went back to the kitchen, looked longingly at the remaining bottles of Grolsch, and fixed a pot of that excessively strong Russian Imperial blend tea. If anything would keep me going, that would.

Sometime in the early hours of the morning, I got an image, the man with the scales in his hand, who immediately rumbled out, "Justice must be done. Justice must be done."

Those were the words I associated with old Goodman Hunsler—that stern and righteous dourness that makes you feel like your whole life has been one unending sin. For a moment, I shivered. The image was definitely far too strong. But it was worse than that, because it wasn't a ghost, just a hollow projection. So why was I so upset? Because I didn't want to deal with the issue of justice?

I really didn't feel up to thinking about that, so I sucked him into storage with the ghost-collecting hardware and turned off the machines and the lights.

"Such weeds are memories of those worser hours; put them off." Carolynne perched on the banister halfway up the stairs. She was wearing a high-necked dress of some sort. I guess the aura of righteousness had gotten to her as well.

"No. I suppose not. But it's hard to take all that righteousness."

"O you kind gods, cure this great breach . . ."

"I know. I know. I've created a lot of mistakes."

"Alack, alack! 'Tis wonder that thy life and wits at once had not concluded all." She was gone, and I looked stupidly into the darkness before walking back into the study and through the kitchen.

"Carolynne?" I called several times, but she didn't reappear. "Carolynne?"

Finally I went up to a cold bed and collapsed, still dreaming about how to make my justice ghost more merciful. Pure justice, I just couldn't take. Who could?

"Cure this great breach?" Who could do that, either?

CHAPTER TWENTY

• • •

Wednesday didn't start much better than Tuesday, and even the feeling of partial success I'd felt four hours before dissolved under the barrage of the alarm's chimes. I finally dug myself out of sleep and pulled on exercise clothes. I even managed to run over the top of the hill and to the end of the ridge, despite the cold mist that pricked my face like fine needles. Each foot hit the ground like an anvil on the way back.

Breakfast wasn't much, not with the state of my larder, but I managed with Russian Imperial tea, the rest of the biscuits, and a pear I reclaimed from the cellar. After leaving the dishes in the sink, I showered and dressed, deciding that I was going to be late. The hell with office hours. I needed to add mercy to justice.

I was standing in the foyer when Marie rapped on the door.

"Good morning, Doctor Eschbach. Have you had the chance to—" Marie had her coat off before I had closed the door.

"Good morning, Marie. No, but I will shop this afternoon. Unhappily, the dishes are merely rinsed."

"A few dishes, that's not much. You leave me too little to earn my pay. But you had best lay in a goodly supply of staples, Doktor. Do you think that you could run down to town for food in a snowstorm anytime?" Her expression was somewhere between a sniff and a snort.

"I will lay in significant supplies. I promise. But this morning I'll be working in the study for an hour or two. I hope that doesn't disturb you."

"Since I cannot bake or prepare food, there being nothing to prepare, I will finish the kitchen and then, if you do not mind, I will reorder the fruit cellar. It has needed cleaning—a good cleaning—for a long time." She looked at me and added, "A very long time." She rolled up the cuffs of her gray long-sleeved blouse. I went into the study and turned on the difference engine.

Adding mercy to justice was far easier said than done, especially with Babbage codes, but when I left at ten-thirty, I had a projected ghost image that felt somewhat softer, with a sense of justice. That had to do, even though it still gave me a chill, knowing that I scarcely measured up to the ideal I'd created. I also wondered if what I felt was merely my imagination or something another person could feel, but I wasn't about to call Marie in for an opinion.

I almost felt guilty when I disassociated the ghost construct, but how could I fill my study with ghosts of justice in various stages of sensibility? And the ethical issues? I just shook my head, imagining that Carolynne was probably doing worse than that, were she even watching. Or *did* she think, or merely quote half-remembered dialogue at me?

When I left for the university, Marie was still in the cellar, mumbling about my various failures. I guess I wasn't quite Dutch enough for her, or perhaps the cleanliness was the feminine aspect of Dutch culture.

Gray and cold—that was still the weather as I drove down Deacon's Lane and into Vanderbraak Centre to pick up the paper at Samaha's. It was more like December than early November, and I hoped that didn't mean a really long winter.

David—Herr Professor Doktor Doniger—was on me as soon as I reached my box. "Johan, I know you've been working hard, but do you suppose you could let Gilda know if you won't make office hours?"

"No. I haven't missed a damned office hour all term."

David swallowed. "It is the policy."

"Bother the policy." I left him standing there even as I realized he would probably be scheming to get me back under control. David liked everything under control, and the results would probably be nasty. At that point I didn't care, but half realized that I would later.

I went up to my office to collect the tests I'd graded so that I could return them.

The wind was blowing again as I walked over to Smythe, although the sky was clearing and showing a coldly cheerful blue. I didn't feel cheerful.

At eleven o'clock I practically threw the greenbooks at the Environmental Economics class. "Someday, ladies and gentlemen, and I use those terms merely as a courtesy, you will come to understand that there are too many unanticipated crises in life for you to postpone what you can do now until the last possible moment. Life often does not give you those moments. Call this a dress rehearsal for life."

Of course, they didn't understand a word of what I meant.

"Sir, how much will this count on our final grade?"

"Is there anyway to obtain some additional credit?"

"Life doesn't provide extra credit," I snapped, "and neither do I." I shouldn't have snapped, but they didn't have the Spazi hanging over their heads. Probably half of them didn't even know who or what the Spazi was.

Somehow I managed to get through the lecture and discussion without snapping or yelling again. That was fine, except Gilda and Constable Gerhardt were both waiting for me back at the department office.

"Constable Gerhardt, this is Doktor Eschbach."

"Thank you." He tipped his hat to her and turned to me. "If I could speak with you . . ."

"Let's go up to my office," I suggested.

He nodded, and up we went. I set aside the still-ungraded Environmental Politics papers.

"This business about professor Branston-Hay . . ."

"What business?"

"His accident, of course."

"I'm sorry, Constable, but I didn't know he'd been in an accident. When did it happen?"

The worthy watch functionary gave me one of those looks that tends to signify disbelief before explaining. "His steamer piled into a tree on Hoecht's Hill late yesterday afternoon. He died before they could get him to the hospital."

"I didn't know."

"The throttle valve jammed open." Constable Gerhardt spread the fingers of his right hand about a half-centimeter apart. "A bolt about this big jammed in the assembly."

"Why didn't he turn the bypass valve?"

"He hit the brakes first, and they failed, corroded lines. By then it was too late. He was probably going too fast and bouncing around too much to reach it. He was driving a Ford, not a Stanley, and on the older models, you have quite a reach."

My father had always said to buy quality, and Branston-Hay's example certainly confirmed that wisdom.

Poor Branston-Hay. He'd had to throttle the old black steamer all the way up to climb Hoecht's Hill, and then the throttle had jammed on the downside. Except it hadn't been an accident.

"Who was chasing him?" I asked, since it was clear the constable was there to deliver a message from Chief Waetjen.

"Chasing him?"

"Professor Branston-Hay was a careful and methodical man. He was headed home, or at least in the direction of home. Why would he be going so fast?"

"I don't know, sir. I only know that Chief Waetjen told me to tell you what happened."

I'd done it for sure. Good stolid Constable Gerhardt would tell Waetjen of my question and, sure as the sun rose, Officer Warbeck would know, and so would vanBecton.

"Thank you." I rose. "I appreciate the courtesy and the information."

"I was just letting you know, sir. The chief said you should be told." The constable rose as he spoke, having done his duty and his inadvertent best to roast my gander.

After that, I wasn't hungry. So I graded papers for almost two hours, not the smartest thing to do, especially on an empty stomach. And I probably shouldn't have bothered with my two o'clock, but . . . you take on obligations, and you become reluctant not to carry them out.

When I dispersed the corrected greenbooks and a sermon similar to the one I had delivered at eleven o'clock, there was just silence, the appalled silence of an entire class that has just realized that Kris Kringle is a myth and that Mother and Father filled the wooden shoes with coal, and they meant it for real.

After class I left the pile of Environmental Politics 2B papers and went shopping at McArdles', since, as Marie had pointed out, there was nothing to fix, not
even for the most industrious and resourceful of Dutch ladies.

Two women in white-trimmed bonnets looked blankly at me as I left the meat
counter, but I heard the whispers after I turned toward the flour and corn and oatmeal.

"Doktor Eschbach . . . say he was once a spy . . ."

"Once a spy, always a spy—that's what I say."

"You know, the foreign woman and him . . ."

I didn't like the term "spy," but "intelligence agent" was even worse, and as for
the other terms . . . I took a deep breath and put the flour in the cart.

Once I got home, it took five trips to unload. Marie had actually been so resourceful that, when I walked into the kitchen, there was some type of tart-strudel
and a pot of barley soup waiting. I didn't know how she had done it. After the chill
of unloading all those packages—they'd filled the trunk and the back seat of the
steamer, since I'm sometimes an extremist—I ladled out a bowlful and sat at the
kitchen table, letting the spicy steam wreathe my face before each spoonful, trying
not to think about vanBecton, Miranda, and poor Gerald. The soup was so good
that I almost managed it.

After supper, I sat for awhile in the dimness before I had company.

"At some hours in the night spirits resort . . . alack, is it not like that I . . .
Oh, look, methinks I saw my cousin's ghost . . ." Carolynne made an effort to sit
on the corner stool, even if she had a tendency to drift around and through it.

"Your cousin's ghost. Probably not. Or did you mean the one I created this
morning? I felt badly about disassociating him, though."

"Thou couldst give no help?"

"How can one help something that was not quite alive?"

"And bid me go and hide me with a dead man in his shroud . . ."

"Wonderful. If I make a better ghost, I'll then qualify for murder."

". . . that did spit his body upon a rapier's point . . . is it not like the horrible
conceit of death and night?"

That was another good question—one I really didn't have a good answer for.
Was sleep a form of death? Was Babbage storage of a synthetic ghost sleep or
death? "I don't know. I feel it's more like sleep, but I couldn't say why."

Unlike most people, who, when you say that you "feel" something, pester you
to give rational and logical reasons, Carolynne did not. She just gave a faint nod before speaking. "So tedious is this day . . ."

"Tedious? In a way. On Monday, I warned a man to be careful that he did not
suffer an accidental death. On Tuesday, he died in a steamer accident that I do not
believe was an accident. I have this feeling that some others are going to try to
prove that I created the accident."

"What storm is this that blows so contrary?"

"Contrary indeed. But that doesn't really count." I forced a smile. "From what I hear, you should know about that."

". . . that murdered me. I would forget it fain, but, oh, it presses to my memory like damned guilty deeds to sinners' minds. . . . How shall that faith return again to earth?"

Faith? Did I even have faith, or was I believing what I wanted? Hearing what I wanted from a demented ghost who at least seemed to listen when no one else did? When I stopped asking questions, Carolynne was gone.

What could I do, even as the noose was tightening? Listen to a half-sentient ghost as if she were alive?

I had enough of Branston-Hay's letterhead to compose a couple of letters, since I could use blank second sheets from our own department's stock; all the second sheets were the same. Sometimes paper helped.

The first letter was to Minister Holmbek, protesting the perversion of the VSU Babbage Center research toward developing "psychic phenomena erasure technologies." The second one was also to Holmbek, protesting the failure to extend the research contract as blackmail. I wrote it more politely than that, suggesting that "the Center's disinclination to pursue psychically destructive technologies has resulted in withdrawal of federal funding contrary to the original letter of agreement."

Branston-Hay hadn't been that courageous, but his family would rather have him a dead hero than a dead coward, and, besides, it just might keep me alive.

I was running out of time, and at least one of the questions was how Waetjen and Warbeck intended to pin Branston-Hay's death on me. Maybe I had nuts or something in my car barn the same size as the one that had seized poor Branston-Hay's throttle.

And then again, maybe I hadn't, but did now. I set down the memos and rummaged in the desk for one of the flashes that I kept putting in safe places and never finding again. There was one behind the Babbage disk case.

I walked out to the car barn through the freezing drizzle and studied the workbench and bolt bins under the dim overhead light and my flash. Was the bin cover at the end less dusty? I opened it. There were two different sizes of nuts in the last bin, and I never mixed sizes. The larger ones were clearly newer.

I pulled them out and pocketed them, then dusted off all the bin covers and the top of the workbench. That way, there would be nothing to indicate that only one bin had been used. I closed the car barn and walked down the lawn in the darkness toward the tangles of black raspberry thickets. There I pocketed two of the nuts and scattered the rest, well back into the thickets where no one would find them unless they were to uproot the entire yard. If they did that . . . I shrugged. Nothing would save me then.

I walked slowly back to the house. My gut reaction was to run, but that was clearly what Warbeck or Waetjen or vanBecton had in mind. Somehow I had to put the light back on them—get suspicions raised about the watch.

I smiled grimly. Perhaps I could plant a rumor or two, get their pot boiling and force them to act hastily. In the meantime, I had a lot to wind up—one hell of a lot.

The first thing I did was polish my prints off the two nuts and put them into the false drawer in the bedroom, the one containing miscellaneous "evidence."

I needed to get my geese in order, so to speak, because I doubted there was much time left before the rotten grain hit the mill wheel. Part of dealing with a problem lies in how you set things up before everything starts flying, and some of that is hard evidence, and some is how you handle the paperwork—and the truth. I decided that my approach would have to be truthful lying, so to speak.

It was late by the time I had finished and printed all four memoranda. After flicking off the difference engine, I began to reread the copies I had printed.

I studied the first memo. Not so polished as I would have liked, but, given the contents, and its accuracy, I doubted that the press would balk too much.

FROM: Ralston McGuiness
TO: WLA
SUBJECT: Psychic Research Budget Reviews
DATE: October 10, 1993

Background
The Budget Review Office has identified more than a dozen concealed university-based psychic research projects, including those which have already been compromised by some form of public disclosure, such as St. Louis . . .

The majority have been funded under Babbage-related research lines within the Defense Ministry budget . . .

This research has identified clear potential for implementing deghosting techniques . . .

Despite public denials, Speaker Hartpence receives regular reports on major projects . . .

Leaders of virtually all major religious orders, but particularly those of the Anglican-Baptists, the Roman Catholic Church, the Spirit of God, the Unified Congregation of the Holy Spirit, and the Latter Day Saints, have taken positions firmly opposing such research . . .

International Considerations

Similar psychic research is ongoing in the Austro-Hungarian Empire, as reported in both international media and by the Spazi . . .

To date, Spazi reports (attached) indicate that agents of Japan, Austro-Hungary, and New France have been definitely identified in conjunction with espionage surrounding Columbian psychic research . . .

Several unsolved murders, including the Vanderbraak State University incident, appear associated with such espionage . . . clear indications that Speaker Hartpence's staff has begun efforts to divert inquiries onto either New French sources or even former government personnel . . .

Recommendations

Since the presidency has no power over the actual composition and disbursement of Defense Ministry funds and since the Speaker has publicly avoided any comment on psychic research, bringing the matter before the national media would probably prove counterproductive at this time. Some media favorable to the Speaker would attribute any exposure of the Speaker's covert psychic research program to pure political motivations.

Likewise, attempting to meet with the Speaker could also prove counterproductive . . .

Recommend that you continue to use budgetary analyses and disclosure in areas where a greater public sympathy and understanding exist, and where the Speaker's policies run counter to that public sympathy, such as the size of naval forces and the need for totally free transoceanic trade . . .

Also recommend that you avoid any discussions or comments about psychic phenomena and research funding. This one is a loser!

I grinned. While it certainly wasn't perfect, it had just the right feel. It even sounded like Ralston, and the twist was, of course, that the disclosure of the memorandum would be totally against its contents, which would reinforce its validity with the press. Even the sensationalist videolink reporters would appreciate that.

The second memo I had composed dealt with the upcoming presidential budget review of the Defense Ministry outlays.

TO: GDvB
FROM: Elrik vanFlaam
           Budget Controller
SUBJECT: Psychic Research Budget Reviews
DATE: October 12, 1993

The new Babbage engines being used by the president's budget examiners have greater integrative capabilities than the earlier models. In
addition, the president's budget task force on program funding distribution now has the capability to cross-index disbursements by program category and amount, and such analyses are proceeding.

A leak from the black side of the budget has also been integrated,
which will reveal psychic research disbursements by region. Plotting
these against the institutions receiving funds will clearly outline the scope
and magnitude of the program.

In view of the Speaker's avowed disavowal of Defense Ministry research on psychic phenomena, the publication of any such analyses could
prove somewhat difficult to reconcile.

The budget controller's memo was almost innocuous, except for the last
line. That was the trick—to make each document as innocuous as possible, but to
have the composite paint a damning picture. That way, it also gave the reporters
away to claim that they had "discovered" the scandal, rather than having it handed
to them.

The third memo, to GH (Gerald Hartpence) from CA (Charles Asquith), apparently just dealt with press office support. Again, the implications were almost
totally between the lines.

TO: GH
FROM: CA
SUBJECT: Press Support Allocations
DATE: October 15, 1993

As discussed, we have reassigned another press officer to provide lo-
gistical and informational support to the psychic research issue . . .

The new fact sheets showing a comparative decline in all psychic research will be ready shortly, as will a full briefing book . . .

We should be ready to brief you on the initiative to assume credit for
the Japanese initiative . . .

"Whither goest thou?" asked Carolynne.

"I'll make these available to the press."

"Is there no pity sitting in the clouds?"

No pity? "The time is past for pity—that is, if I want to keep my head some-where close to my body."

"With treacherous revolt . . . this shall slay them both . . ."

"Probably. Except . . . is a false document which brings out the truth a for-gery or a fraud?"

Carolynne looked at me, and I thought I saw tears in her ghostly eyes, and then she was gone. I wished I could have gone to bed, or held her, or something. But I couldn't do any of those things. Instead, I began to create another false document. Because it was meant to be crude, it didn't take that long. I even printed it up in the cheap-looking Courier style.

WHY DO THE NEW
HEATHEN RAGE
AGAINST THE SPIRITS?

The corrupt government in our federal city has conspired to destroy the spirits of our fathers and forefathers. A man is nothing without his spirit. The haughtiest and the mightiest shall find that their possessions and their worldly attributes shall be for naught, and that their wealth shall avail them nothing . . .

After reading the diatribe of the "Order of Jeremiah" through, I printed ten copies on draft on my cheapest copy paper, addressed the necessary envelopes, then went up to bed and collapsed.

CHAPTER TWENTY-ONE

• • •

On Thursday morning I awoke alone, as was definitely getting to be even more common, in a cold and silent house, with snowflakes drifting lazily in the darkness outside my window. The snowflakes were sporadic and mostly disappeared even before I started my running.

I paused by the door, glancing down at the white enamel of the kitchen win-dowsills, polished virtually every day Marie came. Then I took a deep, cold breath before jogging down the drive. Running in the dark wasn't that much fun, and I had to cut my climb to the hillcrest short of the ridge because I needed to drive to Lebanon to meet a train and return well before my eleven o'clock.

I hurried through making breakfast, deciding to shower and shave after I ate. When I sat down to the hot rolled oats and milk and a strong pot of Russian Imperial tea, I thought about wiring Llysette, but, given her moods in the morning—especially at six o'clock—decided to hold that until later.

After cutting an apple into sections, and slowly chewing, I thought about what else I could do to anticipate whatever disaster would hit, but there's a time to act, and a time to respond. Unhappily, the situation still required me to respond mostly—at least until I could find a lever to unbalance vanBecton. So far, he'd kept pushing, and I hadn't responded until now—with my upcoming distribution of the cheap-looking flier from the "Order of Jeremiah" and the letters from Gerald Branston-Hay.

The memos would come later, and vanBecton wouldn't know that they were from me—assuming everything went as planned, which it wouldn't. In any case, that meant he'd have to push farther. I just hoped I could dodge the next push, or that it wasn't fatal.

In the meantime, delivering my hastily created fliers meant getting them to their destinations without a direct link to Vanderbraak Centre. I did know how to do that. Unfortunately, it meant driving to Lebanon, which was why I had dragged myself up so early.

With that cheerful thought, I rinsed the dishes and headed up for the shower. Pausing at the landing window, I watched a few lazy white flakes drift toward the partly covered lawn before shaking myself back into motion.

I took Route Five south through the scattered flakes before I got on the Ragged Mountain Highway west. I passed Alexandria and the biomass power plant just after seven, slowing for only one hauler filled with wood chips.

The rest of the drive to Lebanon was quiet, with only a few haulers and steamers on the road. I was standing trackside at the station a good ten minutes before the express stopped. I'd already posted the first letter from Gerald to Minister Holmbek in the box outside the station. The second would be posted from Styxx on the way back to the university.

The conductor looked for my ticket as I stepped up.

"No ticket. Need to mail these." I held up the letters.

He smiled, a knowing smile that acknowledged I wasn't supposed to do it, but that he'd seen more than a few men or women who needed faster post service on some debit payments. "Make it quick, sir."

I did, smiling at the conductor on the way down the mail car steps, and resting somewhat more easily knowing that the postmark would be from New Amsterdam.

On the drive back to Vanderbraak Centre, I thought a lot, probably too much, but I did drop the second letter from Branston-Hay into the postbox in Styxx. I doubted either would really get to Holmbek, but they might, although that wasn't their main purpose. The copies I'd kept were the useful ones. Then I reflected and went inside, almost right after the Styxx post center opened, and bought an inordinate amount of postage, knowing that I would certainly need it. If I didn't, the money would be immaterial. The clerk shook her head, her white bonnet bobbing as she did.

With the sun up, I saw a handful more steamers on the way back, mostly battered older farm wagons.

As I finally neared the square in Vanderbraak Centre, I did keep an eye out. A little paranoia never hurts, especially when you know they are out to get you, but there wasn't a local watch steamer in sight, not even when I pulled up in front of Samaha's.

Louie Samaha and another white-haired man glanced briefly at me and lowered their voices—another sign promising trouble—as I retrieved my paper. Wonder of wonders: there were actually two papers in mister Derkin's box, the first time I'd ever seen anything there. Perhaps he did exist.

With a nod to Louie, who nodded back as I left the silver dime on the counter, I scanned the front page of the *Post-Courier,* but the dirigible-turbo fight dominated the ink, and even the charge that Governor vanHasten's son had forged his father's signature to a cheque given to a well-known Asten courtesan was but a tiny story below the fold.

Llysette's Reo was not yet in the car park, but again, that was not especially surprising, not since I was relatively early.

Gilda smiled briefly from the main office.

"Good morning, Gilda. How are you on this wonderfully warm and bright morning?"

"Doktor Eschbach, how kind of you to inquire. Your presence brings light into all of our lives . . . just like a good forest fire brings warmth to the creatures of the wood and vale."

"I do so appreciate your kind words."

"I thought you would. Doktor Doniger is most unhappy, and I think it concerns you, since Dean Er Recchus called him out before he could even finish his coffee, and he was mumbling about former government officials."

"How absolutely cheering." I bestowed an exaggerated smile upon her, and she responded in kind. Then I went upstairs, where my breath almost steamed in the cold of the hall that the overhead glow squares did little to relieve, and unlocked my office.

After getting settled behind my desk, I penned a short note to Llysette, wishing her well with her rehearsals and conveying more than mere affection, then slipped it into an envelope.

By then it was still only a quarter before ten, and, not wanting to waste too much time, I reluctantly dug into the Environmental Politics 2B papers. My reluctance was indeed warranted, given the dismal quality of what I read. Why was it so hard for them to understand that, just because a politician claimed he or she was environmentalist, politicians were still politicians? After all, the subsidies for steamers and the fuel taxes weren't enacted for environmental reasons but strategic ones. Speaker Aspinall never met a tree he didn't think needed to be turned into lumber or a coal mine that he didn't love—but he pushed both the subsidies and the taxes through. Why? Because Ferdinand and Maximilian—the father, not the idiot son who was deGaulle's puppet—would have strangled Columbia if we'd ever become too dependent on foreign oil. Now, the taxes are seen as great environmental initiatives. I tried not to lose my breakfast at the soupy rhetoric asserting such nonsense, and instead contented myself with an excess of red ink.

At ten-thirty I trotted down to the Music and Theatre Department, since I knew Llysette was teaching Diction then. After putting the envelope in her box, I turned to Martha Philips. "Don't tell her it's there. Just let her find it when she will."

"That's mean."

"I hope it's romantic. We need that around here, especially these days."

"These days . . . ? Wasn't that terrible about Dr. Branston-Hay's accident? Such a nice man. And his boys, they are so adorable. And then the fire."

"Fire?"

"Didn't you hear? Last night, the electrical box shorted. It was terrible. They lost everything—all his years of research, and his own Babbage system. At least they escaped."

"At least . . ." I shook my head. "It wasn't in the paper. I didn't know." So much for Branston-Hay's backup disks. VanBecton wasn't leaving much to chance.

"It will be. Poor woman."

"Strange. First Miranda's murder, then this. The watch hasn't been able to do much. You know, after her murder, they even called in the Spazi?"

"They did?"

"There was a big gray Spazi steamer parked right next to the watch office for two days." I shook my head. "Gerald was doing some sort of research for the Ministry of Defense. He didn't like to talk about it. I wouldn't either, I suppose, not with all the other fires and accidents happening at Babbage centers at other schools. Still, the feds won't let on, and probably poor Chief Waetjen will get the blame for not solving the crimes. And another fire." VanBecton liked fires, or this was a way to pin it on Ferdinand.

"Ah, do you think so, Doktor Eschbach?"

I grinned. "Given the federal government, is there any doubt?" I grinned. "I need to go, and please don't tell Doktor duBoise. Let her find it when she picks up her messages."

"I won't." She smiled faintly, as well she might, since her husband was on the town council that had hired Chief Waetjen.

That had been one of the purposes of my visit, that and reminding Llysette that I was still around. She had been reserved, or was it just preoccupied with her opera production coming up? Or was I withdrawing from her?

I waved briefly to Hector as he was placing snow shelters over the bushes beside the music building, but didn't see Gertrude anywhere. Hector waved back, in his somber but friendly manner, and I marched back to the Natural Resources building, where I repeated the same conversation with Gilda, not because she was connected to anyone in particular, but because she talked to almost everyone about everything. Except with Gilda, I added one more twist.

"I wonder if the Spazi have their fingers on the chief."

"Don't they have their fingers on everyone?"

We both laughed, but Gilda's laugh died as the good Doktor Doniger marched toward his office.

"Gilda. Where is the memorandum from the dean?"

I went upstairs, actually reading through the text assignments—novel concept—and reviewing my notes for my eleven o'clock before I trudged through the snow flurries to Smythe Hall for Natural Resources 1A.

"I beg your pardon for my breathless arrival, and I do know that you are waiting breathlessly." I held up my hand. "Unfortunately, a number of matters have retarded my arrival, including a few recent deaths." I waited. "I assume you have heard about the accident that killed Doktor Branston-Hay? I hope it is not part of the unfortunate pattern of accidents involving professors at university Babbage centers across the country." I shrugged.

"Accidents?" finally came a whisper.

"You should read the press more closely. However, in answer to your question, there have been explosions and fires at a number of Babbage centers across the country. I do not know if students have been killed, but several professors and staff have died. There was even one incident in Munich. Now, enough of noncurricular speculation! What about solid deposition?"

I looked around the room. "Mister MacLean? What is solid deposition?"

I got a blank look, but eventually, someone got the idea. We didn't get into carbon, and I had to spend far too much time explaining why it was highly unlikely that significant quantities of VOCs would ever be present in any form of atmospheric deposition, solid or liquid.

A faint glimmer of sunlight graced my departure from Smythe, but it vanished as I entered the bright redbrick walls of the student activities building.

After wolfing down the bowl of bland chicken noodle soup at the counter in the activities building, I returned to my office through another, heavier snow flurry, and finished grading the Environmental Politics 2B papers. The last papers weren't that much better than the first.

Since I hadn't heard anything from Llysette, I dialed her number at about quarter to two, but there was no answer. I shrugged and gathered together the papers.

The grass wore a thin sheet of white flakes, but the brick walkways were merely damp, and the snow had stopped falling before I left the Natural Resources building. Perhaps three students nodded to me as I crossed the green back to Smythe. I nodded in return, but all three looked away. I must have looked grim. Either that or the word was out that Professor Eschbach was flattening all markers, or whatever the current slang on the korfball court was.

My Environmental Politics 2B class almost cowered in their desks, except for one brave soul—Demetri Panos, a Greek exile. What he was doing in New Bruges, I never understood. He shivered more in a classroom under a coat than even Llysette did outside.

"Professor, you will be generous in considering our faults?"

I had to smile.

"If your faults show effort and some minimal degree of perception, Mr. Panos." I felt safe saying that, since he'd actually gotten a B, a low B but a B, one of the few. Then I began handing back the papers, trying to ignore the winces and the mumbles.

". . . not graduate school . . ."

". . . what does he want . . ."

I did answer the second mumble. "What I want from you is thought. You have brains. You should read the material, make some effort to comprehend it, and then attempt to apply what you have learned to one of the topics. For example, take the second topic, the one dealing with whether real environmental progress has been made, or whether most of the environmental improvements of the past generation occurred for other, less altruistic, reasons. Were the petroleum taxes pushed through by Speaker Aspinall for environmental reasons, or because the Defense Ministry pointed out the need to preserve domestic petroleum supplies with the drawdown of the Oklahoma fields and the difficulties in extracting North Slope oil?"

Half of them still looked blank. I wondered if that blank expression were a regional trait common to New Bruges or a generational expression common to all young of the species.

Somehow we struggled through, and I got back to the main office. Still no message from Llysette, and I wondered if she were out on a short tour with her group. But would she be traveling so near a production?

Or had I done something to offend her? Finally I picked up the handset and dialed.

"Hello."

"Is this the distinguished soprano Llysette duBoise?"

"Johan, do not mock me."

"I wasn't. I was just remarking on the quality of your voice."

A sigh followed. I waited.

"A long day it has been."

"So has mine. Would you like dinner?"

"We are still rehearsing, and still I am beating the notes into their thick Dutch heads."

"Chocolate before rehearsal? Now? At Delft's?"

"I do not . . ." She sighed again. "That would be nice."

"I'll be at your door in a few moments."

And I was. And another wonder of wonders, she actually was ready to leave, carefully knotting a scarf over her hair and ears as I rapped on the studio door.

"Johan . . ." I got a kiss. A brief one, but a kiss. "For the note. Sweet and thoughtful it was."

"Sometimes I try. Other times, I'm afraid I'm trying."

We walked down the hill to the center of town.

"How are you coming with rehearsals?" I shook my head. "From what I've seen, you're really pushing them to do *Heinrich Verrückt*. Didn't everyone think Beethoven was totally insane for writing an opera about Henry VIII? From what you've told me, it has the complexity of the Ninth Symphony and the impossibility of Mozart's Queen of the Night in every role."

"Johan," Llysette said with a laugh, "difficult it is, but not *that* difficult. To baby them I am not here."

Delft's was almost empty, and we got the table by the woodstove again.

"Ah, much better this is than my cold studio." She slipped off the scarf even before sitting.

Victor's son Francois arrived and nodded at Llysette. "Chocolate? Tea? Coffee?"

"Chocolate."

"I'll have chocolate also, and please bring a plate of the butter cookies, Dansk style."

As Francois bowed and departed, Llysette shifted her weight in the chair, as if soaking in the warmth from the stove.

"Johan?"

"Yes."

"Well did you know Professor Branston-Hay?"

"I can't say I knew him exceptionally well. We talked occasionally. We had troubles with the same students."

"A tragedy that was." Llysette pursed her lips. "Some, they say that it was not an accident."

I shrugged. "I have my doubts. According to the papers, a lot of Babbage researchers are dying in one way or another."

"Is that not strange? And Miranda, was she not a friend of Professor Branston-Hay?"

I nodded.

"Your country, I do not understand." Llysette's laugh was almost bitter.

"Sometimes I don't, either. Exactly what part don't you understand?"

"A woman is killed, and nothing happens. A man dies in an accident, and the watch, they question many people, and people talk. No one says the accident could be murder. But they question. The woman, she is forgotten."

Except I hadn't forgotten Miranda, and I didn't think vanBecton had, either.

Francois returned with two pots of chocolate and a heavily laden plate of Danish butter cookies. He filled both cups.

The chocolate tasted good, much better than the bland chicken noodle soup that had substituted for lunch. The cookies were even better, and I ate two in a row before taking another small swallow of the steaming chocolate.

"Did they question you?" I asked.

"But of course. They asked about you."

"Me? How odd? I barely knew either one—I mean, not beyond being members of the same faculty."

"I told the chief watch officer that very same." Llysette shrugged. "Perhaps they think it was a ménage à trois."

"Between a broken-down federal official, a spiritualistic piano teacher, and a difference engine researcher with a soul written in Babbage code? They must be under a lot of pressure." I refilled my cup from my pot and hers from the one on her left.

She laughed for a moment, then added, "Governments make strange things happen. People must . . . make hard choices, n'est-ce-pas?"

"*Mais oui, mademoiselle.* Like insisting on producing *Heinrich Verrückt* in New Bruges. Why didn't you just use one of the Perkins adaptations of Vondel?"

"Vondel? Dutch is even more guttural than low German."

"I think it's interesting. Seventeenth-century Dutch plays turned into contemporary operas by a Mormon composer."

Llysette made a face.

"The Dutch think that Vondel was every bit as good as Shakespeare." I took a healthy swallow of chocolate. The second cup was cooler.

"Good plays do not make good operas. Good music and good plays make good opera."

"You have a problem with Perkins?"

"Perkins? No. Good music he writes. The problem, it is with Vondel." Llysette looked at her wrist. "Alas, I must go. A makeup lesson I must do, and then the rehearsals."

I swallowed the last of my chocolate, then left some bills on the table for Francois.

Llysette replaced her scarf before stepping into the wind. A few damp brown leaves swirled by, late-hangers torn from the trees lining the square.

"Makeup lesson?"

"The little dunderheads, sometimes, they have good reasons for missing a lesson."

"Few times, I would guess."

Llysette did not answer, and we proceeded in silence to the door of the Music and Theatre Building. I held it open, and we walked to her empty studio.

"Take care." I bent forward and kissed her cheek.

"You also, Johan." Her lips were cold on my cheek. "The note—I did like it."

I watched for a moment as she took off the scarf and coat, then blew her a kiss before turning away.

As I walked back to my office, I had to frown. Was I getting so preoccupied that Llysette was finding me cold? She still seemed distracted . . . but she had kissed me and thanked me. Was I the distracted one—not that I didn't have more than enough reasons to be distracted—or was something else going on?

I went back to my own office, where I reclaimed my folder before locking up. The main office was empty, although I could see the light shining from under David's closed door. Whatever it was about me that he'd been discussing with the dean apparently was still under wraps. He was probably plotting something. God, I hated campus politics.

The wind continued to gust as I walked to the car park. A watch car was pulled over to the curb on the other side of the street outside the faculty car park. I started the Stanley, then belted in. As my headlamps crossed the dark gray steamer, glinting off the unlit green lenses of the strobes, I could make out Officer Warbeck, clearly watching me. When I got to the bottom of the hill, he had pulled out, following me at a distance. He followed me across the river, but not up Deacon's Lane.

First Llysette, and then the watch.

At least Marie had left me a warm steak pie, and I had eaten most of it when the wireset rang. I swallowed what was in my mouth and picked up the handset.

"Hello?"

"Doktor Eschbach?"

"Yes."

"This is Chief Waetjen. I just had one additional question."

"Oh?"

"Do you recall whether Professor Miller was wearing a long blue scarf the night she was killed?"

I frowned. "I only felt her ghost. So I wouldn't have any way of knowing what she wore. I hadn't seen her since that Friday, I think, and I don't remember what she was wearing then. You might ask one of the women."

"I see. Well, thank you." *Click.*

I looked out into the darkness onto the lawn, barely visible under the stars that had begun to shine in the rapidly clearing skies.

In belated foresight, the situation vanBecton was setting up was clear enough. Johan Eschbach had been under enormous stress, had even received a health-based pension for wounds from a would-be assassin. Now a murder, perhaps one he had committed in his unstable state, would be found to have turned him into a zombie— one of the more severe varieties. And his ghost would never be found. What a pity!

I walked upstairs and looked outside, seeing a few bright and cold stars between the clouds and wondering how long before I got a caller. Then I opened the false drawer in the armoire, taking out a few Austro-Hungarian items—and the two new shiny nuts I had put there just the day before. Of course, the whole thing was ridiculous, since no real agent would carry anything even faintly betraying, but the items were suggestive—a medallion reminiscent of the Emperor's Cross, a fragment of a ticket in German, the sort of thing that could get stuck in a pocket, a pen manufactured only in Vienna, and a square metal gadget which contained a saw and a roll of piano wire, totally anonymous except for the tiny Austrian maker's mark.

As evidence they might be too subtle, but I didn't have much to lose. I put them in my pockets, not that they were any risk to me, since I'd either walk away or be in no shape to do so.

I studied the lawn, but no one was out there, not that I could see. So I walked back downstairs and washed the dishes. Then I went into the study, got the disassociator, and set it in the corner by the door. I got the quilt from the sofa and rolled it up and set it on the chair before the Babbage console, putting a jacket from the closet around it and an old beret on top. I'd never worn it, not since Anna had sent it to me from her trip to New France years earlier, but I doubted any agent knew what I did or didn't wear in my study. In any case, the lights would silhouette the figure, and, from the veranda, it would be hard to distinguish the difference between me and the impromptu dummy from any distance because the Babbage screen assembly would block a head-on view until an intruder was almost at the windows.

I reached forward and turned on the difference engine. After that, I slipped the truncheon from the hidden holder on the table leg into my belt, then turned on the lights, picking up the disassociator.

I didn't have to wait long before a tall figure in a watch uniform glided up the hill and across the veranda. I shook my head. He was relying a lot on his uniform, and I've never had that much respect for cloth and braid and bright buttons.

He fiddled with the door, opened it, and lifted the Colt-Luger.

Crack. crack.

The young Spazi—I was sure the imposter's name wasn't Warbeck, even if I had appreciated his sense of humor—actually fired two shots into the quilt-dummy before he looked around. Metal glinted under his watch helmet. His large Colt-Luger swung toward me.

Crack.

I jumped and pulled the trigger on the disassociator, then dropped it. The room went dark, but I hadn't waited for that, as I had dropped forward and to Warbeck's right. I could feel him ram into the heavy desk, and his hesitation was enough, even if it took me two quick swings with the truncheon. I had to aim for the temple because I didn't know how effective the truncheon would be with Gerald's mesh cap and Warbeck's regular hat over it.

Still, even in the darkness, I could tell I'd hit him too hard, not that it frankly bothered me much. The Colt thudded to the carpet, but did not discharge again. My effort with the truncheon had been quick enough that there would be no ghost, although the disassociator would have taken care of that detail.

I pulled the flash from the desk drawer and played it across him. He was definitely dead.

After placing those few items I had prepared in Warbeck's clothes, I used a handkerchief to replace the Colt in the military holster, then wrapped his cooling fingers around the weapon before dragging the body out the door and onto the veranda. I used the handkerchief to put his hat by him, then waited in the shadows. I've always been good at waiting. It's what separates the real professionals from those who just think they are.

It must have been an hour before the two others slipped up the lawn through the trees. One carried a large body bag. I felt like nodding. Instead, I waited until they found the body.

"Shit. Somebody got him first . . ."

Both lifted their weapons, and that was enough for me. I held down the spring trigger on the disassociator. One collapsed, and the other shrieked. I waited and potted both ghosts with the disassociator, but the second one resisted. The power meter I hadn't paid enough attention to earlier dropped into the red.

I set aside the disassociator, placed the truncheon in the hands of the collapsed zombie, and took Warbeck's truncheon. I also thought about taking the metal hair net, thinking I might be needing it myself. Then I decided it would be more valuable on Warbeck. The other zombie looked at me blankly—still somewhat there probably because the disassociator had run out of power.

"There's been an accident."

"There's been an accident," he repeated.

"Wait here for help."

"I wait here for help." He wasn't quite expressionless in his intonation, but close enough.

I had to hand it to vanBecton. He hadn't even wanted me as a zombie, and he'd set up Warbeck. Poor Warbeck. He'd just thought he was carrying out a removal. If he succeeded, then I was out of the way, and then he would have been killed trying to escape from my murder.

Waetjen's own boys had doubtless been told that Warbeck had gone off the deep end and to bring him back in one piece or many, but not to risk their lives. They'd also been told I was dangerous, and armed, and not to be too gentle there, either. Neither vanBecton nor the chief was in favor of my continued presence, although it would have been hard for me to convince any judge or jury of that.

That was the hell of the position I was in. If I'd waited, I'd have been dead. If I weren't careful, I'd be in jail for murder, because I couldn't prove, and no one outside the intelligence community would understand, that I was being set up.

My knees were weak. As I walked to the study, I was beginning to understand the difference between being an impartial agent and a directly involved victim. I didn't like being the targeted victim, nor what it was doing to my nerves.

In the study, by the light of the flash I dialed the watch number and began screaming. Chief Waetjen got on the line.

"Who is this?" he snapped.

"Johan Eschbach! There's been a terrible fight outside. I think . . . I don't know. Get someone up here."

"There were two men headed there. Have you seen them?"

"There are three men here. One's dead, one's unconscious, and the other's a zombie."

"Oh . . ."

"And, Chief, I think the dead one's an Austro-Hungarian agent."

"You would now, would you?"

"Well," I said carefully, "someone has to be. The way I see it, your men tried to stop him from potting a former government minister when he started shooting at me. I probably owe them a lot. So do you."

After that, I flipped the switch on the difference engine so that it wouldn't come on when the power returned. Then I went to the closet and reset the circuit breakers. I shivered. Had I destroyed Carolynne as well?

A flash of white by the veranda, a glimpse of the recital dress reassured me. With that, I quickly tucked the disassociator back in the closet, and put the quilt, jacket, and beret away. The sirens echoed from across the river as I flicked through the wireset directory until I found the number. I wished I'd cultivated press contacts in New Bruges, but . . .

"Post-Courier."

"News desk, please."

"Vraal, news."

"My name is Johan Eschbach. There's been a murder at my house, and two zombies are walking around the yard. I used to be a government minister under Speaker Michel, but I now teach at Vanderbraak State University in Vanderbraak Centre. The murdered man is an imposter, and the two zombies are local watch officers."

"We don't take crank calls, sir."

"If you look at last year's *Almanac of Columbian Politics,* my name and profile are on page two hundred twenty-nine. If you don't want the story, or if you want it buried, that's your problem."

A long pause followed.

"Who did you say you were?"

"I was, and still am, Johan Anders Eschbach. The Vanderbraak Centre watch chief, Hans Waetjen, is headed to my house at the moment."

"What happened?"

"I heard someone trying to break in. When I went downstairs, someone shot at me, and there were yells and sounds of a struggle. Then I found the body on the veranda and two zombies standing there. One had a bloody truncheon in his hand. The house is off Deacon's Lane across the River Wijk from the main part of Vanderbraak Centre. You might find it worth looking into." While I talked, I found the number for Gelfor Hardin, who edits and prints the *Vanderbraak Weekly Chronicle*.

"I hope this isn't another crank call."

"It is scarcely that, although I must admit that I have little fondness for armed men who shoot at me and bodies appearing behind my house."

"Why did you call the *Courier?*"

"The occupational paranoia of government service stays with one for life, I fear. A good news story is often a deterrent."

"You say that one watch officer tried to break into your house, and he was killed by two others?"

"I don't know that. That is what it looked like."

"Why would someone be after you?"

"I don't know—unless I happen to be a handy scapegoat for something."

"Scapegoat?"

"You might remember the Colonel Nord incident."

"Oh . . . you're *that* Eschbach?"

"How fleeting fame is."

"Can we call you back?"

"Yes." I gave him the number and wired Hardin.

Hardin didn't answer, but another voice, female, did. "*Chronicle* services."

I gave an abbreviated version of the story to the woman, then walked back out on the veranda. By then, Chief Waetjen was standing there with three other officers beside the dead man and the two zombies.

"Who were you wiring?" asked Waetjen.

"The newspapers. I thought they might like the story."

"You know, Doktor, I could end up not appreciating you very much."

"I understand." I bowed slightly. "But you should understand that I don't like finding bodies outside my house, especially bodies in watch uniforms. It's bad for my digestion."

Hans Waetjen wasn't as smart as he thought, because he'd used sirens and brought three watch officers with him. I was grateful for small favors, since those were the only kind I was likely to get.

He bowed politely. "You understand that my digestion also suffers when I find dead officers and officers who are zombies?"

"I can see that we share many of the same concerns, Chief Waetjen."

"Could you tell me what happened?"

I gave him the sanitized version of Warbeck's efforts, concluding with, "I don't know what Officer Warbeck did, but when the shooting stopped, he was on the veranda, and the two others were just like they are now."

"Just like this?" He clearly didn't believe me, and he was certainly correct, but I wasn't about to oblige him.

"I didn't check exactly, but I don't think anything's changed since I called you."

"What about before that?"

"I heard the noise at the door. Then all the lights went out—"

"You didn't mention that."

"Sorry. They did. I reset the breakers after I called you."

"How could you see?"

"I have a flash in my desk." I glanced over my shoulder. "It's on the corner now—right there."

"How convenient."

"No, just practical. I spend most of my time at home in the study or the kitchen. There are flashes in both places. I have a kerosene lamp in the bedroom."

One of the other three watch officers had set up a floodlight and was taking pictures of the scene on the veranda flagstones.

Another siren wailed, and the ambulance glided up the drive and stopped behind the two watch steamers. I watched and waited until the medics carted off the two zombies with a promise to return for the body shortly.

Chief Waetjen finally turned to me. "I could insist you come in with us, Doktor Eschbach."

"You could," I agreed amiably. "But . . ." I looked at the body on the cold stone and thought of the truncheon with one of the zombies' fingerprints all over it. "Arresting me for something someone else clearly did wouldn't look really good. Especially since we both know that Warbeck isn't Warbeck."

"He isn't?" asked one of the officers, who was using some sort of amplified magnifying glass to study the stones around Warbeck's body.

"No." I smiled at Waetjen, who tried not to glower at me.

"You think you're pretty clever, don't you?"

"No. I don't. There are people a lot more clever than either one of us, and I suggest we leave the cleverness to them."

Waetjen paused. Then he turned to the others. "Finish up the standard procedure. Do you have prints, photographs, complete tech search?"

"We're still working on it."

"Don't forget the outside knob on the door there," I suggested. "It should have Warbeck's prints all over it. And there are some bullets and bullet holes somewhere in the study."

Waetjen didn't say a word, just gestured at the watch officer with the print kit.

The wireset bell rang.

"Excuse me, Chief."

I edged the door open by the inside of the frame and went inside to pick up the handset.

"Hello."

"Do you come in, or do we put you in cold storage?" It was Ralston McGuiness's voice. "Think about your friend, too."

"This is somewhat . . . open."

"Christ, all of Columbia will know something's up. Your nominal superior downtown will call you in, and you'll never come out."

"I'll come in. But where?"

"Use the bolthole we discussed." *Click.*

Trouble wasn't quite the word. More like disaster, I thought. And what Ralston had in mind wasn't exactly friendly. Come in or we'll ensure you never go anywhere, and, if you don't understand, we'll take out one Doktor duBoise. That wouldn't happen immediately, because he'd lose leverage, and he'd want me to think about it, but he'd start with her, and then it would be my mother, Anna, Judith, Eric . . .

The wireset rang again.

"Hello."

"This is Garrison vanKleef at the *Post-Courier.* Is this Doktor Eschbach?"

"Yes."

"Do you think this incident has anything to do with the Nord incident?"

"I would hope not. The last time I heard, Colonel Nord was reforesting semi-tropical swamps outside of Eglin. And I don't have another wife and son to lose."

"Have the watch arrived yet?"

"Chief Waetjen is standing about fifteen feet from me with three others. He does not look terribly pleased."

"How does he look?"

"As always, stocky, gray-haired, and not very pleased."

"Why should we be interested in this?"

"Call it a feeling. You also might try to find out, though, why the dead watch officer was wearing a funny metal mesh skullcap."

"A funny metal mesh skullcap, you say?"

"Under his watch helmet. I thought I once saw one in the Babbage research center. A rather odd coincidence, I thought, especially after the recent accident that killed the Babbage research director at the University."

"So do I, Eschbach." A laugh followed. "You have a body and two zombies there. Any thoughts on why this happened to you?"

"One thing I did learn from all my years in Columbia was that speculations are just that. It's Chief Waetjen's job to get to the bottom of the mess."

"Do you think he will?"

"On or off the record?"

"On, of course."

"I think the chief will devote a great deal of effort to this investigation, and I trust that he will discover why one of his officers apparently went beyond the call of duty."

"You spent too much time in Columbia, Eschbach. Good night."

I walked back outside.

"More press?"

"Of course. Isn't the press a man's safeguard?"

"Sometimes. If the feds don't get there first." Waetjen snorted.

I understood. The government can't force retractions, but it can suggest that stories never be printed—if it knows in advance. The press still likes good stories, and they like to scream about direct censorship. It's a delicate balancing game, and I'd tried to upset the balance.

Neither of the other three watch officers said anything. So I stood and watched while they poked, prodded, and photographed everything. What they didn't do was take my prints, and that obviously bothered me, because it wasn't an oversight.

It was well past midnight when the chief left and I locked up the house. After pulling the study drapes closed, I plugged the disassociator into the standard recharging socket, and it seemed to work, just the way Bruce had designed it. That was one reason I liked Bruce. When he built something, it did what it was designed to do.

"These things are beyond all use, and I do fear them." Carolynne floated in the study doorway.

"I have gotten a similar impression. The question is what I should do about it."

"Do not go forth today . . . not go forth today . . ." Carolynne's voice seemed faint.

"Do not go forth? What about the people who sent the false watch officer?"

"Graves have yawned and yield up their dead; fierce fiery warriors fight upon the clouds."

If she meant that both the ghosts and the powers that be in Columbia were after me, she was right, but having a ghost's confirmation on that wouldn't help me in Columbia City. So I began to stack all the materials I would need on the side of the desk.

"When beggars die, there are no comets seen . . . alas, my lord, your wisdom is consumed in confidence."

"Probably, but I'm no Caesar. And I can't fight enemies in the federal city from here. Not any longer."

"Let me, upon my knee, prevail in this."

"All right." I had to laugh. "I probably should leave tonight, but I'm too tired. Besides, if he detained me right now, Chief Waetjen would look as though he were trying to run on foam. He'll need to go through all the procedures, and that will take a day or two, making sure that I am very visible. Of course, if I disappear, then I will be presumed guilty. But if I don't I'll either be charged or killed while resisting arrest."

Carolynne listened, but she said no more as I gathered together identity documents and copied real and false memoranda and all the supporting materials. I carried the whole mess upstairs.

I packed quickly but carefully, with working clothes on the top of the valise and suits in the hanging bag. The top suit was shiny, hard gray wool, a threadbare and very cheap old suit I had kept around in case I might need it. I had always hoped I wouldn't, but you always plan for the worst.

Then there was the equipment bag—all the gadgets I'd collected over the years and never turned in. All of us who worked those jobs have such bags. You never know when you might need them again. Some I knew—and I thought Bruce might have been one—did keep firearms they had picked up. You didn't keep issue weapons, not since they really tallied those. But how could anyone tell if you used eight or eighteen yards of plastique, or an electronics installer's belt, or tree spikes, or mountain gear?

Mine had a coil of thin plastic, nearly ten yards' worth. I had two radio detonators, plus a handful of contact detonators. There was the truncheon, plus a complete Federal District watch uniform, including the Colt revolver I'd never used. I'd been undercover back in 1986 when the French president in exile pleaded for Columbian support against Ferdinand, and the federals were afraid that the Jackal's group might try an assassination. We'd had a tip that they had a plant in the watch. They'd had two, actually, and I'd turned in one's uniform instead of mine. Larceny, I know, but when dealing with thieves total honesty is suicide.

I looked up, but Carolynne was gone. Even ghosts don't like being ignored or being thought of as part of the furniture. I sighed, although I wasn't quite sure why, before pulling out the next item, a set of blue coveralls, almost identical to every electrical installer's in the country, and very useful for a variety of purposes. I shook the dust off them and packed them in the bag.

After laying everything out, I collapsed into bed, setting the alarm for an hour earlier than normal, wishing I could get more than five hours' sleep.

But I did sleep, even if I dreamed about ghosts, and iron bars, and driving endlessly on unmarked roads through rain and fog.

CHAPTER TWENTY-TWO

• • •

Half awake already when the alarm jolted me out of the darkness, I was still exhausted. After putting on the kettle, I showered, shaved, and dressed quickly, then let the Imperial Russian tea steep while I loaded the Stanley.

First, the equipment bag, the disassociator, and the toolbox went in the false back of the Stanley's trunk; then the rest went into the main part, clearly the artifacts of a traveling sales representative, down to the slightly battered sample book and the worn leather order book.

The sky lightened as I sipped tea and ate my way through a too-ripe pear and three slices of Marie's bread slathered with my own blackberry preserves. I actually made them—had ever since I'd returned to Vanderbraak Centre.

Finally I backed the Stanley out of the car barn and headed into town. I went around the square first, just for effect, before stopping in at Samaha's to pick up my paper. Louie didn't look at me when I left my dime on the counter. Neither did Rose, his equally dour wife.

I didn't open the paper until I was back in the Stanley. The story was played straight—too straight.

Last night, a Vanderbraak Centre watch officer was killed, apparently by another officer, as he tried to enter the home of Johan Eschbach, a former Deputy Minister of Environment. Although Eschbach was not hurt, both the officer who was forced to stop the intruder and another attending officer suffered psychic disassociation.

According to unofficial sources, after firing several shots, the intruding officer suffered a fatal skull fracture, apparently inflicted by a watch truncheon.

Eschbach reported that the intruder wore a strange metal cap, a fact confirmed by the Vanderbraak Watch Chief, Hans Waetjen. Neither Waetjen nor Eschbach would speculate on the reason for the apparent attack or the cause of the psychic disassociation of the other two officers.

Chief Waetjen indicated that a complete investigation is ongoing.

I folded the paper and restarted the Stanley. After I pulled away from Samaha's, I waved to Constable Gerhardt through the wind, and headed northward on Route Five, just until past the woolen mill. There I took the covered-bridge turnoff onto the back road that eventually reconnected to Route Five south of Vanderbraak Centre. In the dimness of the woods beyond the Reformed Church's summer retreat, I twisted the knob under the dashboard to get the thermals on. The thermosensitive paint faded from red to maroon to dark gray.

At that point I changed from coat and cravat into comfortable flannels and put the wallet with Vic Nuustrom's license in it in my pocket. The coat and cravat went into the garment bag in the trunk, along with my real identification.

I took Route Five south almost to Borkum, where the Wijk flowed into the Nieumaas, before taking Route Four west. Wider and smoother than the Ragged Mountain Highway that ran from south of Vanderbraak Centre to Lebanon, Route

Four skirted the base of the Grunbergs and entered New Ostend just south and east of Hudson Falls.

Just before I left New Bruges, I ran into a series of snow flurries, but they passed about the time I left Riisville and the girls' seminary there. All the buildings at the seminary were white-painted clapboards, a southern affectation hardly at home in New Bruges.

It was late morning, almost noon, before I crossed into New Ostend and Route Four became the Heisser Parkway. And that was despite some periods where I had the Stanley really moving on the open stretches. One positive sign was that none of the highway watch in New Bruges had stopped me. I had to admit that I began to breathe easier when I saw the sign that said WELCOME TO NEW OSTEND.

By midafternoon I got to the outskirts of New Amsterdam, coming down the new Hudson River Bluffs parkway, two lanes in each direction all the way, with mulched gardens in the median. I even had the now-maroon Stanley close to its red line a few times, but even with the new parkways, driving was definitely not so fast as traveling by train.

I stopped near Nyack to eat and to top off the tanks. I avoided the Royal Dutch stop on principle and pulled into the Standard Oil station. First came the water and kerosene, then the food.

"Both?" asked the attendant, a girl not much older than Waltar would have been.

"Both. Filtered water?"

"It's the only kind we have. Single or double A on the kerosene, sir?"

"Double, please." The double was nearly twenty cents a gallon higher, but the purity more than paid for the price in cleaner burners and, in my case, the ability to redline the Stanley if necessary. Eastern water wasn't usually a problem, but some of the mineralized water in the west played hob with steam turbines, coated the vanes and literally tore them apart.

The flaxen-haired, red-cheeked teenager wore her jacket open over a blue flannel shirt, despite the chill, and whistled something that sounded like the Fiddler's March, well enough that any Brit would have been apoplectic.

Standard Oil or not, the station had a well-mulched flower garden in the shape of an oval that matched the sign. Did the flower patterns spell out "Standard Oil" in the summer? I asked as she racked the kerosene nozzle.

"No, sir. Grosspapa tried, but the blues didn't really work out, and people complained. So I plant whatever suits me now that he can't do the gardening anymore." She smiled. "That came to twenty-five fifty, sir."

I nodded and handed her a twenty and a ten. With the latest round of energy taxes, fuels were running over three dollars a gallon. "Thank you."

"Thank you, sir. Please stop and see us again." She handed me my change in silver.

I drove a quarter-mile down the side road to the Irving Tavern, where I parked and locked the Stanley outside the restaurant. Lace curtains, freshly laundered, graced the windows. On the way into the dark-paneled dining room, where the dark wooden tables still shimmered, their wood set off by glistening white cloths, I picked up a copy of the *New Amsterdam Post*.

"One, sir?"

"Please."

The hostess's white cap could have come from two centuries earlier. She escorted me to a small side table. "We have everything on the menu except for the pork dumplings, and the special is a dark kielbasa with sauerkraut. Would you like coffee or chocolate?"

"Chocolate."

After pouring me a cup, she set the pot in the center of the table and waited as I studied the menu, glancing over the stuffed cabbage while trying to repress a shudder at the list of heavy entrees. If I ate half of what was listed, the Stanley would be carrying double—if I made it out the door.

"I'll have the Dutch almond noodles with the cheeses."

"They're good today." She nodded and departed.

While I waited, I leafed through the *Post* and found the RPI wire story, which I read twice, stopping at the key paragraph.

Although the Vanderbraak Centre watch officer killed in the scuffle outside former minister Eschbach's house has been determined not to be Perkin Warbeck, his true identity remains unknown. Sources who have requested not to be named have indicated that items found on the dead man link him to the Austro-Hungarian Empire.

In Columbia, President Armstrong called for an investigation of the Spazi, asking how the nation's security service could allow a former official to be almost assaulted or murdered.

Speaker Hartpence responded by calling a meeting with top officials of the Sedition Prevention and Security Service.

Ambassador Schikelgruber responded by denying that the dead man had any connection to the Austro-Hungarian Empire.

Public perception—that was the key. It didn't matter what really happened in politics, but what people believed happened. Still, vanBecton would be out to nail my hide, preferably somewhere very dark and unpleasant, that is, if Ralston didn't get me—and Llysette—first. I had to act quickly, but not too stupidly. It's wonderful to be so well liked and wanted. The last paragraph had someone's twist.

Former minister Eschbach, no stranger to controversy from his links to the Colonel Nord incident and the man at the center of the strange occurrences at the university, was not available for comment.

That was disturbing, because I clearly was available when the paper had been put to bed—or had vanBecton and company blocked my wireset? I wouldn't have known. I hadn't tried to call anyone after my comments to the Asten and Vanderbraak papers.

"Here are your noodles," offered the smiling hostess, who apparently doubled as waitress. "And your bread."

Along with the noodles and bread came four thick slabs of cheese—white cheddar, yellow cheddar, Gouda, and a double Gloucester—and cauliflower smothered in processed cheese.

"Thank you."

I forced myself to eat most of the noodles, but I couldn't finish the cheeses or the bread.

"Would you like any dessert? More chocolate?"

"No, thank you."

The heavy lunch came to three-fifty, and I left a dollar tip before I lumbered out to the Stanley.

There really wasn't that much I could do except keep driving, not until I got to the Federal District. Once I left New Ostend and entered New Jersey on the Teaneck Parkway, I had to slow down because the parkway was so rough in spots. That was probably because Speaker Colmer had choked off most road payments to New Jersey more than a decade before, when the incidence of ghosts along newer highways rose as the number of Corsican "family" members precipitously dropped.

Governor Biaggi had protested, but the Speaker refused even to meet with him, politely declining on the grounds that federal grants could not be dictated by local political concerns. That was right after Colmer had met with Governor Espy, the youngest governor ever from the state, and increased the road payments to Mississippi.

It might have been coincidence, but Biaggi dropped his protests and the Spazi dropped their investigation of Governor Biaggi's brother's contracting business.

Around ten that night, my eyes burning, I finally gave up, after winding down past Philadelphia and skirting Baltimore. It had been a long day, after too many days and worries with too little sleep. I wasn't likely to sleep any longer in the future, either, not after I reached my immediate destination.

In a town named Elioak, which I'd never heard of, about forty miles north of Columbia City, I found a motor hotel, not quite seedy, the kind that Vic, my transitional identity, could have afforded. I took a room and walked across the street to the chrome-plated diner meant to be a replica of the Western Zephyr. It wasn't a very good replica. One waitress lounged behind the green-tiled counter, a gray rag in her hand, listlessly watching two white-haired men in the corner booth.

"Fiske could stop any shot, even Ohiri's . . . big lug broke Rissjen's wrists . . ."

"Still remember Summerall . . . got around anybody . . . big reason big Ben never got that hundredth shutout."

"Ben was overrated. Take what's-his-name—the blond guy with the bad legs, played for the New Ostend Yanks for a year. Even he got one in the nets . . ."

I slumped into the worn green leather of a booth for two, on the side where I could watch the door, and glanced at the dark-speckled menu as I waited for the woman to slouch from behind the counter.

"What will you be having, sir?"

"Number four, heavy on the gravy, and make sure it's hot. Black tea." I set the menu back in the holder with a thump.

"Number four, hauler style." A minute later she returned and set down the chipped white mug of tea. "Don't see no rig," she offered.

"No rig. Woolen mill rig, up north. Just on the way to visit my sister. She lives outside pretty city."

"You going to make that tonight?"

"No reason. Don't get along with her man. He's on the road tomorrow. Dumb bastard." I shrugged. "She's happy. I don't mess, but I don't put up with that crap."

"Takes all kinds."

I nodded and sipped the tea—bitter with a coffee aftertaste, just the way most haulers liked it, even in England. I could drink it without wincing, and that was about all I could manage, but the taste made it easy to look sullenly at the smears on the table's varnish.

The fried steak was far better than the tea, and the mashed potatoes didn't even have lumps. The gravy was almost boiling, but the beans looked—and tasted—like soggy green paperboard. I doused them in the gravy and left a clean plate.

"Don't know how you haulers eat them beans. Tried 'em. Taste like green pasteboard to me." The sad-eyed waitress with the incipient jowls shook her head slowly. "You want any dessert?"

"What's good?"

"Banana cream pie. Best thing Al makes."

"One slice and more tea."

"Haulers . . . guts like iron tubs."

Since it had been a long day since my heavy noodle lunch and a light and early breakfast, my stomach hadn't been all that discerning. Then again, maybe lunch had put it in shock. The pie was good, certainly far better than the beans or the tea, and actually had a taste vaguely resembling bananas.

I did manage to lock the room door before dropping almost straight into a too soft bed that felt more like a hammock than a bed. But Vic wouldn't have minded, and I was too tired to care.

CHAPTER TWENTY-THREE

• • •

The Albert Pick House had seen better days, probably back when it had been the Columbian flag hotel of the Statler chain, but it was still clean, and my room was three floors up, high enough to be off the street, low enough for some forms of emergency exit, not that I really wanted that. The videolink set was small. I supposed it worked, but I hadn't bothered to check. Somehow even I wasn't desperate enough to sit and watch video.

With its fake Virginia plates, the steamer was safe enough in the hotel lot. They were actually copies of real plates, but since the originals were still in place on another Stanley, it wasn't likely that anyone would care. I also had Maryland plates and a set from New Ostend racked inside the false trunk, all three sets made up in earlier, even more paranoid days after Elspeth's death and right after I'd purchased the Stanley.

My timing had been lousy, since there was no practical way to do what I needed to on a weekend. So all I could do was scout and plan and ensure that everything would go like clockwork on Monday. It wouldn't, of course, but planning helped reduce the uncertainty—and the worry.

Wearing the nondescript tan trench coat over my cheap, hard gray wool suit, a brush mustache, and a battered gray fedora, I left my closetlike room and walked down the hall. I noted the black plate across the lock of the room two doors down and wondered how long the hotel had been forced to seal it. After all, they couldn't very well rent a haunted room to paying guests.

I entered the elevator, nodding at a young man with lipstick on his cheek and a cravat not quite cinched up to his collar. He hadn't shaved, but he looked happy as he left the elevator in the lobby. I hefted the battered sample case that contained the documents I needed as well as several other items, and strolled across the not-quite-threadbare imitation Persian carpet.

The Bread and Chocolate pastry shop across the street provided two heavy nut rolls and bitter tea. I sipped and chewed until I finished all three and my stomach stopped growling.

Then I slowly walked up Fifteenth Street, turning northwest on New Bruges and pausing for a moment in Ericson Circle. The gray of my clothes fit right in with the sky and my mood. I had plenty of time, and there was no reason to hurry. I could have driven, but you don't get the same feel for things when you're insulated inside a steamer.

The pigeons looked at me from under every gray-painted lamppost, but they were city pigeons and didn't move unless you almost stepped on them. Before long I reached Dupont Circle. The fountain in the circle had been drained and contained only dampened leaves, leaves that would have been removed had the fountain been in the square in Vanderbraak Centre or even in New Amsterdam or Asten, cities that they were. More pigeons skittered around the base of the fountain, and two old men leaned over a stone chess table like weathered statues.

A block up on New Bruges Avenue, holiday-sized flags were flying from both the Chung Kuo embassy and the embassy of Imperial Japan, across the avenue from each other just as they were across the Sea of Japan from each other.

According to my research, vanBecton lived in the upper Bruges area, uphill and behind the embassies. It was a long walk from downtown, but I needed the exercise, and the feel, and sitting around a hotel room would have driven me crazier. So I kept walking, keeping my eyes out for what I needed.

One thing I wanted to find was the local power substation. In Columbia City they're generally disguised as houses, and most passersby don't give them a second thought. You can tell by the power lines, though. On a dead-end half-street off Tracy Place, I found the substation that probably served vanBecton's house before I located the house itself.

At first glance, the substation didn't look much different from a normal, boxy, white-brick attempt at Dutch colonial, but there was a sloppiness in the off-white trim paint, a hopelessness in the way the lace curtains in the false windows were so precisely placed, and an un-lived-in air that permeated everything from the evenly placed azaleas to the cobwebs linking the porch pillars to the white bricks.

To me, those were more apparent than the faint humming or the power lines that spread from the brick-walled backyard.

I paused, resting my left leg on the low stone wall that contained the raised lawn, and balanced my battered case on my leg while I opened it and pretended to check the papers inside. I was actually studying the substation, making a few written notes and a lot more mental ones.

There were definite advantages to working in more affluent areas, and I intended to make use of every one of them. With my notes taken, I walked along the hilly, tree-lined streets.

Some houses had perfectly raked lawns and white-painted trim that gleamed, betraying the more northern origin of their owners. On others, especially those with pillars, the white paint almost seemed designed to peel, giving an aura of the lost South, the time that had begun to fade with Speaker Calhoun's machinations.

Senator Lincoln only applied the last nails to the coffin, nails that had led to his murder by Booth, the Anglophilic actor. And yet, despite the fall of slavery and its lifestyle, vampirelike, the essence of the English south still seemed to drift through the Federal District, especially in fog, twilight, and rain.

On a cold hard fall day, more like winter, those houses seemed as out of place as a painted old courtesan at dawn.

I kept walking until I found Thorton Place, and vanBecton's house. It was about as I had imagined it—an elegant, impeccably manicured, false Georgian town house with real marble pillars and slate walks and steps.

I didn't appear to look at his house, instead sketching his neighbor's side garden on a plain piece of paper while I continued studying the false Georgian. There were sensors mounted inconspicuously in various places. I really wasn't interested in the sensors but in the positions of the wireset and power lines. The large maple with the overhanging limbs offered some intriguing possibilities.

After I finished the sketch and some brief notes, I made my way back down Newfoundland, the other cross artery leading back to Dupont Circle, and a memorial of sorts. The debate over that state's admission had nearly led to war with both England and France, and only the advance of the Austrians on Rome had held off what could have been a catastrophe. Quebec still made threatening sounds about Newfoundland, sounds guaranteed mostly to extract trade concessions from Columbia.

Many of the houses on Newfoundland Avenue date from the fifties, with glass bricks and angular constructions that seem to lean toward the sidewalks. Nothing is so dated as past modernism. The demolition crew working on an old "modern" mansion confirmed that, as did my sneezes at the dust. Two empty steam haulers waited to be loaded with debris, and I had to cross the street to the eastern side to get back down to Dupont Circle.

When I finished sneezing, I stopped by Von Kappel and Sons, Stationers, where I browsed through the rag and parchment specialty items, finally selecting a heavy off-cream paper with a marbled bluish-green border. I also bought two dozen large envelopes, the ten-by-thirteen-inch kind with accordion pleats that can hold nearly a hundred pages of documents. The bill for the fifty sheets of classy marbled paper, two dozen matching envelopes, and the bigger document envelopes totaled $49.37.

The clerk didn't quite sniff at my half-open trench coat and cheap wool suit, but he said as little as possible. "Your change, sir."

"Thank you." I put the bag under my arm and made my way across the circle.

Babbage-Copy was at the corner of Nineteenth and N, and they had machines and printers you could rent by the hour.

The balding young clerk put his thumb in his economics textbook and flipped a switch on his console. "Ten dollars. That's for two hours. Copies are five cents a page on the impact printer." He handed me a metal disk. "Put that in the control panel and bring it back here when you're done. Take machine number six."

He was back taking notes on a yellow lined pad even before I sat down. Why, with all the Babbage machines around, didn't he use one for his notes? There was no telling. Some authors still write longhand, although I can't see why. Maybe they're masochists.

Still, I had to set up the week, and that meant starting with a simple one-page introduction—something to tease the reporters. I had some ideas, but it took me several drafts before I had a usable piece.

WHAT IS THE REAL PSYCHIC RESEARCH STORY?

A worldwide wave of fires and bombings has struck Babbage research centers dealing with psychic research. Every major political and religious figure has publicly deplored this violence, yet violence on such a scale is highly unlikely without the resources of some form of organization. Consider these issues:

What organization(s) or government(s) have an interest in preventing psychic research? Why?

Why are militarily related projects the majority of targets?

What has been the goal of such research?

Why has no information on the specific research projects and their results ever been made public?

What role has the Defense Ministry played?

What have the president's budget examiners discovered, and why has that information not been released?

Further specific information will be forthcoming in response to the crisis.

The Spirit Preservation League

That no Spirit Preservation League existed was immaterial. It would, and certainly none of the organized religions were likely to gainsay its purpose.

Then I drafted the Spirit Preservation League announcements that would precede and follow—I hoped—the coming week's actions, assuming that vanBecton and Ralston didn't find me before I found them.

After I got all those completed, I had to hand-feed the marbled stationery to the printer. It jammed a couple of times, but I managed to get the paper feed straightened out, although it ruined several sheets of the impossibly expensive paper. I kept those—no sense in leaving unnecessary traces anywhere. Then I played with the machine to see if I could get a script facsimile, and it wasn't too bad. So I printed the necessary names on the envelopes.

Coming after the cheap and shoddy diatribe of the Order of Jeremiah, I trusted the contrast in tone and the clearly high-quality, expensive stationery would begin to plant the idea that more than a few individuals, crazy and not so crazy, were concerned about the political games being played around the question of psychic research.

After finishing the high-quality printing, I used the copier to make up ten sets of documents in two separate sets. I could only see a need for six, but if I had an opportunity to distribute extras, I wanted those extras handy. All the documents went in the case. No one looks at papers, and they wouldn't look at mine either, unless they knew who I was. In that case, I was probably dead anyway.

During the whole procedure, the clerk never looked my way. He did check the meters, though, when I returned to the turnstile to leave.

"Those extra runs on the printer are a nickel each."

All in all, another fifteen dollars gone, but money well spent, I trusted. With that cheerful thought in mind, and with very tired feet, I took a cab down to the Smithsonian, but I bypassed the Dutch Masters and went instead to the Museum of Industry and Technology. Even when you've seen it all, there's something incredible about it—Holland's first submersible, the first Curtiss aeroplane, the first flash boiler that made the steamer competitive with the Ford petrol car, the Stanley racer that smashed the two-hundred-mile-per-hour mark, the first steam turbine car pioneered by Hughes.

After I marveled at the wonders of technology, I did cross the Mall, looking past the B&P station to the Capitol, white against the gray clouds, to an art gallery, the Harte, which contained mostly modern works. They had a new exhibit, strange sketches by someone named Warhol. I wasn't that impressed.

So I took a trolley back up to the Albert Pick House and collapsed onto the bed for a nap. I didn't wake up until after sunset, when the comparative silence disturbed me. I took another shower and put on a clean shirt and underclothes but the same hard wool suit, and headed to the elevator, where I joined a couple on the lurching descent to the lobby. They both smelled of cheap cigarettes, and I left them behind almost as rudely as my attire would have dictated, quickly checking the full-length mirror before moving past the desk and toward the street. I looked like Peter Hloddn, all right, worn around the edges, not quite haunted.

Trader Vic's was less than a block away, but it was too expensive and too high-class for Hloddn, the traveling ledger-man. Instead, I walked two blocks to a place whose name was lost in the neon swirls meant to spell it out. Inside, the dark wood and dim lights confirmed my initial impression of a tavern, not quite cheap enough for a bar, nor good enough to be a restaurant. I slipped into a side booth for two.

About half the men in the tavern wore working flannel; the rest wore cheap suits or barely matched coats and trousers. The women wore trousers and short jackets, and their square-cut hair made their faces harder than the men's.

At the far end of the narrow room, two singers, one at the piano and the other a woman with a guitar, crooned out a semblance of a melody.

"Drink?" asked the waitress.

"Food?"

She slipped an oblong of cardboard in front of me. From it, I learned that I was in "The Dive." It didn't take long to decide on what to eat.

"How are the chops?"

"Steak pie's better."

"I'll take it and a light draft." I almost asked for Grolsch, but that would have been out of character. The almost-slip bothered me. It wouldn't have happened ten years earlier.

"Morris all right?"

"Fine."

The beer came immediately, and I took a sip, but not much more. I hadn't eaten anything since the morning, one reason I'd probably collapsed. For once I hadn't even felt that hungry. But not eating was stupid in the current situation, and I intended to eat just about everything that came with the steak pie.

Like all of the men in flannel, and some of those in working suits, I sang the chorus with the singers, careful to slur the edges of the words and swing the heavy glass stein, trying to ignore the incongruity of steins and Old West country songs composed in the last decade or so.

"Favorite rails and dim-lit places,
nine of crowns and spade of aces,
let me drink away the pain,
let me ride that evening train.

"And let those boxcars roll!
Make my point and save my soul . . ."

The pianist was good, but he certainly wasn't any Edo de Waart, either.

"Here you go." The waitress set the steak pie, wide fried potato strips, and boiled brussel sprouts in front of me.

"Thank you." I began to eat, not caring especially that the singing duo had taken a break. The steak pie was good, the potatoes fair, and the brussels sprouts a decent imitation of sawdust dipped in turpentine. I ate it all and finished the amber beer in the process.

No sooner had I set down the stein than the waitress was there. "You want another Morris?"

"Please."

She was back in instants with another stein. "The whole thing comes to ten."

I handed her ten and a silver dollar.

"Thanks, Sarge."

I nodded and looked at the amber liquid, ignoring the "Sarge." The second

Morris had to last for a while. So I sipped it slowly, the only way I could now that my stomach was nearly full.

One of the less square-faced women, probably younger than me but looking older despite the dyed black hair, glanced from an adjoining table.

I smiled sadly and shrugged, implying that I was lonely but not exactly flush. The green-rimmed eyes studied my cheap dark suit, and she slipped away from the other woman and eased into the other side of the booth. She carried her own stein, half-full.

"Lonely, mister?"

"Peter. Peter Hloddn at your service. Best damned ledgerman on the East Coast—no . . . You can see that's not true." I set down the glass stein just hard enough to shake the dark-varnished oak top a bit. "I sell enough to make ends meet, not enough to support a wife, and that's good because I don't have one, and I couldn't support her when I did."

"Thel. Thel Froehle. You come here often?" She set the half-full stein on the damp wood. All the wood was damp, despite the antique hot-air furnace that rumbled from somewhere beneath the bar.

"No. I can't pay for many overpriced beers. The company doesn't pay for much beyond the room, and I can't always sit and look at the videolink."

"You could go down to the Mall and look at the pictures."

"I could. Sometimes I do, like today, when I'm here on Saturdays." I took a sip of warm beer from the stein, and it tasted more like lacquer the warmer it got. I guess I'm not really Dutch, despite the genes, because I'm not fond of warm beer or beer you have to chew. "How many times can you look at pictures?"

"I like pictures." She shook the thick dark hair that was probably blond beneath the color. Blonds had been out of fashion for almost a decade with the reappearance of the "ghost" look—pale skin set off by dark hair.

"So do I, but I like people better. Pictures don't talk."

"Sometimes it's better when people don't talk."

She had me there, and I tried not to shrug, instead taking a gulp from the stein.

"You drink that fast, and that stuff will kill you."

"Something will. Not going to get out of life alive anyway."

"No." Thel took a small swallow from her stein and licked a touch of foam off her lips with the tip of her tongue. "No reason to bury your face in the suds. You ought to look at what's happening on the trip."

"The old life's-a-journey business. My wife always said we should go first class. She tried, and I went broke, and she left."

"You're cheerful."

"Sorry." Except I wasn't, exactly. My problem was that I saw what was happening, and I didn't like it, no matter how it turned out.

"Cheer up. Things could be worse." She took another swallow from her stein.

I forced a smile in return. I didn't feel like it, since it seemed like every time I started to cheer up, things had gotten worse. "They could be. They have been. Suppose I should be grateful." I sipped the Morris. "You grow up around here?"

"No. New Ostend. Came here with the B and P when they closed the New Amsterdam office."

"Still work for them?"

"Hardly. I work for a legal office down on Fifteenth. It pays the rent."

"Why'd you leave the railroad?"

She gave me a sad smile. "Ghosts. You know how many people died in that accident last year? Half of them seem to haunt the offices."

I had to frown. Ghosts usually stayed near where they died.

"See, when the train crashed through the platform, it was a mess, so they carted some of them upstairs into the offices. Maybe three or four died right there." She shivered. "Don't seem right. Poor souls can't even stay near friends or family."

"Maybe it'd be better if they'd died sudden."

"I don't know." This time her swallow was a healthy one.

"Read something about the government trying to stop ghosts. Think that would have helped? Would you have stayed there if the office wasn't haunted?"

"Frig the government. Always messing with people. Ought to leave the damned souls alone. Leave us all alone."

"Yeah." I sighed.

"They don't make it easy, do they?" she asked.

I shook my head. They certainly didn't.

She gave me a smile, and stood, her empty stein in her hand. "See you around, Sarge."

Did I really look like an undercover watch officer? Or was that just familiarity? Did it matter, or would it throw off vanBecton's boys?

Since I didn't know, I staggered back to my small, cold room. I would have liked to call Llysette, but that would have been one of the dumbest things I could have done, and I wasn't that stupid or desperate—not yet.

CHAPTER TWENTY-FOUR

• • •

Waking up with a headache in a crummy small hotel room to the sound of air hammers on the street below is not recommended for health, sanity, or a cheerful outlook on life. Then again, why should my outlook have been particularly cheerful?

Ralston McGuiness and Gillaume vanBecton both wanted me out of the way. Hans Waetjen either had orders to frame me for a pair of murders or was being set up so that it was in his interest to do so. My lover had turned cold toward me, or I thought she had, and the family ghost was quoting Shakespeare and old songs at me, or I thought she was. I really couldn't drink, but I'd eaten and drunk too much the night before, or I thought I had. And now I needed to roam through George-town to set up a rather improbable scenario that I would have instantly rejected if I'd been my own supervisor back in my Spazi days.

Outside, the sky was cheerfully blue, and the light hammered at my closed eyelids when the air hammers didn't. Construction on Sunday? Why not? After all, this was Columbia, land of free enterprise, and a dollar to whoever provided the best service, Lord's day or not.

Finally I staggered into the bathroom in an attempt to deal with attacks on all internal systems. After that, I tried not to groan while I stood under the hot shower. That was hard because the water temperature jumped from lukewarm to scalding and back again, sort of like my life in recent weeks.

I wore flannel and worn khakis when I left the room. No ledgerman would waste his good suit on an off Sunday.

The Bread and Chocolate across the street was closed, but I found a hole-in-the-wall a block up and around the corner, Brother George's. Brother George's poached eggs were just right, and the toast wasn't burned. I still almost choked be-cause the cigarette smoke was so thick, and I burned my tongue with the chocolate because I was trying not to cough from the smoke.

After breakfast, all of two dollars, which you couldn't beat, even for all the smoke that still clung to me, I took the Georgetown trolley out to Thirty-third and M. I should have worn a jacket, but I hadn't brought anything except the trench coat—a definite oversight on my part, but under stress you don't always think of everything you need. I hoped I hadn't left anything really important behind, but I probably had. I just didn't know what it was.

In Georgetown, I had to scout out Ralston McGuiness's place, and then I had to begin my engineering—heavy engineering.

When I got off the trolley, I shivered for the first two blocks uphill, but walk-ing quickly seemed to help, and by the third I was doing all right, and I had no trouble finding Ralston's place. His name had been in the wireset book, unlike vanBecton's, which had taken some creativity to obtain.

His home was a modest town house off P Street, if a three-story brick town house in rococo dress with a screened half-porch off to the side could be classed as modest. That section hadn't really been fully gentrified, and Ralston took the trol-ley to and from the Presidential Palace and walked the four blocks each way virtu-ally every day. He'd mentioned that walk in one of his attempts to prove he was just a normal person.

People like Ralston didn't have to worry about security, mostly because no one knew why they would possibly need it. After all, why would a president's special assistant for fiscal review need security protection? And Ralston certainly wouldn't want to advertise that what he was doing was so vital to the presidency that he needed such protection.

The small yard was landscaped carefully, including an ornate boxwood hedge that paralleled the front walk and a dwarf apple tree only fifteen feet from the low front stoop.

I walked past on the other side of the street and went up far enough to see the edge of Dumbarton Oaks before I turned around. It's a private park now, with an art gallery, and the proceeds go to The University—Mister Jefferson's University.

My feet were beginning to hurt, probably because walking on brick and stone sidewalks is harder than running country lanes. I sat down on a trolley bench—serving the upper Georgetown branch that doesn't connect directly with downtown but swings across to New Bruges Avenue and descends to Dupont Circle where you have to transfer. Was what I planned right? Probably not, but what van-Becton and Ralston planned wasn't either, and while two wrongs don't make a right, they might equal survival.

I snorted, feeling cold again, and stood. I began to walk downhill once more with the determined stride of the serious walker, taking in everything I could as I marched by his house. I nodded to the well-dressed couple entering a Rolls-Royce sedan, clearly headed for church, probably the National Cathedral. They actually nodded back, and the white-haired lady offered me a smile.

That wasn't the end of it. I scouted the alleys a bit, just to make sure, before I walked back to the trolley and headed back toward home away from home—the fabulous Albert Pick House.

After I left the trolley on Pennsylvania and Fifteenth, I got a bratwurst from a street cart outside the Presidential Palace, and ate it as I walked down nearly deserted Pennsylvania Avenue. The bratwurst would lead to more indigestion, probably, but I didn't want to collapse the way I had Saturday.

I paused at vanBuren Place, north of the Presidential Palace, when I saw a flicker of white in the shadows. A man in a formal coat ran through the east gate, literally through the wooden bars—it was a good thing they weren't iron—and stopped on the grass. He turned and lifted his hands, as if to surrender, before exploding into fragments of white.

I frowned. The scene recalled something, but what, I couldn't remember. A man surrendering and being gunned down. Now his ghost seemed doomed to relive it, time after time. But who had it been? I shook my head and turned toward the hotel. I had a few more pressing problems than recalling modern or ancient history.

The doorman at the Albert Pick definitely sniffed as I went through, but who was he kidding?

I had the elevator to myself. Once back in my room, I put on the coveralls and the beard. Then I had to wait for the maids to work their way around the corner before I took the service stairs down to the car park. Since there wasn't any attendant on duty on Sundays, I didn't have to worry about how I looked taking the Stanley out—just so long as I didn't look like me.

This time I drove up New Bruges and took California, winding around and crossing the area several times. I wanted to be more familiar with the street patterns before Monday night. I didn't go near vanBecton's place, but straight to the false Dutch colonial that was the power substation. Out came the toolbox with a few items, like plastique from the equipment bag, carefully eased inside. They say you can do anything with plastique except play with sparks, but I still treat things that can blow you apart with respect. It can't hurt.

The locks, both of them, were straightforward, and I was inside in not too much longer than a key would have taken.

Determining the best way to blow a substation isn't as easy as it sounds, since the walls are thick and I'd have to run an antenna that couldn't be seen to where it could pick up the LF signal from the street. Most probably no one would be by to check the station—detailed inspections don't occur every day—but I couldn't take that chance.

In the end I opted for what you might call hidden overkill, with far more plastique than I needed, because I had to hide it. Then I relocked the door and walked briskly to the Stanley and drove away.

Down on Newfoundland, not too far out, I found a chicken place, Harlan's, which featured a sign caricaturing a southern colonel and food caricaturing fried chicken. I sat at a small plastic-topped table, balancing on a hard stool, and munched through the chicken. What I got was filling, although I wondered how I'd feel later.

I should have taken my time, because I needed to wait until it was dark for the next step, and because I began to feel like combining bratwurst and chicken hadn't been the smartest of gastronomical moves. Instead, I drove out to the zoo, used the public facilities, and looked at penguins. Most people like them, but I feel sorry for them, trapped in their formal wear with nowhere to go and no understanding of what life is all about once they've been removed from their habitat—like a lot of people in the Federal District.

Then I took the Stanley out toward where we had lived, but the firs were taller, and the Gejdensons had added a room and put up a big stone wall around the backyard. I drove by only once, and I didn't slow down. Instead, I turned on the radio to the all-news station.

". . . Mayor Jefferson has requested an increase in federal payments earmarked for crime prevention. The mayor claimed the increases were necessary to combat the growing use of weapons in street crime and in Federal District schools. Speaker Hartpence's office has indicated the Speaker will give the mayor's request full consideration in the next budget."

I shook my head.

". . . at the half, the Redskins are down to Baltimore by two goals. The amazing John Elway scored twice, once from barely past midfield. George stopped more than a dozen shots, but couldn't deny Elway . . ."

Who knew, maybe Elway would replace the legend of Chiri. As the twilight deepened, I turned around and headed toward the Arlington Bridge back into Columbia City.

"Ambassador Schikelgruber will meet with Foreign Minister Gore tomorrow to discuss the issue of placing the second fleet in Portsmouth, England, a step regarded as, quote, 'uniquely hostile,' by the Emperor Ferdinand . . ."

I eased the steamer up California Street and toward vanBecton's house. What I needed to do was simple: just set the plastique in the joint of a tree limb so that it would drop the limb across the power line to the vanBectons'. What I needed was a brace and bit, plastique, a detonator, and no spectators.

The first three were in the trunk. The obstacle to the fourth was a couple parked in an old blue steamer with a huge artificial grille—probably a mideighties DeSoto. Since they were parked practically next to the tree I was targeting, all I could do was drive two blocks away and park . . . and park.

After a while I drove up and down Newfoundland for a time, listening to the all-news radio.

"Elway scored three goals and made the key passes leading to two more as the Redskins lost their fourth straight . . . national korfball team faces the Austro-Hungarian team Monday night in New Amsterdam . . . weather tomorrow, clear and unseasonably cold."

I drove back past the end of the street, but the damned blue DeSoto still sat there. I took another spin out New Bruges Avenue, this time checking out Summer Valley and the new storefronts out that way, still half listening to the radio as I drove.

"To find the additional funds, Mayor Jefferson proposed a reduction in the snow removal budget . . ."

Why not, I reflected. No one in Columbia City could drive on snow anyway.

Then I turned over the back bridge to Georgetown and drove around Ralston's area. I decided to see how I did in the dark. I did fine, and by the time I got back to vanBecton's street, the damned DeSoto was finally gone, and half the upstairs lights in the nearby houses were already off.

After all the driving, setting the plastique was almost anticlimactic. All I did was climb the tree, use the brace and bit, fill the hole and set the detonator, and pat it smooth—and hope that no child found it before the next night.

I was exhausted by the time I climbed the hotel's service stairs and sneaked back into my room. I was also so sweaty that I took a shower. Of course, there were no messages. There seldom were, even at home.

CHAPTER TWENTY-FIVE

• • •

Before I left my hotel room Monday morning, I put together the two press packets. The first contained copies of the two letters from "Branston-Hay" to Minister Holmbek and copies of the news stories with my name in them. They were thin—and that was the purpose. It had to appear to the reporters that I was on to something but just couldn't carry it off myself.

The second was the follow-on package from the "Spirit Preservation League," the one I needed to personally send later in the day, after I'd hand-delivered the first classy set of announcements.

After another breakfast of two too many sweet rolls and more bitter tea from Bread and Chocolate, I returned to my room, pasted a goatee in place, and put on a better, tailored suit, covered with my less reputable trench coat when I left the hotel. Two blocks down the street, I took off the coat and folded it over my arm, hailing a cab.

"Where to, sir?"

"Fifteenth Street entrance of the *Post-Dispatch*."

It took less than an hour for the four quick drops—at the *Post-Dispatch,* the *Evening Star,* the *Monitor,* and the RPI wire service.

Only the *Monitor* reception desk clerk looked at me and asked, "What is it?"

"Purely social, my dear," I answered in my driest and haughtiest accent.

I gave the driver a ten for the entire trip—a five-dollar fare—regretted publicly my lack of dispatch in not dealing with the whole sordid matter earlier, and in general behaved like an overconcerned upper-class ninny.

That done, I put the trench coat back on and walked the two blocks back to the hotel, passing vanBuren Place. The ghost was nowhere to be seen, but two gray-haired men played checkers on one of the stone benches. A young woman, probably a ministry clerk, sat silently sobbing on a corner bench under a juniper. I wanted to console her, but how could I tell a complete stranger things would be all right, especially when I was working to ensure they wouldn't be for some people, just to save my own skin?

I took a deep breath and walked on, reclaiming the Stanley from the hotel lot. I drove out toward Maryland, turning onto Georgia Avenue until I reached the big Woodward and Vandervaal, where I pulled into the public lot. The sky was clouding up, and raindrops sprinkled the windscreen. There was a public wireset in a kiosk behind the hedges, open to the car park but not to Georgia Avenue.

I swallowed and dialed vanBecton's office.

"Minister vanBecton's office."

"This is Doktor Eschbach. Is he in?"

"Ah, well, Doktor . . ."

"Yes or no? If you have time to trace this, so do the people he doesn't want to trace it."

"Just a moment, sir."

The transfer was smooth.

"Where are you, Johan?"

"On my way down to see you, provided I can get there without getting torn up in the process."

"You expect me to believe that?"

"Why not? You know very well who else wants me in out of the cold, so that I can be put coldly away."

"And we're supposed to save you from that folly? Dream on."

"Absolutely. And I have some goodies for you to persuade you to let me do just that. I'll wire you again, and you can let me know."

I hung up, hoping the call would persuade vanBecton to wait just a bit. It also confirmed he was in town. I got back into the Stanley, paid for my brief stint in the car park, and headed back downtown through a misting drizzle. The traffic was heavier than I had recalled, with more horns honking, and even swearing and gestures from neighboring drivers, although not at me. At least, I didn't think so.

A frizzy-blond-haired girl in brown leathers—the country look, I gathered—drove a steam-truck over the median to pass a stalled green Reo. An oncoming hauler sideswiped a boxy old black Williams to avoid her, and she sailed down Georgia with an obscene gesture at the hauler. The rest of us crept by the mess, and I wiped my forehead. Sometimes traffic was worse than the trench-coat-and-wide-brimmed-hat business.

I put the Stanley back in the Pick House's car park and then walked down to the Hay-Adams and found a public wireline booth off the lobby. Like the Albert Pick House, the Hay-Adams had seen better days. Unlike the Pick House, the Adams still retained a touch of class, with the carved woodwork, the polished floors, and the hushed reverence and attentiveness of the staff.

The doorman had even bowed slightly to me, without a trace of condescension to my wrinkled trench coat. Of course, I wasn't wearing a cheap wool suit, either. Even the wireline booth had a wall seat with an upholstered velour cushion—deep green.

With my case in my lap, I put in the dime and dialed one number, but it just rang. So I tried a second. It rattled with a busy sound. The third got me an answer.

"Railley here."

"Matt, this is the Colonel Nord doktor. Don't mention my name out loud. Do you understand?"

"Yes."

"Are you interested in proof that the Speaker is playing both sides against the middle on the psychic research issue? And that the Defense Ministry is up to its eyeballs in this?"

"Shit, yes."

"Fine. You'll get it. In the meantime, ask yourself this question. Why is it that there have been very few of these Babbage bombings and fires until the Speaker formed his new government? Why does he want to use this issue against President Armstrong? What does he gain?"

"Hold it! What do you know about the Order of Jeremiah?"

"The what?" I lied.

"Order of Jeremiah. I got some trash from them claiming that the 'corrupt federal government' is attacking the spirits of their ancestors."

"What else is new?" I asked. "Every organized religion around has protested the government's psychic research efforts. They haven't gotten very far, though. The research seems to be going on." I paused, then added, "I've got to go. Watch for a package."

I hung up.

Then I called two more numbers, including Murtaugh at the *Evening Star,* with essentially the same message. Murtaugh didn't ask me about the Order of Jeremiah, and he'd probably dismissed it without reading it. Either that or he was playing it close to the waistcoat.

Neither asked me about the Spirit Preservation League, but given the volume of Monday offerings they received, I doubted that either had seen the envelopes, classy as they were. I would have liked to space things more, but time was something I just didn't have.

My briefcase felt heavier and heavier as I walked back to the hotel in the light rain that the radio hadn't forecast.

The entire situation was insane. To get out of the mess I was in, I was essentially going to have to give both the Speaker and the President what they wanted—except without my hide flayed over the package for wrapping paper. I didn't like either Speaker Hartpence or President Armstrong, but that wasn't the question. The question was who could do more damage, and the answer to that was clear enough.

Ahead in the shadows of the alley off L, people dodged toward the street, apparently leaving an open space. As I approached, I saw why. The ghost of a child, probably not more than five, screamed for his mother, his hands stretched up toward the iron fire ladder above. My guts twisted, and my eyes burned. I watched tears stream down the face of a heavyset, well-dressed black woman. She just stood and looked, and I wondered if the child had been hers and what had happened.

Finally I walked on, thinking about the child ghost. He was certainly a disruption, probably unwanted by everyone except his mother. Probably all the major powers had some way of getting rid of unwanted ghosts, yet no one was implementing the technology on a wide scale. Why not?

First there was the religious angle. Ferdinand didn't want to offend the Roman Catholic Church or the Lutherans, or take on the Apostolic Eastern Catholic Church. Speaker Hartpence certainly didn't want to take on everyone from the Mormons to the Roman Catholics, and Emperor Akihito wouldn't want to disrupt the ancestor worship that was still prevalent; nor would the warlords and the emperor of Chung Kuo.

Second was the practical angle. Ghosts kept wars smaller and less expensive. The ghost angle probably was one of the things that had restricted the deployment of nuclear weapons.

Third was the fact that the present situation allowed for hidden and selective use of ghosting-related technologies, and a more obvious use of those technologies would not have been exactly well received, particularly in more open societies like Columbia or Great Britain.

In short, nobody wanted the genie out of the box, and that meant nobody was quite sure what was in anyone else's box.

Then there was the personal angle. Ghosts were perhaps the last contact with loved ones. Did any government really want to be perceived as severing that contact? What would the press say if the government wanted to take that child's ghost from his mother?

I stopped by the car park and locked my case in the trunk, after first removing the press packages and the goatee. The doorman at the Albert Pick didn't quite sniff at me and my buttoned-up trench coat as I carried my damp self back into the hotel and to my room. First I turned on the video to the all-news station. The talking heads discussed everything from the upcoming negotiations over Japanese nuclear submersible technology to the federal watch subsidy for Columbia City. There wasn't a word about ghosts or me. Although that wasn't conclusive, it helped settle my stomach, until I thought about what else I had to do. While I listened, I changed into the blue coveralls that could be a uniform for anything and fixed a short beard in place. As two impeccably groomed men exchanged views on the continuing landing-rights controversy between turbojets and dirigibles in every major air park in the country, I clicked off the set and listened at the hallway door.

When it appeared relatively silent, I slipped out carrying the press packages. I took the service stairs down to the lobby, where I just walked out to the street. This time the doorman didn't sniff at me; he merely ignored me.

The first stop was the *Post-Dispatch*. I walked in off Fifteenth Street with my stack of messages and a log sheet bound to the top.

"Envelope for Railley," I announced.

"We'll take it here," answered the bored desk clerk.

I offered the log sheet, which had two bogus entries above a group of empty lines. "Signature here, please."

She signed, and I handed over the envelope, marked CONFIDENTIAL. At least she didn't rip it open while I was standing there.

Then I took a trolley down and along Pennsylvania to the *Star* building, where I repeated the process.

By the time I finished with the press and the four wire services, I was soaked, even though the rain wasn't that heavy, and tired. Still, I took the service stairs back up to my room.

I dried off and changed back into my hard wool suit, except now I wore the special vest that was actually made of thin sheets of plastique covered with a thin coat of vinyl that could be peeled off. Neither odor detectors nor metal detectors will show anything besides a vest. It's hot, hell to wear in the summer, but in late fall, heat wasn't a problem. The plastic timer went into the compartment behind the big belt buckle. Then I reclaimed my trench coat and put the rest of my clothes in the garment bag. I descended officially—without beard—to the lobby, where I checked out, using cash and getting a frown from the clerk. After stowing the garment bag in the Stanley, I had a ham and rye sandwich at Brother George's, with more bitter tea, before getting the Stanley from the car park. In its dull, almost mottled gray guise, it looked rather like a company car, perhaps a shade too good but not that noticeably expensive.

I drove around the north side of the shabby train station—Union Station hadn't been kept up the way the B&P station had been—and parked about four blocks east of the Capitol. Then I stretched out in the back seat and took a nap. I could have done that at the hotel, except that single men who stay in their hotel rooms during the week are extremely suspect. More important, I wanted Peter Hloddn on the road before all hell broke loose. Even if the watch stopped and woke me, I could claim that, as a traveling ledgerman, I was resting between appointments.

Around four I sat up, not that rested, since I hadn't so much slept as dozed with a continuing thought to time. I locked the Stanley and took a trolley. The sky was clear again, and a chill wind blew out of the west.

All the Capitol limousines are housed in the top level of the underground New Jersey Avenue garage, and that is linked to the Roosevelt Office Building by a tunnel off the subbasement. Unlike the ministry buildings, the tunnels aren't guarded, just the outside entrances to the buildings and garages. Congressmen and congressladies don't like being stopped going to and from the Capitol building or anywhere else.

So I only had to get into the Capitol, which was easy enough on the last public tour, and then discard the visitor badge and replace it with my own badge, since guards only looked for government badges, not names, once you were inside. If I'd walked in with my own, I would have had to sign in. As a tourist, I'd had to show the Hloddn ID, but no one ever cross-checked. How could they with all the tourists?

I took the east side steps, the ones that have been restored with marble to replace the shoddy sandstone Washington sold to the first Congress, and I waited in line for fifteen minutes after signing in.

"First we'll be seeing the old court chambers. Now, stay with the group . . . The Capitol is very busy when the Congress is in session."

I lagged behind the group, and, once I was relatively alone in Statuary Hall, I bent down to tie my shoes and changed badges. After straightening, I folded my coat over my arm, adopted the diffident, hurried walk of an overburdened staffer, and marched back toward the Garfield Building.

I nodded politely at Congressman Scheuer, who was almost hobbling now but who refused to give up his seniority in the New Ostend delegation. He just looked blankly at me, wondering if he should know me or not, as I walked by.

The Speaker's day limousine was usually retired at five, and the smaller and less obvious evening one took him to the Speaker's House up at the Naval Observatory, or wherever else he went. Since he did little on Mondays, the odds were that the car would be wiped down and locked by five-thirty.

From the basement of the Garfield Building I took two tunnels until I got to the lower level of the garage, then waited in the corner, occasionally walking from one car to another as various staffers reclaimed their vehicles, until I was sure that limousine maintenance was finished.

Really, the only tricky part was easing myself down the half-wall behind the car. The guard in the front booth by the exit arch couldn't see the rear of the limousine, only the front. I'd figured that out years earlier, even recommended a change to Speaker Michel. That was my last assignment at Spazi headquarters. Michel hadn't paid any attention, not that he paid much attention to anything but the hauling and machine tool industries, and that might have been why he'd lasted one term as Speaker. No Speaker since had paid any attention to the recommendation, either, and that made things easier.

So I crouched behind the dark blue limousine and stripped off my coat and vest. There are two ways to use plastique, and most amateurs don't understand that. Instead, they compensate for their lack of knowledge by using enough to destroy a city block, and sometimes don't even get their target.

If you do it the right way, there's a surprisingly small radius of destruction, but it's rather effective. Then there was what I was doing, which was to create the impression of damage without doing much. After all, my purpose wasn't really to kill anybody—even the Speaker.

Basically it only took a few minutes to turn the vest into a flat sheet of plastique flared around the inside of the rear wheel cover and designed to blow out the wheel and some sheet metal. The gray melded with the undercoat and even covered the timer so that only an expert could tell.

I'd set the timer for about noon on Tuesday, but it wouldn't really matter one way or the other, so long as the plastique actually exploded. Normally the Speaker's limousine was parked right outside "his" door at the Capitol, all day long, guarded, of course, just in case he wanted to go somewhere. It didn't matter to me whether the limousine went anywhere or not. The ostensible point of the explosion was to serve notice on behalf of the Spirit Preservation League that the Speaker was vulnerable if he continued his covert war against ghosts.

The next set of letters to the press would arrive within the day.

After ducking back up to the higher level and wending my way back through one tunnel, I climbed to the main floor of the Garfield Building and exited, lifting my government badge to the bored guard. Nothing ever happens in the Congress; all they ever do is talk. The Speaker really makes the decisions, basically with the help of a few ministers and his personal staff. The guards know most members of Congress have no real power, and it shows.

The guard nodded at me, and I walked out and took a trolley back down Independence.

After walking to the Stanley, I moved it to another side street south of Independence and had an early supper at a Greek bistro I recalled. The memory was better than the food itself, but that's the way it is with memories sometimes. Of course, the waiters were all different, and I certainly looked different.

Then it was time to walk back to the Stanley and get ready. The first piece of business was to get the uniform out of the trunk and change in the back seat. Even if someone saw, what would they see? An off-duty watch officer struggling into his uniform?

The second piece of business was to mail the next set of press announcements at the main post centre. Even if they didn't arrive before the explosion, assuming no one detected the plastique, the postmark would show a degree of planning. If the plastique didn't work, I had more left and would have to cook up something else, probably larger and more deadly, like an explosion somewhere in the Capitol. That I could still manage, although I'd rather not have to try.

Posting the announcements was as simple as driving by the post building next to the shabby Union Station and dropping them in the box. I was becoming ever more glad that I had stocked up on stamps in Styxx before I had left New Bruges. My schedule was getting cramped, to say the least.

After posting the second round of classy announcements, I drove out Newfoundland and parked under a tree about a block from where I could see the approach to vanBecton's house.

It was dark when a limousine pulled up, the driver opened the door, and vanBecton stepped out and walked to the house. The limousine departed, and so did I, driving only a few blocks to the Dutch colonial that wasn't a house but a power substation. There all I had to do was send a signal.

The dull thump, the dust, the puff of smoke, and the house lights going out all around me confirmed that the plastique had done its job, or a reasonable facsimile thereof. But no one went running outside. Cities have so many noises that most people don't notice. Despite the cool evening I was sweating because I had the watch uniform on, except for the hat.

There's always someplace in the city where a big tree overhangs a power line, for all the effort to put the lines underground in conduits. On the hills several blocks north of Dupont Circle, off California Street, where the old money that's gone into government service resides, there are more than a few such trees, like the one I had fixed the night before almost next to vanBecton's house. I triggered the second detonator from a block away, and the tree limb crashed across an already dead power line and a not-so-dead wireline serving the vanBecton residence.

The question was one of speed, as much as anything else. I twisted the thermal switch under the dash, and the Stanley glimmered from dull mottled gray into a lighter, institutional gray. I pulled up in front of the vanBectons' in-city mansion, right where the limousine had been, and donned the watch hat. I left the engine on, walked quickly up the perfect marble-paved steps, and used the knocker, ignoring the bell button.

The door opened a crack.

"I am Officer Wendrew Westen. Are you Herr Gillaume vanBecton?"

Flickering candles backlit the young Federal Protective Officer at the door. "No. Can I help you, Officer?"

I looked doubtful, but answered, "Perhaps. It appears that the power failure . . . There is a large tree . . . Could you at least come and take a look?"

It was his turn to look doubtful. I just waited.

Finally he stepped back and called inside, "There's a problem, something to do with a tree and the power failure."

"Take care of it."

I managed not to grin at vanBecton's less than pleased words.

The young FedPro closed the door behind him and stepped onto the marble under the portico. "What's the problem?"

"It's right at the corner there." I turned and began to walk swiftly in the direction I had pointed.

He hurried after me, and I slipped the blackjack from my belt as I passed the Stanley and stepped around the trimmed yew tree and up to the mass of maple branches.

He never even saw the blackjack coming and went down like a steer in a slaughterhouse. He had a separate key in his belt, which I hoped was the house key, and I extracted the ring and dragged him partly under the tree branch, just to get him out of sight.

With a quick step I jogged back to the house and tried the front door. It wasn't locked. So I opened it and stepped inside. "Hello . . . hello?" I asked in a reasonable facsimile of a lower-toned and less cultured voice.

"What are you doing here?" VanBecton marched toward me. Behind him I could see a plump, silver-haired woman.

"What is the difficulty, William?"

"Officer Wendrew Westen, sir. The FedPro fellow, he tried to move the tree, sir, and he's trapped under it. Thought you'd want to wire for help."

"Wire for help? Isn't the tree what cut off the wireset?"

"Might be, sir," I offered helpfully.

"You idiot, how could I wire for help if the tree is what cut off the wireset?"

I frowned. "Do you want to look, sir?"

"No. I don't want to look. I want you to fix the problem."

Frau vanBecton stepped into the large hall, a space bigger than my study, though not all that much larger than the foyer and staircase had been in my own old Virginia place. She carried a candle lamp.

"Good evening, madame. Terribly sorry." I gave a bow that brought me closer to vanBecton.

VanBecton glowered at me as if I were the problem.

"Perhaps I should run down to the station and get some assistance." I took a step forward and half bowed.

"Dorcas, go check the set again," snapped vanBecton.

"Dear, I just checked it."

"Check it again."

"Yes, dear." She shuffled out of sight.

"Sir. I think you dropped your wallet." I stepped forward and pointed.

VanBecton couldn't help looking down, and I used the blackjack again, right across his temple, almost hard enough to crack his skull and kill him. That was the trouble with political appointees. They still didn't really know the tricks of the trade. All they could do was talk and order people around, and play games with people's lives without ever having paid the price themselves. And there was never any proof; so average citizens would think I was a soulless killer. How could they understand? They didn't want to.

After catching vanBecton and letting him down, I stepped into the parlor next to the briefcase that he had not moved when the power had failed.

"Dear . . . You're not William."

"He told me to wait here. He went upstairs for something."

She looked blank.

"Does the set work?"

"No."

"Are you sure?"

She looked down, and in the dim light I scooped up the case.

"I'm leaving, madame."

After walking into the hall and hoisting vanBecton's limp form, I barely staggered out the steps with him before she started screaming. I ignored the screams and stuffed him and the case in the rear seat of the Stanley and threw myself in front. I guided the steamer out of the small circular drive and away before the neighbors decided to investigate.

The drive out to University and the Woodward and Vandervaal car park was uneventful, as I had hoped. The store was closed on Monday evenings, but the lot was open and vacant. VanBecton was stirring by the time I trained the disassociator on him, but a full jolt to the brain dropped him. When he woke he would be a low-class zombie, and I was effectively a murderer for the fourth time, although the victims all still breathed and talked—if in monosyllables. Until he was ready to walk around, I covered him with the disreputable trench coat and went to work on his briefcase.

Although it took longer, I picked the lock on his case, because I needed the case looking untouched later. I riffled through the papers. Most were useless administrative trivia, not surprisingly since vanBecton would have been far too cautious to put something important on paper, and even if he had, it certainly wouldn't have been in a case he casually carried home.

Surprisingly, there *were* two documents I could use—a set of handwritten notes and the summary budget figures, not those with the line items which could obviously have been very embarrassing but those with the general categories. That would tie very nicely to the material I had already prepared.

The notes were mostly trivial except for one line, the one that read in his clear cursive, *"talks on deghosting—Holmbek and GH."* That just might be enough.

I slipped the cuffs around his wrists, just in case, pulled the lap robe from the holder behind the driver's seat, and threw it across his legs and shoes so that no one could see him. Then I pulled out of the car park and headed out University to the nearest Babbage Copy place.

A dozen copies of the key papers from vanBecton's case would be more than adequate, especially given the relatively selective distribution I would have to use.

There was only one other car behind the copy place, not surprisingly, since students were the big users and most just didn't have it together on Monday nights. That certainly hadn't changed between New Bruges and Maryland.

From the protection of the glassed-in operator's booth, a kinky-haired redhead with bleary eyes peered through her spectacles at the watch uniform. I could see my own faint reflection in the glass of the booth, the goatee and mustache still firmly in place.

I held up the folder. "I need a dozen copies of this."

She looked at the uniform.

"I'm paying. I'm off duty."

"Use machine number three." She handed me a metal counter. "Put that in the control panel and bring it back here when you're done."

I nodded.

She pressed a button, and the turnstile released. I walked into the long room toward the big "3" posted on the wall.

Making the copies and stapling them only took a few minutes. The total came to three dollars. I left her four and went back to the Stanley, still holding its light institutional-gray sheen.

In the lot, I rearranged papers, shuffling some into the next set of press packets from the Spirit Preservation League and saving some for later efforts.

After checking the still unconscious vanBecton, I drove steadily back toward

Georgetown, coming in down New Bruges and cutting across well above the turn in Rock Creek, just to make sure I didn't get anywhere close to the scene of my most immediate crime.

Ralston's neighborhood seemed calm, quiet, and I eased the Stanley under a tree a block away and cracked the window, just listening for a time. Then I drove by, but the place remained calm and quiet, as it should have.

I still didn't like what had to be done—but I liked even less the thought of my own death, and that seemed like the only alternative. Neither the President nor Ralston really wanted me around as an embarrassment. So I had to stop being a potential embarrassment, and that meant making a much bigger mess—and making sure my survival benefited them. Or that my demise would hurt them in ways they couldn't afford to be hurt. It's about the same thing either way.

After a short time, I drove the steamer around the block and parked down the way on the other side of the street, where the shadows partly cloaked the Stanley but from where I could see the house. I had to turn in the seat to watch because I wasn't going to drive past the house again when I left.

Although I would have liked to wait until Ralston headed off for the trolley in the morning, I hoped to be well clear of the capital by then. The one thing I knew was that he wasn't traveling, and that meant he would be home sooner or later, if he weren't already.

I watched for a time, convinced at last that one of the shadows in the house was his. As usual, I hoped to take advantage of human nature—Ralston's, of course. The plan was simple.

First I had to wait until the lower-level lights went out. It was almost midnight when that happened, but vanBecton never stirred, just kept breathing. I still had him trussed, just in case.

When the lights went out, I got out the goodies—the file folder, the disassociator, and the kerosene and wadded paper. Using the cover of the shrubbery, especially the ornate boxwood hedge that ran parallel to the front walk, I edged up to the front door and set the disassociator beside the low front stoop, where it would be concealed by the three steps between door and walk. The file folder with both real and phony papers went next to it.

Then I retreated and, with the watch uniform and thin rubber gloves still on, I took the jug of kerosene and crept up through the azaleas to the corner of the empty screened porch. In the darkness I poured it over the railings and the wood, careful to leave a puddle under the bottom of the railing. Then I wadded up the paper and lit it off, retreating quickly and setting the jug under the neighbor's bushes.

As the flames slowly flicked stronger, I waited between the oak tree and the sidewalk in the shadows. When the fire was going, I ran up to the front door and hammered the knocker. Lights went on upstairs, but nothing happened. I pounded again.

"Who is it?"

"What the devil . . ."

Muffled steps announced someone's arrival at the door, and the glow squares cast a faint light across my goateed and uniform-capped face. The door opened. Ralston stood there. I didn't grin.

"Sir! There's a fire on the porch!"

A frown crossed his face, but the glow squares hadn't reached full power and the orange flames from the porch also had caught his eye. He edged forward, his eyes flickering toward the fire.

I caught his temple with the sap, then broke his fall but let him sprawl across the three steps right onto the front walk. It took only a second to lift the disassociator. My stomach turned, but Ralston had threatened everyone I had left—and meant it. After quickly setting it down by the boxwood well into the shadows away from the door, I dashed back to the steps and yelled through the doorway. "Wire the medics! Get the fire department!"

A youth scrambled down the stairs into the foyer.

"Your father saw the fire and fell. He's hurt. You'd better wire the medics and the fire department."

His eyes flicked to his right, where he could see the orange and red glow through the French doors of the front parlor, and dashed for the wireset.

I ran out front and looked for a hose, and actually found one. After several minutes I was playing water on the blaze, keeping it from spreading too quickly, while a gray-haired woman wept over Ralston and the young man tried to spray water from a second hose which wouldn't quite reach.

When the sirens approached, I motioned to the boy. "Take this one."

He didn't argue, tight as his expression was, and he took the hose.

"Might I use the wireset, madame?" I asked Ralston's wife.

"Go ahead. It's inside the parlor." She didn't even look up, for which I was glad.

I dialed the emergency number for the Georgetown watch. "There's a suspicious fire and an injury at thirty-two thirty-three P Street. Thirty-two thirty-three P Street."

Then I dialed the number for the *Post* and gave a similar message.

"This is the watch. There's a suspicious fire and an injury at thirty-two thirty-three P Street. The injured man is a special assistant to President Armstrong, and there are papers strewn all over the steps."

"What? Who are you?"

I hung up and walked out the front door. The sirens were still several blocks away. Ralston's wife cradled her husband, not looking at me for more than a moment. Their son struggled with the hose, not quite able to keep the blaze in check.

When they looked at each other, I stepped into the shadows, recovered the disassociator, and slipped along the hedge and back down the street to the Stanley.

VanBecton was beginning to stir. After untying him, I left him sprawled on the sidewalk, his case in hand, and guided the Stanley away from the curb, a block later passing both a fire truck and an ambulance careening toward Ralston's.

Then I drove the long way out of the city, circling back to New Bruges and then out to River Road, and eventually onto the Calhoun Parkway with its wrought-iron glow lamps that never shed quite enough light on the pavement.

From where the parkway ended near Damascus and Route Fourteen began, I eased up the Stanley's speed, heading northwest through Maryland toward Pennsylvania, aiming to angle back slowly toward New Amsterdam, continually searching for news broadcasts on the radio.

At one point, beyond Frederick, I pulled off onto a side road and changed out of the watch uniform and into the now wrinkled cheap wool suit, looking over my shoulder all the time. I didn't even see any ghosts, but I felt that I ought to be carrying them in my head, with all the mayhem I'd been creating.

Back on the road, I kept changing radio stations and listening, but mostly I got rehashes of how the Colts had mangled the Redskins.

"Some day Elway had . . . made the Redskins' fullbacks look like stone statues. Jack, they just haven't been the same . . ."

The good news was that what I had done didn't seem to have made the radio news, at least not yet.

After almost weaving off the road twice in ten miles, I finally stopped in a whistlestop called Gettysburg, and took a room at the Sunnyrest Courts, awakening a bearded man who wanted cash in advance.

"You sales types come in at all hours, leave, and don't pay." He put a big fist on the counter and glared.

I was so punchy I wanted to ask if he happened to be a farmer in disguise with a beautiful daughter, but even to me that didn't seem smart. Instead I asked, "How much?"

"Twenty. Checkout is before ten in the morning."

I handed him the bill, and he handed me the key to number eleven.

He watched from the door while I drove the Stanley down to the end. There were only eleven units, and it was the last. As I opened the trunk he slammed his door.

I locked the Stanley, picked up the garment bag, and fumbled open the door to the room. The carpet was bright green, and the spread on the bed was a sicker pale green, and I didn't care.

I bolted the room and struggled out of most of my clothes. I didn't remember much after that, but just before I feel asleep I thought—almost in wonder—about how much easier it used to be.

CHAPTER TWENTY-SIX

• • •

A pounding headache, punctuated by screeching tires, awakened me from dreams I didn't quite recall—except that ghosts were chasing me, spouting Shakespeare and bearing guns that fired real bullets that burned when they went through me. Given that I was sweating and shivering simultaneously, I was certain I didn't want to recall those dreams in any more precise terms. The thin pink blanket and the thinner sick green spread didn't provide much warmth, not when my breath was steaming.

I stumbled over to the wall heater, shivering even more and wondering why it didn't work. Nothing works when it's not turned on. So I punched the button. The wheezing groan as it labored into action, beginning with a jet of even colder air that froze the hair on the back of my forearm, drove me back under the thin covers to regroup. They weren't much help, and I trundled into the small bathroom, the kind where the mortar between the tiles is that gray that is neither clean nor dark enough to convince you it's mildew. The hot water was hot, at least. Of course, I forgot that I was still wearing both goatee and mustache and ruined both, at least temporarily.

Some mornings are like that.

I peeled off both goatee and mustache and set them on the edge of the sink that crowded the shower. Still in the shower, with my shivering finally stopped, I shaved, only cutting myself once.

After drying myself thoroughly, I dressed. Then I remembered to put the soaked mustache and goatee in a waxed paper bag meant for other sanitary uses and slipped it into my garment bag. There wasn't much sense in creating any more of a trail than necessary.

With not much more than a bed, a nightstand, and a lamp, Sunnyrest Courts didn't boast the luxury of videolink. So I had no way to check to see how the Spazi was publicly reacting to the previous day's events, but I doubted that there would be much on the air or in print yet.

The bearded character was looking out the window when I drove off, and he came running into the car space, waving his arms. I just let him, since I had left the key in the lock, and I really didn't want to explain why I was clean-shaven. Besides, he wouldn't get anywhere tracing a gray Stanley with false Virginia plates, and twenty for freezing half a night in a large closet was more than the actual charges. I was confident he'd keep the change.

As I drove down the short main street, I could see there wasn't much choice in the way of places to eat in Gettysburg. I finally stopped at a chain outfit called Mom's Pantry. I'd always avoided chains and places with "Mom" in the name, but I didn't have many options. It was that or the Greasy Spoon. Talk about a scythe or a millstone!

I spent a dime on the local rag, since copies of the *Columbia Post-Dispatch* or the *Evening Star* hadn't arrived. It did contain the story about John Elway and the incredible number of goals he'd inflicted on the hapless Redskins, but nothing about ghosts or violence in the Federal District. Somehow that said something about the whole country.

A heavyset woman with a faint mustache handed me a tattered pasteboard menu and pointed to a booth. "There."

I didn't ask if she were Mom—I didn't want to know.

The waiter took his time getting to my booth, and he was young and unshaven. "Coffee?"

"Tea or chocolate."

"They're extra."

"Chocolate, then. I'll have scrambled eggs and flat sausage, with the potato pancake."

He took the menu and started to pour the coffee.

"Chocolate," I reminded him.

"You get the coffee anyway."

I shrugged and left it.

The sausage and toast were fine, but all I got was grape jelly, and the eggs were like rubber. The chocolate was barely lukewarm and tasted like the instant powder hadn't dissolved. The potato pancake had a vague resemblance to potato—it tasted mostly like soil.

"Is there any other jelly?"

"No, sir. All we have is grape."

I didn't leave a tip. But I didn't feel small about that. How can you leave a tip at Mom's?

When I finally got on the road north, reflecting that the Greasy Spoon would have been a better choice, I turned the radio back on.

"Yesterday the Eagles got a present from Baltimore when John Elway dismembered the Redskins . . ."

I twisted the dial.

". . . when the national korfball team meets the Austro-Hungarian team . . ."

I turned the dial again and got the driving beat of what appeared to be five bass guitars and a bandsaw. So I made another effort.

"At the briefing, Minister Holmbek indicated that the goal is to combine Japanese nuclear technology with the best features of Columbian submersible technology . . ."

With nothing about current political developments, I kept driving through the morning. I managed to find the Mid-Penn Turnpike and headed east toward New Amsterdam.

It was nearly noon when I stopped to fill the tanks in Unity Springs, just west of New Amsterdam. The place didn't have the papers yet, so I was still in the dark. I found the local post centre and mailed the last set of Spirit Preservation League announcements, designed mainly to suggest that the invisible spirits would be watching the Speaker and his government. I was sure that copies would get to both the Speaker and Minister Holmbek, one way or another.

About a half hour after I crossed the Henry Hudson Bridge, on the north side of New Amsterdam, the radio finally offered some relevant news.

"The psychic research issue exploded again today with the bombing of Speaker Hartpence's limousine, just moments after the Speaker had left the car at the Presidential Palace. Although no one was hurt, statements received by the press claim the bombing was the act of the so-called Spirit Preservation League."

That was it. Was it enough? I didn't know and kept driving.

Again, just to vary matters, I came up the river route, following the Blauwasser north as it wound through the hills of Nieubremmen, the state that almost wasn't until the New Ostend delegation had threatened to annex it.

I finally decided I had to find a place to stop in Windsor, north of Haartsford. I was still too tired to push it, and I needed a good dinner and a decent night's sleep. The road was having a tendency not to stay in place, or at least not where my eyes said it was.

That tendency stopped when I stepped out of the Stanley and was hit with the cold. It might have been early November, but it felt like winter—midwinter. Belatedly I noticed that every one else on the streets, even in their cars, was wearing heavy coats. I hurried into the road hotel office, which was far warmer than outside.

"Little cold out there. See you're from Virginia. Should have brought a coat."

"It wasn't that cold when I left. So I packed it."

"Better unpack it, friend. They're talking snow or sleet for tomorrow."

"Just what I need."

"You want to pay now or later?"

"Now's fine."

"Be twenty-five. Make any wire calls, be extra. Pay them before you leave."

"I don't have anyone to wire." I laughed.

"Must be nice."

"Just lonely."

We both laughed for a moment.

The Royal Court was a step up—a short one—from the Sunnyrest, but it did have videolink and a wireset in the rooms, not that I had anyone to wire or anyone that I dared notify. The spread on the double bed was thick and white, and the curtains were lace, clean lace.

Across the street was a small restaurant called Jim's Place. That sounded more honest than Mom's Pantry. I had a steak with French fried potatoes—*pommes frites,* I guess Llysette would have called them—and the steak was actually medium rare, rather than charred or raw. There were white linens on the table, but not white lace in the windows.

The tea was like the Russian Imperial blend in my own kitchen, but you can't have everything. Most important, no one paid any attention to me, except for my waiter, and his youthful enthusiasm was clearly aimed at a tip. I didn't disappoint him, but that might have been because I felt I was probably disappointing everyone at that point.

After my early dinner, I walked down the street to Arrow Pharmacy—they're everywhere in the northeast—and picked up a copy of the local paper, the *Courant* or some such.

The psychic story was on page one, below the fold, but still on page one. I skimmed through it.

PSYCHIC RESEARCH EXPLODES

COLUMBIA CITY (RPI)—An unprecedented bombing of Speaker Hartpence's limousine just moments after he stepped out at the Presidential Palace has put the spotlight directly on the psychic research issue. Speaker Hartpence and his staff were unhurt, and only the rear left corner of the limousine was damaged.

Initial puzzlement turned to anger and then concern when the "Spirit Preservation League" claimed credit in a series of announcements postmarked well before the blast.

"This issue clearly needs the Speaker's attention," affirmed Anglican-Baptist Archbishop Clelland, in a speech from the National Cathedral just hours after the bombing . . .

"We're not dealing with simple terrorists here," announced watch specialist Herrick Reid. "The paper used in these announcements is extraordinarily expensive, and the language is cultured and rational. Equally important, these people are professionals. Two sets of announcements were postmarked before the explosion. The explosion itself was also carefully designed to minimize damage." According to Reid and other specialists, the Spirit Preservation League has delivered a strong message—that it has the money, expertise, and ability to kill the Speaker with impunity if he continues his "covert" war on ghosts.

Acting Deputy Spazi Minister Jerome questioned whether the blast was really a League effort, citing threats by another group, the Order of Jeremiah . . .

In a related development, Deputy Spazi Minister Gillaume vanBecton remains in a complete zombie state after his kidnapping from his posh upper Bruges home in the federal city. He was found wandering in Georgetown, not far from where presidential aide Ralston McGuiness suffered brain damage from a concussion incurred in fighting a fire at his home. Reportedly, papers found in his case and near McGuiness's home support the contentions of both extremist groups that the Speaker has committed significant federal resources to his war against ghosts. Neither the Speaker nor President Armstrong had any comments about the alleged documents . . .

It was all there, all right. I decided to keep reading. The story on the bottom of page two didn't help my digestion. It was also a wire story, but more personally inclined.

A prominent member of Congress released copies of letters protesting the direction and termination of a secret Defense Ministry research project in New Bruges on ghost elimination technology . . .

The letters' writer, a professor in charge of research, died in an accident days after posting the second letter . . . The letters also indicated possible illegal contract practices . . .

Minister Holmbek had no comment on the charges, which were made by Congress-lady Alexander last night . . .

Was it Railley or Murtaugh who knew the congresslady? I had to hand it to whichever one it was. By giving her the letters, the reporter had broken the story without breaking his cover, and no one asked a member of Congress for her sources. But I bet the story had played a lot larger under a byline in either the *Post-Dispatch* or the *Evening Star*.

I leafed through the rest of the paper, and paused on the editorial page. I'd definitely tapped something. The editorial was short, and at the bottom, but it was there.

LEAVE THE GHOSTS BE

For months, this paper and others have been filled with stories hinting that the government has been pursuing technology to destroy ghosts. Now, more proof, and violence, have appeared. Most ghosts are the remnants of poor individuals who died before their time, and apparently the Speaker has decreed that their lingering lifespans should be cut even shorter. Enough is enough. There is no reason to spend federal money on technology to eradicate psychic beings who are all that remain of those once and often still loved. In this time of international tension, there are far better purposes for the money, nor should any government spend funds to exterminate the helpless who cannot harm anyone. Leave the ghosts be!

As I folded the paper and walked quickly back to the Royal Court, trying to keep warm wearing just a suit coat, for some reason I wondered what Herr Professor David Doniger was doing. Then again, what did it matter? For all that had happened, I'd been gone less than a week. I sighed. It seemed longer than that.

I also still had one basic problem. How would I convince Hans Waetjen not to arrest me for murder? Even though I hadn't had a thing, directly anyway, to do with Miranda's and Gerald's murders, the watch clearly didn't have any other suspects. My absence wasn't exactly wonderful, but I hadn't had much choice. Sitting tight would have clearly sealed my fate.

Of course, one of the real murderers might well go unpunished by the watch. The other, I was certain, had to have been the infamous "Perkin Warbeck," and no one could say he'd gone unpunished.

Still . . . one murderer on the loose wasn't the most heartening thought, for a lot of reasons, most of which I really didn't want to think about. So I didn't. I went to bed instead.

CHAPTER TWENTY-SEVEN

• • •

The next morning the weather in Windsor was worse, with a cold rain falling that froze on everything but salted roads. After a quick breakfast of French toast at Jim's Place, with chocolate, I had to warm up the Stanley for almost half an hour to melt off the ice. That was one drawback to thermal paint—you don't want to scrape or chip anything.

Then I headed north, in four-wheel drive. The three-and-a-half-hour drive to Lebanon took almost five, including the blocked bridge at Waaling, with the windshield being pelted with sleet, rain, and occasional snow.

Once I turned east on the Ragged Mountain Highway out of Lebanon, the snow got steadier, except for intermittent ice flakes.

The Stanley had a good heater, and I didn't freeze. The big drawback was that the paint looked like a rainbow of black, gray, purple, and red. So I had to reset the thermals and let it revert to its base red. The big matters might have gone all right, but the little details were hell.

By the time I got to Vanderbraak Centre, the ice had stopped, and only big flakes of snow were falling. The back roads were slippery, and I had to take the Route Five alternate, which I always hated, but I wasn't exactly ready to drive my red Stanley past the watch station and announce, "Your number-one suspect has returned!" Not yet, anyway. I had a few more items to try to square away.

Obviously I didn't go up Deacon's Lane, but took the back road and walked through the lower woods. I left footprints in the three inches of snow, and my dress boots and feet were soaked, and once again I was shivering. More snowfall would take care of my prints, and warmer clothes and boots would remedy the cold—assuming I could get into the house.

The place was dark, sitting on the hillside, without a single print in the light snow. I walked closer, using the car barn as a shield. Surprisingly, no one was at the house, and I saw no signs that anyone had been there recently. Then again, there wasn't any reason for anyone to be. I was certain that vanBecton and Ralston, and their successors, thought they already had all of Gerald Branston-Hay's gadgets, and Waetjen probably hadn't been told about any of them. Plus, the locals had seen me depart, and had watched the house for several days. But how long do you watch an empty house? Besides, gossip would show when I got back.

So I walked back through the woods and drove the Stanley up Deacon's Lane and into the car barn.

Then I went into the kitchen and dug out some old cheese; the bread had molded. After about three bites, I put on the kettle, then went upstairs and stripped off the damned cheap suit and stepped into a hot shower.

I felt almost human after I dressed, and I laced on my heavy insulated boots this time. I took the last box of biscuits from the cellar and treated myself to chocolate.

As the early twilight and the clouds dimmed the natural light, a white figure drifted into the kitchen, halting in the doorway.

"Good evening, Carolynne," I said formally.

She curtsied, but did not speak.

"Are you all right?" I asked.

"How quickly everything dies . . . we see, in this fickle world, change, faster than the waves at the shore."

"And yet, sometimes, nothing changes." She seemed sad, but I really didn't know quite what to say. The silence stretched out, and I asked again, "Are you sure you are all right?"

"One believed in being faithful . . ."

I couldn't figure that one out. So I asked, "Was the watch here?"

"Alas, sad awakenings from dreams . . . give me back your illusions . . . the voice of our despair shall sing . . ."

"I take it all that despair means they were." I forced a wry smile. "It's not over yet, though. I'm going to have to use the difference engine."

"The white moon shines in the forest; from every branch comes forth a voice . . . but the day of farewells will come."

"I know you're a ghost, but using songs as riddles is hard on me. I'm tired. Can't you say what you mean?"

"Ne point passer!"

She was gone, even if I didn't know exactly what she had meant or why she had said "Never to change!" in French. She was a full, real ghost, as close to being a real person as possible, and yet she never could be real. Did she know that? Did I know that?

"Carolynne . . . I'm sorry."

She reappeared. "Let me sleep a while, while you rest . . ." With that, she was gone.

"I'm sorry, Carolynne, and I will talk to you later."

I hoped she heard me. I did cover the windows in the study with both blinds and curtains, and, for good measure, I hung blankets behind them. With the snowfall continuing, I doubted that anyone would see any faint glimmer of light, and the snow might cover the Stanley's tracks as well.

After gulping down the rest of the chocolate, I got to work, making up a complete package on what had happened, naming names and places—the whole business—and providing complete specifications for all the gadgets except the replication projector. That one was mine, and I intended to keep it that way, if I could.

I did have to unload some things from the Stanley, and that left prints in the snow, but if anyone came that close, they'd probably find other signs I'd returned.

Halfway through my efforts, the wireset chimed. I wondered whether to answer it, but finally picked up the handset. "Yes?"

"Johan, where have you been? Your aunt and I have been trying to reach you for almost a week."

"I haven't been at the house much."

"No, dear, you certainly haven't been. It's too late now, but Anna's nephew— Arlan's son, you remember Wilhelm, don't you?—well, he was killed in a steamer crash in Erie, and I wondered if you would be able to come to the funeral and the wake—"

"Mother, where are you?"

"We are in Erie. Where else would we be? That's where the funeral was. I suppose you're still working."

"Of course." I glanced at the difference engine screen.

"Well, do try to take care of yourself. Anna sends her best, and come see us again before too long. I must go, and do try to take care of yourself, dear."

The handset beeped and went dead. I just looked at it before I set it down.

It was nearly midnight before I finished the three complete sets of documents.

Almost as soon as I flicked off the machine, Carolynne reappeared and watched me assemble the packages.

"What have you done, you, who now weeps endlessly?" She seemed to be sitting on the sofa, just like any normal young lady.

"Creating life insurance."

"Down here—*ici-bas*—all men weep for their friendships or their loves . . ."

"Weeping, yes. Blackmail is more like it. I set it up so that this material will be made public if I die. Then the people who know that, and who would suffer if this became known to the press, have a certain desire to preserve my life."

"Down here, all lilacs die; all songs of the birds are short."

"Probably, but I don't have any better ideas."

We sat in the dark for a while, a ghost well over a century old and a man who had done far too much he was not proud of.

"Alas, sad awakening from dreams! Is that all there is? Is that all there is?"

"All what is?"

"Say, what have you done, you, with your youth?"

"I don't know. It's gone, and that is the way it feels." Sometimes—and I thought of Elspeth, and Llysette—it was a blind struggle to preserve someone else's life. Sometimes no one else even saw the struggle.

After a time, I stood. "I have to go for a while."

"Return with your radiance, oh mysterious night."

"I'm scarcely mysterious, but I do plan to return."

"How quickly everything dies, the rose undiscloses . . ."

As her words faded away so did Carolynne, and a heaviness dropped around me.

I put on my coat alone and in the darkness, and carried two of the three folders out to the Stanley. The last went into the hidden cabinet in the study for the time being.

I eased the Stanley down the drive with the lights off, and didn't turn them on until I was well down the lane, skidding slightly even in four-wheel drive. Probably I could have stayed at home, but someone might have seen me and just waited until I went to sleep.

The roads were brutal, and I was in four-wheel drive all the way. The good news was that it was highly unlikely that anyone would bother to follow me.

I still thought about Carolynne's last words: "How quickly everything dies . . ." Were they just in my head, my own subconscious? Was I coming undone psychically? Why had I been put in a situation where murder was the only way to survive? Whatever the reason, the sadness behind the words hammered at me.

What could I do about them? Was this all there was? I knew that was a song, one I had heard, but I knew I didn't know where the other words came from, true as they rang. I tried to concentrate on driving, half realizing that I couldn't keep up the insane pace and irregular schedule. I wasn't a thirty-year-old operative, and hadn't been for all too many years.

After pulling into the public parking in the Zuider train station—one of the places where no one was likely to remark upon a car arriving at odd hours—I slept as well as I could until the sun rose. Except it didn't. The snow had stopped, but the sky was cold gray. I found Suzanne's Diner and had a breakfast larger than my stomach really needed, looking over a copy of the *Asten Post-Courier*.

There were only a few stories about the ghost mess, mostly rehashes of what had been in the *Courant* the night before. There was an editorial more along the Dutch lines of why bother with ghosts, very pragmatic and talking about dollars and the need not to waste them—none of that silly stuff about ghosts being loved or being people. Somehow the editorial bothered me.

I waited until close to nine before I drove over to LBI.

Bruce was actually there when I arrived with my package for him.

"Good morning."

"So, the prodigal returns. And you do look like a prodigal."

"Hardly. He had it better. You want to be in the insurance business?"

"Nope."

"How about the reinsurance business?"

"Do I get a share of the profits?"

"You really don't want a share."

"You know, Johan, did anyone tell you that you look like hell this morning?"

"Did anyone tell you that hell probably feels better?"

"You didn't need to tell me that."

"I know." I held up the package. "This is yours."

"I don't want it, whatever it is." He gave a wry smile and a head shake.

"This is an offer you can't refuse."

"One of those again. I knew you'd do this to me, Johan." He sighed. I felt sorry for him. Still, if he didn't help, I'd be feeling even sorrier for myself. So I waited.

"What do you want?" he finally asked.

"Not much. I just want you to post the envelopes in this big folder if I die anytime in the next four years."

"You know, I really don't like the reinsurance business, either."

"I know. It's hell."

"But . . . I'll do it." He took the folder. "I presume you have another one?"

"Yes. That gets posted to my other reinsurance agent."

"Lucky guy."

"He thinks so, too."

Bruce looked toward the parking lot, empty except for our cars. "You'd better get on with your reinsurance before someone ups the premiums."

"You're all heart."

"I know."

I waved and walked back to the steamer and the other folder, glad I had my good boots and heavy coat. The boiler wasn't even cold when I flipped the switch, despite the freezing temperatures outside.

I found the post centre and sent the second envelope off to Eric and Judith's oldest son, a very junior lawyer with a firm in Atlanta. But he was my godchild and a good kid, a young man, really. To make it perfectly legal, I also enclosed a small check for a retainer, to seal, if you will, the attorney-client privilege. I chose him for one other reason. Young Alfred couldn't have built the devices from the specifications if his life depended on it. He probably wouldn't have understood what they meant without a great deal of study, although I seriously doubted that he would open the sealed inner envelope. He took that sort of thing very seriously. I did post it to his home address in Buckhead, though, so some clerk didn't open the whole thing by mistake.

Two probably weren't enough, but I also really didn't want what was in the packages getting out. The whole mess needed to simmer down, not heat up, and that was what I was working for—that and my own self-preservation. Of course, I still had to deal with Miranda's murder, but one thing at a time. I couldn't resolve the murder if I were in a watch cell.

I was tired, but there was no going home yet, not until I made my calls. The first was from the outside wireset behind Herman's Bar and Grill, and it went to Haarlan Oakes, Ralston's former assistant. They put me right through.

"Johan, where are you?"

"In New Bruges. I've been trying to stay out of the limelight. I read that Ralston had an accident."

"Yes. It was rather remarkable, and embarrassing. There were some papers . . . they got to the press. And then there was the coincidence with vanBecton becoming a zombie. It was all rather astounding."

"I imagine that the president would prefer that things were forgotten quickly."

"He has expressed some concern along those lines."

"I would think so. I'm a little concerned myself. With the accidents that happened to those two . . . well, I visited several, shall we say, insurance agents, in the interests of life insurance, you understand?"

"Did you get a good deal?" His voice was hard.

"Oh, it wasn't that kind of insurance. I like living quietly in New Bruges. As I kept telling people, I'd prefer that things remain very quiet. I never did like the commotion. As a matter of fact, I suspect that things will remain quite quiet, quite forgotten, you understand, at least unless someone has to probate, if you will, my estate. Pardon the pun."

"Oh . . . *that* kind of insurance." There was a pause. "I think the president would be very supportive—at least this time."

"I would hope so, and I would hope he and the Speaker could reach an agreement. I am going to call Asquith next, and discuss insurance with him."

"I didn't know you knew Asquith."

"I met him years ago, but I'm sure he'll recall me."

"I suspect so. Well, I'm due to brief the president shortly, and I'll convey to him your sentiments. Under the circumstances, I'm quite sure that he will be pleased."

"I would hope so. After all, I've always been a supporter."

"At least you didn't say admirer." Haarlan actually laughed.

"No, I didn't. But he'll understand."

"So he will. Good luck, Johan. We look forward to seeing you at one of the next presidential dinners."

I took a deep breath, stamped my feet to warm them, and hurried to the Stanley, driving across Zuider to the public wireset outside Narnes, the department store. I probably could have stayed behind Herman's, but then, who knew? Besides, the drive gave me a chance to warm up.

Asquith was Speaker Hartpence's number-two political aide, and I actually *had* met him. He was the one who had requested my resignation.

Again, the operators connected us immediately.

"Johan, I can't say I exactly expected this."

"Nothing surprises you, Charles. I have been making an effort to avoid too much media exposure. But I did read that vanBecton, the number-two Spazi, had suffered some strange form of amnesia."

"I think the entire world knows that, Johan. They also know that the Speaker has been engaging in covert warfare against psychic phenomena—rather elegant wording. It is so elegant that it is almost professorial."

"It could be. After all, the late Professor Branston-Hay was not only inventive, but elegant. Still, I imagine that the Speaker would prefer that things returned to normal rather more quickly than not . . ."

"He has said very little."

"I would think so. Public utterances can be rather damaging when the press has a few facts to work with."

"Why did you call, Johan?"

"Call it mutual concern. I know the Speaker must be concerned. I'm a little concerned myself. With the accidents that happened to vanBecton and Ralston McGuiness, and all the uproar, well, I visited several, shall we say, insurance agents . . . in the interests of life insurance, you understand?"

"I'm afraid I do. Are the odds good?"

"You'd have to provide the quotes. As you may know, since my retirement, my choice was to live a quiet life. Minister vanBecton, shall we say, wanted to encourage a more active lifestyle. I didn't have much choice, but it just wasn't suitable. I'd prefer to resume a far less ambitious lifestyle, I really would."

"I think the Speaker would appreciate that. Of course, we have no idea what Minister vanBecton's legacy might provide for you, but Minister Jerome will certainly share and respect your wishes for continuing such a quiet lifestyle—teaching and writing public commentaries, is it?"

"Exactly. I would prefer to stay away from technical publications, unless, of course, my estate has to be probated in the near future."

"We understand. You will have to resolve the legacies of Minister vanBecton yourself, though, since some of those were never . . . published. His later efforts were . . . rather independent. And please try to deal with those quietly. That would please the Speaker no end. Like you, he would prefer a subdued result. Pardon my pun."

I hated getting puns back from others, but I wasn't about to complain. "I appreciate your concerns and thoughtfulness. I will certainly try for a quiet and calm return to normal life." I paused, but not enough for him to cut me off. "By the way, I do know of one of Minister vanBecton's, ah, legacies. He seemed to have had a number of conversations with a fellow by the name of Hans Waetjen. Hans is the watch chief in Vanderbraak Centre, and he hired some . . . unusual . . . officers. You might encourage him to return to the fold, so to speak."

"I think something could be managed there. We would all appreciate a certain return to tranquility in New Bruges."

"Thank you, Charles. I will do my best to ensure the same."

"I would appreciate that, Johan. Good day."

I found a quiet bed and breakfast, the Twin Pines, and went to sleep almost as soon as I locked the door and got my boots off.

CHAPTER TWENTY-EIGHT

• • •

Thursday morning—it was hard to believe that so much had happened in a week—I slept in at the Twin Pines, if sleeping in means waking at eight o'clock instead of six. I still felt like I'd been dragged behind a road hauler for a week.

I drove the five blocks to Suzanne's Diner. Most mornings that would have been a warm-up walk, but the sidewalks were icy, and my head ached. I picked up a copy of the *Lakes News,* dreading what I might find, and struggled into a small booth.

"Tea, please," I told the waitress.

"You don't look so good. You want some bayers?"

"That would be nice, thank you."

"Not a problem. Wish everything was that easy." She set two of the white tablets on the table. "Anything to eat?"

"How's the French toast?"

"Not bad if you like rubber. You ought to try the Belgian waffle with blueberries. It's pretty good, and you can get it with sausage for only four bits more." She poured the tea into the big brown mug.

"I'll take it." I handed her the greasy menu and dumped three teaspoons of raw sugar into the tea before I sipped any. It was still bitter, but I took the bayers with the second swallow.

Sitting in the small booth, I watched scattered snowflakes drift outside the streaked window as cars glided past on Union Street. I nursed the tea and my headache until the Belgian waffle came. I didn't have the energy to look at the slim paper.

"Here you go." She set down the plate and a pitcher of syrup with matching thumps. A smaller plate followed with four slices of flat sausage.

"Thank you."

"Not a problem." She refilled the mug with tea.

I nodded again and dumped more raw sugar into it. No matter what my mind said, my body was telling me that I was far too old for what I'd been doing. It wasn't the exercise, but the stress, the looking over the shoulder every other minute. Almost everything had worked out. So why was I exhausted?

The Belgian waffle wasn't quite so good as it looked, but far better than rubber eggs, and the sausage slices had just the right hint of pepper and spices.

When I was finished, I let her refill the mug with tea again. Then I took a deep breath and began to read the *Lakes News*.

There was a tiny blip on the national news page—that was all—about the ongoing investigation of the Spirit Preservation League. The story quoted Speaker Hartpence as saying, "Any attempt to shorten the existence of psychic presences will be opposed. That has always been our policy."

I figured he was half right.

There was also a short editorial—predictably Dutch—that suggested the government in the Federal District should spend more time worrying about the waste of taxes than investing in a psychic destruction technology.

The waitress arrived as I folded the paper to look at the editorial again.

"Leave 'em alone. Leave us alone, too. Government's too big as it is."

I agreed, and I left her a twenty-five-percent tip, both for the bayers and the recommendations, then made my way to the wireset booth in the corner.

I dialed the Vanderbraak Centre watch.

"Watch center."

"This is Johan Eschbach. I'd like to talk with Chief Waetjen."

"I'm sorry, sir. I did not get your name."

"Eschbach. Johan. The fellow whose house you searched. The man you've been chasing for the wrong reason. Could I speak with Chief Waetjen?"

"Yes, sir. Just a moment, sir."

I waited. Were they trying to trace the call? Or was Waetjen on another line?

"Waetjen."

"Johan Eschbach."

"What do you want, Eschbach?"

"I just wanted to know if I headed home whether your people would be inclined to leave me alone."

"You know the answer to that. But let me tell you, Eschbach—"

"I know. I'd better be very helpful, very friendly, and not do anything wrong."

"You understand, I see."

"I understand. I never wanted to do anything in the first place, Chief. Remember that."

"A fellow by the name of Asquith made that point to me. So did another fellow by the name of Jerome."

I could tell Waetjen was angry, not only from the brittle tone but the words. No subtleties. No indirection.

"They can be very persuasive."

"I suspect you were more persuasive. Is that all?"

"That's all, Chief. If I find out anything else that could help you, I'll let you know."

"That would be fine. Good day, Doktor."

Another friend for life. Why did it always seem to end up that way? I'd never even wanted to get involved. All because I'd decided to help Ralston out a year earlier, just let him know what I saw. I'd never even seen that much until Miranda was murdered.

I stepped out of the booth and used the men's room. After that, on the way back through the diner, the waitress smiled. "Thanks, Sarge."

Just because I hadn't shaved that morning and my clothes were wrinkled? Did I really look that tough? Or was she being charitable?

I grinned and left the diner.

Once in the Stanley, I turned back northward. None of the flurrying snow had stuck, and Route Five was clear all the way to Vanderbraak Centre. Deacon's Lane was still icy, though, and I put the Stanley back in four wheel.

Everyone knows everything. By the time I got home around ten, Marie was busy baking, and the house smelled of various good things, including apples and cinnamon.

"Hello, Marie. The wanderer has returned."

"I'm glad everything worked out, Doktor Eschbach. There's an apple pie for later."

"Thank you, Marie. Most things worked out, but I have to tie up a few very loose ends."

"You know, Chief Waetjen sometimes is a little, a little enthusiastic."

"Especially when he's prompted by the Spazi."

"Those people in Columbia City don't know everything." She snorted.

"No, they don't." I certainly hoped they didn't, for a number of reasons.

"You just go off to your study and do whatever you have to. Later I'll fix you a little lunch. You look terrible, Doktor."

"Thank you. Actually, I'm going to take a shower."

Everyone told me I looked terrible. I didn't feel wonderful. Maybe they were right. Maybe a shower would help.

The warm water loosened up a few things, and a shave and the comfort of a big sweater and comfortable trousers helped. I felt recognizably human when I went back down to the study.

I sat down at the desk and put in a call to David, but Gilda answered. "Natural Resources Department."

"Gilda, this is Doktor Eschbach. I've been . . . ill. Is David in?"

"He's over at the dean's office, Doktor Eschbach. When are you likely to be back in?"

"Unless this develops more complications, I should be back on Monday. I would be fine to teach the day after tomorrow, but . . ."

"I don't think Doktor Doniger would want to set a precedent for Saturday classes." She offered a brief laugh.

"I don't think so, either."

"What should I tell your students?"

"Just to make sure they've done their readings. That's all. There weren't any papers or quizzes scheduled." Unfortunately, virtually every class had a paper due in the next two weeks, but I'd deal with that as I could.

"Take care, Doktor Eschbach. I have to go. There's another line ringing."

"Take care. I'll see you soon."

I put down the handset and looked out at the lawn, a blotchwork of snow and brown grass, knowing I was putting off the inevitable. Rather than face it, I finally unloaded all the rest of the equipment and papers from the Stanley and put most of it away, except for the clothes that needed washing or dry cleaning.

Sooner or later I was going to have to deal with the remaining problem. Finally I picked up the handset again.

"*Allo.*"

"Is this the lovely Llysette duBoise, the sweet soprano of New Bruges?"

"Johan." There was a pause. "Where are you?"

"At home. I've been under the weather."

"You have not been home."

"No. I had to take a trip, for reasons of health." More like for reasons of survival. "I'm almost recovered. I was wondering if you'd be interested in dinner tonight."

"Tonight?"

"Why not?"

"Rehearsals, I have—dress rehearsals. Tomorrow we open, and the dunder-heads, I do not know . . ."

"I suppose that means no dinner until Sunday night."

"Free I would be Saturday after the performance."

"Then I'll come to the show, and we can do something afterwards."

"Perhaps a quiet evening at your house. Tired you must be."

"I am tired."

"I will see you Saturday. I must go. Another student she arrives."

"Saturday."

For a time, I looked out the window. Marie had taken down the blankets and opened the curtains, again without commenting upon the strangeness of her employer's actions. A few lazy flakes continued to drift out of the sky, but I could tell that the clouds to the west were breaking.

I yawned and realized that I wouldn't be that much good for anything. Perhaps after lunch . . . and perhaps not.

Lunch was good—some sort of dumpling thing with cabbage and sausage and fresh baked bread. Marie had some, but she stood at the counter and watched me, hovering like a brooding hen.

I couldn't eat that much.

"Too tired to eat, Doktor?"

"Too much of too many things," I conceded.

She gave me one of those "what can you expect?" shrugs, followed by a faint smile.

I struggled through a bit more of the dumpling and a half-slice more of bread before I went back to the study, where I alternated between trying to compose final exams and trying to puzzle out the details of Miranda's murder.

Finally, after Marie left and the light outside dimmed, I clicked off the difference engine and looked at nothing.

"Not to notice, while this dream lasts, the passing of time . . ." Carolynne perched on the corner of the desk in the high-necked dress.

The effect was not quite what she expected because there were a good six inches between her and the desktop, and I had to grin.

"You sound almost surprised."

She gave a little sound, although ghosts didn't really make sounds—I only heard them in my mind, like everyone did, like a sigh. "The large ships, rocked silently by the tide, do not heed the cradles which the hands of the women rock . . . and the inquisitive men must dare the horizons that lure them!"

"You're saying that I'm like all men, off to do great deeds?" I stopped. "I'm sorry. I don't mean to be short with you. I'm still tired, and I'm still worried."

"The large ships, fleeing from the vanishing port, feel their bulk held back by the soul of the faraway cradles. You ask me to be silent, to flee far . . ."

"I know. But it's not quite over."

"Alas, I have in my heart a frightful sadness . . . the woman not even hoped for, the dream pursued in vain . . . cruel one . . ."

I caught the edge in her "voice," not that I could have missed the combination of third-person reference and tone. Jealousy? Concern? "Llysette? I don't know," I repeated. "We're quite a group, aren't we?"

"Not to notice, while the dream lasts, the passage of time, not to choose the world's quarrels, not to grow weary, facing all that grows weary . . ." She glided off the desk and stood in the shadowed space before the bookcase to the right.

I had to swivel the chair to face her. For a time I watched her and thought not only that she had been a beautiful woman and was a beautiful ghost, but that she was wrong. Finally I spoke. "No. I can't make that kind of choice. And neither did you. You had as much choice as any of us. You may not have chosen to fall in love with a married man, but you chose to act on that love. That is a choice. Emotional creatures that we are, we may not choose how we feel, but we do choose what we do."

Another long silence fell between us.

"You ask me to be silent . . . rather ask the stars to fall into the infinite, the night to lose its veils . . ." Her words were somehow choked. "The hand that has touched you shuns my hand forever . . ."

"Whose hand?" But I knew. I had ghosts between me and Llysette, and Llysette between me and Carolynne. Wonderful.

She shook her head and was gone.

"Carolynne?" I called. But she did not reappear, even though I sat in the cold study for almost an hour.

CHAPTER TWENTY-NINE

• • •

Again, I tried to sleep in on Friday morning, but I couldn't. I've never been able to sleep that late. So I dragged myself out, and ran through a misty drizzle that was melting off what remained of the patchy snow. Deacon's Lane itself was clear, with a few icy patches, but the snow on the north side of the stone fence was still boot deep, perhaps because the mist was blowing in from the south.

I only got about two-thirds as far as I had been running, not quite to the top of the hill, perhaps because I was still half looking over my shoulder, feeling that everyone was looking at me—Llysette, the watch, Carolynne, Marie, Asquith, Jerome, David, and scores more.

I knew "Warbeck" was dead. What I didn't know was just how many other little traps vanBecton had set. Probably Waetjen wouldn't go against whatever instructions Jerome and Asquith had given him, but he definitely wasn't in the mood
to go out of his way on my behalf. He'd probably look the other way if he could—
great comfort!

After a small breakfast—the larder was getting empty again, and I had cheated
by eating a slice of Marie's apple pie—I felt good enough to go in to the university
and teach class. But showing up would have accomplished nothing since the students had already been told, via Gilda or the grapevine, that I wouldn't be there,
and they certainly wouldn't be. Anything to avoid Doktor Eschbach's class!

I did drive down to Samaha's and pick up a week's worth of papers. I left Louie
a dollar. He didn't quite look at me, instead just shook his head, as if to ask what the
world had come to.

Then I headed to McArdles' for a few supplies, coming out with three bags
and probably missing half of what I, or Marie, needed. Constable Gerhardt stayed
on the far side of the square as I loaded the Stanley. Coincidence?

I wasn't sure I'd ever believed in that, but I didn't feel like meeting any of the
watch—not then, at least.

My sterling housekeeper met me at the doorway as I carried in the bundles. "I
was afraid you were trying to go back to work." Marie looked sternly at me.

"No, Marie. I did feel well enough to go get the papers."

"Papers?" She turned a stern eye at the grocery bags.

"We did need a few items."

"Are you sure you should be doing that?"

"Yes, Mother Rijn."

"Doktor Eschbach, someone has to act like an adult. You go off to God knows
where. You come back with wet clothes and wet boots—I had to dry those—and
you wonder why you're sick. You did not even take a warm coat."

"You're right, Marie. I should be more careful." At that point I knew better
than to argue. Instead, I retrieved the papers, and retreated to my study.

I had accomplished something—that was clear from the front page stories in
the *Asten Post-Courier*. The Speaker had issued an interim order suspending all federal psychic research contracts and introduced legislation which would simultaneously bar expending federal funds on any research designed to destroy or inhibit
psychic phenomena. The proposed bill would also compensate those holding research contracts, provided all documentation and devices developed were turned
over to the Spazi for destruction. That destruction would be witnessed and attested
to by an impartial committee. The details went on for half a column.

So did the congratulatory comments from most of the world's religious leaders. I was, thankfully, not mentioned anywhere, directly or indirectly. Neither
were poor Ralston or Gillaume vanBecton. So quickly are those behind the scenes
forgotten when great announcements are made.

I laughed harshly. The Speaker already had the ghost destruction technology locked safely away. President Armstrong already had his psychic replicators and psychic brain trusts. Ferdinand already had what he wanted, and no one was looking in that direction anyway. Now the Speaker could safely get rid of selected unwelcome ghosts while still posing as the great hero of spiritual redemption.

Still, it was better than the wholesale elimination of ghosts and the spectre of mass warfare between nations. That really would have been a horror. So politics triumphed again, and sort of did the right thing.

I folded up the paper, turned on the difference engine, and called up the justice ghost program, trying to see how I could twiddle it into a personage a little more merciful and not quite so stiff-necked.

I'd jiggered perhaps three lines of code when the wireset chimed.

"Yes?"

"Is this Doktor Johan Eschbach? This is Susan Picardilli from International Import Services, PLC, in Columbia City. We'd like to verify your address before we send your project completion cheque."

"What do you need?" Project completion cheque? What project?

"Is it still all right to send this to Post Centre Box Fifty-four, Vanderbraak Centre, New Bruges, code zero-three-two-two-six-two?"

"Yes. That's correct."

"Would you give me your mother's maiden name, please?"

"It is—she's still living—Spier. S-P-I-E-R. Spier."

"Thank you, Doktor Eschbach. The cheque, as agreed, is for ten thousand dollars. If you do not receive this within the week, please contact me directly. My name is Susan. Do you have our number?"

"Yes, thank you."

"Thank you very much, Doktor."

I set down the handset slowly. I was being not only compensated but rewarded and bought off simultaneously by the Spazi—but at whose behest? Asquith's? Minister Jerome's? The Speaker's? At the last, I shook my head. The Speaker, even if he had heard my name in a briefing, probably wouldn't have remembered it. Jerome, I guessed, with Asquith's approval—rewarding their broken tool.

The money just added to my pensiveness. I was still bothered about Carolynne—and Llysette—but Carolynne wouldn't appear while Marie was around, and Llysette . . . well, she was clearly tied up with her classes and production of *Heinrich Verrückt,* probably with another not-quite-under-the-table stipend from the Austro-Hungarian Cultural Foundation. I couldn't blame her for that, not after living the high life as an almost-diva in France before the Fall.

Rationally, I couldn't blame her for a lot, but her recent coolness bothered me. Was it really my doing? I'd sort of fit her in between my disasters, and no one likes to be fitted into the spaces in another person's life. It makes you part of the furniture. Yet we were continually doing it to each other.

Was I projecting too much into Carolynne, hearing what I wanted to hear? Losing my sanity? I thought I heard what she said, but had I? I knew she was real—others saw her. But did they hear what I heard?

I took a deep breath. I needed to talk to Llysette, and merely fighting with myself wouldn't change much. I turned back to the program parameters, adding another expression to the code line.

The wireset chimed as I was fiddling with how to transform another code line in the secondary structure of my mercy and justice ghost.

"Yes?"

"Doktor Eschbach, this is Gilda Gurtler. From the Natural Resources Department—"

"My dear Gilda, how formal we are."

"Doktor Doniger would like to know if—"

"He must be standing at your shoulder."

"—you would be well enough to see him if he stopped by in an hour or so."

"I could manage." I wanted to talk, or listen, to David like I wanted to trade places with poor Bill vanBecton.

"He would appreciate just a few moments very much."

"I would be charmed."

"Thank you, Doktor Eschbach."

"Thank you, Gilda."

I got a click in return. That bothered me. Then I got to thinking. I'd made a number of assumptions, and most of them had been wrong. That bothered me, too. I could certainly have read dear David wrong. He was so boring that no one looked beyond, yet . . . he generally did get his way, as with the course-capping business. And he generally persuaded the dean to go along with his proposals. Even outspoken Gilda changed her personality when he was standing nearby. Why?

I turned off the difference engine, did some quick rearranging of my study, and retrieved the handgun I'd never used in Columbia City. It was all too easy to let down before everything was over, and I had the feeling that things were not yet over—unfortunately—and that I might be in for yet another surprise. Just wonderful.

As usual on Fridays, Marie had already left, to get her own house ready for the weekend. I put on the chocolate, and wandered around waiting, not wanting to be surprised. I didn't have to worry. David's steamer whistled all the way up the drive, and I was waiting at the door as he came in from the drizzle that had turned to an almost steady rain.

He shook his umbrella, folded it, and stepped inside. His beady blue eyes raked over me as I ushered him in.

"You do look a bit peaked still, Johan. It's a good thing you have the weekend to recuperate."

"Would you like some chocolate?"

"I wouldn't wish to impose."

"It's no imposition, David. I was already fixing some." I made a pot while he watched and carried it and two mugs into the study. I even supplied biscuits. But I never turned my back on him.

I took the desk chair, turned at an angle, wishing I'd actually used a shoulder holster.

"Johan, the dean and I were talking . . ."

I just nodded, sipping the too-hot chocolate.

". . . about this whole ghost business. Now, on the surface it really doesn't have much to do with Natural Resources, but you do have a doctorate and the political background."

I nodded again.

"As you know, the university faces some severe financial constraints, especially with the new state budget for higher education." David leaned forward and sipped his chocolate with a faint slurp. "This is good chocolate."

"Thank you." I still watched his eyes. Was he at the house just to talk about ghosts, politics, and natural resources? What linked them together?

"The department has had an increasing number of majors. We're over two hundred now, but the political science department is losing majors. They're down to forty-five, and twenty are seniors. Garth Bach is retiring next spring. He's thinking about taking up his country singing full-time." David shrugged. "We have to think about the future."

"You want to consolidate the departments?"

"Create a larger department of environmental and political studies. In a way, your work with the environmental politics courses makes it a natural idea."

"How do ghosts fit into this?" I asked, trying not to glance toward the desk drawer.

"I suppose they don't, exactly. But when all this . . . disruption occurred"— David made a vague gesture, as if he found the whole business somewhat unpleasant—"and the dean looked into your background, she was rather impressed with your political credentials. Of course, those . . . distinctive . . . credentials would be even more impressive in a department in which politics—I mean the study of politics—played a larger role." David smiled.

I returned the smile. "More chocolate?"

"No, thank you."

In short, David was about to use me as the wedge to expand his academic empire. "I'd be interested in the dean's reaction."

"She was most interested. She spoke about perhaps approaching the trustees for an endowed chair of environmental politics." David smiled even more broadly. "She also hoped that you would be most happy with Professor duBoise, and wondered if, perhaps, the arrangement might be made more . . . permanent, at some suitable time, of course."

I tried not to choke. Wonderful, just frigging wonderful. I was being offered an endowed chair and a choice of courses to design and teach, provided Llysette and I got married.

"I do appreciate your sharing this with me. You've obviously thought it out carefully, and so has the dean. You'll have to pardon me, but I'm still not quite up to speed . . ."

"Quite all right. I shouldn't have come, probably, but I did want to share this with you before—"

"I understand, and I certainly won't break any confidences." How could I? I couldn't exactly propose to Llysette on the grounds that I'd get a better position. In fact, how could I propose at all if it would ever come out? Talk about setting up academic blackmail on top of everything else!

It was better that the Colt wasn't that handy. I wanted to shoot him, but that wouldn't have helped matters at all.

"And I would also appreciate your not talking about Garth's retirement. We're setting up quite a ceremony, and we would like it to be a total surprise."

I set down the mug and stood. "I do appreciate the thoughtfulness, David. I'm sorry if I haven't been as enthusiastic as I probably will be, but . . ." I offered a wry smile and a shrug. "It's been a hard week." That much was true.

"I do understand, Johan. With your illness, and all the political goings-on that must have impinged upon your life . . ." He stood also, the perfect gentleman.

I did manage to keep a smile until his steamer whistled back down the drive, but I had trouble relaxing my jaw when I went back into the study and stared at the blank screen of the difference engine.

"That bastard! That unholy . . ."

I paced in front of the bookcases, then stared out into the rain. Not only was he out to surprise poor Garth into public retirement, but he was flat-assed blackmailing me to rearrange my private life.

"And it grieves me, its wretchedness will be blinded." Carolynne's voice was soft.

"That is an understatement. Did you hear?"

"Though deceitful is the sinful world . . . these times are turbulent. They cause distress to heart and mind." Her voice turned bleak.

I understood. She understood that if I asked Llysette to marry me, David could always hint that she owed the marriage to him, or that I didn't love her enough to ask without that. Sometimes it was clear Carolynne had seen all too much—or was it my projection of what I thought she had seen? I rubbed my forehead.

"The last flower, the last love, are both beautiful, yet deadly."

"I'm learning."

Carolynne vanished, and I went back to fiddling with the justice ghost since I felt like I was finding precious little justice or mercy in the real world. Even when I tried to console myself with the $10,000 "consulting" cheque from International

Import Services, PLC, it didn't help, at least not enough to keep the metallic taste of silver from my mouth. As an agent, you could shift some of the blame to those who gave the orders—some, but not all. But I'd acted on my own, against orders, and a lot of people were either dead or zombies, and it wasn't over. I shuddered.

CHAPTER THIRTY

• • •

Saturday wasn't any better for sleeping in, either, but I did manage to do a complete run over the top of the hill and to the end of the ridge. After I got back, I even finished most of the exercises, despite a wind that promised freezing temperatures later, underscored by the clear winter blue of the sky.

The snow by the stone fences remained, now topped with an icy crust that would preserve it for the rest of the winter as more and more snow piled onto it over the weeks and months ahead.

Later, following a more leisurely than normal breakfast of apple pie and Imperial Russian tea, I showered, dressed in a warm green flannel shirt and wool trousers, and went to work on drafting my final exams, trying not to think about Llysette and the evening ahead.

Sometime in late morning, after two exams, with two to go, I shook my head, turned off the difference engine, and grabbed my winter parka. The reliable Stanley started without a hitch, even though I hadn't plugged in the heater.

I did use four-wheel drive on Deacon's Lane, just in case, but didn't see or sense any black ice. My first stop was Samaha's.

Louie wasn't behind the counter at Samaha's when I picked up the paper; his wife Rose stood there instead. She actually smiled.

"Good morning, Doktor Eschbach."

"Good morning." I smiled back.

"You be having a good day, now."

"I hope to." Although I hoped to have a good day, or a good evening, David and the dean notwithstanding, my stomach was still tight. I just folded the paper without looking at it and walked across the square to the post centre. The sky was still clear blue, and cold, but the lack of wind made the day seem warmer than it really was.

Unfortunately, on the steps up to the post centre I almost ran into the dean herself, wearing a heavy black coat and matching scarf and gloves. Her scarf bore an oversized golden cello pin. I stepped back.

"Doktor Eschbach, I am glad to see you up and around. David had told me of your illness, and I certainly wouldn't want one of our rising stars laid low, if you know what I mean. I do hope that we'll be seeing some special announcements before too long." She smiled and batted her eyelashes. "We all will be so pleased."

"I am sure that matters will be resolved in the most satisfactory way possible, Dean Er Recchus, and I do appreciate your interest." Like a loaded gun at my temple I appreciated it, but I bowed and smiled again.

She inclined her head, with an even broader smile, and continued down the steps to her steamer.

My postbox contained three circulars, the NBEI bill, and a reminder that I needed a dental examination. The way things were going I needed a lot more than my teeth examined. I scooped up the envelopes and cards and walked slowly back to the Stanley.

I drove around the square on the way back and waved to Constable Gerhardt, who smiled and returned the wave, looking as clueless as ever.

Back home, I put the steamer in the barn, and even remembered to plug in the heater, since I would be heading back out to watch Llysette's directorial efforts that evening.

By midafternoon, with breaks for lunch and this and that—developing exams was always a lengthy and painful process—I ran off the last exam on the printer, the Environmental Politics 2B exam, and took a deep breath. I flipped off the difference engine and reread each of them a last time. I'd proof them once more in a couple of days, but the more times you read them, the more likely you are to catch stupid mistakes. Professors make stupid mistakes. That I was continuing to learn.

"Do you know, I would quietly slip from the loud circle?"

I looked up at the ghost floating by my elbow. "I didn't know you were interested in environmental politics or tests."

"I saw you pale and fearing. That was in dream, and your soul rang." Carolynne's words were soft, faint.

"I'm sorry. You told me, but . . . I'm sorry. You deserve better."

Was she paler than usual? I walked behind the couch and pressed the boss on the mirror. Had the watch tampered with the lodestone when they had searched the house? I swung out the mirror, but the lodestone appeared unchanged.

"Only a brief time, and I will be free."

"Free?" I shook my head. "I'm not about to stop the lodestone. That would be murder of sorts, and you—no one deserves that. You've suffered enough." I eased the mirror back into position.

"How we push away the person who loves us! No grief will soften us cold ones. What we love is taken away." For a moment she almost looked real in the high-necked recital dress, and I thought I could see colors. First she seemed pale, then more real. Was I losing it? How much was in my mind?

I swallowed hard. "Is it always that way? Do all ghosts feel as you do? I never thought about it, but you could as well ask if all people feel as I do. Thoughtless of me."

"I live by day, full of faith."

Faith, for a ghost? "And by night?" I asked as I turned on the hall light and walked toward the kitchen, since I needed something to eat before I got dressed for the evening.

"And every night I die in holy fire."

I pulled out the butcher's knife and started to slice some ham off the joint to go with the cheddar. Carolynne drifted toward the door, then slipped out of sight. I looked at the knife. I couldn't very well avoid knives, but I could understand her revulsion at the blade.

After I cleaned up the dishes and retrieved a bottle of wine from the cellar for later, I went up to the bedroom to dress. First I tried the light gray suit, but that didn't seem quite right. So I settled on the dark gray pinstripe, the one I'd worn the day I'd resigned as Minister of Environment. The suit seemed looser. Had I lost weight, or was I just in better shape?

"How I loved you even as a child," offered Carolynne, in words that felt more sung than spoken as she appeared in the doorway.

"You are a shameless ghost."

"Ways will I elect that seldom any tread."

"Sorry."

"Never will love be satisfied. The heart will become more thirsty and hungry."

"Are you talking about me, or you?"

"Will she change what she enjoyed?"

"She? Llysette? Are you talking about Llysette?"

"Your splendor is dying on yonder hill." She winked out, probably going back to her lodestone for a recharge, or meal, or whatever.

I shivered at the warning, for it was clearly a warning. Why was I doing this? Was it a last attempt to do what was right? Was that the reason I'd kept persisting with the ghost caricature of justice and mercy? After everything, could I do less than try to set things right?

My stomach tightened more, and my heart raced. Was I having a heart attack? No . . . just an anxiety attack. I took a deep breath.

Before I left the house, I quickly pulled one of the disassociators out of the closet and tucked it in the foot well of the difference engine stand, in case I needed it for demonstration purposes later.

When I got to the university, I parked the Stanley at the end of the row that held Llysette's Reo, and took just about the last space in the faculty car park, although a number of the cars did not have faculty tags. After locking the steamer, I walked down and across to the main entrance. Under the heavy overcoat I was actually too warm, and I wiped my forehead before I walked up the stone steps into the building, unbuttoning the overcoat as I did. I did keep an eye out, just in case I ran into one of vanBecton's "legacies." Then again, if they were good, I probably wouldn't see them until it was far too late. And, who knew, I wondered if that might have been better. I tried to keep upbeat and shook my head, pushing away my fears.

I was earlier than usual, maybe twenty-five minutes before the curtain; except, even in Dutch New Bruges, the curtain never rose on schedule. Only a scattering of people crossed the foyer toward the ramps. There wasn't a wait at the box office, and I showed my faculty card and paid my two dollars.

"It's supposed to be good, Doktor Eschbach."

"I hope so."

After climbing the ramps to the main door of the theatre, I took the program from the usher, a woman student I'd never seen, and glanced at the title page:

Heinrich Verrückt

OR

The Tragedy of Henry VIII

BY

Ludwig von Beethoven
An Opera in Three Acts

I paused at the back of the theatre, two-thirds of the former gymnasium. The renovation had been thorough enough to put in inclined seating, a full stage, and some acoustical renovation, including dull-looking hangings, but Llysette had still complained that the sound reverberation was uneven and that she had to watch for dead spots on the stage.

I settled into a seat halfway back on the left side, right off the aisle, and wiped my forehead again. I was definitely not in top shape, however much I had played at Spazi agent in the weeks preceding. It was a miracle I hadn't gotten killed.

While I waited, I read through the program. I didn't really know any of the cast, except by name. By the time the lights went down, Llysette's players had almost a full house, even if two-thirds of the audience consisted of friends just wanting to claim they'd seen the opera.

The first act was all right—still some jitters in the cast even though Friday had been opening night—but they all settled down in the second act. The student who played Henry was good; he was a solid baritone, and he had Henry's total arrogance down pat.

At the end of Act III, of course, Henry was imprisoned in the Tower, foaming at the mouth and singing fragments of the same aria that he used to proclaim himself as the supreme head of church and state. Beside him were the ghosts of Anne and Catherine, who continued to plead endlessly in their separate songs. None of the three heard the others, just as they hadn't all along. In the foreground, Mary lifted the cross and sang almost the same words as Henry, thanking God for delivering the crown to her. Yet it wasn't chaotic, but a deeper harmony that was almost eerie.

The curtain fell, and the applause was instantaneous. I applauded with the rest. Especially with a student cast, Llysette had done a magnificent job.

As I clapped, my eyes saw a familiar figure down the aisle—Gertrude, the zombie lady. She wasn't applauding, but sat there wracked with sobs. I stopped applauding before the others, puzzling over her reaction. Gertrude, for whom every day was a good day, sobbing? Gertrude attending an opera? Especially an opera by Beethoven?

What had touched her? In a way I envied her, even as I pitied her. That direct expression of feeling was so foreign to all of us more sophisticated souls.

After the initial crowd dispersed, I made my way backstage, noting that I didn't see Dean Er Recchus; but, then, she would have made her presence known on opening night.

Again I realized that I should have brought Llysette chocolates, but I hoped she understood that I had had a lot on my mind in the past several weeks.

I still had to stand in line as a dozen or so admirers told Llysette what a wonderful job she had done. In a green velvet dress, she was stunning, as usual, and her warm professional smile was firmly in place as she responded to each compliment.

"Congratulations," I finally said, giving her a hug and a kiss on the cheek. "I don't know how you did it, but it was wonderful."

"The sound, how was it?"

"The acoustics? You had them standing in the right places. I could hear it all clearly."

"That is good." She shifted her weight from one foot to another, then returned a wave to one of the students, the girl who had played Anne, I thought.

"Are you about ready to go?"

Llysette pursed her lips and nodded. "I will just follow you. Tomorrow, I must sing for the Anglican-Baptists."

"Again? You don't want me to drive?"

"Better it would be for me to have my own vehicle, I think."

After I helped her into her coat, and after we gathered up all her material, we walked out to the car park. I opened the Reo's door, then set the heavy bag behind the seat, and kissed her before closing the door. Her cheek was already cold from the wind.

"You are always gallant."

"I try."

The Stanley was ready several minutes before the Reo. Before long Llysette would need to have the burner assembly retuned, I suspected, but I hadn't said anything because she would have pointed out, most logically, that her income was far from astronomical, while steamer repairs were more than astronomical.

Once she waved, I pulled out of the car park—we were the last ones there—and headed down and around the square. We had to wait for a watch steamer to cross the River Wijk bridge, but saw no other cars on the road.

Llysette was out of the Reo by the time I had opened the car barn and pulled the Stanley inside, and her teeth were chattering even after we got inside the house. I hugged her for a moment, then turned on the kitchen lights. After her shivering stopped, I helped her out of the heavy coat and put it in the closet.

"I assume you would like some wine. Or would you like something warm like chocolate or tea?"

"The wine, I think, that would be good."

"Do you want anything to eat?"

Usually she didn't, at least not right after a performance.

"I think not, but you are kind to ask."

I opened the bottle—still Sebastopol—and brought down two glasses. "We can go into the study."

Llysette nodded and followed me.

As I passed the difference engine I flicked it on. I hoped I wouldn't need it, but a demonstration might not hurt. Then I set her glass on the low table in front of us and half-filled each glass. I bent down and let my lips brush her neck. "I missed you."

"You also I missed."

I shook my head. Where could I begin?

Llysette looked somberly at me. "You are serious."

I nodded. "I'd like to talk about our future. It's past time we laid the tarot cards down and set our own futures." I sat next to her. I knew I was rushing things, but if I didn't, I'd lose my nerve, and I was tired of living lies, even partial lies, that were tearing me apart.

"Tarot cards?"

"Fortune-telling cards. People believe them when they really need to plan their own futures."

"An illusion that is. It is one all you of Columbia share, that of choice." Llysette's voice was sardonic.

"We can choose." I didn't want to ask her to marry me, not until I had explained. "Neither one of us is innocent."

She stiffened.

"I have done terrible deeds, and so have you." I frowned. "I don't know whether it's better to bury the past unrevealed or to face it and then bury it."

Llysette put down the wine glass. She had not even taken a single sip. "Too much truth, I doubt it is good."

"In that, we're different, but I don't know that I can be other than what I am. When I play at something else . . . Hell . . ." I took a deep breath. "All my life I've been talking around things, dealing in suggestions and implications, but I want to stop that with you."

"Why is that?"

"Because neither one of us is innocent, and I don't want to be tied up with a woman who wonders about my past, and I don't want you to have to wonder whether something out of your past will separate us." I could see her lips tightening. "Is honesty so bad?" I asked with a forced smile.

"Honesty? Johan, you do not wish to be honest with me. Yourself you wish to be honest with. An excuse am I. Never have you said you love me, except in the bedroom. That is honest?"

I took a deep breath. "I suppose not. But I am trying to change. And I do love you."

"So . . . now it is convenient to admit that?"

I took a deep breath. "I am trying. It's been hard for me. How do you think I feel about loving someone who committed a murder? You killed Miranda. Why, I don't know, but I, fool that I am, shielded you. The timing I gave the watch was wrong, and you knew that. Doesn't that show something? That I care, that I love you?"

"In sex and in murder, you love me?"

"I said I wasn't perfect." I tried to force a soft laugh, but my throat was dry. Llysette stood and so did I.

"You do not understand, Johan." She half-turned toward the window, to the almost ghostly light of the moon on the lawn outside.

I moved toward the desk, bending and tapping the keys on the difference engine to bring up the program.

"I think I might." In fact, I was afraid I did understand, all too well, but I did not reach for the Colt in the drawer, the more fool I.

"No. No one understands." Llysette turned, and I faced a Colt-Luger, a small one but with a long enough barrel to ensure its accuracy. She had it pointed at me, and the barrel was steady.

"Why?" My voice was surprisingly calm. At least the calm was surprising to me, in finding my lover with a gun designed to drill holes in me.

"Because you remember everything and have learned nothing, Johan. Power must be countered with power."

"So . . . the poor psychic Miranda knew that you were an agent for the Austro-Hungarians . . . the convenient fiction of all that money from the Cultural Foundation."

"The Foundation, it is real."

I was very careful not to move, even though both my own Colt and the disassociator were almost within reach. I still had hopes. Stupid of me.

"You know I could have . . ." I swallowed. If I had turned her in, then the blame would have gone to Ferdinand, and if I hadn't, I would have been framed, and the Speaker would have had a chain of evidence pointing straight to the President's office. Either way, vanBecton would have gotten me, or Llysette, or both of us.

"You do not comprehend, Johan."

"I understand everything—except why you agreed to serve Ferdinand." I knew that, too, but I wanted to hear her explain it.

"Ferdinand's doctors, they are masters of torture. To the last drop of pain they know what will free the soul and what will leave one tied to a screaming body. This I know. You do not."

Thinking of those thin white lines on the inside of her thighs and under her pale white arms, I shivered. No wonder she would not speak of the scars or let my fingers linger there. And yet I had said nothing when it could have changed things. Why was I always too late?

"I need to show you something," I said gently. "After all, that's what Ferdinand hired you for, and what the New French were blackmailing Miranda to find out."

"Miranda, she was not just a meddler?"

"Her son is being held in New France. He was an importer. She would have done anything, I think, to get him released. Could I sit down?"

The Colt-Luger wavered for a moment, but only for a moment. I slipped in front of the keyboard, keeping my hands very visible.

"How did you know this?" she demanded.

"Her other son told me about the detention. He also told me that she was a witch-psychic."

"She was a witch. That I know. She said that she would tell you, and that you would turn me in. Because you were a Spazi agent still. I wanted to love you, Johan. I love you, and you said nothing. Why did you not tell me?"

"I told no one."

"That, it does not change things."

"I am trying to be honest. I retired from the Spazi years ago."

"An agent, he never retires."

She was right about that, and I was wrong. Lord, how I'd been wrong. "Let me touch the keyboard. Maybe this will help. First I'm going to make a ghost appear—even around you."

Llysette raised her eyebrows, and I noticed the sheen of perspiration across her forehead. Damn vanBecton! What I'd done to him hadn't been near enough. And Ralston—threatening her just to move me around.

"That is supposed to prove what?" The muzzle of the Colt-Luger didn't waver, and she was standing just far enough away that I wouldn't have stood a chance.

"If you are going to shoot me, then you should have something to give to Ferdinand. This is what he wants. The way to make and unmake ghosts. I love you enough to give you that." I lifted my fingers from the keys to the flimsy directional antenna. "Now I need to point this. I won't direct it anywhere near you."

"What are you doing?" she asked, adding in a colder tone, "It does not matter."

"Creating a ghost." I turned the trapezoidal tetrahedonal antenna in the general direction of the couch and the mirror and punched the last key to bring up the Carolynne duplicate. The white figure in the recital gown appeared before the love seat, wavering more than I would have liked, but it was only a rough duplicate, a far too simplified version of the real singer, just a caricature of Carolynne.

Llysette looked at me. "I am waiting, Johan."

"Don't you see?"

"See what? That mist?"

Partial ghost-blindness? Was Llysette sensitive only to the strongest ghosts? She'd said ghosts didn't appear around her, but had that just meant she did not sense them? Was that what the torture in Ferdinand's hands had done? I was in trouble.

"Let me try again." I swallowed and touched the keys to the difference engine and called up the justice-and-mercy ghost caricature, hoping my latest efforts had made it very strong indeed. My knee rested against the disassociator, but I didn't want to think about that, not even then.

The wavering figure of justice appeared next to the faint duplicate of Carolynne, and I could feel that one-dimensional sense of justice—almost a cartoon version of the man with the scales in his hand.

"Justice must be done." The ghost voice was a whisper, but a strong whisper. "Justice must be done."

"Something there is. You make images . . . How will they help?"

I wasn't sure anything would help. Was she programmed to kill me as a form of suicide? Or herself? Neither alternative was going to help us.

The justice figure drifted toward Llysette.

"Justice must be done . . ."

She edged back, as though even she could feel the merciless singleness of that judicial caricature.

"No! Stay away! Johan, I will kill you!"

I ducked and snatched for the disassociator.

"Johan!"

I swung the disassociator toward her and twisted out of the chair, just as a third flash of white appeared behind Llysette.

Crack. I could feel the first small-caliber shell rip through my jacket shoulder. I tried to drop behind the difference engine, but Llysette kept firing the damned Colt.

Crack! Crack!

"Llysette!"

"No! No one's puppet . . . will I . . . be."

Crack!

I pulled the spring trigger on the disassociator and held it, then jerked it sideways. Not another murder. Not another lover dying because of me. My head felt like it was splitting apart, like a crowbar was being jammed into my skull and twisted.

The lights went out, of course, even as the disassociator slewed sideways at the mirror and the huge lodestone behind it.

But even in the dimness I could see the stiffening of Llysette's face, the faint flash of white as something—something vital?—left.

"Johan. Why have you killed me?"

The dead tone in the voice hammered at me in the darkness, and I looked at the barrel of the Colt.

Crack!

Her hand dropped, and another line of fire went through me, like the blade of a knife. Her Colt dropped on the floor with a muffled thump.

"No . . . no . . ." Llysette's cry was more of a plea than a command. "Please, no . . . NO!!!"

I lost my grip on the disassociator, and I half tripped and half fell into darkness, my hands skidding across the carpet.

That darkness was punctuated with images: Elspeth lying pale between paler sheets and choking up blood; Waltar's closed coffin; two zombie watch officers looking at me; Ralston sprawled across his steps; Gertrude sobbing at the end of the last act of *Heinrich Verrückt;* Llysette's pale face and deader voice.

And the images spun, twirled on the spindle of that single line spoken by the caricature ghost of justice: "Justice must be done. Justice must be done."

I lay there for a long time. A very long time.

"Johan . . . Johan . . ."

In the flickering light of a single candle, Llysette was bent over me, tears dropping across my face and bare shoulder, shivering even as she bound my wound. I did not recall turning over, and I shuddered. My shoulder seared with the movement.

"Johan, do not leave us . . ." Another tear cascaded across my cheek.

Us? My head ached. Why had I done it all? Had I really had to kill Warbeck? Or zombie all those people, especially the watch officers? But they would have killed me, and their guns had been ready. Why hadn't I just told Llysette I loved her? Did I, or had it just been sexual attraction?

A stabbing sensation, almost burning as much as the gunshot wound, throbbed in my skull, behind my eyes. My head burned, ached, and the images flared . . .

. . . standing on a varnished wooden stage, limelights flooding past me, looking out into a square-faced audience, seeing not a single smile . . .

. . . the glint of an oil lamp on cold steel, and the heavy knife slicing through my shoulder, once, then again, and a man wrestling the blade away, trying to rise, watching blood well across a pale nightgown . . .

. . . drifting through an empty house, watching, waiting . . .

. . . a blond boy sitting before the bookshelves, slowly turning pages, his eyes flickering eagerly across the words, my eyes straining to follow . . .

. . . a man winding copper wire, glancing nervously toward the setting sun, fingers deftly working . . .

. . . a woman staring at me, and saying, "Leave the boy alone, or you'll regret it. You understand, ghost hussy?"

. . . drifting through an empty house, watching, waiting, pausing by the covered shelves in the study . . .

. . . a sandy-haired man standing for hours, looking blankly out a window, then burying his head in his hands . . .

. . . listening to the sandy-haired man saying, "I know you're a ghost, but using songs as riddles is hard on me. I'm tired. Can't you say what you mean?" and singing back words he could only hear as cold words, *"Ne point passer!"*—feeling warmth, love, and anger, all at once . . .

The images kept slashing into me, like dreams, half pleasant, half nightmares, and above it all that same statement hammered at me: "Justice must be done. Justice must be done."

Had anything I'd done been just? Yes . . . no . . . yes . . . no . . . both sides of everything whirled in my head, and each side drew blood.

The blackness or the words, or both, hammered me down again.

Sometime later I swallowed, my mouth dry, and opened my eyes. Llysette sat beside me on the floor, her eyes clinched tight, one hand on mine, and I tried to speak, and had no voice, only questions. She looked at me, and more tears fell, but she trembled, and did not speak, only wept and held my hand.

Why had I shut Judith and Eric out? Why had I used poor Carolynne like some experimental animal? And Branston-Hay, had I driven him to his death? And pushed the Spazi into burning his home? Guilt, like a breaker, crashed over me, and I dropped back into darkness.

Was this ghosting? Was I becoming a ghost myself, or a zombie? Why couldn't I move? Was this death?

Llysette was still there when I awoke the second—or was it the third—time, and the candle was still flickering, though so low that wax lay piled on the desk. I was wrapped in blankets.

I wondered why a clean gunshot wound that hadn't shattered bone or an artery—I'd have been dead long since—had floored me. I also wondered why she hadn't shot me dead, or called the Spazi and revealed what she knew.

Instead, she bent down and kissed my forehead, which didn't make any sense, not after she'd pulled the trigger in the first place. But she was trembling, and her face was blotchy, and for the first time she looked far older than her age.

My own vision blurred—with tears, relief. Was I still there? Was there a chance?

"Johan . . ." She shook her head, then closed her eyes for a moment, squeezing my hand gently. "Please, stay with us."

Some of the pieces fit. In the mess, I'd fired the disassociator right into the lodestone behind the mirror, and that had disassociated something from Llysette. I'd seen something. That I knew. But I didn't know what else that might have done or added to my own disassociation. I had suffered some form of psychic disassociation, perhaps extreme guilt.

And I'd gotten some of Carolynne—probably the duplicate version, although I didn't understand how so comparatively few code lines held so much. Or was it only a framework, and were ghosts, even artificial ones, somehow creations of a merciful god merely tied to biologic or logic codes?

But if Llysette hadn't gotten the integrity program, then why was she taking care of me? Why was she so upset? And why was she alive when her face had been so dead and she had cried that I had killed her?

I looked up. The difference engine was off, and there were no ghosts in the darkness.

Llysette's voice trembled. "Loved you, she did." She started to sing, brokenly, "Put out my eyes . . . can see you still . . . slam ear . . . can hear you yet . . . without feet can go to you at will . . ."

Then she just sobbed.

I did manage to struggle into a sitting position and hold my poor singer, even with the burning in my shoulder and my eyes.

"Loved you, she did, poor ghost," she sniffed. "And I also, but not enough." She sniffed again, trying to blot tears that would not stop and streaked mascara and makeup across her face. "Now, two parts, they make a whole . . . and we both love you, and you must not leave us, not when she loved so much."

The words bubbled up on my tongue, but I could only speak them, not sing them. "I grieved . . . so much. I saw you pale and fearing. That was in dream, and your soul rang. All softly my soul sounded with it, and both souls sang themselves: I suffered. Then peace came deep in me . . ."

"And in me," Llysette sang, a lullaby and a love song. "I lay in the silver heaven between dream and day . . ."

She began to cry again, and so did I, for I, too, was whole, out of many parts, as we shared the song I had never known till then, knowing that Carolynne had given us many songs.

CHAPTER THIRTY-ONE

• • •

Things don't ever end quite the way you thought.

Llysette and I are getting married. In the Dutch Reformed Church in Vanderbraak Centre. Klaus Esterhoos deserves that much, at least. Eric and Judith will be here. So will my mother and Anna, and, of course, Carolynne will be with both Llysette and me, in a way, and there's no way either one of us can repay her . . . except maybe by trying to do it right this time.

We aren't inviting David or the dean, and we've avoided the trap David set, because I just told Llysette first—like she asked me—and we laughed.

"Such a small man he is. He and the dean, they deserve each other."

"Of course they do."

"Their own happiness, that will be hard for them." But her voice was thoughtful, not hard, and she bent over and kissed me.

"And our happiness?"

"Best we keep it, dear man. The price for all, it was high."

I squeezed her hand, and she squeezed mine. "But they don't know that."

"*Non*. They, they will live where we once did, in a shallow sea."

And they will, in a sea of illusion, where they believe, as I did, that everything I did was for a good cause. People like that always do, and despite my best efforts with Babbage code, there was really no way to create a ghost of justice and mercy. What I had gotten was only a caricature of justice. Then, that's what most people want—caricatures.

We'd thought about moving back to the Federal District of Columbia, with all of Bruce's gadgets, and giving lots and lots of dinner parties, small intimate ones where Llysette sang. Despite Judith's words about honesty, there was still one problem—my "insurance" policies would probably have been invalidated if our profiles got too high.

So . . . if Mahomet can't go to the mountain, the mountain has to come to Mahomet. Even all the way to New Bruges.

Llysette's singing is a key part, of course. She can really bring tears to people's eyes now, especially to mine, and I'm sure that, between the two of us, we can actually raise money for a new performing arts hall.

Bruce and I have refined his gadgets so that we can now project small voices—call them angels. It's not possession, not by a long shot. It just gets their attention. And then Llysette sings. Music—the right music to receptive ears—can do much more than soothe the savage beast. I didn't even have to twist Bruce's arms, not too much, anyway. But I think he really wishes we were moving.

You ask, is it ethical? I can only say that if I survived two ghostly possessions, then they can handle a few voices in concert. Call it an examination of conscience. Are we playing gods? Of course, but people always have, and refused to admit it. For the first time in my life, I'm being honest. So is Llysette.

She sings, and I teach. After all, what else can two academics do in up-country New Bruges?

Our daughter will be named Carolynne, but she won't ever know the details, or the reason, and neither will Speaker Hartpence, nor President Armstrong. But we always will.

The
Ghost
of the
Revelator

For Bruce, and for Carol Ann,

who made this possible

CHAPTER ONE

• • •

The Late-October New Bruges drizzle—more liquid ice than rain on that Friday night—clicked off the Stanley's thermal finish all the way down from the house into Vanderbraak Centre. Beside me, Llysette sat, drawn into herself, as she always was before she performed.

When you're a professor and retired spy married to a former diva of old France who's been the toast of a Europe now crumbled under Ferdinand's boots, you always hope for peace and quiet. Especially when you've finally turned the disaster of two ghosts in your life into mere inconvenience. And sometimes you get it, but this time even the ice was only the calm before a bigger storm.

"The ice rains . . . at times, Johan, would that we lived where I did not need two coats and wool garments."

"I know." I'd learned early to say nothing controversial before she sang. "I was thinking that over midterms we might take a vacation in Saint-Martine. There's a weekly dirigible from Asten."

"I will not endure that long a time." Llysette shivered. "And tonight, they will applaud like cows. For what do I sing?"

"Because you're a singer. Singers sing. You sing magnificently—"

"Once I did. Now . . . I do not know."

"You'll be magnificent. I know it." I eased the steamer to a stop right opposite the side door to the old Physical Training building, set the brake, and scurried around with the black umbrella to escort Llysette up and inside. I kissed her on the cheek, again. "You'll be fine."

"Fine is for gold, Johan."

"You'll sing magnificently."

"We shall see." She headed up the half-flight of steps to the practice room where her accompanist, Johanna, waited. She'd already warmed up at the house on the Haaren console grand piano. I'd purchased that for her with part of my "bonus" for resolving the governmental ghost crisis. Given what I'd put Llysette through, she deserved the piano and more. Given what Archduke Ferdinand of the Austro-Hungarian Empire and my own beloved country of Columbia had put her through, even a concert Steinbach wouldn't have been the first installment on true repayment to her, but I was trying.

I went back to move the Stanley into a more legitimate spot in the car park, getting even wetter in the process because it was about four times as far from where I parked to the front of the Music and Theatre building.

"Good evening, Doktor Eschbach." One of Llysette's students was handing out programs, but I didn't recall her name—Emelia van—something or other. Then, most of the students at Vanderbraak State University were from New Bruges. Most had a predominantly Dutch heritage—and that Dutch reserve that made Llysette's teaching an exercise as much in trying to bring emotion to singing as to develop the basics of music.

"Good evening."

To my surprise, the foyer was relatively crowded, and I turned toward the theatre itself, but didn't get that far.

"Doktor Eschbach! Doktor Eschbach . . ." Katrinka Er Recchus had the kind of voice that penetrated, but I supposed that kind of penetration was sometimes useful for the dean of the university. Her bright and overly broad smile was dwarfed by the expanse of a white lace collar that topped her too ample figure. Although the auburn hair was faultless, I suspected the original shade had been mousy brown, but there was nothing mousy about her—ratlike, perhaps, but not mousy.

"Dean Er Recchus." I bowed to her and then to Alois, her even more rotund husband, a retired major in the New Bruges guard, as was obvious from the squared-off nature of his white goatee, the guard pin in his lapel, and the dark gray cravat and suit. He returned the bow without speaking.

"I had heard that your presentation on environmental politics and policies was masterful," the dean continued. "Doktor Doniger was most complimentary."

"I'm glad David was pleased." Doktor David Doniger, my chairman and head of the newly reformed Department of Political and Natural Resource Sciences, was usually a pain in the posterior.

"Johan." Her voice lowered, but not the overpowering quantity of that floral fragrance that some vain and aging women immerse themselves in under the delusion that olfactory stupefaction will result in visual illusion. "The vanEmsdens were so pleased that you are the first professor to occupy their endowed chair. Peter was particularly supportive of your past achievements and your dedication to Columbia. He served in the Singapore incident, in the Republic Air Corps, as you did. I am so glad that all such unpleasantnesses are behind us now." The bright smile indicated that any such unpleasantness had best remain behind us all.

The Singapore mess, when Chung Kuo had devastated the city, had been well before my time, and Peter vanEmsden and I had merely passed pleasantries at the ceremony where I'd been installed as the first vonBehn Professor of Applied Politics and Ecology. I doubted most knew the ironies involved with my selection to establish the formal legacy of Elysia vanEmsden's father's forebear, and I wasn't about to explain. After all, how could I—a spy carrying on the legacy of another spy?

"I am delighted that they were pleased."

Alois merely nodded, as he did frequently when with the dean.

When I finally entered the theatre that had been the sole lecture hall of the old

Physical Training center, I checked the program. At least Llysette no longer had to resort to under-the-table handouts from the Austro-Hungarian Cultural Foundation to make ends meet. Tucked in among the recital pieces, besides *An die Nacht* and Barber's *Monastic Songs,* was Anne Boleyn's aria from *Heinrich Verrückt.* Llysette had wanted to do that aria at her recital the fall before but had done the Mozart Anti-Mass instead. She'd needed the stipend from the Cultural Foundation. The recital had been the night Miranda Miller, the piano professor, had been murdered, and that had started Llysette's and my adventures with several different covert operations, including those of my former employer, the Sedition Prevention and Security Service, more widely and less popularly known as the Spazi.

I shivered a touch. The last thing Llysette and I needed was anything more along those lines.

The house was almost full, with nearly all of the 450 seats filled nearly a half hour before Llysette was due to sing. I paused for a moment before I sat down, about halfway back, on the aisle, still surveying the audience.

In about the tenth row, in the middle, sat a bearded man in dark clothes, not the dark clothes of the Dutch, or even of a conservative southerner, but different, somehow, almost out of the last century. Not too far from the stranger sat Dierk Geoffries, Llysette's chair. On the far side I even saw Marie Rijn, who cleaned the house for us, along with an older man I guessed had to be her husband.

After I seated myself on one of the all too inflexible Dutch colonial hardwood seats, I glanced back at the bearded man. The seats on either side of him had remained empty, even as the house filled.

The lights dimmed.

Llysette stepped onstage, dark hair upswept, almost imperial in the shimmering green gown, and I forgot about the bearded man.

Johanna's fingers caressed the keys of the concert Steinbach, and the sound shimmered into the evening. Then Llysette began, a selection from Perkins, not one from a Vondel opera.

Llysette sang beautifully. She always had, but now there was something else . . . even more of a spark or a lambent flame.

She had the entire audience, even the stolid Dutch burghers, standing and yelling after she finished the encore—something from an opera I'd never heard: *Susannah.* And she smiled back at them. The other thing I'd never heard in Vanderbraak Centre was so much applause from the normally restrained Dutch.

Llysette's department chair—that was Dierk Geoffries—caught me in the aisle. "I didn't think she could get better, she was so good. . . ." He shook his mane of gray-blond hair. "I've heard some of the best—Delligatti, Riciarelli, Rysanek. Tonight she was better than any of them."

I'd never heard better, but I was no expert. From the hypercritical Dierk, that was high praise. "Best you tell her. If I did, she'd just dismiss it as the pride of a smitten spouse."

"I will." Dierk laughed, and I let him head down the aisle first, listening as I did.

". . . better than korfball any day. . . ."

". . . good . . . but . . . don't know about that," murmured the tall blond youth, who probably was on the university korfball team—which had lost badly to Rensselaer the night before.

The bearded man in the old-fashioned suit, except it seemed new, had a broad smile on his face as he bowed to Llysette backstage and murmured something before stepping away and vanishing.

I followed Dierk and a square-faced Hans Waetjen backstage. Waetjen was the chief of the Watch for Vanderbraak Centre, and he'd avoided speaking to me ever since my actions had led to three of his officers being turned into zombies because one had been suborned by an Austrian covert agent. Dierk stepped aside, and the Watch chief bowed to Llysette. "You were magnificent." Then he turned to me. "Almost magnificent enough to forgive you for marrying Doktor Eschbach."

Waetjen nodded and was gone. At least, a year after the unfortunate incident, he was speaking to me, and he hadn't protested, so far as I knew, when the Citizenship Bureau, after years of dithering, had finally granted Llysette her citizen's status. And I'd never known he liked singing.

Dierk shook his head again. "Unbelievable. No wonder you were the toast of the Academie Royale. I was truly blessed tonight." After another incredulous headshake, he, too, slipped away.

"You were wonderful." I hugged her, and I even had remembered chocolates and flowers—but they were waiting for her at home. "You . . . you've never been better."

Llysette smiled . . . shyly, for a moment. "Better we were, and better yet we will be. . . ."

"You, not we."

"We," she corrected me. "And it is good, Johan. Sad . . . but good."

I swallowed and hugged her, knowing my own cheeks were suddenly damp.

"Fräulein duBoise . . ."

With others still arriving to see Llysette, I stepped back to her shoulder, nodding at Johanna and murmuring, "You played well."

"She sang . . . she sang, Johan." The accompanist shook her head slowly. "Singing like that you seldom hear. Seldom? I've *never* heard it before."

"I can see that I have missed too much." Katrinka Er Recchus, Alois stolidly behind her, smiled her broad and false smile. "You were delightful, dear, absolutely delightful." Her eyes went to me. "You have been too modest about her. Far too modest, Johan." As if it were my fault that the former chair of the Music and Theatre Department hadn't bothered to come to Llysette's recitals before?

I forced a smile. "She has always been magnificent."

"Oh, I can tell now . . . but how was I to know?"

I could have asked myself the same. Once I'd thought about enhancing her singing with my ghost-projection equipment, to create supporting "angels," but after what I'd heard, that would have been too great a sin . . . far too great. Then, maybe, any use of the equipment to influence people would have been, and I just hadn't understood then.

"Enchanting," offered Alois, stolidly easing the dean aside, for once. "Wonderfully enchanting." Alois bowed and escorted the dean back toward the foyer.

"Professor duBoise," asked a red-haired student, tears streaming down her face, "how can I ever do the Perkins the way you do?"

Llysette waited.

"Couldn't we change places? I'll never be able to sing like you do."

"You wish to sing, Berthe? Then work you must. I will hear the Perkins on Tuesday." Llysette softened the words with a smile and a pat on the girl's shoulder.

"Your coat," I prompted as the admirers began to thin.

"It is . . . in the practice room."

"Do you need a ride?" I asked Johanna as I started to retrieve the heavy coat.

"Pietr is already getting the steamer." The accompanist smiled briefly at Llysette. "Even he was touched, but he won't admit it."

"That, that is *quelque chose incredible*."

After ensuring that Llysette was wrapped in the coat, I managed to ease the three boxes of chocolates and several sprays of flowers under my free arm and to escort her to the side door. "You wait here, and I'll bring the Stanley around."

"That is fine with me." She shivered, as she often did after heavy exertion, and wrapped the heavy coat around her.

The Stanley started easily, despite the streaks of ice and cold water, and the rain had turned to tiny frozen pellets. Llysette almost slipped getting into the steamer. Before long, the road and car park would be black ice.

The town square was mostly deserted, except for the lights in the Watch station, and I wondered if Chief Waetjen had stopped by on his way home, that is, if he had one besides the station.

"Who was the bearded fellow?" I asked. "I've never seen him before."

"The . . . bearded . . . oh, the man with the ancient cravat?" Llysette shrugged under the heavy wool coat. "Never have I seen him. He offered his name . . . James . . . Jacob . . . Jensen. He said . . . we would be hearing from him. Then he was gone."

"That's all?"

"He said my singing, it was as grand as any."

"It was." I laughed, but I wondered about Herr Jensen. When unknown admirers promise that you'll hear from them, you have to wonder in what context.

The River Wijk was dark even under the new lights from the bridge. On the other side, I had to go into four-wheel drive once we started up Deacon's Lane because the narrow uphill road had a thin layer of ice and slush. I had the feeling we were in for an early and hard winter, unlike the previous year.

I dropped Llysette by the door while I manuevered the steamer into the car barn.

She glanced up the stairs as we stepped into the front foyer. Force of habit, still, I suspected, from the days when Carolynne, the family ghost, had lurked there. That had been before my efforts with ghosting technology had ended up grafting her into both our souls. It hadn't been planned that way, and it had saved us from worse, but it wasn't always easy living with feelings and memories you knew weren't yours. I felt it was even harder for Llysette and, for that reason, didn't mention Carolynne much.

"Good it is for there to be no ghosts looking down the stairs. I would dread looking up there."

"I know. I always looked first." I locked the door and took off my topcoat, then led her back to the sitting room. "You just sit here in front of the stove." Although I'd loaded the woodstove before we'd left and the sitting room off the terrace was warm, I opened the stove door and added another two lengths of oak. The heat welled out, and Llysette leaned forward to get warm.

"I'll get your wine . . . or would you like chocolate?" As I turned, I could see the piano in the rear parlor—I'd never really used that space before, but it had turned out to be the best place for the piano, and the room was warm.

"The wine. . . . I am warmer, already." She looked up at me, her green eyes wide. "You are good to me . . . to us."

"After . . . everything . . . you say that. . . ." I swallowed. It was still hard. "I love you."

A smile crinkled her lips. "Dutch you are. For all your words, *mon ami,* some you find difficult."

She was right. I did.

"The wine?" Her voice was softer now when she spoke, softer than when we had first met, but neither of us needed to discuss that.

I ducked downstairs—there was a relatively new case of Bajan red, a mountain Sebastopol. Probably not so good as a really good French wine, but better than anything else, and the French hadn't been producing good wines for the last fifteen years or so, not since Ferdinand had reduced the French population by more than 30 percent in his infamous March.

Once I'd opened the bottle, I brought her a glass, with my chocolates. They were the fourth box, but how would I have known?

"Here is the wine . . . and my small offering." I didn't tell her about the roses up in the bedroom. She'd see those later.

"Good." She smiled, and her eyes smiled with her mouth. "French it is not—"

"But almost as good," I finished. Llysette would never admit that Columbian wine would match that of her vanquished homeland, but we could laugh about it—about the wine, not about her terrors, nor the torture under Ferdinand, nor the hard years after.

"Almost."

I sat down beside her on the new sofa—we'd redecorated a great deal in the six months since we'd been married—with my own glass of Sebastopol.

Outside, the ice pellets turned into snow, and the wind gusted. I eased back to enjoy warmth of the stove, of the Sebastopol, of the coming weekend, and mostly of Llysette.

CHAPTER TWO

• • •

The ice and snow that had intermittently fallen over the weekend and into Monday had long since vanished under Tuesday's sun. Only a light frost remained on the browned grasses of my neighbor Benjamin's fields as I drove the Stanley across the gray waters of the River Wijk and into Vanderbraak Centre just before nine on Wednesday morning. Llysette and I were cutting it close, since she had a student at nine o'clock for applied voice.

"*Mercredi, c'est le jour du diable.*" Llysette had come to speak a bit more French in the months since we had been married, and I wondered how much strain always speaking English had been.

"The midweek peak," I agreed.

"I talk, and they listen, and still I must beat the notes. Nod they do, but understand they do not."

The ever-present Constable Gerhardt waved and smiled above his sweeping mustaches as we slowed on our way around the square that held the Watch building, the Dutch Reformed church, the post centre, and McArdles', the sole full grocery emporium in the area. Then we were past the good constable and headed uphill toward the Music and Theatre building.

"Lunch at Delft's, right after noon?" I asked.

"*Mais oui, mon cher.*" At least I got a dazzling smile before the more somber look clouded her face as she turned toward the Music and Theatre building and her hapless, and probably clueless, young Dutch student.

Dutch students were no different from any other students in thinking that mere mental effort should effect physical results. It doesn't work that way in singing—or in anything—but that's a lesson that almost never can be passed from generation to generation but must be learned the hard way. As Llysette kept saying, "The head, it is smart, but the muscles are dumb." But all too many students didn't want to put in the mental and physical effort required to train dumb muscles.

Before I headed to my own office, I stopped outside Samaha's to pick up the

Asten Post-Courier. While "Samaha's Factorium and Emporium" had been on the corner opposite the bridge for well over a century, so had far too much of the inventory. The proprietor, one Louis Samaha, not only refused to answer to anything except "Louie," but he was also the only shopkeeper left in town who had individual narrow paper boxes for his special customers. I continued to have a fondness for some traditions, even as I had watched them unravel all around me.

The decor of Samaha's consisted of dark wooden counters and rough-paneled walls that contained fine cracks older than any current living beings in Vanderbraak Centre, perhaps even older than some of the ghosts. The modern glow panels in the ceiling had so far failed to shed light on the store's history or the inventory in the deeper counter shelves.

I ignored the bakery counter and the breads and rolls heavy enough to sink a dreadnought or serve as ballast for a dirigible and pulled my paper from its slot, fifth down in the first row, right below the empty slot labeled: "Derkin." In the three years since I had returned to Vanderbraak Centre, I'd seen Mister Derkin exactly twice.

I left my dime on the counter, since Louie was nowhere to be seen. Although the *Post-Courier* was only seven cents, I kept giving Louie the other three as a fee for saving back issues for me when I was away from Vanderbraak Centre.

The left front-page story above the fold was a rehash—more on the continuing political fight between landing rights at the Asten aerodrome between turbos and dirigibles. I sighed in spite of myself. Some things didn't seem to change.

I folded the paper into my case and climbed back into the Stanley for the short drive to the upper faculty car park, not the lower one where I had dropped Llysette, but the larger one closer to my office. The old Dutch Republican house had been converted to the Offices of the Natural Resources Department—rather, I corrected myself, the expanded and renamed Department of Political and Natural Resource Sciences—dear David's political coup and brainchild.

As I eased the steamer up Highland Street, the clock on the post centre struck nine. Three spaces remained, all in the back row, but what was I to expect when the car park only contained four dozen places and nearly twice that number of faculty lived outside of walking distance? The latecomers parked where they could, but not, of course, around the square. Dean Er Recchus and the town elders had squabbled about that before the magistrates on at least two occasions, and that might recur. The dean's memoranda on the issue threatened to revoke faculty parking privileges for any faculty member so desperate as to occupy a space designed for those shopping at the establishments around the square.

I vented the Stanley before locking it and walking to my office. Gilda, the department secretary, glanced up, her frizzy black hair pulled back into a bun. "Marriage continues to agree with you, Doktor Eschbach. You aren't haunting our halls every waking moment." Her eyes flicked to David's closed and dark door. Gilda never was warm or polite when David was around, but in her position I probably wouldn't have been either.

"I continue to be fortunate." That was true, in more ways than one, and what else could I say?

A single message graced my box, from the esteemed chairman, the most honorable Doktor David Doniger—a reminder of next Monday's faculty meeting, on the special memo paper he used as chairman.

Once in my office, I read through the *Asten Post-Courier* from front to back. Two stories intrigued me particularly. The first was about the reaction of Quebec's president to a fishing rights issue:

MONTREAL (WNS). Pres. Alphonse Duval announced an "agreement in principle" with New France over the allocation of catches from the Grand Banks fisheries in return for approval of the sale of three New French Santa Anna class frigates to the Navy of Quebec. The frigates are currently under construction at the San Diego, Baja, shipyards.

Jacques Chirac, leader of the opposition Democratic Republicans, denounced the proposed agreement as an abrogation of Quebecois sovereignty over the Grand Banks and an invitation to a Columbian invasion.

Columbian Defense Minister Holmbek refused direct comment, but Defense Ministry sources indicated that the idea of military action to deal with fisheries matters was "absurd."

The Alliance for World Peace asked Speaker Hartpence to begin an investigation into the charges that the frigate sale agreement was leaked to the media in order to obtain support for an increase in the Columbian military budget for the coming fiscal year.

For some reason, the article bothered me, but I couldn't say why. I read the WNS story again but still couldn't identify why it bothered me. The second story bothered me, too, but for a different reason:

ASTEN (RPI). The latest development in the Israel Ishmaad murder case is a ghost—the ghost of the child Ishmaad allegedly mutilated and murdered.

Asten City Prosecutor Fridrich Devol yesterday used testimony from Dr. Fitzgerald Warren as key support for his argument that Ish-

maad had tortured his six-year-old stepson for an extended period of time. . . .

"In simple terms," said Devol, "young children raised in a normal and loving atmosphere do not develop an awareness of death until they are much older, usually between eight and twelve. The fact that this boy barely six years old became a ghost is the strongest possible evidence that he had been repeatedly beaten, that he was aware of the possibility of death. Not only was he killed, but he was robbed of his childhood long before his death. . . ."

Those close to defense attorney Edward Quiddik have suggested that Devol's argument is "psychological poppycock with no basis in fact" and predict that Quiddik will address the issue with a battery of poltergeistic experts.

The prosecuting attorney's argument made sense to me. Ghosts came from violent knowledgeable death. My son Waltar had lived for nearly ten minutes on that bloody Federal District street, bleeding from bullets meant for me, and he'd been nearly eleven—and he'd never become a ghost. Elspeth had died instantly, too quickly to become a ghost, and, then, I wished I had too. I'd had to learn to live again, and every day, Llysette—and Carolynne—taught me a little more.

At the knock at my half-open door, I set down the paper. "Come in."

"Johan." Wilhelm Mondriaan still remained the junior member of the expanded department. The shirttail relative of the painter continued to inform all who conversed at length with him, in some fashion or another, that he had received his doctorate from the University of Virginia. He had trouble understanding that I had ceased to worship unquestioningly at that or any other altar of higher education, Thomas Jefferson notwithstanding.

"Yes?"

"You know that David is going to bring up the question of putting a zero cap on registrations on Natural Resources Three B?" Mondriaan eased into my not-terribly-capacious office.

Natural Resources Three B was officially the ecology of wetlands course that all the students hated, because none of them wanted a detailed environmental rationale for preserving wetlands when most of them had a tradition of either developing, filling, or "reclaiming" wetlands. The question of what course to cut back on always came back to wetlands ecology. I just sighed. "Are we back to that again?"

"I do not believe we ever left it." Regner Grimaldi stood in the door, chipper as always, in another of his European-cut suits, this one a dark gray chalk stripe accented by a maroon cravat. "Our Doktor David has the persistence of Ferdinand." Young Grimaldi had little love for Ferdinand, and I suppose I wouldn't have either, not if my father had died under the panzerwagens when Ferdinand had contemptuously disregarded the older Grimaldi's surrender of Monaco.

"I take it that our honored chair is elsewhere this morning?"

"He is having another tooth faultlessly capped," added Grimaldi. "But he will return . . . both to us and the elimination of Three B."

"Unlike Gessler to Singapore." Mondriaan attempted to cultivate a rumbling bass, but a mild baritone was all he could manage.

How could Gessler have returned to Singapore after Chung Kuo had thrown three million crack troops into the peninsula? The Aussies hadn't let Columbia use Subic Bay as a staging area against the Chinese assault, not with both Japan and Chung Kuo exerting pressure. Of course, how long Australia itself, let alone its Philippine Protectorate, would last was another question these days.

Mondriaan looked at Grimaldi. "What is the festive occasion?"

"Festive? This is conservative for me, Wilhelm." Grimaldi laughed. "Johan? Will you say anything about the wetlands course?"

"Me? The chairman's favorite bête noire?"

They both waited.

"I'll make my usual point that wetlands are the pivot point of any integrated ecology . . . and I suppose that will get a grudging acceptance that one section will be taught in the spring, and you two can fight over it."

They both nodded.

"I need to finish preparing for my ten o'clock." Grimaldi vanished from the doorway.

"You are the only one Doktor Doniger must listen to," Mondriaan said before he left. "Like the founders had to heed Jefferson. You do know that, do you not?"

I didn't know anything of the sort, only that David and I always clashed and probably always would and that he had the dean on his side. I wasn't sure who or what was on my side, except two assimilated ghosts and Llysette. Having Carolynne as part of my soul hadn't been too bad, but the ghost of justice I'd created with my equipment was sometimes pretty hard for someone trying to deal with departmental politics that had little reason and less justice.

In fact, the whole ghosting and de-ghosting business was as confusing as departmental politics. Supposedly, Heisler, the Austro-Hungarian scientist, had developed a system for systematically removing part of the electronic ego field that comprised the human spirit. Of course, that was the part of the spirit that became a ghost under the condition of knowledgeable violent death. Then, under contract to the Spazi, Branston-Hay, the late Babbage researcher at Vanderbraak State, had developed a similar de-ghosting technology that could either remove the entire spirit from a live person, rendering him a zombie, or destroy any disembodied spirit that had become a ghost. A technology that could turn a healthy individual into a zombie wasn't something I'd wanted to let loose on the world—and I hadn't.

After Branston-Hay's untimely "accidental" death—because the Spazi had discovered he was also selling his knowledge under the table to President Armstrong's covert operation—I ended up as the sole possessor of all his files on the subject. Of course, I'd had to meddle, not that either the Spazi or the president had given me any choice, and matters had gone from less than sanguine to far worse.

Reminiscing over what Llysette and I had survived wasn't going to get papers corrected. So, in the relative quiet that followed my colleagues' departure, I spent the next hour correcting quizzes from Tuesday's natural resources intro course—and trying not to think about the ghost of the child in Asten. I muttered a lot with almost every paper, especially when I discovered that a third of the class couldn't define the water table.

The wind had picked up when I left the office to cross the grounds to Smith, enough that the two university zombies toiling there—Gertrude and Hector—were having trouble raking the fallen and soggy leaves. I smiled at Gertrude, cheerfully struggling with her rake, perhaps because I still recalled her reaction to *Heinrich Verruckt* the spring before. Zombies were those unfortunate beings who had lost that part of their soul that would have been a ghost, or that part of their soul had left them prematurely to become a ghost. Zombies weren't supposed to feel strong emotions, but Gertrude had sobbed, zombie or no zombie.

Hector inclined his head, and I offered him a smile. Hector, one of the few somber zombies, nodded, but it wasn't quite a smile.

Wednesday was usually a long day. So were Mondays and Fridays, since I taught the same schedule on all three days, but Wednesday felt longer, particularly with my eleven o'clock Environmental Economics 2A class. Smythe 203 was always hot, even in midwinter, and Mondriaan didn't help. He had the room before me, and he made sure it was like an oven. Usually I didn't even have to open the windows because the students had done it first. That was about all they were good for on some days.

The blank looks on the faces of those in the front row indicated what kind of day it was going to be.

I forced a smile. "Mister Rastaal, what are the principal diseconomies of a coal-fired power plant, and how can a market economy ensure that they become real costs of production?"

"Ah, Doktor Eschbach . . . I was on the korfball trip, and somehow, I didn't bring the text. . . ."

I didn't even sigh. "Miss Raalte?"

"Doktor . . . the cost of coal mining?"

"Mister Nijkerk?"

"The . . . ah . . . um . . . cost of transporting the coal to the power plant?"

"Miss Rijssen?"

Elena Rijssen just looked at the weathered desktop in front of her. I had to call on Martaan deVaal—one of the few who read the material faithfully.

All this came after an entire class dealing with external diseconomies. Of course, the class had been two weeks earlier, but I tended to forget that retention of material for more than one period was not a strength of the students at Vanderbraak State University. Or any university, I suspected. Why were there so few who really sought an education?

The combination of difference engines and the videolink had given them all the mistaken idea that everything could be looked up and nothing needed to be retained.

After deVaal finished I did sigh. Loudly. "We discussed external diseconomies two weeks ago." I walked to the chalkboard and wrote the question out. Actually, I printed it, because my handwriting is abysmal. "A two-page essay answering this question is due at the next class. It will be counted the same as a quiz."

A low muttering groan suffused the classroom, and several students glared at Mister Rastaal and Miss Raalte. One glared at deVaal, as if having the temerity to read the material were a mortal sin. I felt sorry for deVaal, but not enough to let the rest of the class go.

"Now . . . Mister Zwolle . . . would you please define the total pollutant load from a coal-fired power plant?"

Most of them didn't know all of that answer, either, except for sulfur dioxide and carbon dioxide.

It was a very long class.

Afterward, I managed to scurry across the windswept grounds of the university, glad to see that Gertrude and Hector had abandoned their raking, and down toward the square. The post centre clock had struck twelve just as I reached the door.

"Your table is ready, Doktor Eschbach." Victor motioned me ahead of several others and toward the table Llysette preferred—close to the woodstove. I was looking at the wine list when my lady arrived, clutching not only a purse but also a large, brown, bulky envelope.

"Good afternoon, Doktor duBoise." I couldn't help grinning at the ritual as I stood.

"Afternoon, I must concede, Herr Doktor Eschbach. And it is good. . . ."

"If it is good . . . some wine to celebrate?"

At the sound of the word "wine," Victor appeared.

"The chocolate, today, I think. And the soup with the croissants." She smiled.

"Chocolate, too," I decided. "The special, chicken and artichoke pasta."

Victor shrugged at our rejection of the wine but bowed and took the menus.

"What is your news? The envelope?"

"This. . . . It arrived just before noon. I cannot believe it."

"Just now? This noon?"

She smiled and nodded again. "An invitation, a contract . . . to sing in the great concert hall of Deseret. Six weeks from now . . . because Dame Brightman has been hospitalized. That is what I have been asked. Did you know that it is one of the largest . . . perhaps like the Arena di Verona. . . ."

I'd never heard of the Arena di Verona, and my face showed it.

"Perhaps, it is not that large . . . but it is certainly as large as Covent Garden." Her eyes glazed over for a moment, and I wondered which singer within that body—Carolynne the ghost soprano or Llysette the former songbird of fallen France—was reminiscing.

"Deseret?"

"The man who came to see me sing—the one in the ancient coat. . . . I think he signed the letter."

"Are they paying?" I asked, all too imprudently, but lately all too many organizations in New Bruges had been requesting that Llysette perform either gratis or for nominal fees.

"You, you should look." She thrust the stack of papers at me.

So I did, while she edged her chair slightly closer to the woodstove and watched. Being married hadn't made her any less susceptible to the chill of New Bruges, but perhaps more willing to let me know. The cover letter praised her performance in New Bruges and extended the invitation to perform in Great Salt Lake City. It was signed by a Bishop Jacob Jensen, on behalf of the Prophets' Foundation for the Arts in Deseret.

I'd never cared much for the Saints of Deseret, even as I'd admired their ability to carve an independent nation out in the western wilderness between New France and Columbia. These days . . . Deseret scarcely qualified as a wilderness, not with its coal and iron, its synthetic fuels technology developed from the northern European refugees, and with its carefully guarded monopoly on naturally colored cottons that needed no dyes.

The political problem was that polygamy, even as restrained as it had become in the last few generations, had not set well with Columbia from the beginning. Nor had Deseret done much to allay my concerns about their not-always-so-environmental actions, but I tried not to let my past as a Subminister for Environmental Protection intrude upon Llysette's career.

The contract seemed generous, very generous—$10,000 for three performances at the Salt Palace Concert Hall and two master classes for the University of Deseret. A $5,000 cheque—Columbian dollars—was included as a retainer, drawn on the Bank of the Federal District of Columbia, plus all transportation, including the offer of a first-class cabin on the *Breckinridge,* of the Columbian Speaker Line.

There was another sheet: "Standard Requirements for Female Performers in Deseret." I read it and then handed it to Llysette.

"*Mais non!* Too much it is. . . . I must have a husband . . . as a . . ."

"Chaperon?" I suggested.

"And the gowns . . . no uncovered arms above the elbow, and the covered shoulders? Do they come out of . . . a seraglio?" She jammed the requirements sheet back into my hand. "This . . . I will not do!"

"You certainly don't have to. I did hear somewhere that the Salt Palace Concert Hall is the largest and most prestigious concert hall in Deseret," I said quietly. "If not in the western part of North America."

"My own words you do not have to throw at me." Llysette thrust out her lower lip in the exaggerated pout that indicated she wasn't totally serious . . . not totally.

Victor hovered in the background with the chocolate, and I nodded. The two mugs of heavy and steaming chocolate were followed with Llysette's soup and my pasta and with the hot, plain, and flaky croissants.

I took a sip of the chocolate. "And you could have a recital gown made to their standards from the retainer cheque—"

"Johan!" sputtered Llysette over her mug.

"You did tell me that once your gowns—"

"You mock me!"

"I am sorry. I didn't mean that. I was teasing you, but . . . sometimes you are even more serious than I am." I offered a long face, and that got a bit of a smile. The pasta wasn't up to Victor's normal standards, too heavy by half, but the sauce was good, and I was hungry.

So was Llysette, and we ate silently for a time.

The contract for Llysette bothered me, though. Yes, she had been one of the top divas in France before it fell to the Austro-Hungarians. Yes, there were few singers in Columbia who could match the performance I had heard on Friday. And yes, the rate offered was probably even a shade cheap for a world-class diva. And yes, it would do her ego, her reputation, her status at the university, and her pocketbook good. But no one had been offering Llysette contracts, ostensibly because of her unsettled status. Why now?

Admittedly, she'd finally gotten her citizenship and gotten married, both of which made her more acceptable to Deseret, but how would the Saints have known that? Or had someone alerted them to it? And why?

None of it made sense, and from the time I'd been a junior pilot in the Republic Naval Air Corps I'd known that coincidences just didn't occur.

"You are thoughtful."

"I wondered about the contract . . . why it arrived now."

Llysette shrugged, then smiled. "Perhaps . . ."

"Perhaps what?"

"You recall the seminars last summer?"

"The ones where all those singers came in?" I did remember them. We'd barely been married a month when dozens of young singers had arrived for Dean Er Recchus's MusikFest, and I'd barely seen Llysette for two weeks.

"A young man there was from the University of Deseret. He was a Saint missionary, but a good bass. The arrangement of the Perkins piece 'Lord of Sand,' he provided that, and I wrote Doktor Perkins. You remember, *n'est-ce pas?*"

I nodded. Perkins had written a note back, sending several other arrangements and professing enthusiasm about her singing his work.

"This Doktor Perkins, he is well known everywhere."

"Well known enough to get you a contract, or to want to?"

"*Non* . . . but could he not recommend?"

A noted Saint composer—yes, he could recommend, and the Saints were so hidebound they probably had sent someone to double-check. I nodded. Put in that light, it made some sense, especially with a performer hospitalized. But I wondered. Then, after what we'd been through, I wondered about everything.

I wanted to chide myself. After everything we'd been through? Llysette had been through far more—imprisonment and torture under Ferdinand after the fall of France, a struggle to get to Columbia even after the interventions of the Japanese ambassador who had loved opera and Llysette's performances, and then the unspoken Spazi injunctions against her performing too publicly.

Llysette glanced out through the window toward the post centre clock, then took a last sip of chocolate.

"Late it is. Notes . . . more notes must I beat."

"Don't you have . . . the good one?"

"Marlena vanHoff . . . she is a joy . . . *mais apres*. . . ." Llysette shook her head.

I motioned to Victor, thrust the banknotes upon him, and we were off—me to prepare for my two o'clock and Llysette for yet another lesson of studio voice.

The wind was stiffer and colder, foreshadowing another storm, probably of ice, rather than snow, the way the winter was beginning.

CHAPTER THREE

• • •

L lysette didn't run with me before breakfast, and she wasn't exactly a morning person, even on Saturdays when we slept in—except sleeping in for me was eight o'clock, still a relatively ungodly hour for Llysette.

After the strenuous efforts required during the previous year, I'd vowed I'd never let myself lapse back into the sedentary professor I'd almost become after I'd been involuntarily retired as Subminister for Environmental Protection. Of course, my nervous overeating didn't help. Still, at times, it hadn't seemed that long since I'd been a flying officer in the Republic Air Corps, and my assignments in the Sedition Prevention and Security Service had certainly required conditioning. Especially with Llysette beside me, though, it took great willpower to lever myself out of bed, not that I was sleepy.

But I ran—hard—up past Benjamin's frosted fields and well over the top of the hill through the second-growth forest that was beginning to resemble what had existed when the Dutch had reached the area from New Amsterdam.

I was still sweating long after I got back to the house and kitchen, even some-what by the time the coffee and chocolate were ready and I called up the stairs, "Your coffee awaits you, young woman!"

"You wake too early, Johan." After a time, she stumbled down the steps wrapped in a thick natural cotton robe, disarrayed, yet lovely, and slumped into the chair, looking blankly at the coffee.

"I've already been—"

"Johan . . ."

I sipped my chocolate, then started on finishing up, preparing the rest of breakfast—some scones, with small omelets, not exactly Dutch, but tasty, and my cooking has always been eclectic.

"Johan?" Llysette did not speak until she had nearly finished her omelet and half a scone.

"Yes."

"For this concert, I will need a number of things."

"I know. We'd agreed that we'd go down to Borkum today, do the shopping, and have dinner there."

She smiled.

Even after the two years we'd known each other, Llysette still had trouble be-lieving that men—or man, in my case—would carry out promises, despite the fact that I always tried to. Most of the time I did, and I was working on those few times when I got sidetracked.

After I showered and dressed, and while Llysette was finishing dressing, I took the Stanley down to Vanderbraak Centre to pick up the paper and check the post. Mr. Derkin was nowhere to be seen at Samaha's, nor was Louie.

The post centre was another matter. I saw the unmarked brown envelope, postmarked from the Federal District, and my guts churned. I'd never wanted to see another one of those.

Maurice grinned from the window, and I forced a smile as I thumbed through the other envelopes, including the electric bill from NBEI and the bill from New Bruges Wireline. They always arrived on the same day, without fail.

"You always grin when the bills arrive, you reprobate," I chastised him.

"And you never give us credit for the good things, Herr Doktor."

"Such as?"

"The chocolates from your mother and the letters from your family."

"Few enough those are, and why should you get the credit?"

"You're a hard, hard man, Doktor." He grinned again.

I had to smile back despite the tension that gripped me.

Out in the Stanley, I opened the plain envelope. As I had feared, it contained only media clips, and I'd have to read them carefully to determine from their con-tent whether they came from my former employer—the Spazi—or from the of-fice of the President. At least, Deputy Minister vanBecton had sent his clippings under the imprint of International Import Services, PLC. That had given me some warning. The new head of Spazi operations was Deputy Minister Jerome, but I'd only met him in passing years ago. My latest separation from the Spazi had been handled through Charles Asquith, Speaker Hartpence's top aide.

In any case, the clips were less than good news, although I waited to read them until I parked the Stanley outside our own car barn. Llysette's Reo was in the other side. I'd had it thoroughly overhauled and the burners tuned after we'd been married.

I sat in the drive and read through the clippings, all from the Federal District's *Columbia Post-Dispatch*:

GREAT SALT LAKE CITY, DESERET (DNS). In presiding over the Saints' Annual Conference on the Family, First Counselor Cannon highlighted the church's concerns about the role of culture in developing morals: "We must provide to our youth the finest examples of culture that uphold the moral fabric of our society. Excellence in art must include moral excellence, not mere technical artistry."

Cannon, owner of the Deseret media empire that includes the *Deseret Star, Deseret Business,* and Unified Deseret VideoLink, is the youngest First Speaker of the Church of Latter-Day Saints since the founding of Deseret. He was selected as a counselor 1988, and he has been one of the Twelve Apostles since 1983.

There was more, but it all related to the rest of the Conference on the Family and the emphasis on the need for upholding the "traditional" values, including, I suspected, that of polygamy.

GREAT SALT LAKE CITY, DESERET (WNS). Former First Diva of old France, Llysette duBoise, will appear in place of Dame Sarah Brightman on November 23, 24, and 25. DuBoise, now a Columbian citizen and performer, is a noted academic as well as a performer. . . . Dame Brightman was hospitalized two weeks ago with an undisclosed ailment. . . .

Doktor duBoise, recently married to a former Subminister of

Natural Resources of the Republic of Columbia, boasts an international reputation for both her technique and her sheer vocal artistry. She performed extensively in Europe prior to the fall of France, and recent concerts in Columbia, according to Jacob Jensen, Director of Salt Palace, have confirmed that "her artistry not only remains unchallenged, but is greater than ever. We are indeed fortunate to be able to secure her performance. . . ."

The article ended with almost a listing of Llysette's credentials, some of it clearly lifted from her recital program. She might be pleased to have been listed as a former First Diva, although I wasn't sure she actually had been—unless it had been while she'd been imprisoned and tortured, simply because the others had fled or been murdered by Archduke Ferdinand's troops.

COLORADO JUNCTION, DESERET (RPI). Upstream from this historic Saint fortress today, Deseret's Secretary of Resource Development christened the second phase of the Colorado Power Project, a linked series of three dams designed to provide water for the industrial development spawned by the Deseret Synthetic Fuels Corporation. . . .

In a prepared statement, Premier Escobar-Moire of New France stated that he was "confident" that Deseret would continue to abide by the terms of the Riverine Compact, including the provisions relating to water quality and quantity. . . .

"Deseret risks ecological disaster by this continued unbridled exploitation of river resources," commented F. Henrik Habicht II, the Columbian Deputy Minister of Natural Resources, following a ministerial meeting at the Capitol. . . . Habicht specifically highlighted the Saint diversions of the Snake River as well as the Green and Colorado rivers.

I shook my head and went into the house and upstairs, where I handed the envelope with the clippings to Llysette. She was doing her hair. "These arrived in the post."

Her eyes widened as she read. "First Diva . . . not I. *Mais, ca.* . . . That I will not deny, not now." Then she paused and looked at me. "You said . . ."

"I did. I didn't ask for these. No one has wired me. They're all about you, and about Deseret." I laughed, harshly. "I guess we've been scrutinized a little more closely than I'd thought. You're now national news. Perhaps you should offer a copy to Dierk."

"Rather I would send one to the dean." Llysette's eyes glittered, and I recalled a time when I'd faced that look—and a Colt-Luger—across my difference engine. Then, of course, she'd still been partially ghost-conditioned—a result of Ferdinand's agents' tender treatment. I'd been lucky to escape with a shoulder wound.

"You could do that. She'd probably use it to pry funding out of someone, but you might actually benefit." I paused. "We'll still need to go to Asten sometime this week to start things rolling on your passport."

"A passport, that would be nice. . . ."

"You're a citizen now, and after that story, you won't have any trouble."

"That I should not." She frowned, then pirouetted in the gray woolen suit with the bright green blouse.

"You look wonderful."

"Good. I am almost ready."

While Llysette finished straightening up the bedroom and selecting jewelry to wear, I went down to the study and sat in front of my SII custom electrofluidic difference engine to squeeze in a few minutes on the business of teaching. I called up the text of the Environmental Politics 2B midterm exam that I'd given the previous spring. The second essay question had been a disaster: "Discuss the rationale for Speaker Aspinall's decision to impose excise taxes on internal combustion engines and petroleum derivatives."

The answers had been dismal, ranging from increased revenue to political payoffs—all general and none showing any understanding of either the readings or the class discussion. I'd used a lot of red ink, and I wondered if it had just been me.

It all seemed simple enough to me. Why was it so hard for them to understand that the fuel taxes weren't enacted for either environmental or revenue reasons—but for strategic ones? Speaker Aspinall never met a tree he didn't first consider as lumber or a coal mine that he didn't embrace. He'd pushed the taxes because Ferdinand and the elder Maximilian—not the idiot son who was deGaulle's puppet—would have strangled Columbia if we'd ever become too dependent on foreign oil and because it was clear Deseret wasn't about to ship its excess oil and the liquid fuels from its synthetic fuels program to Columbia, no matter what the price, not when New France would pay more and allow transhipment on the Eccles Pipeline for sale to Chung Kuo.

Less than a generation later, my Dutch students were claiming the taxes had been needed for revenue when Aspinall's government had run enormous surpluses.

I looked out the window into the gray and icy Saturday morning, listening as Llysette came down the stairs.

"Johan, a steamer arrives."

"Could you get it? I'll be there in a minute." I saved the question for later thought and flicked off the difference engine.

"*Mais oui.* That I can do." I could hear the door open. "Yes?"

A feeling like doom looked over me, along with a sense that the part of my soul that was Carolynne clawed in frustration to get out. With that feeling, I ran toward the front door, knocking back the desk chair and literally careening off the wall.

Llysette was faster. The heavy door with its ancient, almost silvered leaded glass pane shuddered closed, simultaneously with the thin whining of a ghosting device that ripped at my soul, trying to tear it away from my physical body. The whining died into silence, and we were both still whole, unzombied, perhaps because of the leaded glass or the door's thickness or both . . . or our previous encounters with ghosting technology.

I held her for a moment, and she held me—as we both shuddered.

"That . . . like the awful . . . what . . ."

"I know." And I did. The feeling was so similar to the time that I had almost used the ghost disassociator Bruce had built for me on Llysette—except the lodestone and the mirror had meant we'd both got a dosage—ghost-possessed, or enhanced. But the soul-shivering and shuddery feelings were the same.

I eased to the kitchen and peered out the side window.

A man stood there blank-faced—zombied. The dark gray steamer stood unattended in the drive.

We waited.

He stood—expressionless, still holding what looked to be a large box of chocolates.

After even more time, I went back to the door and opened it. The clean-shaven and dark-eyed fellow was clearly a zombie, his soul lifted by the device I knew remained inside the pseudo-box of chocolates.

"I'll take that," I said quietly. "Who are you?" I eased the chocolate box from his hands, the box that held some form of the technology that could tear souls from still-living humans.

"Joshua Korfman, sir." His voice held that flat zombie tone.

"Was anyone else with you?"

"No, sir."

"Do you have a gun?"

"Yes, sir."

"I'll take that, too." I paused, not really wanting my prints on it. "Set it down there."

The gun was' a standard Colt, not a Colt-Luger. I could sense Llysette's wince behind me. The last thing—the very last thing—I wanted to do was wire Hans Waetjen about another zombie at our house. But there wasn't much choice, not as I saw it.

"Would you call Chief Waetjen?" I asked Llysette.

"I should call?"

"Do you know what he would say if I called?"

"That I can guess. The chief . . . what should I tell him?"

"The truth . . . just not all of it. Tell him that the man raised something and you slammed the door and called and I came running. Then we waited."

"And the box?"

"The box is something that the chief doesn't need to know about. The gun is sufficient."

So Llysette called, and the three of us waited . . . after I tucked the box away in the hidden wall chamber under the lodestone in the study.

The chief arrived in the black Watch car, along with Constable Gerhardt, he of the ample mustaches and thin, always-cheerful face.

"Doktor Eschbach." The square-faced and gray-haired chief snorted. "Why do strange things always happen around you? Why couldn't you have retired somewhere else?"

"This is the family home," I pointed out, although it had only been in the family for two generations before me, and that was a short tradition compared to many in Vanderbraak Centre. "Where else would I go?"

"Anywhere," snorted the chief before he turned to the zombie. "What were you doing here?"

"A man gave me five hundred dollars to kill the people who lived here. Something happened."

"What happened?" asked Waetjen.

"I don't know. I remember reaching for my gun, and she slammed the door. That was when it happened."

"What happened?"

"I don't know." Korfman's face and voice remained expressionless.

"Disassociative ghosting," I suggested. "Strong mental block against murder, but not conscious."

"Eschbach . . . I know about that."

"Sorry."

"Did you ever see these people before?"

"No."

"How did you know whom to shoot?"

"The man showed me a picture."

That bothered me—more than a little—since there weren't any pictures of the two of us together, except for the wedding pictures, and we'd given none to anyone, except for the pair we'd sent to my aunt and mother in Schenectady. They'd come to the wedding, but the pictures weren't ready until later. But someone had a picture.

Waetjen glanced toward me.

"There aren't any pictures except our wedding pictures, and no one has any except us and my mother."

"There wasn't one in the paper?"

I nodded. "I hadn't thought about that. It wasn't very good."

"Good enough for this." The chief glared at me, as if it were my fault that someone had been dispatched to kill us, then motioned to Gerhardt. "Drive his steamer down to the post. Use your gloves and don't touch anything. The wheel won't have any prints but his anyway."

We watched as the two steamers departed.

After the chief left, I turned to my dark-haired soprano. "I'd like to invite my friend Bruce up for dinner as soon as we can. Would that be all right with you? You don't have any night rehearsals yet."

"*Mais oui* . . . and you think he could help with . . . what here has happened?"

"I want him to look at that device, and I'm afraid that they'll be watching me more closely." I shrugged. "I don't even know who 'they' are." I thought about the clippings from the Federal District. "With some of those clippings I've received, it could be any one of a number of different groups involved." What I didn't say was that my past experience had taught me that once one group got involved, so did another, and often another.

"Johan . . . with you, nothing it is simple."

I bent over and kissed her cheek. "Nor with you, my dear."

I picked up the handset and wired Bruce. It seemed like I always wired or saw Bruce when I needed technical support. Then, he'd been the only one I'd been able to trust when I'd been doing fieldwork and he had been one of the designers in Spazi technical support. He'd been smart and left the Spazi early. Because of Elspeth's— my first wife's—medical condition, I'd stayed . . . and paid dearly. And in the end, the bullets meant for me had taken both Waltar and Elspeth.

"LBI Difference Designers," answered Bruce.

"Doktor Leveraal, this is your friendly environmental professor."

"I should have guessed. It's been one of those days." There was a pause. "What can I do for you this time? No more insurance, please?"

Bruce remained an "insurer" of sorts, since he had all the files on the ghosting-destruction research project that had almost led to my and Llysette's deaths— along with a large number of other unexplained deaths, zombies, and "accidents" across Columbia, especially in the Federal District and in Vanderbraak Centre. He also had the files on my not-so-well-known technology that could replicate the electric free fields that defined a ghost. Meddling with that, when Llysette had tried to kill me with her Colt-Lugar, had led to our own "ghost possession."

"A dinner invitation, for you to meet my lovely bride."

"That makes you sound almost human, Johan. I won't ask any more. When?"

"I'd hoped this week. Llysette doesn't have night rehearsals until the week after, and then it's going to get hectic. She's been asked to do a big concert in Deseret—Great Salt Lake City."

"You're going with her."

"There isn't any choice. She's female, and they're Saints."

Beside me, Llysette grimaced.

"Tuesday, Thursday, or Friday. Monday and Wednesday nights I'm the one who stays late."

"Tuesday?"

"I was afraid of that. I did want to meet the lady, and your cuisine is superb, but I worry about the technical details."

"What can I say?" I temporized, knowing everything I said was probably being recorded somewhere.

"I'll see you on Tuesday. What time?"

"Seven. I could make it later."

"Seven is fine. Have a pleasant weekend, Johan."

"I will. And thank you."

"Not yet." With a laugh he was gone.

I set down the wireset and turned to Llysette. "We might as well go down to Borkum and go shopping, as we had planned."

"After this?" asked Llysette. "After someone, they wanted to turn us into ghosts?"

"Do you have a better idea to get our minds off this? We've done what we can right now."

After a moment, she gave me a rueful headshake and nodded.

What else could we do?

CHAPTER FOUR

• • •

Marie Rijn shooed us out of our own house that Tuesday, but I was glad she had decided to stay on as my housecleaner, even after Llysette and I had married, because she kept it Dutch-spotless, and for me or Llysette to have done the cleaning would have taken too much time out of schedules that were already too crowded—and getting worse.

"She likes me now, and she did not," observed Llysette as I waited for the Stanley's flash boiler to heat.

"She didn't know you."

"Different this is. I know, Johan."

I wasn't about to get into that argument. We were both different people from those we'd been a year earlier—far different—and I wasn't certain I had yet learned how different. Every so often, I still recalled a memory image that had to have been Carolynne's or had a shivery feeling about justice that hadn't come from me. How long would I continue to process such additions to my soul? Forever? Sometimes I wondered how I'd managed to add two ghosts to my soul and still survive, but I tried not to dwell on it.

"You are thinking. *C'est vrai, n'est-ce pas?*"

"*Oui,*" I finally admitted.

She leaned over and kissed my cheek, and I eased the Stanley down the drive toward Deacon's Lane. Despite the clear winter blue sky, there was a crust of skim ice on the Wijk, and a chill wind gusted around the steamer as we crossed the river bridge into Vanderbraak Centre.

As I usually did, I followed my morning routine, dropping off Llysette and then getting my paper from Samaha's before heading back to my office and holding office hours, of which few-enough students availed themselves. While I waited for their infrequent appearances, I corrected papers or worked on various lectures.

Still, when I looked at my desk and the stack of quizzes remaining from the natural resources intro class, I had to repress a sigh. I knew that they would be depressing. So I looked out the window, toward the Music and Theatre building, and that wasn't terribly encouraging either.

Sometimes I do get premonitions, and I was definitely getting one about Llysette's concert engagement. After five years of relative obscurity, why was she being offered the same fees as Dame Brightman? Or ones that were in the same general area, at least? And why were the Saints making the offer?

That line of speculation didn't go far, because the wireset chimed, and after another deep breath I answered. "Professor Eschbach."

"Professor Eschbach. Chief Waetjen here."

"Yes, Chief. Have you found out anything more?"

"Not much. Have you found anything out of place—or anything that your would-be killer might have left?"

"Might have left? I can't say that I've really looked, Chief. I could search if you want."

"The zombie died this morning—delayed sympathetic bloc, Doktor Jynkstra thinks. But he had mentioned a box of chocolates."

"Chocolates?"

"That's what he said."

"I haven't seen anything like that around lately. I mean I gave Llysette a box after the concert, and there were several she got from admirers, but he couldn't have meant that."

"Eschbach—I know what your real background is, even if no one ever told me. I don't like this sort of thing happening to Vanderbraak Centre."

"I don't either. I give you my word that I don't have the faintest idea what this is all about or even why. I was unconditionally released from all . . . past obligations by the highest possible authority." I paused. "If I learn of anything that will help you, I'll certainly let you know."

"Please do. And I'd appreciate it if you would let me be the judge of whether it is helpful."

"I understand, Chief." My understanding did not mean my agreement, not when two of his Watch officers had previously been suborned into trying to kill me.

Another of my lifelong friends—the chief. I stood and looked out, wondering which was worse, facing the chief or my upcoming intro course in natural resources. Or the ungraded quizzes.

I settled on the quizzes and eased myself behind the desk and took out the pen with the red ink. I needed it. About half of them still hadn't the faintest idea of why food/life complexity distribution was a pyramid or why ancient cities were invariably located on waterways or even of the total extent of the impact of natural resources on the development of human culture.

I groaned after the eleventh quiz. I shouldn't have, because when things get bad, they invariably get even worse. The wireset chimed again.

"Yes?"

"Doktor Eschbach," announced Gilda, "a Harlaan Oakes for you."

My stomach turned at the name—Ralston McGuiness's successor—in essence, the de facto chief of intelligence for President Armstrong, not that the president had too much more than a token operation, but it could be deadly enough, as I had already discovered once before. Had he sent the clippings I'd received on Saturday? Wouldn't Jerome have used the Spazi cover firm?

"Johan here."

"It's good to hear your voice, Johan. The president is having a reception for the arts next week, Wednesday, in fact, and you and your charming wife will be getting a formal invitation. I wanted to let you have some advance warning. He'd like very much to see you both there, and I'd hoped, since you will be in the Federal District, that perhaps we could get together for a few minutes."

"That might be possible," I answered warily.

"The president also wondered if Fräulein duBoise—she still is using that as her performing name, isn't she?—if she might be willing to sing one or two songs."

"I would have to ask her, but I wouldn't see any objection to it . . . so long as she can sing something already in her repertoire. A week's too short notice for something new."

"Anything she would like."

"Should I let you know? She'll need an accompanist and a run-through."

"We can arrange that for the morning of the reception. I can guarantee a good accompanist, perhaps Hatchet or Stewart or even Spillman. We could chat then."

That wasn't a request. I swallowed silently. "I'll wire you later today or in the morning and let you know what she'll sing."

"Good, Johan. Very good. The president would very much like that on the formal program."

"I'll let you know."

"Good. I look forward to seeing you on Wednesday next, Johan."

"I'll be there." As if I had any choice. When the head of government, ceremonial or not, wanted something, it usually meant trouble, especially now that President Armstrong was trying to re-create the stronger Executive Branch once envisioned by Hamilton and using more than a few questionable tactics in his struggle with Speaker Hartpence. Having dealt with the Speaker before, though, I liked his tactics and supporters even less than the president's.

I looked at the wireset. Problems had this way of compounding. If we were to be ready on Wednesday morning, that meant leaving the day before and staying in the Federal District Tuesday night. That brought to the fore another problem that I'd avoided. There are some things you don't want to think about—such as how to deal with former in-laws. But Judith and Eric had been good to me and stuck by me when no one else had. So . . . that was another thing I had to ask and work out with Llysette, and I wasn't exactly looking forward to that either.

With a deep breath and a glance at my watch—ten-fifteen—I picked up the wireset again and tapped out Llysette's extension.

"Is this the charming Llysette duBoise Eschbach? One Herr Doktor Eschbach would like to request your presence at luncheon. He would also like to inform you that word of your talent has spread far and wide."

"Johan . . . I beat notes today. Do not mock me."

"I'm not. You will be receiving an invitation to the big fall arts dinner at the Presidential Palace next week—a week from tomorrow. The president—President Armstrong—has requested that you sing two pieces of your choice at the annual Presidential Arts Awards dinner."

"I do not understand . . . ," she murmured.

"A friend called me. He thought you would like as much advance notice as possible."

"But . . . a week? *Impossible!* I cannot do that."

"I told them it would have to be from your current repertoire. They agreed."

"One year . . . they would forget me. Now, I am to perform before the president?"

"We can talk about it at lunch, but I thought you would like to know. I just got off the wireset."

"Johan . . . what is happening?"

I wished I knew. "You've been rediscovered. That's what. Enjoy it—you've suffered in obscurity all too long." That was all true, and certainly the way I felt, but my guts were still tight.

"Much you have to explain at . . . when we eat. I must beat more notes."

"I love you."

"You are sweet. *Au 'voir.*"

Sweet? That wasn't a word I'd have applied to myself. Devoted, responsible, even hardworking, but not sweet.

Next, I needed to find my hardworking and scheming chair, but Herr Doktor Doniger was out. Gilda promised to let him know I was looking for him. That meant I'd still have to run him down after lunch or after my two o'clock class.

Eleven o'clock came and, with it, Natural Resources 1A, and Mister Ferris.

"Professor Eschbach, will we have to know all of this material about the water cycle for the test?"

"No. About half, but I'm not telling you which half." I turned to the redhead in the third row. "Miss Zand, would you please explain the environmental rationale for avoiding the use of internal combustion vehicles?"

Miss Zand looked blank.

"Mister deRollen . . . why do we use steamers?"

"Professor, that's because when you use a burner, an external combustion engine, you can adjust it so it doesn't pollute, and you get mostly carbon dioxide and water, instead of carbon monoxide. That's really high for a petroleum-fueled internal combustion engine. . . ."

I tried not to smile too broadly, but you have to take your successes and the thoughtful students when you can.

Because of all the questions about the quizzes I handed back at the end of class to avoid too many questions, Llysette actually made it to Delft's before I did and was sipping chocolate.

"You look wonderful, Fräulein duBoise, or Frau Eschbach." And she did, in the gray suit and pale green blouse that she'd found in Asten in August.

"Frau Eschbach . . . in some ways, that I like."

She waited until we had ordered before she finally asked, "This performance . . . at the Presidential Palace . . . you were not joking?"

"No. Harlaan Oakes called me. He said you would be getting a formal invitation. I'll check the post centre after lunch."

"An accompanist . . . I know no one, and Johanna . . . on such short notice—"

"They promised either Hatchet, Spillman, or Stewart."

Llysette's mouth did open at that. "They . . . are . . ."

"The best, I'm sure. You'll have a rehearsal and run-through that morning. Ten o'clock. I'm supposed to give them the pieces, the arrangement details, this afternoon or tomorrow morning."

"Tomorrow morning." Llysette was back to sounding like a diva, if with the softer tone I associated with the overtones from Carolynne. She shook her head slowly. "So strange this is."

"Very strange," I agreed. "I have another problem." And I did—my former wife's sister and her husband.

"A problem?"

"Judith and Eric."

"And?" Llysette raised those dark and fine eyebrows. Was there a twinkle in them?

I wasn't sure, but I'd promised myself—and Llysette—to try not to hide anything. So I didn't. "I normally stay with them in the Federal District . . . but . . . Judith . . ."

"Elspeth's sister she was."

I nodded. "We could stay elsewhere."

Llysette frowned. "Strange it is. . . ." She shook her head. "With that we have no difficulties."

"You don't?" I wasn't sure I wouldn't have.

"Johan, we will stay with them, if they will have us. You are a dear man, and you asked, and that says much."

It said that I was probably stupid, but if I were going to be and stay honest with

Llysette, I didn't have many choices, especially since I had a tendency to be so self-deceptive that there remained too many things I didn't catch.

My soup arrived, as did Llysette's croissant sandwich, and we ate quickly, with scattered bits of conversation.

"The dean . . . now she has declared that we will expand the graduate strings program . . . but we may have no more faculty positions."

"What about voice?"

"The voice area, that remains to be seen. Barton, he has returned from his . . ."

"Sabbatical," I supplied.

"And now he talks about a baritone and a contralto we should have." Llysette took a last sip of her chocolate.

"What does Dierk think?"

"Dr. Geoffries, he is of the opinion that there are no funds."

"He's probably got that right."

She glanced from the woodstove to the post centre clock, and I paid Victor.

After walking Llysette back to the Music Building and her waiting student, I doubled back to the post centre to find three bills and, as promised, a heavy embossed envelope with the presidential seal. I decided to save it for Llysette to open, although it bore both our names.

Gertrude the zombie was raking the leaves away from the walk as I marched back to the department.

"Hello, Gertrude."

"Hello, sir. It's a pleasant day."

For her, it always was, but I still remembered her sobbing her eyes out at Llysette's opera the spring before. A zombie, feeling that much emotion? Perhaps . . . could song rebuild a removed soul or spirit? I didn't know, but that confirmed my decision not to mix music and ghosting equipment.

I'd had the idea of using the equipment I'd developed to create "ghost angels" to influence people, but the more I'd thought about it, the more I'd turned from it. Trying to cope with the internalized ghosts of Carolynne and the abstract ghost of justice and mercy I'd created had often left me on the brink of sanity—and I knew what I'd done and faced.

I did catch Herr Doktor Doniger in the corridor as he was heading out.

"David . . . you recall that you and the dean have insisted that I maintain certain political connections?"

"Why, yes, Johan. It does benefit the university." He still had a wary look.

"Llysette and I have been requested to attend an arts dinner at the Presidential Palace next week. She has been asked to perform, and . . ." I shrugged. "I'll work out something for my classes."

David beamed. "I was going over to the Administration building, and I'm sure the dean will be pleased."

"It hasn't been announced yet," I said. "Probably tomorrow." That would make the honorable Dean Er Recchus even happier—that she knew in advance.

"That will be another achievement she can use in presenting the budget to the state legislature in January." David inclined his head. "Funds are looking tight, and that will help."

"Good."

He went off smiling, and I vaguely wanted to smash his kneecaps, but I didn't feel like I wanted to play any more academic politics.

The less I thought about my two o'clock the better, even afterward. Halfway through the semester was a bad time. The students had realized that they were in trouble, that material was piling up faster than they could or wanted to read it because they hadn't read any of it until right before the midterm. You can't assimilate the type of material I provided in midnight cram sessions, and that meant most of the class had received grades of less than a B. For a Dutch burgher's child, even a B was unacceptable, especially with grade inflation.

So the questions became more and more desperate.

". . . would you please explain, Doktor Eschbach, the relationship of the Escalante Massacre on the Deseret synthetic fuels development . . . ?"

". . . I don't understand how the River Compact. . . ."

". . . still not clear on why Speaker Roosevelt rejected the Green River compromise proposed by Deseret. . . ."

". . . I just don't understand. . . ."

". . . don't understand. . . ."

All the questions translated into either desperate attempts to stall the class or equally desperate attempts to avoid in-depth reading and thinking. I suppose that's always been the effort of young adults, except in the past those who felt that way either never got to college or quickly flunked out. Higher-level technology has created a dubious boon of removing much of the old manual labor and requiring more positions where judgment and some thinking are required. People want the jobs, but not the effort required to hold them. Oh, they say they do, but when it gets right down to it, the average student would rather use the university's difference engines for games than number crunching and the library for assignations than assignments.

"Enough!" I thundered, and you would have thought that I'd whipped them. "I am not here to explain every little thing that you find slightly difficult. You are here to learn. That requires thinking. Thinking means working hard. Your questions show that you stop the minute something gets difficult and requires thinking . . . the minute the answer is not written on the page. And who will be there to answer such questions once you graduate?" Assuming that they did.

I wasn't patient, and I felt as though I were getting less so. When you first start teaching, it's flattering to be looked up to and asked, but after a time, you realize that all too many questions are asked out of thoughtlessness and laziness.

Still, I had to remind myself that there was a thoughtful minority in the class who felt, and looked, as appalled as I did at the desperate questions and the failure to try to learn something. That handful was the group I called on when I needed an answer.

Because of them, I'd almost managed to get over being cross when I picked up Llysette.

"You are angry?"

"I'm getting over it. My day was like some of yours. 'I don't understand. . . . I just don't see how . . . Can't you make it simpler? . . . Why do we have to read so much?' "

"To France perhaps we should send them?"

I laughed. Their questions would have them in Ferdinand's concentration camps—except he called them relocation and training camps. That or selectively part-zombied and turned into killing machines for the invasion of Britain that was sure to come in another decade . . . or less. Unless Ferdinand decided to push over the crumbling remnants of the once-great Romanov dynasty in Russia. But no one ever beat the Russian winter, or the Finnish winter, and most of the Scandinavians were building redoubts in every rocky hill and fjord and peak north of the Baltic. The Finns had turned Vyborg into an armory in the Autumn War and continued to upgrade it against the Hapsburgs.

"Oh. Here's the invitation." I handed her the heavy envelope.

For a moment, she just looked. Then she opened it. "A personal note there is." Her eyes brightened, and I could see the hint of tears.

"You deserve it. You deserved it years ago."

"Johan, what we deserve we do not always receive. Because of you, I receive. Not because—"

"You wouldn't have those invitations if you weren't the best."

"*Non. C'est vrai.*" Her green eyes were deep, almost two shades of green simultaneously, as she turned to me. "I would not have them save for you. We know that, and I am thankful to you, and angered at the way the world is. We cannot change what is." She leaned over and hugged me, then kissed my cheek.

I eased the Stanley out of the car park, around the town square, slowly, because McArdles' was crowded with late-day grocery shoppers, and then over the Wijk bridge and up Deacon's Lane to the now-spotless house.

Marie had even set the dining room table and left a steaming apple pie.

I had to scurry to get dinner started, while Llysette assisted with setting out such details as wineglasses and serving bowls. I'd decided on something relatively simple—a spinach linguine pasta with a chicken fettuccine sauce, hot rolls, and the salad.

Before Bruce arrived, I took a few minutes to close the study draperies and remove the ersatz chocolate box from the hidden wall compartment. After I set it on the ancient desk, I went to look for the Watch report that I'd pried out of Chief

Waetjen. I thought I'd left it in a file in the second drawer—on top—but it wasn't there. I checked the third drawer, then went back to the stack in the second drawer. It was there, about four files down. I shook my head. Even my memory was going. With the sound of something boiling too violently, I dropped the file next to the difference screen and scurried back to the kitchen.

Even while I chopped the roasted almonds for the curried wine vinegar dressing for the salad, I continued to have less than sanguine feelings about Llysette's invitation to Deseret, despite all the papers—and despite the retainer cheque. But what could I say? "Turn down a five-thousand-dollar retainer; turn away from the recognition you deserve?"

Bruce arrived after dark, well after dark, in his ancient Olds ragtop, and I thought I could hear the beating sound of tattered canvas. My imagination, doubtless.

As he entered, Bruce immediately bowed to Llysette, offering a warm smile. "At last, the beautiful chanteuse of whom I have heard so much."

She blushed. "I have heard much of you."

"Try not to believe too much of it."

I took his coat. "Dinner will be ready in just a few minutes after I put in the pasta."

Bruce looked at me. "So, Johan, business before or after dinner?"

I shrugged. "I'd thought before."

The three of us went into the study.

"There it is." I gestured to the box.

"What is?"

I realized I'd never explained. "A gentleman showed up at the door with this for Llysette. She slammed the door in his face, and he turned into a zombie as a result of the gadgetry inside. I wanted your opinion." I paused. "I did take the liberty of disconnecting the power."

"Thoughtful of you, Johan." Bruce eased open the box and peered and nodded and then fingered his mostly black beard. He took out a small screwdriver, the clip kind, from his shirt pocket and fiddled slightly. Then he nodded and straightened.

"It's the same thing as your first gadget to separate soul from body and then destroy the spirit or ghost. But it's a different approach. I prefer your design. It's a great deal more stable than this."

It hadn't been my design, but one I'd stolen from the difference engine of the late Professor Branston-Hay before his untimely death at the hands of the Spazi covert branch. At least, that was my surmise, although the official cause of death had been a faulty steam control valve in his antique Ford. His house—and all his backup disks—had burned in an electrical fire right after the funeral. So the files and designs I had were among the few left, and probably highly illegal after Speaker Hartpence's announced decision to ban all research and development on ghost-related technologies.

"Good," I murmured. While not relieved, I was happy to know that my surmises had been correct and that Llysette and I hadn't panicked at nothing. I picked up the folder. "Here's the Watch report. It doesn't say anything."

Bruce scanned it quickly. "No, it doesn't."

"I thought so, but you have a more skeptical mind than I do."

"Me? How could you think that?"

"Experience." I laughed, and so did he.

"Is that all?" He held up a hand. "Foolish of me to suppose that, of course."

"Actually, I have a request of sorts. You remember that gadget you built me, two of them actually, that preceded the perturbation replicator and resembled this in function?"

There was a long silence. Bruce glanced from me to Llysette.

I nodded. "She knows." Llysette definitely knew about both the ghost-creation technology and the so-called perturbation replicator, or de-ghoster, although I couldn't remember exactly how I'd come up with the name.

"Those . . . ah, yes. Johan, I had hoped you would get beyond playthings once you married, that kind of gimmickry, I meant."

"You know that Llysette has been offered a concert engagement in Great Salt Lake City; one of the conditions, since she is female, is that her husband or other legal guardian accompany her."

"You are skeptical?"

"She has since received an invitation to perform at the Presidential Palace, and I have received several unsolicited materials that could be construed as background briefing materials."

Bruce held up his hand. "That's enough. More I don't need to know. I'm perfectly capable of creating my own problems. That I can do without assistance—"

"I was wondering if there might be any way to package one of those toys into separate components of an innocuous nature and yet be able to reassemble it into a toy—smaller than the original but equally effective for personal meetings, if you will."

"Johan . . . I rather like the insurance business better than any new ventures, and you *know* how I feel about insurance."

I almost smiled wryly. Bruce didn't like at all the fact that he was one of the two individuals who'd have to release all my forbidden technology if anything happened to me—my insurance, I hoped, against an untimely and early death. "I understand. Can you look into it?"

"How soon? Forget that." He shook his head. "It was a foolish question. I'll wire you tomorrow with an estimate."

"I appreciate it. Now . . . I think we should have dinner. I have some very good Californian wines, a Sebastopol you should enjoy."

"I always enjoy good wine . . . and beautiful women." He nodded at Llysette.

"Careful there," I said with a laugh.

"With you, Johan, I would always be careful. But I can look and appreciate your taste, and your luck." He smiled gently.

Llysette blushed again—more than I'd seen since I'd known her. Carolynne?

I eased the pasta into the big kettle and then brought out the 1982 Sebastopol, around its peak, I thought, and filled the glasses. "We can sit down."

"A toast to your upcoming performances," offered Bruce.

I lifted my glass, and, after a moment, so did Llysette.

"This is a beautiful old house," Bruce said after taking a sip from the wine.

"We've made some changes, and there will be more."

Llysette nodded emphatically, but she could have any changes she wanted except in the study.

"Don't take away the atmosphere," Bruce cautioned.

"That, we could not do. *Mais non.*"

I knew the word "we" referred to more than the two of us, but there was no reason to explain. Who would have understood?

I had to get the pasta and drain it before tossing everything together and serving it, with the rolls. "It's simple."

"He does nothing in the kitchen simple," said Llysette.

"She sings nothing in the theatre simple," I countered.

"I know enough to know that neither of you is simple in any way. Johan always said he was simple. He's simple only in the fact that quiet waters are deep and dangerous."

Llysette laughed softly.

"So is she," I pointed out.

"Like I said . . . ," offered Bruce ambiguously before taking a sip of the wine.

I offered the rolls to Llysette, then to Bruce, and then handed him the serving platter.

"How do you find New Bruges . . . and teaching?" asked Bruce. "Is it that much different?"

"New Bruges . . . it is colder than France, and the people, they keep more to themselves." Llysette lifted her shoulders, then dropped them. "Teaching . . ."

"Is hard," I finished the sentence.

"*Tres difficile, quelquefois* . . . the simplest of matters, and they look as though two heads I had. I cannot do my best if accompany them I must. Do they find an accompanist? *Mais non!* They whimper about how their funds are short and how their lives are hard."

"I can see that you are less than impressed," offered Bruce.

"Ferdinand's prisons they have not experienced," answered Llysette, pausing for a sip of the Sebastopol. "Work, *travail vrai,* they do not comprehend. To find an accompanist? Is that so difficult? To learn the notes?"

"Anything is hard if one doesn't work at it," Bruce suggested.

How well I knew that, and I nodded. Even in the simplest of books, if something did not happen to be explained in two-syllable words, or less, or if they had to think, even in novels, I suspected, they were baffled and claiming that someone *had* to explain. Life never worked that way, I had found. So had Llysette.

"*Mais oui.* But still they whimper."

"Some always will," I suggested. "But you have some good students."

"Marlena . . . a joy she is . . . and Jamella . . . she studies so hard." Llysette smiled faintly. "The good ones, they are few."

"That's true in anything."

"Good pasta, Johan," said Bruce. "After all these years, I finally get to sample your cooking."

"Thank you. You will more," I promised. "Even without agendas."

The slightest trace of a frown creased his forehead before he asked, "Why did you decide to bless me this year?"

I shrugged, not willing to tell him that ghosts of joy and justice and mercy did have an effect. Those I had saddled myself with inadvertently were quietly making me a slightly better person. "It seemed like a good idea, even if you are wary of things that seem like good ideas."

That got a laugh. For a time we ate silently. Outside, the cold wind whistled gently and one of the shutters rattled.

"There will be a time when someone needs a ghost . . . badly." Bruce raised his glass of the 1982 Sebastopol, then took a healthy sip. "And I don't want to be around when it happens."

"You, why would you be around?" asked Llysette. "Ghosts, you have said you avoid them."

"Avoid them. What ever gave you that idea? It couldn't be that I never visited Johan until this venerable and ancient dwelling was no longer spectrally inhabited?" Bruce grinned.

Llysette and I smiled back and then at each other. What else could we do? After the fact, it was amusing, not that it had been at the time. Neither Llysette nor I had ever mentioned the details of poor Carolynne's displacement to our own souls. How could we? How could we tell the world that she'd shot me, under a compulsion from Ferdinand's selective soul-sifting technology? Or that I'd turned all my ghost-creation and de-destruction gadgets on her, except a leaded mirror had skewed everything and dumped the real ghost of Carolynne into Llysette's half-shattered soul and a copy, as well as a ghost that was a caricature of justice and mercy, into mine?

All the world of New Bruges and particularly the enclave that was Vanderbraak Centre knew was that Johan Eschbach's family home was no longer haunted, and a good thing it was, too, now that the black sheep had finally married the French soprano. She might be a foreigner, that Llysette duBoise, and it might have taken a bullet in his shoulder to drive out the family ghost, but he'd finally seen the light.

I almost laughed—it had been a lot more complicated than that, and Bruce was right to worry about ghost creation. I still had the equipment he had created that had saddled me with a simplified version of both Carolynne and a ghost of justice. I was still coming to terms with those forms of possession, but at least it hadn't gone the other way and left me a zombie.

"You two . . . in the Spazi . . . one could not believe it today," offered Llysette.

"They make offers that are difficult to refuse," Bruce pointed out wryly. "If one wishes to work in any high-level position later."

"And how is that so different from Ferdinand?" she asked.

"*Most* of the time," Bruce answered, "the Spazi is content with a few years of your life, and they don't tell you what to think, just what to do."

"My life they have asked years of, also."

"That's past." I hoped it was past. At least she could now perform anywhere in Columbia.

"To many years of rewarding song." Bruce lifted his glass again.

That was something I definitely would drink to, and I lifted my glass as well. "To song and singer." I reached under the table and squeezed Llysette's thigh just above the knee.

That got me a shy and sidelong smile, and a sense of warmth.

CHAPTER FIVE

• • •

After my early wirecall to Harlaan Oakes with Llysette's two songs, Wednesday found us in Asten, at the Federal building, and the less said the better about the parking in that convoluted city. The only place we ran into no lines was in the passport office itself.

It was almost as if they were expecting us. They even insisted that, as my spouse, Llysette receive a diplomatic passport—since they had issued one to me when I'd been Subminister for Environmental Protection . . . and let me keep it. Having matching passports with the heavy green covers and the gold stripes offered an additional touch of class on someone's part. The fact that I didn't know whose part twisted my guts more than a little.

We were happy to leave, and even the congested streets of Asten were a relief, despite the excess of dark black steamers that reminded me of the high-tech trupps that controlled the south side around the diminishing back bay.

I took a deep breath once we were clear of the verge-on-verge towns that clustered around Asten and once the Stanley settled into a high-speed glide on the relatively open highway north toward Lochmere.

"You're not only a confirmed Columbian citizen, but you have a passport as well."

"A diplomatic passport—and a year ago they could not find my residence forms." Llysette provided a sound halfway between a snort and a sniff. "Why a diplomatic passport?"

Because that meant that Columbia could scream louder if anything happened to us and because it meant someone expected something to happen. "You are a cultural diplomat, of sorts." My internal ghost of honesty and justice compelled me to add more. "And someone is worried that something might happen. I don't know what."

"My life I thought would be boring in New Bruges. It has not been so."

"There are times I wish it were less exciting." Then, I was beginning to realize that I was never going to escape my past—nor was Llysette.

"Johan?"

"Yes?"

"The zombie who died—was he sent to kill me?"

"I don't know." I eased the steamer around an empty hauler that trailed black smoke, half-wondering why the owner didn't adjust the burners. "He had a gun, and he was told to kill us both. I'd think there are more reasons to kill me . . . but these days, I just don't know."

"A year ago, that you would not have said."

"Said what?"

"You say . . . you have opened your heart more, and I love you for that."

"So have you, and I have loved you longer than I ever let you know." I laughed ruefully. "Matters would have been a lot easier if I had told you."

"*Non, je crois que non* . . . I would have heard the words. The meaning, it would have escaped." Llysette's hand caressed the back of my neck for a time, and I just drove and enjoyed the sensation, trying to forget about assassins, presidential receptions, and the ghost-related technology that was supposed to have been outlawed—and was still being employed.

"We won't know," I said later . . . after leaving two more haulers in the Stanley's wake.

"What will we not know?"

"How things would have turned out."

She laughed, and so did I. We talked the rest of the trip, enjoying just being together—until we drove up Deacon's Lane and into our drive.

Constable Gerhardt was waiting, standing by a Watch steamer, a glum look on his face.

"I'm sorry, Herr Doktor." His eyes went to the house, and he fingered one side of the sweeping mustache.

"Sorry?" I had to shake my head.

Llysette just frowned, her eyes going from Gerhardt to the house and back again.

"Frau Rijn was leaving after her cleaning, and she thought she saw an intruder from the lane. She wired from her house, but by the time we got here, he got away. Smashed the panes in the glass door in back good, he did. Since Frau Rijn said you'd be back this afternoon, the chief had me wait."

"I hope you didn't have to wait too long."

"Less than an hour. Could I wire the chief that you're here?"

"Be my guest." I unlocked the door and let Llysette and the constable enter before me.

The kitchen seemed untouched, the white windowsills clean and gleaming in the late-afternoon light, the floor dust-free, and the faint odor of a meat pie from the warmer filling the room.

"There." I pointed to the wireset on the corner of the counter, the one I seldom used.

The constable dialed something. "Chief, they're here." Gerhardt waited, then said, "Yes, sir." He hung up the handset and turned. "He'll be right up. He asked that you not touch anything."

"I assume we can look?"

"I think so, sir."

"Upstairs, I will check." Llysette scurried up the steps even before she finished speaking.

Gerhardt and I went out into the study. My desk was disarrayed, with the desk drawers pulled out. My custom-designed SII difference engine was on, but only to the directory.

"He ran out the back, we guessed—across the wall," offered Gerhardt. "The Benjamin boy said there was a steamer on the back road there, but he didn't see it very well. He said it was dark-colored."

I walked around the study. Outside of the papers strewn across the Farsi carpet my grandfather had brought back from the Desert Wars and the switched-on difference engine, the room looked as it had when we had left.

The French door to the terrace had a large hole in the double panes next to the lock and glass fragments on the floor and on the stones of the terrace. Print powder lay dusted across the knob and the stones and bare wooden floor just inside the door before where the carpet began.

"Can I?"

"No prints," Gerhardt said. "Not on the glass or knob."

I pushed the door, already ajar, open and stepped onto the terrace, and into the light and cold wind.

The rear yard seemed unchanged—from the compost pile below the garden to the brown grass carpet. The frost-killed tan stalks of the raspberries remained erect, although that would change with the next heavy snow. The only remnant of raspberries until spring would be the frozen pies, freezer jam, and whole frozen berries, more than enough to last through until the next summer.

The second Watch steamer whistled into the drive, and the gray-haired chief piled out, barely pausing at the door long enough for me to open it.

"Doktor Eschbach, you present a problem." Waetjen glared, and I suspected he still didn't care much for me. "When you are here, people get killed and zombied, and when you are not, the same occurs, with thefts as well."

I shrugged. This time, I had done nothing. I tried not to swallow. The last time, when Miranda had been murdered, I hadn't done anything either. Was life trying to tell me that I could not continue being a turtle?

"Is there anything missing?"

"Not down here." I turned to Llysette, who stood in the archway between the sitting room and the study.

"Nothing has moved . . . upstairs." She finished with a gesture.

"Nothing?"

I eased around the chief and let everyone follow me to the study. I pointed toward the desk and the papers scattered across the green Farsi carpet. "I couldn't say that they might have gotten some papers or loose coins or something like that, but there's nothing obviously missing."

"Doktor . . . would there be papers of value here that anyone would know about?" asked the chief.

"Most of the files on the difference engine deal with my writings or my lectures and class notes. I can't imagine any value to anyone but me. I have records for taxes, but why would anyone else care?"

"No valuable manuscripts, anything like that?"

I nodded toward the bookcase. "There are some moderately valuable books there, but it would take a collector to know which."

Waetjen surveyed the long wall of floor-to-ceiling cases. "Are they all there?"

My smile was half-apologetic, half-embarrassed. "I wouldn't know for sure. None seem to be gone, but I couldn't say if a single volume might not be missing."

The square-faced chief touched his gray goatee. "Do you have cash or other valuables in the house?"

"Some of Llysette's jewelry, a few books, some antiques, the silver, some crystal that couldn't be replaced." I tried to think. "The carpet here, the painting in the piano room. But they're all still here."

"You should thank Frau Rijn, then, Doktors. Apparently, we got here before anything of consequence was removed."

"I think so," I answered. "We'll take a closer look to make sure. Did you find any idea who it might have been?"

"The intruder wore gloves, leather gloves. Midheight." The chief shrugged. "Size forty-eight boot—that was in the mud on the far side of the field. Late-model Reo steamer, probably midnight gray."

Constable Gerhardt shifted his weight and looked at Llysette, who boldly returned the look. Gerhardt blushed at being caught and glanced away.

"Let me know if you find anything gone—or added." Chief Waetjen bowed to Llysette, then to me.

After the Watch officers left, I taped cardboard over the broken pane and cleaned up the glass. By then it was dark, and we straggled into the kitchen.

I was getting a good idea what someone was after—but it didn't make sense unless there were two groups involved, because the theft effort came after the attempted de-ghosting/murder.

So . . . someone wanted us removed, but very indirectly, with no connection. That meant it couldn't be the Spazi. Minister Jerome and his minions had ways to remove us without going to low-class thugs. That pointed toward an outside power—someone like the Austro-Hungarians, or the New French, or even Chung Kuo. Quebec could have brought in someone who could pass scrutiny in New Bruges, and Deseret wouldn't go to all the trouble of inviting Llysette, not when such invitations had to be cleared by the Council of Twelve, and then killing her. The Japanese had helped get Llysette released from Ferdinand's prisons and torture . . . and had never called in that favor—or tried.

Someone wanted to steal something I had—that meant they knew or suspected I had ghost-removal technology. That also had to be an outside power, because both the president's office and the Spazi already had such equipment. That bothered me a great deal . . . because no one knew I had that technology, for sure. Jerome and his analysts might suspect—but there wasn't any hard evidence, except in the compartment behind the mirror and in my insurance packages. The file protocols on the difference engine that could capture or create ghosts would have been meaningless, and they were hidden, and the intruder hadn't tripped the counter. But Bruce could have gotten the file without tripping it; so the untripped counter meant only that no amateur had tried.

"How about a salad with the meat pie?"

"*Bien. . . .*" Llysette sat at the kitchen table. "Johan? This is not the same as the zombie, *est-ce que?*"

"*Non,*" I admitted.

"Who are they? What do they want?" She paused.

I continued to shred lettuce into the salad bowl—romaine, not iceberg.

"The creating and destroying of ghosts—is that what they desire? Your knowledge about such?"

I set aside the lettuce and began to work on a cucumber. "I'm not sure. I think we're seeing two different groups. The first wants us out of the way, and the second wants knowledge, but I'd thought it was more about de-ghosting." The Spazi couldn't have known about the ghost-creation gadgetry, nor could Ferdinand's people. Still, the furor that I'd created before and the latest incident pointed out, again, how ghosts were a real phenomenon in our world, with an impact that couldn't be ignored. Ghosts had certainly made a historical difference in our world—from those that had turned William the Unfortunate's conquest of England from a triumph to near-disaster to all those of women who had died in childbirth and thus prevented early remarriages and slowed the world birthrate.

"Ferdinand . . . could it be?"

"What do you think?"

"*Je ne sais pas* . . . the puppets of that devil Heisler. I know nothing, and they must know more than we do."

I nodded. That was my feeling. Why would Ferdinand or his mad scientist Heisler bother? But who else would even care? The Spazi could have us imprisoned or eliminated with less fuss.

I set the salads on the table and retrieved the meat pie from the warmer. "It is a puzzle, and we aren't going to solve it tonight, and it is time to eat. Wine?"

"*S'il vous plaît. . . .*"

"That I can do." I could manage wine, just not the spreading web of intrigue that seemed bound to snare us both.

CHAPTER SIX

• • •

On Thursday morning I was looking at the latest pile of ungraded tests on my desk—these from the Environmental Politics 2A class. I'd persuaded Regner Grimaldi to give it for me while we'd been in Asten. That meant I'd have to return the favor at some point, but I had to admit my schedule was lighter than his. That was always the case with younger faculty. I could afford to tell our honored chair what he could do with an ill-considered idea. Poor Regner couldn't. Nor had Llysette much leverage, and that was another reason why she couldn't afford not to perform in Deseret . . . or in the Federal District—especially when performing might lead to her obtaining such leverage.

I put those thoughts aside, picked up the first test, and began to read: ". . . Speaker Aspinwaald liked mines and lumbermen so he got the excise taxes passed to help them. . . ." I winced at the spelling of the former Speaker's name and the answer, which quickly got worse. I had said that Speaker Aspinall never met a tree or a mine he didn't like, but he pushed through the excise taxes *despite* that. Somehow, about a third of the students never heard the whole story. I picked up the next test, wondering if they had the same problem with whatever else they read, like novels, but before I could concentrate, the wireset chimed.

"It's Watch Chief Waetjen for you, Doktor," said Gilda in the formal tone that indicated David was standing by her elbow.

"Thank you." I waited, then answered, "Yes, Chief?"

"Professor Eschbach, was anything missing?" asked Waetjen.

"Llysette and I have looked, Chief, but neither of us has discovered anything that was missing." I juggled the handset to the other ear and restacked the tests I'd already graded. "There was even a twenty-dollar bill on the corner of the desk—I guess I'd left it half tucked under some papers and the thief fumbled through the papers and uncovered it but left it."

"No thief I ever heard of."

"It could be that was when your officers arrived," I pointed out. "You said that he left in a hurry."

"I have my doubts, Herr Doktor Professor."

"Doubts or not, Chief, we haven't found anything missing yet, and we've looked." Like the chief, I wasn't exactly happy about the missing burglar or what he'd been rummaging through the house to find. I was afraid I knew—he wanted the information and technologies on de-ghosting—and that meant very big problems, especially with our upcoming trip to the Federal District.

"Do you have any idea what he sought?" pressed the chief.

I tried not to pause in answering. "It could have been a number of things, Chief, but he didn't leave any clues."

"You didn't leave your difference engine on while you were gone, did you?"

"No. He must have turned it on, but none of the files were altered, and it didn't look like he'd copied anything. I can't imagine what he'd want with all those academic records."

"Do you keep your financial records there?" pressed the chief.

"No—nothing like that. I don't need anything elaborate. I get a salary and some consulting income and a modest pension. We're comfortable, but hardly wealthy."

"Let me know if you happen to discover anything else."

I promised that I would, which was a safe promise, because I doubted that I'd find out anything more.

Then it was a dash down the stairs and out to Natural Resources 1A, the previously graded quizzes under my arm.

Gertrude and Hector were turning the flower beds in front of Smythe, spreading bark mulch along the base of the hedges by the walk. The two zombies were turned the other way, and I didn't say anything.

The classroom wasn't too hot, probably because the day was gray and cool, not cold . . . not yet, despite the dark clouds looming to the northeast.

Unfortunately, Mister Ferris was waiting. "Professor Eschbach, you said that we should know all of the material on the water cycle on the test. Does that include the stuff on aquifer and recharge zones? And what about radionuclides in water?"

"All of it." I forced a smile as I continued handing out the quizzes and ignoring the groans.

"Oh. . . ."

"It won't all be on the test, Mister Ferris, as I told you the last time. I'm just not telling you what will be." After shuffling away the three quizzes belonging to absentees, I looked at the black-haired sleeping student in the last row. "Miss Gemert!"

"Sir?"

"Perhaps you would be so kind as to tell the class about upland wetlands."

"Upland wetlands?"

I nodded pleasantly.

"Ah . . . sir . . . I'm on the soccer team . . . and we had an away game yesterday . . ."

"Those caravan rides are a good time to read, Miss Gemert. And Coach Haarken isn't the one who takes your tests." I kept a smile on my face. "Mister Andervaal?"

"Uh . . . are those the ones . . . the intermittent wetlands . . . with maples and stuff like that?"

"That's a start. What else can you tell us?"

Young Andervaal glanced desperately around, but no one would meet his eyes. It was going to be one of those classes. I repressed a sigh.

Getting an answer to each discussion question took about three students, and I was sweating under my cravat by the time the bell chimed.

Llysette had a faculty meeting at noon so she wouldn't get lunch, and I wouldn't get to see her. I picked up a nearly inedible sandwich from the student center and, after gulping it down, headed out for the post centre, passing Hector on the green.

The zombie nodded without pausing from his raking, and I returned the gesture.

Another unmarked manila envelope rested in our postbox, and it went into my inside jacket pocket. While I didn't want to open it—more trouble—I did, but only after I got back to the office and closed my door.

Again, only clippings were in the envelope, and there were two.

GREAT SALT LAKE CITY, DESERET (RPI). An unannounced series of police raids in the warehouse district near the Deseret and Western rail yards early this morning resulted in no arrests but the confiscation of "material of a pornographic and objectionable nature," according to police spokesman Jared Bishopp.

Calls to several foreign legations alleged that the raids were designed to harass businesses whose owners had expressed reservations about recent "revelations" made by President Wilford W. Taylor before the Council of Twelve. Among those revelations were language suggesting that multiple conjugal relationships were a matter of individual choice, not an absolute tenet of the first prophet, for those able to support additional familial units.

Of greater concern was the "clarification" referring to the trade language in the *Doctrine and Covenants* laid out by first president Taylor more than a century earlier. Taylor had revealed that "the people of God should trade only with those who neither threaten nor revile them, who accept the kingdom of Zion, and not with Gentiles who would seek to undo our kingdom. . . ." Although this trade proscription has often been honored in the breach for nearly half a century, the clarification language was seen by some observers as easing the way to permit significant synthetic diesel and kerosene exports to Columbia. New France has never been classified as a "Gentile" or an unfriendly nation, possibly because it supported Deseret against Columbia in the Utah War and again in the Caribbean Wars . . . and because it harbors the Colonia Juarez and Dublan enclaves. . . .

Bishopp denied that the raids were of a political nature.

HEBER CITY, DESERET (DNS). "The ideals of the first Prophet must not fall to the Lamanites of the spirit," cautioned First Counselor Cannon in opening the annual Latter-Day Saints conference. "Nor must we cease in bringing light to a darkened continent or in our efforts to return those of Laman into the fold of God. Our kingdom is of God, and it shall stand forever." Cannon went on to praise the role of the arts in opening man to understanding the need for the coming of Zion to the entire world. . . .

Cannon's language turned more practical in his assessment of the state of Deseret. "Energy and technology are the keys to the next century, and the wise use of water facilitates both. We will continue with the headwaters project." The First Speaker went on to pledge additional funding for the advanced natural gas liquification plants, for water reuse technology, and for additional support of the cotton mission initiatives.

I folded the clippings back into the envelope and slipped them into my case. Great—Deseret was building up its liquid hydrocarbon production industry, which certainly needed more water, I suspected, and trying to ease into more normal relations with Columbia despite nearly a century of unease, a century preceded by thirty years of near-war and border skirmishes where Deseret's independence had only been established through the willingness of New France to provide capital and a trade conduit for technology.

That didn't bother me so much as the fact that someone wanted me to know it—and I still didn't know if that someone was the same someone who'd sent me the earlier clips about Llysette and the arts in Deseret. It had the marks of the Spazi, but the lack of cover address continued to worry at me.

I took a deep breath and sat down at my desk, where, in the hour and a half between returning to my office and Environmental Politics 2B at two o'clock, I would try to put a dent in the tests from Environmental Politics 2A.

I hadn't even started grading the short quizzes that I'd given my honors class in environmental studies. Why did I give so many tests? Because too many of the dunderheads wouldn't study the material unless I did. The attitude seemed to be: "If I'm not going to be tested, I won't learn it."

What none of them seemed to understand was that—at least in my life—the world wasn't too forgiving about what you didn't know. You didn't get second chances—like emergency procedures when flying. If I hadn't known them when I'd been in involved in the Panama Standoff, I'd have been somewhere at the bottom of Mosquito Gulf.

Philosophizing didn't grade tests, and I began to read and to apply the red ink. While some of the students actually made sense, a lot more merely tried to parrot what I'd said, whether it was in context or not.

I looked at the next paper: "Speaker Colmer followed the strong environmental example set by Speaker Aspinall. . . ." Environmental example? Hardly! And I'd told them that, but some hadn't gotten the message. The bottom line was that Columbia was starved for liquid hydrocarbons and the strong Speakers—Roosevelt, Messler, Aspinall, and Colmer, particularly—had recognized that fact and eased through taxes and conservation measures that had immense environmental benefits, but not for primarily environmental reasons. The combination of the high turbojet fuel tax and the astronomical landing fees was really what kept the more environmentally sound and energy-efficient dirigibles and the trains competitive. A lot more people would have been taking turbos and old-style aircraft if it weren't for the fact that those fares were nearly ten times as much.

Except for the Louisiana fields, and Hugoton Fields in Kansas and the Cherokee lands bordering Tejas, most of the big North American oil fields lay in either Deseret or New France. Had the Saint wars happened a generation later, I suspected, Deseret would have been a part of Columbia no matter what the cost in lives, but the disasters in the Mexican War, followed by the slavery issue and the *Sally Wright* incident, followed in turn by the first Caribbean War, where the Austro-Hungarians had backed both New France and Deseret, had made a full-scale military effort against Deseret highly unpopular . . . and most impractical. The second and almost abortive 1901 Caribbean War had further reinforced the Deseret-New France ties.

Now . . . with Deseret's chemical and synthfuels industries, and continued militarization, not to mention the so-called Joseph Smith brigades, Columbian military action against Deseret would have been an invitation for deGaulle to strike against the comparatively vulnerable Kansas, Louisiana, and mid-California oil fields, and Columbia couldn't afford that at all, not when Indonesian oil was held by the Rising Sun and the Arabian peninsula by the Austro-Hungarians. There was talk of development in Russia, but the Romanovs didn't have the capital, and Russia was so strife-torn and chaotic outside of Saint Petersburg and Moskva that none of the international bankers would consider it, even with what Columbia and the Brits would have paid for the oil.

Instead, it looked like both President Armstrong and Speaker Hartpence would have to court Deseret for liquid hydrocarbons. Better Deseret than New France, I supposed.

More than a third of the honors class quizzes missed those points. *Honors class?* I wondered as I set the few remaining quizzes aside and headed for Environmental Politics 2B.

They were presenting summaries of their projects, and that meant I just listened and took notes—thankfully.

I got back to the department offices at three-forty-five. Gilda waved before I got to the stairs. "Herr Leveraal called. The number is in your box."

"Thank you."

Once in my office, I closed the door and wired Bruce.

"LBI Difference Designers."

"Bruce?"

"No. This is Curt."

"I'm sorry. This is Johan Eschbach; I'm returning Bruce's call."

"Just a moment."

I waited. Curt—that was Bruce's brother Curtland. I'd never met him, and until now he'd been a shadowy sort of figure, except he'd never been in the Spazi, unlike Bruce and me.

"Herr Doktor," offered Bruce.

"You wired?"

"I have an estimate on your toys. They should be ready Saturday."

"I take it they're not cheap."

"Compared to what?"

Bruce had a point there. "All right. How much?"

"Say . . . roughly three hundred for a pair. Maybe four at the outside."

I didn't quite wince. Then, if they were useful in keeping untoward things from happening to us . . . how much were our lives worth? "They cost what they cost. Anytime Saturday?"

"You're the customer. I'll see you then, and try to stay out of any more trouble."

"You remain all heart, Bruce."

"Always." There was a pause. "I do have a request."

"Oh?"

"I'd really like to hear your lovely bride in concert. So . . . the next time she performs—somewhere in the seminear geographic vicinity—could you inform me?"

"Of course." I cleared my throat. "It might be a little while, because she just did a recital, but I'll certainly let you know. Sometimes she's done concerts around Zuider, but there aren't any scheduled right now."

"I understand."

Why was Bruce interested in Llysette's singing? Was it because he did a lot of work with music systems? I shook my head. I could sense he was interested in her singing, but why? Then, for all the years I'd known Bruce, there was a lot I didn't know, probably because he was private and because I'd never asked. Or was it just that I was getting paranoid about everything?

That raised even more questions I didn't want to consider, not at the moment, although I knew I'd have to, sooner or later.

CHAPTER SEVEN

• • •

On Saturday morning, as we lingered over breakfast, Llysette yawned ever so slightly in the warm light from a sun we had seen too little of in the previous week.

"Are you tired?"

"Tired am I all the time. Tired from teaching Dutch dunderheads who believe that singing the wrong notes many times is practice. Vocalizes I give them, and they do not use them . . . but for a few, and those, they are too few. A written sheet on how to practice they have, and they do not read it. *Non* . . . they sit and pick out one note after another because the piano they cannot play, and accompanists they will not find. Rhythms they do not learn. . . ." She sighed.

"I'm sorry." I didn't know what I could do, but I was sorry. Even with my pension and salary, I couldn't support her in the style she deserved.

"*Quelquefois . . .*"

I refilled her cup with the last of the chocolate from the pot. "I need to go to Zuider to pick up the gadgets from Bruce. You'd said you wanted to do some shopping. I'm game. Are you?"

"Shopping, that I can always do, even in Zuider."

"I know. We could drive on down to Borkum afterward," I suggested.

"That I would like."

I'd thought she would. "I thought I'd get the post while you finish dressing."

Llysette smiled. "You are good to me."

Sometimes, I wondered. I'd almost gotten us both killed, and she was still having to work far too hard.

The Stanley had plenty of kerosene, and the water tanks were nearly full. I had my own water filter system in the car barn, and that saved a lot of trouble. Then I backed out into the sunlight, under a sky with only a few scattered small white clouds—a good day for a drive.

Benjamin had the whole family out, doing something in the orchards beyond the field that bordered Deacon's Lane. None of them looked up, but I knew they'd noticed. They noticed everything, which had certainly been to my benefit recently.

Who had been behind the attack on us? I had no real idea—or, rather, I couldn't narrow down the suspects. With a half-shrug, I stopped on the east side of the bridge to wait for a long lumber hauler, then took the steamer across.

The square was crowded with Saturday shoppers, but I only had to take the Stanley around once before I could pull into a spot by the post centre. The clock chimed ten as I walked up the stone steps.

I opened the postbox gingerly, only to discover that I had cause for my trepidation. Another of the damned manila envelopes from the Federal District lay there like the miniature bomb it was.

Rather than open it in the post centre, I took it and the letter from my mother and a bill from Dunwijk Plumbing for repairing the kitchen sink lines and eased them into my jacket.

The manila envelope exuded heat in my pocket. It didn't, but that was the way it felt, and I opened it once I'd parked the steamer back in our drive. There was but a single clip from the *Columbia Post-Dispatch*:

FEDERAL DISTRICT (RPI). J. Taylor Hunter, assistant president of Deseret, met with Natural Resources Minister Reilly yesterday. The substance of the private meeting was not immediately disclosed, but speculation centered on oil or liquid hydrocarbon exports from Deseret. . . .

The federal stockpile is at an all-time low, less than two months' worth of total Columbian demand, as a result of the refusal of Japan to increase exports from its Indonesian fields to Columbia and the recent oil field explosions in Venezuela, which reduced exports to the Mobile refinery. . . .

The cause of the South American disaster has not yet been established.

I had a good idea about the South American disaster. It had the fine hand of Ferdinand written large upon it.

Since Llysette was still rummaging through the closet upstairs, I set the plumbing bill in the basket for such things on my desk and opened my mother's note:

Johan,

I was sorry that you and your darling Llysette will not be able to come down over harvest.

Both Anna and I were thrilled to hear that she will be performing before more appreciative audiences. . . .

You might recall Romer van Leyden. He passed away after a long bout with cancer last week. His son Georg asked to be remembered to you. He works for the New Ostend Water Authority, but I've forgotten what he does. . . .

All our best . . .

Mother still insisted on both wiring and writing, the writing a relic of a more graceful age that I appreciated—and that gave me some pleasurable anticipation in opening a postbox otherwise filled with the mundane business of bills or the chilling manila envelopes that represented a past I never seemed quite able to escape.

Llysette was dressed in a blue jumper, with a white blouse, except she was trying to decide between two jackets—a tan woolen one or a wool one that seemed to match the jumper.

"Mother sent a note." I extended it to Llysette as she hung up the tan jacket.

She frowned in that way that crinkled her nose, and I laughed.

"You mock me," she said.

"You're cute."

"Baby . . . baby ducks, they are cute."

"You are also beautiful and talented."

"Cute, that you called me first."

I groaned.

She smiled and began to read. "She comprehends the Dutch audiences here."

"Backwater Dutch, she's always called them."

"Backwater?"

"Away from the culture of New Amsterdam or Philadelphia, or even Asten."

"*Backwater* . . . a good term." Llysette nodded and handed the note back to me.

"I'm still getting clippings," I said quietly, easing the latest one to her.

"*Mais qui est-ce qui?*"

"I don't know. It might be Harlaan Oakes—the one who told me about the president's decision to ask you to sing."

"You are not *certain?*" she asked, pronouncing "certain" in French.

"No. The clips and the methods are Spazi, but it doesn't have any of their cover addresses, and I don't know why anyone in the Spazi would be doing this."

This time her frown wasn't cute as she read.

"The oils . . . what have they to do with us?" Her green eyes glinted. "*Quelqu'un crois que* . . . am I to sing for oil?"

"I don't think so. It's more to point out how delicate matters are." I took a deep breath. "Can I explain it on the drive to Zuider?" I forced a grin. "That way we can get through the unpleasant necessities and to the shopping."

"You mock me more. . . ." She gave a pout, lower lip well out, out enough for me to know that she was teasing.

"Absolutely." I hugged her and got a warm embrace in return.

We gathered coats, because despite the sun, there was a chill breeze, and I escorted Llysette out to the steamer, after locking the doors carefully, not that locks would ever stop a real professional. I just hoped they wouldn't break the glass I'd had replaced . . . or worse.

"You would explain?" Llysette said even before I had the Stanley onto Deacon's Lane. The red thermal paint glittered in the bright fall sun, as it should, since I'd washed the steamer the afternoon before while Llysette had held rehearsals for the winter opera.

"About the clippings?" I cleared my throat as we headed down to the bridge. "Columbia is oil-starved. We took certain conservation measures years ago to reduce fuel demands, but there's a cost to all of that. Prices get higher because of the energy component of goods, and higher prices tend to depress investment. Lower investment and higher prices make it harder to develop alternative fuel sources, the way they have in Deseret. We have a lot of natural gas in the Canadian states, but we don't need gas so much as liquids, and liquification and transport are expensive. A good chunk of the western hydropower goes into the aluminum industry." I shrugged. "Sorry. It gets complicated. Higher technology means more energy demand—unless we cut our standard of living. If we could get some oil from Deseret—they're producing a healthy surplus—then we'd have some breathing space to develop our own synthfuels industry more. But Ferdinand doesn't like that, and New France certainly wouldn't like closer ties between Deseret and Columbia. At the same time, I can't believe either New France or the Austro-Hungarians would cooperate in trying to keep Deseret and Columbia from establishing closer relations." I eased the Stanley onto the cutoff leading to Route Five, which would take us to Zuider.

"Cooperate . . . those two? Never," said my soprano.

"Exactly. Deseret wants the best deal it can get. The Saints have been working to become less and less dependent on New France, but it's delicate. We fought four wars with the two of them, but I can see where deGaulle's expansionism would make the Saints very uneasy. If we can open trade more, then deGaulle can't take Deseret's support totally for granted. That also might relieve some of the pressure on the Panamanian Protectorate and the canal."

"And us . . . what of us?" she asked, trying to steer me back to the main point.

"Your singing is a first step. You're now a Columbian citizen, and that one clip pointed out how the Saints see art as a reflection of the world."

"Someone does not wish me to sing in Deseret?"

"Ferdinand, probably. Maybe deGaulle and Maurice-Huizinga, his spy chief. Possibly even the Japanese, since we wouldn't be as dependent on their Indonesian oil." I coughed, then paused to pass one of the ubiquitous and spotless white tank haulers—from vanEmsden's Dairy, of course. "That's the problem. A lot of people have an interest in your singing, and an equal number have an interest in your not singing."

"I thought . . . perhaps they wished for my ability."

"They do." I laughed. "The Saints wanted the best Columbia has. It's a compliment, and the president has reinforced that. It's precisely because you are so good that you're in the middle of this."

"*Jamais pour l'art,*" Llysette murmured and looked out the window. I gave her the space she wanted and kept driving.

After I came off the cutoff onto the new road, Route Five was smooth all the way south to Zuider and Lochmeer, the biggest lake in New Bruges. Route Five shadowed the Wijk south beside fifteen miles of stone-fenced walls enclosing winter-turned fields, stands of sugar maples, and meadows for scattered sheep.

The stone walls exemplified their Dutch heritage, each stone precisely placed and replaced—as Benjamin always had his family doing—almost as soon as the frost heaved it out of position.

After nearly twenty-five minutes, we reached the spot where the Wijk winds west and Route Five swings east toward Lochmeer and Zuider. At the sight of the three Loon Lakes and the well-trimmed apple orchards, I shook my head. I still hadn't gotten around to a proper pruning of my own small orchard.

"*Plus ca change,*" murmured Llysette after her long silence. "So hard you try to stay away from what happens in the world, and still they find you. They find me, and, again, my songs are for those in power. But sing I must, or I will beat notes, all my life, and learn the students will not. I do not beat notes, and the rhythms are not there. Half cannot even accompany themselves."

"Will it get better as you get better students?"

"Who would know? Some, like Marlena, they are good. Or Jamella. The others . . . I give them vocalizes. These to train their voices. The brain it is smart, but the muscles, they are stupid. They will not learn vocalises."

"Is that because they feel stupid singing nonsense syllables?"

Llysette shrugged. "Nonsense is in their heavy skulls."

"Thick skulls?"

"Matters it at all? They will not change."

Was everyone like that? I thought I'd learned, but had I? Or was I repeating the same patterns in a different way?

Even on the new road with its passing lanes, it took almost an hour from Vanderbraak Centre into the car park behind the small structure that housed LBI.

The shop was empty, not surprisingly, since LBI wasn't for browsers but for those who knew what they wanted and who could explain it quickly—for busy people—and desperate ones, I reflected.

Bruce bowed to Llysette, then nodded to me. "I would look forward to all your visits, Johan, if you would bring this lovely lady more often."

"I'll see what I can do, but her schedule is far more cramped than mine."

"Truly a pity." He grinned.

A new SII machine stood on the counter, and my eyes went to it.

"It looks good, but it's not that much better than what you have. I'd wait until next year, or longer if you can."

"I can certainly wait."

"What you requested is in my office."

We followed him. A box with the SII logo stood on his desk, beside the small SII difference engine.

Bruce eased the door closed. "We do take certain precautions here, but they don't work against personal eavesdropping, only against electronics."

I offered a faint smile as he opened the top of the box and extracted two silver cylinders.

"These are a pen and pencil set. They work, but I won't guarantee how well or how long." He lifted a squared-off hand calculator from the box and set it on the desk beside the silvered pen and pencil. "This won't do as much as its size says it should, but it does operate." He smiled wryly. "You put them in the jacks at the bottom and point. The delete key is the activator, but it won't work that way unless both pen and pencil are in place. It uses standard batteries, but they're only good for two uses, three at the outside. I'd suggest bringing some spares."

Llysette shivered, and I understood why. I felt like shivering myself. Firearms, bad as they were, felt cleaner, but there was no way I could carry firearms into Deseret. I squeezed her hand.

"Now this. . . ." Bruce lifted the electric hair blower and bowed to Llysette. "Rechargeable batteries in the base, and they'll recharge if you just plug it in. The batteries only work for the special function." He offered a wry smile. "When the temperature switch is down to the 'C' and pushed in and the blower is on low, when you hold the blower trigger you'll get the de-ghosting or spirit removal effect." He looked at me. "I thought your bride should have some protection also, something . . . appropriate."

Llysette could handle a Colt-Luger. I still had several white scars on my shoulder and back to prove it. So I had no doubts that she could handle Bruce's blower/de-ghoster. "Thank you."

"I also," offered my soprano, with a warm but ginger smile.

"Think nothing of it."

"You haven't lost your touch," I said.

"There are definitely times that I wish I had, Johan."

"Me, too—except about that time, I find I'd be dead if I had." I counted out the bills, eight hundred dollars' worth. "I hope that's enough."

Bruce gave a crooked grin. "So do I. I'd rather not deal with your insurance."

"I'd rather you didn't have to either."

"When do you leave?" Bruce asked as I lifted the box.

"Not for another few weeks. Right now, it looks like we'll be there a bit over a week. Llysette's doing three performances and giving some master classes."

Bruce inclined his head to Llysette. "I wish I could be there to hear you."

"You are kind."

"No . . . selfish. One doesn't get to hear the greatest diva of the generation often."

Llysette blushed, but she needed and deserved the praise—it wasn't flattery, but praise.

"This could lead to closer engagements," I pointed out.

"I certainly hope so."

I looked down at the box. "Thank you . . . again. You've been a great help when no one else cared."

"We aim to please."

I let it go. Bruce didn't seem to want to accept my real gratitude, and I'd have to find another way.

The sun was still shining and the white clouds still puffy as I carried the SII box out to the Stanley and slipped it into the trunk. Then I seated Llysette, and then myself, lighting off the steamer.

"To Borkum . . . shopping and a good meal."

She smiled, and for a time we pushed away the implications of the box the steamer carried.

CHAPTER EIGHT

• • •

On Tuesday, we boarded the early-morning Quebec Express in Lebanon and rode it into New Amsterdam. We had an hour wait there, spent mostly at a corner table at a so-called café off the main station floor, before we boarded the Columbia Special to the capital. At least, I hadn't received any more of the ominous clips and no one had attempted any more burglaries, but I had few doubts that the respite was more than temporary.

The Special went to the Baltimore and Potomac station just off the new Mall, and even with stops, it was less than seven hours after leaving Lebanon that we stepped out into the seemingly perpetual drizzle that covered the Federal District in late fall.

"That is?" asked Llysette, pointing to the mist-shrouded marble obelisk to the west end of the Mall—almost on the edge of the Potomac.

"The Washington Monument. They finished it five years ago, but it was started more than a hundred and forty years ago."

My soprano shook her head. It was hard for me to believe, too, especially since the Congress was talking about a memorial to Jefferson. Why did they think that would be any different?

The drizzle was warm, steamy, unseasonably hot, even in the former swamp that was the Republic's capital, and I wiped my forehead with the cotton handkerchief. Llysette appeared cool and composed in her pale green suit.

"You like it warmer."

"For me, it is pleasant, like Paris."

I glanced around for an electrocab, finally managing to flag down a dark blue one, bearing the hand-painted logo of "Piet's Cabs."

The driver opened the door. "Where you bound?"

"Upper northwest. Spring Valley—Forty-seventh and New Bruges."

"That's a minimum of five."

"It's usually four," I pointed out.

"Cab commission finally upped the rates," said the ginger-bearded driver with an embarrassed smile.

I showed a five. "I won't argue with the commission."

"Me neither, sir." He stepped out and opened the trunk, and I slid the two valises inside—and the long hanging bag that held Llysette's concert gown.

The driver didn't talk as he headed west on Constitution.

"That, *qu'est-ce que c'est?*" Llysette pointed to the heavy-walled marble monstrosity that the Smithsonian had built to house the Dutch Masters—the remnants of the collection of Hendrik, the former Grand Duke of Holland, yet another casualty of Ferdinand VI's armies in their sweep across the Low Countries. When I'd been subminister, I'd objected to the design, but since Columbian Dutch, the oil people, had paid for the building, the Congress had ignored my objections.

"That's the Dutch wing of the Smithsonian Gallery. I've avoided it—call it a protest, not that mine have made much difference."

"A French gallery is there?"

"They have some van Goghs and Degas, but no one volunteered to build a gallery the way Columbian Dutch did."

"Always the money."

That was the way it seemed to me also.

The cab turned onto New Bruges Avenue and headed northwest, north of most of the official sector of the Federal District, past the Ghirardelli Chocolatiers and around Dupont Circle.

We passed up Embassy Row, beginning with the huge structures belonging to Japan and Chung Kuo, facing each other across New Bruges Avenue, and I pointed out each, including the still cordoned-off section of sidewalk where the ghosts of ten Vietnamese monks still wailed—fifteen years after they had immolated themselves there in protest. The Chinese could see the ghosts, especially at twilight—but their continued presence hadn't changed anything. In fact, I wondered if the Chinese secretly enjoyed such a reminder of the futility of protest to their endless expansion.

I swallowed as the cab eased around Ward Circle and into Ward Park beyond the seminary. Within a half-dozen blocks, the driver turned off New Bruges and onto Sedgwick.

"The houses . . . they are large."

"Yes." The upper northwest in the Federal District reeks of money, with tile or slate roofs, manicured lawns, trimmed hedges, sculpted gardens, and shadowed stone walks. Once the upper northwest had been far enough from the capital itself that it served as an interim retreat for Speaker Calhoun, but now such retreats were farther, much, much farther, from the Capitol building.

The Tudor house set on a large corner plot was Eric and Judith's. They'd walled the entire back of the property, not long after Elspeth's death and my notoriety in the Nord case. Their car barn had space for three steamers, and the house was thoroughly alarmed.

"This the place, sir?"

"It is." After I reclaimed the bags, I tipped the driver three dollars. "It's a long ride back."

"Thank you, sir."

Judith opened the Tiffany-paneled front doors even before we were halfway up the walk. She'd cut her silver hair short, but she still wore a blue suit, as she often did, from what I recalled.

"Llysette, this is Judith."

"I am pleased to see you, and I am so glad you could stay with us." Judith sounded glad, but I could sense Llysette's wariness. "You are lovely, and that's without singing a note." As always, Judith's words were genuine and warm, as were her gray eyes, and her smile. "As Johan may have told you, I remember hearing you once in Paris, just before the fall of France. You were at the Academie Royale back when I did my fellowship there—one of the last ones before Ferdinand."

"Few remember those years."

"Few want to," answered Judith, half warmly, half ironically. "It was not our finest hour." She gestured toward the dark blue carpeted circular staircase. "I'll lead the way. Johan was the first guest, and you two are the first couple we've had since we remodeled." With a nod, she turned and slipped up the stairs past the large crystal chandelier that hung in the two-story front foyer. We followed her to the guest rooms at the end of the hall, overlooking the front garden.

Llysette glanced from the triple-width bed with the green satin brocade spread to the pair of upholstered chairs that flanked the wall table and then to Judith. "This . . . c'est magnifique."

She was right; it was. Eric and Judith had always exhibited good taste, and they'd made enough to be able to indulge that taste.

"We like our guests to be comfortable, and I especially wanted you to feel welcome."

"*Pourquoi—*"

"Because you and Johan deserve happiness." Judith inclined her head toward me, ever so slightly. "He has had to worry about too much for too long. From what little I know, so have you. I am so glad you will be singing tomorrow. I hope you are."

"The occurrence is strange." Llysette shrugged, glancing toward the window hangings that matched the spread, then back to Judith. "But a singer must sing when she can. These things we do not choose, and . . ."

"After your engagement in Deseret, you will be able to choose where you sing," the older woman predicted.

"One would hope." Llysette's smile was skeptical. "We will see."

"Would you like some *café,* or tea, or chocolate? Or some wine?"

"The wine I would like, but that must come later." Llysette smiled, more warmly.

"Chocolate?"

"Something warm . . . but tea, perhaps?"

"Tea I can do. You'll want chocolate, Johan?"

"Of course."

"If you want to unpack or get settled, I'll be downstairs. Just come down when you're ready." With another smile, Judith turned and departed.

"Little she holds back," offered Llysette.

"They have been supportive when few were." I opened the closet so that Llysette could hang out the gown she would wear the next night. Then I hung up my own suits—one for meeting with Oakes and the formal wear for the dinner.

Once we hung up anything that would wrinkle, or wrinkle more, we went downstairs.

The chocolate and tea were set out in the nook off the kitchen—sunny there when the sun actually shone in the Federal District, but not under the gray drizzle. The old bone china teapot was also there, steam rising from its spout.

In addition to the two pots, Judith had set out the butter biscuits I was too fond of and *galettes.* Llysette took a *galette* with her tea. I had two biscuits.

"Good this is," murmured Llysette after a sip of tea, but I could see her eyes strayed toward the parlor and the silent Steinbach.

"Something hot is good after traveling, especially when it's so damp." Judith looked at Llysette. "Have you been in the Federal District recently?"

"*Mais non* . . . not since first I arrived in Columbia, and little do I remember."

"I doubt it has changed much."

I agreed silently, taking another biscuit. Nothing happened quickly, not in a city that had taken more than a century to finish the monument to the general who had freed the colonies. "The buildings all look the same."

"They are talking about moving the railway station on the Mall," Judith ventured.

"Again? Where would they put it?"

"They're talking about refurbishing and enlarging Union Station."

"That would take some doing." I reached for another biscuit.

"Johan. . . ." Llysette paused, and I knew what she was thinking. I'd gulped down four biscuits in as many minutes. But that was because I was nervous. I always ate too much when I was stressed or worried—another reason why I needed exercise.

"I know." I grinned.

Llysette smiled faintly. After a moment, her eyes went toward the sitting room, and she shifted her weight in her chair and set down her cup.

I got the message, and since Llysette wouldn't ask, I did. "Could Llysette use the Steinbach in the sitting room to practice a bit?"

"Oh . . . I should have offered. Of course." Judith turned back to face Llysette. "Let me show you. You are welcome to practice anytime you wish. Anytime," she emphasized with a smile. "You can close the doors . . . or not, as you please. We do miss the music. Since Suzanne left, no one plays. The piano is really hers, but she has no place for it, and we keep it tuned."

The two headed for the parlor, and I let them, listening as Judith tried to make Llysette feel welcome.

When Judith returned, after closing off the doors so that we wouldn't distract Llysette, I poured more chocolate. "Would you like some more?"

"A half a cup. Let me check dinner. Eric should be here before long."

I poured the chocolate and waited, listening to Llysette. Even through the doors, she sounded magnificent. She'd finished a run-through of both pieces before Judith slipped back into her seat.

"I hope that didn't get too cool."

"It's fine."

"I appreciate your trying to make her feel welcome. . . ."

"She's beautiful. She plays well, too," Judith added as her eyes went toward the closed French doors.

"She's always telling me that a singer needs keyboard skills, and she's always bemoaning the fact that her students never want to work on the keyboard. I did get her a piano—a Haaren, nothing compared to yours."

"You spent more than you had, knowing you."

I had, but . . . what else was new?

"Most of our students couldn't handle the training she's had," said Judith. "I can tell it wasn't easy for her."

"No. Not much has been, and I've been no bargain in that department, either."

"You've been hard on yourself, Johan."

"With some reason," I pointed out.

"You've never had too many options."

I heard steps and stood as Eric entered the kitchen.

"Like the proverbial clipped coin, you've returned." He held both his case and a folded copy of the *Post-Dispatch* but leaned over and kissed Judith. "You look and smell good."

"You had a hard day, then."

"Such a skeptical woman after all these years."

The piano stopped. Llysette came to the parlor door, and I opened it.

"This is Eric. Eric, Llysette."

"Johan is indeed a lucky chap." He bowed in that charming way he had, with that boyish and disarming grin.

I reseated Llysette and poured more tea into her cup. Eric took the empty chair but did not pour himself anything.

Judith slipped out of the nook and back into the kitchen.

"It's really amazing," Eric continued. "Here I am in my own house, sitting across from one of the great divas of the century. I'd count myself lucky to meet her, let alone find she's married to this . . . shirttail relative."

I suspected Eric had wanted to say more but realized it might raise implications.

Llysette blushed. *"Non . . . pas de tout. . . ."*

"After your last recital, I'd have to agree with Eric," I told her.

"You . . . you favor me, and so you do not listen. You hear what you would hear."

"If Johan says that," Eric interjected, "he means it. He's never been known for undeserved flattery."

"Thank you," I told him. "What other words of welcome do you have?"

"I could have told that you'd arrived." Eric added, more soberly, "Just from the news."

I groaned, half in mock-anguish, half with concern. "Now what?"

"Secret talks between Deseret and the Speaker, the reappearance of the famous Llysette duBoise, and more speculation about the man she married—rumored to have been a top assassin in the Spazi foreign branch. . . ."

"You're kidding, of course." Eric had been known to stretch matters.

"I wish I were, Johan." He shook his head. "They don't want to leave you alone."

I swallowed. "Who . . . when—"

"This afternoon's *Post-Dispatch*."

Llysette glanced at me and smiled, as if to say that it didn't matter, and, now, between us, it didn't. But it wouldn't help her if the rest of the world thought I was a former killer dog.

I forced a shrug. "They can say whatever. An assassin is one of the few things I haven't been, and heaven knows, I've done enough of which I'm not exactly proud." And that was certainly true.

"It's time for dinner," Judith said firmly. "Such serious subjects require nourishment." She glanced to Llysette. "Unless you need more time to practice."

"*Mais non* . . . I have practiced enough."

Dinner consisted of a rack of lamb with a rosemary glaze, potatoes in a cheese soufflé, and green beans amandine, not to mention breads and salads.

At first, the conversation dealt with the trip, passing items, and praise of Judith's cooking. Mostly I ate and listened.

Then Judith asked, "What are you singing?"

"Debussy, the aria of Lia from *L'Enfant du Prodigue,* and Mozart, *Exultate Jubilate.* Two is but what the president requested." Llysette glanced at me.

"I haven't heard the aria," said Judith, "except through the parlor doors, but it sounded beautiful."

"Everything she sings is beautiful."

"You can't tell he's in love or anything," said Eric.

I took refuge in another bite of lamb.

"You're different, Johan. More mellow, I'd say," Judith offered.

"More there is that he feels," opined Llysette. "And he will speak more."

"The original Sphinx—he actually speaks about how he feels?" asked Eric.

"*Quelquefois.*"

"If I don't, she waits until I do." And the waiting had gotten very cold at times before I learned.

"With this trip to Deseret, are you up to being spy, manager, bodyguard, and general flunky?" asked Eric.

"That's about it, isn't it? Except you forgot target. I don't mind the others, but I worry that we're being set up for something, and I don't even know what."

"They won't let you be, will they?" said Judith, shifting her weight in the Jefferson spiral-back chair.

"Not when they need us." I explained why I thought we—Llysette, actually—were being used as one of the cultural pawns to open energy trade.

"It figures," added Eric, turning to Llysette. "The fact that you're French will make it harder for deGaulle to say anything openly."

I wasn't sure about that, but Eric might well have been right.

Llysette yawned.

"You need some rest," suggested Judith. "What time are your engagements tomorrow?"

"Ten," I admitted. "I have a meeting, and she has a rehearsal."

"Then you should be resting or relaxing, not sitting stiffly around a table with a pair of fossils," said Judith.

"Fossils? Hardly."

"You have been most kind, and for that I am grateful." Llysette stood. "Perhaps you could visit us?" She laughed. "You could wait until the spring. The winter in New Bruges I would wish on no one."

"That would be nice," Eric said. "You know, we've never been there. It's strange, but somehow . . ." He shrugged, and I appreciated his words.

"Shoo," said Judith with a laugh. "We'd keep you talking all night, and while Johan wouldn't suffer, Llysette would."

I had to grin.

Llysette used the whirlpool tub in the overlarge guest bath, and I sat on the tiled edge in my undershorts, enjoying the warm steam and the view.

"You . . . are . . . *impossible* . . . ," she said slowly, accenting the French *"impossible."*

"Me?"

"Toi!"

"I'm impossible," I agreed, not averting my eyes. "How was the piano?"

"Magnifique . . . almost a concert instrument it is, and to have no one to play it . . ."

I wished I'd been able to afford one for her that good, but ours—hers, really— was a rebuilt thirty-year-old Haaren, good, serviceable, with a nice tone, but definitely not in the class of the grand Steinbach in the sitting room below. I wished I'd been able to give her something like that.

"You, you have given me . . . us . . . much. Do not worry yourself," she commanded, as if she could read my thoughts, and perhaps she could. Or my face, anyway.

I tried not to, too much, and got her one of the big cream-colored Turkish towels instead.

She didn't need it for long, and I wasn't that impossible. Neither was she.

Later, after I'd turned out the lights and we'd climbed under the covers of the triple-width bed, Llysette snuggled up beside me. "Good people, they are," she murmured sleepily. "I am glad we came."

I was pleased that she was glad, less pleased that my Spazi past had shown up in the *Post-Dispatch,* and even less pleased that I'd been termed an assassin, since I hadn't been. Even though I'd killed, as had most Spazi field agents being hunted by Ferdinand's Gestaats, it had been only for self-preservation. Even as I reflected on that in the darkness, I had to ask myself—or had Carolynne's ghost prompted me?—how much was self-justification. I tried not to shiver and wake Llysette. She needed her sleep.

CHAPTER NINE

• • •

The next morning Eric insisted on dropping us at the Presidential Palace, and Judith insisted—equally firmly—that she would pick us up whenever we wired. Judith's parting words had been: "I've taken the day off, and I expect you two to take full advantage of that."

I presented the government ID I still retained to the guards by the wrought-iron fence that surrounded the Presidential Palace. Llysette proffered her university card.

"One moment, sir and madam."

I glanced eastward, toward the Capitol, the domain of the Speaker, its lower reaches blocked by the turrets of the B&P station on the Mall, the whiteness of the recently restored west front of the Capitol a contrast to the dingier structures that flanked an increasingly run-down Pennsylvania Avenue. The Capitol had been restored three times, but it had taken a century to finish the Washington Monument. Somehow that said something about the relative priorities of the Congress in dealing with politicians and soldiers.

"They're expecting you both, sir and madam."

I didn't know about both of us. When we got to the east entry, a young man in a dark suit, with a goatee that looked glued on, immediately hastened up to Llysette. "Fräulein duBoise?"

Llysette nodded as if there could not possibly be any doubt, and I wanted to grin. Instead, I did the answering, like any good manager. "Yes. Who will be accompanying her?"

"Fräulein Stewart. She is already in the Green Room."

We followed the goateed young fellow, and then I bowed to Llysette as she entered the Green Room, where a full-size concert Steinbach had been set up at one end. "I'll wait somewhere if I'm done first."

"And you, sir?"

"I have an appointment with Harlaan Oakes."

"Very good, sir." The goateed fellow and the functionary in the butler's outfit let me head toward the east entrance, except I doubled back and headed for the lower stairs. I didn't get far before another fresh-faced young man, with the telltale bulge in his jacket, found me. "Minister Eschbach?"

"Yes? I presume Harlaan is where his predecessor was."

"Ah . . . yes, sir. If you would follow me . . ."

No, they weren't about to allow me to wander through the Presidential Palace by myself.

Harlaan, wonder of wonders, was actually standing in the lower hall. Like all political functionaries, he wore a gray suit so dark it was almost black. His maroon cravat blended with the faintest of stripes in the suit. "Johan. You are punctual, as always, as in everything."

That bothered me. "I try. Sometimes circumstances don't allow it, but today worked out."

Harlaan gestured toward the small office that had been Ralston's, and I followed him. His goatee was square, with a hint of gray. No trace remained in the small office of Ralston, the man who was now a zombie, the man I had turned into a zombie to protect Llysette and myself, to cover up one murder, and to, in the end, ensure that I took on the burden of two other souls.

The door closed behind us, seemingly of its own volition, and I took the battered wooden captain's chair on the right of the desk. Harlaan looked at the chair behind the desk, then took the one in front, as if to admit we were equals, another less than wonderful sign.

"I caught a glimpse of your wife. She is beautiful."

"She'll also sing beautifully."

"That will please the president . . . to no end."

"Good. What did you have in mind, Harlaan, since this isn't really a social call?"

The president's adviser cleared his throat. "Johan, you're also going to be contacted by some people on Minister Reilly's staff, and we've been requested to ask if you would visit Deputy Minister Jerome after you're done here. Reilly's people are going to want you to do some sightseeing—or keep your eyes open for violations of the Colorado River Compact."

"And see what else I can steal of environmentally friendly or synthfuels technology?" I shifted my weight in the old chair. "What does my friend Minister Jerome want? Or is it Asquith?"

"Officially, it's Minister Jerome."

I waited.

"And officially, he wishes to apologize for past discomforts."

Worse and worst. That meant even more disasters to come.

"You scarcely look pleased, Johan."

"Would you? In my position?"

Harlaan laughed, once. "Possibly not."

"And why is the Spazi going to such lengths?"

"Because the Prophet, Revelator, and Seer of Deseret has requested your wife's performance, and because Minister Holmbek is disturbed by the disruption of Venezuelan oil exports."

"I presume you have been the one enlarging my exposure to the print media?"

Harlaan shrugged. "One is never sure whether what is printed here reaches New Bruges."

"Do you know who made that attempt on our lives?"

"An attempt on your lives?"

"Harlaan." I waited.

"No. We suspect Maurice-Huizinga or Ferdinand. You might ask Minister Jerome."

That was all I'd get, and I changed the subject. "What else will Minister Reilly's people want?"

"A written report, I am sure. They always want something in writing. I can't imagine you have any problem with that."

Not too much of a problem. Just writing a report doubtless of an adverse nature on a neighboring country for which I wouldn't get paid. And if I did, the amount wouldn't be near enough to cover the real costs.

"What do you want?" I asked, another foolish question.

"A copy of whatever you report would be appreciated, of course, although you're certainly under no compunction to provide one."

"Harlaan . . . a little more, please."

"The president is concerned, Johan, deeply concerned."

"That's apparent. Why?"

"Deseret is almost a closed culture. Great Salt Lake City is the only place where they really allow outsiders, in any meaningful sense, you understand. The world has changed in the last century since the death of Prophet Young, but Deseret has not."

I had to frown at that. "What about their advances in drip farming, the natural cottons, their synthetic fuel plants, their specialty steels? Or the results of their partnerships with the Bajan difference engine suppliers? Or their success in building on the original Fischer-Tropsch designs? Those aren't exactly products of a backward culture."

Harlaan raised his eyebrows. "As you know, all of those are derivatives of others' ideas, not original in nature. That is the essence of Deseret, and why our concerns are social and political. The president is deeply concerned that any measurable unrest in Deseret will invite greater New French involvement under their mutual defense pact."

"Those concerns wouldn't have anything to do with the growing oil shortages, would they?" I asked. "This great interest in lack of Saint creativity and originality seems to have appeared from almost nowhere."

"Those are more concerns of Minister Holmbek and Speaker Hartpence."

"They're real concerns," I pointed out.

Harlaan shrugged. "Our concerns are political."

"How can you have politics as we know them? Deseret is a theocracy, and from what I know, their Prophet, the Twelve, and the First Speaker have close to iron control."

"Exactly." Oakes's smile was anything but pleasant. "And in this modern world, social change is going to occur, either peacefully or from the barrel of a firearm. There have been rumblings about something called the Revealed Twelve. We don't know much about them, except that they feel that the Twelve in power are rejecting the real teachings of their prophets."

"Whereas you and the president hope that Deseret decides to move into the twentieth century before the rest of North America moves into the twenty-first? Perhaps so that you can reduce conflict with Deseret while tensions are building to the north and south—and, of course, with Ferdinand and our commitments to the Brits."

"Something like that."

"I'm somewhat confused, Harlaan. While I may understand the international implications, what does all this have to do with a retired subminister?"

"With a retired subminister . . . nothing. With a former Spazi agent who is familiar with some of the latest developments in . . . shall we say . . . the proliferation or de-proliferation of psychic realities . . . a great deal."

"Oh?" I didn't like his reference to the "proliferation" of psychic realities, not at all.

"We all have our sources, Johan. The decision to offer your Fräulein duBoise a contract to perform was not made purely on artistic grounds." He held up his hand. "She is certainly well qualified, and as a Columbian citizen now, she certainly meets the requirements of the Cultural Exchange Act, which is the ostensible political rationale for the invitation. Artistically, the choice is impeccable, and now that she has married you, the decision conforms to the policies of the Twelve, which restricts female performers to those underage or married and accompanied by their husband. We and Minister Jerome have been offering, and will continue to offer, a modicum of, shall we say, residual and residential oversight, as we have for all of those associated with the recently discontinued projects of former minister vanBecton."

The more I heard, the more superficial sense it made, and the less real logic Harlaan's words held.

"Who is interested in such illegal psychic research?" I pressed, not wishing to admit much of anything. "Ferdinand knew it all to begin with, and vanBecton— and Minister Jerome—certainly knew. As do others." Meaning the president and Harlaan.

"Certain equipment has been traced to Deseret. It's a closed society, as I pointed out. We don't know who or why, but your invitation wasn't exactly by coincidence. Minister Jerome has doubtless come to the same conclusion." Harlaan smiled grimly. "None of us like the idea of advanced psychic technology in a potentially unfriendly theocracy with an energy surplus on our borders—and on New France's borders."

I did wince slightly.

"Now . . . you understand that, under other circumstances, the president merely could have gone to the Speaker and suggested that your trip to Deseret would not have been in the national interest."

I understood. President Armstrong and Speaker Hartpence were waging a silent but ongoing war for control and direction of Columbia, and any concession or request for cooperation would have been seized upon as a weakness. At the same time, they both agreed that anything that could destabilize Deseret or allow greater New French involvement there was in neither's interest.

"So . . . what do you want from me?"

"What you want for yourself, Johan. Peace and quiet. Your pledge to avoid becoming entrapped in the politics of Deseret. That's all." Harlaan rose from his chair with a smile.

That was hardly all—hardly it at all—and we both knew it. Harlaan proved that with his next words.

"Minister Jerome's limousine is waiting for you. They'll bring you back after your meeting."

I could hear Llysette and Fräulein Stewart still practicing as Harlaan escorted me to the less obvious west exit, where a dark gray Spazi car waited.

With just me and the driver, the short trip to the Sixteenth Street Spazi building was silent. I still swallowed when I entered the underground garage of the building officially called the Security Service building, for all that the entire world knew it as the Spazi building. Another young fellow in dark gray, with one of those new ear sets, was waiting for me and escorted me to the elevator and up to the fourth floor.

Neither the flat gray ceramic tiles and light blond wood paneling designed to hide the darkness behind each door had changed. The smell of disinfectant was particularly strong in the garage subbasement. Even in the elevator, the odor of disinfectant, common to jails and security services the world over, lingered, although it vanished when I stepped onto the dark rust carpet on the corridor leading to Deputy Minister Jerome's office.

His clerk, though young, had a narrow, pinched face under wire-rimmed glasses and presided over a large wireline console. She nodded and tapped a stud on the console. "You are expected."

The young Spazi agent waited, and I stepped through the paneled door alone.

Jerome, blond, expansive, and blue-eyed—and younger than vanBecton—stepped forward, extending his hand. "Minister Eschbach—"

"Minister Jerome, those days are past. I'm more of a simple professor, married to a woman far more famous than I am."

"Nonsense, Johan. You two are perhaps the most visible couple in Columbia today."

And whose doing was that? I wondered, considering that no one had even heard of us a month previous.

"Please." He gestured to one of the leather-covered chairs before the desk, then took the other. The blue eyes weren't as friendly as the smile, but I supposed that had been true of every Spazi director I'd known.

"What can I do for you?" I asked.

"I've been reading your file, Johan. I rather suspect you know, in general terms, but I will spell it out. We have reached an ostensible accommodation, tacit in nature, with Ferdinand, on the issues surrounding ghosts. He won't keep it, and he doesn't believe we'll keep it. We need to attain a better energy trade with Deseret, and this performance of your wife is one of the tools for, if you will, de-ogrefying Columbia in Great Salt Lake City. The problem is that Ferdinand's people suspect you know something about the de-ghosting technology." Jerome smiled coldly.

I frowned. "Why is that a problem? Assuming I did, they'd like nothing better than for me to be in Deseret. But if I did, the last people I'd give that technology to would be the Saints."

"I'd hoped that would be your view . . . especially given the sensitivities to, shall we say, psychic proliferation or destruction." The Spazi minister gestured toward the briefcase on the desk. "We would feel more . . . comfortable . . . if you would be willing to borrow what you need. Just take the case. Call it a loan of equipment necessary to protect your lady."

"A loan." Almost the last thing I needed was a loan of that kind of equipment, yet if Jerome was correct, and he probably happened to be, I couldn't afford anything less. "Does this also have to do with the attempt on our lives? Was that Ferdinand?" I waited. "Or Maurice-Huizinga?"

"We don't know."

"Comforting to hear," I said. "Such certainty in this uncertain world."

"There is one other matter."

"Yes?"

"Deputy Minister Habicht—Natural Resources—has requested that you spend a few moments with him."

"I'd been told that was a possibility."

"You can pick up your 'loan' on the way back. His security people might get a little concerned." Jerome stood. "I do sincerely wish your wife well, and look forward to her success. You may not wish to convey that. The blessing of the Spazi is certainly not always looked for, but you two will have it where it can be provided."

I stood as well. "Thank you. I understand." And I did. He honestly wanted Llysette to do well, and he wished I'd drop off the face of the earth, except that no one could afford that because of the "insurance" arrangements I'd made previously, which would release too much ghost technology if I died.

"I'm sure you do, Johan. We all do what we must."

That was that, but I wanted to chew my nails down to the quick.

Since Natural Resources was only across the street, the young Spazi agent and

I took the tunnels. Deputy Minister Habicht's office was on the eighth floor, on the south end of the east side, with an unobstructed view of the Capitol dome.

Habicht looked more like a Spazi chief than Jerome had—with deep-set dark eyes, narrow face, and a smile as false as de-Gaulle's word. He put me on the leather couch, deep blue, and stayed behind his desk.

"It's good to meet you in person, Johan. Minister Watson spoke of how dedicated you were."

Dedicated—that's such a weaseling word. It means someone worked hard but either doesn't agree with you or is ineffective or both.

"I've seen in the paper that you've also obtained a reputation for dedication," I countered.

"According to our records, you were also rather effective at a time when most of your contemporaries were inclined to disregard environmental protection. Would you mind telling me why?"

"Because over time you can't separate environmental protection from either defense or survival." That was obvious enough. "What do you need?"

"A man who gets to the point." Habicht smiled. "We understand Deseret intends to continue massive expansion of both its synthfuel plants and its related chemical industry. Currently, our emissions control technology would not support that kind of expansion. That means that either Deseret is going to increase downriver emissions in the Colorado—which has certain strategic considerations—or they've achieved a better system. Any information you could provide would be more than welcome . . . more than welcome."

I tried not to frown, and that disturbed me. Was it me or the circumstances? I was trying not to frown all the time. "I would think that you would have better sources than a casual visitor to Deseret."

"Let us just say, Johan, that your in-depth technical background has been overlooked by Deseret in the interests of obtaining your wife's services. We're confident that anything you can add will be more than useful." Habicht smiled, and I had to wonder why they all smiled and why I felt very much the opposite.

"I'm not sure I'm as confident as you are, Minister Habicht, but any environmental and technical information I may run across will certainly be yours."

"That is all we could ask."

And all he was going to get.

Then it was back through the tunnels to the Spazi building. The loaned equipment briefcase was waiting with the electrolimousine. I took a quick look before closing it. There actually were a few items I might be able to use, and that was somewhat disconcerting.

Minister Jerome wanted my help and Llysette's success badly. That made me more nervous than I'd been in years—except perhaps when I'd found Llysette pointing a Colt-Luger at my forehead. I wondered just how bad the energy supply situation was getting.

As I rode back to the Presidential Palace, another thought crossed my mind. Should all my equipment on ghost disassociation and replication be removed from the house in our absence? Or would it be safer there in our absence? Either way, that would pose a problem, not insurmountable, but a definite problem. Then again, I had this feeling that what I'd thought secret wasn't nearly so hidden.

When I reentered the Presidential Palace, Llysette stood near the east entrance with a small, dark-haired woman. Small the woman was, but so determined-looking that I could scarcely have called her petite.

"Johan, I would have you meet Terese Stewart."

"Johan Eschbach. I'm pleased to meet you, Fräulein Stewart."

"Terry, please. If for nothing else, I'm glad you married this lady so that the rest of us will be able to hear her sing again." Terry Stewart paused, then fixed me with those intense eyes. "Were you really a spy?"

"That was a long time ago. But . . . yes. Not an assassin, a spy." There wasn't much point in lying. My record had been laid out in the media.

"And they still made you a government minister?"

"What else could I have done?" I asked. "I did have a doctorate in environmental engineering. Were you really young and foolish once?"

She did laugh, and Llysette smothered a frown.

I'd learned, probably too late, that a cheerful attack is a lot better than detailed explication.

"You might have what it takes to be married to a prima donna at that." She turned to Llysette. "Until tonight."

"Tonight," affirmed Llysette.

Even as she finished, one of the functionaries in dark gray eased up. "Your limousine is waiting, Minister Eschbach, Fräulein duBoise."

Indeed it was. A substantial black limousine stood in the side drive of the palace, with a driver holding the door.

"*Comme ca, c'est etrange* . . . last year I cannot sing, and now . . . the limousine of the president . . ."

Put that way, it *was* strange, but we'd already learned how life twisted.

Once again, we were driven up New Bruges, past Dupont Circle and the Japanese and Chinese embassies and the old observatory. The trees were gray in the light drizzle. I felt as though the entire world were gray.

The limousine didn't bother me quite so much as the small gray steamer that was parked back on Sedgwick—just barely in sight of Eric and Judith's. Harlaan hadn't been jesting about protective details.

I wanted to shake my head. VanBecton—Jerome's predecessor—had tried to eliminate me, and now everyone was doing their best to protect us. Protection meant danger, and I still hadn't a very clear idea of exactly what that danger was—except that something in Deseret was very dangerous and everyone wanted Llysette and me there.

Judith opened the door before I had a chance to knock. Her eyes went to the black limousine that slowly pulled away. "That's very impressive. I forgive you for not wiring. Have you eaten?"

We both shook our heads.

"I am famished, also," announced Llysette.

I didn't announce it, just ate everything that Judith put on the table. None of us said anything, really, while we wolfed down the croissants and soup. Then the three of us sat in the sunroom for a time after lunch.

"What did you think of the Presidential Palace?" asked Judith.

"*C'est magnifique, mais triste d'une maniere ou d'une autre . . .*"

Sad somehow?

"In what way?" asked the silver-haired woman who had been my sister-in-law.

Llysette shrugged. "That . . . I could not say. It could have been greater, but I know not how."

It could have been, I supposed, if Washington had not died before taking office, if Adams had been a bigger man . . . if Jefferson had not been so opposed to a strong executive. . . . So many ifs, but we had to live the lives we led, not those that might have been, and that went for those who came before us and for those who would follow. Somehow, that thought made me feel uneasy—or did it make that part of me that was still Carolynne uneasy? Or both of us?

Judith glanced at Llysette. "What would you like to do now?"

"To rest, perhaps . . . ," ventured Llysette.

"Then you should."

I went upstairs with her but, after I tucked her in, came back down. She definitely wanted just rest.

"Beneath that cheerful exterior you're worried," Judith observed. "Would you like some more chocolate?"

"Yes, and please."

We went back to the sunroom, and the warmth of the chocolate was more than welcome. I worked at curbing the appetite engendered by nerves and only had two of the butter biscuits.

"You're thinking like a spy again, Johan. That may be the immediate problem, but it's going to be very small in the future."

"Assuming we get to the future."

"I have every confidence that your talents will see you two through the web of intrigue. Yours and Llysette's talents, anyway."

"What do you mean about the future?" I was afraid I knew, but I asked.

"You've always been the star, so to speak. The spy, the minister, the noted professor and commentator. Llysette could be a far brighter star. How do you plan on dealing with that?"

"I hadn't thought about that. What would you suggest?" I took a long swallow of chocolate and refilled the cup.

"It might not happen, but I think it will. Times are troubled, and people look for heroes. They want a symbol, someone who has triumphed over adversity." Judith shook her head. "She's a singer, possibly without equal. A beautiful singer, a woman who has survived Ferdinand's prisons, married to a handsome war hero, spy, and politician. All of the ingredients are there."

I wanted to protest, to say that Judith didn't know any of that for sure, but I didn't. After having heard Llysette's recital last year and the one weeks earlier, I knew there was no comparison. Good as she had been, now she was outstanding, brilliant . . . and if I—and the Spazi—could keep her safe, the world would find out soon enough.

"You already know it," Judith pointed out. "You're fighting it, but you know it. It makes you nervous. You ate practically half a tray of butter cookies."

She was right, and I had, despite my initial resolve to eat only two. I didn't have any real answers, either. Llysette deserved everything, and I'd have been deceiving myself if I didn't wonder where that would leave me, because I was essentially a has-been.

After a time, I went back upstairs when I heard Llysette getting ready.

Another of the president's black limousines was waiting at five-thirty outside Eric and Judith's.

Llysette wore the shimmering green gown we'd gotten in Borkum, although she'd almost balked at spending that much, retainer or not, until I'd pointed out that she could use it both in Deseret and in the Federal City.

"I'm impressed," I told Llysette as we walked out to where the driver held the door for her. "In all my years in government, I never got a limousine to take me anywhere. You've gotten us two in a single day."

It got worse—or better, depending on the viewpoint.

The limousine took us to the north front entrance of the Presidential Palace, and they'd opened it to the media types—and there were a half-dozen, more, again, than I'd ever seen as a subminister.

"A little to the left, Minister Eschbach. Thank you."

I moved, and that meant they got several shots of Llysette all by herself. She looked radiant, even with the green cloak over the full gown.

We were seated together, midway down the table, but on Llysette's right was Hartson James. Besides being the head of Columbian TransMedia, he'd also bankrolled the president's early campaign when no one ever thought a politician from West Kansas stood a chance of becoming president, whether the office was considered largely ceremonial or not.

James immediately monopolized Llysette.

"You're the one William is so determined to hear sing. Well, if you sing half as good as you look, we're in for a rare treat."

"You are too kind," murmured Llysette politely.

"Kind? Never call a media man kind. We always want something. If you're that good, I'll be badgering you to perform, and if you don't, my commentators will be questioning the president's judgment. Either way, we win." He laughed, and I disliked him.

Llysette continued to listen politely.

I was seated beside the artificially red-haired Deanna Loutrec, otherwise known as Madame D—of the artificial "Madame D's Gems" and the slogan "no one will know but your jeweler." To my surprise, she wore but a single ring, and I would have bet it was real, for all its size and sparkle.

"So you are the mystery minister?" asked Deanna.

"Hardly—just a university professor who was once a junior subminister and who had the fortune to marry a beautiful soprano."

"Beautiful and talented soprano's don't marry nobodies or no-talents," she observed, "even handsome ones."

Handsome? I doubted that.

"No false modesty, Minister Eschbach. You are handsome." Deanna laughed, not quite raucously. "You're also very off-limits. If I batted an eyelash at you, your lovely diva wouldn't leave enough of me for a one-minute commercial."

I almost nodded at that. Of Llysette's determination I had no doubts.

"See? You don't even protest."

How could I?

After a bite of the green salad orange and amandine, I turned to Llysette, who had barely taken one small bite. "How are you feeling?"

"Nervous . . . I feel *tres* . . ." She shook her head.

"You'll do fine." I squeezed her knee under the table. "You will."

Before we finished the fillets, Llysette slipped away to join Terese Stewart. Even I couldn't eat the remainder of my dinner, and I wasn't the one singing.

"I have persuaded one of our guests—the lovely Llysette—to sing a pair of songs for us," the president finally announced, "and I won't even try to pronounce the names of either song, except to say that the first one is by Mozart and the second, naturally, by a French composer. Fräulein Llysette duBoise, accompanied by Terese Stewart."

Llysette said nothing by way of introduction, just nodded to the pianist, waited for the music, and launched into the Mozart. I'm no musician, but it seemed to me that her voice floated, soared, and yet carried a depth that was beyond depth.

The stillness between songs was absolute, the hush of an audience afraid to break a spell, the sort of hush seldom heard, especially in New Bruges, I reflected absently.

Then came the Debussy.

After the Debussy, the entire table was silent. The silence of shock, the silence of having heard something so great that all else paled. Then the staid burghers and astute politicians cheered and clapped . . . and clapped and cheered.

Just before Llysette sat down, Deanna turned to me. "The idiots . . . why did they keep her from singing for so long?"

I shrugged. "We tried. It took a while." A while, two ghosts, and too many zombies and deaths.

Llysette eventually slipped away from the impromptu stage in the corner of the room, and I stood to seat her.

At the end of the table, as we sat, President Armstrong rose, and the clapping died. He held up his water glass—he'd never touched anything alcoholic, the rumor went. "Even if it's water, the thought is champagne. To the greatest singer I've ever heard. . . ."

Another round of applause followed the president's toast.

"You were wonderful," I whispered.

"You were absolutely magnificent! Absolutely!" insisted Hartson James. "You should do a special for TransMedia."

Llysette nodded. "You are too kind."

"I mean it. After your Deseret engagement . . . perhaps something for Christmas . . . at least a few songs for one of the Christmas specials."

I had the sinking feeling that he meant it, really meant it.

Somehow, we got through the rest of the dinner, and Llysette smiled politely again when the President and Frau Armstrong made their way to Llysette as we were departing.

"I meant what I said, young lady. If I were more articulate, I would have said more." His practiced smile was warm.

"I so enjoyed your singing," offered the strawberry blond First Lady, and I trusted the warmth in her voice more than the practiced voice of the President.

Then we were escorted back to the limousine—or another one—for the drive back to Eric and Judith's.

Llysette almost cuddled against me in the limousine on the way through Dupont Circle and up New Bruges.

"Both of us . . . we wanted to sing so much, and . . . we sang for us . . . and for you, Johan."

For me? I could sense the tears, and I just held her. What else could I do?

I kept thinking about Bruce's pen and pencil set and about the case under the wide bed in Eric and Judith's guest suite—and about the deadly words *psychic proliferation*.

CHAPTER TEN

• • •

The Friday after Llysette's appearance at the Presidential Palace was the first full day we were back in Vanderbraak Centre. I dropped her off at the Music and Theatre building, as usual in our routine, and went to Samaha's to pick up the papers that had accumulated in our absence.

I scurried through the fitful drizzle that had replaced the early-morning snow flurries, but, barely four steps into that dark emporium, I ran into the proprietor.

"Doktor Eschbach . . . that was some picture of your lady," offered Louie. "And right on the front page, too. Saved a couple extras for you. Rose says we'd best go to her next recital."

"I'll tell her. Thank you."

"Fancy that—one of the world's greatest, and right here in Vanderbraak Centre."

"You never know," I said as kindly as I could after picking up the papers and paying Louie for the extras. My stomach twisted at the mention of the front page. Even the annual Presidential Arts Award dinner shouldn't have made the front page—unless someone important in the capital wanted it there very badly.

"Right here," Louie repeated.

"It does happen." I slipped the papers under my arm and made my way out into the damp.

Back in the Stanley, I read the story before heading up to the faculty car park. I thought I'd better know what had been said. Louie had understated the press—page 1, if below the fold, of the *Asten Post-Courier,* with the picture taken outside the Presidential Palace, one of the ones that didn't show me.

FEDERAL DISTRICT (RPI). "The greatest singer I've ever heard"—that was how President Armstrong characterized soprano Llysette duBoise after her performance at the National Arts Awards dinner at the Presidential Palace.

"Magnificent performance," commented honorary National Arts chair Benjamin Kubelsky. "I only wish she'd had time to do another piece by Mozart—*L'Amero e Costante.*"

DuBoise's performance marks the return of the French soprano once hailed as the next Soderstrom, and those who heard her were unanimous in their praise. . . .

DuBoise had been imprisoned after the fall of France, released after the intervention of the Japanese ambassador to Vienna, and granted asylum in Columbia. With an earned doctorate from the Sorbonne, rather than return to opera or the concert stage, she took a teaching position at Vanderbraak State University in New Bruges in 1989. Last year, she married another distinguished faculty colleague there, former Subminister for Environmental Protection, Doktor Johan Eschbach. Eschbach, a decorated pilot in the Republic Naval Air Corps and rumored to have once been a Spazi agent, was the most notable figure in the Nord scandal, when a still-undisclosed assassin wounded him and killed both his wife and son.

Sources in the capital indicate that duBoise felt she could not perform publicly in the uncertain status of an artistic refugee, but once she was granted Columbian citizenship earlier this year, the way was open for her return to the stage, and what a return it was and will be.

DuBoise is scheduled to present a demanding and full concert at the Salt Palace Concert Hall in Deseret in early December, where she will be accompanied by the noted composer, arranger, and pianist Daniel Perkins.

I shook my head. The story was nearly a duplicate of the one that had run in the Federal District's papers, both the *Post-Courier* and the *Evening Star,* although there it had merely led off the entertainment and arts sections. Merely? More people read those than the front page.

With all the publicity, someone definitely wanted a target. That was clear. Why they did wasn't so clear, for all the explanations.

I hadn't even gotten inside the office before David practically swarmed over me. "Johan, the dean called over, and she was most pleased about the story."

They both should have been. Although Llysette had gotten top billing, as she deserved, the story had mentioned both of us and suggested that Vanderbraak State University had a distinguished faculty.

"And a spy, Johan? I never would have guessed beneath that scholarly exterior."

That was a purely political disclaimer, but I smiled. "The story noted that it was *rumored* I was a spy, David. I was a pilot and a subminister, however, as you know."

David let my own political statement slide. "We shouldn't go on rumors, I suppose."

"No. The dean wouldn't like it if people insisted that the rumors about her and Marinus Voorster were true."

"Ah . . . no. That is true."

"I'm glad that's understood." I smiled more broadly. "I need to get ready for my classes and talk to Regner and Wilhelm about what happened in the ones they took for me."

"Of course."

The papers in my box were mostly junk—textbook announcements and cards for perusal copies—but there was one envelope in the dean's cream-and-green stationery.

I opened that as I walked up the stairs.

All it said was: "Bravo, Johan!", with a scrawled "K" beneath.

Bravo for what? Having the sense to marry the woman I loved? To let her do what she had been born and trained to do? That merited congratulations?

Regner caught me opening the door to my office. "Oh, that was beautiful. Such a slap in Ferdinand's face."

"What?"

"Llysette's performance. It makes him look like the uncultured barbarian he is." Regner then glanced around the empty hallway. "About what they wrote about you . . ."

"I was a pilot and a subminister, Regner. I am a full-time university professor, and would like to stay as such. Let's leave it at that."

"As you wish, Johan." Unfortunately, the young fellow grinned, but I didn't want to lie outright. So I let it pass.

Nowhere could I escape the questions, not even in my environmental economics class.

"Ah . . . Professor Eschbach . . . is it true you were a spy?"

"Mister Nijkerk, you can't believe everything that the newspapers print. I was a pilot and a subminister, and that's enough for any faculty member." More than enough.

"But they all wrote—"

"I believe what they wrote was that it was *rumored* that I was a spy. That is not quite the same thing," I pointed out, trying to avoid an out-and-out lie but also not wanting it broadcast across the campus that I'd admitted to having been a spy. In my vanity, I'd rather have been classed as a Spazi covert operative, not a common run-of-the-mill spy, but they wouldn't have known the difference. "The newspaper speculations will not assist you in discussing the impact of taxation on the consumption levels of environmentally sensitive goods. Mister Dykstra, what does the location of the Tejas oil fields have to do with the development of the current steamer technology in Columbia?"

Mister Dykstra swallowed.

After forty minutes more on the impact of transport technology on the environment, I escaped to Delft's. I made it there before Llysette.

"Herr Doktor Eschbach, will the lady be joining you?"

"Yes, Victor."

"Then you must have the table by the stove."

I nodded toward the door. "Here she comes."

Victor turned and gave a deep bow to Llysette. "I did not know, but I am pleased that it was a French soprano that the president did praise."

"Merci." Llysette smiled.

Victor ushered us to Llysette's favorite table, and that was a good thing, because she was almost shivering from the damp cold.

"Do you know what you would like?" he asked.

"The New Ostend cheddar soup, with the green salad, and chocolate," I ordered.

"The croissant with the salad, and the wine, the good white."

"With pleasure. With much pleasure, mademoiselle." Victor bowed again, as if Llysette's presence had made his day.

"You are certainly the belle of Vanderbraak Centre," I said with a laugh. "What did Dierk say?"

"I should apply for full professor. That is now before they forget."

"He's probably right. That assumes you want to keep teaching."

"Johan. I have one paying concert."

"So far."

"We shall see."

She was right about that, but she hadn't seen the local paper.

"Here you are, prima donna of Columbia." I passed the newspaper across the table to her.

Llysette still flushed ever so slightly. "This, it is . . . *tres difficile*—"

"Hard to believe? For the diva who was supposed to replace Soderstrom?"

"Long ago, that was so long ago . . . or it seems so."

"Voilà!" Victor presented Llysette with the shimmering white Sebastopol, followed by my chocolate, and flashed another smile. He was clearly enjoying himself.

"Did anyone else say anything?"

"The dean, such a letter she wrote me." Llysette gave a sound that was too feminine for a snort and too ironic for a sniff. "The butter, it would not melt in her mouth."

I got the idea.

"She only told me, 'Bravo.'" I lowered my voice slightly, not that it mattered. "David was worried that it said I'd been a spy."

My diva smiled broadly. "Worry he should, the . . . weasel. He and the dean, they are similar."

Weasel was probably too kind a description, but I was feeling charitable and let it pass.

CHAPTER ELEVEN

• • •

O utside of the gray steamers that appeared in and around Vanderbraak Centre, especially in the vicinity of Deacon's Lane, the next complete week after Llysette's appearance was surprisingly quiet. Both Llysette and I actually managed to catch up on missed teaching and lessons, at least mostly.

No strangers appeared at our door with odd boxes, and the newspapers were temporarily silent on the subject of either Llysette or me.

That lasted until I picked up Llysette the following Friday, a clear late afternoon so cold that her breath was a white fog as she slipped into the Stanley in the twilight.

"I'm glad you don't have any rehearsals tonight," I said casually, easing the steamer out and around the square past McArdles' and toward the Wijk River bridge. "It's been a long week. Anything interesting happen?"

"Doktor Perkins—he sent me an arrangement, a special arrangement, to see if it would I like." Llysette's words ran together, the way she did when she got excited. "And he writes that he looks forward to playing for me, and would I send the arrangements I would prefer. . . ."

"Doktor Perkins?" I pulled up to wait for a hauler to cross the bridge.

"The composer—he is the one who put Vondel to music. But his art songs, they are so much better. I sang the one."

I frowned, trying to recall her recital. For only a few weeks ago, it seemed even longer. *"Fragments of a Conversation?"*

"Exactement!"

"He's a Saint?"

"For me, he wishes to play. . . ."

"He should. Who could he play for that would be any better?" I had to smile. Sometimes she still didn't realize just how good she'd gotten.

"You are kind."

"This time, I'm just accurate." The Stanley slid a bit, and I eased the steamer into four-wheel as we headed up Deacon's Lane in the dimming light.

Llysette swallowed. "And my concert, they wish to record. There is . . . an agreement. . . ."

"A contract?"

"I have it here." She held up what might have been an envelope, but I was concentrating on driving.

"I'll look at it when we get home." I paused as it hit me. "A recording contract? That's wonderful! Maybe you won't have to teach Dutch dunderheads for the rest of your life."

"*Mon cher* . . . sweet you are, but even I, I know that people, they must buy the recordings, and who will buy the songs of an aging French singer?"

"About half the world, once they hear you. And you're certainly not aging. I can attest to that."

Llysette laughed. "You are *impossible*."

I probably was, in more ways than one, but I had this feeling. Llysette had needed only one break, and she'd gotten it. With her determination, she wouldn't fail—not unless someone stopped her. And that led to the other feeling—the one that said she needed protecting more than I did.

Once we were inside, and after I'd stoked up the woodstove against the chill created by the cold and the rising wind, I did read the contract while Llysette sat in front of the stove and watched.

"It looks all right to me. Would you mind if I called Eric? I think they have someone in his law firm that does this sort of thing."

"He would do that for me?"

"I am sure he would be more than happy. More than happy, but I probably can't get an answer until late Monday or Tuesday."

While Llysette changed into more casual—and warmer—trousers and a sweater, I went into the kitchen and started on dinner: a ham angel-hair pasta with broccoli that wouldn't take too long, with biscuits and a small green salad. First came the water, since that took the longest to heat, and then I went to work on the sauce, digging out the butter, a garlic clove, the leftover ham and the horribly expensive broccoli crown. Fresh vegetables were still costly in the winter in New Bruges. Then I got out the milk and the dash of flour I needed.

I had the sauce ready, the biscuits ready to go into the oven, just about the time the kettle was boiling. So in went the angel-hair. I set the kitchen table, but the pasta wasn't ready—still far too al dente.

Because watched pasta never boiled, not for me, I slipped out of the kitchen and into the study for a moment, taking the mail from my jacket pocket and setting it on the desk.

I looked at the mirror on the wall, with the bosses that opened the concealed storage area that contained not only the old artificial lodestone but also the deghosting equipment and, now, the equipment case from Jerome.

Strange . . . a year before I hadn't even known about the hidden area, not until Carolynne—then known only as the silent and enduring family ghost—had pointed it out to me and begun to murmur Shakespeare and art songs. Now, from within me, sometimes I could almost hear the songs in my ears, not just in my thoughts. Llysette, I knew, heard more than I did.

When I'd attempted to develop a copy of Carolynne, assuming that's what you could call a difference engine–generated replication of a ghost of a singer who'd been murdered more than a century earlier, I'd failed until I'd used the scanner to replicate her actual being. Did that mean there had been two Carolynnes until each joined with me and with Llysette? Did that mean technology would someday be able to clone bodies and each body's soul? I wasn't sure. The metaphysics was beyond me, and I didn't want to think about it all that closely.

I shook my head, eyes refocusing on the mirror and the equipment it hid. The Colt-Luger from Jerome wouldn't help at all, but some of the other items might, such as the detector-transparent rope. I had my own plastique, but there was no point in turning down some from Minister Jerome, and the miniature homing beacons might come in useful somehow. I'd have to consider what to take to Deseret— and how I could conceal it, although most of the equipment was radar- and scan-transparent.

My hand brushed the difference engine as I turned. Was it warm? I frowned, checking the desk. I hadn't recalled the stack of papers beside the console being quite so neat.

After the screen cleared, I ran a check, but there was no sign that the machine had been used since the night before. I shook my head. If strange agents with de-ghosters didn't get me, paranoia would. I switched off the SII machine.

With the hiss and smell of pasta water that had boiled over, I hurried back to the kitchen. I still hadn't managed handling both cooking and worrying simultaneously, and I doubted that I ever would, all Llysette's comments about my being a chef to the contrary.

CHAPTER TWELVE

• • •

After another week of chill and occasional snow flurries, the temperature had climbed again until it was nearly springlike, although the scent of damp fallen leaves permeated the entire campus. My nose itched. The clock had struck four o'clock as I'd left Smythe after my last class for the week, and the wind—suddenly colder—gusted around me as I walked downhill toward the post centre.

Most of the parking spaces on the square were taken, and the small car lot beside McArdles' was filled with the steamers of those who wished to do no grocery shopping on the weekend.

"Good afternoon, Constable." I nodded to Gerhardt as I passed the Watch station and turned up the walk.

"Afternoon, Doktor. A good one." He looked to the fast-moving clouds coming in from the north. "So far, but the clouds look nasty."

"They do. Maybe I'll get home before they get here."

The post centre lobby was deserted, and my dress boots echoed hollowly on the stone floor. In our box were three envelopes, and one was manila. The manila envelope was exactly the same as the earlier ones postmarked in the Federal District. From Jerome, I suspected more and more. I shook my head and put it and the two bills into my inside jacket pocket.

On the way back to my office from the post centre, I took a detour. I walked by the Science building, noting that the blackened windows remained where Gerald's concealed laboratory had been. I'd seen the equipment lugged out and even toured the empty spaces that had been refurbished for a new difference engine center for the students.

I'd been so concerned about de-ghosting, but what about creating psychic proliferation, as Minister Jerome had put it? Was there a military application to creating ghosts?

I snorted. There had to be. The military could pervert anything. Then it struck me, and I swallowed. He'd mentioned it. I never had to anyone in the Spazi—ever.

The sky darkened, and I looked up as stiff gusts of cold wind buffeted me. The clouds had swept in and covered all but the lowest part of the western horizon.

Branston-Hay's equipment hadn't been destroyed, no matter what Speaker Hartpence had said. It was doubtless somewhere else, with some other Babbage type attempting to refine the selective de-ghosting procedure already adopted and implemented for Ferdinand's crack commando troops.

Pellets of ice bounced off the stone walk as I headed back to the Natural Resources building.

I also wondered who or what branch of government might be working on Gerald's project to create ghosts. So far as I knew, I'd been the only one to actually implement that feature of his research, but if Bruce and I could, it certainly wouldn't be a problem for any number of researchers, assuming anyone had the material . . . and that was the question. I'd erased the files from Gerald's difference engine, and his backup disks had supposedly gone up in flames with his house. Had anyone else seen his material—all of it? I just didn't know, and wouldn't if or until strange ghosts started popping up places where they shouldn't be.

My own efforts had indicated that matters didn't usually turn out as planned, and while Llysette and I had survived, we certainly weren't the same people we'd once been. Still, those considerations wouldn't stop others, and both Harlaan and Jerome were hinting that they hadn't.

Hunched up in my overcoat, I trudged through the intermittent ice pellets and wind gusts to the Natural Resources building. Gilda's desk was empty, and David's door was shut and locked—not surprising on a Friday afternoon.

I sat at my desk and extracted the manila envelope that held a single clipping:

GREAT SALT LAKE CITY, DESERET (WNS). Denying reports that New France had sent a strongly worded note protesting the planned diversion of more than 10 percent of the annual flow of the Colorado River, First Counselor Cannon reemphasized the close and continuing ties between Deseret and New France. "Allies in the past, and allies in the future . . . there is no room and no reason for discord in a world haunted by the spectre of Austro-Hungarian imperialism."

Cannon refused to discuss specifics of the so-called Green River revitalization program, only saying that the amount of water involved was "vastly overstated". . . .

Usually reliable sources indicated that the First Counselor was delicately suggesting that Deseret needed calm relations with both New France and Columbia.

In a related development, scientists in the water reuse program at the University of Deseret announced an improved metering technology for drip irrigation systems.

Water, diplomacy, and strained relations between Deseret and New France. The clipping seemed to be something that Deputy Minister Habicht would be more interested in than Jerome or Oakes—but the envelope had come from Jerome's operation, and that still bothered me.

Then, everything about Llysette's scheduled performance in Deseret was beginning to bother me, and we still had another three weeks before we got on the dirigible for Great Salt Lake City.

Still . . . there wasn't too much I could do that I hadn't already done, and I had papers to grade. There were always papers to grade. Papers, tests, and quizzes. I almost didn't know which stack to tackle, but I settled on the quizzes from Environmental Politics 2B. That was because I could make a dent in that stack before I was due to pick up Llysette at five o'clock.

By then, we'd be the last on campus. We usually were.

I actually got through the quizzes, but I didn't have time to record the scores in my grade book, so both grade book and quizzes went into my case, as did the other ungraded materials. I had to lock the building and turn out the lights, and that meant it was slightly after five before I pulled the Stanley up to the Music and Theatre building.

Even so, I waited almost ten minutes before Llysette arrived, preceded a few minutes earlier by the dejected form of a student I did not know. I never knew who the first-year students were until close to Christmas.

"That was a discouraged student," I observed as Llysette hoisted herself and two large bags full of papers and books into the front seat.

"Discouraged she is? Ha! I should be the one discouraged."

"Oh?" I waited as she settled herself.

"To sing, that she wishes with but two hours of practice a week."

"Don't they know better?"

"They think they are busy, too busy to practice, yet to learn music, to major . . . they say that they desire." Llysette snorted. "So few understand."

"Most young people have to learn about work," I temporized.

"Work . . . *non* . . . I have talked of school too much. . . ." She shook her head. "So much warmer it was this morning, but now. . . ."

"It didn't last long," I observed. "All of a day and a half. It feels like it's going to get colder, a lot colder, and soon."

Llysette shivered at the thought, even while ice pellets resumed their pinging on the Stanley's thermal finish and glass. The square was half-deserted by the time I drove the steamer past McArdles' and the post centre. Truly amazing how a good ice storm emptied the square so quickly.

After we crossed the river bridge, I glanced at Llysette. "I think we ought to ask Bruce up for dinner."

"*Pourquoi?* You have need of his services?"

"No. I don't need anything. Not that I know of. But I've always contacted him when I wanted something, and that's really not fair or right. Besides, he's got a good sense of humor, and he likes music." I eased the Stanley up Deacon's Lane, taking a little extra care in the heavy gusting winds.

I let Llysette out by the door, then opened the car barn and put the Stanley away. I definitely didn't want to expose the thermal finish to the ravages of an ice storm.

While Llysette changed, I went into the study and lifted the wireset. There was a good chance Bruce was still at the shop. He always was.

"LBI Difference Designers."

"Bruce, this is Johan."

"Don't tell me."

"I'm not telling you anything. Llysette and I wondered if you'd like to come up for dinner on next Friday or Saturday. Not tomorrow. . . . I wouldn't drop an invitation on you with no notice."

"It must be worse than I'd thought." His voice was dry.

Had I been that inconsiderate? Probably. "It's not bad at all. I don't need anything. No one's attacked anyone. No strange messages."

"That might be worse."

"Bruce, it's a dinner invitation. Good food, and I hope good company."

"Saturday would be better."

"Good. We'll see you at seven a week from tomorrow." After I hung up the wireset, I glanced around the study. I swore I could feel heat from the SII machine, but when I checked it, it was cool, although not so cool as I would have thought.

With a sigh, I fired it up and checked the accesses. Nothing. Then, on an off thought, I checked the backups. One was something I hadn't recalled accessing in a while, some notes on the wetlands course. In a moment of whimsy, I'd entitled the notes: "Politics."

Maybe I'd called it up, but I didn't recall it. Besides, how could anyone even get into the house without Jerome's people noticing? And they wouldn't be interested in ecology notes.

I shook my head. Paranoia? Or was Jerome playing a deeper game? Probably, but what, and what could I do about it at the moment?

With a snort, I walked back to the kitchen, wondering what I would fix for dinner. I hadn't really given it the faintest thought.

CHAPTER THIRTEEN

• • •

Friday's ice storm turned to snow, more than a foot, which was followed by rain and then a hard freeze that turned everything to ice on Monday. Tuesday, the wind changed, and by Wednesday morning the temperature was springlike again, not at all like the last days of October, and foggy, but not bad for running. I went all the way to the top of the hill and out into the old woods a ways, my boots crunching through the crusty snow.

After breakfast, a shower, and dressing, I made my way to the car barn to light off the Stanley. Although the day had gotten foggy with the sunlight and warm, moist air, the glare was intense even through the intermittent fog.

Standing outside the car barn, I glanced to the south, across the glittering iced snow and through the leafless trees of the orchard. Between the drifting patches of white, I could see a gray Spazi steamer on the back road. Jerome was certainly keeping his promise about surveillance.

I shook my head and opened the car barn door, then unplugged the heater, before starting the steamer and backing out. I'd closed up the barn, turned the steamer—avoiding Marie's old black deSoto—and even had the Stanley warm inside before Llysette struggled out of the house and into the seat beside me, clutching her bags of music and books.

"Winter, for this I am not prepared." Llysette shivered.

"It's warmer than yesterday." I eased the Stanley onto Deacon's Lane and headed downhill toward the river and Vanderbraak Centre.

"That is like comparing the icebox and the freezer."

"Wait until it really gets cold."

"I cannot believe I leave the stove to beat notes to dunderheads." Llysette half-sniffed, half-shivered in her heavy coat. "Even to the good ones."

"You will. You'll just complain more." I laughed.

"You mock me."

I could feel the pout. "I wasn't mocking you, just stating what I thought would happen." When I stopped at the bridge, I bent sideways and kissed her cheek.

She raised her eyebrows, and I knew what she was thinking.

How did I get out of being condescending when I had been? By not opening my mouth in the first place. "Lunch?"

"*Mais non* . . . auditions we have for the festival. Did I not tell you?"

"You did. I didn't remember that was today."

"Johan. . . ." She shook her head but then spoiled it by smiling shyly, as if to ask how I ever could have been anything other than an absentminded professor. Maybe she was right.

After dropping Llysette off at the Music Building I made my morning pilgrimage to Samaha's for the paper, before heading back to my office to scan it and prepare for my classes. There was little enough in the *Asten Post-Courier,* except a tiny blurb about the Austrian ambassador being recalled to Vienna for consultations. I wondered why, but the story was just a wire blurb without details.

The big story was the latest revelation about the Asten midtrupp ring and the turbo-dirigible controversy. One of the trupp chiefs had invested heavily in the governor's brother's construction business, and lo and behold, the business had been awarded the contract to extend the obsolete aeroplane runways to accommodate turbojets.

After shaking my head, I surveyed the environmental economics papers I had to hand back—not really terrible, but methodically mediocre. They'd all realized that I wanted facts and analysis, and most had gone through the exercise, but without either insight or inspiration. I picked up one.

". . . taxes raise the price payed for fuels, like steamer kerosene so when Speaker Aspinall pushed through the excuse taxes . . ." I couldn't read any farther again after "excuse taxes," not without wanting to add comments about proofreading, assuming Miss Lyyker knew the difference. So I set it aside before I lowered her grade more.

Eleven o'clock came and went, and environmental economics was about as I feared—multiple hidden groans over the grades, followed by sullen glances when they thought I wasn't looking.

The class discussion was subdued, because it had begun to dawn on them that they weren't getting As or, in many cases even Bs—clearly my fault, in their minds. After all, I was there to teach them, to spoon-feed them what they needed to know, if necessary, so that they could obtain the magic diploma and entrance to the occupation or graduate school of their choice.

Did I feel cynical?

The frightening part was that I believed my analyses were objective. So I plunged into trying to ignite some interest.

"Mister Deventer, would you rather be a north woods logger or a New Bruges fishing boat captain?"

"Ah . . . sir?"

"You heard me. A north woods logger or a fishing boat captain?"

"But, sir . . . I would prefer not—"

"To be either? I can understand that. Humor me, Mister Deventer. If you *only* had those choices, which would you choose?" I smiled and waited, ignoring the sigh. If you don't ignore such sighs, you go slightly mad.

Mister Deventer surprised me. "If I had to choose, Doktor, I'd try to be a fishing boat captain. . . ." He went on to explain in logical terms how he could invest more in equipment to seek out fish while as a logger he would be limited in what he could log and where.

"Very good. Now what about the impact of the Blue Water Laws?"

Mister Deventer knew that, too, explaining how the combination of the water and wetlands laws retained the quality and quantity of marshland breeding areas for various species in the food chain and thus increased his putative profitability as a fishing captain.

Somehow, ignoring the handful of sighs and focusing on those students who appeared interested, I struggled through the examples of how environmental issues and changes impact basic economics and even society's structures.

Water from the melting ice and snow covered the stone walks outside Smythe by noon. Given New Bruges's variable weather, the water would probably freeze at night, leaving a death trap for the early-morning classes. I pushed aside that thought.

Instead of lunching with my spouse, since she was otherwise occupied, I went to the post centre. When I opened the postbox, I wished I hadn't, but not totally. Besides a letter from my mother, there was a manila envelope, thicker than any of those I had received earlier. I swallowed and carried it and the letter from my mother back up the hill to my office, stopping to get a sawdust sandwich and powdered chocolate that wasn't quite a uniform solution from the student center.

Between sandwich bites and sips of cool and dusty-tasting chocolate, I read the friendly letter first, not that it said much except that life went on for Anna and my mother and asked, again, when Llysette and I would next visit Schenectady.

I could have worked out some times before semester break, but Llysette couldn't, not with the load and schedule she carried and not with the time she was taking off to sing in Deseret.

Outside my window, I could hear the post centre clock chime the half hour. Twenty-five minutes before I had to go another round. I finally choked down the sandwich before opening the manila envelope:

NEWPORT (FNS). Defense Minister Holmbek represented Speaker Hartpence at the keel-laying ceremony for the *Hudson*. Holmbek's remarks were brief, but he did state that the *Hudson* would provide the first step "to ensure freedom of trade and freedom of passage."

The *Hudson* and the *Washington* will be the first nuclear-electro-submersibles in the Columbian navy and are projected to be launched nearly simultaneously with the second Japanese electrosubmersible, as yet unnamed. . . .

The first Japanese nuclear submersible, *Dragon of the Sea,* completed her maiden voyage more than a year ago, but the three newer ships will incorporate updated technologies from both Columbia and Japan.

The second clip put the first in proper perspective, even if I didn't care for that perspective:

VIENNA (WNS). Minister of State Franz Stepan announced that Ambassador Schikelgruber is being recalled "for consultation" with the emperor and his government. . . .

Sources close to the State Ministry have reported "dissatisfaction" with the Japanese-American technology sharing that resulted in the development of nuclear-electro-submersibles. . . .

In a related development, the Austro-Hungarian Southern Fleet has closed the Arabian peninsula to non-Austrian-flag shipping "indefinitely" in the wake of Islamic fundamentalist riots in Makkah and Madinah. . . .

The closure was protested violently by the Indian Mogul Shaharrez, who suspended iron and textile exports to Europe "indefinitely."

I rubbed my forehead, not that I could do anything about a world situation that seemed to be getting worse and worse, and slowly studied the next clipping:

CITIE DE TENOCHTITLAN (NFWS). "In time of trouble, we of mid-America must help each other." Those were the first words of Marshal deGaulle in announcing a loan of 300 million new pesos to Venezuela for the refurbishing and repair of the fire-ravaged Lagunillas oil depot.

DeGaulle went on to pledge continued New French support for embattled President de Sanches's efforts to strengthen Venezuela's industrial base and trade balance, noting that "we must decide our own destinies, based on the needs of our people, not upon transatlantic agendas."

Reports from the Bolivar naval yard indicate that two New French cruisers and the carrier *Buonaparte* are already on station "somewhere in the vicinity of Aruba."

Great—deGaulle was protecting the South American oil fields, while Ferdinand was exerting complete control over the Middle East and Columbia and Japan were racing to build and deploy technology that would make obsolete conventional miltary vessels, presumably to give them the ability to interrupt oil shipments, among other things. I picked up the last clipping:

FEDERAL DISTRICT (RPI). "The recall of Ambassador Schikelgruber confirms Ferdinand's effort to make Columbia an Austrian dependency," stated Congresslady Alexander (L-MI). . . .

Alexander, known for her outspoken opposition to any form of accommodation or compromise with Austro-Hungary, also released the text of a purported communiqué from the Ministry of State in Vienna. The alleged communiqué orders the ambassador to "take all steps necessary to convince the Columbia government of the severity of the decision to implement a nuclear-powered armaments race." Alexander's revelation was dismissed by Ambassador Schikelgruber as "a political ploy designed to disrupt efforts at peaceful resolution of difficult issues."

I noticed that captivating, charming, and cultured Schikelgruber hadn't actually denied the communiqué. It was an interesting situation, since Alexander and the president were of the same party and these clips had come from Jerome, who was a Reformed Tory to the heart.

At least, there weren't any clips from Deseret . . . this time.

With a look at my watch, I began to gather my notes for my next two classes.

CHAPTER FOURTEEN

• • •

By Saturday, we'd had both another freeze and another thaw, but the drive-way was clear, and so was Deacon's Lane when I headed down to McAr-dles' and the post centre. That gave Llysette time to practice by herself. She continued to fret about the Perkins pieces, probably more than she would have otherwise, because Perkins would be playing for her in Great Salt Lake City.

With the square crowded, I tried the post centre first, using one of the short-time parking slots for the Stanley. Getting out, I slipped on a patch of ice and al-most tripped over the raised stone curb.

The postbox contained a few bills and advertising circulars, no more manila envelopes from the Federal District, and a flat package wrapped in brown paper—addressed only to "J. Eschbach, Vanderbraak Centre, New Bruges," with no post-box or other identifier. The post cancellation was from the Federal District. The return address on the package stated: "International Import Supply, 1440 K Street, Federal District, Columbia," and both address and return labels were plain white with standard-difference printer typefaces. Was this a new Spazi cover firm? The paper wrapping was similar.

I put it in the rear trunk—uneasily, especially since it was heavier than it looked. After that, I had to circle the square twice before there was a space behind McArdles' in the small car park lot.

"Professor Eschbach," said a young woman carrying a baby, someone I should have known but didn't recall.

"Good morning. How are you doing these days?"

"I was going to come back for my master's work." She shrugged and looked down. "But one of us in school is about all we can afford right now. Terrence should finish his premed courses by spring."

"It's hard with children." The reference to Terrence jogged my memory. Ter-rence Maanstra had undergraduate degrees in music, engineering, and political sci-ence. Rachel had been a promising pianist—until she met the intelligent, charming, and totally unfocused Terrence. "But don't wait too long. Professor duBoise thought you could have a good career as a coach-accompanist."

Rachel smiled, almost sadly, as she shifted her weight to catch the child, who had suddenly lurched awake. "We'll see."

"You take care," I told her as I headed into McArdles'.

Her smile faded slightly as she turned away.

Why did so many of them think marriage solved problems or that they could avoid facing themselves by getting married? In my life, at least, marriage had just made facing myself more imperative—and simultaneously harder. Much as I loved and had come to love Llysette more and more, facing up to myself, that part wasn't getting that much easier.

I'd decided to fix flan for dessert for Bruce—and for myself, I admitted, since I was trying to be less self-deceptive—but flan required more in the way of heavy cream and eggs than we had. Picking up a basket, I walked to the back corner of the store. As I lifted the quart of cream and two dozen eggs—not that I needed that many, but better too many than too few for a cook who liked things too rich—I couldn't help overhearing fragments of conversation from two women an aisle over.

". . . that Professor Eschbach . . . the one who was a spy . . ."

". . . you think she was a spy, too . . . why she was imprisoned?"

". . . Delia heard her sing . . . must have been a spy . . . too good for here . . . say she was the mistress of the Japanese emperor once. . . ."

"Patrice said she was doing a big international tour now that she's a citizen . . ."

". . . maybe I'll go the next time she sings."

I tried not to wince as I walked back to the checkout stands. The truth was bad enough without gossipy elaboration.

After I parked the Stanley in the car barn, eased the suspicious package into the empty storage locker on the side of the car barn, and put the cream and eggs into the refrigerator, I pondered what to make for lunch to the strains from the Haaren's keyboard and Llysette's throat. I also wondered if I were being paranoid about the package. Still . . . better paranoid than injured or dead, and I wanted to let my subconscious chew on the problem.

Llysette was still practicing as I puttered around the kitchen—the Perkins piece I thought. It wasn't Latin. That meant it couldn't be the Mozart, and it was an art song in English.

Deciding on a mushroom quiche—dinner would be the lamb that had been marinating for two days—I tried not to clank as I got out a baking dish and the eggs and cheeses. The crust came first, and I was in such a hurry that it was probably going to be too thick and not flaky enough. Once it was in the baking dish, I blotted my forehead with the back of my arm.

The white enamel sills of the kitchen didn't seem quite so sparkling. I'd probably have to get around to repainting them once the spring semester was over. Like my mother, and all the Dutch, much as I muttered about the endless cleaning and painting, I still started squirming at chipped paint and hints of grime.

Instead of worrying about spring cleaning, I threw together a small green salad for each of us, then quickly sliced and sautéed the mushrooms while the oven heated.

Everything took longer, and it was well past one o'clock before I could announce, *"Mademoiselle la chanteuse . . . your midday repast . . . c'est pret."*

The piano stopped. "In a moment, Johan . . . but a moment." Then her fingers went back to the Haaren's keyboard.

I wondered whether to turn the oven on low to hold her lunch. When she practiced, a moment might be a half hour, but that was one of the traits I respected and—sometimes—loved.

Then she bustled into the kitchen.

"The other Perkins. . . ." She shook her head as she sat. "*Tous les annotations* . . . he is less . . . conventional . . ."

From what little I'd heard, the esteemed Doktor Perkins was less than the perfectly conventional Saint. He'd waited to get a doctorate before undertaking his mission, then been asked to leave Finlandia during that mission because he insisted on playing music rather than trying to convert locals. From Vyborg he'd gone to the Netherlands, where he'd dug Vondel's plays out of the depths of the libraries and started turning them into operas, again ignoring the preaching business. After receiving an award and some solid cash from Hendrik—one of the last such grants before Ferdinand and his jackbooted troops arrived, the good Doktor Perkins had trundled home to Deseret, where he had married his childhood sweetheart—and only his childhood sweetheart. He'd been periodically quoted, from what I'd been able to dig out of the Vanderbraak State University library, as saying that music was his mission.

"Did he write anything conventional?"

"*Mais oui* . . . but no longer. The more recent . . . they are better, but *tres difficile.*"

I cut her a healthy wedge of quiche, a second for me, and then opened a bottle—table-grade Sebastopol, but better than tea or chocolate with quiche. I set the glass before her and seated myself.

"A chef you should have been," Llysette said after her first bite.

"I don't know about that. It's hard for me to handle more than a few dishes at once, and chefs have to oversee dozens."

"*Une petite brasserie.* . . ."

"Very *petite.* Such as the size of our kitchen here."

The quiche was good—even if I *had* cooked it.

While I did the dishes and thought, she wandered back into the music room. I wondered what to do about the package. I was 90 percent sure it was trouble, but with the strange mailings I'd had . . . who knew? And if it happened to be trouble, was it an amateur effort or a professional one? Also, did the package contain anything of value if it weren't trouble? There was no way of knowing without opening the package.

Finally, I went out to the car barn and began to fiddle with tools until I had what I wanted.

It took me a long time, but using a mirror and a razor knife fastened to a cross arm attached to a rake, I had a tool I could use around the corner of the stone-walled car barn.

Then, trying to open the package carefully was tricky. I'm one of those people who has trouble directing actions in a mirror. It must have taken me a dozen attempts to make the first cut in the heavy package tape and almost as many for the second.

I only started the third attempt.

Crummtt!

The explosion ripped my rake-tool out of my hands.

There were only fragments of confettilike cardboard and shards of paper-thin metal—those and a depression next to the car-barn wall.

"Johan!" Llysette came running from the house.

"I'm fine. Just stand back."

She didn't.

"The ground explodes, and you are here, and I should stand back?"

"Yes."

"Johan." Her green eyes flashed.

"I didn't want to worry you."

"You still are *impossible*."

"You're right." I had to smile sheepishly. I hadn't been careless, but stupid, and I didn't feel like admitting that totally openly. "I do need to clean up the mess."

"The . . . mess . . . will it explode?"

"There's nothing big enough left to explode."

She shook her head.

She was right about that, too.

After Llysette went back into the house, I searched the area but found little except for a larger assortment of shreds of the thin metal and what looked to be the remnants of some form of pressure sensor. Basically, the idea had been to shred me with the metal, had I been stupid enough to open it. Well, I had been stupid enough, just not in direct range, and I suspected I'd hear from someone, sooner or later.

But I just collected the mess and tucked it into the rubbish bin. There wouldn't be anything traceable, scientific forensic work or not.

Then I went back to the house.

"Johan." Llysette put her arms around me almost before I closed the door. "I did not mean—"

"I know. You were worried, but I was trying to keep the Watch out of this. What would Chief Waetjen say if I'd handed him a bomb?"

"You could have been killed."

"If I'd opened it in the normal way . . . but if it were a professional job, the chances were less, assuming I took precautions." I shrugged. "I did. If there's a next one, we call in someone else." I knew there wouldn't be. There might be something else, but not another bomb. The bomb was almost an admission that Jerome's people in the gray steamers were doing their job very effectively.

"That you promise?"

"I promise."

She kissed me, and the kiss was warm enough that one thing led to another and that Llysette didn't get back to practicing.

As a result, I was still struggling to catch up on dinner when Bruce's ancient Olds convertible whistled through the darkness and up the drive to the side door. I had extracted a promise from Llysette not to mention the explosive nature of the afternoon, the explosive nature of either the early or later afternoon.

Bruce stepped up to the door at six-fifty-eight, with two bottles of wine in a basket. The wind had picked up and was swirling snowflakes across the drive, the light kind of flurries that wouldn't stick.

"Greetings, Johan." He handed me the basket. "And Llysette." He turned his head and smiled.

Standing by the foot of the stairs, she returned the smile. "Good it is to see you."

"Greetings and thank you." I glanced at the wine. "Yountville. You're definitely spoiling us."

"I am not spoiling you, Johan," he said with a grin as I took his coat.

"I wondered about that."

"New Bruges has too few cultural adornments to risk losing one." He inclined his head to Llysette. "This is part of my small effort to persuade her to remain."

The shy smile that crossed her face was part Llysette, part Carolynne, and an expression I treasured.

"Business?" he asked briskly.

"Strictly social." I shook my head. There was no way I was going to tell Bruce about the bomb—no sense in ruining his evening. "Except I'm running a little behind."

They followed me into the kitchen while I checked the pepper-roasted potatoes and the steamed mixed squash and tasted the mint-apple-plum sauce for the lamb.

Somehow, I got it all together, and we sat down at the table by seven-thirty.

Bruce took one bite of the marinated rack of lamb, then a second. "Very good, Johan. Very good."

"Thank you."

After a sip of the Yountville, he tried the potatoes and nodded. "Tasty."

"They are good also," Llysette offered. "In France, Johan, he could have been a chef."

"I don't question his cooking, dear lady." Bruce paused. "Then again, the best chefs have also been known to be handy with knives and other weapons. Perhaps he would have been a well-known chef."

"You are so complimentary," I told him, passing the hot croissant rolls to Llysette.

"With whom else can I be so honest?"

He had a point there.

"Have there been any new . . . developments?" he asked.

"Outside of a few clippings to ensure we are fully informed of the tense international situation? No."

Bruce took a roll and set the basket in the middle of the table. His arm fanned the air, and the three candles in the silver candelabra flickered, then recovered. "Technology interests?"

"More energy and water, from what I can tell. Energy is the big thing."

"With imports up to forty percent of fossil fuel consumption, I would think so. I wonder why it took so long to get the Speaker's attention?" asked Bruce.

"Oh, it might have to do with the Red Sea embargo . . . or the accidents in Venezuela. Or even the Japanese refusal to divert some Oceanic oil to Columbia. Then, it might be that energy is just the issue of the month."

"You also believe that Ferdinand is Kris Kringle and that mechanical brass difference engines represented the peak of computing technology," suggested Bruce.

"Compared to deGaulle, or that fellow in Quebec—Chirac, is it?—he might be."

"Frightening thought."

"The good Saint Nicholas, more coal he should bring to the stockings of Dutch children," added Llysette.

"I agree." Enough of international politics, which none of us could ever control. I refilled her glass, then lifted mine. "To friends and forgetting international disasters."

Bruce nodded, but he drank. After a moment of silence, he asked, "What are you singing in Great Salt Lake City?"

"The pieces . . . they are from many sources." Llysette shrugged. "Mozart, Debussy, Perkins, Barber, Exten—"

"It has to be difficult getting an accompanist," ventured Bruce, his hand touching a dark beard that had rapidly grayed in the past several years. I wondered how much I had contributed to the gray . . . and why he was asking about accompanists. Bruce seldom ventured idle questions. "You said it was a problem the last time I was here."

"Johanna . . . she is . . . good."

"But not outstanding?"

"On some pieces." Llysette shook her head. "The students . . . they . . . they are the difficulty . . . not Johanna."

Bruce frowned, his brows creasing slightly.

"It's hard for Llysette to play for them and teach them, and a lot of the piano students think accompanying is beneath them." I snorted. "There's more demand for accompanists than for virtuoso pianists, but they don't seem to understand that." I paused, then turned to Llysette. "I forgot to tell you. I ran into Rachel . . . the one who married Terrence Maanstra. They have a child."

"A waste. A great accompanist she could have been. Now . . . she will have children and wonder."

That was one of the few things I had learned young. You seldom regretted the opportunities you took that didn't work out, but you always regretted those you turned from.

"Is having children so bad?" murmured Bruce, then added with a smile, "It wasn't so bad for us that our parents did."

Llysette raised both eyebrows momentarily. "An *artiste* who children has before . . . before . . ." She paused. "To turn from the art, that is a choice. *Mais, point de chanter . . .*"

"You're saying that a singer can turn from singing after she knows what singing is all about, but to abandon it before she really starts is wrong?" pressed Bruce.

"It creates a different kind of ghost," I said dryly.

"I respect your opinion on ghosts very deeply," Bruce replied deadpan.

"It's one area where I have a range of experience."

"Assez des revenants . . . ," suggested Llysette, and she was probably right. "The students, they do not understand the need for the accompanist, and too many notes must I play. Wine, lager, they can afford, even steamers, but not the music, not the accompanist."

"Students haven't changed much, I see," answered Bruce with a laugh.

"I suspect they're a bit more spoiled than we were," I suggested.

"Un peu? Spoiled you never were, Johan." Llysette gave me a broad smile.

She was wrong, but I appreciated the support. Compared to her, compared to Bruce, compared to many, I'd been spoiled, though I flattered myself that at least I knew all the advantages I'd had in life.

"You were never spoiled," I finally said.

Bruce remained silent.

"Oh, *mon cher?* And was not to sing before the *Academie,* was that not being spoiled?"

She had a point. There, unlike New Bruges, the audience knew great music when they heard it, but most of those who had heard her then were probably dead, except for those few who had survived Ferdinand, either physically whole or as ghosts.

"Being able to enjoy culture is a form of being spoiled," observed Bruce.

"So is being able to perform without fear of starving," I added. "The highest-paid forms of singing these days are popsingspiel and Philadelphia lip-synch."

"They're reviving *Your Town* again, I saw." Bruce finished his goblet of Yountville, and I refilled it.

"That's because a flop of the thirties is better than anything being written to-day." I hadn't cared much for either Pound's poetry or his sole play, satire as it was of *Our Town.*

"*C'est si triste . . .*"

From there we discussed theatre, poetry, and, of course, music.

The Yountville had long since disappeared when Bruce finally rose. "I don't live around the corner."

"You could come more often if you did," I pointed out.

"I couldn't afford to. No one up here except you, Johan, buys what we sell."

I nodded and reclaimed his coat from the front closet.

"It's been a lovely evening." Bruce looked vaguely puzzled as he paused by the door.

I could understand that, but I couldn't say a word. It was probably the first time I'd offered Bruce something without asking for something, or expecting it, and that bothered him.

"I've enjoyed it," he added, as if he were surprised that he had.

"We're glad."

Llysette nodded with me.

With a nod, he was gone, into the snowflakes that still swirled but hadn't stuck on grass or drive.

"Lonely, he is," said Llysette as we watched Bruce back the Olds around and head out into the darkness, back toward Zuider.

I knew that. I'd been there, and I tightened my fingers around hers, glad that I was no longer lonely, that our ghosts had left us filled and together, rather than empty and alone.

Llysette squeezed my hand in response.

CHAPTER FIFTEEN

• • •

Not a great deal happened over the next week, perhaps because of the pair of ubiquitous gray steamers that parked in out-of-the-way lanes and perhaps because nothing would have happened anyway.

That is, nothing of cosmic import occurred. I did get a brief call from Minister Jerome in which he suggested that the disposal of suspicious packages might be better handled by some of his experts, assuming I preferred not to involve the local Watch.

I thanked him and told him that I would certainly keep that in mind.

Llysette still practiced and beat notes into students, worried about the student opera production she had to leave six weeks or so before it went up, even while the students thought six weeks was an eternity. And she reminded me, more than occasionally, to be aware of suspicious packages. But we didn't get any more, and mostly, her worries centered on the Perkins pieces.

"So . . . so . . . precise . . . they must be."

I'd heard that phrase more than once.

As for me, I continued to struggle with my own Dutch dunderheads, as well as study the occasional clips from various news sources that periodically appeared in our postbox. I had to admit that the clips were interesting and that I'd missed that aspect of my job two positions previously—I did like learning new and differing things . . . and always had.

On that Wednesday, after scanning the local paper, I'd reluctantly plunged into grading papers, half-enjoying the bright sunlight pouring through the window, sunlight that had been rare in recent weeks.

The papers were on the issue of converting external diseconomies into market forces. I had asked each student to come up with one example of government success and one of failure and then compare and contrast them.

I glanced at the top paper and began to read: ". . . the fuel taxes imposed by Speaker Aspinall's government represent a case in point where a successful use of external diseconomies was achieved . . ."

At that point I began to wince. Despite lengthy explanations, Mister Anadahl had apparently failed to grasp the distinction between the specific external diseconomy and the policy designed to remedy the problem.

Several other papers cited fuel taxes as a success without ever explaining the diseconomy they were supposed to remedy. Then I came to a gem, by one of the quiet ones—Miss Gaarlen. She'd actually gone beyond the assignment and compared legislation that had attempted to remedy environmental diseconomies, such as the Wetlands Equalization Act, with other legislation designed for different objects, such as the fuel taxes, that had achieved the same result. Several of the following papers cheered me up with their understanding of the subject.

In a way it puzzled me. They were all in the same class, with the same teacher, yet a disparate handful understood, and another larger group, with no noticeable difference from the first group, hadn't seemed to learn anything and had failed in exactly the same way. Had the second group all worked on their papers together? Who knew? What I did know was that they hadn't had the brains to work with someone who did understand the problem I'd posed. Or they didn't care, which was more disturbing.

I tried to take comfort in the half dozen fairly good and good papers, toiling with papers, and red ink until ten-forty-five and then packing them away and extracting my class notes.

"You're leaving next Friday?" David cornered me as I left my office for Environmental Economics 2A with a stack of papers under my arm.

"Saturday. Friday I teach a full schedule."

He cleared his throat. I waited.

"Johan . . ."

"You're wondering if I have to go the whole time?" I shrugged. "If I don't go, Llysette doesn't sing. Those are the terms of the contract. The Saints don't want unattached attractive females in Great Salt Lake City. Especially singers, I'd guess. So if the dean wants the publicity, I have to go."

"Ah . . . it wasn't that."

I waited again.

"I just received the latest issue of the *Journal*—"

"The one with my article on environmental realities?" I continued to be surprised that the *Journal of Columbian Politics* continued to seek my articles and commentaries, given the outrage they often provoked.

David nodded.

"What was it that disturbed you about this one? My analysis of the practical impossibility of compliance with the legal terms of the Safe Water Sources Act?"

My chair shook his head and cleared his throat. "I was . . . somewhat concerned by the flippant definition—"

"Of an environmentalist? Someone who throws his trash in your backyard and proposes to split the cleanup taxes with you?" I laughed. "I could have used almost the same definition for an industrialist, except he leaves the trash where it is and calls it previously used raw materials. Maybe, in my next article—"

"Johan . . . the vanEmsdens would not be pleased."

"Donors or not, David, they won't read the article. The most they read is the *Dairy News,* or whatever their trade press is." I shouldn't have been so hard on David. I suppose I should have been grateful to occupy the vonBehn Professorship, but I doubted that the legendary and outspoken Aphra would have minded my independence.

"Johan . . . ," he said almost helplessly. "What about the students?"

"They won't have read it either." Had any of my students ever read the *Journal*? If they did, not a one had ever read ever mentioned it or used the material. Besides, why would they ever read anything not assigned? Or read a book that wasn't enjoyable?

Last year, one Mister Paulus had blanched when I'd suggested that the criteria for greatness of a book included far more than the level of enjoyment of the readers. The poor fellow had been honestly shocked.

"You'd say that about our students?" David was honestly distressed, or counterfeiting distress well.

At times, I had to wonder why he got so upset about such comparatively minor things—but I wondered about too many things too often. "We have some good students, David. Then we have the others, and I'd say more than that about them, and you know it. I'm hopelessly outspoken. Use it as an example. . . . On the other hand, you'd better not. None of them regard outspoken honesty as a virtue." I smiled. "I need to go, or I'll be late for class."

I nodded and stepped around him. With the endowed chair had come tenure, and that meant David could rant and rail, but that was about it. I only wished Llysette had tenure, but I hoped, even with all the complications, that her singing in Deseret would give her the stature to negotiate something like that.

Environmental Economics 2A was predictable, especially after having read their papers. Predictable and totally inexplicable. An environmental diseconomy is very simple. It is effectively the negative environmental impact of any cultural or societal action for which no individual or group of individuals bears either the cost or the responsibility—such as air pollution from the old internal combustion engines or wastewater discharges from manufacturing plants before the Blue Water Laws.

So why did I get questions like Miss Fanstaal's? "Professor Eschbach, I don't understand why you said the federal grazing fees created external diseconomies. Can you explain that?"

"Because the fees don't cover the maintenance costs of the grasslands. The degradation isn't anyone's specific responsibility."

She still looked blank. So did four or five others. Miss Gaarlen managed to conceal the same wince I felt.

All in all, it was a long class, and I kept wondering where I'd gone wrong. So much of what I taught seemed simple enough to me—and to about a third of the class—but for the others it was as if I were teaching Boolean algebra in Sanskrit with Greek footnotes to explain the underlying concepts . . . or something.

Llysette was actually coming out of the Music Building before I got there.

We both looked at each other, and then we began to laugh in the mist that wasn't quite a freezing drizzle.

"It's been one of those mornings," I finally said.

"Dunderheads, they are," she agreed.

We walked slowly down to the square, arm in arm.

"The diva and the doktor." Victor bowed deeply as we walked into Delft's.

From his tone, I had the feeling both terms referred to Llysette.

"The doktors and the diva," I replied with a smile.

"But of course." Victor's smile was bland.

We got the table by the stove. That had effectively become Llysette's table once Victor had ascertained that she was *the* diva of Columbia.

"Wine, the good red," said Llysette.

"Chocolate, please," I added.

Victor nodded and hurried away.

I offered the basket of bread to Llysette. She shook her head. I took a piece of the crusty bread and ate it all even before Victor returned with our beverages.

"Your wine, mademoiselle."

"Merci."

"Thank you for the chocolate, Victor."

"It is nothing."

I wanted to add, *"Et comment!"* But I refrained, showing the self-restraint David was convinced I lacked. Instead, I said, "I'll have the small pasta primavera." I didn't need the large serving, not with my battle against midlife bulge.

"The special soup," Llysette added.

Victor bobbed his head and slipped away.

"You had a bad morning?" I prompted.

"They are so slow." She paused to sip the wine, then looked at the glass. "This . . . I should not. *Mais* . . . I dread the afternoon rehearsal. Soon we must go to evenings."

Llysette was doing a short comic opera, something I'd never heard of—*The Spinster and the Swindler,* by a composer I'd also never heard of, Seymour Barab.

"Why?" I thought I knew, but I asked anyway.

"To them, six weeks, eight weeks, it is forever. One week and more I will be gone, and for two they have the holidays. They should be off book, but still they must hold their scores. So . . . we must rehearse more. Only in rehearsal do they look at the music."

"You can't sing with your nose in the score."

"Sing? They cannot sing, except three; they cannot act; they cannot think. And I must beat notes and walk them from the one place to the other." Llysette took another long swallow of the wine, then set the goblet down as Victor reappeared with her cream of broccoli soup and my pasta primavera.

For a time, we ate silently. We were both hungry. We always were, it seemed, or was it nervousness?

Later, I walked Llysette back to the Music Building and her waiting student, then went down to the post centre.

The manila envelope in the postbox was briefing book–sized and thick. Unlike the others, it had a printed return address, the Spazi one, International Import Services, PLC. From the feel, it contained briefing papers and clippings, and I could definitely feel the contents. I swallowed hard but didn't open the package or the two bills. Packages gave me a queasy feeling.

David was out—or still at lunch—when I got back to the department offices.

"Is our esteemed chairman expected back soon?" I almost bowed to Gilda, but that would have been too much of a mockery.

"Doktor Doniger has left to attend a meeting of the Association of Columbian University Professors in New Amsterdam." Gilda smiled. "His return is not imminent."

"But return he will," I predicted.

Gilda nodded, her fingers on the calculator. The sheets of difference engine printouts before her indicated she was trying to catch up on the departmental budget, something she never did while David was around.

I'd never bothered to join ACUP, since the one meeting I'd attended had convinced me that the group catered to the lowest common denominator, and that was complaining. I hadn't regretted the decision, not yet anyway.

For once, I actually locked my office door while I was inside—before I opened the heavy envelope . . . carefully.

More than a dozen clippings lay on top of the stapled document that had no letterhead, nor any identifying marks. After setting aside the clips, I flicked through the document, noting the section heads:

"Deseret: Current Government Structure"
"Deseret: Economic and Market Structure"
"Deseret: Internal Security Forces"
"Deseret: Church Security Forces"
"Deseret: External Security Forces"
"Deseret: Dissident Influences"
"New France: Intelligence Operations in Deseret"
"Quebec: Intelligence Operations in Deseret"
"Austro-Hungary: Intelligence Operations in Deseret"
"Japan: Intelligence Operations in Deseret"

I noted the obvious omission—"Columbia: Intelligence Operations in Deseret."

I had a lot of reading to do in the few days ahead, and I doubted that I'd enjoy any of it.

In the meantime, my two o'clock environmental politics class was nearing, and with it the stunned looks on about half the earnest Dutch faces. What would they look like if I showed them the material I'd received from Jerome? I shook my head—just the same stunned looks. Anything outside their universe was incomprehensible.

Had I been that dense when I'd been their ages? I could ask my mother, but I wasn't sure I really wanted to know.

I slipped the briefing materials back into the envelope and the envelope into my case. The case was going with me to class and everywhere else until its contents reached my study at home.

At least the Spazi was overseeing the house, for which I was becoming increasingly, if reluctantly, grateful.

CHAPTER SIXTEEN

• • •

S unday afternoon before we were due to leave, I finally faced up to the unpleasant task of determining what I should take to Deseret. Of course, if I
decided on Sunday, that also gave me almost a week to reconsider.

The briefing materials from Jerome had given me enough pause, but what they
hadn't addressed was who had made the attack on Llysette and me or sent the package bomb. From what I knew, and from what Jerome had sent, it was clear that the
first attack had to have been directed by either Quebec, New France, or the Austrians. Quebec made no sense, crazy as some of the Quebecois were, unless it was as
a favor to New France.

Most of the operatives on the other sides, the ones I'd known in passing over
the years, wouldn't have used that sort of a high-technology bungle. A good long-
range slug thrower was far more effective and simpler. Only the Austrians seemed
fascinated with the use of de-ghosting devices. But Maurice-Huizinga of New
France was perfectly capable of using that sort of device to implicate Ferdinand's
people—and that would have been foolproof, because the implication didn't require the success of the technology, only its discovery. In fact, it would have been
better if the technology failed, because that would have me and the government
looking.

The bomb was another question, but it fit the same pattern, either Ferdinand
or New France trying to pin it on Ferdinand. Except that I really didn't know. It
was all educated guessing, and guessing was guessing.

The other thing that bothered me was the continuation of subtle signs that
someone had been looking through the study—and that meant Jerome's people.
Why, I didn't know, because they had all the information about ghost technology
that I did, and a lot more besides—that they could have known about. Or had they
figured out more from the supposedly destroyed backup disks of Branston-Hay?
But if they had, again, they didn't need what I had.

I shook my head. I didn't know enough. I never did, it seemed.

The array of equipment and material spread across the study was impressive,
even to me, and I was glad I'd drawn the blinds before I'd started.

Yet after what Jerome had sent me in the briefing package, how would what I
could take possibly be enough? Every major power in the world seemed to have a
presence in the Saint theocracy—and each had an agenda as to who should get the
fuels and chemicals from the Saint factories.

The international situation was worsening, as if it could do no less. DeGaulle had reinforced New France's naval forces in the Azores and Madeira—both seized with the fall of the Iberian Peninsula a generation earlier. An Austro-Hungarian garrison had been bombed in Madinah and another in Aqaba, and nearly six hundred soldiers had died. Claiming that the explosives were of New French manufacture, Ferdinand had extended the prohibition on non-European shipping, and that meant non-Austro-Hungarian ships, in the area around the Arabian oil fields. Ferdinand's Mid-East governor had also rounded up and summarily executed over a hundred known Muslim activists.

I swallowed and shook my head. I couldn't handle the whole world, or even a corner of it. I just needed to figure out what would best protect us in Deseret.

Deseret didn't sound all that stable, from the briefing materials. There was supposedly a schismatic group called the Revealed Twelve, sort of a shadow First Presidency. The First Presidency was the effective governing body of Deseret, composed of the Twelve Apostles. From what I could tell, the president and assistant president were almost religious heads of state, while the real power was the First Counselor, who was also a member of the Twelve.

The Revealed Twelve were underground, the actual names and members unknown, but they had been circulating materials claiming that the First Presidency had corrupted the true teachings of the original Saint prophets. The warehouse crackdown mentioned in one of the clippings had apparently been a Saint government attempt to seize materials printed by the Revealed Twelve. One of the Twelve Apostles had been killed in a steamer accident under mysterious conditions three months earlier and another hospitalized for undisclosed ailments.

Of course, that wasn't all. There was a Women's Party, but they circulated nothing, except a verbal de facto veto of names for replacement elections to the Seventy—equivalent to the Columbian Congress—and to the First Presidency. According to Jerome's materials, the women hadn't been terribly effective in influencing choices for the presidency, but several candidates for the Seventy had, in fact, been rejected. What I still didn't understand was how women could vote in a patriarchal, polygamous society and yet how they clearly voted to support the theocracy.

At the whisper of feet on the floor, I looked up from my reverie.

Llysette stood in the doorway from the sitting room, her eyes going from the case provided by Minister Jerome to the three dusty cases that had rested in wooden wine boxes, each under two layers of bottles of Sebastopol. I hadn't even brought down any of the clothing or taken out some of the special equipment that fit on the difference engine—or the large de-ghosting projectors in the compartment under and behind the mirror.

"That . . . you cannot bring it all."

"Hardly." My voice seemed dry, even to me. "I'm not even sure where to begin, except that metal firearms are out." Of course, that suggested that I should bring the plastic dart gun with the tranquilizer darts—the pieces probably would fit in the special boots. Probably plastique, because I could conceal that in innumerable places and could rig up detonators from common elements obtainable in Deseret. I sifted through Jerome's case and found the vest—the standard-issue Spazi vest that was essentially pure plastique and undetectable. There was also a vest liner—proof against most bullets and sharp objects, provided they were aimed at your torso and not your neck and head. The thin synthetic cord might come in useful, because it always had.

My eyes turned to the difference engine, and I swallowed. Just in case . . . I probably ought to bring some of the codes I'd developed—Bruce had predicted that someone would need a ghost, and I'd always regretted it when I hadn't listened to him. Of course, he'd also said that he didn't want to be anywhere around when that happened.

Even those decisions still left a lot to be determined, and I shook my head.

Llysette's eyes went from case to case, from deadly item to deadly item, and then back to me. A faint smile played across her lips. "If your David . . . or the dean this could see . . ."

"I'd rather they didn't, thank you." David was paranoid enough without absolute proof that I really had been a covert agent.

"If I had seen . . ."

"It wouldn't have changed anything."

"*Mon cher*. . . ." Her tone said I was lovable but deeply mistaken.

I didn't argue. I just walked over and held her for a time.

CHAPTER SEVENTEEN

• • •

In the end, I hired a public limousine to take us to the aerodrome in Asten, since with our newfound visibility I really didn't want to leave the Stanley exposed in the public car park. I did make the limousine reservations in Marie's name, with our street address—a small protection, but better than none, and besides, since I didn't have a published street address anywhere, anyone looking for us was more likely to key on the name.

The driver who pulled up on that cloudy Saturday morning was a sandy-haired woman—she could have been a lady trupp with the hard planes of her face and the gritty voice. "The Rijns here?"

"This is the place. Asten Aerodrome?"

"Be fifty."

I flashed the fifty, and she loaded the four valises and Llysette's hanging bag into the dark gray deSoto, a vehicle far more square than my sleeker Stanley. The faint odor of kerosene emanated from the deSoto, the sign of a mistuned burner.

Rain pelted the deSoto briefly as we passed through Zuider before taking Route Ten southeast.

"You two taking a dirigible or a turbo?"

"Do we look like spendthrifts?" I asked, forcing a laugh.

"Never know these days. If I could afford to go anywhere, I'd take the dirigible—first class. Be nice to sit on that fancy deck and watch the world go by."

"That it would," I answered.

"They have a gourmet café, too. That's what the *Post-Courier* travel section said." The driver's voice was firm.

With a shrug, I let it pass, since I'd never traveled first class on a dirigible, not except for a few short trips between New Amsterdam and the Federal District when someone else paid the freight.

"You think your students will miss you?" Llysette asked somewhat later, just before we entered Zuider.

"I doubt it. What about you?"

"They will be most pleased. For a week, no one will make them practice." Llysette shook her head. "Nor will I beat notes." She smiled.

"You need this time away from teaching," I said.

"*Plus du temps* . . . that I do need."

We talked about teaching and about the weather, but I didn't feel comfortable about much else, not with a strange driver. In the end, neither Llysette nor I said that much, and I kept worrying about all the questions raised by the briefing materials sent by Jerome. A tense international situation, enough domestic unrest in Deseret that the police were conducting raids against the so-called Revealed Twelve, and enough international concern that someone had tried to turn both Llysette and me into zombies and someone else had tried to blow us up, while someone else had been prowling through my study but taking nothing.

With those happy facts constantly intruding into my thoughts, we arrived in Asten around eleven.

The driver deposited us before the white-and-gray awning of the Speaker Line, and a porter appeared with his cart.

"The first-class departure lounge."

"Yes, sir." The porter nodded his square-bearded face, and we followed him to the smooth stone ramp to the second level, past the lower lounges and the smoke that drifted from them.

The landing and loading tower dated back nearly a half-century, although it had certainly been refurbished over the years and doubtless would be again, especially after the dirigible-turbo battles were threshed out.

The first-class lounge was paneled in dark walnut, with heavy but slightly faded green hangings. The windows were clear, shining, spotless, like every window I'd ever seen in New Bruges, and through them I could see the shimmering white length of the *Breckinridge,* with the twin gray stripes. A direct dirigible flight from Asten to Great Salt Lake City, on the Speaker Line yet.

The brunette in the trim gray uniform with the winged dirigible with the "SL" superimposed inclined her head. "Might I see your passages?"

I extended the folder.

She glanced from me to Llysette. "Oh . . . you're the famous singer. The one who sang at the Presidential Palace."

"Mais oui."

The scanners hummed, and I tried not to swallow, hoping that none of the various assorted tools for committing or preventing mayhem would register. The potentially most dangerous "tools" were Babbage code sheets tucked into Llysette's and my professional papers, but they were meaningless to about anyone but me and the late Professor Branston-Hay. Or so I hoped.

"You may board now. We won't be allowing coach travelers on yet." The sniff indicated what she thought of coach travelers, those who would spend days in mere seats.

A first-class cabin on the *Breckinridge,* of the Columbian Speaker Line—clearly, someone had gone to a great deal of trouble for Llysette, or us, although I wondered if I were just being paranoid and jealous of the attention and whether I were really suited to be the spouse of a true diva.

The dirigible was named after the short-termed Speaker who was assassinated more than a century earlier by a disgruntled Irish immigrant whose sister had died in the *Falbourg* disaster, along with nearly a thousand others fleeing the Great Tuber Plague.

Breckinridge had been a compromise Speaker, I recalled, because he had the support of the old Anglo-South. He'd also been a terrible strategist, because he'd misjudged the strength of Santa Anna and ignored the northern provinces of what had then been Mexico, fearful that attempting to annex California would have upset the slave-nonslave state balance. I sometimes wondered what would have happened if General Scott hadn't died of ptomaine poisoning, but wondering didn't change history. What had happened had happened.

The *Breckinridge* was not the largest airship, but it was impressive enough—a shimmering white cigar, floating from the docking tower, visible through the windows as we walked up the circular ramps, the porter following with our luggage.

The steward almost clicked his heels as he studied the passes. "Yes, sir and lady. Lower promenade four—one of the most charming. If you would follow me?"

We did, down the central corridor and up a gentle ramp to the next level, the porter and baggage cart behind us. The corridor walls were a cream damask, probably over thin aluminum sandwich with honeycomb sound barrier between.

At the door, we received an old-fashioned bronze key. "Enjoy your trip with us, lady . . . sir."

I tipped the porter, and Llysette and I were alone, the door ajar. I closed it.

Like all dirigible cabins, ours wasn't terribly large, but the bed, covered in immaculate white lace, was double-sized, and our window was beneath the promenade deck. We stepped up to the double-pane glass, sparkling even in the gray morning light, glass framed with shimmering blond paneling that glistened with care.

"There's the river." The *Breckinridge* seemed to swing into the wind, and I could hear the slow-speed turbine fans whine.

"This . . . I cannot believe . . . *la premiere classes*. . . ."

"You can't? Not even after the praise of the president?"

"Les mots, ce sont seulement les mots. . . ."

She had a definite point there. Words were but words, while the cabin represented another two to four thousand dollars for a round-trip. Rather than dwell on that, I stepped behind her and put my arms around her, then kissed her neck slowly.

"You are *impossible*. . . ."

"Not totally."

For a moment she relaxed; then she opened her eyes as the airship lurched ever so slightly, and the ground began to recede slowly.

"Could we . . . the promenade deck?"

"If it's open. You want to watch as we leave lovely industrial Asten and the mills and factories?"

"Mais oui. . . ."

So I locked the cabin, not that a lock would stop a real professional, and we climbed the circular golden pine staircase to the promenade deck, itself also polished and varnished golden pine. Stowing the luggage could wait. We'd have plenty of time, and then some.

Asten lay spread out beneath us as the *Breckinridge* eased westward and skyward on a level keel. Intermittent drops of rain from the higher clouds splattered against the transparent semipermeable windscreen, and the impact and screen combined to create a thin fog that shifted unpredictably just above the polished wooden railing of the deck.

Most of the spotless and white padded lounge chairs were already taken, but we did find a pair of chairs near the stern, closer to the rushing whine of the turbine-powered airscrews.

A heavyset man in the business brown of a commercial traveler looked across the space between his table and our chairs. His eyes dismissed me and centered on Llysette. I couldn't blame him, but it bothered me. Would it be more and more like that?

I didn't know. So I pointed. "There . . . way down there, you can almost see where the Brit colony failed. I was in charge of that preservation effort, you know?"

Llysette's lips crinkled. "Somewhere, you have told me that."

I got the message. I'd told her more than once. So I laughed.

That got a smile in return.

"You are not so serious now, Johan, not about yourself."

That might have been, but I felt serious about everything else around us. I did notice that the traveler in brown had shifted his attention to a female steward who was half my age, or less, and I didn't know whether to be relieved or concerned.

So I signaled for refreshments, and we got an older male steward who immediately made for Llysette.

"Fräulein?"

"Wine . . . do you have any from Bordeaux?"

"Alas, fräulein . . . no. We do have some excellent Sebastopols and a red Yountville—a cabernet."

"The Yountville."

"Make that two," I added.

The *Breckinridge* continued to climb as it soared westward, well south of Vanderbraak Centre, and even Zuider, and we sipped the Yountville before ordering lunch—also on the promenade deck—although it was really more of a midafternoon chocolate or tea by the time we were served. Still, we weren't exactly in a hurry.

The traveler in brown left, only to be replaced by a wrinkled lady in purple, whose lavender perfume wafted around us intermittently.

CHAPTER EIGHTEEN

• • •

On the second night, with the dirigible soaring across the Columbian midwest after our afternoon stop at the Chicago aerodrome, Llysette and I sat at an outside corner table in the dining salon, with a view of the darkening plains to the south. The salon was small, with a dozen tables, compensated for by three sittings. The menu was equally restricted—four entrées.

The waiter, in his green-trimmed gray coat and gray bow tie, bowed. "Have you decided?"

"*Coq au vin* . . . with the pilaf."

"The same," added Llysette. "And I would like the basil dressing also."

I nodded. "And we'd like a bottle of the chardonnay—the ninety Sebastopol."

"Very good, sir." He bowed and was gone.

At the nearest table—the one behind Llysette—sat the commercial traveler in brown and another younger man in a charcoal gray suit.

". . . probably another fool's errand. The Saints really don't want to buy our stuff, just steal it," said the man in brown, his voice barely carrying to me.

"Hervey, the boss wouldn't send you if he didn't have a reason. Besides, they can't steal something as big as an industrial boiler system."

"They can steal damned near anything, and don't you forget it, Mark. Or copy it." The man in brown snorted. "Try the wine. . . . Worry about the Saints tomorrow."

A smile crossed my face.

"You smile?" asked my singer.

"Singers and salesmen," I whispered. *And spies who don't want to be.* "It's just interesting. You still nervous?"

"I have not sung a concert this large in many years."

"You probably sang for a lot more important people at the palace."

"They would not know a . . . an aria from an art song."

"You have a point there. But do most audiences? Except for the critics?" I stopped as the waiter returned with the wine and poured a bit of it into my wine-glass.

I sipped and nodded, and the waiter half-filled both glasses, leaving the bottle. "It's good."

Llysette took a small swallow. *"Mais—"*

"Not as good as a really good French wine," I finished with a grin.

We both laughed. My eyes rested on her for a moment, then traveled the salon as my singer took another sip of wine.

Dark mahogany arches were draped with green hangings, as were the faintly tinted salon windows that framed the darkness of the night, a darkness broken intermittently by pin lights from the communities below and by the reflected glow of the airship's green and red running lights.

Pale green linen covered the table, and the white bone china and heavy silver glimmered in the muted illumination from the chandeliers. Low voices from the other tables merged, just enough that only a few distinct words emerged, here and there.

On the surface, I reflected absently, little different from a private club anywhere in Columbia—stolid, heavy, ornate, and relatively tasteful—yet a total illusion. The paneling was a thin veneer over plastics, the hangings lightweight and fireproof fabrics, the tables fragile frames bolted in place over a deck that was more cunning braces than solid polished wood. Even from all the conversations came only a few words rising above the rest.

Was the *Breckinridge* a metaphor for all Columbia? I wondered. Or the world? Didn't Columbia have its conflicts, and was the power struggle between President Armstrong and Speaker Hartpence any different from that apparently beginning between the Twelve Apostles of Deseret and the Revealed Twelve?

"You are thinking?" In her teal traveling suit with a green scarf and a cream blouse, Llysette looked cool in the salon's muted light, young, and very beautiful.

"You are beautiful." I could only shake my head.

"*Belle . . . parce que . . .* you said that because you love me."

"I do, but that doesn't mean what I say isn't true. It is."

She shook her head. "Once. . . ."

"Now."

She finally smiled.

Always, behind the clink of silver on china, the low drone of merged voices, behind the walls and hangings, was the thin whistling of the turbine airscrews as they pushed the *Breckinridge* westward across the high plains, through the darkness.

I definitely felt pushed through the darkness, trying to see what would happen before it did, wishing for a better light.

But there wasn't much I could do except enjoy the time. I lifted my wineglass. "To now . . . to us, all of us."

Llysette's eyes weren't even puzzled, but clear, and her lips smiled in acknowledgment as she lifted her glass to touch mine.

CHAPTER NINETEEN

● ● ●

Llysette and I had a continental breakfast on Monday morning—that was all that was available—at a table on the promenade deck.

In the night, we'd passed well north of the Kansas Proving Grounds and the legendary White Sands, so called because the first nuclear device tested there had turned the sand hills white. There hadn't been many atomic tests in Columbia—no place was really suitable, even for the underground tests that had followed.

That problem hadn't hindered either Chung Kuo or Ferdinand. Ferdinand had just cordoned off a section of the Sahara and turned it into various forms of glass. I didn't know exactly what the Chinese had done, but then, few did, even Minister Jerome.

"Would you like some more chocolate?" The steward, in crisp gray, bowed from the waist yet managed to keep the tray level, a tray containing both a teapot and a chocolate pot.

"Yes, please." I glanced toward Llysette. "Chocolate?"

"*Je crois que non.*" Her voice was languid, relaxed as I seldom heard it, and I was glad the trip had been relatively leisurely.

"No more for the lady," I said.

"Yes, sir."

The mug of chocolate, rimmed in gold, and a butter biscuit went on the lightweight wooden table, anchored to the composite deck beside my lounge chair, and

the steward slipped toward the heavyset businessman at the larger table, surrounded by assorted stacks of paper.

Through the transparent and semipermeable windscreen I could see clouds to
the south and feel the slightest hint of a breeze on my face, cooling it from the heat
of the winter sun.

As I sipped the heavy chocolate, reminiscent of my Aunt Anna's, I leaned forward in the chair and looked over the polished blond wooden railing that circled
the *Breckinridge's* promenade deck. Below were the dry lands, another of the flat
plateaus of eastern Deseret, and a thin strip of green that was a river I didn't know.
In the shaded places and on the north sides of the low hills were patches of snow,
apparently remnants of an early winter storm.

"Are we over Deseret yet, Johan?" asked Llysette sleepily, stretching and rub-
bing her eyes as she straightened in her chair.

"I think so. Deseret starts before the Rocky Mountains actually end. In fact," I
pointed back eastward, "all of that is part of Deseret."

"It is not a pleasant-looking land."

"No."

"That, what is it?" She pointed to a squat and sprawling complex of buildings
that sprawled across the hills just west of the peaks we had skirted in coming down
from the north.

"It's probably one of the new synthetic fuels plants."

She wrinkled her nose.

The synthetic fuels plants were just another far-reaching result of the unfortunate Colfax incident, or the circumstances that had led to it, really. Prophet
Young, the second and apparently greatest Saint prophet, had set up fur-trading
stations on the eastern side of Deseret, all along the Colorado River and well into
the Kansas territory of Columbia, at least that part of it claimed by Columbia after the Kansas Compromise, which had averted—along with Lincoln's speeches
and maneuverings—a civil war over the slavery issue.

The Saints had used that time of unrest to consolidate their hold on the
wilderness, but Columbia had protested the fur stations.

The Saints had rejected the protest and sought aid from Santa Anna and his
French advisors. They'd obtained, somehow, Brit-built Gatling guns and secretly
fortified the so-called fur stations. Columbia then sent Colonel Colfax to rout out
the Saint invaders, but Colfax and his troops had disappeared without a trace. So
had most of the soldiers in the ill-fated Custer expedition, except for the strag-
glers who had claimed the Saints and Indians had used a white parley flag as a ruse
to lure the Columbians into a Gatling crossfire.

Looking down on the rugged terrain, I could see how even a large mounted
troop could disappear . . . or fail to see an ambush.

With the later infusion of the French forces behind Maximilian and the threat
of a retaliatory invasion beyond the boundaries of Tejas and into Columbia from

what was becoming New France, despite Maximilian's Austrian origin, the Colfax and Custer incidents were laid aside, if not forgotten, and the Saints retained most of the former Kansas territory west of the Continental Divide—except that Columbia had held onto the headwaters and the first fifty miles or so of the Colorado River.

At the time, no one had known of the oil, coal, and natural gas held there— and now the area accounted for most of the liquid and gaseous hydrocarbon production of Deseret. The Saints had become pioneers in another way, in the development of producing liquid hydrocarbons from both coal and natural gas.

Of course, it hadn't hurt at all that the arms genius John Moses Browning had been a Saint and poured his considerable ingenuity into weapons development.

"Johan, *qu'est-ce que c'est?*"

"Oh, sorry. I'm just thinking about history. How things could have turned out very differently."

"You think that Columbia, it might have conquered Deseret?"

I had to laugh at that. "*Non.* If New France had been weaker, Deseret might control much of Tejas and all of California. Somehow, I can't see Deseret and Columbia in the same political system."

Llysette shrugged. "One never knows."

"That's true." There was a lot I'd never anticipated, and that was in a world I knew, or thought I did. "I suppose we should finish repacking. Then we could come back and watch the landing."

"I would see the landing."

So we abandoned our table and went down to the small but elegant cabin. I had wished it had more than a tiny sink and toilet, but I knew that water had to be limited—it was heavy. Still . . . after three days, I wanted a good hot shower.

Once we'd packed, we made our way back up one level to the promenade deck and an unoccupied set of lounge chairs.

The dirigible had changed course and was approaching Great Salt Lake City from the south, coming over a long, low ridge. Below were houses, and more houses, all set on streets comprising a pattern largely gridlike, except where precluded by the hills and occasional gullies.

We stood at the railing of the promenade deck, not more than a meter from the windscreen, as the *Breckinridge* eased northward. The city lay right under the Wasatch Mountains, far closer than I had realized from my self-gathered briefing materials, and far more polluted, with a thin brownish cloud veiling the city itself. The air pollution bothered me, because it seemed unnecessary. The Saints had advanced water treatment technologies and a chemical industry second to none.

"The air, it is not clean."

"Must be some sort of inversion," I speculated. "I'd bet it's more common in the winter."

"I must sing . . . in that?"

"It looks that way."

Llysette frowned slightly.

Ever so slowly, the *Breckinridge* eased down into the valley, across the miles of houses, and toward the dark iron pylon that was the Great Salt Lake landing tower.

In time, a slight shudder ran through the deck, and then lines sprang from everywhere to steady the dirigible.

Llysette and I exchanged glances.

"I haven't been here before either," I pointed out. "We might as well gather up our luggage."

As we walked down the single set of steps to the lower promenade deck and our cabin again, a crackling hiss came from the corridor speakers, followed by silence.

"We are docked in Great Salt Lake City. Local Deseret time is eleven o'clock. We will be debarking shortly. Please check your seats or cabin to make sure you retain all personal items."

I opened the cabin door. The suitcases and Llysette's long garment bag for her gowns remained as we had left them. Since no porters or stewards appeared, I hoisted three of the bags and managed to tow a fourth.

Llysette struggled with the garment bag—at least until we reached the promenade deck, where someone had lined up some luggage carts, all bearing a strange logo that was comprised of an intertwined "Z" and "M" within a golden oval.

I gratefully commandeered a cart, cutting off a pair of commercial travelers, and stacked the luggage on it. The garment bag went on top.

"First-class passengers are requested to de-board through the left forward doors," crackled over the airship's speakers. "Left forward doors for first-class passengers."

We headed toward the port side, following a handful of others. I could see that while the first-class debarking doors were open, the starboard side doors were not.

"Just first class here," said the steward.

Llysette favored him with a look somewhere between a sneer and a glare, and he swallowed. I didn't blame him.

At the end of the glassed and enclosed ramp to the tower itself, through another set of doors, stood two figures in gray.

"Non-Deseret citizens to the right for customs and immigration clearance, please. To the right, please. Take your luggage with you. Deseret citizens to the left. . . ."

We headed to the right, behind perhaps twenty others, near the rear of the group. We'd taken longer because I'd stopped to load the bags on a luggage cart and because the others traveled lighter. Then they probably weren't bringing concert clothing either.

I stopped the luggage cart on the polished brick floor, and we waited behind a short line of several men.

Llysette had her winter coat, hardly necessary in the warmth of the landing tower, draped over her arm. I was perspiring in mine and took it off, laying it across my arm as we waited. Waiting always reminded me of my time with the government.

Five flat podiums stood at the end of the long room, and behind each was a gray-uniformed figure. All the customs officers were male, and four had square beards.

"They do not look happy," observed Llysette in a low voice.

"I never met a customs official who did," I whispered back.

"You never will," murmured the short man in front of us without turning. "Especially here."

Then, as the Deseret customs types began to ask for the passports of the first-travelers in each of the five lines, a bearded figure in an antique-looking brown suit stepped up to the customs/immigration officer on the far left, whispered something, and pointed. The officer nodded, and the man stepped forward, past the travelers before us, and bowed to Llysette, then nodded to me. "Fräulein duBoise, Minister Eschbach . . . if you would come with me."

Belatedly I recognized the man and grasped mentally for his name. "Herr . . . Jensen, is it?"

"Here it's Brother Jensen," he said with a smile. "But I'm gratified that you did recall me."

"You were most complimentary," said Llysette, "at the recital."

"You deserved every word," answered Jensen. "We need to clear your luggage. I have a steamer waiting below."

As we were escorted past the other travelers, I could catch a few words.

". . . said there was some opera star on board. . . ."

"She looks like an opera star, she does . . . and to think . . ."

". . . called him Minister. . . ."

"Like to get fancy treatment like that. . . ."

Jensen led us out through a side door, and I could sense more than a few eyes on our backs as we followed him into another office with both a desk and chair and a podium, behind which stood an older customs official.

"Your passports, if you please?"

We presented them, and the white-haired official compared pictures and faces, then returned the passports.

"You aren't carrying any firearms, are you? Any religious materials that are not meant for personal use?"

I must have frowned.

"You can bring in a Bible or Koran or that sort of thing for your own use, but commerce in religious publications is restricted," the official explained.

"Music . . . that is all," Llysette said.

A faint smile crossed the white-haired man's lips. "If you would open your bags?"

We might be getting special treatment, but even opera stars apparently weren't exempted from customs. Or maybe opera stars whose husbands were former spies weren't.

The inspection wasn't quite cursory, but the inspector probably felt it didn't have to be more than that, since the platform was actually a scanner of some sort. I didn't worry—not too much—since the valises had passed Columbian scanners of a more sophisticated nature and since every single item I'd brought was scan-transparent.

"Thank you."

The scanners passed us. I managed to keep the same bland smile in place.

"Thank you, Brother Harrison." Jensen smiled, and Harrison smiled back.

"Now . . . to get you settled."

We followed the stocky Jensen down the dull red-carpeted spiral ramp and through the nearly deserted main level and out under a portico. I pushed all the luggage on the cart, walking behind Llysette and Jensen and drawing up when the Saint stopped. The wind was chill, if not quite so cold as it had been in Vander-braak Centre when we'd left, and bore the faint odor of chemicals.

"Here we are." The Deseret official gestured to a shiny brown steamer.

It was a make I'd not seen before, a Browning, and far more square and angular than my Stanley, but effectively the size of a limousine, even if Brother Jensen hadn't called it that. Was it named after another development from the arms makers? I didn't know. I wondered what else I didn't know and would find out.

Jensen opened the square rear door and helped me load the bags. I laid the garment bag on top.

"Performing clothes, I'd wager."

"To Deseret standards," I added.

"Good. Some folks have trouble with that."

"When in Rome . . ."

Jensen closed the rear door. I turned, wondering what to do with the cart, but a man in a brown jumpsuit had already collected it and several others and was wheeling them back inside.

A clean-shaven young man sat behind the steamer's wheel. He wore a dark green jacket, almost a military blouse, but with no brass and no insignia.

Jensen opened the door and inclined his head to Llysette for her to enter.

"Merci."

The Browning had bench seats in the section behind the driver, the kind facing each other. I sat by Llysette, and Jensen sat across from us.

"I'm afraid that the route to the city isn't the most scenic," apologized Brother Jensen. "The aerodrome has to be here in the flat south of the lake. Because of the winds, I'm told." He smiled. "I understand that neither of you has been here before."

"You understand correctly."

"I'd like to go over a few basics. It avoids misunderstandings. I assume you read the background materials I sent with the contract."

"Mais oui," said Llysette politely, not quite coldly.

"Yes."

Jensen turned and nodded to the driver. The Browning eased away from the aerodrome building.

"Good. We won't have to go over those. You'll see women with hats—that's a tradition, but not a requirement."

"Unlike the business of no bare shoulders?"

Jensen nodded. "I should also point out a few other things. Profane language bothers people here, even if it's casual and accepted language elsewhere. Also, although it's common in Columbia, it would be better if "—he inclined his head to Llysette—"you were accompanied in public, by either Minister Eschbach or Doktor Perkins or myself, if they're unavailable."

Llysette's face hardened ever so slightly, although she merely nodded.

"Now." Jensen cleared his throat. "On to a few more mundane items. The city is on a grid system. All the towns and cities in Deseret are. The main north-south street is always Main Street, and the main east-west street is Center Street." Jensen laughed. "Except here in Great Salt Lake. The north-south street is Temple, and the part north of the Temple is North Temple and the part south—"

"Is South Temple?"

"That's right. So if an address is two hundred west, two hundred south, you can tell that it's two blocks south of the center of the city and two blocks west."

I nodded. That seemed simple and logical—too logical for a sect that was supposedly based on mystical revelations translated from golden tablets that only three or four people had ever seen, none of whom had lived past the Nauvoo Massacres.

Then again, given the hostility that had driven the Saints from Columbia out into Deseret, I couldn't say I blamed them for some of what they'd done.

Jensen gestured out the window again. "There is the Temple. The building with the rounded roof is the Tabernacle."

"Is that where the Saints' Choir—?" ventured Llysette.

"Yes. They practice and broadcast from there. Also the General Conferences are broadcast from there as well."

"Once I heard them, in Orleans." Llysette nodded. "Many years ago when I was young."

The Temple was all I had expected, its towers white and shimmering on the hillside, immediately surrounded by what appeared to be white walls, browned grass and leafless trees, and a few evergreens. The Saints had emphasized the Temple's grandeur by keeping the buildings around it low.

The uniformed driver eased the Browning off the expressway and onto a wide boulevard heading north in the general direction of the Temple.

A series of interconnected white stone buildings appeared on the left.

"There's the Salt Palace performing complex, where you'll be singing. The Lion House Inn is where you'll be staying," offered Jensen. "It's straight ahead, but I'm having Heber take you around the Temple just so you can get an idea of the area. The original Lion House is a museum. It was the home of Brigham Young. We'll pass that after the Temple."

"He was the second prophet? The one who founded Deseret?"

Jensen nodded before continuing. "You can change your money, as you need it, at the Inn." He shifted and handed an envelope to me but looked at Llysette. "This is just a hundred dollars, but that should hold you until you get settled." His eyes flicked back and forth, as if he were unsure as to whom he should be addressing.

Since it appeared expected, I opened the envelope. There were ten notes, each ten Deseret dollars. Each note held a picture of the Temple on one side, with a bannered motto beneath that read: "Holiness to the Lord." On the other side was a likeness, but it wasn't that of Joseph Smith or Brigham Young but of someone called Taylor.

"Thank you." I slipped the envelope into my jacket pocket. "We can return it later—"

"Please . . . it's just a courtesy, and we'd feel better about it."

I didn't protest, and I doubted Llysette would either.

The driver turned the Browning again, onto West Temple South. Two blocks later, we passed the Temple, surrounded by white stone walls and heavy wrought-iron gates, all swung wide open.

"Here's the Temple."

The Browning came to a brief halt, and I could see that the Temple wasn't quite so white as it had looked from a distance, but it was impressive nonetheless, especially with the gold angel suspended above one tower. I could see perhaps a hundred figures in groups scattered around the walks and gardens, despite the chill winds. After a moment, Jensen nodded, and the Browning pulled away.

Just beyond the Temple, where the street signs changed from West Temple South to East Temple South, we passed another turn-of-the century complex, with interlocked buildings and covered walkways.

"The Lion House."

Right past the Lion House was a bronze memorial, a monument apparently to a bird, but I didn't want to ask. Abruptly the houses grew larger.

"*Pourquoi* . . . why is that house . . . many houses?" Llysette pointed toward a compound, almost, surrounded by a white iron fence that was head-high. Four good-sized houses surrounded an even larger structure.

"Oh, that's the older Eccles house. Each wife has her own house, but the main house is where the family gathers for home firesides and family home evenings and the like."

I could see the reasoning, particularly if the custom had started with the polygamy of more than a century earlier. Effectively, the ghost of a wife who died would be restricted to her own house.

Llysette's face remained calm, but her hands tightened around her purse and her gloves.

After several blocks more, the driver turned north again.

"Up the hills in that direction"—Jensen pointed generally eastward—"that's where the University of Deseret is."

We passed more of the oversize and well-established dwellings. "A number of the Seventy reside in this area."

"The Seventy?" asked Llysette.

"The Quorum of the Seventy," answered Jensen. "That's the body below the Apostles, in a way."

Llysette offered a Gallic nod.

The Lion Inn was a squarish white marble building, of perhaps six stories, less than three blocks from the Salt Palace complex. The awning under which Heber pulled the Browning was a forest green, trimmed in gold, and a doorman in a green suit, piped in gold, was unloading the bags even as Llysette stepped out onto the polished bricks of the walk.

Another doorman held wide the golden wood and brass-trimmed door that led into the carpeted and hushed lobby.

The concierge looked up expectantly as the three of us neared. "Brother Jensen."

"This is Doktor Llysette duBoise and her husband, Minister Johan Eschbach."

"We are pleased to have you as our guest." The clean-shaven blond concierge nodded to Llysette.

"The performance suite."

"Yes, Brother Jensen. The nonsmoking one?"

Jensen turned to us.

"Definitely," I said.

A faint smile crossed the concierge's face. Approval, I thought.

Even the interior of the elevator was paneled in golden oak and trimmed in shimmering brass. The floor was a white marble tile. Jensen pressed the "six," and the lift hummed upward.

Brother Jensen turned left off the elevator, and we followed. He paused at the door to the suite, then bowed and handed a folder to Llysette. "This has the rehearsal schedules, as well as Doktor Perkins' wireset number, and some information about the hall and an advance copy of the program—the one you and Doktor Perkins approved. The master classes will be held in the small recital hall. It's marked on the map." He unlocked the door, then handed the two keys to me.

We stepped inside and onto a thick pale green carpet. My boots sank into the pile. The walls were a cream damasked rose pattern, and the crown moldings were cream as well.

The performance suite was capacious indeed. The space contained a master bedroom with a triple-width bed and two separate attached bathrooms, a living room, and a small kitchenlike area, with an eating nook overlooking a balcony. From the windows and the balcony it looked almost like I could have thrown a rock and hit the northernmost buildings of the Salt Palace performing complex.

The suite was definitely for performers. There was even a console piano on one wall of the sitting area—a Haaren. I had to smile at that. I just hoped it was tuned.

"I've taken the liberty of including several bottles of wine in the cooler. Alcoholic beverages aren't permitted for Saints, and they're not served in the restaurants, but there is a dispensation for visiting dignitaries."

"We appreciate the consideration," I said politely, "and all your arrangements."

"You have been most kind," Llysette added.

"If you wish to eat in the Inn, just put the meals on the room bill, and we'll take care of them. That is a standard part of the contract. If you wish to eat elsewhere, leave the receipts for me with the concierge, and I'll ensure you're reimbursed—for the two of you." Jensen frowned momentarily, then continued. "I think I've covered everything, but if you have any questions, please feel free to wire at any time." He bowed at the door and was gone.

I glanced around the suite, certainly more palatial than anywhere I'd ever stayed. "They certainly are treating you like royalty."

"No wine?" Llysette snorted.

"You get wine. You'll just have to enjoy it here and not in the restaurants. He even got that right." Except how they had known? . . . That was another question that bothered me, unless they did it for all outsiders. "Do you want to eat, or do you want to clean up?"

"A bath, I would like. Is there any food here in the room?"

I crossed to the kitchen area and opened the cabinet—only a small range of china and glasses. Then came the cooler—where there were five bottles of wine and some cheeses and packages of crackers and two apples wrapped in foil.

"Apples and cheeses and crackers."

"*Assez.* I will bathe, and you can shower in your own bath."

"I forgot that."

So I started slicing apples and cheese to the background noise of running water.

CHAPTER TWENTY

• • •

L lysette's first rehearsal was scheduled for ten o'clock, and that meant not sleeping too late on Tuesday. She wore a dark green dress with a tan jacket, both tailored, but loose-fitting enough for her to sing. She'd end up removing the jacket. I knew how hot she got once she was really working.

Singing was athletic, and I'd never appreciated that until I'd met Llysette and watched her work.

"Are you ready?" I glanced toward the door of the suite.

"*Mais oui.*"

"Do you mind eating downstairs?"

"*Non.* I do not like staying in a room, even one as large as this."

I understood. She even hesitated about closing the bedroom door, or any door. At times, I hated, really hated, Ferdinand. Then, probably a third of Europe still did.

She smiled. "You wish to observe?"

She was right about that. We hadn't observed much the day before, just taken a short walk in the wind up to the Temple, only to find the grounds were closed on Monday afternoons for maintenance. So we'd just wandered back to the hotel and taken a nap and eaten and slept. The dirigible trip shouldn't have been that tiring, but it had been. I could tell that because nothing seemed quite real, foreign country or not, despite all my worries and all the Spazi briefing materials.

No one else was about on the sixth floor where we waited for the elevator. Perhaps no one else was staying on what seemed to be the suite floor—or they weren't up yet.

Then, I had noticed the black seals on one door. I wondered how having a ghost-inhabited suite impacted on the bottom line of the Lion Inn. Hotels might provide a good market for de-ghosting equipment. I pushed that thought away. The last thing anyone needed was de-ghosting equipment available to everyone—since it also had the property of turning healthy individuals into zombies. My hand strayed to the calculator in my jacket pocket. The silver pens were in my breast pocket.

Llysette frowned but said nothing.

When we stepped out of the elevator into the lobby, I looked around for a moment before spotting the brass letters that spelled out: "The Refuge."

"There."

Llysette's heels clicked on the marble as we crossed the long lobby to the Inn's restaurant. The Refuge was white-walled, with dark green upholstered chairs and a dark gray carpet.

We didn't even have to wait.

"This way, Fräulein duBoise."

"Someone's briefed them," I whispered as we trailed the young woman to a corner booth, and a table with crisp white linens and shining silver, and a serving tray with six covered silver dishes of assorted jellies.

The menu, as expected, contained no references to coffee or tea, but they did have chocolate, for which I was grateful.

"Chocolate?" asked a smiling waiter, also fairly young, perhaps the age Walter might have been.

"Please," I answered, gesturing to the cups.

He filled both and left the pot on the table.

The dining area was half-filled, but whether that was because it was nearly a quarter past eight or because the Lion Inn was not filled on a Tuesday—or because the food was not that good—who knew?

"Have you decided, Fräulein duBoise?"

"The second breakfast, if you please."

"The Deseret Delight? How would you like the eggs?"

"Poached."

He turned to me.

"I'd like the number four, but could I have eggs Bruges instead of eggs Benedict?"

The waiter raised his eyebrows. "Sir?"

"Béarnaise instead of hollandaise."

"I can ask, sir."

No promises there.

He returned immediately with two large orange juices and a plate of croissants. "Your breakfast won't be long."

"Thank you."

Llysette sipped her orange juice and glanced around the dining room area. I had more chocolate and refilled my cup.

"There are no men with two women," said Llysette.

She was right. There were men alone, men with other men, and men with a single woman, and one family that appeared to be traditional—husband, wife, and three children.

"I can't explain that one way or another." I offered a smile. "There's probably a lot I couldn't explain about Deseret."

Llysette sipped her chocolate, then lowered her voice. "The women . . . I do not understand them."

I didn't either. They had secret ballots and the right to vote, but they seemed to accept a secondary status. Then, maybe the elections were a sham, except

Jerome's briefing materials indicated that the elections for the Seventy—a sort of theocratic parliament—were real and that the unofficial Women's Party had effectively blocked several candidates.

"Your breakfast, fräulein, Doktor." The waiter's smile seemed pasted in place as he set the orders before us.

I had eggs Bruges—they actually had them. A lot of restaurants think that béarnaise goes only with meat, but the Lion Inn either didn't or was under orders to cater to us.

"Thank you," I said.

"Is there anything else?"

Llysette and I looked at each other.

"No, thank you."

We were both hungry, and we didn't talk that much.

After breakfast, we went back upstairs.

As Llysette washed up, I glanced through the *Deseret Star*—"Proclaiming the News of Zion and the World." The paper had been laid out on the table outside our door.

In the Arts section, there was actually a small article:

. . . the noted Columbian soprano arrived in Great Salt Lake yesterday to prepare for a series of concerts with Doktor Daniel Perkins, the world-famed composer and accompanist. . . . The first concert will be Thursday evening at 8:00. . . . Among the works presented will be several of Doktor Perkins's compositions, including the well-known *Lord of Sand* . . . based on a poem by F. George Evans. . . . First Counselor Cannon hailed the concert as a "widening of cultural horizons" . . . he is expected to be present.

Another article also caught my eye:

GREAT SALT LAKE CITY (DNS). Police arrested yesterday two men wanted in connection with the vehicular homicide of Second Counselor Leavitt last September. Pending full identification, their names were not released.

Although the two were arrested in a hideout in the warehouse district, police spokesman Jared Bishopp denied that the arrests had anything to do with the "pornographic material" raids that have been ongoing in the area. . . .

Bishopp also denied that the raids had any connection with the death of Deseret University professor R. Jedediah Grant. Grant, a difference systems expert, burned to death in a mysterious fire in his steamer last week.

"I'll bet," I murmured to myself. "All coincidence." I couldn't help but think about the fact that the press had referred to Llysette, again, as a noted Columbian soprano.

After she touched up her makeup, I got out our overcoats—it was still cloudy and cold-looking outside. Then we took the elevator down to the lobby.

Llysette tucked the black leather music folder under her arm, not that she'd need the music, except to go over with her accompanist, who was supposed to be the composer. I wondered if he'd use music for his own pieces.

The morning was gray, with brown overtones from the polluted air, and a cold wind whipped around us as we walked down First Street West. According to the maps Brother Jensen had left, we would enter the concert hall through the second door.

A single white-haired guard in green sat at a kiosk just inside the single unlocked glass door. "Hall's closed, sir."

"This is Llysette duBoise. She has a rehearsal this morning with Doktor Perkins." I offered a smile.

"Be a moment." The guard straightened, then rummaged through a folder and looked at something, then at Llysette. "Looks like you, miss." He smiled. "I'll bet you sing as good as you look, little lady."

I could feel Llysette stiffen, but she managed a smile. "We do try."

The foyer inside the doors stretched nearly fifty meters in each direction and was covered in a green pile carpet. The dimness of the light and the Corinthian pillars, mixed with what I would have sworn were Egyptian half-obelisks, imparted an air of a museum—or a ruin.

I guided Llysette toward the one door to the hall that was propped open. The concert hall proper was enormous, big enough for nearly three thousand people, I guessed, as we walked down the maroon carpet past dark upholstered seats toward the lighted stage where two men stood.

I strained to listen as we neared.

". . . don't care . . . let the music be good and so will the concert . . ."

". . . make it good, Brother Perkins . . . too much rides on this . . ."

"If I could make . . . that should not . . ." The clean-shaven Perkins shook his head and turned. "Doktor duBoise!"

Llysette acknowledged his words with a nod.

"There's a set of temporary steps at the side there."

We took them and met the two men by the end of the concert Steinbach.

"And this must be the famous Minister Eschbach." Perkins smiled warmly.

"Scarcely famous," I protested.

"I'm Dan Perkins. It's so good to meet you, Mademoiselle duBoise." He looked first at Llysette and then in my direction. "Or is it Fräulein or Frau?"

"She sings as Fräulein or Mademoiselle, but technically she's both a doktor and a professor." Somehow I'd thought he'd be bigger, but I was nearly half a head taller than he was.

"A professional in every sense of the word." He offered a boyish smile that belied the tinge of white in his blond hair and gestured toward the man with the blond beard beside him. "This is Brother Hansen. James V. Hansen. He's with the culture people for now."

Hansen bowed from the waist. "A pleasure to meet you both." His smile was friendly and almost as practiced as a politician's. "You are punctual . . . unlike some . . . artists. . . ."

I took Llysette's overcoat, and she opened the folder.

"Some questions . . . before we commence?"

"Of course." Perkins almost sounded happy that she had questions.

I retreated back down to the hall. Standing around would only make them, or me, uncomfortable and slow things down.

I sat in the darkened third row, just out of the lights. Hansen sat on the end of the front row, where he could survey both the empty hall and the stage, and his eyes were never still. He was solid, blond-haired like so many of the Saints seemed to be, and wore a gray suit that was conservative in cut but with a fine green stripe that would have been considered almost frivolous in Asten. I hadn't missed the slight bulge in the coat either or the thickness around the waist. He was also older, possibly even older than I was, and that bothered me.

Good covert agents, and I'd liked to think I had been one, had to go on feelings as much as on cold logic, but that was always hard to explain in debriefs. I'd have hated to explain in writing, even in something as frivolous as a spy novel. They always make spies out as either cold calculators or dashing romantics, when most of us were men trying to handle impossible jobs any way we could—like Hansen apparently was.

Brother Hansen, for all his charming smiles, was the Saint equivalent of a Spazi agent, and he'd been talking to the composer and waiting for us. I tried to think as Llysette and Perkins began to go through the concert schedule but found myself drawn into the music. I could tell Perkins was as good an accompanist as I'd ever heard, and even after a few minutes I could tell the concert was going to be something special.

When they got to his pieces, several times he stopped and talked to her, but I couldn't really catch the words, except that he seemed to be explaining what he'd had in mind. Like most artists, he explained with his hands and his intonations, perhaps more than with his words.

Once, right after we'd been married, I'd wondered what would happen, what could possibly happen, to two upcountry academics. Well . . . something had, and I wasn't quite sure I was ready for it. The rehearsal just reemphasized the feeling I had that Llysette duBoise was about to be rediscovered—and then some.

Hansen sat and listened and watched, seemingly ignoring me, and I sat and listened and watched all three.

After they finished, and it must have taken nearly three hours, Llysette turned backstage, apparently heading for a dressing room or a ladies' room or both. After a moment, Hansen walked up to Perkins. I listened in the darkness at the side of the stage, just short of the temporary stairs. I had both overcoats across my arm.

". . . you were right. . . ."

Perkins grinned boyishly again and shook his head. ". . . better even than . . . they've got quite a surprise coming. Wait until she has an audience. I can tell."

"There may be a few surprises all around."

Perkins looked hard at the older man. "They had better all be pleasant ones, *Brother* Hansen." He stressed the word "Brother."

"The First Counselor has already told me the same thing, Doktor." Hansen cleared his throat. "I only meant that sopranos are supposed to be boring. I enjoyed it, and this was a rehearsal."

"She's got the artistic soul or spirit of two singers—and the artistry. She could look like . . . a duck . . . and no one would notice."

"She's no duck, Brother Perkins. Like I said, surprises all around."

I could hear Llysette's heels coming from backstage, and the two stopped talking. She was pulling on her jacket as she walked into the light, and I stepped up onto the stage, holding her coat.

Hansen frowned as he saw me, as though he'd forgotten I was there. I held in my own smile. One trick I had learned in the Spazi was blending into the background when I wanted to. Sometimes, though, I felt I blended whether I wanted to or not.

"This afternoon, then?" Llysette asked as she neared the big Steinbach.

"At four," Perkins answered.

I wondered if they'd scheduled another rehearsal, but I didn't ask. Llysette would tell me, and it was her voice and concert.

Llysette didn't speak until we were outside, walking back toward the Lion Inn. "Doktor Perkins, he is not what I expected."

"How is that?"

A messenger in a heavy coat dodged around us and kept running south.

"He is not cold, the way his letters were, and he says what he thinks."

I had to wonder how Perkins had survived in a theocracy. Through absolute talent? If so, that said something about Deseret, but exactly what . . . I wasn't sure. Then, I was getting less and less sure about more and more—like who wanted whom dead and who wanted Llysette to succeed and who to fail. I saw too many possibilities—one of the dubious benefits of age and experience.

"We practice again this afternoon—at four. A short time."

"Here?"

"*Non.* In our room. I wished . . . the phrasing in two of his songs. I must think. He played them, and we were not together . . . not how I would like."

"That's fine with me."

"You are good."

I still doubted that but didn't speak for a moment, as a fiercer gust of wind whipped around us and tossed scattered snowflakes along First Street West.

We turned the corner toward the Lion Inn, and I added, "I forgot to tell you. There was another article in the local paper about you and the concert. Brother Hansen reminded me about it when he talked to Perkins while you were backstage. Hansen was talking about a surprise, and I got to thinking about a different kind of surprise. There's one thing you haven't really prepared for. It might not happen." I shrugged. "But it might."

"*Qu'est-ce que c'est?*"

"What if some reporter or videolink type corners you?"

"*Moi?*"

"Don't be coy, my lady. You're getting better and better known, and even the First Counselor here apparently wants a success. What better way than some sort of interview?"

"And they would ask what?"

"Anything." I laughed, then coughed from the cold wind. The hotel was less than a half-block away. "Something like . . . why are you returning to performing now? Or . . . what do you make of singing in two national capitals in less than a month? How do you like Deseret? Was your husband really a spy?"

Llysette shook her head. "Those, they will ask, you think?"

"Some of them have no shame. Most of them," I added.

"I am performing now because they have let me."

I winced. "*Non. . . .*"

Llysette grinned, and I realized she'd just been teasing. "That, I would not say, save to you. What I will say . . . A person who has no country has few choices. I am happy now. I will perform so long as people wish to hear."

"What about the spy business?"

"*Mon cher* . . . he is a very good professor, and he was a war hero, and he is a good man. He is no spy."

That was true as far as it went. "If they ask more?"

"I will say that they should ask you if they do not like my words."

"What is the message behind your concert, Fräulein duBoise?" I asked in the snide way I'd heard from too many linkers.

"Message?" Llysette shook her head. "You have suffered from them, Johan."

"Probably. But it's the kind of question some will ask."

"Then I would say that music is beauty, and there is too little beauty in a cold world." She paused, and I could see that her face had lost most of its color.

"You need something to eat."

"*Je crois que oui.*"

"Is the hotel all right?"

"What is close is best."

We made it to The Refuge, and Llysette had chicken noodle soup, while wait-ing for a salad, and I munched on crackers.

"The soup is good." Her face was still pale.

"I'm glad." We didn't have a corner booth, but, again, no one was seated at the adjacent tables, although we had a waitress, an older and gray-haired woman.

"He is a good accompanist."

"As good as he is a composer?"

"At both he is good. His art songs, they are better than the Vondel operas."

"The lyrics are better than Vondel's?"

"Dutch . . . it has the charm of Russian and the efficiency of Italian."

My Dutch ancestors would have protested, but Llysette remained pale, and I had more to worry about than Dutch opera lyrics composed centuries earlier and set to music by Doktor Perkins.

"Like French, you mean?" I said with a grin.

"You. . . ." Then she shook her head and smiled back.

As she took another spoonful of soup, I glanced around the dining area. Most of the diners were male, in groups of two to four, and most wore gray or brown suits, especially dark brown. None looked in our direction.

The color was beginning to return to Llysette's face by the time the salads ar-rived. I'd eaten three large soda crackers. Would I have been better off with the soup? Probably, but I'd had too much soup as a sickly child.

The salads disappeared quickly, as did the rolls that came with them. I'd barely finished when the gray-haired waitress reappeared.

"Would you like some dessert? The lime gelatin pie is good. So is the double chocolate death cake."

I passed on the lime gelatin pie, and my waistline wouldn't have stood the cake.

"Do you want to see the Temple grounds?" I asked after signing the bill for lunch with: "duBoise/Eschbach, Room 603."

Llysette shrugged, then answered, "I ate too much, and a walk would be good."

The wind had died down by the time we left the Inn's lobby, and with the sun out, I ended up loosening my coat after the first block. Llysette did not do the same, but she wasn't shivering either. I did not point out the snow on the moun-tains to the southeast.

To the east of the Lion Inn rose the white stone spires of the Temple and, be-low them, white stone walls. The air easing in from the northwest carried the faint tang of petrochemicals and of salt.

I squeezed Llysette's gloved hand, and she squeezed mine.

We slowed at the corner, behind a woman with a double stroller carriage.

Both fair-cheeked children smiled at Llysette as she bent over. "They are beau-tiful."

"Thank you." The woman smiled, then pushed the stroller across South Temple.

I caught the brightness in Llysette's eyes as we waited for the signal to turn to allow us to cross the street. "I'm sorry."

A flash of green blotted away the incipient tears. "You did not—"

"I can be sorry." I reached out and put my arm around her shoulders as we walked and squeezed her gently.

"That . . . it was not meant to be."

I didn't know about that, only that Ferdinand had a lot to answer for, and that there wasn't much I could do about that either. My neck twitched, an unpleasant and too-familiar feeling, and I casually looked toward the street and the maroon Browning that steamed by silently.

Two men wearing green jackets, from what I could see, under their gray trench coats eased up the street after us, keeping well back, but you never lose the feeling of eyes on your back.

More Danites? I kept the half-smile on my face as we crossed to the walkway that bordered the park surrounding the Temple square proper.

Although Great Salt Lake City had to hold more than a quarter-million souls, the streets were not thronged with steamers or steam buses. I craned but saw no haulers. Were they banned from the area around the Temple?

The browning grass in the park around the Temple was trimmed and raked and without leaves, despite the winds of the morning and the day before. Nowhere did I see even the smallest bit of litter.

A small group of young adults, less than a dozen, followed a young man in a charcoal gray suit, without an overcoat, who periodically stopped. For a time, we trailed the group, discretely back.

"The building here is the genealogy center." He gestured toward the two-story gray stone structure that bordered the street on the north side of the square. "The difference engines there have everyone's ancestry on record. You'll learn more about that later."

Then came a churchlike building.

"This is now the performing hall. It's called Assembly Hall. There are three concerts a week broadcast from here all over Deseret. . . ."

Llysette shook her head and looked at me.

"I know," I whispered.

The group marched toward another building, with a keystone declaring it the "Visitor Center," but I didn't feel like declaring us as visitors, even though we were.

I glanced back. The two Danites had split up, but they were clearly continuing their vigil.

A higher stone wall encircled the Temple proper, and those gates were barred with black iron gratework. The dome-roofed Tabernacle squatted across a flat rectangular area, half-filled with raised stone enclosures that were turned bare-earth flower beds. The flower beds were bordered with low juniper hedges.

We walked up to one of the Tabernacle doors, where a too-hefty young man in a charcoal black suit stood. He wore a rectangular name tag that proclaimed him as "Brother Marsden."

"Can we look in?" I asked.

He smiled and opened the door. "The choir won't be practicing until tonight. There are some schedules and pamphlets on the ledge along the wall."

The Tabernacle was impressive—essentially an amphitheatre around a series of tiered risers and a huge organ. The walls were white and gold, and the wood-work glistened under the dome. The recording equipment was still in place, with microphones hung strategically.

I could hear the whispers from a couple standing just before the front row of seats, a good ten feet lower than where we stood at the rear, and more than a hundred feet away.

". . . Prophet Young preached right here . . . before they built the Temple. . . ."

". . . so did Jedediah Grant and Cannon."

"Good acoustics," I murmured to Llysette.

She nodded, her eyes still on the massive organ pipes and the tiered seats for the Saints' Choir.

". . . booms when the Saints' Choir sings—"

"I would go," Llysette said abruptly.

I took her arm. "The Tabernacle bothers you."

"For singing it should be, not for the preaching."

"I don't know how much preaching they do there now."

She shook her head.

We walked slowly back to the hotel and our suite, where Llysette eased off her shoes and stretched out on the bed. I found the hotel-provided *Guide to Great Salt Lake* and began to read.

I got as far as the winter recreation areas by the time four o'clock came. The rap on the suite door was firm, and I opened it. Doktor, or Brother, Perkins stood there.

"Come on in. She's expecting you."

Beyond the composer, where the corridor turned toward the elevator, I saw a gray coat with a fine green stripe and a blond-haired head vanish around the corner.

Perkins saw my eyes and nodded.

I shut the door without comment. "Could I take your coat?" I wanted to see what the composer said.

"Brother Hansen is concerned. He insisted on ensuring that I arrived . . . without incident. He worries that admirers will waylay me—as if any of them would recognize me outside of formal wear." The composer's laugh was ironic, with a hint of what I would have called self-mockery, as he turned to Llysette. "You, lady, will reinvent my career. If you sing as you did this morning . . ." He shook his head.

Llysette's slight frown disappeared with his words, and she said, "I am but a singer, not a composer."

"People listen to singers, not composers."

Llysette shrugged, indicating that she didn't agree, but that she wasn't going to argue.

I retreated to the corner chair when the slender blond man sat at the piano and played several bars—something I didn't recognize. "It's even in tune." He opened one of the folders he had brought in and set the opened music on the piano's rack.

"Good," answered my lovely wife, and I wished I could play. But whatever gods or ghosts determine our heritage ensured musical talent was something I lacked.

"I thought we might try the 'Fragments' part first. Here. . . ."

"*Oui*. . . ."

There was a difference between their efforts in the concert hall and the suite, but one so slight to my ears that I wouldn't have caught it without Llysette's explanation, and I wondered how many people really would have caught the difference.

They continued for a time, then switched to the second song. After two attempts, Perkins paused and turned to Llysette. "Could you hold this just a little longer?"

"I did not read the phrase so. Could we sing that phrase both ways?"

"Of course."

So they did.

Afterward, the composer frowned.

Llysette remained straight-faced.

"I think you were right," Perkins said. "It sounds better. That could be because no one else has . . . the vibrancy you do."

Llysette looked down. Sometimes, she still didn't fully understand what she had become. "*Encore* . . ."

They went back to working on the song—*Lord of Sand,* I thought, the Evans poem.

In time, Perkins stopped playing and stood, stretching.

Llysette almost shook herself and glanced toward me. "I feel better," she said with a faint smile.

"I am glad you do," the composer answered, bending over and folding up the music. "I think a great number of listeners, even those few who heard you years ago, will be surprised." He looked at me.

"I haven't doubted that," I said, "but I'm not a musician."

"I am, and I know that they will be surprised." He offered that boyish grin again.

I brought him his coat.

"How have you found Deseret?"

"We've not seen that much, except what we saw on the airship and the Temple grounds."

"And the Salt Palace," added Llysette.

"I hope you get to see more after the concerts. You might ask if you can get farther south. There's so much there—Cedar Breaks, Ankakuwasit . . ."

Llysette nodded.

I decided to ask. "We're strangers here, and some things aren't obvious. When Herr Jensen picked us up, he had a driver who wore a green jacket. The coat looked like a uniform, but it had no insignia." I spread my hands. "I might be mistaken, and I would dislike having an incorrect impression."

"I doubt your impression was incorrect." The composer smiled wryly. "The Danites wear green, and I wouldn't be surprised if Brother Jensen's driver were a Danite." He turned to Llysette. "The Danites were the original militia in the first Saint war back in Columbia. Now . . . they're more of a . . . something like the Masons in Columbia."

According to Jerome's briefing papers, they were far more than a fraternal order, more like a paramilitary order, if not a secret but official arm of the church.

I didn't have to force the frown. "That seems odd."

Perkins laughed. "Why would it be odd? Deseret is surrounded by Columbia and New France. Until comparatively recently, Columbia kept trying to annex us, and now Marshal DeGaulle has the same idea. We can't afford a large standing army. That's why the First Presidency has always supported the Danites and the Joseph Smith Brigades."

I shook my head, then decided to push a little more. "No, I didn't mean that. I meant his having a driver who was a Danite."

"That's no more strange than my having Brother Hansen as an escort." Perkins paused. "Surely you understand that we all want this concert to go well and no one wants either this lovely lady—or, unfortunately, me—to be distracted. Music is far more highly regarded here in Deseret than in Columbia." He smiled. "This lady would not have had to wait for citizenship to have sung here. Her concerts would have been mobbed."

I got the message and felt guilty for pushing so far. "I guess I didn't realize just how celebrated you two are here. I got into the arts business late, and by marriage." I put on a sheepish grin and looked at Llysette. "In New Bruges, people are not exactly the most enthusiastic of music lovers. Sometimes . . . I'm not so bright . . . as I should be."

"My lady." Perkins turned to Llysette. "You are indeed fortunate to have a husband who is not a musician."

"That I know." She smiled fondly at me. "He worries about me, not about the notes."

I tried not to sigh. I just hoped she wouldn't analyze the conversation too closely, praying she was still thinking about the music.

"My wife is probably asking where I am." Perkins turned to Llysette. "Tomorrow at ten?"

"That would be good."

With a last boyish smile, the composer left. The gray coat and blond hair told me that Brother Hansen was waiting by the elevator.

I closed the door and turned to Llysette. She'd slumped into one of the armchairs.

"You're tired."

"*Oui.*"

"And hungry."

She nodded.

"I'll dig out some of the cheese and crackers. It's hard working with a composer."

"*Non* . . . he is easy to follow, but to sing his words . . . as well as one can . . . *c'est tres difficile.*"

"Do you want to rest? A glass of wine before we find somewhere to eat? Or should I order dinner up here?"

"The wine. Then I will decide."

I went to extract one of the bottles from the cooler and to get her some cheese and crackers. Perkins was honest, and he didn't want Llysette worried, and he was worried, and we were definitely under protective surveillance—all of us. All in all, a pattern was emerging, and I didn't care for its shape in the slightest.

"Do you think you have . . . whatever it was . . . worked out?"

"I should think so. Tomorrow, then we will see."

That we would, except I knew tomorrow was but the beginning.

CHAPTER TWENTY-ONE

• • •

After breakfast on Wednesday, while Llysette reviewed her music again and warmed up some, I went through both local scandal sheets. In addition to a small article about the decision by Escobar-Moire to send another New French naval battle group to the Azores, the *Deseret News* contained an article mentioning the concert. That meant both papers were being fed material. I had my doubts that they had teams of reporters seeking it out.

Great Salt Lake City (DNS). A select number of University of Deseret voice students will get the chance of a lifetime this coming Friday and Saturday—an opportunity to show off their talents to world-famous Columbian soprano Llysette duBoise. . . .

In addition to her three concerts this week at the Salt Palace (see Entertainment Calendar) with Deseret's own world-renowned Daniel Perkins, duBoise will be conducting two master classes for the top female voice students at Deseret University.

"It's a great opportunity for our students," said Joanne Axley, the Director of Voice Studies for Women at Deseret University. "They're really looking forward to working with Doktor duBoise. . . ."

I flipped to the Entertainment Calendar, and, as indicated on the front part of the Arts section, all three concerts were listed, with three stars, presumably indicating a recommendation of some sort. I pondered the story, carefully placed below the fold, but on the front page of the Arts section in the lower right corner. Neither the place nor the times for the classes were mentioned, either.

The *Deseret Star* only mentioned the concerts in the section headed "Upcoming Cultural Events"—in bold type—but the *Star* had offered the earlier story.

"Johan?"

"I'm ready any time you are." I stood and handed the section that had the *News* article to Llysette. "You're getting even more famous. Show this to Dierk and the dean. 'World-famous Columbian soprano.' "

She read the story slowly, then looked up. "I am not good enough for their men?"

"I don't know that it was meant that way," I said. "They seem to keep men and women almost separate." I picked up my coat and donned it, then extracted hers from the closet.

"Women are not so good as men?" There was a glint in her green eyes.

"I don't believe that, but I can't control what the Saints do or believe," I pointed out.

"So long as you do not become a Saint. . . ."

"There's not much chance of that." And there wasn't. Who wanted to join a faith based on imaginary gold tablets translated by a prophet who had never been to school? While the idea of dying and becoming God sounded all right, I had my doubts about what it really might be like. Besides, I was having enough trouble learning how to be a real person with one wife, and polygamy had to be even harder. Then, maybe I was spiritually polygamous, with the fragments of Carolynne's ghost welded to my soul and being married to a singer who was somewhere between one and two separate women trying to be one. And people out there were considering creating more ghosts?

"Quiet you are," said Llysette.

"Sometimes . . . I just have to think." I held her coat for her, then opened the suite door.

Llysette shook her head at herself and walked over to the piano and picked up the black folder with the music and then her handbag.

The concierge nodded as we stepped out into the lobby, and I returned the nod, although I wondered if his gesture was really for us.

Outside, even under the canopy, the wind was chill again. The sky was clear and a chilling blue. Cold as the air was, it smelled clean for the first time since we'd arrived, and for that I was grateful.

Llysette fumbled the top buttons of her heavy coat closed and clutched her music.

A green steam bus, trimmed in gold paint, hissed by and stopped at the corner ahead and disgorged several dozen people. All were fairly young, less than thirty, and most were men. The younger men were uniformly clean-shaven. Did beards come with marriage? Doktor Perkins was clean-shaven, but he had a reputation for being a nonconformist. On the other hand, Brother Hansen was bearded and he was definitely older and, given the Saint culture, probably just as definitely married for, as they put it, "time and eternity."

A different pair of Danites followed us to the concert hall. I didn't mention them to Llysette. What was the point in possibly upsetting her before her first big concert in years? Especially when they seemed to be there to protect her?

Still, my fingers curled toward the calculator in my jacket pocket, and I wanted to touch the pen and pencil set. There was also the plastic blade in the belt, but that would have taken too long to get out.

"Good morning . . . Doktor," offered the white-haired guard. He struggled slightly with the "Doktor," but someone had clearly briefed him.

"Good morning," said Llysette cheerfully.

"They're waiting for you."

"Thank you." She bestowed a dazzling smile.

I held the door for her, noting the slightest of headshakes on the part of the guard, almost as if he felt someone that beautiful didn't belong in public—or something like that.

The two Danites had dropped back as we'd entered the Salt Palace complex, and I lost sight of them as we headed through the dimness toward the hall itself.

Doktor Perkins and Brother Hansen were waiting at the base of the stage, at the waist-high dark green curtain that circled the pit.

"Are you ready?" asked the composer.

"Yes." Llysette started to unbutton the heavy black coat, and I stepped forward to help her out of it. "It is cold today."

"We're in for some snow later, only an inch or two, they say." Perkins grinned. "Just so it's over by noon tomorrow."

Llysette shivered.

"It's not any warmer here, or not much," I pointed out as I folded her coat over my arm.

"That explanation, Johan, I could do without."

I shut up. She was tense enough.

"What would you prefer?" asked the composer. "Would you like to warm up?"

"*Non* . . . already have I. . . . The two songs . . . first. Then the program as we would sing it."

Perkins nodded, and I backed away as silently as I could, followed by Hansen. Llysette and the composer/accompanist moved toward the big Steinbach.

"How do you find Deseret?" asked Hansen, smiling his politician's smile, when we reached the space at the foot of the temporary steps.

"With Llysette's rehearsals and practice, we really haven't had much time to sightsee. We did tour the Temple grounds and the Tabernacle, and the small performing hall and the park and the gardens. They're all very impressive." I smiled. "It's always been amazing to me to read about how much you Saints have accomplished. To see it is even more amazing."

"People work hard here." Hansen paused, his eyes going to the stage, where Llysette and Perkins stood by the Steinbach. The composer gestured to the music, then seated himself and played several bars before looking up. Llysette nodded.

"You're a professor now, aren't you? Have you published many books?"

"Environment and natural resources. And no, I haven't published many books, just a handful of articles. Most of them upset people." I laughed softly, not wanting the sound to carry, but I supposed it did anyway, because Llysette looked in my direction.

"Time to sit down and be quiet," I said wryly, moving back up the aisle and into the darkness.

Hansen again took a position in a seat on the end of the first row, from where he could watch both stage and seats.

I watched, but it took only a few attempts before Llysette and the composer appeared satisfied with the two sections they'd rehearsed the night before. Then they went into the program itself. Although it was only a rehearsal, it was still better. I wanted to cry and shake my head, understanding a little bit more why not performing had hurt Llysette so deeply.

Before I really knew it, the rehearsal was over.

As Brother Hansen stood in the open area below the stage, Perkins gestured to me. So I climbed up the temporary steps on the right-hand side, carrying Llysette's coat with me.

Because she was perspiring slightly, I just held the coat.

"I realize that it is very short notice, but Jillian and I would like to know if you both would join us for dinner this evening." Perkins's eyes went fleetingly in the direction of Hansen, so fleetingly that I wouldn't have caught the movement if I hadn't been watching. "A very bland meal, a chicken pasta, if that's all right," he added. "I wouldn't want to upset a singer."

"That would be wonderful," said Llysette. "Johan and I would enjoy that." She paused. "I would prefer . . . cilantro I do not like."

"This recipe doesn't feature cilantro or much garlic."

I supposed we could enjoy a dinner away from the Lion Inn. "Would you care to have lunch with us?"

"I wish I could." He shook his head and checked his watch. "I still have a class to teach."

"You teach also?"

"At the university." He grinned again at Llysette. "I'm the one who set up the master classes for you. I hope you don't mind if a few of my students sit in."

"Mais non." Llysette smothered a frown.

"If that would bother you . . ."

"Non . . . I enjoy teaching men."

"Tonight. I'll pick you up at the Inn just before seven?"

"That would be fine."

He nodded and then gathered up his music and headed down the steps and for the open hall door, his strides long and quick, as if he were already late. Hansen looked at us, then hurried after the composer.

"Do you want your coat?"

"Pas encore . . ."

We walked slowly out of the hall, not because Llysette was tired, but because she wanted to cool off before going out into the cold. My thoughts kept flitting to the business about his teaching and his students and the newspaper article that mentioned only female students—yet more pieces to a puzzle that got more and more complicated.

"Lunch?"

"Please."

The two new Danites, or whatever they were, followed us back to the Lion Inn and The Refuge, where we were escorted back to the corner table—again with a healthy space around us.

Llysette didn't feel like talking, and I didn't press. As every performance neared, she drew more and more into herself. That was one reason why I'd been surprised that she'd accepted the dinner invitation. But her instincts were good, and if she accepted, I'd follow her lead—with a look over our shoulders.

The rest of the day was uneventful. After lunch, Llysette napped, and then . . . well . . . we both napped after that.

When we woke, she took a bath, and then I showered and dressed and she fussed over one of the songs at the piano before she dressed. I opened another bottle of wine, but she only had one glass while she dressed, and I read the hotel-provided guidebook from cover to cover once more.

At five to seven, we were down in the lobby. At three before the hour, a red steamer pulled up under the canopy—unsurprisingly, a Browning—and we stepped into the night air.

Despite their ornate wrought-iron shapes, the streetlights were energy-efficient glow throwers that penetrated the gloom without searing the eyeballs. Again, as I sniffed and smelled chemicals and air pollutants, I had to wonder why the Saints had installed the most environmentally friendly and energy-efficient lights while only undertaking considerably less effective air pollution controls.

As Perkins guided the steamer eastward and uphill, I glanced back through the twilight, convinced that the same pair of headlights that had pulled out from the Lion Inn was still behind us, if a block back. There's a thin line between occupational caution and paranoia. I wondered if I was crossing that line.

Doktor Perkins drove quickly, except when he neared what seemed to be a school, where he slowed down. That seemed odd, since it was well past any normal school hours.

"There's a ghost of a young woman there. She was killed in a steamer accident several months ago, and her family visits her every night."

We peered through the darkness. Sure enough, several figures seemed to group around a white shadow. I shivered, and Llysette reached out and squeezed my hand. How many ghosts were on my soul? I tried not to think about it.

Perkins turned right, downhill, then pulled into a bricked driveway another hundred yards past the turn.

The two-story house was nearly a century old, made of hand-formed yellow-brown bricks. The light on the wide front porch revealed that the trim was almost a forest green, accented with gold-painted gingerbread.

A double car barn had been added later, although some attempt had been made to match the house brick.

I held the steamer door for Llysette, feeling dampness on my face. Scattered flakes swirled down around us for a moment, then vanished.

Perkins led the way up the antique brick steps and across a wide-planked and roofed porch to a golden oak door, which opened as we neared.

"That didn't take long," the petite blonde woman said to the composer.

"They were waiting." He gestured, and we stepped inside. "This is my wife, Jillian. She's a pianist."

"When I get time." Like the composer, Jillian Perkins was blonde and slender, except her hair was more of a strawberry blonde shade and very curly. She had a pixielike face, and her eyes sparkled. She wore a tailored blue dress that set off her eyes and hair. I liked her.

"If you'd say good night to the children, Dan? They're waiting."

"Excuse me." The composer bowed and headed up the narrow staircase, shedding his overcoat as he hurried upstairs, his shoes slapping on the polished wood steps.

"We can sit down for a moment." Jillian nodded toward the front sitting room, which contained a couch and two armchairs, as well as a small grand piano, something called a Ballem, but I didn't recognize the name. I walked over and studied the piano.

"We inherited that. Dan hates it. It's good furniture, but the internal works leave a little to be desired." Jillian offered a short laugh. "I teach youngsters on it. It's hard to keep in tune, but it's good practice for my tuning business. The good piano is in the study."

I sat on the couch beside Llysette, our backs to the filmy lace-trimmed curtains that framed the small bay window overlooking the front yard and street.

"How do you like Deseret?"

"It is . . . different." Llysette smiled gently. "Very . . . clean."

"The Temple is impressive. So is your husband," I added. "Llysette had told me about his music. She's sung some of it for years. But he's much younger than I expected."

"Dan does have that boyish look," Jillian replied, brushing a strand of curly hair off her forehead. "Would you like something to drink? We have hot or cold cider, hot chocolate, and orange and grapefruit juice."

Llysette smiled. "The hot chocolate, if you please."

"The same, thank you."

"Make yourselves at home. I'll be right back."

Alone momentarily, we glanced around the sitting room. From what I could see, it was the largest space in the house, and the only one capable of holding even a small grand piano. The house was actually smaller than ours in New Bruges. A large brick fireplace stood in the middle of the outside wall at the end of the room away from the small entry space and stairs. On each side of the fireplace were built-in bookcases.

I scanned the titles, those I could read, starting with the shelves on the left side. The few titles I could read told of the subject matter clearly enough— *History of the Latter-Day Saints, Witness of the Light, Sisters in Spirit, The Gathering of Zion, Brigham Young: American Moses,* and several volumes entitled *Doctrine and Covenants.*

The books on the right side were radically different: *Principles of Voice Production, Dynamics in Scoring, A Brief History of Music, The Complete Pianist, Vondel: A Guide, Henry Purcell,* and two shelves of what looked to be scores, some hand-bound.

The mahogany side tables, while akin to Columbian revival, were more spare and were scarcely new. Neither were the chairs and the couch on which we sat, although the room was as spotless as any well-kept Dutch dwelling. I definitely got the impression that composers, at least in Deseret, were not all that well compensated. And from what Llysette had indicated, Perkins was one of the better-known North American composers.

From the couch, we looked into a dining room not much larger than the eating space in my kitchen, at an oval table set for four.

"Modest . . . ," I murmured to Llysette.

She nodded.

Doktor Daniel Perkins needed Llysette as much as she needed him, perhaps more, and the recording contract made a great deal more sense—a great deal.

"Here's your chocolate." Jillian returned with a small tray and four cups, all steaming.

"*Merci.*"

"Thank you."

At the sound of shoes on the steps, she turned.

"They're all tucked in," Perkins explained as he passed the piano.

"It's cold out. I thought you might like some, too."

"Thank you, dear." He took the cup and settled himself into one of the chairs.

She set the tray on the side table and took the other chair but perched on the front.

"How many children do you have?"

"Three," answered Jillian. "Two boys and a girl."

"Ages ten, six, and two," he added. "And they're going on forty, fourteen, and two."

I must have frowned slightly.

"You wonder about the stories of large Saint families? And multiple spouses?" asked Perkins with a smile.

"It had crossed my mind," I admitted, "but you really never know, and it hasn't been that easy to learn more than the basics about Deseret. At least until recently." I was pushing it, but too many loose ends were dangling about, with too much at stake.

"Deseret is no longer a farming nation. We're growing, and we need more hands, but they have to be guided by an educated mind. Minds take longer to train than bodies."

"So the 'magic number' is no longer five?" I asked blandly.

Jillian winced, but Perkins grinned, a little self-consciously, before answering. "The church believes that while five children is an ideal, ideals don't necessarily fit all families."

I got that message—immense social pressure to have large families, but not an absolute written declaration.

"I'm curious. We saw a large house near the temple—with separate dwellings. . . ."

"The old Eccles house. It's almost a museum," Perkins said with a nod. "There were more housing complexes like that even twenty-five years ago." He shrugged. "Times change." Then he stood. "I need to finish up with the dinner."

"Dan's a far better cook than I am," Jillian said with a smile as the composer vanished in the direction of the kitchen. "He's not totally traditional."

Not totally? I was definitely getting the impression that Perkins was very untraditional in a traditional society, maintaining the mask while straining against it. Was that the reason why Brother Hansen was trailing Dan Perkins? "Are any composers traditional?"

"I don't know any others personally." Jillian smiled. "Most biographies of composers show they have a certain . . . flair."

"That is true," averred Llysette.

I would have had to agree.

"Here it is." Perkins held a large serving dish, then lowered it onto the small oval table.

We rose and inched toward the archway to the dining room.

"If you two would sit here and here," said Jillian, pointing to the two chairs away from the archway to the living room and the door to the kitchen. "That way, we can get to the kitchen."

I held the chair and seated her, and Perkins seated Llysette.

The dinner was simple—the chicken pasta with portabella mushrooms, flaky rolls, and a green salad.

"The white pitcher has ice water, the gold one cider," Jillian added.

I decided to try the cider and lifted the pitcher, looking at Llysette.

"Mais oui. . . ."

Then I tried the pasta. Not only was Perkins a composer, but he was also a good cook. Straight-faced, I asked Llysette, "Do you think he should have been a chef, too?"

"Together, you should open a bistro."

"And you'd sing?"

"The café songs, I heard them first, and when I was small, *tres petite,* a café singer I wanted to be." Llysette took a swallow of the too-sweet cider and managed to get it down straight-faced.

"You've come a long way," I pointed out.

"She really has," added Perkins.

"Your husband said you were a pianist," I said to Jillian.

"He is much better, but I teach part-time at the university, and I play at the ward services." She smiled. "I enjoy it."

"I wish I had that kind of talent," I answered.

"You have other talents, *mon cher.*"

"Listen to your lady," suggested Perkins.

"I always do."

"Maintenant . . ."

"It took a little while, but not long, to realize I got into trouble for not listening."

That got a smile from both Perkinses.

"So," I asked, after a moment, "how do you think the concert will go?"

Llysette frowned over a mouthful of salad at my boldness.

Perkins finished chewing before he answered. "If our rehearsals are any indication, it should be good."

"What about the recording?"

"That's easy. The hall has a permanent recording system. Deseret Media will record all three performances, and we'll take the best version of each song.

Hopefully . . . everyone in Deseret and Columbia will want a disk, and we'll all make lots of money."

Jillian nodded. "At least to cover the deposits."

"You made deposits?" I asked.

"Even in Deseret, artists have to pay," he pointed out. "It seemed like a good idea."

"Everywhere we pay," added Llysette.

I wondered if Llysette and I could get the loudmouthed media type at the presidential dinner—Hartson James, had that been his name?—to push Llysette's disks in Columbia. That would have to wait. "Artists pay everywhere."

"So true," said Jillian wryly.

I reached for the rolls, then offered them to Llysette. She declined.

"Maybe you could answer a few questions for me," I offered tentatively. "I've been a few places, but I've never been here, and Deseret is strange because, on the one hand, it's very familiar, I suppose because we speak the same language, dress similarly. On the other hand, words and terms don't quite fit."

"Such as?" The composer held his cider glass without drinking.

"Well . . . don't you call steamers Brownings?"

Jillian smiled.

"We generally call them steamers, or sometimes Stanleys, even though there are other kinds in Columbia." I took a small sip of the cider, very sweet. "And you have chocolate, but not tea or *café*. You have cider, but not wine." I shrugged. "I suppose I could come up with others, except I don't know enough yet to point them out." I offered a laugh. "A measure of my ignorance."

"You said you had questions . . . ," prompted Perkins.

"I suppose I do," I said ruefully, "but it's hard even to ask what you don't know. I guess I feel like I have some, but when you ask me . . ." Actually, the problem was even more basic than that. I needed to know things, but I didn't want to upset any of the three before the concerts. Yet I'd not have this chance again. It was frustrating, and I've never been that good at drawing people out. Llysette could be, when she wasn't worried about performing, but she was worried now.

My words—or my acting—got smiles from the others.

"Maybe . . . it's just that all the terms I read in the papers are confusing. I read about counselors and presidents and a presidency and apostles, and I see the same name being so many things." I shrugged.

"The same name?" asked the composer.

"Cannon, I think. He talks about culture, and he's a counselor to someone, and then I read that he's an apostle, or one of the Twelve. But he's also a businessman." I shrugged, then grinned. "I've done a lot of things, but I don't think I've ever done four separate jobs all at once—and been in the media as well."

Perkins nodded, an amused nod. "He does get around, but it's simpler than you think. The same people are members of the Twelve and the First Presidency.

Counselor is one of the titles within the Presidency. We've never really had a full-time government separate from the church and business. For Deseret, they all go together."

"So the Twelve Apostles are like the apostles of Christ, except that they're more of a government, like, say the ministers of government in Columbia?" I paused, then added, "But what's the difference between the First Presidency and the Twelve Apostles?"

"Same people, but different functions," answered the composer. "As the apostles, they guide the church. As the Presidency, they guide the country."

I frowned, not dissembling in the slightest. "Is the President also the . . . Prophet, Seer, and . . . ?"

"Revelator?" Perkins took a sip of cider. "Actually, the First President—that's the official title—is usually the head of the church, the Prophet, Seer, and Revelator, but in his government role, he's more like the president of Columbia."

"The head of state? Then who functions as the real head of government?"

"That's the First Counselor."

I shook my head. "So the same people wear different hats." I added another frown. "Now what's the difference between the Twelve and the Revealed Twelve? Is that another set of hats, too?"

Both Jillian and Llysette exchanged puzzled glances, then looked to the composer.

"No," he said. "The Revealed Twelve . . . that's some sort of underground schismatic religious movement. No one seems to know much about them, except they're claiming that they're the true Saints and that the current Apostles have betrayed the Prophet. I've seen some fliers around the university, but they don't last long. The Danites get rid of them pretty quickly." Perkins grinned wryly. "Some people always think the rest of the world is out of tune."

Somehow I wasn't certain whether he was referring to the Danites or the schismatics.

"Oh," I answered. "I just thought . . . with all those interlocking names . . ."

He shook his head. "The Revealed Twelve, or whatever else they call themselves, are just disgruntled outsiders afraid to appear in public and make their case."

I nodded. From what little I'd seen, I wouldn't have given much for their chances if they did appear.

From there we talked of cabbages and queens, ships and sailing wax, so to speak, through a heavy chocolate cake for dessert and more chocolate to end the dinner.

In the end, Perkins drove us back to the Inn, and I noted that another pair of Danites watched us from the back of the lobby.

CHAPTER TWENTY-TWO

• • •

The less said about the hours before the first Deseret concert the better. Llysette was as touchy as a caged cougar, not that I expected any less, with
all that was riding on her performance.

The fewer words I offered in such circumstances, the smoother matters went.
So I massaged her very tight shoulders and then confined my conversations to inquiries about what and when she wanted to eat, any chores I could run for her, and
reading the favorable story in the *Deseret News.*

"The headline is good—'World-Renowned Pair Open Concert Season.'"

"They did not write our names?" said Llysette from the piano bench, where
she looked at the music.

"The rest of the story is good, too." I began to read:

"'Great Salt Lake City (DNS). With one of the world's top vocal piano and
vocal duos in Llysette duBoise and Daniel Perkins, the Salt Palace performing complex opens its fiftieth consecutive season tonight.

"'Perkins, recently awarded the Rachmaninov Award by Czar Alexi, is also
the recipient of numerous other honors, including the Hearst Arts Medallion and
honorary degrees from the Curtiss Institute, the University of Virginia, and the
Saint Petersburg Conservatory. His arrangements and compositions have been
played by every major symphony orchestra in the world. He is the composer in
residence at Deseret University.

"'DuBoise, most recently featured at the Columbian Presidential Arts Awards
dinner, where she won rave reviews, has returned to an active performing career,
interrupted for several years as a result of the instability in France. Former First
Diva of France and featured soloist at the Academie Royale in Paris, she has appeared in most of the major opera houses of Europe. With a doctorate from the
Sorbonne, she is director of vocal studies and opera at Vanderbraak State University in New Bruges, Columbia. Last year, she married former Columbian Subminister for Environmental Protection Johan Eschbach.

"'The program will feature works by Mozart, Strauss, and Handel, as well as
several new arrangements of Perkins's own work written specifically for Fräulein
deBoise. The concert will begin at 8:00 P.M.'"

"About the Debussy they said nothing."

"They didn't," I agreed. "That's one of your best pieces."

"You do not like the *An die Nacht?*"

"You know I love that, and you do it beautifully. But," I sighed, "you do so much so well that I'd spend all day categorizing them." I shouldn't have mentioned anything by name, not before a performance.

"I am difficult. *Je sais ça. Mais . . .* "

"I know. There's a lot at stake."

"Trop . . ."

We had eaten a late breakfast—room service—and from what I knew, a late lunch/early dinner would be the order.

"A short walk might do us good."

"Peut-etre." Llysette didn't sound convinced.

"There were some shops on the other side of the street from the Temple, a woolen shop for one."

She pursed her lips. "A short walk?"

"Three blocks each way."

"Three. I can do that."

We stopped by the concierge's desk and converted 300 Columbian dollars into Deseret dollars. The two red hundreds also had the "Holiness to the Lord" motto, but the face on the bills was of someone called Grant.

It had snowed or rained earlier, and the streets were wet under high gray clouds. A steady cold wind blew from the northwest. Llysette fastened her collar.

Another pair of young and bearded Danites followed as we walked eastward on West Temple South.

Deseret Woolen Mills occupied a small red brick building practically across from the Temple grounds. In the window were woolen coats and brown and black woolen scarves.

Llysette wrinkled her nose. "Brown is for cows."

"They might have other colors inside."

"Peut-etre." That was one of the more dubious "perhapses" I'd heard, but she consented to turn toward the door, which I opened for her.

"The ladies' section is to the right," offered a woman with braided gray hair, although I doubted she was much older than I.

Llysette marched in the direction indicated, as if to determine quickly that the Deseret Woolen Mills had little to offer her.

I paused by a small rack of men's coats—jackets without matching trousers, almost blazers, except they were tweed and the upper part of the chest and back were covered with soft gray leather.

"Those are popular with the ranchers." A gray-haired bearded man eased up beside me.

"Ranchers?" I hadn't thought there were many left, with the energy developments.

"They do wear jackets, but they're particular about what they wear. Why don't you try one on?"

The jacket was comfortable and probably warm—definitely necessary in New

Bruges. In the end, though, somehow I just couldn't see myself wearing tweed and leather to class or anywhere else.

I replaced the jacket on its hanger, put my own suit coat back on, and went to find Llysette.

She was in the rear corner of the store, holding a woman's suit. She glanced at the pale green woolen skirt, then finally took off her own coat and tried the jacket.

"Looks good." I tried to keep my voice enthusiastic, even as I saw the Danites on the sidewalk, waiting. "Why don't you put on the skirt?"

"I do not know. The skirt is long."

"Try it on. I think it would look good."

The saleslady, the only other woman in the store, nodded.

While Llysette was in the fitting room, I walked toward the front of the store and studied the pair outside. Young, short-haired, but bearded, wearing the dark green overcoats, eyes hard with that look common to all too many fanatics.

At the creak of the ancient fitting room door, I turned and stepped back toward the women's section.

Llysette pirouetted in front of the full-length flat mirror. Although the skirt was long, slightly below midcalf, the lines flattered her.

"You look spectacular."

"*Le prix,* that also is spectacular."

"You deserve it."

"I do not know."

"I'll buy it."

She shook her head. "Now . . . should I wish, I can purchase my own clothes."

The outfit took most of our cash, but I had pressed because it was warm and looked good on Llysette and she needed both, particularly with another cold New Bruges winter nearing.

The streets were still damp as we walked back to the Lion Inn, but the air seemed even colder.

After hanging up the green woolen outfit in the closet, Llysette took out the music again and sat on the piano bench.

My stomach growled.

After checking the menu and running it by Llysette, earning a raised eyebrow for interrupting her, I ordered the plainest form of pasta from room service, with the sauce on the side, to be safe about the whole thing.

Nearly forty-five minutes later, Llysette glared at me. "*Le dejuener* . . . it is where?"

"It's supposed to be here." I picked up the wireset and dialed in the number.

"Lion Inn, room service. May we help you?"

"Yes. This is Johan Eschbach. I ordered a dinner nearly an hour ago, and we still haven't seen it. Suite six-oh-three."

"Yes, sir. Just a moment, sir."

I waited.

"He's already left, sir. Let us know if he's not there in five minutes."

"I will."

I turned to Llysette. "It's on the way."

"On the way? And how proceeds it—by airship from Paris?"

"By Brit rail—wide slow gauge."

"Humorous that is not."

A rap on the door saved me from having to make further attempts at humor. The server wore the livery of the hotel and pushed a cart table.

"I'll take it in," I told him.

"But—"

"I'll do it." I smiled.

He backed away.

Llysette watched as I set up the table, then went to the cooler and extracted a bottle of wine and set a glass beside her plate.

She looked at the wineglass, then shook her head. "A half a glass, that is all."

"You can have the rest when you celebrate later." *Unwind,* that would be more like it.

"Then, I will need the wine."

After we ate, Llysette started on her hair.

In the end, I opted for the formal concert dress, black coat and black tie. As the consort to the star, it was better to be overdressed than underdressed.

I still brought the plastic blade, and the calculator and pens, as well as a few other items, such as the dart gun sections in my boot heels.

Llysette warmed up and did her makeup. She didn't put on the performing gown at the inn but wore a plain dress. I carried the garment bag, and we walked the block and a half through the gray gloom to the hall—a good hour before Llysette's curtain time.

Her dressing room was marked—in large red letters—and there were two flower arrangements there.

She read the cards and handed them to me with a smile:

Break a leg, or whatever—Bruce.

Best wishes. Jacob Jensen.

Then I helped her into the gown, and she went back to a few slow warmups. I stood in the corner, slightly away from the waist-high and oversize ventilation grate, half-wondering if that much cooling were necessary in the summer in Great Salt Lake. I shook my head. The big grate covered an air return. The inbound air register was near the ceiling and about one-tenth the size of the big return duct.

I'd seen several of the large grates as we wandered around looking for her dressing room, and I supposed, with the heat from the stage lights, at times there was a need to suck out that hot air quickly.

A knock echoed from Llysette's dressing room door. I walked over and eased it ajar to see who was there.

The brown-bearded Jacob Jensen stood outside, wearing a formal outfit. I was glad I'd worn my own formal dress. Jensen bowed, then extended an envelope to me. "Your tickets, Minister Eschbach."

Strange as it seemed, I hadn't really thought about tickets. For a moment, I just stared.

"The fifteenth row. After I heard your lady . . ." He paused and shook his head. "Her voice is too powerful to sit too close. There are two tickets. That's so you don't have to sit next to anyone if you'd rather not."

"Thank you." Why two and not three? Still, it was Llysette's show, and I wasn't about to upset anything.

"Does she need anything?"

I looked toward Llysette. She shook her head.

"No." I added, "But thank you for the flowers."

"I'm most grateful she's here." Jensen cleared his throat. "If she does need anything, let me know. I'm in the small office at the corner there." With a nod and a smile, he walked briskly toward the back of the stage, behind the rear wall of the stage.

Llysette looked at me, and I got the message. "You're ready to be alone."

That got a nod.

I stepped over to her, hugged her, and whispered, "I love you. You'll be wonderful." Then I left, closing the door behind me.

I hadn't realized just how big the concert hall was until I saw it lit. Llysette hadn't been exaggerating, not much. There had to have been two thousand seats in the three tiers. Even a half hour before the performance, more than half were taken. It was strange to think that more people would hear her in one night in Deseret than had heard her in six years in Columbia. Strange and wondrous and sad all at once.

My seat was beside Jillian Perkins, who wore a maroon dress with a white lace collar. The seat on the far side of her was vacant, and I understood why I'd gotten two tickets, rather than three.

"Good evening," I said as I eased in beside her.

She smiled, an expression pasted on under concerned eyes.

"Worried? They'll do fine."

"Dan . . . he's worked very hard for this."

I understood, I thought. Everyone needed the concert, for very different reasons. Llysette needed it to rehabilitate her career and give her leverage toward more security and tenure . . . and financial independence. Dan Perkins needed it because . . . I suspected he and Jillian required the money for a growing family, and he needed another boost for his career, perhaps because his music wasn't simple singspiel trash or lip-synch monotony, but complex composition based on good verse and possibly better music. The Saint theocracy needed the concert as an opening wedge toward wider relations with Columbia, and Columbia needed Saint oil and energy exports.

Then . . . there had to be others who needed a disruption, like deGaulle, or Ferdinand. I hoped the Danites and the others were up to containing anything along those lines.

Jillian blotted her forehead.

"He's invested a lot in this?"

"Not in the concert, but in the recordings."

"Llysette will sing well."

"He says she is the only one who can do justice to his art songs." She swallowed.

I patted her shoulder, just once. "She says he's the only one that understands the music and the piano enough to let her sing her best." Llysette hadn't actually said it, but I understood that was how she felt. Llysette didn't have to say it, not to me.

Either my words or gesture triggered the slightest frown.

"I wish I could play for her." I laughed ruefully. "But I've got as much musical talent as a frog. It's hard to watch her, to be able to appreciate it, and to add nothing."

"You have done a great deal, Dan says. Weren't you an important government official?"

"It's not quite the same," I protested.

"You love her . . . almost more than time and eternity." Her words were not quite a question.

I nodded.

"That makes it hard. Very hard," she said.

We understood, sitting there as the hall filled, each of us wishing for the best for someone we could do little to help. I'd liked Jillian from the moment I'd seen her—almost like the sister I'd never had, and never would.

The stage remained empty until nearly ten minutes past eight, when the doors to the hall were closed and the lights dimmed. The house wasn't quite filled, but close to it.

My eyes took in the suspended microphones, and I swallowed.

Then two figures stepped forward and bowed. The applause was polite, modest, but certainly not overwhelming.

First there was a light, but florid, aria by Handel—light for Llysette, anyway, *Lusinghe piu care*. After a brief silence, the applause was strong, much stronger. Then came the Mozart, *Exultate Jubilate*.

Llysette's voice intertwined with the notes from the piano yet remained separate, floated yet dropped inside my head, separated me almost from breathing. I wasn't the only one, because when she finished there was a gasp from the entire audience. The applause was thunderous, or close to it.

During the applause, more Saints filed in, filling many of the remaining seats.

Then came the Debussy aria, Lia's air from *L'Enfant du Prodigue,* and there wasn't any doubt about the volume of the applause. A few more listeners straggled in, and I began to wonder about Saint punctuality.

All in all, by intermission I was sweating, and the hall was still slightly chill. Beside me, Jillian was equally damp, and her teeth fretted on the linen handkerchief clutched in her hands. Then I understood. The Perkins pieces were after the intermission.

"They're better," I offered.

"What?" Her eyes weren't really focused.

"Dan's pieces. They're every bit as good as the last Strauss and the Mozart. They could be better. You'll have to see."

She offered a faint smile and went back to worrying the linen.

I tried to listen to the whispers and low voices around us, despite wondering whether I really wanted to know what they were saying.

". . . heard Rysanek once . . . said she was the greatest. Not anymore . . . and I'll bet we haven't heard the best yet. . . ."

"I don't understand. Where did she come from? Why is she here?"

"Don't fret, Jefferson. Just enjoy the music. You won't hear this again, not when the rest of the world finds out."

". . . get tickets for your folks?"

"Never heard Debussy sung like that, and Debussy never did either, poor man."

My guts were tight, and I wished I had something to chew on. I wanted to go backstage, but that was the last thing Llysette needed.

Finally, I stood up, just before my seat, to stretch my legs. I looked at Jillian, but she didn't even glance up.

Then the lights flashed, and people began to file back into the hall, and I sat down.

Jillian fretted with her handkerchief again and twisted in her seat, her eyes downcast.

The first song after intermission was from Puccini's *La Boheme,* in Italian about Paris, and then came a short and humorous Wolf piece, *Mausfallen spruchlein,* before Llysette launched into the three Perkins pieces.

They got another resounding ovation, and she completed the concert with *An die Nacht.*

The last piece wasn't the end, though, not after the audience kept applauding and standing and screaming.

Jillian and I just stood with them. I think we were both numb, in the way that you get when the emotional overload is too great to feel any more.

Finally, the audience sat, and Perkins settled himself at the piano.

The encore had to be partly Carolynne's, although only two of us would have known that as Llysette finished and as the applause and cacophony cascaded around me.

Jillian and I didn't speak. What could we have said that wouldn't have been banal after the performance of our spouses?

Bright lights surrounded Llysette's dressing room, and I had to ease around the crowd, but I wasn't getting very far.

"There's Minister Eschbach!" boomed a voice, and Jacob Jensen and his driver, Heber, pushed aside some of the well-wishers and their bouquets of flowers—just flowers; apparently chocolates weren't *de rigueur* in Deseret—and escorted me behind the videolinkers and their lights, all focused on Llysette.

"Fräulein duBoise, why did you wait so long to return to the stage?"

"For many years I had no country. A person who has no country has few choices. I am happy now in Columbia. I will perform so long as people wish to hear."

"Some people have said your husband was a spy, and that he still might be."

"*Mon cher* . . . he is a very good professor, and he was a war hero, and he is a good man. He is no spy." She offered a wide and sparkling smile, and I thought she had seen me.

"But do you know if he once was a spy?"

Llysette smiled. "You do not like my words, then you should ask Johan. He is there." She gestured toward me.

I had to give one of the young linkers credit. He dodged around Heber and had the videocamera in my face.

"It's said you were a spy. Is it true?"

"I don't think it's any great secret that I once was employed by the Sedition Prevention Service—that was a long time ago. I was also once a military pilot, and a government minister, and my family was killed, and I was wounded for that service." I forced a smile. "But all of that was a long time ago, and I'm a professor of environmental studies married to one of the greatest singers of the age. She's your story. You'll see a lot of retired officials. There's only one of her."

Surprisingly, the young fellow smiled and turned the camera back toward Llysette.

"You've sung in two national capitals in less than a month after years of no public performances. How did this happen?"

"Doktor Perkins. He sent a student to a clinic. There I sang one of his songs. He sent me arrangements." Llysette shrugged. "He is a great composer, and his student led to the concert."

"Is there any message behind your concert, Miss duBoise?"

"Message?" Llysette laughed. "The beauty of the music will last when we are gone."

"How do you like Deseret?"

"Many of the people, they are friendly. I have not seen much. I have prepared for the concert."

"That's enough!" announced a bass voice, and the lights dimmed, and the media scuffled away, slowly.

Blinking in the comparative gloom, I stepped forward and hugged my wife, gently, then kissed her cheek. *"Magnifique!"* I whispered. "And that's understating it."

A few steps away, Dan Perkins was hugging Jillian. Her eyes were wet. After a moment, they stepped toward us.

"There aren't many nights . . . like this." His voice barely carried over the noise of another group that seemed headed toward us and the mutterings of the departing videolinkers.

"Non." Llysette squared her shoulders. "But twice more we must perform."

Perkins nodded, then grinned. "We'd better enjoy it."

"Here they are!" boomed the bass voice again, which I finally attached to a blocky man not much taller than my shoulder who gestured toward an older man at the head of the new group.

"This is the First Counselor, the Most Honorable J. Press Cannon." The bass-voiced man gestured.

First Counselor Cannon had white hair and beard, a cherubic face marred slightly by childhood acne that had never totally healed, and warm bluish-brown eyes. He inclined his head. "You were absolutely superb, Miss duBoise."

His voice was full and concerned, and I distrusted him on sight. He was the kind of man who was always honest, forthright, supportive, and able to use all three traits to his own advantage to be deadlier than most villains.

"I thank you."

"Don't thank me. I'm thanking you for an experience that comes all too infrequently, if ever."

Llysette flushed.

He turned to me. "You have had some experience with the media, I notice."

"Me?" I shook my head.

Cannon laughed. "Minister Eschbach, someday we'll talk." He turned back to Llysette. "Unlike your president, I have heard many singers. I've never heard one like you." He shook his head. "We have been truly doubly blessed with your presence. I will be here tomorrow and Saturday." With a last cherubic smile he nodded, and he and his entourage marched off like some religious band ready for another revival.

Eventually, most drifted away, and Llysette changed back into the simple dress. I eased her performance gown into the bag.

The Danites, and there were four now, escorted us both back to the Lion Inn, right from the dressing room. One carried the half-dozen bouquets that had been pressed upon Llysette.

Outside the concert hall, a dozen people stood in the swirling snowflakes that weren't sticking to the sidewalk or the street.

"Miss duBoise . . . please . . . would you please sign my program?" The girl barely came to my shoulder. "Please?"

I fumbled in my pocket and found a pen, not one of Bruce's set, and extended it to her.

Llysette smiled and asked, "Do you sing?"

"After hearing you . . . I . . . I'm afraid to try."

"So was I once, when I heard Tebaldi. Learn to sing, child."

The girl looked down, then slipped away.

A white-haired woman eased a book toward Llysette—open to a picture of a much younger Llysette duBoise. "I never thought . . . You're better than all of them, and I've heard them all."

"You are kind." I could see the moistness in my diva's eyes as she signed the picture, moistness that glistened in the reflections of the street glow throwers.

When the woman closed the book, I caught the title—*Prima Donnas: Past and Future.*

Llysette signed all fifteen programs, with a kind word and a smile for each. But she was silent, withdrawn deeply into herself, as we walked the last half-block to the Lion Inn and took the elevator up to the suite.

The Danites followed silently, and I wondered why, half-musingly, still in a detached state myself, until we reached our door.

"Miss duBoise? The flowers, ma'am?" asked the Danite who had carried them all the way from the dressing room.

We both looked at the flowers held by the Saint. What could Llysette do with them?

Finally, she took the one bouquet with the pale white roses, barely more than buds, and looked at the young Danite. "Have you a wife?"

He nodded.

"And the others?"

"Some do, Miss duBoise."

Llysette smiled. "I cannot have too many flowers around me. Perhaps you could take them . . . if you would wish . . . for all of you, and for watching out for us."

"Thank you." A momentary smile cracked the pale face under the blond hair.

"We thank you," she said.

After they left, I closed the door and took Llysette's coat, then hung up her gown.

She stood almost where I had left her, in the sitting room area, staring blankly in the general direction of the windows.

"Johan . . . you have not said much."

I shook my head, and my eyes burned again. "What could I say? I've never heard . . . no one had ever heard . . ." I looked into her green eyes, saw the pride and the incredible pain. "I don't have the words. I feel anything I say is so little to describe how you sang." What could I have said that would have been adequate to describe that incredible performance?

"You know."

"I know." And I did.

"Some wine. It might help."

I filled her wineglass, and she took it and nearly drained it in one swallow.

I wanted to tell her to take it easy, but I didn't. Instead, I set the bottle on the table and stood behind her and squeezed her shoulders, sort of an awkward hug, then kissed her neck.

"The critics, they are not the audience." She stood, unsteadily, and walked to the window, looking out at the snow-flurried and misted lights of Great Salt Lake.

Well I knew that. The critics were like David and the dean, unable to do much, but always faulting everyone else. "Even the critics were impressed." *Enough, I hope . . . enough.*

"Never like this . . . and I must sing tomorrow . . . and Saturday."

I understood the pressure more, now. She had conquered, and she had to do it again . . . and again, never letting down, never letting up, and every critic would be wondering, first, if her performances were just a singular occurrence and, then, when she would fail.

"You'll do it." I put my arms around her, gently.

She sobbed softly, and I held her for a time, a long, long time.

CHAPTER TWENTY-THREE

• • •

The next morning, while Llysette was still sleeping, after running through my exercises as quietly as I could, I sneaked down to the lobby and bought copies of both Great Salt Lake City papers, each one in its polished wood stand. No plastic or metal in Deseret, almost a throwback in some ways to the New Bruges of a half-century earlier.

The news stories—if there were any—should have been favorable, but I'd learned a long time ago that critics were a species alien to reason, common sense, or public appeal.

Llysette was still asleep when I got back to the suite, and I eased the bedroom door closed and sat down in the wide-armed and overupholstered chair that almost resembled a padded throne. After opening the *Deseret News,* I turned to the Arts section, holding my breath as I saw a picture of Llysette and Dan Perkins just after taking a bow, Llysette with one bouquet of flowers in her arms. I'd been there, but

I hadn't even seen those flowers. Then I read, slowly, waiting for some bombshell. There wasn't one. Were the Great Salt Lake City critics a species slightly less alien than their Columbian brethren?

> GREAT SALT LAKE CITY. "Magnificent is too weak a word to describe the performance of Llysette duBoise and Daniel Perkins," said Salt Palace concertmeister Jensen. For once, if possible for a man who praises everything, Jensen underpraised the artists he hired for the Cultural Series.
>
> "Never has Deseret heard such a presentation of classic and art songs!" added Grant Johannsen, conductor of the Deseret Symphony. They were both right, even conservative, in their praise.
>
> DuBoise offered depths, shadings, tones, textures in a shimmering and seamless weave of sound that melded perfectly with Perkins's sure touch on the keys. So perfect was the match of keyboard and voice that every number ended with stunned silence—followed by thunderous applause.

My eyes burned as I struggled to the end. It hadn't just been me. Everyone had sensed and felt that impossible energy, that emotional torrent encased in sheer perfected discipline.

The *Star* commentary was of the same timbre, and both ended with the recommendation that would-be listeners sell their dearest possession, if need be, to get one of the few tickets remaining.

Like all critics, the *News* reviewer did have a few nasty digs after the one at Jensen:

> While the concert itself was an unimaginable improvement over past offerings, so much that Jensen will be hard-pressed to repeat such a triumph, even should he live so long as Methuselah, the Salt Palace management still manifests a carelessness of detail in other ways. There were far too few souvenir programs, and the concession areas were grossly understaffed. Likewise the warning bells for the intermission were weak and lost in the hubbub as listeners rhapsodized happily about the music. Fortunately, the warning lights were adequate, if barely.

The *Star* reviewer attacked the parking and the lack of concert-related transport and the lack of programs. I was just glad that everything about the performance itself was glowing.

I took a deep breath.

The bedroom door opened, and Llysette, tousled and beautiful in her robe, stood there. She squinted against the light pouring through the wide window. Then her eyes went to the paper.

"What said they?" She frowned. "*Non.* Do not tell me."

I couldn't help but grin from ear to ear. "No one has ever gotten a review this good. Ever."

"You jest."

"Not about this." I folded back the *News* review, stood, and handed it to her, then went to heat water for the chocolate that was apparently the only warm morning beverage permitted in Deseret. The suite had the powdered kind, but it was better than the alternative, which was nothing at all.

"Non, c'est impossible."

"That's what they wrote. It might even sell a few of those disks your friend Doktor Perkins is having recorded."

"He is having all three nights recorded."

"That's good, but he won't need them—unless it's because of technical problems." All problems were technical in one way or another, as I'd learned in the Spazi.

The wireline chimed.

"Hello," I answered cautiously.

"Minister Eschbach . . . this is Orab on the front desk. Ah . . . we've received a considerable number of flowers. . . ."

"How considerable?"

"Fifteen arrangements, but the florist said there would be more coming."

"Could I wire you back in a moment? I'll need to talk to Fräulein duBoise."

"Yes, sir."

"Now does someone want what?"

I turned to Llysette. "You were a hit. The concierge reports that you have more than a dozen flower arrangements and bouquets downstairs."

"Oh."

"That many flowers. . . ." I paused. "And the florists told him more were coming.

"With so many, I will sneeze and not sing." Her eyes went to the pale white roses, barely opening, that I'd placed in a glass pitcher taken from the minuscule corner that substituted for a kitchen.

I nodded.

"What will I do?"

I shrugged. "Keep the cards or notes. Maybe you could donate the flowers to a hospital or home or something."

"You do what you think best, Johan." She reached for the *Star,* stopping short of the paper.

"It's just as good," I reassured her, picking the handset back up.

"Concierge."

"Orab? This is Minister Eschbach."

"Yes, sir?"

"Fräulein duBoise is overwhelmed at the thought of all those flowers. Unfortunately, she's also somewhat allergic to many of them. She wondered if she could have any cards or notes that went with them, but if we could send the flowers to a hospital—for children or for older people?" I paused. "We'd be happy to pay the florists or the hotel for the transportation. It's just not something we can do personally, and it would be a shame to waste such a lovely gesture."

A brief silence followed. "Why, yes, sir. I'm sure we could arrange that. Would you want to send cards from Miss duBoise?"

"No. Make it anonymous."

Llysette nodded from across the room, her eyes lifting from the *Star* Entertainment section.

I took the liberty of ordering breakfast that was half-lunch from room service, getting another nod as I did.

Llysette read each review several times.

After a meal that was probably too hearty, Llysette decided to immerse herself in hot water. She liked it hot enough almost to boil lobsters. Once she was safely in the tub, I experimented with the videolink set. I did find a noon news program after a half hour or so.

". . . speaking on behalf of the First Presidency, Counselor Cannon was clear about the path Deseret must follow." The screen shifted to the white-bearded Cannon.

"Deseret deplores the Austro-Hungarian action in further militarizing Tenerife, but neither can we condone the seizure of the Cape Verdes by New France. . . ."

I winced. That action hadn't gotten into the papers yet.

"In related news, another squadron of the Columbian navy has been deployed to the Bermuda Naval Station. The Austrian ambassador to Columbia made his protest to Columbian Speaker Hartpence simultaneously with a protest by Ambassador Rommel to British Prime Minister Blair. Schikelgruber's protest came immediately upon his return to the Federal District. Austro-Hungary claims the action violates the Neutrality Treaty of 1980 between Great Britain and Austro-Hungary." The videoscreen showed a Columbian cruiser, accompanied by two frigates, in a blue expanse that could have been any warm-water ocean.

Abruptly the screen shifted to a happy family, five children gathered around a table, with a clean-scrubbed woman serving them and the beaming bearded father.

"For that special family time . . ."

From the family image, the screen shifted to a blue book lying on a white cloth. The gold letters proclaimed *The Book of Mormon, Another Testimony of Jesus Christ.*

"Help your family better understand the eternal truths of the Book of Mormon."

The screen shifted to an oblong box, bearing a stylized figure in a white robe and another set of gold lettering: *The Book of Mormon Family Game.*

"Bring the values of faith into your home in a fun and cheerful game the entire family can play. *The Book of Mormon Family Game.* Sold at LDS Bookstores everywhere. Here's how to bring the Scriptures to life for the whole family."

Another oblong game box appeared on the videoscreen, one with what seemed to be two stylized cobalt roads meeting at a golden intersection.

"The Missionary Game! Exciting and entertaining for Saints of all ages. A fun way to teach your younger children about missionary work. Everyone will catch missionary fever from this entertaining new game for the whole family."

I had to wonder where the Saint missionaries were going. It couldn't be to Europe. Ferdinand and his crew had treated the Saints as badly as the Gypsies and other dissidents. There were some Saints in the western parts of Columbia and in New France and in Oceania and South America. But were they trying to convert New France? Or would the loosening of relations with Deseret mean an influx of Saint missionaries?

Another video cut revealed still one more family, this time with four children, two boys and two girls, all blond, all seated around a table, caught laughing with bowls of popcorn in their hands, and an open blue-covered book on the table. A set of chimes rang, and a cheerful voice proclaimed: "Family . . . more important now than ever."

With that, the video flicked back to the news studio and a bespectacled man in a dark blue suit and a cravat wider than the Mississippi.

"That classical concert at the Salt Palace last night? The one featuring our own Daniel Perkins and Llysette duBoise. Some had questioned, quietly, just how good it was going to be, since Miss duBoise hadn't performed before a large audience in more than five years.

"No one's questioning now. This is the first time in five years a classical performance has generated the level of enthusiasm that approached—no, it almost exceeded that of gospel music in the Cannon Center. Word's gone out, though. The remaining tickets were gone in less than a half hour after the box office opened this morning.

"She can sing, and he can play, and it's just that simple. Of course, it doesn't hurt that she's beautiful. Here . . . take a look."

The image shifted from the announcer to one of Llysette before the interviewers.

"Is there any message behind your concert, Miss duBoise?"

"Message?" Llysette laughed. "The beauty of the music will last when we are gone."

"How do you like Deseret?"

"Many of the people, they are friendly. I have not seen much. I have prepared for the concert."

Llysette's smiling image remained on the screen, frozen, as the commentator added, "For those of you who haven't any idea of how beautiful this music truly is, here's a brief excerpt."

Of course, the excerpt was from Perkins's *Fragments of a Conversation,* but even over the degraded videolink speakers, Llysette sounded gorgeous.

The one news announcer looked to the other. "She seems very gracious."

"She is. After she sang last night, she signed programs and talked to admirers waiting outside in the snow. And if you think all entertainers are elitists, she walked— that's right, walked—back to her hotel. No limousines. If you haven't seen her and Doktor Perkins, beg a ticket if you can. You sure can't buy one now."

"Oh." Llysette's voice was somehow very small.

I turned and flicked off the set, then walked toward her, but she sat in the other armchair before I could give her a hug.

"Are you all right?"

"To get ready for the master class I must."

"That, my lady, didn't exactly answer the question."

She smiled, wistfully, sadly, and with restrained happiness— all at once. "So many I . . . we . . . would have liked to see this, and now it happens in a foreign land. Only you understand, and that is sad."

"Your father?" I asked.

She nodded.

"Your mother?" I didn't ask about the deacon—Carolynne's deacon. I knew.

"She loved me. She did not understand." Llysette stood.

I did hug her—tightly—and for a moment, we clung together. Then she blotted her eyes. "Still I must ready myself for the classes."

"What do you do at these classes?"

"I must listen, and then I must offer instructions. You will see."

She dressed, and I showered and dressed, and we were ready about the same time.

We walked the short distance to the complex, and I held the map in my hand, occasionally noting that the Danites continued to trail us. How were they different from the Spazi? I wasn't sure, only that it felt like we'd been shadowed for half our lives when, in reality, it had been something like two months. Or had it? Weren't we shadowed by government most of our lives, one way or the other?

Outside, the sky was mostly clear, but the wind blew, far more than in New Bruges, but not quite so cold. Llysette still shivered within her coat.

An oval-faced woman was waiting in the lower hall outside the lecture room, neither pacing nor totally composed but worrying her lower lip. A smile of relief crossed her face as she stepped forward. Her long blue skirt nearly swept the floor, but I could see that she wore stylish boots that matched the belt that was mostly covered by the short suit jacket. Her cream blouse was silklike.

"I'm Joanne Axley, professor of voice at Deseret University."

"Llysette duBoise," I said for my diva, "and I'm her husband and escort, Johan Eschbach."

"I'm so glad you could spend the time with us, Doktor duBoise. I've limited this group to graduate students in voice." She smiled apologetically. "Doktor Perkins did prevail on me to let several of his graduate students sit in as well."

"I would be happy to hear all, and offer what I might." Llysette's smile was professional, her voice slightly warmer than cordial.

The procedure was relatively simple. A student got up. Llysette was given a copy of the music and a little time to glance over it. Then the student went over beside the piano and sang one song and then stood and waited for Llysette's comments.

Llysette wasn't at a loss for words, not in teaching.

"Your dipthongs, you are letting them change the pitch."

The blonde young woman nodded.

"When you shift to the second vowel, the pitch changes. Stay on the first vowel. . . . Touch lightly only the second."

That got another nod, but I wondered about the comprehension.

"One more time. . . ."

The blonde cleared her throat gently and then sang.

"*Non!* . . . Like this. . . ."

Llysette sang the same phrase, and even I could sense the difference.

After a time, Llysette gestured toward the next student. The dark-haired girl/woman almost trembled as she stood beside the piano. I could tell that the student's tone was good, better than that of most of the students Llysette had at Vanderbraak State, but there was no life in the song.

Apparently Llysette agreed. "Stop!" My singer shook her head sadly. "What does this verse mean?"

"It's in Italian."

"*Ca,* we know. But what do the words mean? Tell me with your own words . . . what does this mean?"

"Ah . . . Doktor . . . she's singing about how she is sick and everything is hopeless."

"Do you sound hopeless?" asked Llysette with a smile.

The dark-haired student looked confused. In the background, Joanne Axley nodded, and I understood one of the reasons for master classes. After a while students tune out their instructors. When someone famous and important says it . . . then the teacher—sometimes—regains credence.

"You must sing the words *and* the emotions. A voice, it is not a piano. It is not . . . a drum."

The next student had trouble with something that Llysette called "the anticipation of the consonant."

"The body . . . it knows the next sound is the consonant, and it desires to sing that consonant. That closes off the vowel. You must stay on the vowel longer. . . ."

The comments continued with each student.

"You squeeze your breath too much here. . . ."

"A nice touch there . . . delicate, and that it should be. . . ."

"Do you know the style? How must one sing this style . . ."

"Your neck, it is tight like a wire cable, and you have no breath on the long phrases. . . ."

What got me was that these were *good* students. I almost shuddered at what Llysette—or most voice teachers—had to go through with the others.

She motioned to one of the young men, dark-haired. "You, have you a song?"

"Ah . . . yes, Doktor."

"Then sing it for me."

She nodded as he launched into some aria I didn't recognize, but, then, I wouldn't have recognized most of them.

The "one-hour" master class lasted more than an hour and a half before Llysette heard the last song from the last male graduate student and Joanne Axley walked with us to the door of the lecture room.

"You've been very gracious . . . and very helpful." Joanne Axley's smile was warmer than the one she had offered when Llysette had arrived. Another case of Jensen—or someone—leaning hard and people being surprised after the fact?

"I would try," Llysette said. "You have taught them well."

"Thank you. I try."

"They do not always listen," Llysette added dryly. "That I know."

"You made quite an impression." Axley smiled brightly. "Gerald and I will be at your recital tonight. We're looking forward to it."

"Thank you."

We stepped into the hall, and Axley turned back to the group, perhaps for some summary comments.

"She's nice, but a little on edge." I was trying to be diplomatic.

"That I understand. She is a singer. She has worked hard. She has told her students much of what I tell them. More than that, I do not doubt. They do not listen *toujours*. I come, and they listen." Llysette shook her head slowly. "The students, they are so stupid at times."

"They are, and you need to eat," I said as we walked up the carpeted stairs to the main level.

"I must rest, and I worry about the second piece of Doktor Perkins. Last night . . . I was not my best."

For a singer, I'd decided, or for Llysette, nothing short of perfection was acceptable, even when a performance was close to fantastic.

So we walked back to the Lion Inn and the performing suite, where she sat at the Haaren with the music while I ordered a lunch/dinner from room service.

I did manage to drag her from the piano when the cart table was wheeled in, partly by starting to pour some wine.

"Half a glass. That is all."

That was all she got. I took a full glass—just one.

Llysette went through several mouthfuls of pasta before she paused.

"That class took a lot out of you? Why did you agree to it?"

"The opportunity . . . the performance. . . ." She sipped the half-glass of wine she had allowed herself.

I understood that part. It had been presented as a package deal. "But did you have to work so hard?"

"How could I not? When I was their age, no one would listen to me, not someone . . . like I am now."

"You?"

"Then, in France, in the provinces . . . every girl would be a diva. My parents could not afford the best in teachers, and I learned the piano too late." She paused and took a mouthful of pasta.

"At what, age twelve?"

"Twelve," she affirmed. "Eight, it would have been better. So you see, that is why I must teach—"

"And why you get irritated with students who aren't serious."

"*Mais oui.* . . . They waste my time, and that time I could give to others."

Others like little Llysette duBoise had been dying for a chance. I just swallowed and took a small sip of wine.

Between one thing and another, we got backstage at the concert hall forty-five minutes before curtain time.

Dan Perkins met us with a smile as we went backstage. "Joanne wired me," he said. "She was pleasantly surprised at your master class. Very pleasantly surprised."

"She should not be surprised," said Llysette.

"I told her that." His smile widened to a boyish grin. "And I told her that I'd told her earlier that I'd be telling her just that."

That got me smiling, and Llysette as well.

"James B. Bird, one of my students, wired me to tell me you were outstanding."

"Your students were better," Llysette said.

"Don't tell Joanne that." He glanced toward the stage. "I need to warm up."

"Then you should."

He bowed and departed.

Once Llysette was settled in her dressing room and once that look crossed her face, I kissed her and eased myself out. From somewhere, I could hear the sounds of a piano—Doktor Perkins warming up.

After hearing Llysette from the audience the first night, I decided to view the proceedings from backstage the second night, although I couldn't quite have said why. A feeling, more or less. I hoped Herr, or Brother, Jensen wouldn't be too displeased.

I found a stool, which I appropriated, and stationed myself in the wings on the left side of the performing area, on the left looking at the audience.

Of course, I couldn't stay on it and found myself pacing in tight circles behind the angled partitions that provided slit views of the performing area.

Brother Jensen paused as he walked past. "Just stay behind the tape that marks the sight lines, Minister Eschbach."

I glanced down. The stool was a good ten feet in back of the red tape on the stage. "I think we're well clear."

He nodded, then walked on to continue his survey of the backstage area. About that time, I heard the murmurs and rustles that signified that they'd opened the house to the audience.

In time, the five-minute lights blinked, and then the chimes warbled. But the murmurs continued from the hall as more Saints filed in—late—and it was nearly fifteen minutes later before Llysette came out from the corridor from the dressing rooms, accompanied by Dan Perkins. I smiled as they neared and got a warm but puzzled smile in return. "You are here?"

"I thought I'd watch from here. Less company." I grinned. "Your admiring public is waiting."

"Jillian didn't come tonight," said Perkins. "She said it was too nerve-racking, with all the crowds. It's easier to perform than watch." He offered that boyish grin. "For me, anyway."

"I don't know. I can't perform." I reached out and squeezed Llysette's hand.

As they stepped toward the stage, I had to wonder why they'd both gotten tied up with people who weren't thrilled with crowds. Then, my experience with the Spazi and in politics had inevitably led me to the conclusion that crowds tended to bring out the worst in people.

Llysette and Perkins stepped into the light, and the applause built and slowly died away. They waited until the hall was perfectly still before his fingers drew the first notes of the Handel from the big Steinbach.

I turned to my left, where a stagehand had eased up slightly more than a dozen feet away, partly shielded by one of the side partitions, apparently to watch the concert. He wore, like most of them, dark trousers and shirt and the ubiquitous leather equipment belt.

Llysette's voice rose with and over the Steinbach, but I couldn't concentrate on her singing.

The stagehand was dark-haired, and he watched Llysette intently. Too intently. Even with my poor sense of rhythm I could tell he wasn't following the music.

He eased forward, still well out of sight of the audience.

My fingers felt like thumbs as I got out the calculator and fumbled the pen and pencil into the rubber-screened holes, even while I slipped from my stool and edged toward the blackshirted figure, slow step by slow step.

Llysette's voice glided across the Handel and toward the end.

With the applause, the dark-haired stagehand took another step toward the stage, his hand straying toward the shirt that was too loose, Deseret or not.

With the glint of metal and the thundering applause, I jammed the calculator's delete key.

The thump of his body and the dull clunk of the dropped revolver were lost in the applause, for which I was thankful. Bruce's disassociator beam was so tight I didn't even feel that shuddery twisting. I hoped Llysette didn't either, but I hadn't had much choice.

The calculator went into my jacket pocket after I reached the unconscious figure and bent down. I shook my head—another zombie.

A dark-suited figure appeared beside me, one with that air that signified professionalism. His fingers checked the prone stagehand. "Neatly done, Doktor," he said in a low voice. "I didn't think you'd reach him in time. He'll have quite a headache, I imagine."

"Who are you?" I asked, keeping my voice low but straightening and stepping back. Who knew who else might be around?

"Danite Johnson. First Counselor Cannon asked us to keep a watch on the performances. This one slipped by." His eyes continued to survey the backstage area.

Two more Danites appeared and quietly carted the intruder off.

Llysette went to the Mozart, apparently undisturbed—and that got another powerful ovation. So did the Debussy.

After the first half, I slipped out of sight, back along the rear wall, still watching Llysette's dressing room, but placed so it would be hard for her to see me. I didn't want to interrupt her concentration or to let her see me too closely. She'd know that I was upset. One of the uniformed guards remained by her door from the entire time she entered until she headed back toward the stage with Dan Perkins.

The audience got more and more enthused with each song in the second part of the program, and it wasn't clear if the ovations after the encore would ever end.

I hugged Llysette once she cleared the stage. "You were wonderful." And I meant it.

"I wasn't sure how it could be better than last night," added Perkins, "but she was. We've got some incredible recordings, if they didn't have technical problems."

That was about as far we got at that moment, because people began appearing from everywhere. There were more admirers and a lot more guards, both those in serge blue uniforms and Danites. And I could see the hidden and portable scanners. While I admired the efficiency, I got an even colder feeling, because it was clear someone had let the presumed Austro-Hungarian agent in. Then, he could have been one of deGaulle's as well. Either way, his presence had been permitted, and that meant Deseret was no different from Columbia or anywhere else.

When the last admirers finally left and Llysette was beginning to sniffle amid another pile of flowers, I looked at her.

Should I tell her? If someone else did, that would upset her even more. I took a deep breath.

"You had another fan backstage," I finally said.

"A fan?"

"I think he was invited by your former friend Ferdinand. He's now getting a rest cure, courtesy of the Saints."

Llysette's eyes widened. "Backstage you were. . . . Was that why?"

"Just a feeling," I admitted. "I didn't think anyone would try something opening night. People let down their guards after opening night. So. . . ." I shrugged.

"There was a coldness after the Handel, but I sang."

Brother Jensen, nearing with a pair of Danites, frowned at her words.

"I tried to be quiet, and I hoped it wouldn't upset you."

"What drew you to the intruder?" asked Brother Jensen.

"He just didn't feel right." What I didn't want to say was that, for some reason, the Saint security had let him into the backstage area. Were they watching me? If so, I'd fallen for the trap, and that meant trouble . . . but how could I have risked letting Llysette get shot?

Someone clearly knew that, as well, and that left me feeling even more helpless.

"Tonight, you must take the steamer," Jensen insisted.

Neither of us was about to argue and after Llysette changed, we followed him down a long ramp, flanked by Danites, two of them carrying more of the flowers. With Llysette's garment bag over my shoulder and my fingers concealed by it, I checked the hidden belt knife, then the calculator components.

We needed neither. A shimmering Browning—brown, of course—waited below with Heber at the wheel.

We sat back in the dark leather seats of the Browning as it crept from the garage underneath the performing complex up a concrete ramp and around two corners and onto the street, going around the block to bring us in under the canopy of the Lion Inn.

"It is sad. One concert, and now I can no longer walk a few meters."

It was more than sad. I nodded.

CHAPTER TWENTY-FOUR

• • •

I t was awake well before eight, and I finally eased out of bed before nine, leaving Llysette to get the sleep she needed. My back was stiff from trying to be quiet and still when I was wide eyed. I never could sleep as late as Llysette, but I wasn't under the same kind of strain that she was, nor was I undertaking the more strenuous kind of workout that a full recital or concert happened to be.

After closing the bedroom door, I did struggle my way through my exercises again—twice. They weren't a substitute for the running up the hill and through the woods, but the mild workout helped both body and mind. I wasn't about to go running off, literally or figuratively, not while she was sleeping or after the various attempts on either or both of us.

I did go downstairs and retrieve the papers, but no stories appeared in either daily, even concealed, about the assault by the phony stagehand or about Llysette. Most of the news that wasn't local was focused on the Atlantic naval buildups and the increasing tension between the Austrians and New France and Columbia, although Ambassador Schikelgruber had met with Minister Holmbek to assure him that Austro-Hungary had no intention of beginning a naval war in the Atlantic.

"Just like Ferdinand had no intention of annexing France or the Low Countries . . . ," I murmured to myself.

I had two cups of the powdered hot chocolate while I studied the papers, even the advertising, but there wasn't even a hint in the police reports about the attack on Llysette. Should I have been grateful? I wasn't sure.

Then I read through the cards that had come with the flowers. A few were recognizable, one way or another, like the formal card from Walter Klein, the Columbian ambassador. He was one of President Armstrong's few political cronies who had actually gotten rewarded. I might have met him once or twice. There was one from Hartson James, the TransMedia mogul, who definitely saw something in Llysette. I just hoped his interest was purely commercial. The rest were from people, presumably Saints, whose names were unfamiliar.

Finally, I flicked on the videolink, keeping the volume down, and sampled the five channels, trying to avoid the endless family-centered commercials and to find something resembling either news or a cultural program.

Llysette kept sleeping and I kept switching channels. After probably another hour, I picked up the wireset to order a brunch for us—Llysette needed to get up before long and eat.

As I did, I thought I saw a video image of the Salt Palace, and I put down the wireset and eased the video volume back up.

". . . Columbian soprano Llysette duBoise, in the midst of an acclaimed series of performances at the Salt Palace, has shown a side that most women in Deseret would find closer to their hearts than navigating the treacherous slopes to a high C. DuBoise was apparently inundated with flowers from admirers. While she has kept the cards, she sent all but a single bouquet to those in hospitals and homes."

The video showed the same clip of a flushed Llysette taking a bow with Perkins and then one of the interview clips with Llysette speaking.

"The beauty of the music will last when we are gone. . . . Many of the people, they are friendly."

The video went back to a group of three around a low table in a studio setting designed to resemble a sitting room. A blond man sat with a redheaded woman on his right and a brunette on his left.

"She sounds like a woman who has her heart in the right place," commented the redhead.

"She probably does," answered the man. "What's more interesting is that she insisted on paying for the transportation of the flowers and that the donations of the flowers be anonymous."

"Does she have any children?" asked the brunette.

"No . . . her marriage to Minister Eschbach is her first, and they've been married only about a year." The blond announcer paused. "For those of you who only know that she's a high-paid diva and sings beautifully, you might also be interested to know that she spent several years in an Austrian prison. Reportedly she was tortured before she was released."

"So . . . you're saying, Daniel, that this is one singer who isn't just an image and a pretty face?"

"Does it sound that way?" asked the smiling blond man.

"No. She sounds like quite a lady. Have you heard her?"

"Last night. She and Perkins are wonderful. You're going tonight?"

"I already was, but after hearing all this, I really wouldn't miss it."

"You won't regret it. Now . . . we'll be right back with a heartwarming story on the Heber City playground."

With that, the video cut to another smiling Saint family and a sickeningly perky jingle. I switched stations, then turned the videolink off.

The story on Llysette was planted, so firmly I could smell the odor of manure seeping from the silent video set. I hadn't checked the station, but I would have bet that it was the one owned by First Counselor Cannon.

The story was pitched to women, in a sickening way, and even cleverly suggested that Llysette was both to be admired and pitied—admired because of her pluck and talent and pitied because of her childlessness.

I almost wanted to retch. How many other stories were out there—ones I hadn't seen? And why? Was this a crash effort in humanizing the former enemies? Or something else?

The silence about the intruder was deafening. No one had wired, and there was nothing on the videolink news or in either paper.

I felt isolated.

The bedroom door opened, and Llysette stepped out, eyes squinting even in the indirect light of the cloudy late morning.

"Johan . . . how you can chirp like the bird so early, that I do not know."

"Heredity. You should see my Aunt Anna."

"*Toute la famille?*"

"Not all. My father was more like you." I glanced toward the window. "I was about to order something to eat."

"Another meal in this room . . . *non* . . . that will not do."

"That's fine. Do you want me to wire Jensen and find another restaurant?"

"*Non* . . . the bird in the cage will I be." She sighed. "But the cage downstairs, *du moins*. I will not be long."

Her definition of *long* was another comparative I let go, especially since I also needed to shower and to get dressed. First, I did fix Llysette a cup of chocolate, before I climbed into the shower. The hot water felt good, and despite the chocolate I'd had, my stomach was growling by the time we stepped into the elevator.

The lobby was more crowded, but no one gave us more than a passing glance, and a tall blond waiter escorted us to a corner booth in the Refuge—not the same one we'd had before, but a corner booth that was relatively isolated, and I got hot and steaming nonpowdered chocolate, which I sipped most gratefully.

The family at the long table nearest our corner of the Refuge kept looking at us. I tried to concentrate on whatever a Deseret skillet was—a concoction of red potatoes, various peppers, eggs, and slabs of ham all served in a miniature cast-iron skillet set on a wooden holder or plate.

"That's her . . . know it is . . . saw her on the link."

"Must be her bodyguard with her. . . ."

I winced at that.

"Her husband . . . say he was a spy once."

". . . looks pleasant enough."

I felt like glaring but didn't.

"Do you expect a spy to look like a Lamanite, Ellie?"

"A spy you do not look like." Llysette's eyes twinkled, and she raised her water glass. "Even when you are spying."

I decided to eat more and eavesdrop less.

The Saturday afternoon master class was nearly a repeat of the Friday one, except the students were more nervous and Joanne Axley gave Llysette a more glowing introduction.

Afterward, several of them clustered around.

". . . will you be back to give more recitals here?"

"I must be asked," said Llysette politely. "The arrangements are made years before, at times. This was not planned."

I'd almost forgotten that.

"You were so good. . . ."

Llysette nodded toward Joanne Axley, who stood talking to a redheaded young man. "Your professor, she is very wise. You are fortunate."

The slightest frown crossed the student's forehead.

"So easy it is," Llysette continued, an edge to her voice, "to forget. Do you know of Madame Rocza?"

"Ah . . . no, Miss duBoise. Is she a singer?"

Llysette shook her head. "She taught many of the best when they were young. Now . . . some, they scarcely know her. Do not do that." She smiled politely.

"Ah . . . thank you."

"You are welcome."

Joanne Axley slipped over toward Llysette as the conference room emptied. "I overheard your words to Bronwin," she said to Llysette with a small laugh. "I appreciate the thought, but I don't know if she'll listen."

"The students, they are dense."

I could vouch for that.

"Weren't we all?" asked Axley.

Somehow I doubted that either of them had been. I had been, and I knew it, and I'd had to learn far too much the hard way. My only grace in that department was that I knew I'd been dense and spoiled—and fortunate enough to survive both.

After the master class, we walked eastward, through the light and chilly gusting breeze. I glanced ahead toward a large building taking up an entire block. "Zion Mercantile" was spelled out in shimmering bronze letters.

"Shall we?" I asked.

"Mais out."

The first stop was the dress section.

Llysette frowned at the long-sleeved, almost dowdy, dress on the mannequin, then went to the next one—equally conservative, with another ankle-length skirt. Her eyes went to the shoppers.

A tall, graying redhead passed us, her camel overcoat open to show a high-necked cream silk blouse and dark woolen trousers. With her was a younger woman, also a redhead. After them came a stocky blonde, with a wide, if pretty, face and sparkling blue eyes. Each hand grasped a child's hand—both blond and blue-eyed like their mother—and neither boy was over five or six. The mother wore a blue turtlenecked blouse, also of silk, and a skirt that reached nearly to her ankles. Under the skirt I could see blue leather boots. All three women had their hair in French braids. In fact, most of the women in Deseret had long, braided hair, I realized.

Silk blouses? They didn't look synthetic, unless the Saints' synthetic fibres were far better than those of Columbia. Then, the Saints had developed a silk industry early in south Deseret.

I followed Llysette into the coat department, where a well-dressed and gray-haired woman stood with three girls who looked to be of secondary school age. All four had their hair braided, and the girls tried on coats.

Llysette picked up several coats, among them a dark green woolen one.

"That looks nice."

"At least, you do not tell me when I sing that it is nice."

I winced. Llysette hated the word *nice,* but I didn't always remember.

She handed me her coat and tried on the green, then walked over to the flat

mirror on the wall before shaking her head. I handed her back her coat and returned the green one to the rack.

The next stop was lingerie, and I tried not to frown at the filmy garments in
every shade of the rainbow. While the coats and dresses had been solid and conservative, not even the theatre district of Philadelphia showed undergarments like
some of the Zion Mercantile offerings.

Llysette saw my face, clearly, and a wide smile crossed her lips as she lifted a
black lace teddy from a rack. "This one . . . you would like?"

I could feel myself flushing.

"*Oui*. . . ."

I had to grin.

"About some things, Johan, Dutch you are still."

She was probably right about that, too, and I wasn't sure whether I was relieved or disappointed that she didn't buy any of the lingerie. Nor anything else except a small jar of a body cream. All in all, we spent nearly an hour roaming
through the store, and I spent as much time thinking as looking.

The store bothered me, and I wasn't sure why, exactly. There hadn't been
more than a handful of men anywhere, and the women in the store were well
dressed and well groomed, and a number of them were smiling. Not exactly what
I would have expected in a rigid theocracy.

"Johan?"

"Oh . . . sorry. I was just thinking."

"We can go. I have found nothing that I could not do without *absoluement*."

As we walked slowly back to the Lion Inn, toward a sun low in the sky, with
the wind ruffling my hair, I watched the people even more closely. A woman with
braided blonde hair coiled into a knot at the back of her neck walked with an older
white-haired and bearded man. Neither looked at the other. She wore a long camel
coat, as did he. Two women in short wool jackets and ankle-length skirts shep-
herded six children, all fresh-faced and scrubbed, in the direction of the Temple
park. A young man, clean-shaven, strode briskly past us.

"Downstairs or upstairs?" I asked when he stepped into the inn's lobby.

Llysette shrugged.

"Are you hungry? Pasta? Soup?"

"To finish the concerts, that is what I wish." She marched toward the elevator.

I followed but said nothing until the couple with the three children exited at
the fourth floor. "Are you angry with me?"

"*Mais non* . . . I am angry with this place."

"It is different. It—"

"Did you not see?"

"What? That there weren't any women by themselves, unless they had children?"

"You did see," she answered with that tone that indicated that what she meant was perfectly obvious.

With a slight *cling,* the elevator stopped at the sixth floor.

"You're angry that the only place you're getting a chance to sing is one where women are treated this way." I paused, then decided against pointing out that the women I'd seen hadn't seemed depressed or oppressed. It could have been that I wasn't seeing those women.

"I cannot sing in France. It is no more. I cannot sing in Columbia, except to make . . . someone look good." She left the elevator with a shake of her head. "These things . . . I must wait. Tonight, I will sing."

"Did I do something?" What had I missed?

"It is not you."

I wondered, but she did smile, and I opened the door. A large stack of cards lay on the small side table under the mirror—more, I supposed, from flowers sent to Llysette.

With my diva's touchiness, I tried to remain in the background, guessing at the pasta she wanted for dinner and making the arrangements, fielding Jensen's wire-call to notify Llysette that a limousine would be waiting to avoid problems.

The Browning limousine, with Heber at the wheel, was waiting, and we rode silently the long block to the underground entrance.

"Thank you." I opened the door for Llysette one-handed, her gown in the bag I carried in the other.

"You're welcome," answered the driver.

We followed another functionary in a green coat up the ramps.

"How do you feel?"

Llysette didn't answer, and I didn't press. Once she wanted me out of her dressing room, I went to find Jensen. He wasn't in the corner office, but I tracked him to a lower level where he was talking to three men in gray jumpsuits carrying tools and wearing equipment belts.

When he saw me, he turned and hurried over.

"No matter how you plan, some technical thing always goes wrong in a concert hall." He laughed. "What can I do for you, Minister Eschbach?"

"I wondered if anyone has found out anything about the man who tried to attack Llysette last night."

"No. We haven't heard anything much. One of the . . . security types . . . said something about his being zombied." He shrugged. "I just don't know." After a pause, he added, "We've put on another fifty guards, half in plainclothes, and the city police have doubled their patrols in the area around the complex."

"Is there any other reason to worry?" I asked pleasantly. "Besides last night?"

"Not that I know of." He glanced back toward the workmen.

"I won't keep you."

I decided to remain backstage, but I positioned my stool a little differently—where I could watch the approach area to Llysette's dressing room, and the stage. That meant I would see Llysette performing from the side and behind.

Despite the dimming lights and the chimes, the concert was even later in starting than the previous two nights. Saints seemed to have this proclivity to be somewhat tardy. I had peeked earlier, and the hall was going to be standing room only. It made me wish that Llysette were getting a percentage of the tickets, because someone was going to make quite a stash.

With the lights down, the notes rose from the Steinbach, and Llysette's, and Carolynne's, voice shimmered out of the light and into the darkened space. I could almost imagine the notes lighting the darkness.

The Handel was good, the Mozart better, and the Debussy extraordinary.

Again, I kept out of the way at intermission.

The second half was every bit as good as, if not better than, the night before. Llysette's voice seemed at times to rip my heart from my chest and at others to coax tears from me—or from a statue.

If I'd thought the applause the previous two nights had been thunderous, I'd been mistaken. The stolid Saints stood and clapped and clapped and clapped, and clapped some more.

Llysette and Dan Perkins finally capitulated and did a second encore—another Perkins song, simpler, but it didn't matter to the crowd. They stood and cheered and clapped, and they kept doing it.

Llysette deserved it—more than deserved it—both for what she'd endured to get there and for the sheer artistry of what she had delivered.

I met her at the back of the stage. "You were wonderful. More wonderful than before."

"My head, you will turn, but you love me."

"You were wonderful," added Dan Perkins. "And I'm not married to you."

At that she did flush, and the blush hadn't quite cleared when the admirers began to appear.

After several anonymous well-wishers, a familiar face appeared.

"You were wonderful." Joanne Axley smiled at Llysette, then turned to Dan Perkins. "You were right."

"Magnificent," added the short man with the Deseret University voice professor.

"I wish more of my students could have heard you," added Axley.

"They should listen to you," said Llysette. "I told them all those things which you—"

"Thank you." Joanne Axley and her husband slipped away.

Was she upset? I wasn't certain. I just stood back of Llysette's shoulder and surveyed the small crowd lining up to say a few words to either Perkins or Llysette.

"I'm sorry about Joanne," Perkins said quietly.

"I would be upset, were I her," answered Llysette quietly. "She has sung here?"

"A number of times, but she's never moved people the way you did."

"That is sad."

A heavyset woman with white hair stepped up. "You remind me of that Norwegian. You were wonderful. Are you any relation?"

"Thank you. I do not think so. All my family, they come from France."

"Magnifique, mademoiselle, magnifique!" That was the thin man with a trimmed mustache. "Claude Ruelle, the former French ambassador here in Deseret. After the Fall . . . I stayed. You, you have brought back all that vanished." With a few more words along those lines, and a sad smile, he was gone.

Counselor Cannon appeared at the very end of the line of well-wishers, and he bowed to Llysette. "You have sung magnificently, and your warmth and charitable nature will do much for all of us. Thank you." The voice and eyes were warm, but I still didn't trust him.

Beside him were two other men I hadn't met before. The dark-haired one bowed to Llysette, marginally. "You were outstanding." The other nodded.

"Thank you."

"Might we have a word with you, Minister Eschbach?" asked Cannon.

"Ah . . . of course."

Llysette raised an eyebrow. "I will be changing."

"I'm sure I won't be long."

She slipped toward the dressing room, not quite in step with Dan Perkins, and I watched for a moment.

"Minister Eschbach?"

"Oh, I'm sorry. You were saying?"

"She is truly amazing," said the First Counselor. "You must be very proud of her."

The idea behind Cannon's words nagged at me. Was all of Deseret like that? Llysette was amazing and I certainly respected and admired her and loved her, but it really wasn't my place to be proud. Her parents should have been proud, but I hadn't done anything to create her talents or determination or to give her the will to succeed.

"Minister Eschbach . . . now that your wife's concerts are completed . . . we had hoped that you would be willing to tour the prototype of the Great Salt Lake City wastewater tertiary treatment plant," suggested the heavier-set man beside Counselor Cannon. "That way, you could report to Minister Reilly on our progress in water reuse and the continued progress on meeting the goals of the riverine agreements."

Wastewater treatment? Minister Reilly might like that, but did I really care? "What did you have in mind?"

"Perhaps early tomorrow. We understand that you will not be leaving until Wednesday."

"That might be possible."

"We had also hoped," suggested the thinner, unnamed man, "that you might be free to see the water reuse section of the new stage-three synthfuels plant near Colorado Junction."

What half of the Columbian government wouldn't give for me to see that. "I hadn't even considered that possibility."

"We would be honored," added Counselor Cannon.

At that instant, I heard—or felt or sensed—something chill and menacing. A faint scream? A cold feeling gripped me. "Excuse me."

"Minister Eschbach . . . but . . ."

I pushed past the wastewater man, sprinting forward and right into Llysette's dressing room. I also ran into something else, barely getting an arm up in time, and that was enough to send me reeling back into the door.

I staggered up, but the dark-shadowed figure literally disappeared.

My head throbbed, and Llysette's dressing room was empty. Her gown lay on the floor, and her dress was gone. So was she. A few drops of blood led toward or away from the corner of the room.

I stood there fuzzily for a moment. No one had gone past me. Then I saw the air return grate, unattached and leaning against the wall. A man-sized section of the metal on the left side of the air grate ductwork beyond and behind where the grate cover had been cut out.

I didn't bother to wait for whoever it was who charged into the dressing room behind me but scrambled through the grate aperture and then through the opening in the air return duct and into a room filled with pallets of paper products or something. I almost tripped but half-ran, half-tumbled out that door into a back corridor—just in time to see two black figures sprinting down a ramp.

I sprinted after them, but by the time I got to the lower garage, a steam van had hissed up the ramp and vanished into the darkness.

A pair of Danites and a uniformed policeman pounded up behind me.

"They're gone." I wanted to shake my head, but it might have fallen off if I had. I touched my forehead, and my hand came away bloody.

I followed them back to a small conference room in the center, where Brother Hansen and two other blue-uniformed officers waited. I didn't wait to be asked but dropped into one of the chairs. I just looked at Hansen. "I couldn't catch them."

"This was on her dressing table." A grim-faced Brother Hansen handed me an envelope. It had been opened, and that bothered me in a way.

I looked at it. In block letters that could have come from any of a dozen difference-engine printers was inscribed: "MINISTER ESCHBACH."

The message inside was short—very short.

You will be contacted. Be ready. We do not want your wife.

I had a good idea what they wanted, and someone knew me well enough to understand that I was far more vulnerable through Llysette.

"What has anyone discovered?" I asked tiredly.

"Brother Jensen was surprised, bound, and gagged," said Hansen coldly. "His keys were taken, with all the master keys." Hansen seemed to have taken over the investigation, and the uniformed officers looked at him as he talked. "The steamer the kidnappers took was a common blue 1990 Browning, and the tags were covered. There are more than ten thousand blue 1990 Browning in Deseret. They wore gloves, it seems, and the security system was disabled on a lower garage door. Bypassed, actually. They wore standard staff working uniforms, and we think they wore flesh masks as well."

"In short," I said, "they left no traces at all. What about the tools?"

"They were all taken from the cribs on the lower levels. That was why they made the attempt tonight. They probably had all afternoon to get organized."

"No working on Saturday afternoons?"

"Right. When did you last talk to Brother Jensen?"

"Before the concert, I talked to him briefly, but he had some problems. Maintenance problems, I gathered, because he was briefing or listening to several workmen."

"Do you have any idea what they want from you?"

That was the question I'd been dreading, in a way. I took a deep breath. "It could be anything. Something about government in Columbia, information about . . . people I've worked with." I shook my head. "Most of that I'd think they could get from other sources. I've been out of government long enough that things have certainly changed. And why they'd kidnap Llysette I don't know."

"There are some indications that they settled for her," Hansen said. "You can't think of anything else?"

I could think of plenty. "Let me think about it. There's probably something, but my wife's been taken, and I'm not thinking too clearly." That part was definitely true. It's different when matters are personal. I'd found that out with the Nord incident and with vanBecton's games last year.

I stood. "So far as I can figure out, I'm not going to be contacted here, and I don't know what else I can add." My eyes went to Hansen. "How do I reach you?"

He extended a card. I read it—"James V. Hansen, Bishop for Security," and a wireset number. "I think we should meet tomorrow, Minister Eschbach. Perhaps around eleven tomorrow."

"Where?"

"We could come to your suite. That might be easier."

"Fine. Eleven. Unless you find out something sooner."

"I'll have Officer Young escort you back to your room."

I nodded and heaved myself to my feet. *Fine operative you are, Eschbach. You can't even protect your own wife when you knew there was trouble.*

Dan Perkins stood outside the conference room. He'd been waiting. "No one told me, and it took a while to find someone who knew." He swallowed. "Minister

Eschbach . . . I'm sorry. If I had known . . . this would happen . . . They wanted the concert . . . so badly. I just don't see." He shook his head.

"It wasn't your doing." I shook my head.

"I told them she was the best in Columbia."

"She is. But that's not exactly your fault."

"I don't know about that." He paused again. "Can I do anything?"

Somehow, I didn't think so. I had the feeling that he was probably the only honest one in the bunch, and there was no sense in getting him tangled up. "Just make sure you put together the best recording that you can."

He looked puzzled.

"I *think* Llysette will be all right. One way or another, though, the singing was important, almost everything at times, and she'll want the recording." I was trying to be positive, hoping that the kidnappers would keep Llysette alive long enough for me to ensure that she'd remain so. The fact that it was a kidnapping, rather than another assassination, gave me some hope.

"I understand." He worried his lower lip. "Are you sure there's nothing I can do?"

Something he'd said earlier . . . I frowned. "You said *they* had wanted the concert so badly."

"When Brother Jensen found out that Dame Brighton was unavailable—she'd agreed, less willingly than Llysette, to sing two of my songs—he wired me. I wasn't going to be the accompanist for Dame Brightman, you see. She has her own, some fellow named . . . I don't recall. Jensen wanted to know who the best singer in Columbia was that he could get who could also sing at least a couple of my songs. I thought of Llysette, because of James Bird."

I waited. The name was familiar, but I didn't recall why.

"He attended one of her master classes in New Bruges last year. James has a good ear, and he was impressed. I knew her by reputation, and she'd written asking for one of my arrangements. So I told Jensen all that. He asked if I would play for her." Perkins shrugged. "When he mentioned the fee, I couldn't say no, but I did push for the recording rights for us."

"Us?"

"It was in the contract. Llysette and I split them fifty-fifty. He agreed without even a murmur, and that was unusual. Then I didn't hear anything for a few weeks. He wired and sent a contract, with the notation that I'd definitely understated her ability and that the First Counselor would surely be pleased with the concert."

"I take it that such effusiveness isn't exactly normal in their past dealings with you?"

A wry smile crossed the composer's face, and I got the picture. Daniel Perkins wasn't exactly *persona grata* with the hierarchy in Deseret, but he was just well enough known that they'd had to tolerate him.

"Your songs are well received elsewhere," I pointed out. "And your operas."

"Elsewhere—that's true."

More pieces fell into place—or more confirmation of what I'd already suspected.

"I'd even bet that you haven't had much trouble lining up international distribution for the recordings."

That brought another wintry smile. "I see you understand."

"I'm getting there."

"I shouldn't be keeping you." He shook his head. "I'm sorry. But if there's anything Jillian or I can do." He handed me a card. "Anything."

"Hold good thoughts." *Very good thoughts.*

It had clearly been an inside job. Why had Llysette been given that particular dressing room? Jensen? Hansen? Cannon? Someone from the Revealed Twelve? But what did any of them have to gain? The problem was that I didn't know Deseret politics well enough. I did know one thing. More than one person was playing for high stakes, very high stakes.

CHAPTER TWENTY-FIVE

• • •

The suite was empty—very empty. The *thunk* of the door echoed hollowly, but the sound of my boots was swallowed by the thick carpet as I walked to the bedroom. I took Llysette's performing gown from the garment bag, holding it for a moment and wishing she were in it and I could hold her as well. Then I hung it up.

I walked back to the sitting area and stood by the window, looking at the points of light. Great Salt Lake City—where Llysette's career was supposed to have taken off. Great Salt Lake City—where events had confirmed, once more, that we never escaped our past, that we had to vanquish it again and again. And yet again.

I closed my eyes. That didn't help, and I opened them again.

My thoughts were whirling because nothing added up—or, rather, too much added up. Hansen was in charge of security, apparently fairly high up, although I had no idea how high a bishop for security was, and he'd been involved from the beginning. That argued that someone had been worried early on. That worry was confirmed by our Danite followers and the constant surveillance.

Yet someone had clearly bypassed everything, and Hansen wasn't happy about it. That shone through, and it argued that if it were an inside job, he wasn't on that part of the inside. The fact that Hansen had personally been half-watching Dan Perkins was another confirmation that Perkins wasn't on the inside. Besides,

Perkins had everything to lose from a plot that would hurt Llysette. She was literally his ticket back to respectability and financial security.

The clippings and Counselor Cannon's words indicated that he wanted to use
Llysette—and me—as a lever for closer relations with Columbia. So who didn't?
The manner of Llysette's disappearance argued that someone in the power structure didn't agree with the counselor—either that or someone was awfully good at
evading all the precautions set up by Jensen and Cannon and Hansen.

Among my problems was that I didn't know the power structure. Oh, Jerome
had kindly provided me with names and bios, but they didn't say much. The head
of the LDS church, the "Prophet, Seer, and Revelator," was Wilford W. Taylor. He
was also the President of the Kingdom of God in Deseret. Then there were the
Twelve Apostles—or the First Presidency—depending on which hat they wore.
But the real power there appeared to be the First Counselor, who, as speaker for
the Quorum of Seventy and as counselor to the Apostles and the First Presidency,
wielded power equivalent to that of, say, the Speaker of the House or a prime minister. His deputy was someone named C. Heber Kimball, who, as Second Counselor, ranked something like deputy prime minister.

The other Apostles, as I recalled, had names like Smith, Young, Sherratt, Lee,
Monson, Owens, and Orton. Some had biblical first names, others rather English
varieties. Unfortunately, Jerome's biographies didn't provide many hints, and
Cannon was the only one I'd met face-to-face—that I knew. I'd never been introduced to the pair with him at the Salt Palace. I should have asked, but I hadn't been
thinking. My head had been hurting—and still ached.

With that reminder, I went into the bathroom and blotted away the dried
blood . . . gently. The area around the cut was already swelling and would be very
black and blue.

The bedroom was just as empty as the sitting room.

Finally, since I couldn't sleep, tired as I was, and couldn't seem to piece together much, I started assembling items, including Llysette's hair dryer.

Once I had what I thought I needed together, including fresh batteries in
Bruce's calculator gadget, I undressed slowly and climbed into bed. The faint scent
of Llysette's perfume didn't help me sleep.

Neither did thoughts and dreams about various terrorists I'd known. In the
end, that part of me that was still Carolynne pleaded in Shakespearean quotes for
me to seek refuge in sleep.

I guess I did—for awhile—but I was awake with the sun, gray as it was through
the inversion layer that again blanketed Great Salt Lake.

After showering, shaving, and dressing, I looked at the silent wireset, then at
the door. No calls. No notes. Then, it was Sunday, and no doubt a time of worship
for all good—or radical—Saints.

I was to be contacted. Wonderful. No one was going to contact me in my
suite—that I doubted. So I went down to breakfast in The Refuge early on that

Sunday morning. Two Danites waited in the lobby, one talking to the concierge, the other ostensibly using the wireset in the alcove off the registration desk.

I was escorted quietly to a corner booth of The Refuge. For a moment, I sat there, not picking up the menu, but thinking of Llysette sitting across from me.

Thinking about Llysette confined or tied up in some dark space or room didn't help much, nor did the waiting. Lord, I hated waiting, good as I'd gotten at it in the Spazi. But it was different when it was personal.

Special breakfast number two—a cheese and mushroom omelet—was what I settled on, sipping chocolate as I awaited my order.

"Minister Eschbach?" The dark-haired man in the continental-cut suit smiled broadly as he slipped into the other side of the booth, seemingly oblivious to the Danites three tables away. His face was familiar, and he carried a small flat case scarcely larger than a folder full of maps or papers as he sat at the table. The case went on the linen between our places as he dropped into the chair across from me.

I wanted to shake my head but forced a smile. "I should have guessed. What do you want?"

"It wasn't us, Johan."

"You didn't take her?"

"No. This was local, as you'll find out in, I'd say, somewhere over an hour or so." He smiled sadly. "Believe it or not, Johan, I had nothing to do with it. We don't deal with families."

"And I suppose you had nothing to do with the attempts in New Bruges?"

"I had nothing to do with that, either." He poured water from the pitcher into the empty glass across from me, then took a long swallow.

"Careful choice of the pronoun, Dietre."

Dietre shrugged. "I can't stay long. I'd suggest you tell the Saints that I recognized you from the concert and was congratulating you. By the way, she is the finest I've ever heard. And I have heard the finest. It is a pity that they must deal in such a . . . roundabout fashion." He paused as the waiter set down my breakfast.

"Would you like anything else, sir?"

"Another pot of chocolate, thank you."

The waiter inclined his head and departed.

"Always so Dutch you are, Johan."

"I could remark on your ancestry, but I'll refrain. Still . . . it's rather hard to believe that your . . . group . . ." I glanced toward the door but didn't see any more Danites—or any motion from the pair at the nearby table. Then, they probably had orders to watch and not act unless I appeared threatened.

"My . . . superior . . . doesn't care much for you personally, Johan, but he's no fool. Neither is his . . . leader, if you understand. They'd prefer that the present situation remain stable, but some accommodations could be made." Dietre's smile was wry. "These days, naval actions are all the rage, but some rumors have surfaced that General Lobos-Villas could have the south Kansas oilfields in less than

forty-eight hours. Over the long run . . . not exactly desirable . . . except for en-
thusiasts of a 'Greater Europe.' Even our interests must bend to those of cultural
diplomacy."

"You're not here officially." My stomach growled, and I took a small bite of the
omelet, impolite as it may have been.

"In Deseret, as officially as I can be. I'm an accredited representative of FrancoPetEx." He nodded toward the folder lying on the table. "I believe you left that
in the concert hall in your distress."

I looked at the plain black leather gingerly. "And?"

"I found the contents most interesting, as I'm sure you did."

"This isn't for free, Dietre. What do you want?"

"As little disruption as possible—double or nothing is the way to go." He
shrugged. "I have great faith in you, Johan. So does your Minister Jerome, and
quite a few others. The problem is that you solve problems, shall we say, in a rather
unique way. On behalf of our . . . group, as you put it, I would like this solution
confined to the recovery of your lovely bride." He nodded toward the not-so-thin
leather case I held. "That will help us all."

Both my ghosts—and I—sensed that Dietre was telling the truth, and that
scared me.

"And, by the way, I suspect that in the group that will contact you is someone
who was tied into the unfortunate attempt in New Bruges. I don't know who that
might be, but it doesn't make sense any other way."

The more I heard, the less I liked it.

"Now . . . our group did agree to pass a message to you. We're still playing both
sides of the fence, much as I would prefer otherwise. You're to take a walk through
the Temple grounds between one and one-thirty. Thirteen hundred Republic military time." He laughed at that reminder.

I didn't.

"You'll be contacted. You won't recognize whoever it is. I wouldn't either."
With a broad smile he rose and said loudly enough for his voice to carry, "Give your
lovely wife my congratulations, Minister Eschbach!"

"Thank you. Best wishes on your new venture." I stood as he left.

The Danites watched, but that was all.

I sat and took a sip of chocolate and several bites more of the breakfast I really
didn't taste before opening the folder.

The thick file contained detailed engineering drawings—from what I could
tell—for the stage III synthfuels plants, the materials specifications, and the highly
proprietary information on the Saint catalysts. I closed the leather folder casually,
and for a time I sat there forcing myself to eat and sipping chocolate, trying to sort
it through.

Dietre was one of Maurice-Huizinga's top operatives. Some of what he said was
false as a lead schilling—like the business of not involving families. Maurice-Huizinga

had effectively held poor Miranda Miller's son hostage to get Miranda to spy on me and Llysette on behalf of New France. So I couldn't believe that somehow they had a soft spot for families or Llysette.

Yet if what he'd said were true and the plans and specifications were accurate, it meant that my first assumptions had been correct, that Llysette had been taken by agents of the Revealed Twelve.

Why the synthfuels specifications, specifications for which Reilly and his staff would have sacrificed dozens of operatives? Dietre, or, more precisely, Maurice-Huizinga, wanted something, and Dietre had said double or nothing. Then, Dietre had referred to "the unfortunate attempt in New Bruges." "The"—as in singular—and that meant, first, he only knew of one and, second, New France hadn't been involved in either. There was a possibility, as always, that he was lying, but, again, I didn't see much point in a lie on that point, although I'd have probably been hard-pressed to explain why.

After a time, I nodded to myself. Double or nothing. If I managed to pull it off, somehow, and I didn't have more than the vaguest idea of what was involved, then Columbia would have the plans that represented years of trial and error engineering based on the original Austrian research—effectively reducing over time the Saint energy and chemical monopoly.

If I didn't pull it off, I'd be dead, probably linked to spying to devastate the Saints' energy industry, with chances of Columbia getting energy supplies from Deseret close to nil for another decade—or longer.

For all that, Dietre's efforts were weighted toward helping me. Why? Altruism wasn't exactly the watchword of New France, and the sale of Deseret oils to Columbia would probably deprive someone else.

I took another sip of cold chocolate and checked my watch—still only slightly past nine-thirty. Then I swallowed. How had Dietre known I'd been in The Refuge? I shook my head. I wasn't sure I wanted to know.

That just illustrated how unclear everything was. How was Llysette's kidnapping tied into what had to be domestic Deseret politics? How would helping me resolve the problem, with a bonus of sorts, and benefit New France?

I smiled grimly. By playing messenger to the schismatics, Dietre was implying New French support, and he could build on that if they won. By assisting me, if I managed to turn the tables on the schismatics, he was implying support for Columbia and the established Deseret government. His connections to the loser would never come out.

Equally important, someone had figured out that stiff-necked Columbia hated to be in anyone's debt. But Columbia couldn't afford not to build some synthfuels plants, and Ferdinand would certainly not be pleased to see them because it would eventually reduce the effect of his control of the Arabian peninsula oil, and the Austrians planned far into the future. That was exactly how they'd taken Europe and were taking over the Mid-East.

I signed the check and stood. I had a meeting in an hour and a half and then a rendezvous. I wasn't looking forward to either.

The lobby smelled of perfume, an unfamiliar brand, as I crossed to the elevators. The concierge offered a brief smile.

Up in the performing suite, I made more preparations, ensuring the scan-proof dart gun was ready and that the blade was easily reachable. Brother Hansen arrived at closer to ten-thirty, accompanied by two policemen in uniform and another man in a conservative brown suit.

"Minister Eschbach."

"Brother Hansen. Have you discovered anything?"

"No. Have you been contacted?"

"Indirectly." I glanced toward the door. "I thought Counselor Cannon would be here."

"Counselor Cannon and Second Counselor Kimball are scheduled to meet us at eleven."

"I'd prefer not to explain it all twice."

"As you wish." Hansen glanced toward the bedroom door, half-ajar. "Do you mind if we look around? There might be some . . . indications."

"Be my guest." Nothing I'd put in my suitcase looked terribly suspicious, and anyone who would recognize certain items should know that I was going to need them. I hoped they wouldn't be foolish enough to make an issue out of them.

I made some of the powdered chocolate and sipped it slowly as they wandered through the suite. The chocolate was so bad I had to sip it. I couldn't have gotten it down any other way.

Hansen stepped over several minutes into their search. "Your wife is dark-haired, is she not? With long hair?"

"Yes."

"Then it's likely these are her hairs, and we'll be taking what we can find just in case."

"Fine." I didn't want to discuss the implications of "just in case."

Besides the hair, they found nothing—nothing that they wanted to talk about, at least—and that was fine with me. Close to eleven, the four gathered in the sitting room. Hansen looked at his watch. "Counselor Cannon and Second Counselor Kimball should be here before long."

Unlike the audiences at the Salt Palace performing complex, the two counselors were punctual. They came into the suite unaccompanied, but I saw at least two Danites or other plainclothes security types station themselves in the corridor outside.

Cannon looked at Hansen's three subordinates. Hansen nodded, and they bowed and left.

The four of us sat around the small table.

"Minister Eschbach," Cannon said sonorously and with concern dripping from his voice, "I deeply regret this unfortunate situation, and I want you to know that we will do whatever is necessary to ensure your wife's safety." He shrugged. "Unfortunately, we have little to go on." His eyes went to Hansen. "Have you anything to add, Brother Hansen?"

"We have some indications that the kidnappers had scouted the complex earlier. We also have confirmed that the Browning they used was stolen. It was recovered early this morning near Point of the Mountain. We have recovered several strands of dark hair that may match samples we've taken from here."

"Are there any other signs?" asked Counselor Kimball.

"Nothing that the forensics people are willing to talk about yet," Hansen said. "Would you have been in the dressing room with your wife normally?"

"Probably." I shrugged. "Probably. She wasn't too interested in listening to me talk about water reuse treatment systems, and she was tired. I usually help her after she performs."

"So, based on your actions of the first two nights of the concerts, the kidnappers would have expected you to be there?" pressed Hansen.

"Probably."

"Is there anything else that might lend support to the idea they were after you? Besides the note itself?"

The three looked at me.

"I've already had a message," I said, cradling the empty chocolate cup for lack of anything better to do with my hands.

"The gentleman who visited you at breakfast?" asked Hansen.

"Yes."

"What did he say?"

"He was an intermediary—just told to tell me where I should be to be contacted." I waited. "On the Temple grounds early this afternoon."

"That would make sense," mused Hansen. "The grounds and the park are crowded then. Did he say anything else?"

"He said that Llysette gave an exceptional concert."

"Nothing else?" pressed Hansen.

"He said to congratulate her, and that he was sorry to have been contacted as an intermediary for such a sorry situation—or words to that effect."

"Dietre Treholme," Hansen said crisply. "He's supposedly the accredited Franco-PetEx representative here. He knew you personally, Minister Eschbach. From old times, I take it."

"I have met him before. FrancoPetEx has operations in Columbia, and they had environmental concerns." All of that was true.

"He's the chief operative of the New French intelligence service here."

"I can imagine that," I answered. "He's always seemed mysterious, and he did hint that his organization had nothing to do with Llysette's disappearance, but I couldn't imagine that the state oil company would, energy politics or not."

Counselor Cannon cleared his throat softly. Hansen paused.

"Bishop Hansen, do we have any indication that this Dietre Treholme is acting as anything other than an intermediary?" The First Counselor's eyes remained warm, interested.

"No, sir."

"The note said they did not want your wife, Minister Eschbach," interjected the Second Counselor. "That would mean they want you for some reason or another."

"Either that," I answered, "or they want me to do something. Or obtain something."

"What might that be?" asked Kimball.

That had me stumped. I wasn't about to discuss ghosting and de-ghosting technology, and I hadn't the faintest idea what else they might want.

"Embarrassment," suggested the First Counselor. "If we cannot protect visiting artists and government officials in our own capital, how can Deseret be trusted to keep other agreements?"

"How can we claim . . . ," began Kimball, but stopped as Cannon eyed him.

"Exactly," said Cannon quietly.

I got the message anyway. The problem with being a theocracy is that if too many bad things happen, either God has turned away or the leaders have turned from God.

"The Revealed Twelve?" I asked, stirring the pot a little.

Kimball's face twisted. Hansen offered a frigid poker face.

"What do you know about the so-called Revealed Twelve, Minister Eschbach?" asked Cannon.

"Very little except that they exist. I've read some news clippings that suggest you've been waging a covert war or opposition to the group." I picked up the empty cup again.

"You are well-informed. I would not expect otherwise," answered Cannon dryly, so dryly it was clear he'd been well briefed on my background. "And, yes, if this effort is the creation of the Revealed Twelve, and if it succeeds, it will cause a certain . . . reassessment of the policies of the First Presidency. Such a reassessment would not be in the interests of Columbia, I must admit."

"I had already come to that conclusion. That means I have to do what they want, especially until they release Llysette."

"We cannot accept the schismatics' terms," announced Hansen.

"I do not believe that was precisely what Doktor Eschbach proposed," said Cannon quietly.

What had I proposed? Had I proposed anything, really, except getting Llysette back? My head ached, still, I realized, and my thoughts were fuzzy. Fine secret agent and spy I was, letting my own wife get kidnapped out of her own dressing room.

"I want my wife back, safe and unharmed. So do you," I finally managed.

Hansen frowned. "We want the schismatics. Or whoever did this."

I had to look at Cannon. He nodded cherubically, and that meant I got to explain.

"You've trumpeted to the world that Deseret is a cultural capital, and that it is a modern city. Exactly how are you going to explain to the world that a world-class diva has been abducted by a group of religious extremists? And if you try to hush it up, how will you explain the disappearance of a Columbian Subminister for Environmental Protection and his wife, a world-class diva?" I waited.

Hansen still looked blank.

"That plays into their hands. You give Columbia an excuse to make demands you can't or don't want to meet. Then they divert all the headwaters of the Colorado into their Aspinall tunnel project, citing the fact that you broke the Reciprocity Agreement. The schismatic group then has you on two counts—you aren't following the Prophet, and you're bringing harm to Deseret."

Kimball turned to the First Counselor. Cannon nodded. "Doktor Eschbach has a point there. What do you suggest, Doktor?"

I swallowed. "Let me do what they *think* they want."

"Why?"

In for a penny, in for a sovereign. I swallowed. "Right now, you have a missing diva. If I can work a trade for her . . ."

"Who are you trading?" asked Kimball.

"Me." I'd thought that was obvious, but maybe it wasn't in a society that still clung to polygamy. Or maybe it was just Kimball.

"What is our advantage there?" asked Cannon quietly. "We still have a prominent Columbian in the hands of a . . . radical organization."

"If something happens to a singer, it's an outrage," I pointed out. "If something happens to a former official of a powerful neighbor, who in Deseret can fault you for taking whatever steps are necessary to bring the malefactors to justice?"

Even Kimball nodded.

"You seem anxious to do this," said Hansen.

"I'm not looking forward to putting myself in the hands of a bunch of religious screwballs." *Especially screwballs funded by either Ferdinand or someone else.* "But I'd rather act sooner than later."

Cannon smiled almost benevolently. The smile vanished with my next words.

"I'll also need a solid briefing on the Prophet and where you feel that the schismatics diverged from his teaching or whatever."

Cannon winced at the term "or whatever," but his face smoothed over.

"What does doctrine have to do with it?" asked Hansen.

"With fanatics, doctrine is everything," I answered. "The last thing I want is to say the wrong thing and push the wrong button. It also might give me some insight."

"Minister Eschbach seems determined to meet their demands. What do you want me to do?" Hansen's voice did not quite conceal a bitterness.

"Wait to see how matters develop," suggested Cannon. "Offer Minister Esch-bach the support he needs."

And above all, I reflected, *keep things quiet.* But that seemed to be understood in the Saint culture. No one was going to be happy with the solution, no matter what First Counselor Cannon said.

I turned to Hansen. "I'd appreciate it if you would get together all the con-densed and direct quotes of a theological nature from your first two prophets—and the current codified doctrine, or whatever you call it. I'll need it by the time I get back."

"How do you know you'll come back?" asked Hansen.

"I don't, but I have to plan as though I will." I forced the smile. "I need to get ready." I also wanted time to think.

After a nod from the First Counselor, the other three stood.

"Good luck," offered Counselor Cannon warmly as he left. "Please let us know if there is any way in which we can assist."

"I will." I hoped I wouldn't have to ask Cannon for anything, but I wasn't burning bridges I might have to cross. He'd probably give me what I needed. After all, it was clear by his presence that a satisfactory resolution was important to him. I had the feeling that our definitions of *satisfactory* might differ considerably.

I left the suite not much after the dignitaries, taking too-long strides toward the Temple area and trying to breathe deeply and maintain some semblance of relax-ation. While I carried a number of items that Brother Hansen might not have ap-proved of, I hoped I wouldn't have to use them.

The faint odor of late fall, molding leaves, a mustiness, ebbed and rose around me in the intermittent wind.

Despite the partly overcast skies, the Temple park was filled with families and a large number of young couples. Were such family outings where young Saints met? Or, like all young adults, were they just taking advantage of the opportunities?

To my right, a slender dark-haired girl in a dark blue wool coat, braided hair swinging slightly, looked down at the stones of the walk when a sandy-haired youth murmured something. She raised those green eyes, and he flushed slightly. Would Llysette and I have been like those two, had we been raised in Deseret?

After a half hour or so, while I loitered reading the week's concert program posted outside the Assembly Hall, a heavyset and bearded man in a checked brown suit that had gone out of fashion a half-century before even in Deseret eased up be-side me and peered at the program.

"Minister Eschbach, if you wish to see your wife again, please follow me down South Temple. Keep walking until you are picked up."

"No," I said. "You need me, not her. I'm not interested in dealing until I know she's safe." I hoped my words were cooler than I felt.

His bearded jaw dropped open. "We have your wife."

"I'm sure you do. There are two possibilities: you've already murdered her, or she's safe. If she's dead, then there's no point in my negotiating with you. If she's safe, I will."

He looked confused, and that worried me, because it meant he was another courier or the group were amateurs, and amateurs could do anything.

"But . . . we have your wife."

"Exactly. I happen to love her, and I'm perfectly willing to trade myself for her. But I'm the only leverage I have, and I'm a stubborn Dutchman. If you know me at all, or of your superiors do, you know I keep my word. You need my knowledge, but you won't get it until Llysette is safe within the walls of the Columbian embassy."

There was silence.

"I'm perfectly willing to take a steamer to some isolated place on my own, provided it has a portable wireset or a radio. Or some other similar arrangement. Once I talk to her and know she's safe, then I'll be willing to accompany you."

"You're in no position to bargain."

"Neither are you. You don't need Llysette. You need me."

I could see the frustration mounting in his eyes—another disturbing indication.

He lunged, and I moved, my hands reacting with patterns acquired years earlier. His arm snapped, and he cradled it, eyes watering.

I stepped closer. "If she is hurt . . . even scratched, what I did to your arm will look like a pleasure cruise in the Sandwich Islands compared to what I'll do to everyone of your sorry group."

"You wouldn't . . . You couldn't. . . ."

"You don't think so." I forced a hard smile. "You don't think so? Ask your superiors what I've done."

"You'll be sorry."

I already was, but that was beside the point. Already, people around us were drawing away, and silence was radiating from where I stood like ripples in a pond.

Abruptly, brown-suit turned. I watched as he headed toward the building in which the Deseret Woolen Mills store was housed, but he merged into the people once he was more than fifty yards away.

I was shaking by the time I started to walk back to the Lion Inn. Logically, I knew what I'd done was my only chance. I was the only option in town—literally—but I still shivered and sweated all the way back. What if they'd already killed Llysette? It didn't feel like they had, but I'd been wrong before—and that had killed Elspeth and Waltar.

I'd been wrong before and taken a bullet through the shoulder. I couldn't afford to be wrong again, and yet I wondered if I already happened to be—and just didn't know it.

CHAPTER TWENTY-SIX

• • •

H ansen was waiting when I returned to the Lion Inn. He got on the elevator with me, and he looked as tired as I felt. His eyes were bloodshot, and he carried a heavy-looking satchel.

"I don't know," I told him after the well-dressed couple with their three blond children got off on the fourth floor. "They wanted me to come with them."

"They?"

"A bearded man in a very out-of-style brown-checked suit and a nasty temper. He tried to assault me when I told him I wasn't about to go with him."

"You said that?" Hansen raised his eyebrows, then touched the beard shaded with white.

"Look. Either Llysette's dead already"—I swallowed, even though I hadn't meant to—"or she's not. If she's not, and I go with them, then she will be dead before it's all over."

"You don't know that."

I just looked at him, and he looked down.

We got off the elevator and walked to the suite. I opened the door and held it for him, then wandered through the place. The rooms were still empty, the piano silent, Llysette's robe still draped over the stool in the bathroom she'd used.

The faint aroma of Ivoire lingered. Llysette loved it, even if it was manufactured in New France these days and cost twice what it once had. The old price had been close to fifty Republic dollars an ounce, and that had been back before the impact of energy costs had run up everything.

I went back to the sitting room, where Hansen had stacked four books on the table.

"You realize what you're saying, don't you? That there's a good chance you won't make it through whatever you have in mind."

"I have a chance. If I don't do it this way, Llysette has very little chance." I picked up one of the volumes—*Doctrine and Covenants* a fairly new printing. Did the Saints revise their theology all the time?

"You think she does?"

"Someone knows my background, or I hope they do. *If* they do, they'd know how I'd approach it. I have to hope that they do. They know a great deal already."

"How do you know that?"

"Because they clearly want me. Because they're using Llysette as the lever."

Hansen frowned. I didn't clarify that.

"Can you tell me anything more about your contact?"

"Young—early thirties, dark-haired, fair-skinned, bearded, no white or gray in the beard, pale gray eyes, thin lips, broad nose, nose once broken, I'd guess. Fine hair, thin eyebrows. Could probably be a dozen like him."

"Anything else?"

"He's amateur. He found it hard to believe I wouldn't accept their terms."

"So would I. You're a hard man, Eschbach."

"No. Hopeful, hoping, wishing, but not hard. One of the things they pointed out years ago when I was a pilot . . ." I shook my head. "Old history doesn't matter now."

"Go ahead. It might." But he didn't look at me as he spoke.

"It always made sense. If you're captured, once you do what the enemy wants, or say what he tells you to, your value is diminished. If they're honorable, they won't kill you whether you tell or not. If they're not, then withholding knowledge until you can do something is all you have. It may not be enough, but it's all you have."

I found myself pursing my lips together too tightly, wishing I hadn't injured the idiot who'd jumped me, but trained reactions don't always give you much choice, especially when you're emotionally involved, and with Llysette's life at stake I definitely was far too emotionally involved to be dispassionate, no matter what Hansen thought.

"What's the matter?"

"Oh . . . he also has a broken arm. I wish I hadn't, but he jumped me, and I didn't have time to think."

A moment of silence followed. "Just like that, he jumped you and you broke his arm?"

"I reacted. I didn't think, and then I had to act as though it were planned to show they'd better understand who they were dealing with." I shrugged. "You can't show weakness."

"The more I learn about you, Minister Eschbach . . ." Hansen glanced toward the window, then back at the books on the table. "There's a lot more here than anyone's saying."

"There always is, or things like this wouldn't happen." How much more I really didn't want to explain.

Brother Hansen actually sighed. "We will check the hospitals and doctors, but I doubt we'll find anything." Hansen half-stroked his beard again. "Do you think you'll be contacted?"

"There isn't much doubt about that." My only doubts were about Llysette's health.

"How soon?"

"Several hours, I'd guess. Maybe longer. I'd want to make me sweat, but they also don't want to give you—or any Deseret authority—too much time."

He nodded. "We'll keep in touch."

I was sure he would. I was also sure every wireline to the room was monitored and every hall snooped.

When Hansen left, I ordered a room service meal and really got to work, forcing myself through the *Doctrine and Covenants,* writing down passages or derivations of passages that I thought would be useful if I had to use my knowledge. The first prophet had definitely been both a man of vision and a shrewd politician, so shrewd I had to wonder how he'd gotten himself murdered. By a shrewder politician? Bad luck? Either could happen to anyone. There's always someone smarter and tougher, and luck doesn't necessarily favor the skillful or the bold, and Smith had to have been bold, whatever else he had or hadn't been.

The words *psychic proliferation* came back—Jerome's words. I felt they tied in, but I didn't know why . . . yet. I tried not to think of bad luck as I read, and noted, and, later, ate through the same chicken pasta dish I'd had earlier from room service.

Then came *The Book of Mormon* itself. Some of it I could skip, because it was historical. For my purposes, Lehi's flight from Jerusalem wasn't much use, nor was Lehi's death or the wanderings of his son Nephi in the wilderness. It was interesting to see the parallels between Nephi and Laman and Cain and Abel, except in *The Book of Mormon* the younger son prevails—in his own lifetime, anyway. There were some interesting quotes in the second book of Nephi, which I jotted down, wishing I had a difference engine as I did. Writing was always laborious.

Then came the section named "The Words of Mormon," and that was followed by another 250 pages of Saint theological and temporal history as recounted by the personages of Mosiah, Alma, and Helaman. That brought me to another book of Nephi, except it was a different Nephi. From what I could figure, racing through the text, the second Nephi, who presumably wrote the third book of Nephi, presided over a religious rebirth of the Nephites—those were the good Saints, I figured—except that the rebirth and godliness didn't last, and pretty soon there wasn't much difference between the Nephites and the Lamanites. After that, almost all the Nephites eventually perished under the swords of the Lamanites, and *The Book of Mormon* ended with a cautionary and advisory chapter from Moroni, who appeared to have buried the golden plates on which his and all his predecessors' words were inscribed and then expired in turn.

Just like that—over five hundred pages chronicling a religious history, and all the good followers of the Lord are wiped out because, from what I could figure out, they forsook him and indulged in wickedness. That meant to me, in practical terms, that the whole Saint "bible" was cautionary. It also implied that the Revealed Twelve were claiming that the current Saint leadership was like the ancient Nephites, rejecting the "true" vision of the Lord.

Of course, "truth" tends to be rather subjective, as I'd already had confirmed once again from reading the *Doctrine* book. An awful lot of what the first prophet had written could have been interpreted in more than one way, and that might have been why the Saint faith continued to rely on further "revelations"—to keep it on track.

I rubbed my forehead as I sat there at the table.

Then, the Revealed Twelve could certainly claim that later "revelations" had not come from God, but from Satan.

For a moment, I wanted to rip up everything in sight. One or both sides were playing with words and theology to gain temporal power—but that was exactly what the entire *Book of Mormon* effectively warned against. Yet each side would doubtless claim that they were on the side of the Lord. And unless there was a major miracle . . . who would know?

I also had this sinking feeling that the Revealed Twelve wanted me to create something along those lines—and that they'd gotten a little boost from Ferdinand along the way. The misplaced papers, the warmth of the difference engine—both took on a new significance, perhaps a terrible significance. Why did they want a ghost? That they wanted one seemed inescapable. That *someone* knew I could create one seemed equally inescapable. I just wasn't sure who knew—or who had told them.

I opened my case and looked at the folder with the difference engine codes and the code lines. How was I going to translate them into what I needed?

At that point, the wireset chimed. I looked at it. It chimed again. I picked it up. "Eschbach here."

"We accept your terms. Details will be given to you on the public wireset outside the north door to the Salt Palace. Be there at eight tonight."

Click.

That left me with less than three hours to finish preparing what I needed, and all I had was several sheets full of scattered quotes, and even more scattered ideas.

Should I start on the applications side, assuming that was what my soon-to-be-captors would have in mind? I reached for the sheets of code that I had brought.

Thrap! The knock echoed through the sitting room. I closed my case, sealing away the Babbage code lines I'd hoped to be able to forget. Why was it I never had a chance to put anything behind me?

I peered through the peephole. Hansen stood there.

Even before he got inside, he spoke. "You got a call."

"Why don't you come in and sit down for a moment?" The last thing I needed was an angry bishop of security, and I needed Hansen on my side or, at least, not against me. "Can I offer you anything?"

"Water would be fine." He sank into one of the chairs. His eyes were still bloodshot, his suit rumpled, and his shoes dusty. What I looked like was probably worse.

He drained the entire glass, and I refilled it before sitting down.

"I suppose you've digested all of this?" He gestured toward the table and the books and the stacks of paper.

"No. I've got enough—or I will."

"Eschbach, you puzzle me. Why haven't you contacted your embassy?"

"What point would there have been if the kidnappers didn't agree? The embassy types would just get upset. You don't contact them until you know what you want them to do. And why."

"Experience speaking again?"

I shrugged.

"Do you mind if we tap the wireset by the Salt Palace?"

"Did you find out where this call was made?"

"No. It was from somewhere in Great Salt Lake, but it was too short. The equipment can trace a call in about four seconds, but it takes a few moments to get it on the right line. The operator fumbled, and—"

"They were off."

"Right. If they have to give more detailed directions, it will take longer."

"I'm sure that they'll wire from a public set."

"They will, but what else do we have?"

"If you can tap the line without getting near it, I don't have any problem, but I'm not too keen if it means people swarming all over the area."

"We can do that. What are you going to do now?" Hansen finished his second glass of water and blotted his forehead.

"Contact the embassy. Finish my notes."

"Would you mind telling me what the notes are for?"

"Background for what I think the kidnappers want me to provide."

"Couldn't you just provide written material?" The bishop for security had a glint in his eye as he set his glass on the table.

I picked up the nearly empty and cold cup of chocolate from my dinner, then set it back down without drinking. "Actually . . . no. The material has to be applied . . . shall we say." I offered a hard smile. "It's better that I don't get too specific."

"How can we help you when you won't even tell us what the kidnappers want?"

It was a fair question and deserved the best answer I could give without endangering a lot of people. "First, I don't know what they want. They haven't said. I'm guessing, just like Counselor Cannon and you are. Second, it's dangerous enough that the fewer people that know, the safer everyone will be. Third, I'm fairly convinced that the Austrians have a hand in this, as well as a few others, but I can't prove it. Finally, to the best of my knowledge, I'm probably the only person not under government lock and key with the expertise to handle this." I paused. "That doesn't exactly answer your question, but it's why the Counselor ordered you to help. I'm probably skirting the bounds of things to say that if you knew more of the story, you might not be so willing. If you knew the entire story, you wouldn't hesitate, but I wouldn't give much for your life expectancy."

"You're protecting *me*?"

"I'd like to think so." I looked at the books on the table.

So did Hansen. Then he got up. "I think you're being more honest than many, but I cannot say I'm pleased. I intend to stay nearby. My number will get me in a few minutes or less if you need me."

"I'm sorry. I'm doing the best I can." I stood and walked to the door with him. "I really am."

Once the door was closed, and locked, I wired the embassy but could only get the duty clerk. I impressed on him the need for the First or Second Secretary to contact me as soon as possible. He promised to try to find them.

I had my doubts and suspected I'd have to storm the embassy in the morning. I tried the telephone book, but as I did not know their names, it wasn't much help.

Again . . . I should have been more assiduous in gathering that sort of information, but you don't expect to have to run down people on Sundays. You should figure it could happen, but I was out of practice and, once more, it showed. Espionage was like athletics: you have to stay in shape, and paranoia helps.

I'd have to wire the embassy again later.

I glanced at the closed case. Babbage codes or quotes? I decided on codes, at least until I had a better formulation on the structure I had in mind. My last ghost from scratch hadn't been all that successful.

In two hours plus, I had something on paper. What it would do was another question, and that assumed that the Revealed Twelve had the necessary hardware. What scared me was that I thought they did.

At seven-forty, I closed the case and left it on the table. The codes by themselves meant nothing, and I couldn't carry everything everywhere. I washed my hands and face quickly, trying to ignore the remaining scent of Ivoire, and hurried out to the elevator.

I was walking south on 100 West Street at quarter to eight. Ahead, the Salt Palace performing complex loomed like a dark abandoned ruin. Slightly behind and to the east, the Temple shone in a cocoon of shimmering white light. Personally, I'd have preferred the reverse, but that might have been my skepticism about the overall benefit of religions based on true believers.

Several figures—all Danites or Hansen's men or both—lurked in the shadows while I lounged less than a dozen feet from the public communications booth.

Finally, at three past the hour, the wireset rang, and I picked it up. "Eschbach."

"There is another wireset two blocks south of where you are." The voice was disguised and electronically resonant, and that spoke of more sophisticated communications technology than that used by an average terrorist or kidnapper. The technology level reassured me, but only slightly. "It is the only booth with a red façade. Tomorrow at eleven you will receive final instructions. You will park a steamer there, rented from a commercial establishment. We trust you will make your own communications arrangements with your embassy.

"You will be given directions where to drive and for how long. At the end of that time, you will contact the embassy to confirm your wife's safety. Then you will be picked up."

"I can accept that."

"Good. Eleven tomorrow morning."

Click.

I hung up the handset and walked back to the Lion Inn. Again, Hansen was waiting by my door. We walked inside before I spoke. "Eleven tomorrow."

He nodded.

"Any luck on tracing the wire?"

"A public set outside a grocery in South Great Salt Lake City. Right beside the south expressway. No one will be there, but I sent a steamer to check."

"Speaking of steamers, we'll need to rent a steamer in the morning."

"I heard."

"I assume there's no commercial establishment open now."

"This is Sunday, Minister Eschbach."

I wanted to shake my head. What did they do about babies, heart attacks, and other inconveniences that occurred on the holy day?

After he left, I wired the embassy again.

"This is Minister Eschbach. Have you had any luck in finding the Second Secretary?"

"No, sir. We've put a message on his service and on the system and posted it in his box. He's not at home, or he's not answering."

"Tell him it's urgent."

"Yes, sir."

"Tell him Deputy Minister Jerome thinks it's urgent also."

"Ah . . . yes, sir. I'll try again right away."

"Thank you. Both Minister Jerome and I would appreciate it."

I really didn't want to say more—not yet. If need be, I could have Hansen wait outside the embassy with a radio. He'd do it. He'd do anything ethical and legal not to have the blame for the mess dropped in his lap.

CHAPTER TWENTY-SEVEN

• • •

R oom service delivered breakfast to the suite at seven. By seven-thirty I had talked to Hansen. He'd pick me up at the embassy at eight-thirty. Before eight I was dressed, wearing, among other things, the gray vest that looked like leather and was, in fact, little more than textured plastique. I had everything ready to go.

I had packed what I needed into the case—the professional papers, the code lines, the notes and quotes, and *The Book of Mormon*. I took the engineering drawings Dietre had supplied with me. Double or nothing, because if I got killed with the schismatics and they were found there'd be hell to pay. But if I left them behind they wouldn't be there when I returned, and I deserved some payoff for the mess Harlaan and Jerome and all the others had gotten us into. Besides, it was almost a matter of principle. I needed to do more than expected, and I might need every bit of leverage I had once we got back to Columbia. If we got back.

No sense dwelling on that. So I checked my watch. Eight o'clock. Of course, the Second Secretary hadn't called back. So I put in another call to the embassy.

"Ah . . . he's not available at the moment."

"This is Minister Eschbach, and I strongly suggest you find him—this moment. Or the First Secretary. The name is Eschbach, and neither President Armstrong nor Speaker Hartpence or a fellow by the name of Asquith will be very pleased if you don't. Nor will Ambassador Klein or Minister Jerome."

It took a few moments more—more than a few—on the wireset, with a few more helpful suggestions, before I put it down flatly.

"I'll be there in ten minutes to see either the First or Second Secretary."

"We can't do that."

"If you don't, you're all likely to be on a turbo to the Federal District by tonight. By the way, tell them it's Hamilton's Whiskey Revolt."

"Would you hold for a moment, sir?"

"I'd be happy to." I wasn't in the slightest happy to hold.

"This is Second Secretary Trumbull-Hull."

"Johan Eschbach. You have a condition red-two facing you. Hamilton Whiskey Revolt. Status amber, going red at eleven. I'll be there to see you in ten minutes."

"Eschbach? *The* Eschbach?"

"Yes. I'm back where I didn't want to be."

"I'll be here." He sounded less than pleased. I couldn't blame him.

Someone had clearly briefed him, however, by the time I arrived by a steamer cab—a Reo, not a Browning. The embassy was on the hill, between Deseret University and the Temple, in a huge old complex that had probably housed some former patriarch's establishment. The oak door was golden, with spotless brass furnishings, and it opened before I reached it.

Two Republic marines in blues stood back. "Minister Eschbach, sir?"

"That's me." I had out both the diplomatic passport and the government ID.

The shorter marine nodded. "This way, sir."

The Second Secretary's office was on the first floor on the back side, overlooking a garden. The conversion into an office had left an ancient fireplace, faced with blue and cream ceramic tile, with a hearth of the same tile, and a dark walnut mantel that held the picture of a handsome brunette and two children.

Trumbull-Hull was in his midthirties, taller than I was, and balding. His forehead was damp, and he stood behind an antique walnut desk as if it were a rampart under siege.

"Please have a seat." He motioned to the chair in front of the desk.

"I take it that my concerns were reinforced?" I asked pleasantly.

He nodded stiffly. "I was told to offer any assistance within the power of the embassy."

"Good. It isn't that bad from your point of view." How much should I tell him? Too much and he'd muck it up. Too little and he'd manage to obstruct everything.

"It's rather simple. A contact went bad. The wrong people got involved, and they hold my wife. They want me. I need your help in a small way in ensuring her safety and the successful conclusion of the operation."

"Your wife? The singer?" His mouth almost opened.

I nodded.

"The news media——"

"They don't know yet, and I hope they never know. So do you. If this goes right, she'll be here on your doorstep sometime after eleven—probably around noon, but the time could vary."

"Here?"

"Here."

"We'll do what is possible." His words were careful, calculated. "What, exactly, do you need from us?"

"Very little. We reached an accommodation—of sorts: Llysette is delivered here. I talk to her before going with them, but I have to be close to their reach. So what I need from you is a radio or the equivalent and someone listening constantly from eleven onward—a shortwave or similar unit that will reach from anywhere in several hundred miles to the embassy."

"You're going to do that?"

"You can't defuse a bomb long-distance." I laughed hoarsely. "Anyway, my wife is supposed to arrive here sometime after they contact me at eleven. I'll need confirmation of that, and I'll need to speak to her personally. If, and I hope this is not the case, she cannot speak, or she doesn't arrive, I want you on the other end." I smiled. It wasn't a totally pleasant smile.

"Ah . . . I think we can do that. Is there anything else?"

"Once I've resolved the situation, we both get immediate turbo passage to the Federal District and guards to the aerodrome to ensure we get home."

"And?" Trumbull-Hull asked warily.

"You may be contacted by a Bishop Hansen."

"The Saint security chief? You are moving in . . . interesting circles, Minister Eschbach."

"You can tell him one of two things—either that you have Llysette or you don't."

"Are you sure you want to go through with this?" he asked, almost perfunctorily.

"You don't want an incident, and I don't want one. I'd prefer things be kept very quiet. I was trained for this, and I doubt you have anyone acceptable." I cleared my throat. "I'm sure you people can find a cover story if something happens to me. You can't if it happens to her. Not exactly easily." That probably wasn't true. With enough effort, anything can be covered up, especially in a nation that would want it covered, but I didn't want Second Secretary Trumbull-Hull thinking along those lines.

In the end, he saw it my way, not that I really had to press much, probably because he didn't have many choices. Second Secretaries were often more self-serving and rational than the political appointees. More cowardly, often, too. The brave ones usually didn't last, as was the case in so many other fields as well.

Still, I didn't get back outside the embassy until eight-forty, lugging a small radio with a long collapsible antenna and my datacase. Brother Hansen was waiting in a dark green Browning with a young clean-shaven driver.

The day was gray and cold, and even my overcoat didn't seem that warm.

Hansen held the door open from inside, and I climbed out of the wind.

"I see you persuaded Trumbull-Hull to part with a radio."

"It wasn't too hard."

"You talk a good game, Eschbach, but do you really know what they want?"

"I don't have an absolute confirmation, but almost anything would be better than what I've prepared for." I laughed hoarsely. "Then, I'll probably find out that what they want is even worse than that. It usually works that way."

I was guessing, of course, but the kidnappers had agreed to my terms, and that meant I was the *only* one who could do what they wanted—and that was either to destroy or create a ghost. Since there were no rumors about ghosts in existence, that meant creating one, and I had a good idea what that meant.

The security limousine hissed to a stop outside a sandstone-type building. In the car park were a double handful of fresh-washed steamers. The sign read: "Deseret Rentals."

Hansen almost choked at the invoice for renting the steamer. "Three hundred . . . and not even a Browning."

"Groundnuts," I said quietly, deciding he needed a reminder of what was at stake. "You want deGaulle's Foreign Legions marshaling in Santa Fe for a quick march toward the San Juan gasification plants?"

Hansen looked puzzled and I really didn't feel like explaining, but at this point some explanation—or speculation—wouldn't hurt too much.

"Escobar-Moire and deGaulle need diesel for those fleets, and they really don't want to pay your prices. Columbia does, and Ferdinand wants a civil war here and unrest all over North America. If Llysette disappears, you'll get trouble with Columbia and problems from your schismatics. A rental steamer is cheap insurance."

Of course, that was only part of the story, but a part that was true and certainly wouldn't hurt for Brother Hansen to hear. I would have paid for it, if necessary, but with all the risks Llysette and I were taking, I preferred that the Saints, and Counselor Cannon, paid as many of the bills as possible. I'd end up paying more than my share no matter how well matters turned out, and I didn't even want to consider the costs if they didn't.

With all the paperwork—every country had it—it was almost nine-forty-five before I fired up the rental steamer, a small brown Reno, barely big enough for four people.

"Let's go back to the Inn," Hansen suggested. "We haven't finished."

He was right about that, and I worried about what he had in mind.

Because I needed to eat, we sat in the corner booth in The Refuge, which confirmed, indirectly, that Hansen had had a lot to do with our seating and that the table was probably snooped to the gills and Hansen wanted my words on record. I'd have to be careful how I said what I said.

Hansen's eyes met mine over the chocolate. "Would you mind telling me what is really going on?"

"An attempt to use religion as a weapon to alienate Columbia and Deseret forever by playing on the simplistic side of people's faith in a time when life is too complex for many of them to handle."

"My, you sound superior."

"I don't mean it that way, but that's what I see." With a sigh, I refilled my mug.

"You're saying that the schismatics have no real faith and that they're using their disputes as a cover to gain temporal power?"

"Not exactly." How could I put it? "I have no reason to disbelieve the sincerity of what the schismatics believe. I do believe that they are being supported by outsiders who see the schismatics' beliefs as more in the interests of the outsiders."

"Very politely put. One can tell you were a politician."

"A very bad politician, Brother Hansen."

"So, Deseret's . . . furor over faith . . . is being used for political goals."

"That's my guess. It's only a guess."

"And what's in this for you, since you're not exactly a Saint?"

He was right about that in both senses. "The first is obvious. I want my wife safe."

"You love her. That is obvious, and praiseworthy. I do not believe that is the only reason."

"No. I'd like to put a stop to those who would use people's beliefs in ways that aren't in their own interests."

"High-sounding rhetoric, Minister Eschbach."

"Probably, but I've noted that disruption fueled by religious disputes gets extraordinarily ugly, especially when the . . . temporal . . . stakes are high. I happen to think that Columbia and Deseret need to work out an arrangement that's less adversarial. That won't be possible if the schismatics succeed."

Hansen stroked his beard. "That makes sense, but I'm still not totally convinced."

I wasn't either. So I sipped more chocolate and had another bite of the dry ham sandwich.

"There has to be more," he prodded.

"There is. I really want to be left alone. I really want Llysette to be able to sing without fear or concern."

He nodded, and he apparently understood enough that he asked a different question. "Are you certain you don't want a close tail?"

"Look," I said. "They won't do anything until they're convinced no one is following me. That's why they want a rental steamer. I don't want a tracker or a tail."

"Then you'll have to tell us where you're headed."

I laughed. "It's all a blind. I'll be back in Great Salt Lake City by tonight. Where in Great Salt Lake City I haven't the faintest idea. This whole business is designed to make a transfer where you can't get too close. But the best place to hide remains a city."

"You don't want us too close, do you?"

"Yes and no. I'd prefer to be rescued, but the problem is that the problem won't stay solved if it's not played out." I'd only thought the problem had been played out the first time around. Self-deception can be so comforting, until you're called on it. How could I have thought Branston-Hay's theoretical formulations on creating ghosts would have stayed buried? I'd applied them. Probably Minister Jerome had people working on applying them.

"It's your neck."

Unfortunately, it was, but a lot of other necks were stretched under the knife as well. They just didn't understand that.

At quarter to eleven I pulled the Reo up beside the red-faced wireset booth. No one was using the unit, and I walked over to it. No sense in letting someone decide to use it when Llysette's life was possibly hanging on it.

At eleven-eleven the set chimed.

"Eschbach."

"Take a steamer south on the expressway. When you get to Beehive Route Three, take it east. Once you see another steamer flying a purple banner, you may contact the Columbian embassy. When you're satisfied, get back in the steamer and keep heading east. Follow the steamer with another purple banner. Stop when it does, and you will be contacted. Do you have that?"

"Expressway south to Beehive Three. East on Three, until I see the purple banner. Contact the embassy. Confirm Llysette's safety. Then head east again. Stop when the next steamer with the banner does."

"Correct."

The line went dead.

Simple enough. What wasn't spoken was equally simple. Once Llysette was free, my life was forfeit if at any point I tried to double-cross them. Somehow, I'd feel better, a lot better, once Llysette got into the Columbian embassy.

I wiped my forehead, damp despite the chill, looked at the pitifully small Reno, swallowed, and walked back to the steamer.

It sounded simple. I got to drive a small steamer south on the expressway and then out into the Fastness of Zion, along some back road, with no one following, not closely anyway.

Once the radio confirmed that Llysette was safe and I talked to her, then I would get back in the steamer and follow the first steamer I saw with another purple flag.

I followed 300 East south for three blocks, then turned east. Another five blocks found me turning onto the expressway south.

The traffic, for Deseret, was heavy, a mix of haulers, battered steamers, and glistening new Brownings, and I had to concentrate on driving, more than I had anticipated.

Beehive Route Three almost crept by me, and I had to take the ramp at a higher speed than I'd figured. The poor Reo shuddered as I applied the brakes to make the stop at the top of the incline.

I waited for a westbound tanker bearing the logo "Deseret Fuels" and easily several dozen times the size of the Reo. Then I turned behind a gray Browning that left me in the dust of the two-lane road that angled toward the mountains.

To my right, I could see a second flat lake, surrounded by factories, with smoke and steam pouring into the chill early-winter air. The higher reaches of the mountains framed by the front windscreen were mostly white.

I drove for more than a quarter of an hour, intermittently being passed, and drawing closer and closer to the mountains, taller than I realized. A glance in the rearview mirror told me that a glistening red steamer was sweeping up behind. The road on the other side was clear, and the red Browning swept past, then slowed. A purple flag popped from the side window and fluttered there. I just watched for a moment, then finally lowered my window and waved. What else was I supposed to do?

The red Browning accelerated out of sight even before I pulled out into a wide turnout on the right side.

I glanced around. The turnout was empty, except for a painted green metal drum for trash.

After opening the door and setting the radio on the roof, I cranked up the collapsible antenna. The frequencies were already set. I cleared my throat, my heart pounding.

"Embassy, this is Eschbach. Do you read me?"

After a moment of static, an answer squawked through the speaker: "Say again, please."

"Embassy, this is Eschbach. Do you read me?"

"We read you, Minister. A little weak, but we read you. There's someone who wants to talk to you."

I hoped it was Llysette. Lord, I hoped!

"Johan?"

"Llysette?"

"Mais oui, mon cher. . . ." Her voice was tired, but it sounded like her voice, despite the static.

"How is Carolynne?" No one else would know what I meant, and I hoped that she wasn't too tired to understand.

"Ah, she and I are well. Did you know that once she sang for the First Prophet?"

I frowned and tried to call up a memory or an image . . . but only got a hazy sense of limelights. "I don't recall that."

"That was before she met the deacon."

"Are you all right?"

"I am tired. I have some bruises. This was not bad. This was not so bad as the Fall of France." She laughed gently. "It was not so bad as when you and I came to know Carolynne better."

"You're sure."

"Certain I am."

I nodded. "You take care, and stay in the Columbian embassy until this is over."

"Mais oui. I do not like what you do."

Neither did I. "I'll be fine," I lied.

"You must take care. You, we want you back safely."

"I wanted you back safely."

"We know. Take care, *mon cher."*

"You, too. I'll do the best I can. Just keep yourself safe."

I finally flicked off the radio and glanced around the turnout. A battered black hauler rumbled past, its front hood wreathed in steam, then another new Browning, this one blue.

The radio antenna went down, the unit back into the seat beside me, and I eased the Reo out back onto Route Three, still headed east. All I could do was hope . . . hope that everything went right, knowing that, once again, it probably wouldn't.

I drove steadily east for another ten minutes, until I needed a side road. Abruptly a cargo hauler pulled out in front of me, a square purple banner flying from the black-painted door mirror frame. I slowed to follow the big steamhauler.

Five minutes later, the hauler turned left, back north, along Beehive Six, and in less than ten minutes we were back on the expressway, headed north.

Perhaps three miles farther north, the hauler slowed and stopped under a bridge. I swallowed and stopped right behind it, then picked up the case, leaving the radio behind but triggering the transmitter with a blank signal. That might help.

I walked toward the hauler, the kind with a double cab and without windows in the back. The rear cab door on the shoulder side was open. I saw no one, and the front window was blackened.

I stepped up into the rear seat, empty, and with a partition between the front seats and the rear.

Nothing happened.

I sighed and closed the door, sitting there in the gray gloom of the enclosed space, unable to see who was driving, where I was headed, and where I was going. With a hiss, the hauler eased out into the traffic I couldn't see.

CHAPTER TWENTY-EIGHT

• • •

On the narrow bench seat in the back of the hauler I bounced, occasionally steadying myself, as the vehicle turned off the expressway and began to wind through streets, presumably of Great Salt Lake City. The single door had no window. The odor of oil and heated metal seeped up around me, and the space was hot, especially with a wool suit coat and the plastique vest that didn't really breathe. Even after taking off my overcoat, I felt faintly nauseated without any fresh air.

After a time, the hauler slowed, then stopped, and a rumbling screech followed. Then the hauler inched forward and lurched to a second stop. The screech of ill-lubricated metal punctuated more rumbling. The hiss of escaping steam indicated a shutdown. I waited.

Finally, a figure in a gray jumpsuit, wearing a gauzy sort of black hood over his head that concealed all but his general head shape, opened the door. "Minister Eschbach?"

"That's me."

"Follow me, please."

Without much choice, I followed the fellow. He didn't think much of me or my abilities—or knew I wouldn't do much—because he scarcely looked in my direction as we walked through what seemed to be an industrial garage and down a narrow corridor to a door, which he unlocked.

"If you would."

I stepped into the room—more like a prison cell, I supposed. No windows, a pallet bed, a shower nozzle over a drain surrounded by a curtain, and an exposed toilet. No sink. One towel hung on a wooden bracket on the wall, a bar of soap on the back of the toilet.

He stepped inside after me. "What's in the case?"

"Material I thought I might need."

"You might. Would you open it, please, and leave it on the floor?"

I did and stepped back, trying to sniff the air, which smelled like industrial solvents and chlorine combined.

He leafed through the papers. Despite the hood, I had the feeling his eyes were half on me—alert but very amateurish. Then he stood.

"What exactly do you want?" I asked. No sense in assuming too much.

"The ghost of the first Revelator. Your skills should be sufficient to locate and recall up his ghost."

"Not Prophet Young?"

"He was the antiprophet who turned the Saints from the true path to Zion."

I didn't pretend to know that much about Brigham Young, but I had to wonder how the prophet who had built an independent nation out of the wilderness had set the Saints on the wrong path. "I'm not sure I understand. . . ."

"They've hidden it, but it's there," answered the tall figure. He shifted his weight and stated, as if he were quoting, "Verily, verily, I say unto thee, no one shall be appointed to receive my commandments and revelations in this church excepting my servant Joseph Smith, Junior."

I waited, and I wasn't disappointed.

"And if thou art led at any time by the Comforter to speak or teach, or at all times by the way of the commandment unto the church, thou must do it. But thou shalt not write by way of commandment, but by wisdom; and thou shalt not command him who is at thy head, and the head of the church."

"I take it that means that there are no other prophets but Joseph Smith?" I tried to ask casually.

"Even an unbeliever understands that, and yet those hypocrites who strut in the Temple do not. ´

I couldn't imagine First Counselor J. Press Cannon strutting anywhere but kept my mouth shut.

"Even the Danites have forgotten the meaning of their motto."

"I'm afraid I don't know the motto."

"It's from the Book of Daniel: 'They shall take the kingdom and possess it forever.' President Taylor's weaknesses will turn Deseret back to the Lamanites of the south and the Zoramites of Columbia."

"And?" I asked gently.

"All that the prophet strove for will be lost. Once again, Sampson shall rise.

You wouldn't know that, Gentile, but Sampson always rises again. Sampson Avard was one of the pillars of the early Saints, until the followers of Satan turned the prophet against him."

"That's all very well, but how do you expect me to locate a ghost that vanished more than a century ago?"

"You have that knowledge." Abruptly he stepped back and closed the door. The lock clicked.

I closed the datacase and set it on the foot of the pallet bed and began to study the room, or converted toolroom. The walls were cinder or cement block, the floor ancient concrete. So was the ceiling. I checked the door—metal, solid core, steel-framed, with the hinges on the outside. Not impossible to get out of in a pinch, assuming there was some steel in the bed frame or that a few things on my person might assist, but the work would be laborious and noisy. A single lightbulb was set in a bracket above the door, but no switch was visible in the room.

The area had been prepared well, and in advance. I went and sniffed around the pallet bed. No scent of Ivoire, and that probably meant they'd held Llysette elsewhere. Good for her, not so good for me.

"You have that knowledge." The certainty of those words chilled me. They weren't asking me to create a ghost. They'd been told that I could find a ghost that had once existed, a very specific ghost. That was impossible. The first Revelator's electromagnetic spirit field had long since dissipated, if it had even survived his assassination. Yet to escape, to have any chance of surviving, I had to do that. And that meant creating an "old" ghost from scratch. Subconsciously I'd figured out something along that line, but I'd thought the Revealed Twelve were political opportunists who'd wanted me to create a ghost for political purposes. Instead, I had theological fanatics who'd been set up by someone else. They still needed a ghost, but . . . fooling them would be hard, far harder than what I'd anticipated.

With a shrug I sat on the end of the pallet bed. I didn't touch the scan-transparent blade that remained in my belt or anything else. There was no reason to, yet.

Perhaps a half hour passed, and I finally checked my watch—twenty minutes. I opened the case and began to study the notes I'd taken.

Some time later, the door clicked, and a shorter figure stood there.

"If you would come this way, it's time to begin your work."

I didn't ask if the work was mandatory.

The second door in the corridor was open. He gestured, and I stepped inside. Light poured down from a bank of ceiling glow strips. The walls were generally the same blocks, and there was a large glass mirror inset on one wall. Next to the single door was a booth or shield of sorts, which was topped with two feet of leaded glass. Another figure, also in a gray jumpsuit and hooded, stood there. The side of the shield facing the difference engine shimmered.

The more I saw, the less I liked it. In the middle of the room were an oak table and chair. On the table were several items I recognized.

In fact, I had to swallow. The difference engine on the table was almost an exact clone of my own SII machine, and it was fitted with the gadgetry Bruce and I had developed—that is, the projection/collection antennae, but nothing that resembled the de-ghosting projector.

"I take it you find this familiar?" There was a laugh.

"I have to compliment you on your thoroughness."

"Take a seat, Minister Eschbach."

I saw no reason not to, even though he didn't sit, probably since there was only the single chair, except for the stool for the guard behind the booth shield.

"Let's make it simple," I suggested. "What do you want?"

"You know that already. We want you to bring back the ghost of the first prophet, the Revelator of Truth."

"That might be possible," I conceded.

"We've been led to believe that it is very possible."

"Do you have any real timetable for all this?"

"We had hoped you could bring back the ghost of the Revelator within a week."

"I'll need some help from you."

"You're the expert."

"Not on the prophet. To . . . recall . . . his ghost I'll need some help on what teachings and sayings you feel are the most important."

"Why?"

"The more information I have, the easier the location will be." That was as close to the truth as I could get.

"That might be possible." My escort gestured toward the difference engine. "You can begin anytime. It would be more useful if you didn't attempt to direct any of the antennae in this direction." His hand went to the mirror set into the wall facing the difference engine. "That is two-way glass. You'll be under constant surveillance from at least two points."

With a cough and then a click of the door, he was gone. The click told me another thing: it was locked from the outside as well, locking one guard in with me.

They'd had some briefing on my background. Not only that, but somehow, I felt they didn't trust me.

I looked around the gray room. Everything was gray or reflective gray. There was too much money and preparation for simple fanatics, and that bothered me. It bothered me a lot.

Finally, I took out one of Bruce's pens and some paper. Then I flicked on the difference engine. It called up my own directory. I swallowed again, when I saw the disk case by the keyboard—with the backups for the hidden files for ghost creation.

No . . . I wasn't dealing with just a bunch of political schismatics. The combination of religious fanatics and an unknown political manipulator was even worse. I swallowed and looked around at the gray once more. My forehead was very damp, and I felt flushed all over.

CHAPTER TWENTY-NINE

• • •

Early tuesday morning found me back in front of the equipment that effectively duplicated my own, looking at a stack of my own notes and shifting back and forth between three profile configurations, with another hooded and silent guard watching everything.

The concrete-walled and -ceilinged room still smelled of ancient oil and dusty concrete and of heated synthetics being cured in the new difference engine before me.

One stack of notes blurred into another, and I massaged my stiff neck.

When I'd tried to create the first replica of Carolynne, the whole profile had collapsed. I never did really create her ghost doppelgänger from scratch—if *doppelgänger* were the term for a copy of a ghost of a singer who'd been killed a century earlier. I'd actually ended up making a duplicate of the real ghost of Carolynne. The ghost of justice and mercy had never been more than a caricature—enough to still give me shivers when he/it surfaced inside my soul, but a caricature. Now I had to create a "real" complete ghost, when I'd never accomplished that before, while pretending that I was only "finding" an existing ghost. And I had to get it done in a way in which I could walk away from the results.

Would three separate profile configurations be enough? I shook my head. Not for what I had in mind. My eyes went to the gray screen and the pointer poised there.

Finally, I called up what I'd been working on and took a deep breath, looking at the smeared mirror surface of the two-way glass across the top of the difference engine from me. All I saw was the reflection of a stubbled professor, once again in over his head.

The guard remained silent.

I started to set up the sketchy profile files for loading, but when I did try the loading, the machine locked.

The guard leaned forward. I reset the difference engine and waited. The same thing happened again. So I took out the empty auxiliary disk and studied it.

I could tell, as usual, nothing was going quite as planned, either for my captors or for me. They hadn't bothered to get SII auxiliary disks, or the generic equivalent, and I needed the auxiliaries because the equipment was designed to use both the fixed disk and the auxiliary simultaneously or actually in rapid switch succession. That wouldn't have been a problem in Columbia, but Deseret used the New French standards, with a different balance and spin rate.

Purists would say that you can vary the auxiliary disk spin rate and it makes no difference. In fact, some claim you can get better performance that way. Maybe . . . but my system—or the clone set up by the Revealed Twelve—wouldn't take standard Deseret disks. I was finding that out early on.

I reset the difference engine, cleared the screen, and tried a disk format.

"Not reading auxiliary drive" scripted out on the screen.

For a moment, I sat there looking at the machine. Finally, I turned to the guard behind the shield.

"I need standard Colombian auxiliary disks. These don't work, and I can't reformat them, and they'll only foul up the system."

"Keep working."

"I'll do what I can, but I can't finish the project without at least one auxiliary disk." I rubbed my stubbly chin. The shower, such as it was, kept me clean, but my clothes weren't getting any fresher, and I hadn't brought even spare underwear—another one of those stupid oversights. I was making entirely too many of those.

The guard mumbled or grunted.

I touched the cover of the difference engine.

"You don't need to do that," he snapped.

So . . . they didn't want me monkeying with the equipment. That also triggered my suspicious mind.

I played around with Bruce's calculator and diddled some figures, then put it back in my pocket and wrote out some more code lines to build up the profile that I'd eventually have to transfer to the disks I didn't have.

Another guard stepped into the room, and the two mumbled for a moment, low enough that I couldn't hear, before the second disappeared and the lock clicked.

I spent another hour or so building up the quote files, selectively speaking, and trying to design a structure to create parallel interlocking files that the antennae could project in close to real-time simultaneity.

Just about the time I thought I had something, the door to my small section of the blockhouse opened and a tall figure stepped inside. He didn't move far from the booth/shield.

"You said you needed more disks. Why? Why do you need them to recall a ghost that already exists?"

I managed to keep my jaw shut while my thoughts whirled. He really meant it.

"It's hard to explain," I temporized. "Let me put it this way. In our world, which is a temporal world and not primarily a spiritual one, we rely on physical structure to hold us together—our skeletons, for example. A ghost is held together by an energy structure, an energy profile. When the profile loses energy, it collapses." I cleared my throat. "I have to re-create the profile, and that means a lot of storage capacity. Once the profile is re-created and energized, the ghost reappears, but the profile has to be as accurate as possible, in order to ensure that the reenergized ghost is the correct one." I felt proud of myself—momentarily—until I realized the rest of the implications.

After a moment of silence, I pointed to the notes and *The Book of Mormon*. "You can see. I'm using verified statements of the prophet as keys to the profile."

After a long silence, the tall man spoke. "How many disks do you need?" He seemed to be the same one who had led me into the blockhouse—that's what it felt like—and who seemed to be in charge of the group.

"I *might* be able to get by with one, but three, in case of problems—"

"Problems?"

I did sigh, turning in the chair to face him. "I don't know what anyone told you, but this is a new and fairly experimental procedure. This is something where some government research laboratories have failed for years. You want me to duplicate that kind of work with minimal equipment." I didn't tell him that I wouldn't have been able to do it at all without the years of work from one of those laboratories—or the genius of the late Professor Branston-Hay.

"Why aren't you using the antennae?"

I frowned at the change of subject. "Because that's the last stage, when you project the profiles and the fields."

"How much delay will this cause?" he asked.

"Very little if you can get the disks within the next day. I would have liked to load them incrementally, but that's not absolutely necessary."

I had another thought. "If you can get an image scanner and a likeness of the prophet that you think is the most representative, those would also help."

Another period of silence, and then the mesh hood nodded and the door opened and he departed.

As the hours went by, I tended to lose track of time until I checked my watch and found that when I was thinking time sped and when I was wool-gathering, trying to puzzle out vague conceptualizations for the refinements I knew I needed, it dragged.

Every four hours or so, I got something to eat—basically a slab of meat, some bread, a piece of fruit, and some powdered chocolate in a mug. Another guard delivered it. That is, he set it on the floor, and I got it and had to put it back there when I was done.

It was close enough to the booth that I probably could have disabled the guard—but why? I still couldn't have gotten out of the place.

Someone always watched me from the booth, but seldom the same person for more than a few hours, although each wore a gray jumpsuit with no markings and one of the fine loose mesh hoods.

In working out the code lines, I made a point of apparently using one of the pens Bruce had provided and the calculator. I wanted both to be familiar to all the Revealed Twelve people.

I tried not to think about Llysette or much of anything else except what I wanted and needed to do, and that was to create the most powerful ghost image possible—the stronger and more imposing the better. That had been one reason I'd wanted to check the hardware early.

The graphics images would be the hardest, because all the Saints had an in-grained visual concept of Joseph Smith and I'd never really done that much with that side of ghost file creation. In my previous efforts I'd let the internal substance create the image, and that wouldn't be enough for a really strong ghost image of the prophet. I hoped that they'd come up with a scanner, but . . . that remained to be seen.

I took a deep breath and looked at the third—or fourth—guard. The eyes behind the veiled or mesh hood could have been open, closed, or glaring. I wouldn't have known.

After standing and stretching, I sat down again and looked at some of the quotations I had to incorporate into what I would have called the dialogue profile:

All things unto me are spiritual, and not at any time have I given unto you a law which is temporal. . . .

Behold, verily, I say unto you that there are many spirits which are false spirits, which have gone forth in the earth, deceiving the world. And also Satan hath sought to deceive you, that he might overthrow you. . . .

Wherefore, for this cause I gave unto you . . . and I will give unto you my law, and there you shall be endowed with power from on high. . . .

Then there were those that I'd modified, that I hoped would be close enough to the structure and yet would reinforce the current "regime" and its efforts. Neither I nor Columbia wanted a government in Deseret controlled by religious fanatics basing their actions on a century-and-a-half-old code that hadn't been that workable then. Like it or not, I had to support First Speaker Cannon, and I wasn't thrilled about it. I was just less thrilled about the alternatives.

As the angel Moroni said, do not anger so exceedingly that you have lost thy love, one towards another. Do not thirst after blood and revenge continually. . . .

How can a people delight in abomination—and in killing our neighbors and those who have not lifted a hand against us—how can we expect that God will stay his hand in judgment against us? . . .

For behold, a bitter fountain cannot bring forth good water; neither can a bitter man bring forth good works. . . .

Condemn not your brother because of his imperfections, neither his father, because of his imperfection, neither them who have written before him, but rather give thanks unto God that he hath made manifest unto you those imperfections that ye may learn to be more wise than we have been. . . .

Cursed is he who puts his trust in man. More cursed is he that puts his trust in a man's false interpretation of what I have said. Trust rather the Revelations of thy Father in heaven than the man who twists my words. . . .

Unto each generation cometh the Revelations of God; harken unto them, for the Lord will provide, both counsel and providence for those who listen. . . .

I had to hope that no one was going to go through thousands of lines of code, but I had this feeling that they wouldn't, that *any* image of the prophet would serve the purposes of the Revealed Twelve.

I swallowed and looked at the difference engine screen. It was going to be a long day, with at least several more to come.

CHAPTER THIRTY

• • •

Tuesday, I stayed in the blockhouse difference engine room working Babbage code lines until close to midnight. Why? Because the only way out was to create what they wanted, and more. At least, that was the only way I saw it, and worry wouldn't allow me to sleep until I was exhausted. So why not work?

I did, and I was so tired that the continual drip from the shower nozzle didn't keep me from sleeping. Nor did the rock-hard pallet bed, nor the clamminess of the de facto cell, nor just about any of the inconveniences.

Wednesday morning, I struggled through a cold shower—the nozzle was piped only to a cold water line. I felt grubby enough to suffer through it before shivering dry and pulling back on dirty clothes.

Still thinking about whether my captors could or would come up with a compatible scanner and the SII-style auxiliary disks, I took *The Book of Mormon* and began to read through it.

Parts of it struck me as strange—strange because I had to wonder. How could a barely literate farm boy who followed a vision from Virginia backcountry to upstate New Ostend ever even transcribe a five-hundred-page printed manuscript, let alone keep it consistent? Or was it consistent? I wasn't enough of a biblical scholar to tell.

How did he manage to convert thousands to a new religion—or a new manifestation of the old? Would he have managed it if things had been different? If the English colony at Plymouth had succeeded?

I pursed my lips and blinked. Those kinds of speculations weren't exactly useful in my situation.

I had only read another few pages when the door opened and another of the hooded figures stood there, waiting.

When the lock clicked on the difference engine room, in addition to a tray with bread, cheese, and fruit on the floor, a number of objects had been added to my occupational prison.

On the table beside the difference engine was an SII scanner—used, it seemed. In addition to the scanner, the cabling, and the manual, three blank SII disks lay beside the difference engine—as if to suggest that I would have no excuses for failure. In a way, I was more worried about the aftermath of success.

I picked up the portrait of the prophet—a size that would fit entirely on the screen of the flat-bed scanner, allowing me to get it in one pass, assuming I could make the codes match, and that was a big assumption.

Although I wanted to shake my head, I didn't. The heavy gray concrete slab ceiling seemed poised to collapse on me—like everything else. For a moment, I felt very sorry for myself. All I'd really wanted after Elspeth's and Waltar's deaths had been to retreat, to gain some quiet. I'd been lucky enough to find love and respect with Llysette—and Carolynne—but my past seemed to dog me . . . and them.

Why couldn't the powers that be leave us alone? Why couldn't Llysette be allowed to perform without being used as a pawn in a four-sided—or who knew how many-sided—diplomatic and military chess game? Other retired Spazi agents didn't have their lives turned upside down. Other singers, with less talent than Llysette, got to perform and be recognized and make money without risking life and limb.

My eyes burned, and I did shake my head. Self-pity wasn't going to do the slightest for me.

So I coughed, cleared my throat, and ate most of what was on the tray. Not particularly hungry, I still ate, because I didn't think well with low blood sugar and I needed to be able to think.

I definitely needed to think, since what I was attempting was insane. If I succeeded, I'd have to create a ghost that wasn't too apparently distinguishable from a real ghost. Was there theoretically any difference? I didn't know. And if I succeeded in my wild scheme, the ghost had to support the doctrine of the current Saint church leaders, and I had to develop that right under the eyes of the leaders of the Revealed Twelve. That wasn't a problem. Escaping the Twelve would be, and then I'd have to find a way to escape Cannon. Why? Like a lot of things, I couldn't explain why, but I didn't trust the First Speaker, and I hadn't survived all those years as a Spazi agent by ignoring my feelings.

When I finished eating, I set the tray back on the floor and opened the installation manual for the scanner, ignoring the guard and the reflection of a tired and haggard-looking man who had no business doing what he was doing.

Physically connecting everything was easy enough, and so was installing the conversion programs—on a disk I hadn't seen at first.

Once it looked like the system and scanner worked, I eased the image onto the scanner and toggled the scanner on, waiting until it stopped humming and the codes had been fed to the file. Then I called up the receiving file on the screen. Half of what should have been code lines was gibberish.

When I ran the file back through a conversion protocol to get a screen image, all that popped into place was something like a blueprint.

As I had feared, obtaining a graphics image compatible with the ghost file protocols was going to be the problem. In my earlier efforts, the internal substance had effectively created the image, and that wouldn't be enough for a really strong ghost image of the prophet that resembled his image.

In the end, I reverted to doing it by trial and error, using the image scanner on gray-scale and edging the contrast as high as possible. Then I started jiggering the codes into a matrix of sorts.

By the time the midday tray arrived with beef, bread, fruit, and fifth-rate chocolate, I was still working on the codes for the top third of the image.

Midafternoon found me, after two breaks to use the facilities in my cell, with a complete set of codes for the image profile, but codes probably not defined enough. Still, I saved the file on one of the auxiliary disks, then called the image onto the screen.

What I got was a ghostly image on the screen. I compared it to the copy of the painting and shook my head. I needed more definition, and I wasn't sure how to get it.

"How are you doing?"

I jumped a foot from the chair. I hadn't even heard the tall man enter.

"You work hard."

"It's hard work."

"Why is the image so important?" He actually sounded curious.

"Because I have to recall the entire ghost," I answered, trying not to lie too egregiously. "It's hard in the case of the prophet because so many others have spoken his words." That was certainly true enough.

The hood bobbed as though he had nodded. Then he took the tray and left, and the lock clicked. I hadn't even noticed, but a new and shorter guard had taken the place of the former guard.

Sometime after what might have been dinnertime, I ran a second image. Clearer, but still, I felt, not strong enough to carry what I had to load onto it and into it.

I tried second subroutines below the codes, cross-linked, and that improved the image, but the improvement in the areas that were double-coded showed the deficiencies where I hadn't tried subroutines.

By then, my eyes burned and my head ached and I couldn't even think.

I glanced toward the guard. "I can't do anything more."

There was no response. I just put my head down on the table and closed my eyes.

Within minutes, the lock clicked and the tall figure was back.

"What have you accomplished?"

"I've got a basic image to which I can tie the recall programs." My voice was hoarse, even if I hadn't spoken much. Maybe it was rusty from disuse.

"How do we know this will work?"

"When I've got everything ready, I'll give you a test run." I took a deep breath. "Look at the screen. Is this beginning to look like Prophet Smith?"

I called up the image.

"It is similar."

"But not close enough. Well, that's what I need to work more on, but I can't even see the screen in front of me at the moment. I'm calling it a night."

He didn't object as he led me back to my cell-like quarters, and that confirmed, in my mind, a few more suspicions. I was too tired to examine the implications in any depth, and once I was on the pallet bed, my eyes closed despite the dripping from the shower nozzle, despite the odor of oil and dusty concrete.

CHAPTER THIRTY-ONE

• • •

I lurched awake, drenched in sweat from running through endless corridors papered in difference engine printouts, banging at doors that were only images plastered over steel walls, blood running from fingers raw from trying to claw my way through solid steel.

Sitting, breathing heavily, on the edge of the pallet bed, I rubbed my eyes and looked at my hands. No blood. Then, I studied the four walls again.

Nothing had changed. The bulb over the gray metal door still bathed my cell quarters in dim light. The shower nozzle dripped. I still smelled old oil and cement dust. My datacase stood by the side of the bed, and my head ached.

Finally I checked my watch—six o'clock Thursday morning, less than three days, and I was both exhausted and ready to murder the whole lot of them. Llysette was safe, at least, provided Second Secretary Trumbull-Hull hadn't reneged, provided . . . provided . . . I didn't want to think about all the things that could have gone wrong. That way lay even greater insanity.

Instead, I took a cold shower and washed away the worst of the stink of my own fears.

Then I forced myself to write out more codes and ideas while I waited to be retrieved for more work.

It was becoming clear, all too clear, that unless I could resolve this problem, the next one would be worse—I wouldn't stand a chance because I'd simply get potted with a sniper rifle. Then everyone would deny everything, wonder publicly, and I'd be an entry on the obituary page. Llysette would mourn—for awhile—but no one mourns forever.

That line of thought made me even angrier, especially at those who had set me up, and the list included the oh-so-helpful Minister Jerome—for who else could have allowed a search of my house?—Speaker Cannon, Brother Jensen, and possibly even Harlaan Oakes. I was convinced, for some reason I couldn't nail down yet, that Cannon wanted me in the hands of the Revealed Twelve. If they killed me, then he had a civil hook, so to speak, to eliminate them. If I succeeded in somehow disrupting their plans or escaping, then that proved that God was not on their side—at the very least. And . . . miracle of miracles, if I pulled off creating a ghost that supported the existing order, all would be well for Cannon, Deseret, and Columbia . . . and who would care about the wear and tear on the poor Eschbachs?

I went back to work, grimly, and had three pages in longhand before they got me at eight o'clock. The timing confirmed yet other suspicions about their status and class—all good family men maintaining a hidden retreat manned by younger disciples. I wouldn't have been totally surprised if the entire place were locked and deserted while I slept—except for one or two of the new faithful—but I really didn't see the point in trying to escape, not yet.

My escort to the difference engine part of the redoubt was someone new, slightly more rotund—also in the gray jumpsuit and mesh hood.

The difference engine area hadn't changed either—gray concrete, shimmering booth shield, and smeared one-way glass that reflected a man whose beard was coming in mostly white. I knew there was a reason I preferred to be clean-shaven, against the Dutch tradition or not.

I wolfed down the half-breakfast while the difference engine went through its checks. Then I entered all the code lines I'd written over the hours preceding.

The prophet's image was sharper, perhaps sharp enough, because the other profile sections would further refine that image. Time to go back to text.

Sometime after midday the door opened to admit four people. The three figures behind the tall leader turned their hooded visages toward me but did not speak. All three wore dark cloaks under the hoods, so voluminous that their shapes were indistinct even under the gently unforgiving light of the blockhouse's—or warehouse's—glow strips.

"Report on your progress, Minister Eschbach." The word "Minister" was almost mocking.

I ignored that.

"I might have something. . . . Actually, I could show you something now."

"How do we know this will work?"

How many times had I heard that question?

"It will work. I could provide a demonstration."

"Good. After that, we will give you the coordinates where the prophet will be recalled."

I had to force the laugh, but I managed, and then it wasn't forced because the sheer ludicrousness of the demand became all too hysterical.

When I finally choked off the laughter, the tall man snapped, "Explain."

"Don't you understand? You can't do this from a distance. Where this equipment is—that's where the prophet's ghost will . . . reappear." I almost choked on that. "You're lucky I can do that."

"How does that allow a demonstration?"

"I'll manifest the profile, then collapse it before it recalls the actual prophet's ghost."

"Then do so."

I shrugged and began to work, checking the projection antennae and then the auxiliary disk before loading the one I wanted . . . the incomplete one that didn't draw full power. I also set up the program run to trigger only three of the eight profile configurations.

"Are you ready?" I asked after about ten minutes. They were beginning to fidget—no patience at all. If they'd known what I was thinking I'd have died three times over.

Almost immediately, at the focus of the antennae appeared the hazy patriarchal image—from the waist up, since I hadn't bothered with lower limbs on the partial disk—wavering into place, white-limned and slightly flickering, but strong enough to cast a faint reflection in the mirror of the two-way glass.

"It is the Revelator." Even the tall man's voice was hushed.

"This is only a partial retrieval, and I need to collapse it." I turned off the entire difference engine—safer and quicker that way.

The image vanished like the flame of a quick-snuffed candle.

"Why?"

"You don't want the Revelator to be anchored here, do you?"

The fact that there was no answer was answer enough.

"That will not affect his ghost, will it?" His voice was almost anguished.

"The full ghost was never called. That was just the ghost profile. That's why it was hazy." That was a lie, of course. The figure was hazy because I'd inhibited the full projection. "You didn't want him locked here, did you?"

"That is not clear," rasped one of the three behind the tall man.

"Look," I explained. "I told you earlier, where a ghost is created or recalled, that's where the ghost remains. You can see that when a ghost is created by violent death anywhere in Deseret. The ghost doesn't move. If I call up the ghost of the Revelator here, his ghost will be locked here, and I don't think that's what you want." I gestured toward the equipment before me. "This has to be set up where you want the Revelator to be recalled and where you want his ghost to remain."

"Can one of us do it?"

I laughed, easily. "I know what I'm doing, and it's taken me years to get this far." That was true. It was also largely irrelevant.

Figures looked at each other.

"Then make the equipment ready. You will have less than two hours to re-assemble it and call the Revelator."

They all left, except for the guard. Once again, I had the feeling that whoever had briefed them had left out a few details—like I was creating ghosts and not re-calling them, like ghosts of all sorts had limited capabilities.

Why had those details been left out? Either to ensure that one Johan Eschbach got eliminated in anger or to give me a chance? Or both? Ferdinand's agent, and there had to be one in the group, wanted me dead. Maurice-Huizinga's agent—or Dietre's—wanted me to escape. Cannon wanted me to escape, and I was convinced he had his own agents in the Revealed Twelve. Any government worth its salt has agents among the dissidents, and Cannon was too capable not to. I didn't know who was who, just that they had to be there.

That was another reason why I'd pushed myself to get the ghost file done so quickly. I had to get it done before people started comparing notes, and they'd do that if I took too long.

Undoing cables and setting drives for transport was much quicker and easier than writing and checking codes. I doubt it took even a half hour.

"I'm done for today," I finally said. "Everything's ready to go whenever you are."

They led me back to my cell. I even got an earlier dinner there. But I didn't digest it very well. I knew what was coming, and there was little I could do but wait and prepare, wondering if I were really prepared, if my ghost of the Revelator would be as stunning as I'd planned.

The shower nozzle dripped, and the dim bulb shed minimal light, and I waited and sniffed old oil and cement dust—and tried not to think about all that could go wrong.

CHAPTER THIRTY-TWO

• • •

I actually found myself dozing when they came. It was quarter past midnight, and they didn't bother to knock. They still wore hoods, but not the gray jumpsuits—regular dark gray or navy blue suits and polished shoes.

"It's time to go."

I grabbed the datacase.

"You won't need that," said the tall man.

"Unless something goes wrong," I snapped.

"Let him keep it."

They let me keep the case, with the quotes and the engineering drawings, and the definite conclusion that they had absolutely no intention of seeing me walk away from my efforts.

For the first time, their weapons were obvious—all Lugers, straight Austro-Hungarian version, and all of very recent manufacture, and that confirmed that Ferdinand's people had placed one agent, very openly.

The tall man pointed toward the corridor by which I'd entered. "Straight ahead."

"Where's the difference engine?" I asked.

"In the hauler. You'll travel with it."

I let my steps drag slightly so that I edged back toward the guards who followed, enough so that I had a chance . . . a faint one, but one against an untrained fanatic.

The hauler wasn't the commercial kind that had brought me but a square city van, with double doors on the rear. All of us went into the cargo space, except for whoever was driving and one other figure.

The ride wasn't that long, no more than ten minutes, really, before the hauler backed up to some sort of loading dock. Someone opened the double doors.

"You carry the equipment case, Eschbach."

As requested, I picked it up, and set the datacase on top of it.

Two more slender figures carried the difference engine.

I got the faintest glimpse of white light—the Temple, I suspected—in the crack between the van doors and the loading dock doors. Even the quick breath of cold air smelled clean, compared to the way I smelled and felt and the oil and cement dust I had been breathing for days.

I followed the two men with the difference engine down a narrow staircase to a ventilation duct that had been removed. The Twelve people liked ventilation ducts, I gathered.

I didn't like carrying anything but resolved to throw both cases or drop them strategically at the slightest provocation.

I didn't have any.

Three more of them walked behind me, carrying the long-barreled Lugers pointed in my direction as we walked along the empty tunnel, leading presumably to the Tabernacle.

It had to be the Tabernacle, because the Temple hadn't been consecrated until well after the death of Joseph Smith. Hard to imagine how a Virginia farm boy ended up in New Ostend, called to a mystical hill among skeptical Dutch, proclaiming a new religion that had turned into a sovereign and powerful nation in little more than a century.

The Tabernacle made sense for several other reasons. It was open to outsiders, and thus the ghost of the prophet would reinforce their claims not just in the Temple, but to all. And of course, everyone would understand his words just as they did. I almost laughed at that but instead kept lugging the equipment box and my datacase.

The tunnel smelled faintly of dust and of a sickly-sweet odor I would rather not have identified and hoped represented the remains of smaller rather than larger animal matter. The only sounds were those of eight men breathing—strange how most armed fanatic organizations are predominantly male—and the echoes of steps in the tunnel that my head almost brushed.

At the other end of the tunnel was an ancient wrought-iron gate whose lock had been previously drilled out. How many tunnels were there beneath the Temple square? Probably not so many as there would have been if Columbia had been successful in the Saint wars.

Then, there might not have been a Temple or Tabernacle at all. Who could tell what might have been?

"Up the stairs."

The stone steps looked ancient, but they couldn't have been. The centers were barely hollowed, and the stone walls were rough. I followed the two with the difference engine, and we exited from a closet into an arched foyer, gloomy and dark.

I waited, since the others did. The tall man eased up beside me. "How close does it have to be to where you recall the ghost?"

"Five to ten feet."

There was a sense of a nod, and he stepped in front of the men with the difference engine. "Follow me."

They did, and I did, too, my booted feet nearly silent where the carpet lay over the stone floor.

In the dimness, they set the difference engine on the floor in the open space between where the Choir of the Saints normally sat in the high raised seats and the lower seats occupied by worshipers or whoever came to hear speakers or the choir.

One of the younger men laid a power cord from somewhere in the back.

With a hooded figure holding a flash wand, I reconnected the difference engine cabling and then set the antennae in place. Without waiting for any sort of approval, I flicked the power switch and monitored the machine as it self-checked.

I kept checking the positions of the various schismatics, knowing that I'd have only instants once the Revelator's ghost materialized, knowing that I wouldn't have a chance to recheck when the time came. I'd just have to act, and hope the old training held enough to immobilize those necessary to escape.

My mouth was dry as I set up the programs and profiles and laid the auxiliary disk and its backup out. Theoretically, what I had in mind would work. It had worked before, but not quite so much had been riding on it, and I'd be really pushing the power parameters with my modifications, not that I had any choice.

First I made sure all eight profile sections were keyed to be projected; then I loaded the auxiliary disk. Then I gave the execute command and prayed . . . but not for long. While the power built and the antennae almost hummed and vibrated, I eased the calculator from my jacket pocket—I'd left my overcoat behind—then waited until a ghostly shape began to appear in the darkness. Ghosts are slightly phosphorescent and far more impressive in near-total darkness than in daylight or artificial light. Glow strips, especially, tend to wash them out, but the Tabernacle was dark.

The face, and the expressive eyes, appeared first, and then the figure in antique clothes.

The difference engine began to whine, ever so slightly, and I could smell the overload, the odor of ozone and overheating plastics and circuit boards.

"Wherefore, hear my voice and follow me, and you shall be a free people, and ye shall have no laws but my laws when I come, for I am your lawgiver, and what can stay my hand?"

Even the voice was stronger than ghost-normal, except it was more like a mental voice—that was true of all ghosts. People tended to hear the kind of voice they expected, and that should help slow the reactions of those around me.

The eight stood there, stunned.

I had to admit—the ghost was pretty impressive, turning his head from side to side in midair, as if to judge them. The beard was white, patriarchal, definitely patriarchal, and the eyes seemed to burn.

I slipped the pens into the calculator and slowly stood, as silently as possible, angling to one side, so that the disassociator wouldn't impact the ghost of the Revelator.

"That if the day cometh that the power and the gifts of God shall be done away among you, it shall be because of unbelief. . . . To believe in man, any man, prophet or man, rather than in the living God and his Revelations, that is idolatry, and marks the idolator as the spawn of Laman. I did not bring your forefathers to Zion to be idolators."

I winced. That had come out more strongly than I'd expected.

Seven of the eight still looked stunned, perhaps because the ghost aura was overpowering. Number eight turned, and he had something cold and metallic in his hand.

I knew what was coming and pressed the delete key on the pseudocalculator. Bruce's toy made no sound, but the guard, reformed apostle, whoever he was, shuddered and lowered the Luger, but only momentarily. He staggered, and that was enough.

He was fighting ghosts, a disassociator, and me. I was fighting him and fatigue. The Luger clattered on the floor, and one of the other schismatics shook his head and turned slowly.

Beyond us, that sonorous voice rolled forth into their minds, seemingly turning their reflexes into molasses.

"The Lamanites shall destroy this people, for they do not repent. All peoples who do not follow the Revelations of the living God shall be destroyed."

I stepped inside his guard and crushed his throat with my elbow. He struggled for a time more, then slowly crumpled. People forget how deadly a well-placed elbow can be, and an elbow's good close up, extremely good.

Staggering back as the second schismatic moved toward me in slow motion, in my own slow motion, I bent and recovered the calculator, replaced the loose pen, and touched the delete key. The schismatic jerked like a marionette with spastic strings. His face smoothed, and a phantasm of white lifted from him and vanished. Another zombie.

I replaced the batteries in the calculator and focused it in turn on each of the six remaining figures who were entranced by the ghost of the Revelator. I had to replace the batteries once more in the process, and yet no one turned. Shooting fish in a barrel would have been more of a challenge, caught as they were in the power of the ghost that continued to become ever more real- and solid-looking even as the smell of burning insulation grew stronger.

In the end, there were also seven zombies and a body. The body was that of the first man, who had to have been Ferdinand's agent. I bent down and ripped off the wig, toupee, whatever you called it, and underneath was one of the flexible metallic-mesh helmets that Branston-Hay's team at Vanderbraak State had worn. My guts churned. I collapsed the mesh helmet and pocketed it. That evidence would have implicated Columbia, even if it had been planted by Ferdinand, and I wasn't about to let that happen.

Behind me, the ghost intoned, "Cursed is he who puts his trust in man. More cursed is he that puts his trust in a man's false interpretation of what I have said. Trust rather the Revelations of thy Father in heaven than the man who twists my words. . . ."

Even after all I'd done, it was hard to believe he wasn't talking to me. Then maybe he was.

Sometimes age and treachery are enough to overcome skill. Anyway, this time they had been. But I wasn't done. I stripped off the vest and molded the plastique in place quickly around the difference engine, then connected the wires.

I scooped up my datacase and sprinted toward the door.

I didn't quite make it before there were difference engine parts everywhere . . . some embedded in the wooden supports for the balcony. For a moment, I leaned against the outside door and gasped, before opening it and stumbling out.

Since it might have been a good idea to yell, I did: "Help!"

Nothing happened. I yelled again.

A guard in a blue uniform hurried across the lighted stones as I stepped out into the open air for the first time in what seemed forever. Behind the guard, the light-sheathed Temple towered into the dark night sky. I could even see the brighter stars, and a faint smile cracked my lips as I took a deep breath of the city's polluted air, which seemed so clean at that moment.

"Who are you? The Tabernacle's locked. What were you doing there?" His words were cold, brusque.

"I'm Columbian Minister Eschbach. I was kidnapped by . . . those people. The ones inside. You'd better contact Bishop Hansen of Saint security and the First Counselor."

"Why?" The policeman clearly didn't like my unshaven countenance.

At that point there was a second small explosion from within the Tabernacle, and I wondered what one of the zombied schismatics had been carrying. "Go see for yourself."

He didn't but waited until two compatriots arrived, and they started in on me while he eased into the Tabernacle through the smoke. I hoped some of the zombied Revealed Twelve had survived the explosion. I had no doubts that the ghost of the Revelator had.

"Can you prove you're Minister Eschbach?"

"The real Minister Eschbach is at the Columbian embassy."

I dug out my passport. "You will note, gentlemen, that I possess this passport. You will also note that it contains my picture."

Sometime around that point, Bishop Hansen trotted up. "Eschbach! Are you all right?"

The two police officers drew back and exchanged glances.

"I'm tired, and it's been a long week. I've got a few bruises, I think, but I'm in far better shape than I expected."

"Minister Eschbach was detained by the schismatics," Hansen said crisply. "Not another word."

They nodded.

I turned to him and lowered my voice. "There's some exploded equipment in there, and some very stunned schismatics. They're not going anywhere. I'd strongly suggest you get the pieces of the equipment out of there immediately and swear everyone to secrecy."

"Why?"

"There's also the ghost of the Revelator—the first prophet. You'd better see for yourself. I'll explain later. Just take care of it."

He took my arm, and we walked back through the dust into the Tabernacle. I still hung onto my datacase. Better that no one saw that, or its contents, now.

"Holy God . . . ," he murmured.

The ghost image that resembled Joseph Smith turned in midair. "Oh, the vainness, and the frailties, and the foolishness of men! When they are learned they think they are wise, and they harken not unto the counsel of God, for they set it aside, supposing they know of themselves, wherefore, their wisdom is foolishness and it profiteth them not."

The first police guard stood transfixed before us. Five of the seven zombies were still standing there as well.

Hansen swallowed and turned to me. "I knew you were trouble."

"No trouble. The Revelator—any ghost—can only say what he once said." I shrugged. "It may even convince a few people. It certainly won't help the schismatics."

"I don't know," murmured the bishop for security.

The ghost turned toward Hansen. "Unto each generation cometh the Revelations of God; harken unto them, for the Lord will provide, both counsel and providence for those who listen. . . ."

I nodded. Those words came out right, and even Counselor Cannon would like them. He'd better, the double-dealing weasel.

"I'm not sure I want to know." Hansen tapped the policeman on the arm. "Christensen! Seal the Tabernacle until we can check for damage! We don't want anyone hurt. We'll need a detail for the injured."

The ghost image winked out, then reappeared on the far side of the open space. ". . . thou shalt not write by way of commandment, but by wisdom; and thou shalt not command him who is at thy head, and the head of the church."

I stood and listened to Hansen organize the local forces, then followed him outside and listened some more while the building was cordoned off. I almost smiled. I'd done a hell of a good job.

Before long, another entourage arrived—that of First Counselor Cannon. He almost frowned when he saw me, but I smiled tiredly.

He drew me aside, away from Hansen. "What happened?"

"I'm afraid that the prophet was too much for them." I nodded toward the Tabernacle.

"You did what they wanted?"

"I'm afraid they got what they wanted. They asked me to recall the ghost of the Revelator. I didn't have much choice, as you must know. They didn't realize that they'd get the Revelator as he was, not as they thought he should be." I had to cough. My throat was raspy, my mouth dry.

Cannon's mouth opened. Behind his shoulder, Hansen smiled tightly.

I smiled more tightly. "Seven are zombies. One's dead, maybe more. I suggest you check the dead man's background very closely. That's the one with the crushed throat. I'd suspect a certain Austrian connection. They all had very new Austrian Lugers."

Cannon stepped closer. "The Tabernacle?" His voice was more curious than upset, and that, unfortunately, didn't surprise me in the slightest.

"I'm afraid the ghost of the Revelator has returned to set straight the record. Of course, I'm an outsider, but it sounds a great deal like what was recorded in the *Doctrine and Covenants.*"

"What will happen?" snapped Hansen.

I shrugged. "I'd guess what usually happens. Most ghosts fade in time."

"You believe this is the ghost of the prophet?" asked Counselor Cannon.

"I'm not equipped to judge that, Counselor," I pointed out. "All I can say is that I'd be very surprised if the ghost says anything new or radical. Ghosts don't, as a rule."

Cannon offered a warm smile, the one I really mistrusted. "Then the people will hear and believe, as they should. And I thank you."

"As they should," I reinforced. Of course, I'd chosen what words had been taken from the *Doctrine and Covenants,* and I'd been pretty careful. Cannon wouldn't like all of them. No, he wouldn't, but . . . none of us likes everything in our chosen faiths. That's what makes life interesting for a believer. "I have a small favor to ask in return, Counselor. A very small favor."

"Even the powers of a counselor are limited, as you know, Minister Eschbach."

"This is within your power. You've already offered it, and I was unable to take advantage of it. I would like you to confirm it in writing, and by immediate message to Speaker Hartpence and President Armstrong." I forced a smile. "An invitation to bring a technical team, headed by me, to study your advances in wastewater tertiary treatment and, if you will, a strong hint that the team would not be welcome without me. I think that's only fair, after all that's happened."

It was more than fair, and it was another form of insurance. Minister Reilly *wanted* that information, and I wanted the Speaker and the president to get the impression that not only was Llysette's survival important for Columbia's future and ability to obtain resources from Deseret, but mine was also. I needed every little angle I could find, especially since it was clear Jerome had betrayed me.

Cannon touched his beard, then nodded with a slow smile. "Yes, Minister Eschbach, that is something within my powers, and in all of our interests. I might also suggest it be coupled with the next performance of your wife. She might be a tremendous draw to open the summer season at the St. George opera house."

I returned the smile. "I think we would both be delighted with that offer."

"They will have the message in the morning—or later this morning. Have a good trip, Minister Eschbach, and give my best to your lovely wife."

Hansen glanced from Cannon to me, and the shock in Hansen's eyes was palpable. I couldn't say I blamed him. He was a true believer who'd just discovered that his leader not only had feet of clay but also had trafficked with the schismatics.

I touched Hansen's arm before he could speak. "I'd like to go to the Columbian embassy. I presume that's where Llysette still is."

Hansen nodded. "Unless your people moved her." His eyes went to the First Counselor.

"Will you take me, Bishop Hansen?"

Cannon cleared his throat. "Go ahead, Brother Hansen. And thank you, Minister Eschbach. Minister Jerome had said you were a man of your word, and your actions have confirmed that."

Good of them, both. I, unlike Hansen, managed to keep from swallowing as his words confirmed both his and Jerome's role. Jerome had supplied the information about psychic proliferation technologies, just enough that it couldn't be used without me, and Cannon had had it funneled to the Revealed Twelve. Very neat, even if I didn't know exactly how.

That also confirmed that Jensen had definitely been Cannon's agent in ensuring that Llysette and I had gotten into the hands of the Revealed Twelve. Not that I had a shred of real proof, which was why it would have been a mistake to say anything, but I knew . . . and Cannon knew I knew, and neither of us needed to say a word. Sometimes, that's for the best.

Hansen and I finally walked toward the south side of the Temple, where the shining Browning was waiting, amid several police steamers and two red fire steamers.

"I'll drive, Heber." Hansen motioned for the driver to get out of the Browning. "You wait here for me. I won't be too long."

Hansen said nothing until the steamer was clear of the square. "Why did you insist I escort you? My job isn't done there."

"To keep you from cutting your throat, Brother Hansen. Just think about things for a while." I meant it. Hansen was honest, and I respected that honesty. He'd been chosen as head of security because he was honest. Cannon couldn't afford a dishonest security chief; no head of government can. But that meant Hansen had been really shocked to discover the extent to which the First Counselor had manipulated the situation and had used me and the schismatics to reinforce the current Saint regime and its efforts to reduce the conflicts with Columbia.

Hansen's eyes narrowed, but the Browning kept heading east, uphill, at least in the general direction of the Columbian embassy.

After he pulled up into the "No Standing" area reserved for official vehicles, he turned in the seat. "Why do you care about me?"

"Because you're honest and, while we'll never agree on many things, I won't be party to seeing an honest man take the blame for something. So don't. Just accept it as it appears—the schismatics were overcome by the reappearance of the ghost of the Revelator."

He frowned again. I would have, in his position, but there wasn't much else I could do except give him a chance to cool off.

We walked up the stone walk and steps to the main entrance to the embassy. The guard post in the front archway was an oasis of light in a dark structure. The marine guard looked sleepily at me, frowning at my disheveled condition.

"I'm Minister Eschbach."

To my surprise, he straightened. "Sir? You're back!"

"I'm here. Probably Second Secretary Trumbull-Hull wants to know that, and I'm certain my wife does."

"Yes, sir. She's in the guest wing suite. Ah . . . and . . . just a moment." He fiddled with the wireset at his post. "Madame Eschbach . . . your husband, he's here—he appears safe. . . . Yes, madame. . . ." He shook his head. "She'll be right here." Then he looked at the list and punched out another number.

Hansen looked from the marine to me. "I think a number of people underestimated you, Eschbach."

"If so, for that I'm quite grateful."

"Sir, Minister Eschbach has just returned." The guard looked at Hansen, then at me.

"With Bishop Hansen of Saint security," I supplied, adding in a lower voice to Hansen, "You need some credit in this."

"Kind of you," he said dryly.

"With Bishop Hansen of Saint security," the marine parroted. "Yes, sir. I'll get them right in." He hung up the wireset receiver and used a key to open the front door. "Please step in, sir. Secretary Trumbull-Hull will be right down. He's been sleeping in the duty quarters."

Hansen followed me in gingerly, then eased closer. "You had the connections figured out before you left."

"No. I only knew there had to be connections. When I saw the counselor's face and when I realized you didn't know, it was obvious." I didn't mention Minister Jerome. That was my problem.

He shook his head. "This . . . is going to take some getting used to."

I felt sorry for him, but all I could say was, "This sort of thing does." Then I added, "I left my overcoat in their blockhouse. I'd guess it's a concrete building in the northeast warehouse district. Where exactly, I don't know."

"Did you leave anything else there? Anything explosive, for example?" His voice was bitter, and I didn't blame him.

"No. I doubt there's much trace of anything anywhere, now."

"Convenient."

Expedient, but I didn't voice that, and didn't have to.

Llysette, with another guard leading the way, charged past him and down the side corridor, launching herself into my arms. She had thrown a robe over a night-gown, and she looked and felt like diva, beauty, and queen, all in one.

I could feel the dampness on my cheeks, but my own eyes were wet as well, and I realized that I really hadn't been sure I'd ever see her again. I held her for a long, long time.

When I let go, Trumbull-Hull stood there, just in his shirt and trousers, bare-foot, and I'd never seen a Columbian diplomat unshod.

"It's over," I said, turning but not letting go of Llysette. "Here in Great Salt Lake City, anyway. Saint security has most of the key schismatics, and I'm sure that they'll find most of the others."

"What happened?" he asked.

"The schismatics had this idea that the ghost of their prophet would lead them, and that I'd be a useful hostage. The only problem was that when he appeared, he didn't have quite the same ideas as they did, and in their confusion, I managed to put several out of commision and escape. That allowed Saint security"—I nodded to Hansen—"to collar a bunch of the others, and I imagine they'll have everything pretty well in hand in the next few days."

"We believe so," Hansen said on cue.

"It sounds rather traumatic," observed Trumbull-Hull. "Are you certain you're all right?"

"There's nothing wrong with me that some food, a hot shower, and several nights' sleep won't go a long way toward remedying," I lied—because there was still one enormous loose end to tie up before I got hung by it. I was somewhat re-lieved, because the loose end didn't threaten Llysette, not directly, anyway. "But we'd still like to leave tomorrow."

Both Trumbull-Hull and Hansen nodded. It was clear they'd both like the Eschbachs on the way back to Columbia.

That was fine with us.

CHAPTER THIRTY-THREE

• • •

The olive drab bulk of the Republic turbojet squatted on the tarmac like a brooding eagle, being refueled. Llysette and I stood in the VIP lounge, where generals and the like waited, as, it appeared, did government ministers.

The chocolate was nearly decent, and I was on my third mug when a lieutenant in formal drabs stepped up to our escort, Colonel Borlaam, who'd been somewhere close ever since I reappeared.

"There's a blond fellow—says he's Doktor Perkins and that he'd like to see either Minister Eschbach or Mademoiselle duBoise."

"Could you let him in?" I asked Colonel Borlaam. "He was Llysette's accompanist at the concerts, and he's one of the greatest living composers. He's also been on our side."

The colonel looked doubtful.

I glared. I was tired of everyone else calling the shots—literally and figuratively.

"If you would . . ." Llysette's smile would have dissolved even the ghost of the Revelator.

The colonel nodded at the lieutenant.

Dan Perkins hurried in, silver-blond hair drooping over his forehead, but with an enormous grin. "I'm so glad I could get here." He looked from Llysette to me. "Congratulations on the commendation from Counselor Cannon. Both the *Deseret Star* and the morning news had stories about you, something about how you had helped resolve, informally, a major obstacle to talks between Columbia and Deseret."

The colonel raised his eyebrows but said nothing. Neither did I. The commendation was something I hadn't asked for, or expected, but sometimes good things happened, especially if they were in other people's best interests. First Speaker Cannon had once again pushed his media empire into releasing the story he wanted.

I held back a frown, realizing something else I should have caught earlier. Cannon had warned me about Jerome. He was too good a politician to have let Jerome's name slip. He'd wanted me to know that. He also wanted me to do something about Minister Jerome. I would have anyway, but it was reassuring to know I wasn't the only one who felt that way.

"Anyway," Perkins rushed on, turning back to Llysette and handing her the case, "I brought you the first disks from the concert. I could only get ten. We'd pressed five thousand." He shook his head. "They're gone. The distributor says there are orders with deposits for another ten thousand."

The disks showed a picture of Llysette and Perkins—one of the pictures snapped as they'd taken a bow. The title read modestly: *The Incredible Salt Palace Concert: DuBoise & Perkins.*

Colonel Borlaam leaned forward slightly, and I stepped sideways so that he could see the disk cover as well.

"It is incredible," Perkins said. "After all these years . . ."

I understood perfectly. Besides the artistic side, the disks represented freedom—for both him and Llysette.

I couldn't help but calculate. Llysette got almost a Columbian dollar for each one. Fifteen thousand dollars at a minimum, and that was without any sales in Columbia. Strangely, in a way, I felt even happier for the poor Saint composer.

"Le pauvre homme . . . ," Llysette murmured after Perkins had waved and departed.

I nodded. Still, I thought things would improve.

"He's famous, isn't he?" asked the colonel.

"One of the more famous living composers," I said. "You can probably boast about it to friends and family in a few years."

That got an awkward smile, I suppose because colonels couldn't ever admit to boasting.

A figure in a flight suit opened the door to the tarmac, and the odor of distillate and hot metal wafted in.

"We're ready, Colonel."

We walked across the tarmac, through the wind, chill enough for me because I still hadn't gotten back my overcoat, and probably wouldn't, and up the steps into the middle cabin.

"This is where I leave you, Minister," said the colonel, "and head back to the embassy."

"Thank you for everything, and for taking good care of my wife in my absence."

He cleared his throat. "We've enjoyed it, but from what I've heard, Minister Eschbach, no one could take better care of her than you. She's a lovely lady." He saluted and stepped back.

I nodded, and we stepped fully inside the military VIP transport. The decor was military brown, but I didn't care. As the hatch closed, we settled into the pair of plush leather seats before a low table bolted in place—the only passengers in a cabin designed for a dozen.

"You're going to be very famous," I told Llysette, squeezing her hand and then leaning over and kissing her cheek, drawing in the scent of Ivoire again. Lord, at times over the past days I'd never thought I'd see her again.

"Ca, ce n'est pas finis, n'est-ce pas?"

"No. I sometimes wonder if it ever is."

"Is it Ferdinand?"

"In a way, but there's nothing we can do until we reach the Federal District." And there wasn't. I'd sent a message to Harlaan Oakes, strongly suggesting, if he valued his life and his career, he meet us. I didn't make a habit of that sort of thing, and I suspected he'd be waiting. Angry, upset, and ready to rip me apart. But he would be there, and that was fine with me.

In the words of a southern Anglicism, it was his turn to be the hunting dog.

In the meantime, I intended to enjoy every moment with my bride. I squeezed her hand again as the turbos roared and the big aeroplane rolled toward the long runway.

After a moment, her face cleared, and she kissed me.

CHAPTER THIRTY-FOUR

• • •

Harlaan oakes was indeed waiting at the foot of the steps to the landing area once the Republic turbo squeaked to a lurching stop at VanBuren Field, outside of the Federal District and once we walked down the steps and into the cold misting rain. He looked at Llysette.

Her eyes were cold as she returned his glance.

Harlaan looked to me.

"No," I said coldly. "Her life has been played with enough. She knows. You and Minister Jerome's replacement are going to protect her even more than before. She's going to be doing international tours, now, I imagine. A cultural ambassador, for President Armstrong."

"You're presuming a great deal, Johan." He glanced back at the turbo.

"I don't presume, Harlaan, and I don't play games. Haven't you figured that out yet? Have you gotten the follow-up invitation from First Counselor Cannon?" I offered a smile.

He winced slightly. "Speaker Hartpence isn't pleased."

"He'll be less pleased as events unfold. The president should be happy, and that should be your concern." I paused. "I presume you have transportation for us to the B&P station. We're ready to go home after we've debriefed you." This time I was doing the debriefing, rather than being debriefed. It felt good.

"I thought it might be something like this. I have a secure limousine."

Two soldiers carried our luggage to the limousine, and I enjoyed that a great deal. I kept a tight grip on my datacase, although I had prevailed on the embassy to use their duplicating equipment to make a second set of plans, now in the lining of Llysette's luggage.

None of us spoke, not until the limousine was steaming back toward the Presidential Palace—or the B&P station on the Mall. The panel between us and the driver was closed, and Harlaan sat with his back to the front of the limousine.

I held out the flexible mesh helmet. "Do you know what that is?"

Harlaan winced, almost in spite of himself.

"I take it you recognize this. Ferdinand's agent in Deseret was wearing it. He had orders to kill me, and probably Llysette. According to Ralston's briefings," I lied, "only Branson-Hay had figured out the helmets. I never had one. I only saw them once, in his laboratory, and his research was totally funded through the Spazi. They were supposed to be destroyed, as I recall, by Minister Jerome." I pocketed the helmet.

"Johan, there could be other explanations. . . ." He paused. "What happened to him?"

"He's dead, but the Deseret security chief knows he was an Austrian agent."

"There could be a dozen explanations. . . ."

I waved off his words. "Now, the other thing is that there was a complete duplicate of my home SII system waiting for me in Deseret—in the hands of the Revealed Twelve. The system had to have been duplicated when the Spazi had my house under complete surveillance. Even the files were there, as well as some equipment duplicated from a hidden storage room in my house."

"That's a serious charge, Johan. I know the Spazi and you have not gotten on well, but that seems beyond anything anyone would expect."

I was getting tired of his explanations. "Also, the schismatics were all armed with Austrian weapons, new Austrian weapons."

"That would figure," he admitted. "It's to their interest to keep us at odds."

"Something else of interest was a pressure switch bomb that I detonated at our house in New Bruges. Jerome wired me the next morning and suggested I leave such matters to the Spazi, but the problem is that where I detonated the bomb wasn't visible to his observers. So how could they have known what it was that exploded? He didn't ask, by the way—he told me."

Harlaan's mouth twisted.

"Needless to say, Harlaan, I'm not very happy with these events, nor would I be thrilled if I were President Armstrong, because it looks like someone wanted us both dead, with a trail back to you and the president." I smiled. "There's also one other small problem."

"Oh, Johan?"

"There's a very smart head of security in Deseret who is very close to the First Counselor and who won't be very happy dealing with Minister Jerome. The First Counselor has also indicated that he would not be pleased to deal with a

government whose minister of security would support Austrian agents in Deseret."
I was elaborating slightly, but Cannon had conveyed almost that much indirectly.

"Why is that a problem?"

"Because if I were the president, I wouldn't be very happy if the First Speaker
of Deseret were to stall negotiations because of Jerome's actions, especially given
his Austrian . . . contacts. And the message both the president and the Speaker received this morning offers a far better option."

"All this is surmise."

"Come now, Harlaan," I chided him.

"Minister Eschbach, what do you want of me? I am merely an advisor to the
head of state, not a cabinet minister."

"In practical terms, Harlaan, I want the Spazi to stop trying to eliminate me—
and Llysette—whenever they think they might be able to get away with it." I
paused. Time for another push. "There's also one other thing."

"I'm not sure Columbia can stand one more thing," he said disgustedly.

Llysette's eyes narrowed, and she smiled coldly. "You have not been in Ferdinand's prisons. You have not watched your husband sacrifice himself for his wife
and his country. You, do you plan to silence me? You, do you plan to put me away
for small politics? Do you wish to upset the head of Deseret? He *would* be upset, if
anything happened to me." Her green eyes were as hot as the sun, as cold as midwinter eve in New Bruges, and as deadly as when she had held a Colt-Luger to my
forehead.

Harlaan's forehead beaded sweat, and he wiped it. "I can't promise anything."

"Harlaan," I said gently, "you don't have to promise. Just do what needs to be
done. Now, there is one other matter. I'm working out some arrangements with
FrancoPetEx."

"Yes."

"It appears that there is some New French interest in Columbia becoming
more energy-independent. Through some personal contacts, of the type not available to Minister Jerome, I have finalized the agreement."

"What did you agree to?"

"For services already rendered in Deseret, once they are confirmed officially, I
will receive the entire plans, specifications, and design drawings, including proprietary technology, of a stage-three Saint synthetic fuel plant."

"What services?" Harlaan asked tiredly.

"The murder of Ferdinand's agent among the Revealed Twelve."

Harlaan winced again. "Just how many bodies did you leave behind this time,
Minister Eschbach?"

"None that will ever be attributed to Columbia. That's all that counts, isn't it?"

"You will do what is necessary, *n'est-ce pas?*" asked Llysette, a chill smile on her
lips.

The president's advisor shrugged tiredly. "Have events left me much choice?"

"No."

"*Non.*"

"When can I promise delivery of those plans?" Harlaan asked after a time.

"When the Spazi situation is resolved," I said. "I don't think my contacts would feel comfortable with Minister Jerome's attitude or position."

"You drive a hard bargain, Minister Eschbach."

I shook my head. "You and the president set the price when you drafted us. It's only fair that it be paid."

"This is going to change everything," he mused.

Even Harlaan didn't understand exactly how much, and I wasn't about to tell him. After all, the journey is the fun, not the destination. Death is always the eventual destination, so there's no point in hurrying the trip.

I smiled at Llysette and leaned back. She put her head on my shoulder, and the faint scent of her, and Ivoire, surrounded me.

CHAPTER THIRTY-FIVE

• • •

I glanced out the kitchen window into the darkness of Saturday night. Less than three months had passed since Llysette had given a recital attended by the Deseret concertmeister, and our lives had changed dramatically.

Hartson James—the TransMedia mogul who'd been entranced at the Presidential Art Awards dinner—had indeed plugged Llysette and Dan Perkins's disk, and it continued to sell briskly in Columbia. The indications were that the trustees of Vanderbraak State University would grant Llysette tenure at their next meeting, and Llysette had three upcoming concerts scheduled—one in New Amsterdam and one a week later in Philadelphia and, of course, the opening of the spring season in St. George in Deseret. The guarantees for each were triple her annual income from teaching.

There were a few more gowns in her closet and quite a few more dresses, but the Haaren remained in the music room because "a good instrument it is, and given with love." And she was paying for our trip to Saint-Martine.

I could accept that.

Harder to accept was that Llysette had suddenly become as well-off as I, and shortly would become very well-off, I suspected, from what I saw through my activities as her de facto business manager—with Eric's assistance. My former brother-in-law's legal advice had also been most helpful.

Hartson James had recently written about the possibility of using an Irish subsidiary as the vehicle for marketing the disk in Austro-Hungary, and if anyone could work those angles, I suspected the media magnate could. I also suspected that the royalties on a good-selling disk in a market of over 200 million people would be considerable.

"Johan, I have been thinking." Llysette slipped up behind me and put her arms around my waist.

"Yes?"

"So skeptical you sound."

I laughed.

"Was it not strange that the deputy minister, he committed suicide so soon after your return?"

"Do you really think so?" I asked.

"Suicide, it was not. Non?"

"No," I admitted. "Not from what I know about the Speaker and the president." Jerome's "suicide" had made it very simple for them; it had all been the deceased Spazi chief's fault. If I hadn't pressed, though, I would have been the corpse . . . and possibly Llysette, in some terrible "tragedy."

"Was he not the one who sent the bomb?"

"I think so." I looked out the window. Bruce was a little late.

"Did he not work with the agents of Ferdinand?"

"He slipped them some information about us, and that sort of thing doesn't set well even in the Federal District, not at that high a level. There's no deniability."

"Why did he dislike you so much, Johan?"

"Because spymasters dislike anyone who knows their operations and is not under some control and because Jerome was too young. He took my actions personally."

"You think Minister Oakes, he will do better?"

"At least, Harlaan understands both sides of the fence, and can operate as a bridge between the Speaker and the president. The Speaker wasn't happy about it, but given Jerome's indiscretions, he preferred it not become public, and accepted the president's compromise. Since Harlaan never wanted the position . . ." I shrugged. "The synthfuel plans confirmed that Jerome's approach was too paranoid for this new and changing world."

The world changed more slowly than our lives, but changes were coming. FrancoPetEx was actually talking about a joint venture on the first Columbian synthfuel plant—designed to convert northlands natural gas into kerosene—and with those kinds of cooperation between the North American nations, Ferdinand's rhetoric had toned down. I snorted to myself. All that meant was that the Austro-Hungarians would expand southward, rather than westward.

As the flapping of Bruce's Olds ragtop preceded the venerable steamer up the drive, I stopped mental philosophizing and hugged Llysette. We watched Bruce for a moment while the snowflakes swirled around him. He extracted a large box from the passenger side, then went to the door and opened it.

"Greetings and congratulations!" Bruce shook off the scattered snow and stamped his feet. "And happy something." He extended the enormous box, then grinned. "This should go in the music room . . . for now."

So we followed him there, after I checked the oven to make sure the green bean casserole wouldn't overbrown.

He opened the box and extracted a small box that looked like a miniature difference engine, with two disk slots. Then came two DGA speakers, relatively expensive, followed by a scanner. "There!"

"It is . . . what?" asked Llysette.

"You had mentioned the problem with accompanists for students." Bruce beamed. "This solves that problem for practice, at least. You use this to scan the music, and then you can set whatever modifications to the tempo that you need. I figured that you need to stop at any time, too, given what I know about students, and this little gadget here"—he pointed to another little box with a stick—"lets you stop and back up to wherever you like."

"Now, I know there's no substitute for a real accompanist for performing, but this might help with practicing and with students."

Llysette looked at the equipment, half-bewildered, half-bemused.

I drew Bruce aside. "How much . . . I mean . . . this was scarcely inexpensive."

"Johan," and Bruce smiled at me. "This is my treat. I get to solve a problem in a positive way and see a pretty woman smile."

I also understood what he wasn't saying, that things had changed and that we had to be equals, that he was no longer, if he ever had been, merely a contract employee.

"Fair enough." I paused. "Just a moment. I'll be right back."

Bruce's brows furrowed before I headed down to the cellar. Let them.

I brought back up six bottles.

"You liked the Sebastopol. Take these with you."

"I couldn't."

I got to grin. "If we're truly friends and not just business partners, then I get to give things, too."

He smiled back. "It's been a long time."

And it had been, in so many ways. Then, I had to run to the kitchen because something was overcooking, but that was life, too.

AFTERWORD

The fundamental premise of the "ghost" books is simple and obvious enough: In the alternate reality in which the events in the book occur, ghosts are real and can be seen, as well as measured and verified by scientific instruments. As technology advances, of course, human beings being human beings, scientists are attempting to replicate the effect, to modify it, and even to undo it, as depicted in various sections of the books.

While the basic premise seems simple, it has also become painfully clear in the years since the first publication of *Of Tangible Ghosts* that all of the ramifications of the premise, which seemed so obvious to me, were not nearly so obvious to many readers, and I have received a wide range of inquiries about the alternate history behind the three books. Because of these inquiries, and at the suggestion of David Hartwell and Moshe Feder, I have written this elaboration of some of the underpinnings of the books. I am most certain that it will raise as many questions as it lays to rest, but it will at the least explain the structure and presumptions I used in constructing the world of Johan and Llysette.

In particular, the most common inquiry is a combination of question and complaint from "traditional" alternate history buffs, who are looking for the single "point of departure" that seems to define a great deal of alternate history fiction—if Lincoln or Kennedy had not been assassinated, if Babbage had had the funding to build and apply his full-scale difference engine, if Hitler had not chosen to invade Russia. These kinds of points of departure are always interesting to debate, but the problem of the puzzled individuals who have contacted me is that they cannot find such a point of departure. That is because there is no single point of departure. The differences between Johan Eschbach's world and ours arise out of the existence of ghosts, and those differences begin as very minor—with some few exceptions—and slowly build as history unfolds. But why should this be?

History is a process of action and reaction, and it is in the reaction where ghosts have their greatest impact, because, while ghosts are real physical manifestations in Johan's world, their ability to impact the physical world is minimal, but their impact on human beings is far from minimal. Even in our world, virtually all pretechnological and low technological societies have had varying degrees of belief in ghosts, particularly the ghosts of ancestors. Today, all our high technology can find no replicable and verifiable trace of ghosts, but millions of people still believe in them. In older myths and legends, ghosts often have a powerful role and an effect upon conduct. In the world of the ghost books, they still do.

History is not just based upon what happened, but upon what we believe and what we believe occurred. Until several centuries ago, the belief in ghosts was strong even in Western cultures. Shakespeare's *Hamlet* is *not* a ghost story. It is a drama based on a revelation by a being who is as real to Hamlet as any other actor upon the stage, and Hamlet is moved—eventually—to act by his father's ghost. In our own past history, and still in the world of Johan and Llysette, it is the reaction inspired by these ghosts that changes history.

Once science began to suggest in our world that ghosts did not have a physical reality, the strength of belief in ghosts began to wane, and there was a greater emphasis on the physical and verifiable. In Johan's world, ghosts remain an influence, because they are indeed physical and verifiable.

Wars and massacres are fewer, not because humans in Johan's world are better, but because, while you can hide the bodies, you cannot hide the ghosts—at least not until the late twentieth century. This reduces the ability of a ruler to murder large numbers of his subjects undetected and also retain their affection or their tolerance—because the ghosts are there all the time. It does not change the impacts of barbarians and raiders like Tamerlane, Genghis Khan, or many of the Vikings who wanted to plunder and create terror at times, rather than conquer and rule.

Ghosts are visible and often verbal reminders of death and tragedy, and they take years, if not longer, to fade from view. It becomes harder to escape unpleasant history. Thus, ghost formation affects the entire culture because it makes violence, whether created by war or crime, more obvious and harder to conceal. Successful murders and other forms of lethal skullduggery have to be far more indirect, or at least staged so that the victim cannot be in a position to know he or she is being murdered and by whom. Because the ghost is tied relatively closely to the physical place of death, it is far easier to discover certain types of spontaneous murder and far harder to conceal them.

There is also a greater sense of being watched. All of these factors lead to all cultures being far less direct than our Western cultures today and to institutionalizing deviousness, while overtly recognizing and praising directness and peacefulness. Conquest must be plotted more carefully, and bold strokes are less often successful. Even when they are, the trail of evidence is longer and more visible.

Another significant difference between Johan and Llysette's world and ours is displayed indirectly, but never mentioned or explained. The cities are smaller, and the population of all countries tends to be lower than in our world. The reason, of course, lies in the ghosts and the means of their creation and manifestation. Ghosts are naturally created by the knowledgeable and violent death of an aware individual. As explained in the books, this is why there are few ghosts of children below a certain age. The full awareness of what is happening does not exist. This is also the reason for a lower population growth, particularly in more economically and technically advanced countries in the period prior to roughly 1900.

Statistics are rough and only general, but surveys of medical records indicate that prior to the twentieth century, the leading cause of death among women, accounting for perhaps as much as 60 percent of all female deaths, was childbirth. Childbirth is, according to all the women in my life and from my own personal observations, both an exceedingly painful process, and one in which the woman would be particularly self-aware prior to the development of anesthetics. Therefore, death in and from childbirth would result in large numbers of ghosts of wives. Since the majority of births took place at home in this historical period, the high mortality rate would result in a fair number of dwellings being haunted by former wives. My own experiences at having been married more than once suggested most strongly that second and/or third wives would be rather reluctant to move into a house haunted by a former inhabitant, at least until the ghost faded enough to appear infrequently. Since very few individuals could afford to build or move to new houses, and since most houses were small enough that it was impossible to close off the haunted chambers, this ghosting effect reduced the birth rate. It also led to a great deal more domestic strife for those men unwise enough to marry too soon after the death of their first wife.

There are also a number of specific historical references about which many have asked for greater explanation than occurs in the book, and I will briefly address some of those.

The failure of the Plymouth Colony is mentioned but never fully explained. Recent historical studies suggest that the captain of the *Mayflower* was paid to land those troublesome Puritans in New England—or at least somewhere a goodly distance from the English colonies in the more southern areas of North America. However, excerpts from diaries of the colonists indicate that the beaches of Cape Cod were littered with bones—bones from those Indians who died in the deadly measles epidemic roughly a year before, an epidemic beginning with exposures from the colonists in Virginia. Measles in an unprotected Native American (or Hawaiian) population is deadly, with a fever so high that any source of coolness is welcome, including the cold waters off Massachusetts. When the Indians died, their ghosts remained. The ghosts made Massachusetts far less hospitable, and they also made the remaining Indians far less helpful toward the settlers. In our world, the colony barely survived. In Johan and Llysette's, it did not, and in time, the Dutch settlers in the Hudson Valley moved eastward and northward, making the northeast New Bruges, rather than New England.

There was a revolution in which Columbia wrested independence from England, because even the Dutch of New Bruges distrusted the British, and the British still wanted to exploit their new world colonies. The Dutch Columbians were better generals, as were the French of the north, and when the smoke cleared, there was no remaining British presence in North America. The Columbians took Newfoundland and the Maritimes, while Quebec took the remainder of eastern Canada.

The aftermath of the revolution was different, however, since George Washington died of pneumonia before taking office as president, an illness to which he was more susceptible because of an earlier bout with influenza in the last days of the Continental Congress. Because of the changes in the slave trade discussed below, Alexander Hamilton never appeared in Columbia, and Washington had to take a more active—and less effective—role in the debates in the Continental Congress over the emerging nation's financial structure and policies.

There was a President Adams, but from Philadelphia, and ineffectual. He was followed by Thomas Jefferson, who was adamantly opposed to a strong executive. Since the Columbian culture was always more conducive to a less direct exercise of power, Columbia effectively and practically adopted a more parliamentary form of representative democracy with a largely ceremonial presidency.

Slavery existed in Columbia, as it did in our world, but it never took hold as deeply for several reasons. First, the deplorable conditions of the slave ships were less miserable because, when the first slavers arrived off the coasts of Virginia and the Carolinas, their decks crowded with ghosts, planters tended to worry about the health of the slaves. That reduced prices, and in turn encouraged the slavers not to crowd their vessels so much, which reduced the mortality. The numbers of slaves imported were less, and they were better treated in most cases, because the most violent forms of mistreatment resulted in ghosts, and human beings always are more cruel when they do not have to confront the results of their cruelty.

With the slightly later development of the north industrially and a population in the northern states of Columbia more spread out, including the eastern sections of what is Canada in our world, and the French-dominated Quebec, as well as British interests in southern cotton, there was less pressure toward immediate abolition of slavery and more for an indirect political solution. That pressure intensified when a slave ship—the *Sally Wright*—ported in Charleston with so many ghosts that they could not be accurately counted—and no living slaves. While this was an exception, the *Wright* incident was reported all across Columbia and the world, and the reaction was outrage. This outrage was compounded by Speaker Calhoun's failure to deal immediately with the incident, and the popular dissatisfaction resulted in such a substantial loss of seats in the House that Calhoun's position as Speaker was jeopardized. He engineered the so-called Calhoun compromise that limited the number of slaves that could be imported and established a significant tariff on all numbers above that. Although the tariff was often evaded, it did reduce slave trading. The facet of the compromise that had a greater long-run effect were the provisions that required "humane treatment" of slaves. Again, although these provisions were initially widely ignored, abolitionists began to infiltrate the South and document abuses. After a number of Pennsylvania Quakers were murdered in 1859 while investigating slave conditions in Alabama, their ghosts identified the son of one of the largest planters in the state as the murderer. Senator Lincoln used the murders as a vehicle to national prominence and, by focusing on the need to stop slave abuse, avoided a civil war over the slavery issue. Eventually, nearly ten years later, before his later assassination by Booth, he was able to push through the amendments to the national charter that led to the phasing out of slavery in Columbia, otherwise called the Codification of the Rights of Man.

With a lower population in Columbia, pressure for westward and southern settlement was lower and later. Likewise, the ghost "pressure" in Mexico resulted in a slightly less violent conquest and settlement and a somewhat stronger central government, allowing more effective Mexican consolidation in Tejas and the southwest. Not only did Santa Anna take the Alamo, but he crushed all opposition in Tejas because settlers from Columbia were fewer and less organized than in our world. In the disastrous Mexican War, Columbia sent a small force into northern Tejas, but the force was annihilated by Santa Anna, with the aid of some very effective French artillery. The Mexicans early on ceded their claims to West Kansas (Colorado east of the continental divide) and in northern California to Columbia in order to strengthen their hold on what they thought most valuable. Taking advantage of the stronger Mexican position in the southwest, Brigham Young brought his followers to the Great Basin area of the west, obtained a treaty and firm borders with the Mexican government to the south and west, and established the sovereign nation of Deseret.

Despite being faced with a growing threat of Quebec in the north and increasing French influence in the southwest, Columbia attempted several undersupplied, underfunded—and unsuccessful—invasions of Deseret in the Saint Wars of 1860 and 1862. When those failed, Columbia adopted a policy of containment, establishing military posts and settlements all along the eastern and northern borders of Deseret and then sending troops and money to seize western Canada before Quebec could.

The overextension of Mexican power led Mexico to seek a stronger alliance with the French, but the alliance and the shaky state of Mexican finances and increasing corruption led to the imposition of Maximilian and Carlotta upon Mexico by a France deeply concerned about the growing power of Austro-Hungary and seeking both compromises and resources in the New World. By 1890, Mexico had become New France, and the growing production of Tejas oil fueled both prosperity and social reforms that continued to strengthen New France. In turn, Maximilian—or his advisers—played off Austro-Hungary against the French. Fearful of Columbia and seeking to isolate old France, Austro-Hungary backed both Deseret and New France in the small-scale Caribbean Wars (1896 and 1901) as a result of which New France effectively took control of the majority of Central America.

Although the Great Irish Tuber Famine occurred, the lower Irish population and the adverse publicity from the *Falbourg* disaster—when Speaker Breckinridge quarantined the steamer in Long Island Sound, and more than five-hundred men, women, and children died—resulted in less Irish emigration to Columbia and more to Deseret and New France, especially to Tejas and Baja (Southern California).

Afterword

All these factors combined to weaken the industrial and military development of Columbia. Because wars tended to be smaller and shorter in Johan's world, a number of military innovations were developed later, or by different cultures. John Moses Browning was from Deseret and, consequently, with his genius and because of Deseret's precarious geographic position, Deseret developed an arms industry out of proportion to its size and population. It also monopolized the majority of water from the Colorado River to support iron and coal development and use. Unlike monogamous Columbia, Deseret instituted customs that allowed a higher birthrate, because each plural wife retained her own quarters, for example, and girls were married younger. After the ineffectual and costly Saint Wars that effectively wiped out most of the Columbian units attacking Deseret, Columbia avoided direct military action against Deseret, often citing the higher birthrate in Deseret, a somewhat fanatical population, a solid arms industry, and New French backing as reasons for comparative inaction.

With the split in energy resources between Columbia, Deseret, and New France, all face pressures to use more energy-effective technologies, resulting in greater reliance upon trains, dirigibles, and even steamers. Turbojets are reserved primarily for military purpose, and liquid hydrocarbon fuels are expensive and heavily taxed.

And all this . . . just because ghosts are real.

L. E. MODESITT, JR.
Cedar City, Utah (Iron Mission, Deseret)
August 23, 2004